Mountain Gods

By Archie Kregear

Rich,
Enjoy!
Archie Kregear

Mountain Gods

This is a work of fiction. References to real people, events, establishments, organizations or locales are intended to provide a sense of authenticity, and are used fictitiously. All other characters, incidents and dialogue, are drawn from the author's imagination and are not to be construed as real.

Amazon Print Edition ISBN: 9781711872230

Cover design by: Andrew Michaels

Acknowledgements

During the writing of this book I have had the support of many people. First and foremost is the support of my wife Bonnie who supported me throughout the years of writing and editing. This book could not have been written without her patience, encouragement, and allowing me to spend countless hours on the deck pounding on my computer.

To my Daughters, Jennifer and Erica who initially encouraged me to write this tome and helped me refine many of the ideas and themes in the story.

Over the four years of writing I have been blessed to be part of two writing groups. The first in San Jose, California who read over some of the early drafts and helped me tremendously. The Kitsap Writers Group provided wonderful support and beta read the manuscript offering a multitude of suggestions. I am in debt to the members of these groups for their willingness to share their expertise.

I give credit to my editors who corrected a multitude of things for me. Any remaining mistakes are mine.

Lastly I must mention my dog Jasper who laid by my chair providing companionship throughout the writing process.

Table of Contents

Part One - Yangseongso

1 — The Test - May 12 - 13, 1950

Cha Sue-dae scurried down the narrow dirt path between the fields. Long shadows of herself and the dress she held waved wildly over the ankle-high rows of green maize. Her countenance glowed in the golden light of the setting sun, anticipating her daughter's reaction to the dress.

"Sun-hee, I have a surprise for you," Sue-dae said, pulling open the door to their hut while kicking off her sandals.

Her daughter looked up from a book. Her eyes lit up. "A dress!" she exclaimed. "Where did you get it?"

Sun-hee shot up from the floor mat she sat upon, bounced to her mother, and pinched the shoulders of the dress. She admired the light-gray Joseon-ot—a traditional Korean dress—with pink trim around the collar, wrists, and hem. Embroidered red and yellow hibiscus flowers decorated the skirt.

"Oh, Mother, it's so pretty!" Sun-hee said, her feet running in place as her arms shook with anticipation. She pulled her linen blouse over her head and yanked her arms out of the sleeves, while the bamboo floor chattered to the rhythm of her prancing.

A wide grin spread over Sue-dae's face. "I told Mrs. Pae you were nominated by your teachers to take the national test for fifteen-year-old students tomorrow. She thought you might need something better to wear and loaned us this dress."

Sue-dae removed the dress from the wooden hanger and held it over Sun-hee who raised her hands and closed her eyes. The dress slipped down over her lithe frame.

She tugged at the ends of the sleeves, which fit perfectly. The hem was a little long, but not overly so. The dress hung loosely on Sun-hee's shoulders and fit a bit larger at the chest and waist. Mrs. Pae's daughter was two years older than Sun-hee, thus Sue-dae expected some slack.

Sue-dae cleared Sun-hee's shoulder-length hair as she reached around to adjust the shoulders and button the collar. Sun-hee renewed her prancing.

"I want to see! I want to see!" Sun-hee blurted without opening her eyes. Her feet were a blur of energy.

Sue-dae took a couple of steps to retrieve a small mirror from the wall. It was large enough to see one's face, but not anywhere near full-length. She held it in front of Sun-hee. "You can look now," she said softly.

Opening her eyes, Sun-hee reached for the mirror. Her hands shook so much she couldn't grasp it. She forced her feet to stop. The chattering ceased. She seized the mirror, centering it on her face. Her breath stilled and her eyes locked on to her reflection as she examined every detail. Black bangs hung a finger width above narrow eyebrows. The pink collar framed her round chin, and her bulging cheeks enhanced her smile. Panning down with the mirror, she admired the gray dress and sighed, "Oh." She turned, twirled, and danced around the hut while watching herself. Then she stopped.

"Here, Mother. Please hold the mirror."

Sue-dae held the mirror so her daughter could see herself posing, making every move a fifteen-year-old in a new dress could make. She watched Sun-hee stroke the smoothness of the delicate silk bow, caress the threads of the flowers, make faces at the mirror, and dance around the hut.

Tears trickled over Sue-dae's cheeks and into the ends of her broad smile. "My little darling, you look majestic in this dress!"

"Thank you, *Eomeoni*!" Sun-hee said as she threw her arms around her mother.

Sue-dae relished the moment. Then she took her daughter's shoulders, pushing her back, looking into her eyes. "The dress and sandals are on loan. After the test, we must give them back. Tomorrow, you will look as beautiful as you are smart. You will look like you deserve the prize."

Taking her mother's hands, Sun-hee said, "I will do my best, Mother! I will win!"

"Your best is all I ask for."

Sun-hee drew away and spun around, saying, "Unbutton me, Mother. If I have any chance of winning the award, I need to spend every moment I have studying."

With trembling fingers, Sue-dae undid the buttons. "Enough studying for today. It's time to wash and get a good night's sleep. You will need to be well-rested for tomorrow." She lifted the dress over Sun-hee's head, carefully placing it back on the hanger and straightening out the fabric to make sure there were no wrinkles.

Sun-hee took three steps across the hut and poured water into a basin. She washed, using a threadbare cloth and a sliver of soap, before slipping into her nightshirt. Donning her sandals by the door, she ran to the privy.

Sue-dae closed the math books Sun-hee had been reading, picked them up, and closed her eyes. *I wish her father were still alive; he would be so proud.* She took a deep breath and released it slowly while placing the book next to others on a shelf.

Sun-hee entered, skipped across the room, and lay on the mat where she and her mother both slept. "I'm too excited to sleep."

"Close your eyes and dream of what Kim Il-sung will give you for being the smartest girl in the country," Sue-dae said, kneeling to kiss Sun-hee on the cheek. Then she proceeded with her pre-slumber routine, similar to what Sun-hee had finished minutes ago.

Sue-dae blew out the lamp and lay next to her daughter. Her mind wandered through all the years of teaching language and literature, including Korean, Russian, Chinese, Japanese, and English. None of her students had learned as well as Sun-hee. She recalled her teacher at the college in Pyongyang, saying, "Sue-dae, you are a prodigy when it comes to languages."

Her mind flashed back sixteen years to when they had moved to Yonggwang. The Japanese magistrate had ordered, "Speak only Japanese. Teach only Japanese, or I will have your head!" She did so in public while privately teaching all the languages she knew to her daughter. Now the new government decreed everyone was to learn and speak only Korean, and Sun-hee knew as much as she did.

Sun-hee will do well on the language parts of the test. I wish her father were here to teach her mathematics.

She thought about the announcement two weeks ago of the national test for fifteen-year-old students. Since then, Sun-hee had been poring over her father's math books, studying algebra, trigonometry, and geometry.

I hope it will be enough.

Forcing herself to lay still next to her daughter, she stared into the darkness. *Can I ever regain favor and teach again?*

The regional governor's words haunted her. "Where do your loyalties lie?" he'd said as he had written "Denied" on her last teaching application.

Will they deny Sun-hee the prize because of my past? For teaching? For interpreting for the Japanese? What will our future be if she wins? Or if she does not win? What more can I do to show loyalty to the new government? There is so much mistrust.

The rumors of the new government sending people who opposed them to labor camps or executing them went through her mind. *I have always expressed loyalty to the government; they must be better than the Japanese. How long will it take to be accepted?*

It seemed a long time before she sensed Sun-hee fall asleep. But for her, sleep would not come. She remained still, fearing she would wake Sun-hee and prevent her from getting the rest she needed. Her mind dwelt on their life: her work on the farms when they needed help, cleaning houses for some of the wealthy, helping vendors in town when they had jobs. The blessing of knowing Mrs. Pae who had her in once a week to clean house and tutor her daughters. The work paid her enough to buy food and meet their basic needs.

When will living day to day end? Sun-hee must win. For her future. A shudder went through her body. *Where have I gone wrong? Maybe if we had stayed in Pyongyang after we married? We were so idealistic. Teaching in the rural areas of Korea was a chance to make a difference. Has it? Why do I deserve a life of poverty?* She lay there in her thoughts. *Will the fates allow Sun-hee to win? What is the prize?* The same thoughts went over and over in her mind until she dozed off.

***

A rooster's crow broke the cricket melody, signaling the start of test day. A hint of morning light flowed through the window, erasing the darkness in the hut. Sue-dae rose, trying to make as little noise as possible. She prepared all the rice they had and added the last of the goat milk. Sun-hee would get all the food, giving her energy for the test.

Sun-hee awoke and went about getting ready with hardly a sound. She ate, put on the stunning gray floral dress, and combed her straight black hair without saying a word. Sue-dae picked up the loaned sandals and nodded to the old pair by the door. Sun-hee slipped them on. They walked down the footpath and took the dirt road to town, past farms and orchards. Fluffy clouds burned orange against the blue morning sky in stunning contrast to the greens of the newly sprouting fields and leaves on the fruit trees.

Sue-dae tugged on her daughter's arm and picked up the pace. They walked through town, active in the early morning with merchants loading or unloading goods, livery-stable boys feeding horses and mules, and workers moving in various directions across their path.

Four boys and a girl were waiting with their families near a bus at the south edge of town. Two men in army fatigues stood near the bus smoking cigarettes. Rifles were slung over their shoulders. The rusting, peanut-brown Japanese bus was dirty and faded. There was an assortment of dents along the side, one front fender was missing, and the tires were bald.

As they approached, Sue-dae glanced at the neighbors, storekeepers, and local farmers who were waiting. She knew them all, parents and children. Since the fathers were with their families, she bowed to the group collectively. It was not proper for her to approach or speak.

A couple of the mothers fired off questions to their children, drilling them up until the last minute. Sue-dae heard Sun-hee whispering the answers. She glanced at her daughter who smiled back with a look of overwhelming confidence, and her poise calmed the butterflies in Sue-dae's stomach.

A soldier holding a clipboard looked at his watch and flicked the butt of his cigarette toward the back end of the bus. "Time to board. When I call your name get on the bus."

Cha Sun-hee was the fourth name called of the six children.

Sue-dae put the new sandals down. Sun-hee stepped from her old worn sandals into the new ones. Sue-dae put her hand on her daughter's shoulder and said, "Do your best."

Sun-hee wrapped her arms around her mother's waist. "I will, Mother." Then she skipped toward the bus, took the big step to enter, gave a small wave, and sat in the front seat.

Sue-dae looked at her through a cracked window, watching as her daughter put her hands in her lap and stared straight ahead.

The bus roared to life in a cloud of belching blue smoke, causing parents to step back. With a loud grinding of the gears and a sudden lurch, the bus moved off just as the sun rose fully above the hills. Sue-dae, with an undoubting heart and a modest grin, waved at the bus until the dust dissipated.

She strode briskly to a farm where she spent the day laboring in the fields. She hated the work, but it was necessary. After Kim Il-sung had taken over leadership of the country, he instituted socialistic land reform, forcing out the feudal landowners and redistributing the land to individual farmers. This provided an opportunity for men and women without a steady job to work when the farmers needed help. She tried to work harder than other laborers, which usually resulted in enough food for her and Sun-hee for a day or two.

***

The sun was near the western horizon when the farmer brought a bag of food to Sue-dae as payment for her work. It held rice, cornmeal, two apples, and a jar of fresh goat milk. Sue-dae bowed saying, "Thank you for allowing me to work for you."

She picked up Sun-hee's sandals and began to eat an apple, the first food she'd eaten all day. She forced her tired legs to take long strides. *I hope Sun-hee is on her way home, so I do not have to walk through town.*

The sun had set by the time Sue-dae saw the other families mingling. She slowed her pace, stopping a few meters from the others to wait, anxious to hear about her daughter's day.

It was almost dark when the headlights appeared down the road. The parents stood, with a few young children, as the noise of the bus slowly grew louder. Sue-dae told herself to accept whatever Sun-hee achieved this day, yet internally, she knew not winning would be crushing.

With brakes squealing, the school bus came to a stop. The driver gestured with his right hand while yelling, "Children off."

The boys exited first, all with their heads down. They looked dejected like they had just lost a championship game. Sun-hee stepped off. Her hair was a mess. Her face revealed eroding canyons made by tears in the dust caking her cheeks. From a scrape on her right knee ran a dried line of blood almost to her ankle. Sun-hee held her right hand on her left shoulder as she ran barefoot to her mother, holding the sandals in her left hand.

"They tore the dress!" Sun-hee cried, burying her head into Sue-dae's bosom. "They tore the dress! I am sorry, *Eomeoni.* I could not stop them from making us fight."

Sue-dae's heart dropped like a rock. *How could they do this to my little girl? She never hurt anyone in her life.*

Words filled with naked emotion formed on Sue-dae's lips, but the lump in her throat blocked their way. All she could do was hold her daughter tight as the other families walked silently away, demoralized by the demeanor of their children. Sue-dae stooped, checked the scrape on Sun-hee's knee, and held her sobbing daughter while she slipped on her old sandals. Arm in arm, they walked home.

Sue-dae lit the lantern before helping her daughter out of the dress, its left sleeve half torn off and the collar torn in the back. As Sun-hee washed, Sue-dae prepared dinner from the food she had earned that day. Sun-hee finished washing and went to a corner of the room where she sat, put her arms around her legs, and buried her face in her knees.

Placing two plates on the small table, Sue-dae said, "Time to eat."

"I'm not hungry," came a muted reply from a head between knees.

Sue-dae moved to the corner and took her daughter's arms gently, raising her. "Come, eat with me. Tell me the story of today so that I can share your sorrow." Slowly, they moved to the table and sat down on the floor mats. Sue-dae began to eat, taking small bites to encourage her daughter to eat.

"They made me fight. I did not want to," she said, with tears rolling down her cheeks. "They made everyone fight. The soldiers told me to fight a boy from Hanju. I kept running. I could not stay far enough away. He grabbed the dress, and it ripped. I'm so sorry!"

"The dress can be fixed and will be as good as new," said Sue-dae in a soothing tone.

"I got angry! I slapped him over and over. He tripped and fell. I jumped on him and kept slapping him until two soldiers grabbed me and dragged me away. He could not breathe. I hurt him, *eomeoni*! I didn't want to! I didn't!"

Kneeling by Sun-hee, Sue-dae put her arms around her. "Why don't you start at the beginning of the day with the bus ride, and tell me everything?"

Sun-hee sniffed. Sue-dae took her hanky and wiped her daughter's tears.

It took a few minutes before Sun-hee began to talk. "The bus ride was okay, just a little cold when the wind came in the broken windows. We drove to the old Japanese base in Hamhung. A lady assigned each person a desk." She said, taking a sip of water and a bite of food.

Sue-dae sat back down and took a bite.

"The written test took all morning," Sun-hee continued. "I thought it was easy. I knew how to work all the math problems. I think I did very well in math. The language portion of the test was super easy, and I finished before anyone else." She took another bite. "They served us kimchee, rice, and tea for lunch. Then there were more questions that did not seem to have right or wrong answers. The officer giving the test said this was a personality evaluation."

"Next, they had some physical tests," she said, taking bites of her dinner between sentences. "We were measured for height and weight. The nurse said I was average height but too thin. Two doctors looked carefully at our faces. They said it was to evaluate our symmetry and beauty. Then there were running races, pull-ups, and long jumping. I was third in my group of ten runners. I could only do two pull-ups, and I jumped almost two meters, but I do not think it was very far compared to the others.

"It was late in the afternoon when they made us fight," Sun-hee said as she started to sob. "Two soldiers would grab someone and push them into the middle of a circle. The officer who ran the whole thing yelled at us to fight. 'To win the prize you have to win a fight,' he said."

She wiped at her eyes and took a deep breath. "I had made up my mind I would not fight. I did not want to hurt anyone to win the prize. A boy from Hanju tore my dress and made me mad! I'm so sorry."

Sue-dae placed her hand on Sun-hee's arm and said in a consoling voice, "The fight may have been a contest to see who could fight rather than to hurt the opponent. When you ran away, the boy became desperate to obey the soldiers. I'm proud of you for trying to avoid fighting. You did nothing wrong. I'm sure the boy will be fine. I will mend the dress."

"You are not mad at me?"

"Not at all. I'm very proud of you," Sue-dae said with warmth in her voice. "You were selected to take part in a national test. From what you told me, you did very well. I'm very pleased with my little empress."

2 — The Prize - May 25 - 26, 1950

Sue-dae arched her back, right hand pressed on her hip to absorb the ache. Her spirits were high because of the bag of rice and kimchi she carried, enough for two days.

The silhouette of a sedan with wisps of cigarette smoke swirling over it caught her eye. Stories of soldiers taking away people named as disloyal to the government invaded her mind, and her steps slowed. Confident she had never done wrong, she tilted her head, letting the wide brim hat shield her eyes and plodded on.

A deep voice interrupted the clopping of her sandals. "Pardon me, do you know where a Cha Sun-hee or Cha Sue-dae lives?"

A twinge ran down her spine, ending with a shot of pain in her lower back. She lifted her head to see who had spoken and found deep brown eyes focused on her. A scar ran from the middle of the man's forehead across his right eye and down his cheek. Bars on his shoulder revealed a man of rank. The other soldier took a drag on his cigarette.

Sue-dae moistened her mouth and swallowed. "I am Cha Sue-dae. How can I help you?"

"Ah, great!" he said, dropping his cigarette then grinding out the butt. "I am Lieutenant Rim Seung-Gin. I have a letter for you."

She reached out to take the envelope and opened the letter.

> *CONGRATULATIONS!*
>
> *WITH AN OUTSTANDING PERFORMANCE ON THE NATIONAL TEST HELD ON MAY 13, 1950, CHA SUN-HEE IS A PRIZE WINNER.*
>
> *THE PRIZE IS ACCEPTANCE AT A BOARDING SCHOOL ESTABLISHED BY KIM IL-SUNG FOR THE GLORY OF THE DEMOCRATIC PEOPLE'S REPUBLIC OF KOREA.*
>
> *SINCERELY,*
> *PROVISIONAL PEOPLE'S COMMITTEE FOR NORTH KOREA*
>
> *THE DELIVERER OF THIS LETTER WILL PROVIDE TRANSPORTATION TO THE SCHOOL.*

Her heart leaped to her throat with a momentum that nearly brought Sue-dae's feet off the ground. "Sun-hee should be home right now," she said. "I will get her."

She began a half run along the footpath towards their hut. She called out, "Sun-hee! Sun-hee! Are you home?"

The wooden door of the hut swept open, smacking the side with a bang. Sun-hee bounded out. "I'm here. What's wrong?"

"Here, read this letter!" she said, holding out the paper with a shaking hand. "It says you won the prize. You are the winner! These men are here to award you the prize."

Sun-hee took the letter and read the first sentence. "I won? I won?" she said, then her head lifted to see her mom's wide grin. "I won!" she shouted, raising her arms in victory, prancing in the dirt. She bounded into her mother's arms.

Lt. Rim interrupted. "If you could get Sun-hee's things together, we must be leaving."

"Leaving now?" Sue-dae blurted without thinking.

"Yes. I will provide transportation to the boarding school. Please get Sun-hee's things."

Sue-dae froze with a glazed look on her face. She focused on her daughter, who had grown from a baby to a young woman, becoming her only companion. She took a deep breath and let it out slowly. "Come, let's get you packed and not keep these men waiting."

Getting Sun-hee's clothes, coat, and other items wrapped in a linen cloth took only a moment. Sun-hee's hands shook so wildly she could not tie it into a bundle.

"Here, let me," said Sue-dae as she wiped tears from her eyes with her sleeve.

"I'm so excited, but I don't want to leave you," said Sun-hee.

"This is a fantastic opportunity. I will be fine. I'm sure I will see you soon."

Sue-dae moved to a wooden box in the corner and took out a blue silk scarf. "There is something I want you to have. This scarf was given to me by my mother when I went to college. Whenever I got lonely, I put it on. It made me feel like my mother was there with me."

She wrapped the blue scarf around Sun-hee's neck, looped it, and pulled it straight before stepping back to admire her daughter. Sun-hee wrapped her arms around her mother. Sue-dae wiped the tear running down her daughter's cheek.

Sun-hee grabbed her bundle, took her mother's hand, and together they walked out of the hut. They followed Lt. Rim to the car, blinking through silent tears neither could hold back.

"I will be an excellent student," Sun-hee said to her mother around the lump in her throat as she climbed into the back seat.

"I know you will," choked out Sue-dae.

Lt. Rim closed the door. The driver placed Sun-hee's bundle in the trunk.

Her daughter placed her fingertips on the car window. Sue-dae did the same from outside, longing for one last touch. They held them there until the car pulled away.

Sue-dae watched the car's dust trail as the light breeze dispersed it into the fields. *My little girl has broken out of our woe.*

She returned to her hut, put the food away, and made herself a cup of tea. After rearranging the books on the shelf, she sat, staring at the walls long after the light of day vanished.

***

Sun-hee turned to wave out the back window, only to lose sight of her mother in the dust illuminated by the setting sun's rays. She turned and sat straight, trying to hold back her tears.

Where will this new adventure take me? Where is the boarding school? What will I learn?

She watched as they drove through Yonggwang, passing Mrs. Pae's house and the school. She waved to one of her teachers on the street, but he did not look her way. Then there were farms, lit on one side by the setting sun, in shadow on the other.

I have won! I am a winner. I won a prize. A smile grew across her face as her chest expanded. She watched the world she had known grow smaller in her periphery.

It was twilight as they drove through Hamhung. They passed the building where she had taken the test, but they did not stop.

Am I the only winner of those who took the test there?

They drove northeast along a winding, bumpy road. Soon it was too dark to see. Sun-hee laid her head back and closed her eyes, dreaming about what the future would hold.

The car stopped abruptly, startling Sun-hee awake.

"Stay in the car," Lt. Rim said as he got out of the car.

What town is this? She sat forward, viewing light in a few windows. *Are we picking up another winner?*

Nothing moved in her view out the side window. She checked the other directions but could not see any movement. Moments later, the trunk opened and closed with a thump. The door opened across from her. A boy entered the car, slammed the door, and turned to wave at the window. Within a few seconds, the car was moving into the darkness.

They made three more stops, adding another boy and then a girl to the back seat. Then one stop to refuel and visit a privy.

Sun-hee had never sat this long next to a boy her age. She tried to make some space by holding her left arm with her right hand. She had so many questions she wanted to ask the girl next to her. But when the boys began talking, Lt. Rim turned and said, "Be quiet."

She turned her head towards the girl, a hint of citrus entered her nose. She laid her head back. Sleep came off and on, only to be interrupted when they hit a pothole or when the car stopped, giving way to convoys of military trucks going the opposite direction. The headlights illuminated glimpses of the road between the men in front of her. The moonless night left everything else a mystery.

Where are we going? What is north of Hamhung? Maybe the school will be near the ocean. That would be nice.

The winding road seemed endless. Again, she laid her head back, closed her eyes, and slept.

Another pothole jarred the car, and she cracked open her eyes. She observed the girl next to her who always faced the window. She wore a nice wool jacket and had long braided hair tied at the ends with a pink ribbon.

Out of the window, Sun-hee caught a foretaste of the light of a new day hovering above the ocean. A moment later, the driver turned left, away from the morning light, into the mountains.

Tires crunched on the gravel, and the washboards vibrated through the leather seat. Sun-hee sat up to better see where they were going. The driver shifted down, and Sun-hee caught glimpses of a fast-flowing stream on the left while a cliff rose straight up on the right.

Higher they went, around turns and switchbacks, until finally, they crested a pass revealing a view of a valley opening into a broad area of farmland. They drove down the mountain, through a wooded area, until the road met a rumbling brook. The car crossed on a one-lane wooden bridge and stopped at a gate. Four soldiers stood, aiming rifles at them. Sun-hee shuddered but did not sense fear in the men in front of her.

Lt. Rim handed a document out the window to one of the soldiers who signaled to open the gate. The car passed through.

Sun-hee sat forward to see where they were going. High fences topped with barbed wire surrounded the area. She saw wooden and cement buildings, military vehicles, soldiers, and other people in the early morning light.

We are in a military camp, Sun-hee realized. The car halted at another gate. *Why are we stopping here?*

A soldier peeked inside before signaling, and the gate opened. They drove in, and the driver turned off the engine.

"Last stop, everyone out," said Lt. Rim as he exited the car.

This place looks more like a prison than a boarding school, thought Sun-hee as she inspected the fences and buildings.

The driver opened the trunk and placed the bags on the ground. Lt. Rim went into a wooden house a few meters away.

Sun-hee shivered in the crisp morning air. She stooped to retrieve her tattered coat and put it on. Her companions stood over their bags, looking at their new surroundings.

The sun broke over a mountain ridge beyond the gate they had just entered. Sun-hee noted that way was east. Her eyes trailed along the high chain-link fence topped with curled barbed wire around the enclosed area. There were four buildings: the weathered wooden house Lt. Rim had gone into, two cement buildings, maybe four times the size of her home, with thatched roofs and a two-meter cement structure between them. On the other side of the fence to the south were more rectangle cement buildings. On the north was an open field, and a brush-covered hillside was to the west.

Sun-hee turned to the sound of a door opening and saw Lt. Rim come out with a middle-aged woman. Her shoulder-length hair was uncombed, and she was buttoning a woolen military coat.

"Hello," she said in a cheery but commanding voice. "I am Sergeant Kua Eun-young. Boys are in the right dorm, and girls are on the left. The privy is in the middle. There are mats and blankets for you inside the door. I will call you for breakfast."

Sun-hee took her bundle and walked with the other girl to the left building. After picking up a mat and blanket, Sun-hee paused a moment to let her eyes adjust and think about what to do. Two girls sitting against the right wall stared at them. The other girls seemed to be sleeping. The sound of sobs came from someone on the left.

Counting seven mats on her left and three to the right, Sun-hee decided to balance the room out. She stepped softly and laid her things next to the farthest one. The other girl followed, putting her mat next to hers. Sun-hee sat down, leaned back, felt the damp cold emanating from the walls, and covered her legs with the blanket.

She closed her eyes. *Why are we at a military camp? This place must be a temporary stop before traveling on to the school.*

Two more girls entered the room. They each picked up a mat and blanket, selecting places along the wall across from her. Sun-hee watched, but she did not move.

A moment later, Sgt. Kua walked in. "Time to get up girls. Fifteen minutes to assembly."

Deciding this was the time to use the privy, Sun-hee was out the door first. The girl who rode with her all night followed close. They got in line behind several boys. The rest of the girls soon lined up.

She turned and said with a polite bow, "Hi, my name is Cha Sun-hee."

"I am Lim Joo-yun," the girl said in a soft voice, bowing towards Sun-hee. Then she cleared her throat and spoke more strongly. "I am pleased to meet you."

Sun-hee noticed the shine in Joo-yun's long hair, parted in the middle, flowing over a full, round face.

"I am from Yonggwang," said Sun-hee. "I was not able to see our location in the dark when you joined me in the car."

"I live in Kimchaek. My father is the harbormaster," said Joo-yun with a slight squint of her eyes and a charming smile. "What does your father do?"

Sun-hee's attention turned to the stylish woolen coat Joo-yun wore. She wrapped her arms over her old coat. "My father was a teacher of mathematics. He died a few years ago," Sun-hee replied.

"Oh, that is too bad."

A boy came out of the privy, saving Sun-hee from the awkward moment. She was next to enter the building. It had four cement walls and an opening to enter and exit. She pursed her nose at the overwhelming stench coming from the fifteen-centimeter-deep channel in the cement floor. She hurried, took notice of the showerhead on the back wall, then joined the line at the sink outside. Taking a moment to wash her hands and face in the chilly water, she tried to look presentable by straightening the scarf around her neck.

I hope the boarding school has a better privy.

Sun-hee waited for Joo-yun before walking back to the girl's dorm. She combed her hair, straightened her mat and blanket, and placed her things against the wall before going back outside. The bright sun dispatched the morning chill.

Sgt. Kua came out of the house dressed in army fatigues and marched to a position facing the two buildings. An army green cloth cap, pointed at both ends, sat atop her hair.

"Everyone out," she ordered. "First thing to learn is how to line up. I want six boys to stand a meter apart in a straight line, the rest of you in rows behind them. Girls do the same."

Sun-hee, being farthest out, took up the first position in the front line of girls, with Joo-yun to her right. The rest got in place within a few seconds.

"This formation is how we will line up from now on," Sgt. Kua said. "We will dispense with exercises as we are expecting more students to arrive today. Follow me. Single file. Boys first, then girls." She turned and began walking toward the gate.

A soldier opened the gate for the procession. Sun-hee observed soldiers moving about in various directions and took note of the olive-green military vehicles parked here and there on the other side of a fence. The buildings were like others she had seen in the military camps built by the Japanese during the occupation, cement walls with wooden and thatched roofs.

They walked in line—but not in step—along a road for a short distance to another gate, which a soldier opened to let them through. The sergeant stopped at a three-walled building joining a line of soldiers. Women handed steaming bowls ladled from pots that were larger than any Sun-hee had seen before. Soldiers squatted or stood in small groups, eating and talking. Some pointed at the queue of boys and girls without uniforms. Sun-hee pulled her coat tight, taking in the scene while keeping up with the boy in front of her.

Sgt. Kua took her bowl, moved to an open space, sat on her heals, and began to eat. The boys followed, grouping themselves to her right. Sun-hee waited for Joo-yun then went to the sergeant's left. The bowl contained a mixture of cooked grains that tasted bland, but it was warm and filling. Since she had missed dinner the night before, she ate faster than she should. Joo-yun took a couple of bites and put her bowl down.

As the last girl joined the group with her bowl, one spoke in a cheery voice. "We might as well get to know each other. My name is Young-ja."

They went around saying their names: Soo-hy, Choe-me, Kyung-hee, Jong-hui, Son-yong, Kum-ja, Sun-hee, Joo-yun, Eun-seong, Mi-na, Kyuung-hwa, Yu-min, and Sang-me.

Sun-hee tried to repeat all the names to herself, memorizing something about them. *Choe-me is the prettiest, Eun-seong is tallest, Joo-yun is the best dressed, Young-ja is outgoing and charismatic,* and so on. *I must work to get to know them. Where are they from? What were their lives like before yesterday?*

Sgt. Kua went to chat with one of the kitchen staff. After a few minutes, she took a few steps towards the students and said, "Put your dishes in the basins and line up. Follow me." She started walking while everyone scrambled to get into a single-file line.

As they entered the dorm area, Sgt. Kua barked, "Back into formation!" It took very little time for the students to get into lines. She looked over the students for a moment before saying, "I have nothing for you until the others get here. Dismissed."

Sun-hee went into the girls' dorm and stood by her mat.

Joo-yun broke the silence. "This place stinks! There is too much dirt on this floor to sleep here."

"And look at all the cobwebs. I hate spiders!" said Choe-me.

"The windows are so dirty, I wonder how the light gets in," added Eun-seong.

"I do not see a broom. If anyone finds a broom, I will sweep," said Young-ja.

Everyone stood, looking at the dust and dirt. Sun-hee spoke up. "I will go ask Sergeant Kua for a broom." She strode out, walking to the house, and knocked softly.

Sgt. Kua opened the door, put her hands on her hips, and with narrow eyes focused on Sun-hee, she said, "What do you want?"

Bowing, Sun-hee said, "I beg your pardon, Sergeant Kua. We were wondering if there might be a broom and some towels we could use to clean our building."

Sgt. Kua's stern look made Sun-hee shiver. "Good idea. I'll get what you need."

"Thank you, Sergeant Kua," Sun-hee said. She returned to the dorm where the rest of the girls stood looking on.

"We will have brooms soon," she said to the cluster of girls in front of the building. She took off her coat and scarf, carefully folding and placing them in her bundle. She sat down on her mat with her knees up to her chest, arms around her legs.

Was I too bold? What does Sergeant Kua think of me?

Joo-yun sat down on her mat next to Sun-hee and said, "I don't think we can make this room clean enough to sleep in."

"We can make it better, Joo-yon. If this is where we are to sleep, we must do what we can."

"If my mother had known I'd be brought to an old Japanese Army camp, she would have kept me home."

"Aren't you excited about winning the prize and going to the boarding school?"

"Only because my father promised he would take me on a trip to the Sea of Okhotsk if I won. When I left, he said we would go in August or September. My mother heard it was a boarding school and insisted I come. She didn't know I was going to a Japanese prison."

"I think this is temporary. I can't imagine this camp as our boarding school." *Would mother have let me go if she had known I was coming to a prison camp?* Sun-hee thought about what her mother's response would be. *This place is better than our hut.*

A shout came from outside. "Brooms!"

Sun-hee jumped up and ran out of the dorm to see two men with wheelbarrows full of brooms, shovels, rakes, and other hand tools coming into the compound.

Most of the girls began to walk towards the tools until Sgt. Kua intervened. "It only takes two of you to get the wheelbarrows," she barked. All the girls stopped. "You and you," commanded the Sgt. "The rest of you and the boys get into formation!"

Everyone jumped into position while the two girls retrieved the wheelbarrows.

"You requested to clean up your buildings, so this is what you will do," said Sgt. Kua. "There are too many holes, rocks, and weeds. I want the area we are standing on to be level. This place will become muddy when it rains. Make some walkways. Dismissed!"

"Cleaning time girls," said Young-ja as she took a broom from the wheelbarrow and started towards the girls' building.

None of the boys moved. They all had dumbfounded looks on their faces. One boy spoke up, "What did you ask for?"

"We asked for a broom," replied Young-ja, raising it in her hand. "Time to get to work." She went into the girl's dorm and kept a running chatter about what she was sweeping up.

Sun-hee looked around again at the barbed wire fences. *While we are here, we can make it livable.* The rest of the students took items from the wheelbarrows. Selecting two rags, Sun-hee went to wash the windows.

***

I have taken a foolish girl's request and made it a task they can work on all day, Sgt. Kua thought. She felt good about the lesson she was teaching these students. She returned to her quarters to wait for lunch.

Sgt. Kua Eun-young had spent most of her life helping refugees flee the Japanese, keeping people safe, meeting their needs, telling them what to do and what not to do to get to safety. She was not a part of the resistance, even though she had contact with them. Helping civilians gave her a purpose. She had been ecstatic when the Japanese left.

To her amazement, she had been given the rank of sergeant four years ago and tasked with training recruits. She had not seen Dr. Park, now Gen. Park, until he had approached her a month ago with orders assigning her to this camp under his command. Now she was here, not to oversee military recruits, but students.

From the window of her new home, Kua watched the students work. *Why did General Park collect these students? Why am I, a fifty-year-old woman, put in charge? Where is the general?*

***

Sun-hee teamed up with Eun-seong to wash windows. Eun-seong, being the tallest, could reach the top on the outside. Sun-hee cleaned the inside. On the fourth window, there was a big cobweb. Sun-hee asked, "Young-ja, can you sweep this cobweb out of the corner of this window?"

"Glad to," replied Young-ja. She swept the broom over the window

A spider ran across the inside of the window right where Eun-seong washed the outside. She let out a piercing scream, stumbled back, and fell on her butt.

With her rag in hand, Sun-hee smashed the spider against the window. Everyone stopped and stared as she snatched her hand away, letting the rag drop, leaving the splattered spider on the window. She stepped back, grabbing her pounding chest.

"Oh, my," exclaimed Choe-me.

"You got him Sun-hee!" yelled Young-ja, holding her arms and broom in the air. "One less spider to haunt us."

Sun-hee beheld the squished spider on the window, took a couple of deep breaths, picked up the rag, and carefully wiped away the spider guts. Then she went to the sink to rinse the cloth and get her heartrate back to normal.

Eun-seong, having been helped to her feet, joined Sun-hee at the sink. "Thank you for getting that spider," Eun-seong said to Sun-hee, rinsing her rag. "I wouldn't have slept if it were still alive."

"I hope there are no more," replied Sun-hee. "None of us would sleep until we get to the boarding school."

"Do you know where the school is?" Eun-seong asked.

"No, but I don't think this is the school the letter referred to," said

Sun-hee. "It doesn't look like a school. I'm hoping it is only temporary."

"At least we can make it a safe place to sleep tonight," said Eun-seong.

As Sun-hee went into the dorm to continue washing, she noticed Joo-yun standing by herself, stroking one of her pigtails, and staring at the ground. Sun-hee stopped to ask, "Are you alright, Joo-yun?"

"I am fine."

"Is there a reason why you are not helping to clean up the dorm?"

"My mother would not allow me to use a broom. We hired women to clean," said Joo-yun.

"I hope the rest of us clean well enough for you to sleep tonight," said Sun-hee, and she bounded off.

***

The sun was high overhead when Sgt. Kua walked out of her house and yelled, "Get in line!"

Everyone dropped what they were doing and ran to line up. Sgt. Kua marched back and forth, looking sternly at each person. Then she went into each of the buildings and walked around the area.

Sun-hee's knees twitched. She had started this cleanup. Now she felt she would be the focus of any criticism. She tried to stand still, wanting to watch the Sgt. but forcing herself to face away from the dorms.

Finally, Sgt. Kua returned to her place in front of the formation and cast a glare at Sun-hee. "Everyone wash-up and return to formation. Then we will go to lunch."

Sun-hee turned, realized she would be last in line to use the sink, and headed to the privy.

The trough is clear of feces and urine. Someone figured out how to flush the waste. As she waited to use the sink, she noticed rocks outlining paths from the boy's dorm to the privy. *Their feet will not be in the mud. The boys have dug channels to allow rainwater to drain. We did a lot this morning.* She was the last to wash and took a position in the back row. As soon as she looked up, the Sgt. turned, leading them to lunch.

***

Late in the afternoon, a car entered the gate to the dorm area, followed by a bus. Sgt. Kua came out and saluted as a uniformed man stepped out of the vehicle. "Get these students situated," the man ordered before he walked into the house.

"Formation," the sergeant yelled and began walking towards the dorm.

Boys and girls stepped off the bus with their bags and bundles. They seemed lost as they got off the bus. Some looked around, others stared at the line of students staring at them.

Sgt. Kua pointed at some of the boys and commanded, "Each of you help the new boys to get their things situated. Eight of you girls do the same for the new girls. The rest of you, gather up the tools and place them in the wheelbarrows."

The students scattered about, accomplishing their appointed tasks, while the bus rumbled to life and backed out of the compound followed by the car.

One by one, the students got into line, filling up the formation of six rows of four boys and the same for the girls. The last of the new boys came running out of the privy. Another boy pointed to where he should line up.

Sgt. Kua proceeded to walk around, examining each student.

Sun-hee's knees trembled. She noticed the students around her fidgeting. Dust acquired during the day of cleaning covered the arms and clothes of the girl in front of her. Moon Choe-me had a streak of dirt across her perfectly formed cheek.

Do I look as dirty as they do?

Sgt. Kua made another loop and stopped at Sun-hee. "What is your name?"

"Cha Sun-hee," she replied in a quiet voice while trying to still her trembling hands.

"Are you satisfied with the cleanup you requested?"

"We have made progress, Sergeant Kua. There is much more to do."

The sergeant. stared into Sun-hee's eyes. The song of a distant bird pierced the silence.

Sun-hee looked straight ahead at the point in the sergeant's hat while her stomach tied itself in a knot. A door opened. Sgt. Kua turned on a toe and shouted, "Forty-eight recruits ready for your inspection General."

Sun-hee released a deep breath as Sgt. Kua moved to a place midway in front of the students and stood at attention.

The man of average build strode directly towards them. Red and gold bands on his shoulders revealed the rank of a general. Four large polished buttons on his jacket flashed in the sunlight. A wide bowl-shaped hat was pulled low on his forehead, the brim casting a shadow over his deep-set eyes.

When the man reached Sgt. Kua, he slowed, walking back and forth in front of the formation of boys and girls. Sun-hee stood tall and straight. The heads of those in front of her followed his movements.

He stopped his pacing in front of Sgt. Kua and held out his arms towards the students. His booming voice shattered the tense silence. "You have WON! By scoring the highest on the test you took two weeks ago, you have won a most amazing prize. A chance to make a difference in the future of our new nation, the Democratic People's Republic of Korea." He spoke with great enthusiasm. "YOU are the BEST and BRIGHTEST youth of our NATION."

Sun-hee felt her heart beat faster. *Finally, we get to know what the prize is.*

"As winners, you will receive training, education, and leadership!" the General said. "You and your offspring will become the leaders of Korea. Welcome to *Yangseongso.*"

He calls this the training school. We must be staying here. The man paused for a moment, his head moving from side to side, eyes focused on the students.

"Let me introduce myself. I'm General Park. I am a Doctor. Our Premier, the illustrious Kim Il-sung, has appointed me the Director of Medicine in North Korea. My purpose in life is to make our people healthy and our nation great."

Sun-hee felt relief. *This man is the director of medicine, not an army officer.*

"I have instituted the prize and this program for the glory of the Democratic People's Republic of Korea."

Sun-hee's knees stopped shaking. Her heartbeat slowed, her chest expanded, and she stood taller, honored to be among Gen. Park's prize winners.

"To make any difference in our new society, we must be loyal. Your total loyalty must be to our sacred leader Premier Kim Il-sung. Secondly, you must be loyal to the Democratic People's Republic of Korea. Thirdly, you must be loyal to me and the program you are now part of." He paused, studying each of the faces.

"If you cannot swear to these loyalties, you will be escorted out the gate." He pointed back with his right hand. "And you will be taken home." The general walked back and forth, glaring at the children as he paced.

"Does anyone wish to leave?" He paused, studying the expressions on each child before him.

Sun-hee stayed where she was, knowing her mother would want her to stay and serve the premier, her country, and Gen. Park. She glanced over at Joo-Yun, who lifted her right foot, then put it back down.

"Now repeat after me, 'I am loyal to Kim Il-sung!'" said Gen. Park loudly.

The forty-eight replied, "I am loyal to Kim Il-sung."

"I am loyal to the Democratic People's Republic of Korea!" barked the general.

"I am loyal to the Democratic People's Republic of Korea," echoed the forty-eight, louder and in better unison.

"I am loyal to General Park!"

"I am loyal to General Park," the students said in almost perfect unison.

"Look around at each other." He paused. Sun-hee looked at those in front of her. No one moved. "*You* are the prize," he said, pausing again. "You have the privilege to work together and become the foundation of our nation." He started slowly pacing in front of the students. "Maintain your loyalty, and you will attain more than you ever thought possible."

Then he stopped and looked back and forth at the youth lined up before him. "This is a top-secret program. You will tell no one about this place. You will not leave this camp, and only those of us here know what we will be doing. If your loyalty should ever falter, I will remove you from this program." The general paused to look at the faces, and in a stern voice said, "Removal is by execution."

Sun-hee caught her breath, and her knees wobbled. *I must be loyal.*

Gen. Park turned, whispering something to the sergeant.

"Yes, sir," Sgt. Kua replied. The students stood at attention until Gen. Park entered the house. When the door closed, Sgt. Kua barked, "Get cleaned up. Be standing in formation in thirty minutes. Dismissed!"

***

Sgt. Kua stood motionless, watching the students scurry. *I'm glad Park has arrived. I am sure his plans will benefit Korea. Why did he emphasize secrecy?*

The last words he had whispered to her ran through her mind. "You are part of this program. I expect your absolute loyalty."

What is Park doing?

She recalled how she had brought the sick and wounded to Dr. Park, trusting he would care for them.

Now he has chosen me to care for forty-eight teenagers who passed a test to be here. An ominous feeling of responsibility turned her stomach.

She muttered, "I don't want to be anywhere else."

Illustration - Layout of the training camp.

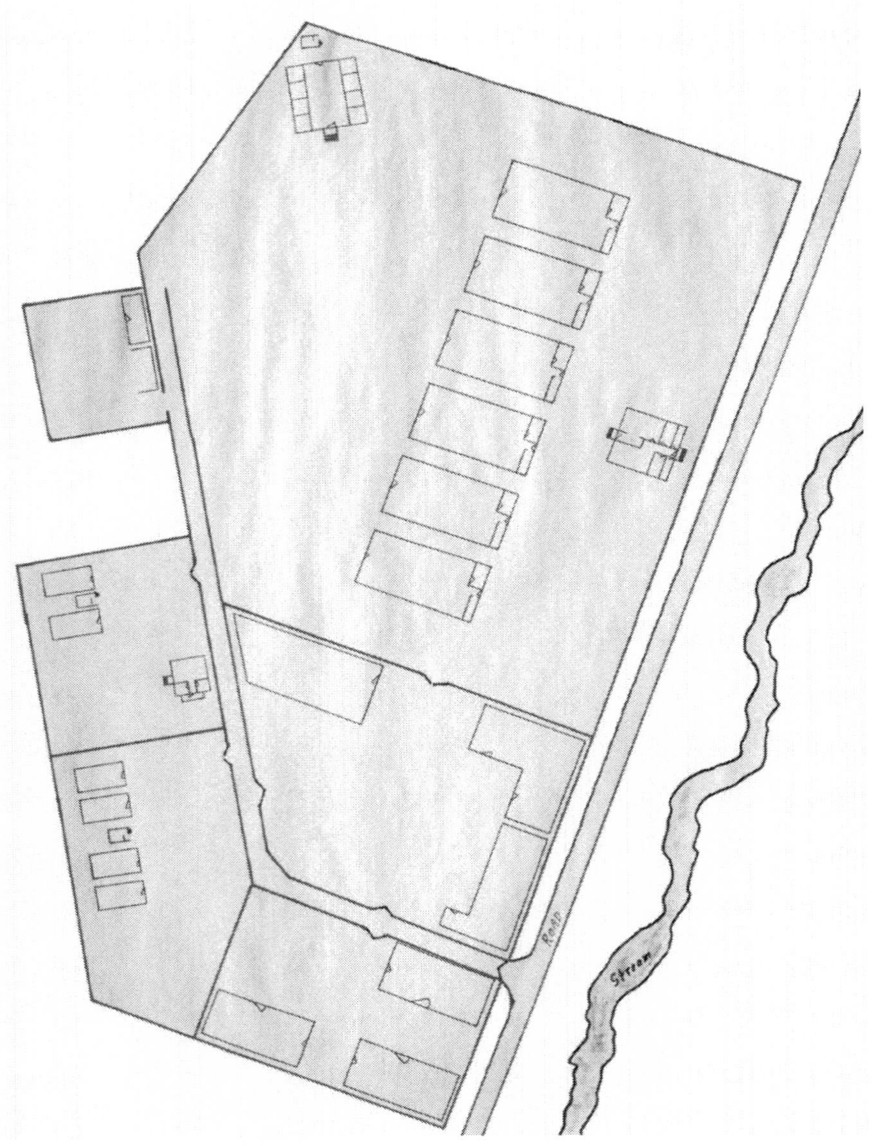

3 — Yangseongso - May 27 - 28, 1950

As Sun-hee shuffled into the dorm with the other girls, Gen. Park's words replayed in her mind. She sat straight-legged on her mat and stared at her feet.

I won a prize but cannot tell anyone. Why is Yangseongso top secret?

Joo-yun, sitting cross-legged on her mat facing Sun-hee, whispered through a sob, "What did General Park mean? Will we be able to see our families again? Have we been brought to a prison?" She glanced around to make sure no one was eavesdropping. Her eyes stopped to focus on Choe-me sitting on her haunches on the other side of Sun-hee.

Catching the gaze, Sun-hee looked over at Choe-me.

"I, too, feel trapped, but I know this is where I belong. I will follow," said Choe-me in a meek voice.

Sun-hee turned to look at Joo-yun and said in a soft voice, "I can't imagine we are captives Joo-yun. We will see our families soon. Everyone must be loyal to the state."

"I have never been away from home. I should have left when General Park said we could," Joo-yun said, following her words with a sniffle.

"You wanted to. I saw you start to move. Why didn't you leave?" questioned Sun-hee.

"I…I was…I just want to go home."

"This is my first time away from my mother. I know she would want me to stay and work to make her proud. To leave would dishonor her."

"What are we going to do?" asked Choe-me.

Sun-hee sat in thought for a moment, before saying, "What can we do? Are there options?"

Eun-seong crawled over from her mat in the corner. "Right now, we are here. We can only do the right thing and hope someday our families will hear about how we served our country with honor."

Sun-hee added, "I think you are right, Eun-seong. We do what we must do. We will be loyal to our Premier, our country, and General Park. As General Park said, our loyalty will lead to great things. You will do wonderful things, Joo-yun. You will make your family proud." Her voice gained strength as she spoke.

"How can we make our families proud if we can't tell them?" Joo-yun said, rubbing a tear from her cheek.

Sun-hee replied, "I don't know. My mother expects me to do my best, which is all I can do. She did her best to provide for me after my father died. I am proud of her." Her voice cracked, and she hung her head low. "It will be hard for my mother if she never hears from me again. Had I known winning this prize would mean never seeing her again, I would have failed the test." Tears crept out and meandered down her cheeks.

"I was always taught to be loyal to my family," said Joo-yun. "Loyalty to General Park does not feel right!"

Eun-seong handed a handkerchief to Joo-yun. She placed her hands over Joo-yun's and Sun-hee's hands. "I have heard of people put to death because they cannot pledge their loyalty to the Premier and our nation. Life is better here than in the south. Communists are put to death there."

Sun-hee raised her head to look at Eun-seong. "Where are you from?"

"Kaesong, near the border. When the country split, there were lots of people going south and just as many people were coming into the north. I'm glad to be away from the turmoil the refugees were causing. I think my father was glad to have me go to a safer place, away from the border. I'm sure he didn't think it would be this far."

"What are we going to do?" asked Joo-yun in a pleading tone.

"Let us get ready to learn how to become leaders who can change our country. What this means right now is getting ready for dinner," Sun-hee said, reaching into her bag, pulling out a clean shirt and changing into it. Joo-yun, Choe-me, and Eun-seong did the same. Together they went to wash. They were the last ones to get into formation before marching off to eat.

Dinner consisted of stew made up of little bits of pork, potatoes, lots of cabbage, and a few other mushy, overcooked vegetables all mixed in a sauce thickened with cornstarch.

After dinner, Sgt. Kua led the recruits back to the dorms, calling them into formation and starting exercises.

Soon, Sun-hee felt like the rag doll she played with as a child. Her legs and arms flopped, her mind wandered, and she could not catch her breath. Choe-me stopped and put her hands on her knees, panting. Other girls were exercising at half the pace Sgt. Kua was keeping. Sun-hee went on autopilot, not thinking, just trying to follow instructions.

The sun slipped behind a mountain, casting the camp in shadow.

She heard the words, "Put hands together in front of you. Breathe in. Feel the fresh air in your lungs. Breath out." She let her body relax, catching herself before she crumpled.

Sgt. Kua barked, "I am loyal to Premier Kim Il-sung."

Together the students repeated the chant. It was followed by, "I am loyal to the Democratic People's Republic of Korea. I am loyal to General Park." The last chant Sun-hee said with a big sigh. Exercises were over.

"Breathe deeply, take in life, and go rest. We are all together. Tomorrow will be a challenging day," concluded Sgt. Kua.

Sun-hee noticed the smile on Sgt. Kua's face. *What will General Park have for us tomorrow?*

"I am loyal to my family," said Joo-yun loud enough for only Sun-hee to hear. They made their way to their mats. Sun-hee laid down and was asleep before a worry could cross her mind.

***

"Time to get up. One hour to get ready," Sgt. Kua's voice rang out.

The dorm room came alive as twenty-four girls went about getting ready for the day. Sun-hee and Choe-me walked out together into a steady rain. The boys were ahead of them in the privy line, so they retreated inside and arranged their things.

"This is too early to get up," complained Joo-yun.

"We need this time for everyone to use the privy," said Eun-seong.

"I have this hat that keeps the rain off my head," said Young-ja. "When I was younger, I liked to dance in puddles and tried to catch drops on my tongue. Actually, I do not like rain. But I don't care, I have my hat."

Sun-hee smiled and noticed the grins of the other girls around her.

A couple of girls came in dripping wet. Sun-hee decided it was time to get in line and headed out the door. She watched the rain runoff in the channels carved into the ground the day before. The stone pathways still needed work, but they kept her feet from sinking into the muck.

If this is where we are to be, we have a lot of work to make it livable.

The steady rain soaked her hair, and her muscles ached during exercises. At breakfast, she watched the drops form on her bangs and then splash into her bowl.

"You look funny, staring cross-eyed at your hair," said Young-ja, chuckling.

Sun-hee refocused before shaking her head side to side, spraying Young-ja.

Young-ja leaped back, and they both laughed.

Following the long line back to the compound, she heard Sgt. Kua yell, "Formation! Quickly! Do not keep General Park waiting any longer."

Sun-hee ran to get in place. She skidded in the mud and caught herself. Others also slipped as they ran, but no one fell.

Once in line, Sun-hee labored to catch her breath before hearing Gen. Park say, "Today, we begin your education. I will be your teacher this morning. In the future, we will have teachers from the new university in Chongjin." His attention shifted. "Sergeant Kua, have them assemble in front of the library in thirty minutes." He turned and walked away, leaving footprints in the mud.

Sgt. Kua commanded, "Return in fifteen minutes." Then she trotted out of the gate. Everyone scattered to get ready for the day.

The rain had diminished to a sprinkle by the time Sgt. Kua returned. She motioned from the gate at the formation of students and called, "Follow me, double file."

As she walked down the road through the middle of the compound, Sun-hee observed the soldiers, jeeps, artillery, trucks, and other military equipment on the other side of a fence to her right.

Will we become soldiers?

They passed the kitchen and marched towards the north end of the compound.

They approached a two-story white building and got into formation. Gen. Park removed his muddy boots on the steps and climbed to the wide porch. From this position above the students, he addressed them.

"We are in the process of turning this building into an education center for you and the officers on this base. The books and references inside are what I could assemble in a short amount of time. Come in, and we will begin."

Sun-hee removed her muddy sandals, placing them on the bottom step before entering the building.

Is this the boarding school? Why here? Why not at a college or university? Where in North Korea am I?

The double doorway opened into a large room with stairs in the middle, climbing towards the back of the building. A walkway went all the way around the upstairs, open to the room below. There were four closed doors on each side of the lower great room. She counted four doors on each side of the second story, a total of sixteen side rooms.

Scattered around the great room were tables piled with books, chairs here and there. Boxes were stacked along walls and dispersed on the floor. All were obstacles for the forty-eight students moving into the room.

Gen. Park took a couple of steps up the stairs and said, "As you can see, we need to put this room in order, get shelves built and the books sorted out. Today we will start with a subject I know well, anatomy and physiology. Find a chair or space on the floor."

Sun-hee sat, leaning against boxes piled against a wall. She listened as Gen. Park explained the systems of human anatomy, reviewing the organs involved, and their roles. She found the instruction stimulating. The general's ability to explain anatomy was easy to follow.

After a while, he crossed the room to stand by the front door. He opened a large pull-down chart of the skeletal system mounted on the wall. He pointed to each bone and described its function.

Sun-hee had no idea how long they sat listening to the lecture. She focused on Gen. Park's words, enjoying learning from an expert. When he got to the last of the bones, he paused and looked outside before saying, "There must be some books around here on anatomy. Find them, get together in groups, and memorize the bones and systems of the human body." He turned and went out to the porch. Sun-hee began to search through the boxes next to her.

***

Gen. Park lit a cigarette and took a long draw while scanning the camp before him.

Lt. Rim hustled over from the southeast, holding a letter. Park took a couple of steps down to meet him.

"You have chosen a good location, lieutenant. This compound is isolated, away from the distractions of a city. The parents can't interfere like last year, and we eliminated children of high officials this time. Next year we will be more prepared."

Gen. Park opened the letter and took a few moments to read.

"This letter says we are going to war with the south. I need to go to Pyongyang. Continue to keep an eye on this group. If any of the students try to leave, make sure they do not get home. Do not let the army interfere with them. Who knows what these young soldiers might do to these students."

"Yes, sir."

"As you were," said Gen. Park. They exchanged salutes before the lieutenant jogged back to stand in the shadow of a building where he could watch the library.

Park flashed back to the day Rim Seung-gin was carried to the clinic over the Russian border with severe wounds. Park spent two days working to save his life and a month nursing him back to health. The story of the massacre of Rim's family by the Japanese touched him, so he took Rim on as an assistant. Rim's expertise in street bartering and a knack for accounting made him a valuable asset to have around. Without a family, Rim was a good soldier, loyal, and followed orders without question.

The general stepped up to the porch and looked inside for Kua. She sat on the stairs, overseeing his students. "Sergeant," Gen. Park said, motioning her to meet him by the door. He was entrusting these students to a woman who had led families, often carrying their children, out of the war zone.

She is tough, and she cares. When she knows my plan, can I trust her?

Once she was outside, Park said, "I have to leave for a few days. In the mornings, have the students work on the compound. Start a garden; we will need all the food we can grow. In the afternoons bring them here to the library. Have them study the sciences: anatomy, physiology, medicine, physics, math, engineering, chemistry, and geology. Let them read and work with each other. Also, language is important. The decree is to use only Korean. They should also learn Russian. I will be back in a week to provide further instructions." He turned towards the steps, then stopped, "One more thing…I need to know the menstrual cycle of the girls. Write down the day each starts bleeding. Any questions?"

"No, General," she answered.

"Dismissed," he said.

Sgt. Kua responded with a bow and returned to the library.

Park lit another cigarette, took the letter from his pocket, and reread it. Most of the two pages were bureaucratic babble. It was the last line he focused on: "Prepare medical staff for war. Must remain a secret."

The country is going to war. Never in the history of humanity have doctors been prepared for war. Damnit! I must make Yangseongso work. It is the future of Korea. Damn the rest of the world.

The general took the steps down to where his boots lay, put them on, and trudged across the muddy grounds.

Kim Il-sung had approved of a school for gifted students. Last year's attempt in Pyongyang had failed due to the interference of parents and government officials. Park hoped they would not discover his ultimate plan.

Even though he and the Premier had grown up together, there was no way the Premier would accept what he wanted to do. He remembered the games they played as children, always by Il-sung's rules. When a group of boys rejected Il-sung's directions for making paper lanterns, he tore up all the paper in a tantrum so that no one could make lanterns. A couple of weeks later, Il-sung and his family had vanished.

A month later, Park's father led his family over the mountains across the Yalu River to China and then north to the Soviet Union. He had been fortunate to get into a Russian school, even luckier to attend the University of Moscow to study medicine. The fates were with him when he returned to the Soviet border. He became reacquainted with his childhood playmate, now a leader in the Korean resistance against the Japanese.

***

The next morning, Sgt. Kua made her way to the small town near the compound, just a cluster of huts amid small farms.

Why does Gen. Park need to know the timing of the girl's flow? Sgt. Kua wondered. She had tasked the students with continuing to improve the grounds and starting a garden, allowing her to get to town. Kua found a vendor and purchased all the menstrual rags and belts available, a total of five, then ordered another nineteen. The vendor told her they would be available in a couple of days.

That evening, after all the girls returned to their dorm, she entered and said, "Girls. I have a supply of menstrual rags. Let me know when you start your flow, and I will provide you with one."

4 — Introductions - May 28 - June 20, 1950

Sun-hee enjoyed working with the other girls in the garden. They talked and giggled, mostly at the comments of Young-ja, as they labored together. Sun-hee tried to get to know where the girls were from, what they liked, their voices and mannerisms. The girls and boys were like land and air: both present, but they did not interact. Sun-hee had not even heard the boy's names.

That afternoon, a book on meteorology caught Sun-hee's eye as she entered the library. She picked it up and sat at an empty table to the right of the stairs. Joo-yun sat down next to her.

Eun-seong came over and put her hand on the chair across from Sun-hee. "May I sit here?"

"Please join us," replied Sun-hee.

A moment later, Choe-me sat next to Eun-seong.

Laughter erupted from a gaggle of girls across the room. Sun-hee looked up to see Young-ja, with a wide grin, walking towards her.

"I need a quiet group if I am going to study," said Young-ja as she pulled a chair to the end of the table and sat between Eun-seong and Sun-hee.

"I am glad to have you join us," said Eun-seong. "I see Sun-hee has a book on the weather. I will go look for other books on meteorology, so we can all study the same thing." She stood and began to browse.

Sun-hee turned to a chapter on clouds and began to read aloud. "There are ten basic types of clouds: Altocumulus, Altostratus, Cirrus, Cirrocumulus, Cirrostratus, Cumulus, Cumulonimbus, Nimbostratus, Stratus, and Stratocumulus." She went on to read aloud about each one as the other three girls listened. Eun-seong returned with three other books, handing one to Young-ja and Joo-yun.

"Choe-me and I can share this one," she said.

They read silently for a while. Then Young-ja asked, "Who can tell me what types of clouds produce rain?"

"Nimbostratus are the clouds that rained on us yesterday," said Eun-seong.

"Cumulonimbus produce thunderstorms and downpours," said Joo-yun. "These are the ones sailors avoid as they can have high winds."

"One more," said Young-ja.

"Mist and dew come from altostratus," said Choe-me.

"All correct," said Young-ja.

In this way, their study group formed. These were the girls who slept near Sun-hee in the dorm. Joo-yun, seeming to need her friendship, was never far away. Young-ja would dominate their conversation, start a discussion, and verbally quiz everyone on what they were learning. Eun-seong had a knack for speaking up when there was a disagreement, offering a resolution to the conflict. She always had a kind word to offer. Choe-me was the quiet one. Shy, yet so pretty she did not have to say anything to dominate a room. Sun-hee translated for the group when needed. Together they focused on learning.

That evening as they lay on their mats, Sun-hee said to Joo-yun, "I liked working with our study group today."

"The instruction at my school was limited," Joo-yun replied.

"Everyone seems to understand what we read," Sun-hee said.

"There are no slow kids here to make the teacher repeat herself," said Joo-yun. "I mostly understood the Russian book I was reading. Your translation was a great help."

"The text I read was in Mandarin. There were only a couple of characters I could not make out. I am glad my mother spent all those nights teaching me various languages," said Sun-hee. "I also know some English, but I have not seen any books written in English here. It doesn't seem to be useful."

"Wow! You know five languages! I know three: Korean, Japanese, and Russian. But I cannot speak in Russian," said Joo-yun.

"I can speak and read Mandarin," interrupted Choe-me. "But I have trouble reading the technical books."

"I was exposed only to Japanese until the war was over," said Eun-seong. "Now I am struggling to get up to speed in Korean."

"We all know Japanese. They were assimilating us," said Young-ja as she crawled to the end of Choe-me's mat. "My grandparents made sure I knew Korean. Every evening they would take my sisters and me into their room and teach us to read, write, and speak Korean. They made me tell them what I was doing as I went around our home."

"That explains why you talk all the time," said Choe-me.

"Here, it looks like Korean and Russian are most important," said Sun-hee. "Joo-yun and I will teach you Russian in the evenings."

Thus, language sessions began.

***

A few days later, a uniformed man stood on the porch of the library as the herd of students arrived for their afternoon study session.

"Are you Sergeant Kua?" he asked when they got close.

"Yes," she said.

"I am Professor Li Jong-soon from the University of Pyongyang. I was in Chongjin interviewing potential professors. General Park asked me to teach mathematics today. Are these the students I am to instruct?"

"Yes, professor," Sgt. Kua said. Then she turned. "Students, inside quickly. Professor Li will lead."

Sun-hee found a place and sat cross-legged on the floor facing a blackboard. Professor Li covered the basics of geometry and algebra. Sun-hee felt she already knew everything the professor taught. She made mental notes of the few things she did not understand or were different from what she previously understood. Professor Li drew a trapezoid, using right angles to find the height. Then he explained the equation to find the area.

This equation would not work for trapezoids with non-parallel ends, thought Sun-hee.

But she remained silent like everyone else, not asking questions. The students did not take notes because there was no paper, so they sat attentively and listened.

It was not until they were ready for bed that Joo-yun spoke up. "Did everyone understand all the professor's instructions today? I thought I knew a lot about geometry, but a few things were different than I learned in school."

Young-ja exclaimed, "I have always been horrible at math, and now I'm more confused than I ever was. I am going to need some help with this math stuff."

"Me too," said Eun-seong.

"What a relief," sighed Young-ja. "I thought I was the only one who didn't understand geometry. We will have to find a math expert tomorrow and beg them for help."

"I think we all have a lot to learn, Young-ja," added Eun-seong. "There is a lot to know, and we should think of ourselves as a collective of knowledge rather than a lot of individuals. There is too much to know for all of us to know everything. Over time we need to specialize."

Joo-yun said, "We could be learning at a university, but we are here in this camp for some reason I do not understand. I expected a formal school."

"Until someone tells me differently, I will learn about everything," said Choe-me. "We have not been told to specialize. Even though I hate math, I will work extra hard."

"Tomorrow, I will try to help with what I know," Sun-hee said. "Maybe someone knows more than I do and can explain it better. We must help each other."

After she sat down, Joo-yun said, "Algebra confuses me, Sun-hee. I used to help my dad with his navigation work at the harbor, so I understand geometry."

"My father was a math teacher. All I know is from school and reading his books. Books explained the concepts but gave no practical application. Will you show me how to use geometry in navigation?"

"Yes, I will show you how to apply geometry if you help me with algebra."

"That's a deal," said Sun-hee.

***

The next afternoon, when the whole group was in the library, Sun-hee said to everyone, "We need to review what Professor Li taught us yesterday and make sure everyone understands. I am looking for a book on algebra to help me review."

One of the boys spoke up. "The books will help, but we need to correct some things Professor Li said. He made some mistakes. Easy for a person to do when teaching for so long without notes."

Sun-hee smiled. She wasn't the only one who had caught some errors.

Ahn Ching-ying showed confidence in his math knowledge. He was not very tall, maybe a centimeter more than Sun-hee. His clothes hung on him like they were on a hook on the wall. He was one of the least attractive boys, but he did know math. He explained the concepts and then found problems in math books for everyone to work on. When he spoke about math, he spoke in a way that made it sound simple, yet only a few of the students could do the problems he put on the blackboard. Sun-hee spent some time reviewing algebra with Joo-yun, who then explained how geometry is used to navigate. By the end of the afternoon, Sun-hee thought she had made considerable progress.

As they returned to the camp, Sun-hee walked next to Young-ja and commented, "That boy sure knows his math."

"I am going to call him *beonho*," she said. "I like to give nicknames to people. He is now *beonho*."

"Numbers is a good nickname," said Sun-hee. "What is my nickname?"

"Only boys get nicknames," Young-ja said. "You will always be Sun-hee. Never anything else."

"What other nicknames have you devised?"

"None that I am sure of yet. I have some ideas, but I need to make sure they are the right names before I start using them."

"You will tell me when you name someone?"

"You will be the first to know unless I tell someone else first," replied Young-ja with a big grin.

***

A few mornings later, Sun-hee went to work in the garden. She looked at the plot of ground and said, "What else is there to do? This garden looks like we're ready for planting."

One of the boys spoke up. "There are four things we need to do. Terrace the hillside as it is still too steep, figure out the irrigation, add fertilizer, and make furrows. The width of the furrows depends on what we will plant. For fertilizer, we need to start relieving ourselves in buckets that we can dump on the garden."

"Ew," said Young-ja, scrunching up her nose.

Sun-hee's stomach turned over.

Young-ja whispered into Sun-hee's ear. "His nickname is Naemsae naneun."

Sun-hee nodded. "Stinky fits perfectly." She snickered.

"We needed a son of a farmer to take over," Joo-yun said to Sun-hee. "Too much work for too little food. I hate working with dirt."

"I have one other nickname for you Sun-hee," said Young-ja. "The boy over there who is always digging. He picks up and looks at each rock he uncovers."

"Yes, I have noticed him."

"He is a *Dol*."

"Stone?"

"He has never said a word, always by himself, so I named him Stone."

"Good choice,"

After lunch, the students trooped to the library. When they arrived, they noticed a stack of boards and wooden strips laying on the ground near the steps. Two men in dirty gray work clothes stood next to the wood, arguing about how to make a bookcase. As she entered the library, Sun-hee realized why they argued. On the right side of the main room lay a few boards amongst a pile of books, a failed attempt to make a bookcase.

"They do not know what they are doing," said one of the good-looking boys who had previously caught Sun-hee's eye. "There is no base and no back. Of course, it will fall over."

Sgt. Kua inquired, "Could you do better, Ho Hon-yong?"

"This is easy stuff, Sergeant Kua," he said with a respectful bow. "My father is a carpenter in Pyongyang. He taught me carpentry since I was a boy. With a few tools, I could make bookcases from the wood outside." He stood straight, straining the buttons across his chest.

"Good," said Sgt. Kua, walking outside. She yelled at the two men, "Go and leave the tools. We will make the bookcases." Then she called, "Mr. Ho!" Hon-yong ran out of the library. Sun-hee followed to see what was going on.

"Are these tools adequate for the task?" asked Sgt. Kua.

Hon-yong looked around, making a note of the hand saw, hammer, string, a bag of nails, and two sawhorses. "Yes, honorable Sergeant, these tools are adequate," he said. "I would prefer a better quality saw. This one looks quite worn," he replied respectfully.

"Work with the rest of the students to make a plan for making the bookcases. I will see if I can find better tools," she said and marched off into the compound.

Hon-yong showed everyone how to make a solid bookcase with cross boards and a sturdy base. He taught them how to measure with string and how to cut wood and nail it together. Everyone went to work moving books and boxes, clearing space by the walls.

Sgt. Kua entered the library. She handed some tools to the first student she met. "Mr. Ho," she barked, "what is the plan?"

Hon-yong explained the plan in detail, having others show where the bookcases would go, the bookcase dimensions, and how the books would fit into them.

The results of her request were apparently beyond her expectations. She cut off Hon-yong's explanation. "Build them!" She sat down on the steps to watch.

Hon-yong was in his element. He demonstrated how to saw boards straight, not an easy task for those who had never handled a saw.

Sun-hee tried sawing a board. She struggled to keep the saw straight, and her arm was soon limp. She handed the saw to a boy.

Hon-yong showed how to hammer nails. No one found it as easy as

Hon-yong made it look. Many nails were bent or went in at wrong angles. Someone smashed their thumb.

Hon-yong demanded each measurement be made twice by different people before cutting the wood. Some students sorted books by topic and then filled the completed shelves.

Young-ja commented on the way to dinner, "I can't believe we made so many bookcases. Half the books are in place in one afternoon."

"What is Hon-yong's nickname?" asked Sun-hee.

"I was thinking about naming him Namu but changed it today to Mangchi."

"The name Hammer fits him perfectly," replied Sun-hee. "Much better than Tree."

***

The sun was blazing at breakfast, and Sun-hee motioned to Eun-seong saying, "It is too hot to work in the garden today. Let's go to the library."

"Good idea. I am tired of digging our dung into the soil. Stinky has the garden under control. He doesn't need us," said Eun-seong as the two went the opposite way of the rest of the students.

"Ew the dust," exclaimed Sun-hee as she tried to wave away the dirt kicked up by the soldiers performing drills. "I am glad we made paths in our area."

"We can get them some rocks from the hill," said Eun-seong, pointing through the fence to the left.

"I'm not picking up any more rocks," said Sun-hee.

They kicked off their shoes on the steps and entered the library. "Do you remember how jumbled this place was the first day we were here?" asked Sun-hee.

"It was a nightmare. I was cramped in the front corner. Halfway through Park's lecture I had to pee. I wish I'd known there was a privy out back," said Eun-seong.

"I went out there to get away from the geology lecture," said Sun-hee. "That professor taught us like we were in grade school."

"Do you remember how Stone cornered the geology professor afterward? I didn't know Stone could talk, but he asked question after question."

"Then Chou Sung-man asked me to translate the English chemistry book after the lecture on the elements. So many of the terms have no Korean equivalent. I am glad I found the English dictionary."

"Is that when you moved all the dictionaries to the bookcase next to our table?" Eun-seong said as she patted the table before her and sat down.

"If I have to translate, I need the references," said Sun-hee.

"What are we going to study today?" asked Eun-seong.

"I think I will find a long novel."

"I could use a story with action and adventure. If it were not for making new friends like you, I would hate this place."

"We have settled into a tedious routine after three weeks. Let me get a vision of another part of the world," said Sun-hee. She picked up *A Room with a View* and *Howards End* and began to read.

Eun-seong said, "Time for some adventure." She opened *Story of the Bandit.*

***

Sgt. Kua paced around the main room of her house. Three girls had requested rags during the week, only one the week before. By her simple calculations, twice as many should have started their periods. She would have to watch to see if anyone showed signs but did not request rags or had their own.

She heard the gate opening behind her. General Park was walking through it. It had been three weeks since he'd left.

She yelled, "Formation!"

Students stopped what they were doing and ran to get in place.

Gen. Park strolled around, inspecting the compound, pausing to view the garden before circling the student formation. He stopped in front.

"Thank you for looking after this group in my absence, Sergeant Kua," he said in her direction, but loud enough for all to hear. "I must apologize for being away so long."

He turned to address the students. "Today, we will perform a health physical. To assist me are a doctor and his assistants." He gestured towards a man and two women by the gate wearing white lab coats. "Please cooperate with them. You three, go now," he said, pointing to the closest boys. "When you finish, come back and send someone else."

"Come, Sergeant," he said as he started towards the house.

"Back to work," Sgt. Kua commanded before she turned to follow the general.

***

The main room of the house had a wooden table in the middle, surrounded by four wooden chairs. Two padded leather chairs were in the corners to the left of the door. In the middle of the right wall was a hallway leading to a privy, and doors on each side of the hall opened to small bedrooms. Sergeant Kua had taken over the bedroom towards the front of the house. The back room was empty. There was one light bulb hanging from the ceiling in each room with a string to turn it on.

Gen. Park sat at the table saying, "Take a seat, Sergeant. Tell me, how are the students doing?"

She spoke about the daily routine she had set up. She explained their study habits and admitted she usually had no idea what they were discussing. They helped each other learn.

"Have you been monitoring the girls' monthly cycles, Sergeant?"

"Yes, sir." She pulled out a paper from her pocket, listing the girls and dates they had requested menstrual rags.

"Only four?" he questioned.

"Yes, sir. There should be more. I have watched them closely to see if they show signs, but no others have approached me for rags," she explained nervously, wondering if she had the right plan to discover this information.

"Their physicals will tell me more," he said while standing and gathering his things. "I must meet with Lieutenant Rim. Make sure everyone is examined by the doctor today. Again, I am sorry that events in the rest of the country have kept me away." He walked out the door as he finished talking.

The student physicals lasted until after dark. Sgt. Kua sat in the comfortable chair in the corner of her quarters, knitting a new pair of socks. If only she could get some new boots that were not so hard on socks, she wouldn't have to spend so much time mending and knitting.

The door opened, and Gen. Park strode up to the table. She stood, dropping her knitting and needles on the floor beside the chair.

Gen. Park placed a large pile of papers onto the desk and pulled out a chair. "Please join me, Sergeant," he said, motioning to a chair on the other side of the table. "There are a couple of things we need to discuss. The first is the physicals done today show the recruits are all undernourished. They are in good shape but need to eat more.

"Arrangements have been made for them to have double servings at every meal. Each student is to eat twice as much. Most of the girls have not had their first menses, probably due to not having adequate body fat." He showed her a list. "Many of those who have started are irregular. Continue to monitor the girls as you have been doing."

Sgt. Kua inhaled slowly, letting her breath out even slower.

"Second, education will be focused on medicine from now on. To protect the students, they are now officially medical staff directly under my command. You are still in charge of their day-to-day lives. Keep a sharp eye on them. Deal with any disloyalty at once," he said with a firm voice.

"There will be other changes in this compound soon. In a week or two, Lieutenant Rim will take charge. Report to him any issues with the students. Are there any questions?" he asked staring directly into her eyes to see her response.

"They are a wonderful group of young men and women, General Park," she blurted out. "They show great ability and initiative. They work very well together on the tasks given to them. I am most grateful you have chosen me for this honor," she said and ended with a bow from her chair.

Park stood and began to pick up his papers while commenting, "I must get back to Chongjin tonight. I bought some seeds. Make sure the students get the garden growing. Also, increase the exercise program," he said as he opened the door. Then he turned back to look at her. "And one more thing…I am trusting you with the lives of these students and the success of what I have planned. Thank you for your dedication."

Sgt. Kua strolled to the porch and watched the unloading of bags of seeds. She sighed. The burden of responsibility placed on her shoulders for overseeing the students was huge, and at the same time so effortless.

5 — Captain Kwang - June 20 - 21, 1950

The next morning, Sun-hee was eating her second bowl of breakfast gruel when Capt. Kwang, commander of the military compound, approached the students. Four armed Korean soldiers accompanied him. Sun-hee and the rest of the students became still and quiet.

Sgt. Kua stood and bowed. Capt. Kwang commanded, "Sergeant, make your students ready to transport. Report to the front gate at noon."

Bowing deeper, Sgt. Kua replied, "General Park has ordered me to remain here, Captain."

"My orders from the Premier are to have the entire compound packed up and on trucks today. That includes you and these medical students," Capt. Kwang retorted in a booming voice, then he turned and marched away, followed by the soldiers accompanying him.

"Yes, Captain," replied Sgt. Kua to the men's backs.

Sgt. Kua did not move until Capt. Kwang was out of sight, then she took off running towards the dorms. Sun-hee and the students scrambled to place their dishes in the washbasin and sprinted to catch up then pass her. They were in formation as Sgt. Kua arrived to face them. She took a couple of deep breaths, then said, "You heard Captain Kwang. Pack your things. Get ready to leave."

***

Sun-hee laid her clothes out and began to arrange them to be rolled up in her mat. She stroked her blue scarf for a moment before folding it carefully and laying it among her things.

"Where are we being taken?" Joo-yun asked as she stood over her mat, stroking her braids.

"I do not think anyone knows, but we are going with the rest of the soldiers in the camp," said Sun-hee.

"Sergeant Kua was surprised by Captain Kwang's order," Eun-seong said from behind Sun-hee.

"I will be glad to get out of this place," said Choe-me.

"Do we take our mats and blankets?" asked Young-ja. "I will be taking mine even if it is a lot more to carry. We get to ride in a truck, which should be fun. Now I need to figure out the best way to bundle all this together. Roll things in the mat? Or bundle everything in the blanket?"

Sun-hee finished packing by rolling her mat around her possessions and tying the blanket to make a bundle. She stood to see that Joo-yun had not moved. "Let me help you. We need to get ready to leave." She knelt and helped arrange Joo-yun's clothes.

"I want to go home," said Joo-yun, pulling away. "I will stay here until everyone is gone and then walk home."

"You can't do that. It'll be too risky," said Eun-seong as she joined Sun-hee in packing Joo-yun's things. "The captain is closing this compound. You must come along. It's where they are taking us that worries me."

"I'm worried, too," replied Sun-hee as she finished tying up Joo-yun's things. "I wonder if General Park knows we are leaving?"

Eun-seong whispered to Sun-hee, "We need to stay close to Joo-yun, so she does not say or do the wrong thing."

"You're right. One of us needs to be with her all the time." She looked up at Eun-seong, who pinched her lips and narrowed her eyes to slits.

Eun-seong and Sun-hee took Joo-yun's arms and walked her out of the dorm.

The three got in the back row of formation.

Sgt. Kua said, "Work in the garden until they come for us."

Sun-hee and her friends went into the garden where one of the boys said, "Yong-gak, you're into political history. What is going on?"

Yong-gak pointed at the boy who had asked the question. "As you know, the Americans and Soviets divided up Korea after the Japanese left, with the 38th parallel as the dividing line." He drew a line in front of him with his right hand. "America supports South Korea with the objective of stopping the spread of communism. The Democratic People's Republic of Korea is communist, aligned with the Soviets."

He gestured with his hands as he talked, but his elbows stayed firmly by his side. "There is a lot of turmoil in South Korea. A couple of years ago, there was an uprising on the island of Jeju. Soldiers slaughtered thousands of protestors. The president of South Korea, Syngman Rhee, is killing all communists and rules by fear. He too wants to unify Korea but under his control.

"It is obvious to me, sending the army of the DRPK into South Korea first, to eliminate the oppression of the South Korean government, is a good thing. Korea will be reunited under Kim Il-sung and be an independent nation for the first time in forty-five years. To me, this is the right decision. Attack South Korea. Our army is much stronger, and with help from the Soviets, there will be one Korea again." He finished by clasping his hands together in front of his chest.

"What about South Korea's ally, the United States?" asked another boy.

"America has only a few troops in South Korea. It will take them too long to get an army across the Pacific Ocean. By the time they are mobilized to fight, the war will be over. Korea will be united," replied Yong-gak.

"We are not going to have to fight, are we?" said another boy.

"We are not trained to fight. I think we are moving because this camp is closing. No idea where we are going."

"Just as we get the garden planted, we must leave," said Stinky as he dropped a shovel and made a disgusted face.

Sun-hee picked up his shovel and said, "We might as well keep busy while we wait." She went to work weeding the garden while most of the students just stood around, chatting and waiting.

Young-ja came over and said, "I thought it was interesting what his hands had to say." She mimicked the boy's hand movements.

With a big smile on her face, Sun-hee asked in a whisper, "Nickname?"

"*Jeonlyagga*," replied Young-ja, raising her eyebrows.

"He is a strategist," agreed Sun-hee, while admiring him. He was taller than most of the boys, broad-shouldered but with skinny legs and arms. His medium-length hair was in disarray like he had never combed it. His pointed nose was the most prominent feature of his face.

"Formation!" yelled one of the boys.

Sgt. Kua was carrying a large duffle bag towards the dorms. She stopped in the rock area made for her and put down her bag. The students ran to get their bundles and soon stood in formation, belongings at their side. Sun-hee escorted Joo-yun to make sure she got in line.

Sgt. Kua turned and marched down the road, towards the garages and workshops to the main gate, where the trucks were loading. Sun-hee, Choe-me, Eun-seong, and Young-ja surrounded Joo-yun, forcing her to walk with them. The only sound breaking the silence of the empty camp was their footsteps.

Sun-hee's focus darted around the compound, and her mind raced.

Something is wrong. What can I do? Nothing. Follow the sergeant.

They passed the metal shop and garage, arriving at the main gate.

Sgt. Kua marched the students up to Capt. Kwang who stood at the edge of the road outside the compound. The line of students stopped a few meters behind her and became more of a cluster.

"Load the students into those trucks, Sergeant," said Capt. Kwang, pointing to four trucks to his left.

"Captain!" yelled Lt. Rim from inside the gate as he trotted towards them. "I see you are about loaded. I have orders to take over this camp after you depart." He handed a piece of paper to the captain.

"Whose orders? My orders are to take everyone with me. That would include you."

"As you can see, my orders are to remain here and take charge of this camp."

Capt. Kwang glanced at the paper for a moment, then glared at Lt. Rim saying, "We are leaving in a few minutes, Lieutenant. The empty camp is yours." He waved his hand towards the camp.

"Thank you, Captain. Sergeant Kua and these students are to remain here at this camp with me," said Rim in a firm voice.

"We will need these medical students, Lieutenant. They must come with me per my orders from the Premier."

"You may find them useful where you are going, but for the long-term benefit of the Democratic People's Republic of Korea, they must remain in this compound."

"Lieutenant, are you saying my orders to get everyone from this camp to the border with South Korea are invalid?"

"No, sir," replied Lt. Rim. "To your superiors, these students do not exist. They only exist to you because you have seen them. To my superior, General Park, these students are important. They are in my camp now, and they will stay here."

Capt. Kwang stepped forward to stare eye to eye with Lt. Rim. Lt. Rim stared back, the scar over his right eye quivering.

Sun-hee held her breath, taking small steps back, eyes fixed on the two men. Capt. Kwang broke the tension.

"I must leave immediately and do not have a moment to waste. When I return, I will have you court-martialed for disobeying orders." He then turned and walked to a car, motioning to the four trucks to drive on.

The lieutenant motioned with his right arm towards the camp. "Sergeant Kua, double-time these students back to their quarters!"

Sun-hee ran with the rest of the students, listening to the trucks rumble off behind her. She funneled through the door with the other girls, carrying all she owned, falling out of breath in the area of the floor that had become her 'space.' Joo-yun stumbled in last, dropped her bundle, and stood stroking her hair.

"I thought we were going to head off to South Korea," said Choe-me between heavy breaths.

"Me too," said Joo-yun. "That is why I wanted to go home. I have never been south of Hamhung on land. On the water, I have been to the end of the peninsula."

Sun-hee said, "I remember going to Pyongyang as a child, but never farther south. I have never been on a boat. Someday I want to sail on the ocean."

"We should dream of where we would sail," said Choe-me.

"For now, we are safe," added Eun-seong.

"Who is the lieutenant in charge?" asked Choe-me. "I have not seen him before."

"He is Lieutenant Rim, the man who brought my letter telling me I won the prize," said Sun-hee. "I have seen him a few other times."

"Formation!" yelled Sgt. Kua from outside. The girls scrambled to their feet and hustled to join ranks outside.

A few minutes later, they were in the library poised over books at a table. Eun-seong leaned into the group and said, "Captain Kwang referred to us as 'medical students.' Is General Park going to have all of us become doctors?"

"Not me," said Joo-yun. "I cannot stand the sight of blood."

"Not my idea of fun," said Choe-me.

"Helping others in need is wonderful," added Eun-seong. "I am sure I can raise the spirits of those who are sick and injured. I am looking forward to it."

"I don't know enough about medicine to treat a person," said Sun-hee. "There is so much to know, and what we have been learning has not prepared me."

"And we are back to our studies, making ourselves into doctors," said Young-ja, opening the book before her. "What is the treatment for the flu?" she asked.

"The flu?" Sun-hee said. "Captain Kwang was taking us with him to battle. He wanted us to treat injured men."

"Let me find a chapter on severe injuries," said Young-ja.

The five girls dove into the medical texts before them. The hardest part of learning medicine for Sun-hee and her friends was not its complexity but understanding what they read. Books in different languages described medical conditions in various terms. Treatments were different in Chinese, Russian, and Japanese medicine. Korean medicine was a compilation of folk remedies and therapies from other cultures, some ancient and some modern. Comparing the different medical books was both confusing and time-consuming.

***

Lt. Rim stood outside the gate as the dust settled. He sauntered into the empty camp. Yesterday, it had contained over a thousand soldiers. Now there were fifty residents plus the civilian support staff. He closed the gate and lowered the boards, securing it from the inside.

I hope Park will approve of what I just did. He told me to find a way to keep the students here. If Kwang ever finds out I wrote my orders to take command, he will have me in front of a firing squad. He took a deep breath and let it out slowly. *For now, these students and I will not be going to war.*

The next couple of days were quiet. Rim kept a few women to run the kitchen and do laundry. The rest of the staff were released. He would post notices when he needed help. He would have to guard the compound by himself.

6 — The Program - June 24, 1950

Lt. Rim sat on a wooden chair near the main gate, a rifle across his lap. For the umpteenth time, he removed his hat and wiped the sweat from his brow with his forearm. A car drove up and sounded its horn. He stood and peered through the gate. An arm waved out of the back window. It was Gen. Park.

Lt. Rim opened the gate and let the car in. After closing the gate, Gen. Park held the car door open, inviting him to get in the car.

"I see you are in charge, Lieutenant," said Gen. Park.

"I am, sir. Captain Kwang ordered us to leave with him. With no disrespect, General, I typed up orders from you giving me command of the compound and keeping the students here."

Gen. Park gave a hearty laugh and said, "Wonderful job, Lieutenant. Wonderful!"

***

Shouting from the library doorway jolted Sun-hee out of her book.

"General Park is here."

She ran with others as fast as she could, panting heavily by the time she got in line. Working to catch her breath, she kept her eyes focused on Gen. Park conversing with Sgt. Kua.

Through the spaces between the girls in front of her, she watched Gen. Park grind out his cigarette butt, then walk up to the boys. He began to ask the boys medical questions, moving up and down the rows.

Sweat trickled down Sun-hee's face, but she did not want to attract attention by wiping the drops away with her sleeve. Her stomach fluttered in anticipation of what he would ask her.

When he stepped in front of her, she could smell his smoky breath as he asked, "What do you know about mumps and how to treat it?"

She explained what she knew about the symptoms of the disease and how treatment options differed between the Chinese, Soviet, Japanese, and Western medicine. She finished with, "Treating the fever reduces the chances of fatality."

"What about mumps in adults?" he followed up.

"I do not know if it is different in adults, General Park," she replied, ashamed at not knowing the answer.

"Bedrest for five days after diagnosis; also treat the fever in adults," replied Gen. Park before moving on.

She stood at attention, lips quivering.

Was I supposed to know about adult mumps?

She reviewed in her mind what she had read about mumps but did not remember seeing anything about adults. She hated not knowing the answer.

Gen. Park's booming voice brought her attention back to him. "Excellent answers everyone. You are an amazing group of students. In less than a month, you know more about anatomy, the treatment of diseases, and injury than the medical students in Pyongyang. Impressive. The only thing you lack to be real interns is patients."

He continued, "Right now, I wish I had more to offer you than this compound. Over the next few years, *Yangseongso* will become a place of great promise. Tomorrow starts the reunification of Korea. Together, we will be a great nation. I expect each of you will have a significant role to play in the future. For now, I have new shirts and pants for all of you." He turned to his driver. "Open the trunk and get out the clothes for the students. Sergeant Kua, come with me."

"Get washed up and put on your new clothes for dinner," said Sgt. Kua before hurrying to catch up to Gen. Park, who walked quickly towards her house.

***

Once inside the house, Gen. Park turned to Sgt. Kua. "We are going to need to use this house as a place for students to be alone. Prepare a bedroom for the students to fornicate in. I have brought robes, towels, and additional mats." His eyes focused on her face.

"Yes, sir!" was her obedient reply without showing any reaction.

"I'll take the students to dinner while you prepare," he said.

***

Sun-hee ate slowly, making it easier to consume the double rations.

Gen. Park circulated among the students while they ate, asking more medical questions. He praised them when they were correct and explained further when their answers were lacking.

Yong-gak, the strategist, said, "Pardon me, General Park, did I hear you correctly when you said we are going to war to unify Korea?"

"Yes, our armies will be attacking in a few days to make the two nations into one," said Gen. Park proudly.

"Whoohoo!" exclaimed Yong-gak, raising a fist but not letting his elbow leave his side.

Sun-hee got a nudge from Young-ja who then mimicked the fist gesture. They giggled.

When Gen. Park came to Young-ja, she took the initiative and asked, "Would it be possible to write to our families? I am sure they are worried about us."

"This program must remain secret," he said, pausing for a moment, eyes looking upward in contemplation. "You may write letters to your families to put their worries to rest. I will review the letters and make sure they are delivered."

Gen. Park moved on. "Is there a way, General Park, we could have better living quarters?" inquired Eun-seong.

"The rest of the camp is not any better than the two buildings you are in," Gen. Park replied. "In the long term, I will try to find a way to make improvements. You have done a lot already to improve your compound. Together, we will make *Yangseongso* comfortable."

He continued to talk to the students as they ate. When Gen. Park got to So Jung-sip, he winked at him and said, "Tonight I have something special for you."

Jung-sip got wide-eyed, shrugged his shoulders, and held his hands out to the other boys.

Sun-hee noticed a smirk on Gen. Park's face.

The general left, returning a few minutes later with paper, fountain pens, and ink. "Write letters to your families. I will collect them in a couple of hours."

***

"What are you writing, Joo-yun?" asked Sun-hee.

"Writing about this place is hard. I do not like it here, and there are no fun things to do. The good is that we are studying every day, and we will be far from the war. But I miss my mother's cooking and the room I had to myself. Not that living with you is bad, but there is no place to be alone," said Joo-yun. "And I miss the ocean. We always had fresh seafood."

"I think the food is good," said Sun-hee, recalling living day-to-day with her mother. "I can write that I'm learning a lot of new things, and the library has a lot of good books. I like my new friends, and the boys are...I better not mention the boys to my mother. I do not want her to worry." She smiled as Joo-yun chuckled.

"General Park is going to read our letters, so I can't say what I want," said Joo-yun. "My mother will want to know how I am doing, so I will write a letter that will look good to the general but not good to my mother. And I will not complain about these new clothes, even though they are the worst garments I have ever been given to wear."

"I think I'll mention the new clothes. The general will see I appreciate new clothes," said Sun-hee.

***

Sgt. Kua stood on her porch, the sun was disappearing behind the hills to the west, which for the end of June this far north, meant it was about eight o'clock. She sucked in a breath. She was not looking forward to doing what she was now ordered to do. She made her feet walk towards the dorms.

Halfway there she called out, "Formation. Bring your letters." Then she watched the students pour from the dorms and get in line. She made a note of where Jung-sip and Choe-me stood.

"Hand your letters forward," she said and began to walk across the front-line, collecting letters in silence.

Returning to the pad of rocks the students had made for her, she turned to look over the youth before her. Taking a deep breath, she said, "Jung-sip and Choe-me step forward. The rest of you are dismissed for the evening."

"You two follow me," Kua said in a solemn voice and turned, walking with her head down to her house.

I do not like this. Objecting will not stop him and might get me sent to the war. I am so sorry, Choe-me. You are so pretty.

Sgt. Kua held the door for the stunningly beautiful girl, whose slight widow's peak started perfect archways, allowing her silky black hair to frame her face. The lanky boy, whose arms were too long for his sleeves, while his shoulders were too narrow to fill out his shirt, followed her.

They entered the house. Gen. Park sat at the square table with the bare lightbulb overhead casting their shadows on the floor.

7 — Trapped - June 25 - 30, 1950

A sniffle woke Sun-hee. The sound of sobbing was coming from the mat next to her. Moonlight flowing through the windows offered enough light for Sun-hee to see Choe-me changing into her nightclothes and wiping her eyes every few seconds. Sun-hee sat up and said in a soft voice, "Are you alright? Can I help?"

"No! You can't help," Choe-me said in a stern, quiet voice. She laid down, curled up, and covered her head. "Leave me alone," came her muted voice from under the blanket.

Sun-hee peered at the mound of blanket and Choe-me. She wondered what might have happened that caused her to be so upset. Every sniffle and sob from Choe-me roused her. She spent the night watching the window-shaped moonbeam move across the room like the movement of an hour hand on a clock.

***

"Time to get up," boomed Sgt. Kua.

Sun-hee's eyes opened and went directly to see if her friend had moved. She hadn't. She motioned to everyone to be quiet and then dressed for the day.

The other girls went outside. Sun-hee sat down on her mat and reached out to put her hand on Choe-me's shoulder. Young-ja stuck her head inside the door and said in a whisper, "We are getting lined up."

Sun-hee quickly walked out and took her place.

Sgt. Kua looked over the girls, then stated, "There is one empty place."

Sun-hee responded, "Choe-me does not seem to be feeling well this morning, Sergeant Kua. We have let her sleep."

"Very well. Kwong-ku, lead the exercises."

Kwong-ku led them through the routine. After the loyalty chant, Sgt. Kua said, "Sun-hee, stay and look after Choe-me. I will send breakfast for the two of you." The sergeant turned and jogged towards the gate. The other students followed.

Sun-hee returned to the girl's dorm.

"How are you feeling, Choe-me?" Sun-hee asked. Choe-me moved only her swollen, red-rimmed eyes to look at her. Sun-hee reached over and felt her forehead. "You do not feel warm; you do not have a fever," said Sun-hee. "Are you ill?"

"No. Just go away!" Choe-me snapped. "I don't want anyone to know!"

What does she not want me to know?

Sun-hee leaned over and rubbed her friend's shoulder lightly for a few moments then sat back, wishing she could share whatever was troubling her friend and lessen it for her.

Suddenly, Choe-me sat up, her wide-eyes focused on Sun-hee. She gripped Sun-hee's shoulders. "I must tell you what they are doing," she blurted, followed by a sniffle.

Sun-hee pulled back, startled, frozen. Choe-me's lips and round chin were quivering. Sun-hee's mind raced as she thought of all kinds of things Choe-me might tell her. She waited for her to share her troubles, and when it did not come, she said, "What is it Choe-me? You can talk to me."

"We are here to have babies." The words fired from her mouth. "He made me have sex with Jung-sip," she said while wiping her eyes and nose. "General Park said it is like breeding dogs to get the traits you want. He said, 'We are the best of the DPRK. And our children will be better.'"

"Oh, no," said Sun-hee.

"He wants a race of super children. We are his…" Choe-me choked on the words, "his breeding experiment! When he said we are special, here to do great things for Korea, he meant we were to have children." She curled into a fetal position with her back to Sun-hee, burying her head under her covers and wept.

"Oh, no. I'm so sorry for you, Choe-me." Sun-hee said, rubbing her blanket lightly.

Sun-hee had not considered this possibility.

Choe-me is too young. I am too young. I am not ready. She shivered in fear. *We did not win a prize. What is this program?* She clasped her shaking hands together on her lap.

For the next few minutes, Sun-hee sat in silence, considering Gen. Park's plan. Like breeding dogs, our children will be the best in Korea.

And if the best of those children were to have children, they will be the smartest children in the entire country. I know what he is doing. Park is a manipulative beast to bring us together to breed. But why are we being forced this soon to have children?

"Why did General Park force you to mate?" she said aloud.

A muffled voice poured out from Choe-me's blanket. "He said the program was urgent. Without marriage, we are like comfort women," responded Choe-me crossly. "It's Mongolic!"

"Yes," Sun-hee said, processing Choe-me's words and voicing her train of thought. "His method is like the Mongols who raped women, thinking their seed was superior."

Just then, Young-ja and Eun-seong came in each juggling two bowls and tea. "How's Choe-me?" said Young-ja as she knelt at the end of the mat. She sat breakfast down as if offering it at a shrine. "The boys told us what happened last night."

"I am so sorry," said Eun-seong as she placed her hand on Choe-me's shoulder. "Is there anything I can do?"

"No," came the angry response from under the blanket.

"She is very distraught," said Sun-hee. "Thank you for bringing breakfast. I will see you later at the library." She motioned to Young-ja and Eun-seong to leave, even though she could tell they wanted to stay and help.

"Sit up and try to eat some breakfast," Sun-hee said and began to eat her breakfast slowly. Choe-me sat up, took a sip of tea, staring into her cup.

"This is all wrong," said Choe-me. "In a year, all of us might have fallen in love. General Park could have a joint marriage ceremony. Our families could attend. He would have lots of babies. The children would still be great leaders."

Sun-hee wrapped her arms around Choe-me. "I'm so sorry this happened to you."

"I will make General Park pay for what he did to me," Choe-me said through her tears.

Sun-hee sat back, held Choe-me's hands, trying to feel her pain.

I will be like her soon. She closed her eyes and choked back a vision of her future, and her thoughts rambled out. "Thank you for warning me, us." She took a bite of breakfast and chewed slowly while thinking of what to do next.

Choe-me took a nibble of her breakfast, then another. Slowly they ate, lost in their thoughts and emotions.

Sun-hee stayed at Choe-me's side while she washed and dressed in clean clothes. As they walked to the library, she saw the camp differently. The barbed wire on top of the tall fences fueled her claustrophobia. The locks on all the gates stealing her freedom. It was a prison!

She took a full turn from the porch of the library, scanning the compound. There was Lt. Rim staring at her. *This Japanese prison camp is now our prison, and there is the guard.* She entered the library, looked up at the rooms on the second floor. *Is my fate any different from the comfort women the Japanese kept here?*

Choe-me took Sun-hee's arm, leading her into an empty side room, then she shut the door behind them.

"They were all staring at me!" she said, as she burst out in tears.

"They are concerned because they care for you, as I do. May I go tell the others you are going to be okay?"

Choe-me's head lowered to look at her feet, and she said meekly, "Yes. Physically I will recover."

Sun-hee hugged Choe-me and went out to talk to the rest of the students. She reassured them Choe-me was fine physically, but extremely upset. She approached Jung-sip, who was sitting by himself in the corner.

"I did not want to hurt her," Jung-sip blurted out. "I was only obeying. I didn't know what I was doing."

"She is distressed. You need to figure out what you are doing." She looked over her shoulder into the fixed eyes of Sgt. Kua, sitting on the steps, watching her every move. Sun-hee turned, took two medical books off a bookshelf, went back into the side room, and closed the door. She put the books on the table.

Sun-hee became lost in her thoughts. The importance of marriage, the stable bonds of love in a family, and loyalty to one's mate were shown to her by her parents. She had experienced her mother's grief when her father had died. She recalled her mother telling the story of the day of her marriage. The family had spent days preparing their home for the ceremony, buying new rugs, placing flowers around the house, inside and out. Sue-dae's grandmother had made a stunning wedding dress for the occasion.

Her mother had laughed as she told about how she stood by the window all afternoon, wanting to get a glimpse of the man who would be her husband before he saw her. Sun-hee remembered how her mother's eyes lit up when she told about her father riding up on a horse with a goose under his arm. His whole family had paraded behind him.

I will never have a traditional marriage. Mother will not select my mate. General Park is the arranger. There will be no ceremony, no celebration. No window to stand behind. No groom on a horse leading his family parade. No union of families. Park is stealing my happiness.

Young-ja stuck her head in the door. "Can you help translate some Russian?"

"Yes," replied Sun-hee. "Come in."

The chapter of the Russian medical book was about reproduction. It spoke about abnormalities, complications, and dysfunctions, not on normal relations.

Then Eun-seong peered in saying, "One of the boys found a book in English. It has lots of drawings. I remember you said you could read English.

Sun-hee took the book. On the title page was, *Kama Sutra, Translated from Hindi to English by Sir Richard Burton 1883*. She was too embarrassed to translate or explain what she read.

She looked at Eun-seong, "Why?"

"Everyone is trying to find out about human reproduction," said Eun-seong. "The Korean books tell stories of marriages all based on respect and admiration, but there is no information on…the act."

Choe-me looked up at Eun-seong. "It's emotional more than physical."

"I…I am trying to understand that," Eun-seong said, wrapping her arms around her, tears forming in her eyes.

Sun-hee put the Kama Sutra aside.

***

After dinner back in the dorm, Sun-hee eavesdropped as the girls talked about what had occurred the night before. They knew what had happened, but they did not know why Choe-me had been forced to have sex. Jung-sip had said little all day, and Choe-me had confided only to Sun-hee.

She decided to take this moment to explain what was happening. "Listen up, everyone. Choe-me explained to me why General Park brought together the healthiest and smartest children in Korea. He told Choe-me and Jung-sip we are to be parents of a great generation. He is our matchmaker, and we are being forced to have children."

"I am not going to obey the general," exclaimed Youj Mung-jo stomping her foot. "I will not bear children without a proper traditional marriage. I would rather die."

Intense discussion flooded the room.

"Why should we do what he wants?" said a girl from across the room.

"Why don't we all leave?" shouted another.

Someone questioned, "Will the boys leave with us? Or will they want to stay here?"

"What will the general do if we try to leave?"

"He said if we are disloyal, he will execute us."

"I don't want to die."

Sun-hee looked at the faces around the room. Fear was in their eyes. She tuned out the emotion in their voices, the anger, the confusion, and assembled what had been running around in her mind all day. She gathered herself, stood up, looked around the room, and said, "I have thought about this all day. We have three options. First, we can refuse to obey and suffer the consequences. I am uncertain how far the general will go if we are all disloyal. Next, we can attempt an escape, but I have not seen an easy way to get out of the compound. Last, we obey and survive."

"I don't like any of the options," came a voice across the room.

"I want to go home," said Joo-yun, sitting on her mat, pulling on her braids.

A voice in the crowd said, "Then get up and go."

Joo-yun did not move.

Sun-hee paused and swallowed. "Unless we find a way out of here, obedience is our only option. I do not want to die. I do not want any of you to die." She sat down on her mat, put her knees up, and her head down. Her hand reached into her clothes bundle and stroked her silk scarf.

"So, you think the best thing we can do is obey General Park?" said Mi-na.

"Only a little better than being dead," said Choe-me meekly.

Sgt. Kua's voice commanded from outside the dorm, "Formation!"

When everyone was in line, Sgt. Kua said, "Ho Hon-yong, lead us in exercises."

Gen. Park and Lt. Rim stood on the porch of the house, smoking cigarettes and watching.

Sun-hee performed the exercises while her mind reviewed their predicament.

What is right? What should I do when someone in power makes me do what I know is wrong? Even more, what should I do when a friend is forced to do something immoral? I could rebel. Would it be worth the risk? What makes people risk their lives to revolt or take a position against those in power?

Her thoughts turned to the dissenters exiled to internment camps.

Was the benefit worth losing their lives? Death only removes me from the fight. If we are the best and brightest of all the children in Korea, we must live to find a solution.

Sgt Kua's voice brought her back to the moment. "Choe-me and Jung-sip, report to General Park. Everyone else, return to the dorms."

Choe-me put her head down. Sun-hee and her friends gave her a supportive hug before she pulled away and staggered submissively to Kua's house.

Sun-hee got ready for bed. Her stomach felt like it was full of rocks. No position on the matt felt comfortable. The throbbing in her head forced her eyes closed. She slept.

When the light went on, she first noticed Choe-me sitting quietly next to her, dressed and ready for the day. She rolled onto her hands and knees and asked, "How are you?" Everyone else in the room stopped to listen.

"Fine," she replied, without raising her head. She waited a bit and continued. "You were right. If we resist, we will die. Jung-sip told the general he did not want to go in the room with me."

"What did the general do?" asked Young-ja.

"The general stood and slapped Jung-sip, almost knocking him off the chair. Then he yelled, 'Are you loyal to the Premier, to Korea and the Program?' Jung-sip said, 'Yes.' Then the general pushed him saying, 'Then get in the room and make a baby.'" Choe-me's quivering lips cascaded into weeping.

Sun-hee reached out and put her hand on Choe-me's shoulder. Others reached out and put their hands on her shoulder or head. A moment later, all the girls were in a blubbering group hug.

"You are all wonderful," said Young-ja while wiping a tear from her cheek. "The only way we will get through this is to support each other." Slowly the girls peeled off to go about their day.

While getting ready, Sun-hee noticed she had started her first menses. Taking a deep breath, she went and knocked on the door of Sgt. Kua's house.

The door opened. Sgt. Kua said, "Yes?"

Swallowing hard, Sun-hee spoke, "I am here to request menstrual rags. My menses has begun."

Sergeant Kua pressed her lips together, sighed through her nose, then said, "Just a moment."

As Sun-hee received the rags, she bowed and remarked, "In two weeks, it will be my turn."

"Yes, Sun-hee," said Sgt. Kua, her eyebrows raised. "Does everyone understand the plan?"

"I think so," said Sun-hee. "It is an amazing prize, a chance to make babies for the Premier," she said, turning and walking away, hoping the sergeant did not catch her sarcasm.

***

As exercises started the next morning, there was an empty place in the back row. "Who is missing?" said Sgt. Kua with concern in her voice.

The girls all looked around. Young-ja called out, "Youj Mung-jo. Youj Mung-jo are you here?" There was no response.

"Has anyone seen her?" Sgt. Kua asked.

Heads shook side to side. Everyone stood in silence. Sun-hee recalled Mung-jo's words from last night, 'I would rather die' and a lump formed in her throat.

Just then, Lt. Rim came through the gate with a bundle in his hands. The sergeant must have seen their eyes looking past her, and she turned to look at the lieutenant.

The sound of the soles of the lieutenant's boots grinding gravel into the dirt filled Sun-hee's ears.

He handed the bundle to Sgt. Kua and spoke quietly to her. Sun-hee, being in the front row, overheard his words. "A girl dropped this as she went out of the gate last night. She will not be returning."

Sun-hee felt a bump against her arm as another girl ran past her, bringing her back to reality. The other students were running towards the kitchen. She started to jog after them while watching Sgt. Kua detour to toss the bag on her doorstep.

Youj Mung-jo must have gotten away. She is going home.

They ate breakfast, staring into their bowls or past their dishes to the ground. The lack of conversation carried on throughout the day, while they worked in the garden, eating lunch, and studying. Sun-hee did not know how to break the silence. What could she say? How could she put into words what she was feeling? When she looked at others, they looked away. She noticed she turned her eyes away from the glances of others. Why was she afraid? What would she say if she spoke? She tried to focus on reading a book on the circulatory system, but images of Mung-jo kept leaping into her thoughts: her smile, her laugh, the way she parted her long hair.

What will happen when Mung-jo tells her parents what is going on here? Maybe, she will send help. She will be a hero.

After dinner, Sgt. Kua escorted Choe-me to the house for a third evening with Jung-sip.

Sun-hee settled on her mat to wait for her to return.

"Do you think Mung-jo got away?" asked Joo-yun as she sat down beside Sun-hee.

"I do not know," replied Sun-hee. "It is troubling not to know. I hope Mung-jo escaped and made it home. Like everyone else, I fear she is dead."

"This is like the fishermen who do not return. Their wives and families have hope that they will return but fear they have died. Not knowing is the worst. There is no grieving, no moving on, no relief of their emotions."

"All this has made me angry," said Sun-hee. "I feel helpless."

"Me too. I do not know what to do," said Joo-yun.

Sun-hee stared at the ceiling with visions of Mung-jo reuniting with her family.

Choe-me walked into the dorm, returning from her third night in the sergeant's house. Everyone embraced her in a group hug.

"How are you?" said Sun-hee.

"Just fine. Jung-sip tried to be gentle and nice tonight. We did have a chance to talk. Some of the boys want to leave, but others are afraid to try to escape. Jung-sip told me about the rifle Sergeant Kua keeps in the corner of the main room. Maybe we could get it and use it to help our escape."

"If we tried to escape, would Sergeant Kua use it against us?" asked Young-ja.

"The sergeant cares a lot for us. But I think she would shoot at us if we tried to escape," said Choe-me.

As they settled back onto their mats, Mi-na said. "Mung-jo got away last night. We can too."

"Mung-jo did not get away," said Choe-me.

"How do you know they caught her?" said Eun-seong to Choe-me.

"I saw the bundle of her clothes up close. It looked like all her clothes and her coat. She would not leave them!" said Choe-me.

"No! She dropped her bag and ran. She could be to the ocean by now," said Rhee Son-yong.

"Did you see her body or blood?" said Mi-na.

"No, only her things," replied Choe-me.

"She was disloyal! We know what they said they would do to us if we were disloyal," said Han Soo-hy.

"That is why we must leave tonight," said Joo-yun, who was

arranging her belongings on her blanket.

"We can all leave. If we travel light, we can run away if they chase us."

"There are two men with rifles by the main gate. One of the boys saw them."

"Not tonight but soon we will get out of here," said Young-ja. "We need to have a good plan to assure our survival."

"What if we cut a hole in the back fence?" asked Han Soo-hy.

"What will you cut the wires with?" said Young-ja.

"There are tools to cut wire," replied Han Soo-hy.

Voices added to the discussion.

"Do you have any tools? Or know where to get them?" someone asked.

"No. But we have shovels and can dig under the fence," said another girl.

"That would take too long," came another voice.

"Can we climb over the fence?" Eun-seong asked.

"We would be spotted. And when would we have time?" responded a voice.

"Quiet," said Mi-na in a loud whisper. Someone is at the door.

Clank

Young-ja tried the door. It would not open. "We are locked in," she said. "That rules out escaping tonight. Unless we climb out the windows."

"What about the boys?" asked Eun-seong. "We must coordinate with them."

"Why don't we make a list of the escape options?" said Young-ja. "So far, we have cut a hole in the fence, dig under or climb over it, make a run for the gates, and I'll add revolt and fight our way out. Any other ideas?"

"I wonder if any prisoners the Japanese held here escaped?" said Choe-me.

"What will we do if we can't get out of here?" asked Mi-na.

Sun-hee stood and said, "We will care for one another and do what is right. I don't know after that. What I do know is I will not be a part of any plan that risks our lives." She laid down on her mat and considered the stand she had just taken with the girls.

The light was turned off. Sun-hee stared again at the slivers of moonlight creeping around the room, marking the passing of the night. Thoughts whirled and twisted in her mind, causing her pulse to race.

She felt her face flush with anger, and the cold chill of helplessness made her shiver.

I cannot be impulsive. Stay in control. Keep everyone else from doing something stupid. Develop a plan.

She thought about the escape options, but all had the risk of someone dying.

The next morning, she noticed Lt. Rim removing a chain on the gate to their compound. Sgt. Kua counted them as they took their positions. They exercised and went to eat breakfast. Sgt. Kua walked around and through them as they ate in silence.

At the library, Sgt. Kua strolled around, kept the doors to the side rooms wide open, squelching private discussion. As they returned from lunch, she spotted Lt. Rim, holding a rifle, watching them.

We can't revolt, even if we outnumber them.

8 — The Letter - July 4 - 9, 1950

At the end of exercises on the evening of the fourth of July, Sgt. Kua invited a second couple, Mi-na and Chulsoon, to her house. The girls formed around Mi-na to give her a group hug. The boys pushed and punched Chulsoon in their show of support.

Mi-na returned thirty minutes later in shock and collapsed on her mat sobbing. The girls moved around her in a show of concern. They heard the locking of the door.

A few minutes after the lights went out, Mi-na sat up, wiped her eyes and nose, then said, "Thank you for your support tonight. Since I knew I would be selected, I prepared myself mentally, and Chulsoon is a nice guy." She sniffled and rubbed her eyes again. "I don't want any of you to suffer like this. I asked Chulsoon if the boys talked about escaping."

"Have the guys come up with anything?" asked Young-ja.

"Chulsoon said the best idea is cutting a hole in the fence. But we need to find wire cutters. Then we could run up the hill where the brush and boulders will give us some cover. Stone estimates it would take two days to dig under the fence with the tools we have. To get all forty-seven of us over the barbed wire, they estimated it would expose us for a couple of minutes. In that time, Lieutenant Rim would shoot many of us with his rifle, so that is too risky. If we can create a diversion, like a fire, we might have more time. The boys discarded the idea of a revolt. Lieutenant Rim is never close enough to be attacked before getting off a few shots, and there are the other guards at the main gate."

"We could start a fire in the library then run here and climb over the fence," said Young-ja.

"Chulsoon said they wouldn't support a plan that puts the girls at risk. And since they don't see a safe way for all of us to get out of the camp, we're stuck." Then she crawled back to her mat and curled up.

***

The next day, Sun-hee watched some of the boys laughing and exchanging coins. "What is so humorous?" she asked.

"We were paying off our wagers," one said.

"What were you betting on?"

"Who would be selected next."

"This is not a game! It is very traumatic for the girls," she yelled and walked away.

That evening, she realized the girls were not much different. They continually discussed the boys and which one they wanted for a partner. They argued about who was better looking, who would make a good husband, who would father the best children. She listened and chuckled at the jokes but did not add to the discussion. She preferred to focus on what she could control: her actions, supporting others, and staying focused on her studies. She stuffed her feelings as deep as she could.

The mood between the sexes changed over the next few days. To the girls, the boys were no longer boys. They were potential fathers of their children.

***

Sun-hee counted down the days, wondering which boy Gen. Park had selected for her.

The stress of knowing when she would visit Sgt. Kua's house grew with each passing day. Her time was coming. What she read, she did not remember. She avoided her friends, only doing the next thing that needed to be done. Her thoughts and emotions were in constant battle.

Am I doing the right thing? What are the right things? If I had only gotten to know Mung-jo *better, would she still be here? If I had taken her threat seriously, could I have kept her in the dorm? If I could be better, I could figure out a plan to free all the students from this camp. If I had wings, I could fly home. If I could breathe fire. If I were invisible. Why am I here?*

***

Sgt. Kua called out more couples to visit her house precisely two weeks after the start of the girl's last menses. Everyone who returned from the house would get a group hug. There were tears, traumatic outbursts, and a cold realization that their lives had become controlled. No one could figure out a safe way to escape or a way to change their fate.

On the afternoon of the eighth of July, Sun-hee was in the library reading a chapter on whooping cough for the third or fourth time. It was not sinking in. The only thing she thought about was the two-day countdown before her turn to visit the sergeant's house.

A voice yelled into the library, "General Park is here."

She ran out. The dark storm clouds threatened a monsoon downpour. She sprinted partly out of obedience and partly due to the energy the pent-up anger infused into her muscles. She took a position in the back row, lips pursed and eyes penetrating Gen. Park. She could feel the tension in the other girls. Choe-me clenched and unclenched her fists in front of her.

She watched as Sgt. Kua praised the group for their studies and cooperating with the mating plan. Gen. Park smiled broadly, showing off his tobacco-stained teeth, and then clapped his hands.

"Prizewinners," he began, "today I bring you some great news. The Korean People's Army has won many battles against South Korea and advanced nearly to the end of the peninsula. Before the summer ends, we will see a unified Korea. Many of our fellow citizens are sacrificing to win the war. I am grateful for your sacrifice. Your cooperation is the first step in a new generation who will be leaders in our united country."

She looked past the general to see Lt. Rim next to the house with a rifle in his hands. She hoped everyone would control their anger and not do something foolish.

"One more thing, I have a surprise for everyone. In this bag, I have letters from home."

Sun-hee's heart flip-flopped as Sgt. Kua passed out envelopes and packages. She received her letter. The lid of emotion she had suppressed for the last couple of weeks erupted in tears while her feet began to dance in place. She struggled to get the letter out of the envelope. She forced her feet to be still, wiped her eyes on her sleeves, and started reading:

> *My Dearest Daughter,*
>
> *I am so proud of you. The whole town is proud of you. Please forgive me for bragging, but I showed the Prize-Winning letter to everyone. They all think you are magnificent! I tell them you are my little empress.*
>
> *The four weeks since you left have been the longest weeks of my life. I miss you. Every moment of every day I wish I could give you a big hug. HUG! I am delighted you are doing well at school. You have made me the proudest parent in Yonggwang.*
>
> *The magistrate offered me a position at the adult school teaching Korean. I immediately became the most requested teacher. My days are filled doing what I love, teaching language, all because you won the prize. One student brought me a few baeksalgu that were so sweet and flavorful. I wish I could have shared them with you.*

Construction started on new houses on the south end of town. I took the risk and requested one for us. The magistrate approved the request. Hopefully, I will be in a new house this winter. They have electric lights and furnaces. No longer will I need to scour the hillsides for wood. No more freezing during winter in a grass-roofed hut. I am so excited!

The first chance I get, I am coming to Wonsan to see you. If you get a chance to come home, borrow money for a train ticket. I will reimburse them.

I hope to see you soon!

Love, Mom.

Sun-hee sat down on her mat and re-read her mother's letter over and over through blurred watery eyes. She recalled the time, five years ago, when her mother was so excited to have enough money, after bartering a merchant down, to buy two *baeksalgu* — one apricot each.

Her mother had wiped the juice off her chin with her finger, saying, "We can't let any of the fruit go to waste." Then she had licked her finger.

The general must have used a return address in Wonsan. He kept our location a secret. He has considered everything in keeping us prisoners.

Young-ja and two other girls handed out *hangwa* from the packages they received. She placed the candies aside as she felt more trapped than ever before.

If I can leave the camp and get home safely, everything mother has gained will be lost.

She looked up, seeing the tears of others, their hugs, their joys, the sharing of hangwa. San Hien-jin wept uncontrollably. Her brother had been killed in the fighting. Others shared their letters and talked about their families. Sun-hee folded her letter, put it under her mat, and shared nothing.

I'm trapped in this camp and cannot return to my mother. I'm like water swirling in a funnel, leading to an unknown future.

***

The next day, Sgt. Kua handed out writing paper, ink, and pens so they could write back to their families. Sun-hee wrote a letter her mother could show off. It was all lies, but it would make her mother's life better. She placed her unsealed envelope on the pile, knowing the general would review them before mailing them out. She did not care how he felt about her message of lies.

After dinner, Gen. Park called them into formation. "Tomorrow, this camp will become a hospital," he said. "Soldiers are returning from battle injured. I trust you will do your best to give them the care they deserve. Get a good night's sleep. Tomorrow will be a busy day."

He walked away as a couple of men unloaded bundles of pants and white smocks. She took the clothes, joined the group hug, and prepared for bed.

Sun-hee laid down and wondered which boy Gen. Park would select for her. She thought about each of the boys, trying to think of something positive about each one.

"Sun-hee, are you asleep?" whispered Joo-yun.

"No. I was thinking about who Park selected for me."

"You're ready to do this, aren't you, Sun-hee."

"Not really, just mentally preparing for the inevitable."

"I do not know how to prepare, Sun-hee. My mother always talked about finding me a husband and how I would love him. Now we are being forced together like breeding dogs."

"The choice I made is to view all the boys as our husbands. General Park is the matchmaker. All we can do is accept the boy as our husband." She was scrambling for the right words as she spoke. "If we were still at home, our parents would have a difficult time finding such good fathers for our children. I know I am not ready to be a mother or to even have sex, but we must prepare ourselves. Choe-me was not emotionally ready for what happened to her. I am preparing myself. We can hate General Park while accepting the boys as our family."

"We are more than this," Joo-yun said.

"I hope we are, Joo-yun. I hope we are."

In a few minutes, she fell into a restless sleep.

9 — War and Love - July 10, 1950

The clatter of the door unlocking woke Sun-hee. The lightbulbs flashed on, blinding her eyes. Sun-hee dressed in her new smocks and stepped outside into a light rain. Sgt. Kua made a quick count before turning to jog out the gate.

We don't have exercises this morning.

Sun-hee ran to breakfast, only to stop to help Joo-yun who had slipped and fell in the mud.

While eating her second bowl of gruel, trucks rumbled into the compound. Lt. Rim began barking orders in the distance.

Sgt. Kua yelled, "Let's go, time to go to work!" She waved her hand, tossed her dish into the washbasin, and took off in a run towards the trucks which were rolling to a stop on the other side of the fence by the barracks.

Throwing her bowl in the basin, Sun-hee sprinted after the sergeant. The energy in her legs carried her to the new challenge. One she was willing but not prepared to face. Together with Joo-yun and two other girls, they unload a stretcher from a truck.

"Take the men into the barracks," commanded Lt. Rim while pointing at the first of the six identical buildings.

They carefully set the man onto the floor. Bandages circled the man's head and upper left arm. More covered the man's entire abdomen. The pungent stench of body odor, urine, and feces filled Sun-hee's nostrils. She gagged, swallowed hard, and barely held her breakfast down. She heard some of the boys razzing Numbers as he lost his breakfast.

Gen. Park knelt next to Sun-hee, looked the man over, and said, "This man needs bandages and clothes removed. Call me when you have him clean, then I can evaluate his wounds." He moved on.

Joo-yun helped Sun-hee unwind the bandage on his head. When the gash across the side of his head was exposed, Joo-yun covered her mouth and ran. Sun-hee finished removing the man's bandages, revealing a deep cut on his arm and an inflamed stomach wound full of pus. She had read about infection, but never had she seen it up close. It made her skin crawl.

The man was warm to Sun-hee's touch. He had a fever, which meant infection had set in. A woman she had never seen came over with a bowl of warm water and some rags. Together, they washed the dried blood from around the man's wounds. When finished, she stood and looked around.

"Doctor Park," she yelled.

I called him a doctor, not general.

"In a minute, Sun-hee," came the reply from across the room.

The room was full of students kneeling around wounded men. For the first time, the moans, groans, and screams of the men in pain invaded her ears. She heard the shouts of fellow students as they attended to the patients before them.

Gen. Park came up and examined the man. "We need to clean the stomach wound and stitch up the head and arm. Cover him, but no bandages. Cool compresses on the head, chest, and legs to reduce the fever."

"Yes, General Park," she said, emphasizing the word general.

"Right now, I am a doctor. Referring to me as such is preferred," he said as he moved to another injured soldier.

A few minutes later, she saw Eun-seong by a stretcher that had just been brought in. She went to help her friend. A couple of sticks wrapped with cloth formed a brace on the man's leg. Together, they carefully removed the splint as Dr. Park came up.

"Here is how to set a broken leg. Hold the man down. It is painful."

Eun-seong grabbed one arm. Sun-hee grabbed the other.

"Bite down hard," the doctor said while placing a stick in the man's mouth. "Sun-hee and Eun-seong, observe so you can do this next time."

Sun-hee struggled to hold the man still as she watched the doctor manipulate bones through the man's flesh, pushing them into position. With every move, Park described what he was doing. In a couple of minutes, he said, "Put the splint back on, and we will add a cast when the swelling goes down. The next one you can do."

She reached over and took the stick from the man's mouth, noticing the teeth marks. She said to him, "We will get your leg splinted, and you will be fine." Eun-seong helped her immobilize the leg and make the man comfortable before moving on.

Dr. Park showed the students how to clean wounds, apply bandages, set bones, and fight infection. He would take a patient and a few students, explaining to them what was needed, then leave to care for another patient.

As Sun-hee listened to him explain another procedure, the fog of her hate for him diminished, slowly buried by the needs of the soldiers. She helped one wounded man after another, casting aside the gore of maimed bodies, trying to speak kindly and encourage them.

Dr. Park worked and taught with a sense of urgency. The reason became clear as more trucks, full of wounded men, arrived before lunch. Sun-hee knelt by one man who had just been carried in. She started to remove the bandages, but he did not move. He did not seem to be breathing.

She called Dr. Park over to help. He knelt beside him, checked for a pulse, then listened for his heartbeat.

"This man is dead. Take him outside," he said and moved on.

She looked at the dead man before her for a moment, the dirt on his whiskers, his greasy, disheveled hair.

Where was this man from? What was his name?

She grabbed one of the boys walking by. "Give me a hand in moving this man." They lifted the stretcher and carried him out.

As they walked out, Sun-hee, blinded by the sunlight, paused and wondered what to do with the burden she carried.

Lt. Rim yelled out, "Is that man dead?"

"Yes, Lieutenant," Sun-hee said.

"Place him over there near the northeast corner with the others," he said, pointing the way.

She struggled to carry the load. The sky had cleared, and the sun was blazing. By the time they got to the corner, sweat crawled off her forehead and down her face. The man they carried was the sixth to be laid in this corner of the compound. They placed him next to the others. Her hands were free. She wiped the sweat, mingled with tears, from her eyes and face. As she walked back, she tried to remove the image of the dead man. There were others still alive and needing help, but the image of death endured.

She had no desire to eat, but Dr. Park insisted they go in groups of twelve to eat lunch, telling them to drink lots of water because of the heat.

As she ate, her mind returned to the man in the corner of the camp.

Who would prepare him for burial?

She recalled how her mother was kept from her father the last day before he passed, as tradition demanded.

Women must not watch men die.

Had she broken tradition by being the first person with the man after his death?

With no family here to perform a ceremony, will he wander forever as a ghost? Her spoon grated against her empty bowl. *I must help.*

When she returned, Sun-hee began to attend to the soldiers who had just arrived. In her peripheral vision, Dr. Park entered to stroll among the patients, picking out ones needing shrapnel removed, bones repaired, a body part amputated, or some other form of operation. She saw the red-faced man with the stomach wound receiving special attention. She felt relieved he was going to get help.

The doctor selected four of the boys to aid in surgery. She turned, focused on cleaning dried blood from the leg wound before her.

One injury after another, Sun-hee and the other students worked throughout the afternoon. She ignored the screams when she cleaned infected wounds or set bones to the best of her novice ability. The pain she invoked was to treat, not to harm, she kept telling herself. She could not keep her hands clean, continually wiping them on unused areas of her smock until there was no clean spot left.

The students who could stomach the sights and smells had no time to waste. Trucks kept coming. By the time the sun had set, Sun-hee counted seventy men in the building she worked in, and three other barracks were filled with more injured men. She wondered how many more men were lying in the corner of the camp.

It was almost dark when Gen. Park called the students together in front of one of the barracks. Sun-he held her head down and took deep breaths of the cool evening breeze flowing off the mountains. Her legs felt like limp seaweed, and her arms hung like wilted flowers. Her knees ached from repeatedly kneeling beside patients, and she badly needed to pee. Exhaustion blocked any emotion that quivered up from inside her.

"We must divide up so we can provide care around the clock," said Gen. Park. He pulled out a paper and read off twelve names. "You will continue to work until midnight. Get some food and return." Then he called out twelve more. "You go eat and get some sleep. You will return at midnight and work until noon. Suk Jong-hui and Ki-young, report to Sergeant Kua. Han Young-soo and Cha Sun-hee, also report to the sergeant. The rest stay here until the first group returns from dinner and then eat and rest until morning."

The girls gathered around Sun-hee. She barely felt their warm embrace. Then they left. She stood alone, breathing shallowly, staring at the ground.

When she looked up, Stone was standing about ten meters away.

Everyone else was scurrying to their appointed tasks. Their eyes locked. He gave her a sheepish smile.

Sun-hee had prepared her emotions for this moment. Now, she didn't have the energy to care. She scanned the boy Park had chosen for her. Blood and who knew what other bodily excretions stained his clothes. Crescent moons of sweat rimmed each armpit.

She looked down at herself, horrorstruck at her filthy smock. She bit her lower lip, started to brush her hair out of her face with her arm but stopped when she saw the ooze covering her sleeve.

Stone stepped slowly over to her. His short black hair laid down around his head except for the cowlick at the top, which stood on end, pointing at her when he bowed.

She returned the bow as custom dictated, hesitating at the bottom to show her respect.

Stone strode off. Sun-hee forced her legs to follow, and slowly, a distance grew between them. The sound of her footsteps plodded in her ears. She was glad for the silence and lack of conversation. She could only think: *this is the worst day.*

Sgt. Kua met them at the door. Alarmed by the soiled clothes, she stepped back, and said, "Take your smocks off outside and take a seat. We'll get you two cleaned up after the others finish with the shower."

Young-soo sat, folded his arms, and laid his head on them.

Sun-hee sat, folded her hands in her lap, and stared at them. Her mind's eye saw the wounds she had treated and the dead dumped in the corner of the compound. So many wounded men brought to this camp so far from the fighting. She remembered Lt. Rim not allowing Capt. Kwang to take them away. She made a mental note to thank him someday. She shivered as she imagined what it would be like to see men being injured and killed in battle. A door opened, and she turned to see Ki-young entering a bedroom.

Sergeant Kua handed Sun-hee a robe and said, "You're next in the shower."

The water was cold. Cleansing her body from the crud from the day was her only goal. She washed, then washed again. Coming down the hallway, she could see that Stone still had his head on the table.

Sgt. Kua put her arm out, guiding Sun-hee into an empty bedroom. "I'll get Young-soo to clean up and send him in," she said.

The door closed. The air was musty from the humidity and unpainted wood walls. Sun-hee's head swirled from the day of chaos in the stillness of the room. On the far side of the room, there was a mat on the floor, with a brown wool army blanket and a couple of towels folded neatly on one end. A vase with two small, yellow sunflowers sat on a shelf above the mat. A naked light bulb hung from the center of the ceiling, illuminating the room. She placed her garments near the door, lay down on the mat, arranged her robe, and pulled the blanket over her. In an instant, she fell sound asleep.

10 — Max and Alek - July 11 - Mid August, 1950

Knocking on the door startled her awake.

"Sun-hee. Young-soo," said Sgt. Kua.

She sat up and noticed it was light outside of the window. Young-soo sat up beside her, with a startled look on his face.

"Are you decent?" Sgt. Kua asked.

She glanced around and said, "Yes, Sergeant."

The sergeant stuck her head into the room. "It is morning, and you need to return to your quarters."

Sun-hee looked at the sergeant and then at Young-soo. "We must have fallen asleep. Give us a few minutes to complete our task," Sun-hee said.

The sergeant closed the door. Sun-hee pushed the blanket off her and let her robe fall open at the waist.

Stone untied his robe.

She closed her eyes and gritted her teeth as Stone moved on top of her. His body pressed between her legs. Her chin shot up with the pain. They held still for a moment. He moved away, wrapping his robe around himself and swiftly exiting the room.

She took a deep breath and let it out slowly. The morning sunlight came in through the window, creating a crossed square on the wall by the door. She had wondered for the last two weeks how she would feel at this moment. Her only sense was emptiness.

She waited until she heard footsteps run down the hall. Wrapping the robe around her thin body, she winced as she got to her feet. She gathered her things and opened the door. Sgt. Kua handed her clean pants and a smock with one hand and motioned her down the hall with the other.

The cold water stimulated her aching muscles. She put her face to the flow, allowing the water to stream down her body. Shaking her head to break through the cobwebs holding her consciousness hostage, she failed to set it free. Her breath was heavy as she dressed and scampered back to the dorm.

"Sun-hee! We were so worried," said Eun-seong as she entered. "Are you okay? What happened?"

"I'm fine. We fell asleep." The few girls in the dorm joined in a group hug around her.

Am I fine? If feeling nothing is fine.

"We need to get ready and go to breakfast as our shift is about to start," said Eun-seong.

A minute later, Eun-seong, Joo-yun, and Sun-hee left for breakfast.

During breakfast, Eun-seong asked, "How are you feeling?"

"After seeing dead men yesterday, I am overwhelmed. The moment with Stone is overcast by the fog of death."

"I am always available to talk," said Eun-seong.

"Everything in this place makes me mad," said Joo-yun.

The three finished their breakfast in silence.

Together they entered one of the barracks, now a makeshift hospital. Joo-yun stood at the entrance and pulled on her pigtails. Sun-hee and Eun-seong knelt by a man on a cot and started to unravel bandages.

Gen. Park's voice boomed through the room. "I would like to introduce two Soviet doctors who arrived this morning. Doctor Maxim Bogdanov." He pointed to the man on his right. "And this is Doctor Aleksey Zaytesev," he said, pointing to his left.

"I need four of you who are fluent in Russian. Kwong-ku and Chulsoon, assist Doctor Zaytesev. Joo-yun and Sun-hee, assist Doctor Bogdanov."

Joo-yun said, "But, General Park."

"No excuses, Joo-yen," said the general as he grabbed her arm and thrust her towards Sun-hee.

Dr. Bogdanov approached and examined the wounds on the man Sun-hee knelt next to. The doctor was a head taller than Sun-hee. His square chin was cleanly shaven. Thick eyebrows formed umbrellas over his deep-set eyes, and his tea-brown hair was combed straight back over his head.

"Shrapnel wounds to the leg and torso," he said in Russian. "We will start with him. Let's move him to the operating room."

They picked the man up and carried him to the back of the barracks into the small room designed for the unit commander. A new metal table was in the center. Small tables, covered in supplies, were spaced around the sides.

"Place him in the center of the table."

Sun-hee bowed. "Yes, Doctor Bougndove," she said in Russian, struggling to pronounce his name.

"Call me Max. Much easier and is more efficient when in the operating room," he responded in Russian.

Sun-hee bowed and said, "Yes, Doctor Max."

"Max only," he said sternly. "And do not bow as it takes your eyes off what you are doing." Sun-hee froze, her eyes fixed on Max's blue eyes. "I will call you Sun and you Joo." He pointed at each girl. "First lesson, poor communication in the operating room can kill patients. Second is how to wash up." He showed them how to scrub and prepare for surgery.

As soon as Max uncovered the open wound, Joo-yun's eyes rolled into her head. She collapsed to the floor with a thud.

"Joo-yun!" exclaimed Sun-hee, moving to her side.

"Some people can't be in an operating room," said Max as he picked up Joo-yun. He carried her to the main room and laid her on the floor.

Sun-hee yelled at Eun-seong, "Come help in the operating room. Joo-yun can't handle it."

Eun-seong rushed to kneel by Joo-yun. "Is she all right?"

"She fainted. She will be fine in a few minutes. We need to help Max," said Sun-hee, taking Eun-seong to wash up.

They joined Max, who was already working. He explained his movements as he made them. "I make a cut on his side large enough to stick in a finger, then feel for shrapnel."

Max took a glance at Eun-seong who had paled.

Eun-seong took deep breaths and held onto the end of the table.

Max continued, "Even though the wound is in the front, the metal is deeper, so I make a cut where I think it is, and…it is here. Tweezers." He looked up, flashed a grin, and raised his eyebrows at Sun-hee.

Sun-hee translated Max's Russian to Korean for Eun-seong while handing him tweezers. Max removed the shrapnel and held it at eye-level towards Eun-seong's face. "If you do not faint now, then you are good," said Max.

Sun-hee translated.

Eun-seong smiled and said, "I will not faint, but I may cry." She flicked her eyelids a couple of times, sniffled, and forced back tears. "To see these men in this condition is crushing my heart."

Sun-hee translated Eun-seong's words.

"Block feelings out," Max said, looking directly at Eun-seong. Then he turned to Sun-hee, "You must block them out."

For the rest of the day, the two were with Max, operating on wounded soldiers. Max constantly talked, explaining what he was doing, why he was doing it, and how the girls could help him. He told them the vital signs to look for in the patients and what could go wrong. Sun-hee kept up a running translation.

Sun-hee absorbed as much as she could. She made a game with Eun-seong, naming the bones, muscles, and other body parts in different languages. It helped to distract from the smells and sights of the wounds and most importantly, tune out the moans and screams.

Now and then, between Max's running dialogue of explanations, he would say, "Block feelings out." By the end of the day, Sun-hee had walled them in.

Students who had slept all day began to arrive. Max left. As Sun-hee started to go, she walked by Gen. Park. He sat on a stool, leaning his head against the wall, his shirt soaked in sweat.

"Sun-hee, just a moment," he said, sitting up.

She halted as he took a piece of paper out of his pocket. "You and Han Young-soo have a second night together. Please tell Seo Young-ja and Shon In-jung to report to Sergeant Kua."

"Yes, General. I will inform them," she said.

Gen. Park folded up the paper and placed it back into his pocket. He leaned back and closed his eyes. Sun-hee began to walk away when she heard, "And Sun-hee, tell everyone I am very proud of the work they have done for these soldiers. Very proud."

"Yes, sir! If only we could have done more," she said politely, then walked away.

General Park commended me. How can he praise me after telling me to make a baby? He compromises morals to achieve his ends. Sun Tzu said, "Know thy enemies." I must understand Park better. I must know his goals.

She headed off to eat dinner.

Sun-hee took a bite of the bland tofu stew and nearly spat it out. Park's words pounded in her head.

He twists my emotions. For what reason? He is so pleased we are complying with everything he wants. He will not use me as a messenger of his exploitation.

A slight grin crossed her face, and she resumed eating.

She found Young-ja. "General Park told me it is your turn tonight."

"Why did you tell me? I was going to hide from the sergeant. Now I can't say having sex slipped out of my mind."

Sun-hee smiled.

"I got you to smile. I like it better than the frown you wear most of the time. You are always too serious. I wonder which lucky guy will be with me tonight."

"You are so positive, Young-ja."

Young-ja looked Sun-hee in the eye, the ends of her mouth curled up slightly, while her eyes sunk back into her head. "To be honest, Sun-hee. I want to run. I want to scream. I want to get out of here. I can't do what I want, Sun-hee. We are trapped, and I am so tired."

Sun-hee wrapped her arms around Young-ja. They held each other tightly. After a moment, Young-ja said, "Here I am complaining when you also have to visit the house tonight. How were things with you and Stone?" she asked. "You were with him all night. Did he tell you all about his rock collection?"

"I was so exhausted. I fell asleep as soon as I laid down. Stone did not wake me, so we did not do have sex until we woke up this morning."

Young-ja began to chuckle, causing Sun-hee to smile.

"Maybe I can get my guy to fall asleep and then sneak out. I wonder who I am going to fool?" Young-ja said.

"I'll go find him and tell him to report to the sergeant," Sun-hee said teasingly.

"You know?" Young-ja grabbed Sun-hee by the shoulders and looked her in the eye. "Tell me, Sun-hee! Now!"

Sun-hee snickered. She had gotten Young-ja to react. "You will know soon."

"I am not going to let you go until you tell me."

Sun-hee enjoyed keeping Young-ja in suspense. Finally, she said, "Shon In-jung."

"In-jung," Young-ja yelled. "The Skinny Beast?" In-jung, being tall and skinny, with a square head and short straight hair that stuck out all over, fit the name. "I can't do it with him. I will start laughing when I see him naked. Sex with him will not work," she went on and started to chuckle. "Just thinking of him naked makes me laugh."

They both giggled and went looking for In-jung.

Outside the boy's quarters, Sun-hee asked Chulsoon if he had seen In-jung.

"He is in there," Chulsoon said, pointing to the boy's dorm. "I will go get him if you like."

"Yes, please. I need to tell him something."

"I will go get ready," said Young-ja.

A couple of minutes later, In-jung came out, "Hi Sun-hee, what do you want?"

"I have a message from General Park. You are to report to the sergeant's house tonight. It is your turn."

"M-m-me," he stammered, eyes darting. "I…I must wash up." He turned as pale as Joo-yun before she fainted. Then he sprinted to the privy, stumbling along the way.

Sun-hee's head sunk as she turned. *I am going to enjoy the shower and getting the grime off before my agony.* She grabbed some clean clothes and sauntered towards the house.

"Young-soo is waiting for you," said Sgt. Kua when she walked in. "Robes are on the hooks. Young-ja is in the shower."

Young-ja came out. "I'm ready for Skinny Beast," she said. They snickered.

Sun-hee took her time in the shower, letting the ugliness of the day wash off. She donned her robe, walked out, and placed her soiled clothes in a pile with Young-ja's and Young-soo's. Sgt. Kua picked them up and took them outside. In-jung entered at the same time.

"You get that room In-jung," Sun-hee said, pointing at the door. Then she opened the other door and stepped inside.

Stone was sitting against the wall away from the mat with his knees up and arms around his legs. Without looking up, he said, "I'm sorry, Sun-hee."

"Me too, Young-soo."

"I was already promised. My parents arranged for my wife last year. I was to be married when I turned seventeen."

"None of us want this. We have considered the options, and if we want to live, this is what we have to do."

"It shouldn't be this way. It seems so wrong. I wanted to tell you, I am sorry."

"I am tired. Let's get this over with." Sun-hee laid down on the mat, allowing the robe which had been tightly around her to lie loose. Stone crawled across the room and lay on top of her. She grimaced, then heard Young-ja's loud laugh from across the hall.

Stone rolled over on his back, covered himself with his robe, and stared at the ceiling. His task complete.

Sun-hee put her hand on his arm. "Apology accepted."

Stone pulled away and turned his head away from her.

Her eyes closed for a moment before she startled awake. Not wanting to spend the night again, she hopped up, showered, and returned to the dorm, receiving comforting hugs.

When the lights went out, Choe-me pulled herself next to Sun-hee, wrapped her arm around, and whispered, "You were here for me. I'll be here for you." They held each other through the night.

The next day there were more wounded men, more operations. Eun-seong and Sun-hee worked with Max as fast and as efficiently as they could. One injured man after another, in the heat and humidity of the summer, drained their energy. Max insisted they drink water between each surgery. Past, future, and periphery were a blur. She saw the men before her, nothing else.

Morphine was in short supply; the doctors administered it only during surgery. The injured suffered in their pain. More soldiers died, mostly due to infection. She lost count, but it seemed at the end of the day, there were twice as many wounded men in the makeshift hospital. Trucks continued to arrive.

Lt. Rim recruited local people to help. There were more cooks and people feeding the wounded. Women whisked dirty clothes off to the wash. Men were continuously cleaning floors. The smell of bleach overpowered the stench of the wounds.

More medical supplies arrived, including lots of medical pants and smocks. Sun-hee was relieved to be able to change a few times a day. Each time she passed by Stone, he did not look at her nor acknowledge she was there.

When Max quit for the night, Sun-hee went directly to the house. Young-soo came in, performed mechanically without saying a word, then left, all within a couple of minutes.

She lay on the mat.

What is my mother doing tonight?

She imagined her mother sitting next to her, listening while she shared about the camp, the girls, her studies, and treating the wounded. She stopped, realizing she was avoiding telling her mother the real story.

I can never tell mother the truth. It would destroy her. I can never go home. I wished I had failed. I have failed.

She rolled over and cried.

She had no idea how long she shed tears before getting up. She took some clean clothes off the table, taking care not to wake the sergeant who lay sleeping on a mat in the corner. She showered and started to leave only to meet Young-ja in the hallway. Tears flowed down Young-ja's cheeks, and they fell into each other's arms.

Sun-hee stepped over to gather some clothes for Young-ja. She handed them to her, saying, "I will wait for you." They walked back to the girls building arm-in-arm.

Life seemed so empty on this moonless night. All she had was the other girls. All she wanted was sleep, blanking her mind to the horrors of the last few days. She pulled out her silk scarf and stroked it. Choe-me's comforting arm wrapped over her. She fell into a deep slumber.

Another twelve-hour day went by, caring for the injured. She cleaned up and returned to the dorm. Some of the girls had a calendar and were writing names on it. Her name, with Young-soo's, was written in the previous three days. She read the other names on the chart. The names in the past were the couples which had already been together, only girl's names were in the future, placed three days in a row, two weeks after their last period.

"We found this calendar," said San Sang-me. "Now we can keep track of the schedule ourselves. When you start your period, record it on the date with your initials."

The next few days went by quickly. The wounded brought stories of the war. The army captured Seoul. Many South Koreans were surrendering or defecting; the North was winning.

July ended. Sun-hee's period had not arrived. She worried about being pregnant but accepted her fate. There was nothing she could do about it. August was hot and muggy with monsoon rains most of the days. The camp was muddy, except around the student dorms where they had built rock paths.

The number of new patients slowed to a trickle. Some of the men recovered, able to return to their units or families. Lt. Rim put some of the men to work around the base. Soldiers who could hold a rifle reestablished the military force. Sun-hee was happy to see the men she had operated on walk out of the camp. Something she could not do.

Sgt. Kua discovered the calendar on the wall. The girls watched her check her list with the calendar. She turned, scanned them, and said, "Keep it accurate." Then she tore up her paper and walked out.

The second week of August, Gen. Park left to tour the medical facilities in the rest of the country. He returned ten days later, strutting around proudly, proclaiming the Korean People's Army was pushing the Republic of Korea's Army down the peninsula. The South Korean Army was holed up in the southeast corner of The District of Pusan. Everyone felt the worst of the war was over.

Sun-hee stayed with Max when he made his rounds in the mornings. Max played cards and drank vodka with Alek in the afternoons.

Sun-hee spent her afternoons in the library. Her studies of medicine held new significance. What she was learning could help save a life.

11 — Changes - Late August & Early September, 1950

"We should refer to Sergeant Kua's house as the 'comfort rooms,'" said Choe-me.

"I do not like the connotation," said Eun-seong.

"I will name it Sergeant Kua's guesthouse," said Young-ja.

The name stuck. Eight weeks after the start of Park's baby-making efforts, the guesthouse was busy every night.

Six girls were now late, including Sun-hee. Six weeks had passed since she had been with Stone, and she thought she was pregnant. Since no one had gone through childbirth before, the girls scoured the medical books to tell them what was happening.

However, on the twentieth of August, Sun-hee's period arrived. She wondered if irregular periods were a part of Park's plan. He had told them the pairings would be the same until each girl was pregnant. Sun-hee avoided telling Stone, leaving their next meeting in the guesthouse a surprise.

The wounded informed the students on the progress of the war. North Korea dominated the battles. With the war farther away, there were fewer wounded arriving. A low patient count and the joy of releasing them from the hospital improved everyone's morale.

Farmers lined up, delivering food to the compound. The land reform of the new government had made this military camp the local collection point for food. Lt. Rim was seen running around and coordinating the storage of the crops.

A significant amount of building materials such as lumber, cement, and bricks arrived. Lt. Rim employed some of the former patients as workers to repair the existing buildings and build new storage for supplies. The camp was once again becoming a vibrant working community.

***

On a bright sunny day in the first week of September, Sun-hee was hoeing weeds in the garden between rows of carrots and potatoes. Suk Jong-hui was picking tomatoes and green beans while complaining about being pregnant. "How can I raise a child in this cement block of a building. We are doctors, and we get this cold box while they are doing construction in other parts of the compound. Are we not important? If we do not get a better place to live, I am walking out of here and going home!"

About twenty meters behind Jong-hui stood Sgt. Kua, hands on her hips, listening to the tirade. "You are correct, Jong-hui," interrupted Sgt. Kua. "You deserve better living quarters. However, you know if you try to leave, you will not make it home." Then she turned and walked out the gate.

The girls stopped and stared. When Sgt. Kua was out of hearing range, Young-ja spoke up. "Hon-yong, you know carpentry. Can you build us a new building?"

"I know woodworking," replied Hon-yong. "When they finish a new building, I can make furniture, hang the doors, and build cabinets. A whole structure is beyond my ability."

A half-hour later, Sgt. Kua returned and called the students into formation. A few of the students were helping at the hospital, so not all were present.

"General Park has decided to have a new dorm built in this compound to house students. The materials are available. We need someone who can design a building larger than a barrack. Lt. Rim will be inquiring around the area for someone who can design and oversee the project."

This news lifted everyone's spirits. There was hope for better living quarters.

Three days later, during lunch, Gen. Park and Lt. Rim were seen outside the fence between the kitchen and the student dorms. Accompanying them was a grey-haired man who walked with two canes. There was a wooden stump on the man's right foot.

Gen. Park spoke loud enough that everyone could hear. "Mr. Yun, I have asked you here because we need to build some proper quarters for our medical students. I envision this camp will be a learning facility apart from the distractions of a city. Building materials are available, and more are to come from the Soviet Union. Lieutenant Rim runs the camp and will work with you to provide what you need. Thank you for coming out of retirement to direct this task for the glory of Korea."

"I have had nothing better to do lately," said Mr. Yun. "I am ready to get started."

"Excellent," said Gen. Park.

Sun-hee watched as Mr. Yun and the general walked around the kitchen on the hillside. She turned to Young-ja. "I think the general was talking to us and not the man with the canes."

"We think alike, Sun-hee," said Young-ja. "We may get a new place to sleep, but it only chains us tighter in this prison."

"Park is cunning in his control over us. We need to get our lives back," said Sun-hee.

"How can we do that?" asked Young-ja.

"Another question I can't answer."

"You're frowning again, Sun-hee."

"My lunch has turned sour in my stomach." She got up and put her half-eaten bowl in the washbasin.

The next day, work started on a new section of fence to enclose the area for the new dorms. Trenches were dug to lay pipes. Some pipes would bring water from an earthen dam up the valley, others would take waste to the stream down the valley. Recovered soldiers became workers. There were more men than Mr. Yun could put to work.

***

The time for Sun-hee's second round of meetings at the guesthouse arrived. She endured the first two visits, hating the coldness of having sex with Stone. She wanted a feeling of closeness, a sense of comfort together. All she got was a boy who performed like he was eating a bowl of gruel: gulp it down, throw the dish in the sink, and vanish.

The third night, Stone was late. Sun-hee pinched herself continually to stay awake. When he did come in, he smelled of earth and sweat. His clothes were dirty. He had not bathed. He fumbled with the ties on his clothes.

Impatiently, Sun-hee blurted out, "Hurry up! Get me pregnant, so I will not have to endure you any longer."

Stone grabbed the string on his pants, yanked, and broke it. He pushed his pants to his ankles and fell as he tried to move forward.

Grabbing him under the armpits, Sun-hee pulled him on top of her. His face was flush. He fumbled about, adjusted, then let out a grunt. Sun-hee pushed him aside and got to her feet, wrapping the robe around her body. The two met at the door, both in a hurry—he like a scolded puppy, and she like an angry cat. Young-soo backed away, letting Sun-hee leave first.

She met Young-ja, returning from dinner, who reached out to hug her, saying, "How was your time with Stone?"

"I…" She burst into tears.

Young-ja held her tight and let the tears flow on her shoulder.

"The only way we get through this is to support each other," said

Young-ja. "My shoulder is always available."

"Thank you," she said between sniffles. "The name Stone fits his personality perfectly."

After a moment, they released their hug. "How was Skinny Beast?"

A smile came over Young-ja's face. "I shouldn't tell you."

"I am here to support you as you supported me. Why are you smiling?"

"I referred to him as 'skinny beast' the last night we were together. He looked down and said, 'good name for it.' I laughed so hard, I farted."

Sun-hee doubled over, releasing her emotion in hilarity until her sides hurt.

The next night, Sgt. Kua came to get Joo-yun and took her to the guesthouse even though her name was not on the calendar.

When Joo-yun returned, Sun-hee sensed her stiffness during the group hug. Joo-yun pulled herself away and went to her mat. Sun-hee followed. "Are you alright?"

"I am good," said Joo-yun, who started getting ready for bed.

"Your name was not on the calendar."

"My time is private. That woman shouldn't have known."

"You hid your menses from everyone?" Sun-hee inquired.

"That is what I was taught to do."

"What boy were you with?"

"I refused Kwang Byeoung-keun. We did nothing." Joo-yun laid down and turned her head away from Sun-hee.

Sgt. Kua escorted Joo-yun out of the dorm the next evening. Sun-hee and her friends stepped out a moment later. A gust of wind hit them in the face as they stopped in front of the dorm. Sgt. Kua had Joo-yun by the arm. Byeoung-keun followed a couple of meters behind.

"I don't have a good feeling about what is going to happen in the guesthouse tonight," said Eun-seong.

"Me either," said Choe-me in a quiet voice.

"That is an ugly storm cloud to the east," said Young-ja.

Just then, a bolt of lightning lept out of the cloud, striking the mountain across the road from the compound.

Raindrops began to fall. The gusts of wind forced the girls back inside the dorm. They waited in worried silence.

Rain began to pelt the roof in waves. The windows shook. The girls huddled together in groups around the room.

The door flung open. Joo-yun stumbled in and fell to her hands and knees. Water dripped from her unbraided hair.

Sun-hee and Eun-seong lifted Joo-yun to her feet.

Joo-yun pushed them away and crossed the room to her mat and pounded on the wall with her fists. "That woman is a chameleon," she said with anger. "She called me a snobbish aristocrat." Her fists hit the wall again. "How did she know we didn't have sex last night?" Joo-yun turned around and slid down the wall onto her haunches. "Kua had the nerve to check me after Byeoung-keun left," she shrieked and gritted her teeth.

Eun-seong reached out to comfort Joo-yun who batted away Eun-seong's arms.

"I don't want your comfort. I don't want to belong. I'm not like the rest of you," said Joo-yun, eyes glaring at the rest of the girls.

"We are here when you need us," said Eun-seong.

The girls went to bed. Sun-hee kept an eye on Joo-yun who sat against the wall all night.

Joo-yun went to the guesthouse for the next two evenings. She remained angry, resisting any comfort, and never shed a tear.

***

For weeks, Sgt. Kua had been feeling more like a maid than a sergeant in the army. She would get the students up in the mornings and make sure they had clean smocks. In the evening, she made sure the rooms in her house were neat with fresh towels and robes available. She put the laundry on her porch for one of the civilians to take away. The girls seemed to show up when they should, and the boys arrived when called.

One day, Kua had noticed Joo-yun rinsing rags at the sink. She had made a note of it. She had never liked Joo-yun's attitude and lack of effort compared to the rest of the students. And hiding her menses was a disappointment. Kua felt like she had been lax in her duties in working with Joo-yun.

Two weeks later, Kua invited Joo-yun to her house. When Joo-yun left, her demeanor was different than the other girls. She knew the girl had been disobedient. Her anger came out the next evening when she confronted Joo-yun. She had to be sure Joo-yun did what they were commanded to do. Joo-yun gave her a new purpose, someone who needed her training.

Kua sat down in the chair in the corner. She didn't like her role in the program, yet she was glad not to be with the rest of Korea's soldiers. She thought of her future. The plans for the new building did not have a place for her. She had moved her mat to the main room, as the students were using both bedrooms. Where else would she go and what else would she do?

She did what she could; she started knitting baby booties.

12 — Choices - Late September, 1950

Choe-me jumped onto her mat and knelt, looking at Sun-hee wide-eyed. "Sun-hee, did you see they have a wall of the new building standing?"

"I did," said Sun-hee. "Since we are captives in this place, I am looking forward to having a better place to live. Hopefully, the lighting will be better than these hanging bulbs. Reading in the dorm hurts my eyes." She closed her book. "And thyroid disorders are not the most interesting subject to read in poor light."

"I hope the new building has stoves," said Choe-me. I don't want to be in this cement room in the cold of winter. It's only September, and the nights are already getting chilly."

The door opened, and Sun-hee looked up. The last returnee from the guesthouse this evening arrived. It was time for a group hug. She pushed off her blanket and got up to join the rest of the girls in offering support. Then it was back to bed and lights out.

The next morning at breakfast, Sun-hee said to Eun-seong, "The sliced pears and berries are a wonderful change."

"I mixed them in with the mush to make it taste better. I think we are getting the best of the local farms. I noticed carts full of food coming into the storage area yesterday afternoon," replied Eun-seong.

After breakfast, Sun-hee and Eun-seong made the rounds with Max. For once, no one needed surgery. Max left to play cards with Alek. Since it was a beautiful fall day, the two girls went to work in the student garden, digging up onions and carrots. They loaded a cart and took the food to the storage area. They watched the workers prepare the food for canning.

Sun-hee took a deep sniff of the air. "I love the sweet/sour aroma of kimchi."

"I like the garlic smell. The aroma wafting around makes my mouth water," said Eun-seong.

They stepped aside to let cartloads of clay pots enter the storage area. They watched women fill the containers to the brim with kimchi, seal the tops, and stack them in the buildings.

"Lots of food for the winter," said Eun-seong. "We may have to double our rations again to eat it all."

"I've gained a lot of weight," said Sun-hee. "You're still too thin."

There was a roar over the camp. The girls stopped to watch two jet planes pass over the compound.

"Wow, those planes are fast and loud," said Sun-hee.

"What?" said Eun-seong as she removed her hands from her ears.

Sun-hee leaned towards Eun-seong and yelled, "I said those planes were loud."

Eun-seong stepped back a little and laughed. "Do you think the planes were American?" she asked.

"I think they were Soviet planes. I couldn't tell," replied Sun-hee.

"Let's go ask Strategist."

They found Yong-gak and asked him, "Were the two planes that flew over the camp American or Soviet?"

The Strategist replied, "The United States has come to the aid of the South. They have jet planes like the two that flew over the camp. We are far north of where the Americans are fighting in the south, and I presume they are planes from the Soviet Union."

"Have you heard how the war is going?" asked Sun-hee.

"The Americans have stopped the advances of the North's army. I am afraid we did not defeat the South fast enough," Strategist said with his typical hand gestures. "Our success depends on the resolve of the Americans to fight."

"Thank you for the update," said Eun-seong.

"My pleasure."

The girls started off to the library. They scurried off the road and hugged the fence as Gen. Park's car sped by.

"Where do you think he is going?" said Sun-hee.

"At that speed, it looked like he was trying to chase the airplanes," answered Eun-seong.

***

The next morning, Sun-hee went to Max as she entered the hospital building. She appreciated working with him and having the opportunity to improve her Russian language skills. After translating instructions to another student, Sun-hee said, "Would you like to learn Korean, Max. I could teach you."

"No, Sun. Adding another language would add confusion to my brain," Max replied in Russian.

They continue their rounds. "We need more penicillin," Max said. "Infections are winning. Look at this man, Sun. The wounds in his leg are infected." Max placed his hand on the man's forehead. "He has a fever. The red streaks on his thigh show the infection moving into the rest of his body. An amputation will not save him. I have enough Penicillin for one patient today. Do I give it to him or one of the other men? Who do I save?"

Sun-hee looked at the man's leg. The calf had a bullet wound they had repaired the day before. "How do you choose who lives and dies Max?" she said.

"At Stalingrad, there was a captain who sorted out the wounded for the doctors. He made the tough choices of who received treatment first and who received antibiotics. Those he did not choose were moved outside into the cold where they froze. I did not care why he chose as he did. I treated the men he sent to me. Why must I choose, Sun? How can I know which of these Korean men is more important? Without more penicillin, the infection will kill this man, and that man, and the man over there. Choose, Sun. Select one to live. If we get more penicillin soon, the others will live."

Sun-hee hesitated, eyes darting between the three men. Her feet marched in place.

Why must such a choice be made? I am not a captain in the army. I am just a fifteen-year-old girl.

She rubbed her fingers across her palms. "I cannot choose which of these men are to die, Max," Sun-hee said, holding up her hands in surrender.

Max took a step towards her, being over fifteen centimeters taller, he looked down as she looked up into his face. "You look at this wrong, Sun. How I see it is like this: When Kim Il-sung declared war, he picked these men to die. They are the lucky ones who have made it back to us to receive treatment for their wounds. All we are doing is adding to the luck one of them has. As doctors, the only way we could save them all is to prevent the war. That would make us politicians. But politicians never seem to be able to prevent war." He got a big grin on his face then took a step back. "I take a patient and do what I can for him. Maybe I do not have the supplies for the next. I make one man lucky at a time. Then, I drink vodka to forget the rest."

He took a syringe from his right pocket and a small bottle from his left pocket, then he sucked out the contents of the bottle into the syringe. "Only enough to treat one. Who is it, Sun?"

Sun-hee studied the three men. She pointed to a small man they had operated on the day before, removing shrapnel from his neck. His weathered face held a wide smile, showing off his stained, crooked teeth. His deep brown eyes met hers.

He is thin but seems hearty. With the infected neck wound, he will die first if he does not get the antibiotic. He needs a little more luck.

"This one, Max," she said as she pointed. Max stuck the syringe in the man's arm, pushed the plunger to the bottom, removed it, and walked away.

She turned and bowed slightly to the Korean soldier. "We have given you something to help with the infection. It will make you better in a couple of days. What is your name?"

The man pulled out a piece of paper from his pants pocket and wrote, "I am Jo Jin-taek. Thank you."

"You're welcome," said Sun-hee. She turned, looked for Max, and hurried to catch up to him as he was already examining another patient.

Have I saved the right man? What will he do with his life? I hope more penicillin arrives soon.

The day continued. She thought of what the future would hold for each patient she treated.

That night, as she sat down on her mat next to Choe-me, she said, "Max made me choose who should die today."

"How was it your choice for men to die?

"He made me choose which man received the last dose of penicillin."

"There is no more penicillin?" Choe-me exclaimed. "Then many will die of infections. Who did you save with the last dose?"

"A small man named Jo Jin-taek. Max pointed out three men who will die soon without antibiotics. He only had one dose of penicillin left. He made me choose who got the shot. I hate making decisions on who gets to live. It means I choose for someone else to die."

"How did you choose?" said Choe-me.

"I chose a man with a neck injury. The other two men have leg injuries and may live long enough for more penicillin to arrive."

"Infection is the main reason soldiers in our care are dying. We must get more soon."

"They are dying because of the war, Choe-me. We cannot stop the war. Max said, 'we can only help those who are lucky enough to reach us.'"

She rolled over and tried to go to sleep. Her dreams were of Jo Jin-taek. She dreamt he would be a hero.

The next day, she looked in on Jo Jin-taek and watched his health improve. She also cared for the other two men she did not choose. She watched their infections spread, slowly making them weaker. Every time she heard a truck, she checked to see if more penicillin had arrived. On the third day, one of the men was missing. He had died during the night. The next morning, she held the hand of the other as he succumbed to his infection. She pulled the blanket over his head and walked out of the hospital ward. She went to the side of the building, buried her face into the cold cement wall, and cried.

I don't like watching people die. Why do I have to be here? Nothing is worse than this! She pounded the wall as she wept.

The next few days, she spent in the library, avoiding everyone else.

***

Late in the afternoon of September twenty-first, Gen. Park returned. He gathered the students and others in the camp together to update everyone on the war. "The Americans landed their army at Inchon on the fifteenth. Most of our army was in the deep south, and our soldiers were surrounded. The American Air Force is bombing our troops and supply lines day and night. The hospital at Pyongyang is getting lots of new wounded. I have arranged for them to be transported here. Be ready," he ended in a depressing tone. He turned, put his hands in his pockets, and walked away.

Eun-seong turned to Sun-hee and said, "Strategist was right. The war is not close to ending."

"No, it's not. General Park looked very troubled. I do not want to treat more wounded. I wish this war were over," Sun-hee said and walked off to dinner. She ate by herself, not wanting to talk about the possibilities of the future. Then she went straight to bed; her dreams were visions of a unified Korea.

A knock on the door woke Sun-hee. She opened her eyes, but it was still dark. She heard Sgt. Kua's voice. "Everyone up! Trucks with wounded have arrived. You have soldiers to attend to."

She closed her eyes and pulled the covers over her head. She took a deep breath and let it out slowly.

I must do this.

She pulled back her blanket. The lights were on.

Sun-hee ran with other girls towards the line of truck headlights stretching as far as she could see. She grabbed a stretcher.

This will be a busy day, Focus!

Midmorning, she heard the roar of planes flying low over the camp, and this time there was no debate. They were American planes. Patients cried out as they flew over, fearing American bombs.

"Sun!" she heard Max call out. "Choose a patient who needs an operation. I will wash up."

"How can I choose, Max? So many need help!"

"You learn this lesson slowly, Sun," he said. Then in a more commanding voice, he said, "Choose!"

"I can't!"

"Then bring this man," Max said, pointing to his left and walking to the operating room.

She got some help and moved the man to the operating area. As they washed, she asked, "Why did you choose this man, Max? What was it about him that made him the person we should help first?"

"He was the man at the end of my finger," said Max.

As she prepped the patient, she thought, *There is no reason. He is the next lucky man.*

She shook the logic from her head and focused on helping Max remove shrapnel from the man's legs and arm. Five clinks of metal into a pan followed by some quick stitches in each wound. Max's ability to find and remove the metal in a body amazed her.

When Max finished the last stitch, he looked at her and said, "Sun, go choose the next man?"

"I will try," she replied.

As she walked out, she asked the other students who needed surgery.

Young-ja pointed and said, "The captain is over there. He has a badly damaged foot. It is infected and needs attention."

She moved to where Young-ja pointed and noticed Capt. Kwang on the floor. "Welcome back, Captain," she said, trying to be pleasant. "Please relax. We will take good care of you. Your foot looks infected. I will have you moved into the operating room where the doctor can evaluate your wounds."

Once in the operating room, she removed the bandages and saw his mangled foot. It was bright red. The wound was filled with pus, and maggots crawled around his toes. She gagged and closed her eyes momentarily, forcing her stomach back under control.

Focus!

Max came in, looked at the foot, and said one Russian word, "Amputate." Then he selected a syringe and picked up a bottle of morphine.

Sun-hee turned and spoke, "Captain Kwang, your foot is badly infected. We need to remove it, or the infection will spread. The doctor will give you some morphine for the pain."

"We lacked medical staff on the front lines and could have used you there," said Capt. Kwang. "If you and the others had been there, many men would be alive.

The bitterness in his voice sent a shudder through Sun-hee. She thought for a moment before responding, "We have been able to serve Korea here as we would have served if we were at the front lines. All of us have committed to learn medicine and do what we can to help the heroes who have fought to unify Korea. We will be of service today and, hopefully, for many years in the future."

"When I find Lieutenant Rim, I will shoot him!" said Capt. Kwang. "Too many soldiers died because he disobeyed me."

"We need to cut here, just below the knee," Max said in Russian while pointing to where he described. "Secure the restraints, so he does not move."

"We need to make sure you do not move during surgery, Captain," said Sun-hee in her gentlest voice. "Please lie back and remain still. The morphine will deaden your leg. You will not feel a thing."

Sun-hee proceeded to strap the captain to the table, making sure he could not move his arms and good leg. Then she secured the upper part of the leg they were going to amputate, adding a tourniquet above the knee.

"Cut around the bone with the scalpel. I will cauterize the blood vessels as you cut," said Max, handing her the scalpel.

For the first time, Sun-hee wielded the scalpel during an amputation. She shuddered. For the first time, she knew the name of the patient on the table before her. She began to cut the leg, but Capt. Kwang's words about the lieutenant came into her head, fighting for her attention.

Focus!

The stench of infected flesh crept in. She gagged and nearly threw up. Max gave her step-by-step instructions.

"Cut here, cut there…focus!" she heard him say.

She cut around the leg just below the knee, one side and then the other. Max cauterized blood vessels to stop the bleeding. The smell of burnt flesh permeated the air. She fought to breathe through her mouth. Her eyes watered.

She struggled to cut through the hamstring ligaments, forcing the scalpel down with all her strength. The ligament snapped, and she smashed her knuckles into the table.

"OUCH." Sweat dripped off her forehead, plopping into the pool of blood under the nearly severed leg. She looked at the bonesaw in Max's hand, sighing in relief when he did not give it to her. Her eyes fixed on the back and forth movement, yet her vision was void.

"Dispose of this," Max said, startling her back to reality. He held out a lower leg like he was presenting a gift. "I will finish. When you return, bring help to move the patient."

She wanted to wipe the sweat from her face as she walked through the ward, holding the leg in a towel, but Capt. Kwang's blood covered her hands and arms. The sweat would have to take care of itself. She walked outside to a gate in the north fence. A man came up to the gate and held up a bucket. She dropped the leg into the bucket, then watched as he walked about thirty meters away and dumped the leg in a hole. She turned, felt the breeze blowing from the south, and enjoyed the coolness on her face.

She brought two of the civilian staff to help move the captain to a bed. She undid the restraints, reviewing in her mind what had just occurred. Capt. Kwang stirred as she made him comfortable.

"Captain Kwang," she said as she bent over him. "Let someone know when the morphine wears off. We can get you some more to help with the pain."

All day the words, "When I find Lieutenant Rim, I will shoot him!" kept entering her mind. She worked with Max until well after dark, then walked back alone to get some sleep. She saw Sgt. Kua on the porch of her house and approached her. "Sergeant Kua, I thought you might like to know Captain Kwang has returned as a patient. I assisted in the amputation of his left leg this afternoon."

"Do you think he will recover Sun-hee?" asked Sgt. Kua.

"Yes, Sergeant. The surgery went well. He is now resting."

"Did he say anything about the war?"

"He said our medical talents would have been helpful on the front lines. I assured him we serve Korea here as we would have done with him." She started to turn but then stopped to add, "Captain Kwang said he would shoot Lieutenant Rim when he saw him. We must keep them apart."

"Goodnight, Sun-hee," said the sergeant, ending the conversation.

As she was getting ready for bed, Choe-me said, "Did you hear Captain Kwang was back?"

"Yes, we…I mean I…" she swallowed. "I amputated his foot today."

"You operated on the captain?"

"Max made me do the cutting today. Since it was Captain Kwang, I was shaking the whole time. I had a hard time staying focused."

"Everyone was talking about him at dinner. We wondered if he will take over the camp again. If he does, how will things be different?"

"It will be a while before he is ready to take charge. If he does take command, maybe our lives will change."

***

Sgt. Kua made sure the rooms in her house were empty, and nothing needed her immediate attention. Her mind was on what Sun-hee had said earlier.

Park needs to know Kwang is back.

She headed over to the command building. A half-dozen wooden steps led up to a porch at the front door.

The lieutenant and the general might think I am disloyal if I do not tell them about what Kwang said to Sun-hee.

She knocked on the door.

When a soldier answered, she said, "Sergeant Kua here to see General Park."

"I will inform the general. Wait here." A moment later, the door reopened. "General Park will see you now."

The door to the left of the entryway led to a room where the general sat in a cushioned armchair. "Come in, Sergeant," said Gen. Park without getting up. "What can I do for you tonight?"

She stood at attention and said, "I have received word the former commander of this camp, Captain Kwang, has returned as a patient. Sun-hee told me the captain threatened to shoot Lieutenant Rim."

"Valuable information, Sergeant. Anyone as high of a rank as a captain deserves my personal attention. I shall have him moved into our spare bedroom at once. Anything else, Sergeant?"

"No, sir," she said, and let herself out. As she walked back to her house, she considered Gen. Park's response.

I hope I did the right thing.

13 — River of Blood - End of September to October, 1950

"Line up patients in need of surgery outside the operating room. The more urgent patients move to the head of the line," Sun-hee directed the other students.

I will not have to choose the next lucky patient.

All-day Eun-seong and Sun-hee worked with Max. The line of men needing surgery was never-ending. When they finished operating on one man, Sun-hee pointed to the next man. The only time they paused was to drink or pee. The blood, moans, smells, and sights no longer affected Sun-hee. She focused on helping the men.

"It is late," Max said. "Enough for today. Time to rest."

"There are so many who need treatment, Max. How can we rest?" said Sun-hee.

"When I first arrived at Stalingrad, straight from the university, there was an endless supply of wounded men. For days, I operated one man after another. On the third day, I dozed while removing a bullet from a man's belly. Before I could catch myself, the scalpel in my hand cut deep into his liver. We could not stop the bleeding." He paused, eyebrows clenched together, a deep breath filled his chest, "War always brings a river of blood, Sun. It never stops. Channel some off. It helps the crops grow. Too much, the field is flooded, and the crops are ruined. I am not good with illustration. Get rest each day. The river of blood will be here tomorrow."

Max walked away.

As Max had said, the next few days brought a flood of injured from the war. Sun-hee and Eun-seong assisted Max from breakfast until after sundown. New arrivals brought news of fighting around Seoul. The American Air Force was bombing everything, destroying railroads, bridges, and towns. The North Korean army was in retreat, and there were no reinforcements.

The sound of American planes flying over the camp panicked the wounded.

***

September ended. October arrived. Rain fell off and on, making the ground sloppy. Chilly winds came off the ocean from the northeast. The pregnant girls harvested the garden, adding to the camp food supplies. The camp swelled with the wounded and civilians recruited by Lt. Rim.

On the fifteenth of October, Joo-yun bounded into the dorm later than usual. "Guess what happened today?" she said with excitement in her voice.

The girls turned their attention to her. Young-ja spoke up, "Tell us. We are too tired to guess."

"Eleven trucks full of books arrived today. Gen. Park retrieved the contents of the library in Pyongyang. The library is full of boxes."

"I wish I had time to read," said Sun-hee.

"I wish you would help in the hospital, Joo-yun," said Mi-na.

"I am. Sergeant Kua is making me help with rehabilitation," she said, pulling a pigtail.

***

Two days later, Sun-hee and Max were in the operating room. "I hope we can give this man the ability to use his hand again," said Max. "He may then be able to work and support himself and his future family."

"Sun-hee, we need Max!" yelled Young-ja into the room.

"She says we are needed," she translated for Max.

"Always men in need. Tell her we come when we are finished," Max replied.

"We will be there as soon as we finish with this man's hand," Sun-hee said to Young-ja in Korean.

"There are children! They have burns!" Young-ja cried out.

Sun-hee turned to Max. "Children with burns have arrived Max."

"This man will live," he said calmly. "Focus, Sun! We must remain focused."

She realized, for the first time, Max told her to focus when he fought to keep his emotions in check. No amount of focus allowed her to deal with the women and children who were arriving this morning. American planes had firebombed nearby cities.

Max gathered the students together. "Use morphine only if necessary. We are in short supply. Remove the burnt and dead tissue. Clean up the wound." Sun-hee started translating but gagged at the sight of Max peeling the dead flesh off a child's arm. She ran out of the building, regurgitating from the horrible sight.

Two boys stood next to her, also puking their stomach contents. She knew she needed to translate, so she took a few deep breaths to calm herself and went back in.

Max had finished cleaning the wound and said, "Use only clean bandages to slow infection." She translated. "If they are over a third burnt, they will not survive. Make them comfortable."

"Stay with me, Sun. We will walk around and help."

Following around and translating gave Sun-hee the benefit of Max's instruction for each patient. She found herself telling students what to do and not waiting for Max to tell her what to say. She avoided looking at the people, not wanting their faces in her memory. Breathing through her mouth to escape the putrid smell of burnt flesh, tuning out the screams, listening only to Max's voice, she focused on the task. She kept her hands by her side, not wanting to touch the scorched flesh. The commotion made her dizzy.

Focus! she said to herself. *Do not feel! FOCUS!*

Still, the burns of each patient seared her heart.

The rest of the day and into the night, victims of American firebombs arrived. It was late in the night when Sun-hee remembered Max's words—taking Eun-seong's arm, calling Choe-me and Young-ja over, together they went to eat and sleep.

***

Days of treating burns, working with Max, and trying to remain focused passed slowly. So many died. The only relief was exhausted sleep each night. Sun-hee lost track of the days, who she treated, who she talked to, her mind blocked out the scenes of the suffering and dying.

Late one afternoon, Gen. Park went from one new patient to the next demanding to know where they were from and what had happened. They told him story after story of bombs falling, fires burning for days, people fleeing to the mountains. General Park asked each person if they saw an American. Nobody had.

Gen. Park yelled, "Damn Americans! Couldn't they leave us alone?" He pushed Sun-hee aside as he stomped out of the hospital.

Sun-hee backed up to a wall and used it for support. She gazed around the room and felt overwhelmed by the needs of the patients. All Sun-hee had left to give were her actions: no more kind words, no soothing touches, unlike Eun-seong who poured out her heart, making each patient feel special.

Max came in from another barrack and handed Sun-hee a bottle of morphine, saying, "Don't let the children suffer."

Moving from patient to patient, Sun-hee tried to do something for each one. She administered the morphine, especially to the children, until she realized she was giving it to them to stop their crying more than easing their pain.

Kwang-ku came for the night shift. He assisted Alek in surgery during the day, took a nap with dinner, and then returned for the night. Of all the students, he was the best doctor. Chulsoon was not far behind.

Sun-hee caught herself falling asleep on her feet. She handed the morphine bottle to Kwang-ku and went out the barrack door. She began trudging through mud, leaning into the wind and pelting rain. Lightning flashed, revealing the silhouette of a figure on the ground between two buildings. She slogged over to investigate only to find Gen. Park laying in the muck, an empty vodka bottle next to his hand. She bent and felt for a pulse. His heartbeat was good, but her own heart stuttered with the image lying before her.

She turned to get help, and her feet slipped. When her hands hit the ground, they slid apart, leaving her face to fall into the mire. She struggled to her hands and knees and spit out mud, but the wall around her emotions ruptured, and she wailed uncontrollably.

Rain pelted her back and head, streaming off her hair and into the mud that buried her hands. She crawled to the side of the building and used it for stability to climb to her feet. Standing for a moment, face to the sky, she let the pounding rain wash the filth from her face until she could see. One step at a time, keeping her hands on the wall, she slipped and squished back to the hospital ward.

She entered and yelled, "I need some help!"

"Sun-hee," yelled Kwong-ku. "Where are you hurt?"

"Oh my, Sun-hee!" said Eun-seong as she came running over.

"I am not hurt. Park needs our help. Come with me." She turned and led them to the general.

Sun-hee yelled over the storm. "I think he passed out. If we can carry him to the command house, we can get help to get him inside."

The three of them pulled the general, slipping and sliding in the mud, to the stairs of the command house. Sun-hee climbed up the steps and pounded on the door.

Lt. Rim opened the door. "The General needs help," she blurted out. "We got him here but can't carry him up the steps."

Lt. Rim moved quickly down the steps to the general's side.

"The general is unconscious. There was a vodka bottle next to him," said Kwong-ku.

"I smell the alcohol," said Lt. Rim. He pulled a whistle out of his shirt and gave one short burst. Within a few seconds, three soldiers ran up and carried the general into the command house.

Sun-hee bent over to catch her breath.

"Let me go with you to the dorm," said Eun-seong, placing a hand under Sun-hee's shoulder.

"I better return to the hospital," said Kwong-ku.

The two girls sloshed across the compound, holding one another for comfort and stability. The cold rain assaulting their heads combined with tears to wash the mud off Sun-hee's cheeks.

Sun-hee stopped, grabbed the front of Eun-seong's coat, and pulled her close. "Lieutenant Rim was wearing Captain Kwang's uniform. I saved the captain. For what? Another man dead. The general's program goes on while he has no hope. What future is there for us?"

Eun-seong sobbed. "I…I do not know. I live to care for you and the others. Right now that means getting out of this rain."

The two went to the sink, took off their smocks, and tried to wash off the mud. They failed miserably. They turned on the shower in the privy, and a flow of icy cold water poured out. They stripped and let the frigid water rinse away the dirt. Standing naked, shivering, Sun-hee and Eun-seong washed the mire from their clothes, wrung them out, and put them back on.

They entered their barren cement hut dripping wet. Everyone was asleep, cuddled in blankets. They changed while shivering uncontrollably. Sun-hee put on all her clothes in layers, hoping it would help her get warm. She sneezed.

"Are you two okay?" whispered Choe-me.

"No. I'm cold," Sun-hee said, teeth chattering. "I slipped in the mud and needed to shower. I hate this place!"

"Come, share my blanket and my warmth," invited Choe-me, holding up both sides of her blanket. Sun-hee and Eun-seong scooted together and wrapped their blankets around the three of them. "Your hands are freezing, Eun-seong," exclaimed Choe-me.

"We found General Park passed out drunk in the mud," Eun-seong muttered. "Kwong-ku helped us drag him to the command house."

"I am not surprised. The general was so upset today," said Choe-me.

"I am worried. The future is so uncertain. If General Park has no hope, what will he do?" Sun-hee said. Then she added, "Captain Kwang is dead. Lieutenant Rim was wearing his uniform."

"Do you think Lieutenant Rim killed Captain Kwang?" said Choe-me.

"One was going to kill the other. I told Sergeant Kua about Captain Kwang's threat to kill Lieutenant Rim. Tonight, he's wearing Captain Kwang's uniform. It's my fault that Captain Kwang is dead."

"You did the right thing, Sun-hee. You always do. You make the right choices for who lives. It is up to others to decide who dies," said Choe-me. "Right now, get warm and get some rest." Choe-me put her arm around Sun-hee, more for comfort than warmth.

As she closed her eyes, Sun-hee's mind flashed back to the vision of Captain Kwang's leg in her hands. She saw herself dropping it into the bucket, and the leg dumped into the burial pit. Following the leg, the faces of all the men, women, and children she had treated flowed out of the bucket into the hole in the ground. She sobbed until she fell asleep.

Light streamed into the windows when she woke. Only the girls who worked the night shift were sleeping. She dressed and headed off to the kitchen, where she discovered it was lunchtime. She looked up at the puffy white clouds drifting across the blue sky.

What would it be like to be a cloud floating without a care through the air? They look so lovely, each one silvery and fluffy, dancing in the heavens with each other.

Sun-hee ate and went to the hospital. Stopping at the door, she took a deep breath.

What can a little fluffy cloud do here today?

***

A couple of days later, Sun-hee's period came. She went to the calendar on the wall. October twenty-sixth was crossed out.

This must be the twenty-seventh. At least I am not pregnant. But I need to schedule Stone for a few nights in the guesthouse.

She thought about the girls with morning sickness who avoided treating patients. They could not cope with the sights and smells of burnt flesh.

Being pregnant might be an excuse to not deal with the injured.

She started to write her name on the calendar and noticed Eun-seong standing behind her.

"So, you are not pregnant, Sun-hee," said Eun-seong. "How do you feel?"

"I feel that Park's plan to get us all pregnant is no longer relevant. With all that is going on, I don't know if I care anymore," Sun-hee said in a depressed tone. "How are you?"

"A little scared and a little excited," said Eun-seong. "I must put my name on the calendar for the first time. I'm last and was beginning to feel left out. I have had four months to accept we are being mated and think about the boys who might father my children. Three remain. One to go with Bok-soon who put her name here." She pointed to the calendar a week earlier. "One of the other two boys for me. All are good men. I am not afraid." Sun-hee put her arms around Eun-seong, and they hugged.

"Have you seen the general?" Sun-hee asked.

"Not since we carried him to the command house, but I will ask around," said Eun-seong. "He worries about the war. I hope it ends soon. I hate watching people suffer." She stared blankly at the calendar. "I do not care who wins. I want the wounded to stop coming. I am glad I can help, but there is no end. The suffering has drained me."

"Max called it the river of blood," Sun-hee said. "I hope this war is like the monsoon rains; they end as winter arrives."

14 — Exhaustion & Waiting - Early November, 1950

The weather turned as November arrived. Sun-hee helped Choe-me pull her smock down over her coat. Choe-me did the same for her.

"If you two had white hair, you would look like snowmen," said Young-ja. The girls stepped outside. Snow blew by from right to left, and they locked arms to fight the wind together.

"If we keep eating like this, we will look like snowmen without our coats under the smocks," said Choe-me.

"If there were no fences, I could jump and ride the wind to the hospital. With a kite, I might make it to the sea," said Sun-hee.

They grabbed their bowls of food and ate as fast as they could before heading to their shift in the hospital. The barracks door opened as they arrived. Sun-hee and Eun-seong struggled to hold the door open. Two men carried a body out. One of the men slipped slightly in the snow. The wind caught the stretcher, tossing the dead man onto the ground. Sun-hee and Eun-seong helped the men get the body back on the stretcher so the men could carry him to a frozen grave.

"I treated him yesterday. I wish I knew his name," said Eun-seong as they entered the hospital. Sun-hee clasped Eun-seong's hand, giving it a comforting squeeze. Eun-seong let go and moved to a man lying nearby. "Let's see what injuries this man has…"

Sun-hee made her way to the operating room and held her wet hands in front of the stove.

The dead man looked so young. He came in alone and died alone. There was no one to weep, no one to be sad, no one to fold the clothes and point them to the north on the roof, and no one to speak the name of the deceased three times. No one knows their names. War does not allow time for seup; no washing, hair combing, or nail trimming. They die, and minutes later they are laid to rest. Do those who die in this prison camp hospital, die alone to be kaekkvi and wander as ghosts for eternity? Are we enough to channel the dead to the world of the ancestors where they can look over their loved ones? Is there any meaning in so much death?

Max joined her by the stove. "Finally, it is cold," he said.

Sun-hee looked up with a questioning gaze, rubbing her hands together over the stove to get them warm. "Why do you like the cold, Max?"

"The cold will slow infections. It gives patients an extra day or two to fight off the bacteria."

Sun-hee went to get their first patient for the day. They worked steadily until mid-afternoon when the line of patients for surgery stopped. The snow and cold had slowed the river of blood to a trickle.

For the next few days, only a few men, women, and children arrived. The new arrivals were all suffering wounds from bombs and had somehow survived long enough in the freezing weather to get to the hospital. She spent time talking to patients, learning their names, hearing their stories, which were all similar. They heard planes, bombs fell, or bullets came from the air.

With fewer wounded, the students had more time to study and read in the library. The night shift was only a handful of boys.

***

Early on the morning of the seventh of November, while it was still dark, horse-drawn carts arrived at the gates with more patients. Their wounds were fresh. American bombs had fallen all along the coastal road between Chongjin and Sungam. The port at Sungam was reduced to rubble. The only option for the wounded and refugees was to travel over the snow-covered pass through the mountains. Sun-hee remembered the winding dirt road Lt. Rim had taken the morning she arrived, and she cringed at the thought of walking up the road in the cold.

The wounds and burns caused by bombs and shrapnel were as gruesome as the students had seen. The untreated wounds seared her mind with images of women, children, and the elderly mangled by war. Americans were not accurate with their bombs. The explosives missed the port, landing in the residential area. The river of blood was a torrent. Everyone, including Dr. Park, worked frantically to save lives.

Patients yelled, screamed, and ducked for cover at the roar of planes overhead.

Yong-gak assisted Sun-hee by holding a patient still while she stitched up a wound.

"He needs to be very still for me to stitch this right," Sun-hee said.

Strategist has the worst medical abilities of all of us. He is always so distracted.

"Focus, Yong-gak. What is on your mind, you cannot keep this man still?"

"I noticed Lieutenant Rim giving orders and mobilizing the soldiers. He is preparing to defend the compound when the Americans attack. I fear they will try a beach landing at Sungam to secure the northern part of the country. This is the only military facility in the area and will be an objective when the Americans get here. The lieutenant is sending a messenger to Musan, requesting tanks and artillery."

He is always thinking about the big picture. I wish he could keep this patient still.

She messed up a stitch because the patient moved.

Maybe we will be attacked soon.

She shuddered at the thought, resulting in another sloppy stitch.

If bombs fall, we are prisoners inside the fences; we will not be able to run.

"Hold the patient still. Focus, Yong-gak," she demanded.

Now I am telling others to focus when I need more focus.

"We must not try to defend this camp," Gen. Park said from across the room. "They will bomb us. They will set up artillery along the pass and shell us. Then they will come down the road with tanks. This camp will be in ruins before we even see an American if we live that long. I would rather let the Americans have this camp without a fight than have it bombed to rubble. I need to talk to Lieutenant Rim." He stormed out.

A few minutes later, Gen. Park returned to the hospital and addressed the students. "Everyone is to wear white gowns when outside. The planes must see this is a hospital. There is no advantage to dying from bombs dropping on our heads."

On the way to lunch, Sun-hee saw men on roofs painting red crosses. Soldiers who had recovered from their wounds were packing. As the sun set, a large column of soldiers marched north from the camp.

Many times during the night, Sun-hee startled awake, interrupting nightmares of bombs falling around the camp.

More wounded arrived with the dawn, many with fresh burn wounds. Incendiary bombs had fallen on the city of Sungam, burning the city to the ground.

"Why?" Young-ja cried, catching Sun-hee's attention. Young-ja held a bundle of bandages, a little arm protruding out. "Why?" she pleaded. "Why would any civilized society use firebombs on a city and burn children?"

Sun-hee went over and tried to console her. "Let me take the child," she said to Young-ja quietly.

"No!" she yelled back.

"It is war," said Gen. Park. "This is how Americans wage war. They bombed Japan and Germany. They bombed Pyongyang and other cities. Now they bomb little towns like Sungam. They win by destroying their opponent. We can only help the wounded and hope the Americans show mercy to this camp."

That evening, when Sun-hee returned to the dorm, Eun-seong took her arm and whispered, "I am worried about Young-ja. She came in crying before lunch, and when we tried to comfort her, she yelled at everyone. Then she lay down and covered herself up, striking at anyone who tried to comfort her. She has been there since."

Sun-hee knelt beside Young-ja and put her left arm on her shoulder. She caught the hand that reached out to strike her and slowly moved it back to her side. "I am with you, Young-ja. I want to join you in hiding from what we face. I wish I could tell you how to block out the horror you have seen. But I do not know how. All we can do is survive one day and one moment at a time. Please survive with me. I need you."

Sun-hee rolled back onto her mat and pulled her blanket over her head. She had succeeded in becoming so exhausted, sleep came without difficulty.

***

The next day on her way to lunch, more jets flew over the compound. Sun-hee grabbed two children and held them close. They trembled together, hoping bombs were not going to fall. She ate lunch with them, finding out they were orphans. There were staying in the building which was once a garage.

That night, light snow fell as Sun-hee made her way to the dorm. As she started to get ready for bed, Young-ja came over and sat on Sun-hee's mat.

"Thank you, Sun-hee," Young-ja said. "Everyone else asked me what was wrong. You understood. I cannot cope with this place anymore. The suffering is too much for me to block out. I am going to try what you do. Work until I am so tired, I fall asleep easily."

Sun-hee hugged Young-ja and said, "I wish I could change the world. If we survive, maybe we will be able to. First, we must survive. Time for me to sleep." Then she laid down and pulled her blanket up, closing her eyes.

Choe-me was lying on the mat next to Sun-hee's, and she reached over to hug her. "How was your time with Stone?"

"I…I forgot it was my night tonight," Sun-hee said. She sighed and started to put her clothes back on. She looked at the other girls in the room, blank stares on their faces: so much despair and depression.

Choe-me took Sun-hee's hand. "If I could take your place tonight, I would. For your sake, I hope Stone is quick." They hugged.

Sun-hee felt they needed her strength. She found none to give. She reached out to them, clasping hands and arms with compassion, drawing energy from their concern. She took a deep breath, brushed her hair behind her ears, and made her way out the door. She heard Max's words in her head.

Focus. Block feelings out. You must block them out.

Sun-hee entered the guesthouse to see Stone sitting at the table in a robe. Sgt. Kua was in the corner knitting. "I will be just a minute," she said while turning towards the shower. When she came out, Eun-seong was waiting, her head down and arms folded over her breasts.

Eun-seong started sobbing. Sun-hee could do nothing else but hold her for a minute. "Are you OK?" Sun-hee asked.

"Yes, I think so," said Eun-seong. "Dae-suk is a nice boy. I like him. I think he likes me. It is the wrong time. So many emotions. Hurt, joy, hatred of this program and the war. He tried to be gentle." Eun-seong cried.

The minute turned into at least five, maybe ten. "Stone is waiting for me. Go wash up and go to bed. I hope to be there soon." Sun-hee opened the door.

Stone sat against the opposite wall from the mat. She pulled the string, casting the room in darkness. The joining of bodies took a few seconds.

As Young-soo rolled off, Sun-hee said, "I am worn-out and am going to get some sleep."

The next day was one of the most strenuous days of her life. The constant movement, increasing demands of patients, helping Max, all done without thinking, without feeling, took every bit of energy from her. It was late when she arrived at the guesthouse. She fell asleep on the mat, waiting for Stone. She woke when he came in. He paced a couple of times, his hands clasping and unclasping. He stopped and looked directly at her.

"I am beginning to accept you as my wife." He paused. She felt trapped in the moment of silence. "You will make a good wife. I believe you would take care of a household very well."

Sun-hee wanted to be blunt and say; *I am not and will not be your wife.* Instead, she chose her words. "You are a good man, Young-soo. I am not ready to be anyone's wife. I only accept you will be the father of my first child. The situation in this camp is such that thinking about marriage is as remote as thinking about walking on the moon. Come here. Do what General Park commands so I can get some rest."

He reached up and pulled the string. Five minutes later, Sun-hee was lying down on her mat. She shuddered at the thought of being married to a Stone.

The next night she was on time, and they started their task without speaking. Stone tried to kiss her, but she turned her head to the side.

"Don't you like me, Sun-hee?" he asked while thrusting.

"We have been forced together in this very unnatural way during a war," she said. "It is not a time or place to fall in love. If our parents had arranged our union in a peaceful time, I would learn to have feelings for you. But not here in this camp; not forced together like this. Give me a baby so the general will be proud of you." She closed her eyes, turned her face to the wall, and survived the moment.

15 — Surrender - Mid-November, 1950

"Your incision looks good. There is no infection," Sun-hee said to a patient she had operated on the day before. The rumble of jet engines roared overhead and was immediately drowned out by panicked screams. The patient reached out and grabbed her smock, pulling her on top of him. She braced herself, listening for the sound of explosions which never came. The roar of jets cycled, getting closer and then farther away, only to return.

Max walked out of the hospital. She wondered what was going on, so she followed him out into the frigid morning air. Across the sky, contrails were tying together the puffy clouds.

There were four jets shooting at each other.

If I were that fluffy cloud, the planes would seem like flies buzzing around me. Sun-hee shuddered. *What if a plane flew right through me?* One plane caught fire. *Would a burning plane hurt me if I were a cloud?*

Another plane went silent. She watched the one on fire go over the hill to the south, and a few seconds later she heard a distant explosion. The other glided for a moment above the camp, two seats ejected from the plane. The seats hovered in the air as the plane spiraled down to the west.

As a cloud, I could reach out and catch them. Parachutes unfolded into large white cones, the seats separated and fell. *Two parachutes floating below her, white circles above the camp, carried, as she was, by the wind. She drifted, watching the falling parachutes.*

She was brought back to earth by loud yelling. Sgt. Kua and a few soldiers were running towards the main gate, carrying rifles. Jung-sip and Hung Young-jee ran by her.

"Someone may be injured," Young-jee said.

They are going after the Russian or American pilots, but none of those running out of the gate speak Russian or English.

Impulsively, Sun-hee dashed to follow the others, chasing drifting parachutes up the hill to the southwest of the camp.

Sun-hee was breathing heavily, far behind everyone except Sgt. Kua whom she passed soon after she started running. Hearing a gunshot, she dropped to the ground, her hands breaking through the crusted snow. She heard more shots.

Lt. Rim yelled, "Stop shooting."

She lifted her head over some bushes. White parachutes were flapping in the breeze higher on the hill.

Lt. Rim commanded, "Do not fire. We need to take the American pilots alive."

"Come on, you commies," she heard in English.

What does 'commies' mean? It does not sound nice.

Lt. Rim shouted, "Surround the parachutes. Do not fire. Americans. Put down your weapons and surrender."

He is yelling at the Americans in Korean. They will not understand.

In a crouch, she made her way through the bushes to the lieutenant. She was out of breath. Her heart pounded with the adrenalin rush of the moment.

"May I speak to them, Lieutenant Rim?" she asked.

"You know English?" he asked in a surprised voice.

"Yes, sir. A little."

"Tell them to surrender," he said.

She swallowed, trying to get some moisture in her dry throat. "Americans. You surrender," she yelled in English.

I hope I am saying things correctly.

"Come and get me," was the reply.

"Soldiers are in all direction," Sun-hee said and then added, "They have guns. You do not get out." *There is another word that starts with an 'E.' What is it?* "You not run. You will not get away." *Why didn't they run? Maybe they are hurt.* "Are you hurt?" she asked.

"I am fine, but if you come this way, you won't be!" the American yelled back.

"What are they saying?" Lt. Rim said while grabbing her arm for attention.

"They do not want to surrender," she said in Korean. "They must be hurt, or they would have run."

"You are not fine. Or you would run," she yelled in English. "We are medical students. We can treat wounds."

"I have heard how the North Koreans treat prisoners," he replied. "I will not be your prisoner."

"We have no prisoners here. We have not treated Americans. I have never seen an American," she yelled. "You must surrender. You have no hope. Men are all around with guns."

"Lieutenant Rim, the American does not wish to surrender," she said quietly in Korean so only the lieutenant could hear.

"Convince them to surrender!" yelled Lt. Rim at Sun-hee.

"Mister American, my superiors are impatient. You surrender now!" Sun-hee yelled, feeling the pressure from Lt. Rim.

"If he does not surrender, I will kill him," said Lt. Rim.

"If you do not surrender, we will shoot you," Sun-hee said in English.

"You are going to have to come and get me," the American replied.

"If I come to get you, will you surrender?"

"I will shoot any Korean who comes this way,"

"Why do Americans want to kill Koreans?"

"You are the enemy," said the American.

"My eyes have seen the results of your bombs, Mister American."

"Then you know you have no hope of winning this war. Let me go, and I will tell my superiors to spare your hospital."

"We have no hope of defeating America. When will your bombs fall on us? When will you kill me?"

"Let me go. Nobody dies."

"Surrender now. You live. The honor of our soldiers will not let you get away. I am tired of watching my people die. I do not want to see anyone die today."

"If you try to get me, you will die."

"Why do Americans desire to kill? I have seen enough death. I am tired of pain and suffering. I am tired of treating women and children, burnt and mangled by your bombs." Sun-hee yelled. The vision of the little hand dangling from the bandages in Young-ja's arms filled her mind.

"More of you will die if you try to capture me," came the voice from up the hill.

Sun-hee clinched her hands and yelled out in a rage. "You are worse than Japanese! They kill many people. We see them do it. Americans kill people. We never see an American. I will not watch another person killed by unseen American. I do not want to watch you kill all the people in Korea?" She was yelling as loud as she was able. "When will you bomb our hospital, Mister American? When bombs fall, we will die. I will not watch my friends die!" Her pent-up anger got the best of her. She stood up.

"Get down, Sun-hee!" shouted Lt. Rim.

"I want to see what an American looks like before I die," she said, first in Korean and then in English. She began to move up the hill through the scattered bushes, her feet crunching in the snow towards the American's voice.

"Sun-hee!" screamed Sgt. Kua, "Get down!"

"If I am to die at the hands of Americans, you can look at me when you shoot me," Sun-hee said in English, her hands held out wide as she walked towards the parachutes. "Can you see me, Mister American? I am coming to look at you."

Lt. Rim yelled out, "If he shoots her, we will butcher him."

Sun-hee saw one American lying about twenty meters to her left. He was not moving.

The American I have been talking to must be on the other side of these rocks.

"Your friend looks hurt. I can help him," she said.

She looked up to see her cloud. *As a spirit, I will watch over all of Korea.*

She took a deep breath, held her arms out straight, and climbed onto the rocks in front of her. She looked down. The American was sitting among the boulders with his gun pointed at her. Their stares met, the breeze flipped her bangs back and forth across her forehead. She stood on the uneven rocks, fighting her balance in the winter wind, feeling the rapid beat of her heart, waiting for the American to fire and she could become one with the cloud.

"Shit!" the American said as he threw his gun to the ground beyond his feet.

"Hello, Mister American," said Sun-hee. "What does 'shit' mean? It is a word I not know."

"Hello, Miss Korean," the American said with a half-smile, staring directly at Sun-hee. "I am your prisoner."

Sun-hee dropped her arms to her side and said, "You can bomb us like a child stomping on an anthill, but you can't look me in the eye and shoot."

Why do I feel so calm?

"Lieutenant Rim, the American has thrown down his gun and surrendered. Jung-sip, Young-jee, one American is over there. He is not moving. See to him," she said, pointing to her left.

Then she saw Jo Jin-taek, the man she had chosen to receive the last dose of antibiotics a few weeks ago, standing on a rock beyond the American, holding his rifle with a big grin on his face.

She climbed down next to the American. Soldiers were quickly around her, aiming their guns at the American. Lt. Rim climbed up onto the rock and looked down at the scene. One of the soldiers held his rifle on his forearm. His left hand was missing.

She squatted next to the American. "Where are you hurt?" Sun-hee asked in English.

"My ankle. It is either broken or badly sprained," said the American while holding his hands up, pointing with one finger at his foot.

"Get back, Sun-hee," Lt. Rim barked. "Search him for weapons," he said to the men.

"They want weapons. Please give to soldiers," Sun-hee said in English as she reached for the American's ankle.

The American pointed to a knife on his belt and said, "There is a knife in my belt and another in my boot." Sun-hee translated. Jo Jin-taek took the visible knife attached to the belt and removed the American's helmet. Then he patted the American down.

Sun-hee felt his boots, located the knife, and removed it. She looked at it for a second and handed it to Jin-taek.

"Secure those parachutes, men," said Lt. Rim, still standing above them on the rocks. "We do not want planes to see them from the air. You two, go get stretchers and rope," he said, pointing to two soldiers.

"We will leave the boot on. We will treat your ankle at the hospital," Sun-hee said to the American in English. In Korean, she said, "We can do nothing for the ankle here. We should get him to the hospital."

She stood, "Young-jee, status?" she said in a commanding voice that startled her after she said it.

"A bullet hit his helmet. There is a head wound with lots of blood," Young-jee said. "It is not deep, but he is unconscious. I think he broke both femurs."

Sun-hee turned to the American and spoke in English, "Mr. American, your partner has a head wound. His legs are broken." Then she stood. "I can do no more here. Now, I can say I have seen an American." She started to walk away.

"Miss Korean, what is your name," the American asked.

She stopped and looked back. "Sun-hee," she replied and looked at him like it was his turn.

"I am Theodore. Theodore Reed," he said.

In Korean, she said to Lt. Rim, "His name is Theodore Reed."

Sun-hee started walking towards the compound. Sgt. Kua walked with her. Then she turned and screamed in English. "It was not a pleasure to meet you, Theodore. It was not a pleasure to meet an American. I wish you were not here. I wish Americans were not in Korea. I wish this war did not happen. I wish I never won this lousy prize."

"What are you yelling? And why did you act so foolishly?" said Sgt. Kua.

Before Sun-hee thought of a response, two jets flew low and fast overhead. Sgt. Kua dove down to the ground. Sun-hee looked up and watched them go by.

There I am. That cloud is me, drifting southwest towards home.

"I told him what I think of Americans. It would not be polite to say in Korean," she said calmly to Sgt. Kua.

Twice more jets flew over the area as they walked down the hillside. Each time, Sun-hee stood and watched them go by.

They cannot hurt me as I am floating above them.

They walked on down the hill picking their way through the snow and bare bushes.

I am out of the barbed wire fences. For the first time in six months, I am free. Would I be shot if I walked home? Here is the road. I can turn south and walk away. Would Sergeant Kua shoot me when the American did not?

She slowed her pace, stopped, looked up at the clouds, took a deep breath, and exhaled slowly.

No. I cannot leave the other girls. I cannot ignore the patients who need help.

She turned north and followed Sgt. Kua. As she walked through the gate, she looked up. The fluffy white clouds were merging into a giant billowy cloud.

Sun-hee walked behind the sergeant in silence to the kitchen. She ate quickly without saying a word. When she finished, she went to care for the women and children, severely wounded by Americans, like the one she had captured.

16 — Americans - Mid-November, 1950

Sun-hee stepped into the hospital.

Max called to her, "Come, Sun, assist me in treating the American pilot."

She made her way through the room, the faces of the injured men, women, and children jumped into her vision. Entering the operating room, she halted, her breath stopped.

Why is this man lucky today?

Max was examining the American pilot on the table. "The bullet broke the skull but did not penetrate to the brain. We can't know if the brain is damaged until he wakes up. That is, if he wakes up."

Sun-hee returned to the moment and went to wash up.

"Clean up the head wound. I will work on the legs," said Max.

Sun-hee shaved the short red hair around the head wound. She could see the break in the skull through the gash across the side of the American's head. She picked up a scalpel, holding it by the wound

"This man is the enemy," said Max. "Wounded enemies have been known to die on the operating table."

Sun-hee turned to look at Max. "No, I am not a killer. You told me that anyone who arrives for treatment is lucky. As doctors, we choose to help them live. Others determine who will die." She put the scalpel down, picked up a needle, and threaded it.

"You learn well," said Max. He began to set the bones in the American's legs and applied splints while Sun-hee stitched the wound and applied bandages to the head.

When she finished, Sun-hee went to get some workers to move the American. She passed Theodore who was tied to a stretcher and guarded by Jin-taek and another soldier who had a cast on his leg.

Gen. Park walked up behind her and said, "The American broke his ankle. Set it while I figure out what to do with him."

Sun-hee looked around and saw Young-ja. "Can you help me with the American?"

"If I do not have to be nice," she said.

Sun-hee sniggered.

They walked over to Theodore and looked at the ankle.

"We are going to treat your ankle, Theodore," Sun-hee said in English. "Your foot is swollen inside the boot."

"I have an idea," said Young-ja. "I'll be right back."

"Have you seen my partner, Sunny?" Theodore asked.

"I stitched and bandaged his head."

"You operated on him?" asked Theodore.

"The head wound was not deep. Only stitching and bandages were needed. He is still unconscious. His broken legs are set and in splints."

Young-ja returned with a flask of oil. She started talking. "We will pour the oil into the boot to lubricate it, and hopefully, it will be easy to slip off." She picked up the leg and moved it, letting the foot hang down off the cot. "Pour the oil into the boot. Move it around, move it around. Get the oil all over and let it soak in."

"Sunny, what are you doing?" said Theodore.

"We poured oil into your boot. Hopefully, the boot will slide off."

"Time to give the man a stick, Sun-hee," said Young-ja. "He is not going to like this, but it will be less dangerous than getting a knife out and trying to cut off this high-quality boot."

Sun-hee took a stick that already had many bite marks and put it in Theodore's mouth. "Bite down," she told him.

"Can you give me a shot of morphine for the pain?"

"Morphine is for injured women and children. Burns are more painful than a broken ankle," said Sun-hee. "Bite down hard."

"Round and round we go, get the foot dizzy..." Young-ja was saying over and over as she slowly rotated the foot. "Round and round, round and yank." She pulled with all her might. The boot came off.

Theodore spit out the stick and yelled, "Ahhhh...SHIT, SUNNY!" He fought against the restraints. His knuckles white on his fists.

Sun-hee did not reply to Theodore. "He says you are too nice, Young-ja," she said in Korean.

"That was easy," Young-ja said. "Now we peel the sock off. Did you like that, Mr. American? Oh, that looks nice and red."

Sun-hee knelt at the end of the cot. Together they felt the ankle bones looking for breaks.

Young-ja continued to talk to Theodore in Korean. "Not as bad as that woman over there who's side looks more colorful than this. She must move her side to breathe. I bet her pain during each breath is greater than what we did to you. Does this bone hurt?"

"OW! Where did you study medicine?" Theodore yelled.

Young-ja held her finger to her lips, "Shhhhh."

"She says, 'stay quiet, Theodore,'" Sun-hee said in English.

Theodore started to talk again, and Sun-hee held her finger to her lips. "Shhhh." Young-ja moved his ankle just enough to cause pain.

The American looked at Sun-hee angrily.

Young-ja then sang in a joyful tune, "Wrap the foot with plaster and gauze, put on a cast, put on a cast," over and over for the fifteen minutes it took.

When they finished, Sun-hee said to Theodore in English, "You have broken bone and a bad stretch of tissues. I don't know the correct word in English. You will heal."

"Can I use a restroom, Sunny?" said Theodore.

"You rest here, Theodore, with the other patients."

"Is there a bathroom I can use?" said Theodore.

"We have no place for a bath," Sun-hee said with a slight twist of her head.

"I need to pee, Sunny. Pass water. Urinate."

"Oh, you need privy, Theodore."

She said to Young-ja, "He needs to relieve himself. Help me undo the restraints."

"Undo this, undo that," Young-ja said as they untied the arm and waist restraints. "Now, the legs. Help him up, and we can go pee-pee."

Jin-taek kept his rifle pointed at Theodore with a stern look on his face.

"We must help him to the privy," Sun-hee said to Jin-taek. When they got him standing, she realized Theodore was the tallest man she had ever seen. She hardly came up to his shoulder. She stepped under one arm, and Young-ja stepped under the other.

"Jump, Theodore. We will steady you."

"Just point the way," replied Theodore.

They supported Theodore as he hopped. Young-ja kept up her running commentary. "This lady was burned by firebombs. That man has shrapnel wounds. This boy has burns on over half his body. He will die soon."

A few patients yelled at the American, and a couple of others spit in his direction. Someone threw a shoe, hitting Theodore in the chest. Young-ja kept talking about the other patients. When they got to the privy, Young-ja gestured to the trough, took a step back, and folded her arms. Sun-hee did the same. She watched Theodore look around.

"Can I do this in private?" he said.

Sun-hee motioned to Young-ja. They took a couple of steps back behind Jin-taek, who was a couple of centimeters shorter than Sun-hee.

"The American is tall and very strong. When he leaned on me, I thought I was going to fall," said Young-ja.

"I wonder if all Americans are this big. No wonder we are losing the war. We are fighting monsters." Jin-taek adjusted his stance ready for any wrong movement.

"These soldiers would like the American to try something. I think they are looking for a reason to shoot him even though General Park told them not to," said Young-ja.

"Jin-taek will protect us," she said, looking at the grinning man next to her as he nodded his head in agreement.

Thump, thump. "I hear Theodore hopping. Time to get him back to the stretcher," said Young-ja.

As they returned, Lt. Rim stood near the cot. "Get him restrained."

"Lay down, Theodore. We will strap you," said Sun-hee in English.

Jin-taek and the other soldier strapped him to the cot. Lt. Rim tested each strap while staring sternly at Theodore.

Max, Alek, and two men with Soviet flag patches on the upper arms of their flight suits walked in. They scrutinized Theodore. Sun-hee could smell the vodka on their breaths. She listened to their jokes, their laugh, and drunken antics.

Lt. Rim stood tall and said in Russian, "We need the prisoner for information, no one but me will hurt him."

One of the Russian pilots made a gun with his hand and pointed it at Theodore, then shot with his thumb. The Russians all laughed and started to walk out. The other pilot said in Russian, "Dumb American. He let himself be captured by a little girl!" They gave a hearty laugh as they went out the door.

Max has been drinking. We will not be operating anymore today.

Sun-hee walked around, helping where she could. She paused to watch Lt. Rim instruct soldiers to carry Theodore away.

I captured him. What will happen to him now? Should I care?

***

As she had done so many nights now, Sergeant Kua watched the last couple go back to their respective dorms. Then she looked to her left at the guards standing at the gate to the south. There was now an American prisoner in the second building; she would have to be more alert.

She did not lock the doors of the dorms anymore even though she had not received orders to stop. If they tried to leave, she would stop them. The students were not capable of surviving in a war-torn countryside. They were her recruits, and she would protect them with her life.

She went into her house and picked up her knitting. Making one booty a night had resulted in a bag full of booties in the corner. The room went dark. She felt for the windowsill where she kept matches and a candle. She lit the candle, placed it on the table in the middle of the room, and resumed her knitting. Then she felt under her chair for the canvas bag where she had placed a set of civilian clothes and some rice. When the Americans came, she hoped to slip away with other refugees.

17 — Cold & War - Late November, 1950

Sun-hee finished helping Max with a few minor surgeries and wondered what she could do in the hospital, mainly because she wanted to stay in a warm place.

The door opened, and Sgt. Kua said, "Sun-hee, General Park would like to see you at once."

Sun-hee grabbed her coat on the way out the door and followed the sergeant down an icy path. A cold front from the northeast dumped a thick layer of snow over the camp during the night. Keeping her balance on the slippery, uneven surface was a challenge.

Sgt. Kua led her across the camp, past the gate to the student dorms, and on to the next gate. Four soldiers stood at attention, all disabled, but still able to hold a rifle. The sergeant led her through the gate where they walked in the deep snow towards Gen. Park, who stood by the door of the closest building to the dorms.

Gen. Park said as she approached. "Sun-hee, I need to question the prisoner. Since you are the only person here who knows English, I need you to translate." She bowed in acknowledgment. "The American prisoner is in a chair facing away from the door. You will sit in front of him and be able to see me. Do not make any references to my name or rank. He must not see me or know who I am. Do you understand?"

"Yes, General Park," Sun-hee said. She straightened her smock, took a deep breath, and followed Jin-taek into the building which was like the dorm where she slept.

Jin-taek being here is a good omen.

Theodore sat with his back towards the door. A strap around his chest held him firmly in the chair. Straps around his forearms held them against the arms of the chair. His shins were tied to the legs of the chair in a way his feet were not able to touch the floor. She bent to examine the cast she had helped put onto the ankle, making sure it was intact. The empty chair was about two meters in front of Theodore. She turned and sat down on its front edge, placing her hands in her lap.

"Sunny," Theodore said, "I expected I might see you here."

Sun-hee sat still, trying not to show emotion. She focused on the back of the room where Gen. Park entered, followed by a soldier. She wished she had some water as her mouth had become dry.

Gen. Park waited for about a minute before speaking, "Ask him why he was flying over this hospital."

"Why were you flying over this hospital?" Sun-hee asked in English.

"Theodore Reid, captain, United States Air Force, 493 72 82," was Theodore's reply.

"The prisoner replied by giving his name, Theodore Reid. He is a captain in the United States Air Force, 493 72 82," said Sun-hee in Korean.

"Tell me your mission," said Gen. Park.

"Tell me your mission," Sun-hee repeated, in English.

"Theodore Reid, captain, U.S. Air Force, 493 72 82," was Theodore's reply.

Sun-hee repeated in Korean.

"Ask him why he is not answering our questions directly?" said Gen. Park.

"Why do you not answer our questions, Theodore?" asked Sun-hee.

"Our training limits what we can say to the enemy," Theodore said. "We can only give our name, rank, and serial number."

Sun-hee translated the answer.

Gen. Park went on to ask more questions, trying to discover why American jets were flying over this hospital. Theodore answered all the questions about his mission with his name, rank, and serial number. Sun-hee could see Gen. Park was getting impatient.

"What is the name of your partner?" Gen. Park asked.

Sun-hee translated.

"How is he doing, Sunny? Is he alive?" said Theodore.

Sun-hee thought for a moment and then addressed Gen. Park in Korean, "How is he doing, Sun-hee? Is he alive?"

"Give me his name, and I will tell you how he is doing."

Sun-hee again translated. She tried to force the shakes in her chest to stop.

"Jeremy Mcleod," said Theodore.

Sun-hee translated. "Theodore says his partner's name is Jeremy Mcleod."

"If he tells me his mission and when the Americans will attack, I will let him know more about the other pilot," said Gen. Park.

Theodore's answer was name, rank, and serial number.

"Why did America attack the Democratic People's Republic of Korea?" asked the general.

Sun-hee sighed and looked deeply into Theodore's eyes as she asked this question in English.

Sun-hee noticed how Theodore focused his eyes on her, pausing for a long moment before he finally said, "To remove the communist government."

The response was passed on by Sun-hee.

"Who would the Americans replace Premier Kim Il-sung with?" Gen. Park went on.

"The South Korean Government," said Theodore matter-of-factly.

"Do you know, captain, how many people were killed and imprisoned by the government of Rhee Syngman? Tens of thousands. He killed anyone who spoke badly about the government of the Republic Of Korea." Gen. Park went into lecture mode. Sun-hee struggled to keep up. "…And the Americans supported him just because he was not communist." Gen. Park said, waving his hands. "Kim Il-sung was trying to liberate the Korean people from the evil of Rhee Syngman and his oppressive rule. What will the Americans do when Rhee begins to slaughter thousands of North Koreans after you have handed it to him?"

Sun-hee knew what Gen. Park was saying, but had difficulty translating due to her rusty English skills. She did not imitate his hand gestures.

Theodore sat, staring at Sun-hee.

"Answer me, Captain!" Gen. Park shouted, waving his arms.

She translated but was unable to reflect the anger of the general. She clenched her hands in her lap.

"I have no answer," said Theodore.

"I can tell you, Captain Theodore Reed," yelled Gen. Park. "Americans came to Korea to stop the Soviets and the Chinese. To do this, you are killing North Koreans."

Sun-hee translated in a steady voice.

"Our blood will be on your hands, Captain!" screamed Gen. Park.

Sun-hee translated.

The general turned to a soldier on his left and commanded him to break the captain's hand.

Sun-hee sat back in her chair to move from the violence. A soldier took his rifle and slammed the butt of it into Theodore's left hand, smashing it on the arm of the chair. Theodore grimaced in pain while keeping his eyes focused on Sun-hee.

"An example of your brutality, Sunny," Theodore said in a stern voice.

Sun-hee saw in Theodore's eyes that his comment wasn't meant for her. She translated the words for Gen. Park.

"Do you mock me, Captain?" said Gen. Park while motioning to Jin-taek on his right to smash the other hand.

Sun-hee was barely able to finish the translation before Jin-taek smashed his rifle butt into Theodore's right hand. Jin-taek smiled towards her as if he acted for her benefit.

He seemed pleased with himself.

Theodore's eyes closed, his teeth held tightly together.

More senseless pain. War only brings pain. Injured people, injuring people.

Gen. Park continued. "Our blood is on your hands and the hands of every American. Now tell me, when will the Americans bomb this hospital?"

Sun-hee translated the best she could, hoping Theodore was getting the emotion of the general.

Theodore's eyes focused on his hands. The rest of his body shook. "I truly do not know," was his reply.

Sun-hee translated.

"When will they land at the beaches of Sunham?" Gen. Park asked.

"I would not know until the day of the landing," said Theodore.

"Where were you going to bomb when you were shot down?"

Theodore shook his head and repeated his name, rank, and serial number.

Gen. Park paced back and forth across the room a couple of times. "Sun-hee, tell him I will be back tomorrow and that I expect better answers." Then he stormed out of the room.

Sun-hee stood and began to walk out.

"Are you going to leave me here, Sunny?"

"I have no say in leaving you here."

"Is my partner still alive?"

Sun-hee stepped back to look Theodore in the face. "Sun-hee, medical student, we don't number people."

"I only want to know if Jeremy is alive. Can't you tell me that?" pleaded Theodore.

"We only want to know when to flee, so we can stay alive when the American's attack," Sun-hee replied.

Theodore paused for a moment, and then replied, "We were a reconnaissance plane. We carried no bombs."

"What is reconsass…?"

"My mission was to gather information by taking photographs," Theodore said.

"When will the Americans come here?" Sun-hee begged. "I want my friends to stay alive. I have seen too many mangled and burnt bodies." Her eyes began to water. "Help me save my friends from the same fate." She started to cry.

"I would never know about an attack ahead of time," said Theodore. "I am told where to fly an hour before I take off. My plane cannot carry bombs, just cameras. I only take photographs. Pilots do not get information on attacks because they might be shot down and questioned like you are questioning me now."

Sun-hee looked carefully at Theodore and said in anger, "You couldn't put me out of my misery of having to treat victims of American bombs. And now you can't save me from American bombs. What use are you if you won't help me live or die?"

"I'm sorry, Sunny," Theodore said followed by a deep exhale, and his chin dropped to his chest.

Sun-hee looked at the American she had verbally conquered. She said in a confident tone, "I checked on Jeremy this morning. He has not regained consciousness. His broken legs are in casts."

"Thank you, Sunny," Theodore said without lifting his head.

She looked at Theodore's hands. His right hand was swelling. A bone was sticking out of his left hand, and blood dripped onto the floor. "I am not your enemy, Theodore. We are not your enemy," she said. Then she stood and walked out. Jin-taek followed, leaving Theodore strapped to the chair.

The rest of the day, Sun-hee helped the wounded and tried to spend time comforting children. Sgt. Kua came to her after dinner and said, "You are needed with the prisoner again."

When she entered the cement building where the questioning took place, Kwong-ku and Hien-jin were there with bandages along with Jin-taek and three other soldiers.

"We were told to wait for you," said Kwong-ku.

"These men and I will examine your hands. Do not resist," Sun-hee said to Theodore while observing next to the bowl-sized circle of blood drying on the floor.

Kwong-ku and Hien-jin loosened the arm restraints and attended to Theodore's left hand. Theodore winced in pain as the boys set the bones.

Sun-hee took Theodore's right hand and used her fingers to search for the broken bones. Then she applied pressure in the right places to put them back in line.

Jin-taek watched faithfully, ready to protect them if Theodore made a wrong move.

They used sticks taken from the bushes on the hillsides to keep Theodore's hands immobile. Hien-jin and Kwang-ku helped Theodore pee into the bucket, something they had done for many injured Korean soldiers over the last few months.

When the bandages were in place, the soldiers removed the rest of the restraints. Theodore stood on his left leg and said to Sun-hee, "Did you really want me to shoot you, Sunny?"

"I am tired of seeing people maimed by war. I expect that the Americans will kill all of us," said Sun-hee before the soldiers led Theodore away.

Sun-hee returned to the dorm and got ready for bed.

"How is the American?" asked Joo-yun.

"He will be fine. General Park did not punish him as much as I thought he would."

"What did General Park do?" asked Choe-me.

"He had the American's hands smashed," said Sun-hee. "Blood of the Korean people were placed on his hands."

"Compared to the children we have been treating, the American got off easy," said Choe-me. "I would have done much worse."

"Is he the one who should feel our pain? Are the people who are laying in the hospital the people the American's are fighting?" Sun-hee said and lay down, covering herself with her blanket. Someone blew out the last candle.

Sun-hee woke, shivering uncontrollably. She felt Joo-yun next to her. She must have joined her under her blanket during the night. Still, she was freezing, and her eyes could see nothing in the total darkness.

How long until morning when I can get up, go to the hospital, and get warm? The only warm place I know is filled with blood, moans, screams, burnt flesh, broken bodies, and death.

"It is too cold," said Joo-yun in her ear. "I can't stop shivering."

"Cuddle with others," came a voice from the lightless room.

"We are," said Joo-yun.

"I need someone to keep me warm," said a voice. Sun-hee heard shuffling across the room.

"Me too," said another.

"Everyone gather over here." She recognized Young-ja's voice.

In a couple of minutes, twenty-three girls had spooned together under their blankets. Sun-hee fell back asleep.

"Time to get up," the sergeant said while lighting a candle by the door. Since everyone had worn their clothes and coats to bed, they were ready for the day.

As Sun-hee walked to breakfast, she looked at the building that, when finished, would be their home. She longed for a warm place to sleep. The walls were up, and the wood frame for the roof poked into the sky. She gobbled breakfast and ran for the warmth of the hospital wards.

The day seemed colder than any previous. She did not look forward to sleeping in a cold dorm. It was well after sunset when Choe-me grabbed her for dinner. They huddled by the fires in the kitchen to keep warm on the outside and warmed their insides with a hot stew. She lingered for a while with other girls before facing the cold. When they arrived in the dorm, they saw a tent made by Hammer from boards and blankets. It was a meter high, four meters wide, and six meters long. They arranged their mats and belongings inside the tent, leaving the rest of the room bare. Soon the tent was warmed by their body heat. Sun-hee quickly fell fast asleep.

The next morning as she entered the hospital, the Hammer stood near the door making splints out of boards.

Sun-hee approached. "I wanted to thank you for making the tent. It is much warmer inside."

"I made one for the guys and thought the girls could use one, too," he said. "I am glad you like it."

"I wonder if we should make a small one for the prisoner. So he does not freeze to death," said Sun-hee.

"I will put one together and tell Sergeant Kua it is available."

That night, when she lay down, Eun-seong asked, "How are you, Sun-hee?"

"I am tired of this place and what the war has brought us. I wish I could go home."

"Where is home?"

"Yonggwang," she replied. "The Americans have advanced past there."

"I hope your mother is okay," Eun-seong said.

"Our hut is outside of town and hopefully away from the bombs. My mother will find a way to survive," she said, reassuring herself. "She had a new teaching job and was to get a new house because I was a prize winner. Nothing matters now! Nothing matters!" She broke down in tears.

Eun-seong tried to console her.

"I heard today the Americans had captured Kimchaek, where my parents are. I hope they got out," said Joo-yun.

"Nampo is my home," said Eun-seong. "I hope the Americans left it alone on the way to Pyongyang,"

Then another girl joined the conversation and another. For the next couple of hours, they talked about their families, expressed their worry, and comforted one another.

18 — Despair - November 20th, 1950

"First or second bowl, Sun-hee?" Sgt. Kua inquired.

Holding the bowl of warm stew against her chest with her knees, Sun-hee looked up from her huddled position. "My first, Sergeant Kua." She held her spoon in the sleeve of her coat wrapped over her hand.

"Finish lunch and report to my house," Sgt. Kua said. "Your help is needed with the prisoner today."

What do I need to do this time?

She had not seen Theodore since they had bandaged his hands a week ago. She scraped out the last spoonful and rose to get her second bowl of warmth. The stew was not that tasty, but it was hot. She held the stew with both hands, allowing the warmth to relieve the tingling in her fingers. She rushed to fill her belly, to conserve the heat in the food, not to report to Sgt. Kua any faster.

At least I have enough to eat. I think I am starting to get fat. Am I pregnant? I have no other symptoms. I should go see what they are doing to Theodore today.

She arrived at the guesthouse and knocked. Sgt. Kua let her in, pointed to the table, and said, "Put these things on. Here are some long socks to keep your feet warm, a sweater to wear under your coat, and a wool hat. There are some mittens to keep your hands warm. I cut the fingers out as you will be doing some writing. Follow me and be quiet." She led Sun-hee out the door.

Lt. Rim stood with Jin-taek and three soldiers, holding a stretcher inside the prisoner compound. A blanket covered the man, revealing only boots, like the ones Theodore wore. Sgt. Kua looked towards Sun-hee, holding a finger to her lips. She stepped slowly past the soldiers and between buildings where a table and chair sat in the snow.

A wire dangled from the window above the table to a set of headphones hanging on the back of the chair. Sergeant Kua motioned Sun-hee to sit, then pulled a notebook and two pencils from her coat, placed them on the table, and whispered, "You are to listen to what is said by the Americans, translate, and write it all down. Can you do this?"

"I will do my best," Sun-hee whispered.

Sgt. Kua stepped back and waved to Lt. Rim. The soldiers brought up the stretcher and entered the building. Sun-hee heard the door opening through the headphones. Theodore shouted, "Jeremy!" There was some shuffling noise. "Thank God, you are alive."

She began to write down the Korean translation of Theodore and Jeremy's conversation.

"Theo, good to see you, buddy. Where are we?" said Jeremy.

"A mountain medical facility with mostly young medical students," said Theodore. "I have seen two Russian doctors and lots of injured Koreans. Even the soldiers are walking wounded. They patched up my ankle by torture and seemed to enjoy it. The girl putting on my cast sang to me the whole time. The next day they put me in here. They questioned me the day after that and smashed both of my hands. Since then, I have seen soldiers twice a day. They bring me food and hold me while I piss and shit. Other than that, I try to keep warm. How are you?"

"I woke up a couple of days ago," Jeremy said. "My head hurt, and my legs throbbed in these casts. I was wondering where I was when this pretty young Korean girl in a doctor's smock comes up and starts feeling my feet. I said that tickles and she jumped about six feet. Then she started blabbing and lifted my blanket, which I grabbed back from her. She gave me the dirtiest look, grabbed her nose, and lifted it again. A few minutes later, I was restrained and got a sponge bath from a couple of old Korean women."

Sun-hee wrote, *they laughed.*

"When do you think we will get out of here?" Jeremy asked.

"I think our boys know where we're at, but, if they were going to come and get us, they would have been here already," said Theodore. "Either we are in a place they cannot get to easily and figured the mission too risky, or they think this hotel is a lovely place for us to spend the winter."

Sun-hee wrote as fast as she could, trying to keep up with translating and writing was not easy.

"This is not like the Moana Surfrider," said Jeremy. "Now that was a wonderful place. All the Hawaiian girls."

"Those girls at the luau with the coconut shells were really something!" said Theodore. "With this cold, it's more like a fleabag hotel in Fargo."

Sun-hee wrote English or put question marks for the words she did not know. She began to use the first letter of their names to note who spoke.

J – "Anyone else here?"

T – "None I have seen. One girl speaks English. She said I was the first American she had seen."

J – "With only two guests, this fleabag hotel will be going broke."

T – "They don't change the sheets, the service is lousy, but the food is edible."

For the next six hours, Sun-hee sat writing what the Americans said. They talked about how they were treated, life at home, their wives, and children. They spoke of foods she had never heard of like Peatza. Some she just had to guess how to spell, and no concept of others like a juicy steak, and hamburgers. The men discussed each other's wounds and concluded that all things considered, they had been treated okay. They talked through the ordeal of helping each other to piss and shit.

There is that word again. Now I know what it means from the context. Why did Theodore say it when he threw down his gun?

She enjoyed the story Theodore told of their capture. How Sunny, a young girl dressed in medical garments, stood above him and told him to shoot her or surrender. She was careful to write his recounting of the interrogation accurately. However, she did not write down their conversation after Gen Park left. Theodore repeated it to Jeremy, "Sunny said, 'I am not your enemy. We are not your enemy.'"

"What do you think Sunny meant?" asked Jeremy.

"I can only guess the Koreans in this camp may be friendlier than the rest of the country," said Theodore.

The hours passed. Sun-hee's hands quivered with the rest of her body, and her feet pained her. She stomped them to get more blood flowing to them, but it only intensified the pain. She swung them back and forth and side to side instead.

As darkness came, she bent closer to the paper to see her marks. A frigid gust swirled around the building and caught her notes. She slammed her hand on the desk to keep them from blowing away.

Did they hear that? No sign from inside. My teeth chatter louder than the American's voices.

She had never stayed out in the cold this long. Her fingers would not move.

I cannot write anymore. I need to pee. Soon! Should I do it here? No. Hold it for a while longer.

The shakes and her bladder stole her concentration. She jumped as a hand took her shoulder. She exhaled, seeing Sgt. Kua with a finger to her lips, motioning to come.

Half-doubled over, wincing with each step, Sun-hee followed Sgt.

Kua to the guesthouse, barged through the door, and headed straight to the privy. When she came out, she was still shivering, stomping her feet and rubbing her hands. Sgt. Kua was flipping the pages of the notebook. Lt. Rim walked in.

"Who said she could leave her post?" he yelled.

"I did," said Sgt. Kua in a calm voice. "She was freezing out there."

Sun-hee tried to stand at attention, but she just shivered.

"My men are out on guard duty all night in this cold," said Lt. Rim in an angry tone.

"This is a young girl, not a man, and they can move around. She sat still writing all afternoon." Sgt. Kua waved the notebook.

Lt. Rim grabbed it out of her hand. "Who gave you permission to read this?" he shouted.

"I do not know how to read," she said in a quiet voice, looking down at the floor.

Lt. Rim turned to Sun-hee. "Anything in here you think is important?"

"Yes, Lt. Rim," Sun-hee said. She licked her lips and swallowed. "The Americans spoke of being rescued but mentioned rescue usually occurs in the first day or two after a pilot is shot down. It has been almost two weeks, and they do not expect a rescue attempt."

"Is it all here?" he asked, holding up the notebook.

"Yes, sir. I may need to rewrite some of it. I used shorthand and transliteration to keep up."

"We will talk later, Sergeant," Lt. Rim said sternly and left with the notebook.

"Go back to the dorm. I will have food and hot tea brought to you," said Sgt. Kua.

When Sun-hee arrived in the dorm, with the woolen cap still on her head, she crawled into the tent and headed to her mat.

"And just where have you been? And where did you get that nice woolen hat?" asked Young-ja.

"I have been out in the cold. That is all I should tell you," she said, pulling the blanket tight around her while shivering. "I am freezing, and my feet hurt."

"Your face is all red. Let me warm your feet." Eun-seong pulled the socks off Sun-hee's feet and started rubbing them. "Your feet are like ice," she pulled up her shirt, placed Sun-hee's feet on her belly, and rubbed them. "Ohhh, they are cold. My mother did this when my feet were cold. Does it feel good, Sun-hee?"

"They hurt," replied Sun-hee.

"Check for frostbite," said Young-ja.

"Is there any white on the toes?" asked Moon Choe."

Eun-seong held Sun-hee's feet up while everyone tried to look. "Just bright red, no frostbite." And she put the feet back on her belly.

One of the cooks came in with a tray of food and two cups of hot tea.

Sun-hee grabbed a cup to warm her hands. She sipped the hot tea and ate while her feet slowly began to feel normal. She laid back, grateful for the warmth of good friends and to be out of the cold. Soon, she was asleep.

The sky was bright orange when she woke.

A beautiful sunrise is a good omen.

She lingered over breakfast before continuing to the hospital. The frigid air turned her breath into clouds as she walked. Gen. Park was talking with men near the command house. From a distance, the discussion did not seem to be going well.

A minute later, Lt. Rim was barking orders for his men to escort Chinese soldiers into buildings. Groups of Chinese soldiers ran into each building. She watched as at least fifty went into each of the student dorms and more into the nearly completed building the students hoped to occupy. She estimated that a couple of thousand Chinese soldiers invaded the compound. During the day, Chinese men seemed to be laying everywhere, most of them slept except when they were using the privy or eating the meals brought to them. She noticed they ate ravenously, pleased to get a hot meal. They did not talk and stayed to themselves.

After the sun went down, the Chinese soldiers left, faster than they had arrived.

Sun-hee was eating dinner when she saw Strategist and asked, "What were the Chinese doing here?"

"I believe we are seeing a part of the Chinese Army, which is moving to attack the Americans. They hid here during the day, so American airplanes would not see them. They travel at night."

"What do you think will happen?" asked Joo-yun.

"There are three possibilities," said Yong-gak raising three fingers, talking with his forearms. "First, the American air force will bomb the Chinese Army, and they will not make any difference. The Chinese will be more causalities of war. Second, the Chinese will push the Americans out of Korea, and we become part of China. Third, the

Soviet Union decides they want this as their territory and takes it from both the Americans and Chinese."

"Your possibilities do not include the Korean nation in the future," said Sun-hee.

"We defeated the South's army, and America has defeated the North. There is not enough left of either Korean Army to fight for unity," said Yong-gak in a disappointed tone. "I suspect Kim Il-sung has fled the country or has been killed by the bombing. When this war is over, America, China, or the Soviet Union will control Korea. Our history is one of being conquered by other nations, and this is no different. The United States and the Soviet Union are the most powerful nations in the world. China has fifty times as many people as we do. Their communist government is presently in a land acquisition mode. Maybe two thousand Chinese soldiers stayed here last night. If we searched all of North Korea, I doubt we could find that many Korean soldiers. If we survive, I hope whoever wins sees us as doctors, and we are needed."

***

The next week was calm. A few people made their way from Chongjin on foot, reporting the Americans had bombed the road. Except for a jet flying over now and then, it was too quiet for a country at war.

The next afternoon, a soldier with a fresh gunshot wound was carried in. They called for Sun-hee and Max to save his life. "Focus and work quickly!" Max said. The bullet had punctured a lung and the man's liver.

Who shot this man? Why? wondered Sun-hee as they worked frantically for over an hour, trying to save the man. They could not stop the bleeding.

Max kicked the table. "Another unlucky man!" he said and stomped out.

She stood by herself for a moment, took a sheet, and laid it over the soldier. She walked out of the operating room, sat on an empty cot, and looked at the bloody hands in her lap.

Just another unlucky man.

Choe-me walked over, sat beside her, and asked, "Is he alive?"

"No. We failed to save him. Shot in the wrong place to survive."

"He was stealing food. Lieutenant Rim shot him."

Sun-hee bent over and buried her face in her hands. "We failed to save a soldier who was hungry enough to steal food. I could have saved him by giving him half of what I am forced to eat to be healthy enough to have a baby that will die when the bombs fall."

"I have no more words of comfort. When will this nightmare end?" said Choe-me as she held Sun-hee.

Sun-hee got up without saying a word and walked out, bloody handprints around her eyes.

19 — Arrivals - End of November - December, 1950

The twenty-seventh of November was clear, but the sun did not put a dent in the cold. The day started with the roar of jets, then many planes leaving contrails high in the sky. Eun-seong, with severe morning sickness, was in tears most of the day. Young-ja did not talk. Max and Alek were drunk before noon. For the first time, Mr. Yun did not venture out into the frigid air to work on the new building. Sun-hee sat in the hospital, responding only when a patient cried out. After sunset, it was snowing lightly. Sun-hee, wanting warmth at dinner, found lukewarm stew and silence broken only by the clanking of spoons.

The word "wounded" meshed into Sun-hee's dream and did not cause her to wake.

"Wake-up, Sun-hee. There are wounded," Choe-me said while shaking Sun-hee, rousing her from her deep sleep.

Sun-hee put on her shoes. Joo-yun sat with her arms around her knees, rocking back and forth. Eun-seong ran out, trying to catch her heave. Choe-me and Young-ja went with Sun-hee to the hospital where ox carts were lined up, loaded with Chinese.

The hospital was out of every medical item needed to treat patients. There was no more morphine or antibiotics. All available cloth was ripped up and boiled for bandages. Hong-yong spent his time making custom splints and crutches for patients from scraps of building materials. The only good thing was that the hospital buildings were warm enough to be tolerable. Young-ja and Choe-me maintained a full line of men to be operated on. Sun-hee did not have to choose the next lucky man.

More Chinese wounded arrived over the next few days. They adored Choe-me and Young-ja, who both spoke Mandarin. Young-ja kept up a running conversation with the Chinese soldiers and got news of the fighting. The Chinese told of attacking the Americans in waves. Many died, but they were winning.

The next morning, Sun-hee was up early. She noticed it was the first day of December on the calendar by the door. The line of men ready to be touched by the lucky hands of Max and Sun-hee was a long one.

She was cutting a leg off a patient when Sgt. Kua stepped into the operating room and said. "Your English is needed again. Report to the prisoner area."

"May I finish with this patient, Sergeant Kua?" she asked while holding up a bloody scalpel.

"Yes. The Chinese are more important than Americans," Sgt. Kua replied. "Come to the prisoner compound when you finish."

What will I be doing with the two Americans today? I hope I will not be sitting out in the cold again.

They finished the amputation on a Chinese soldier. Without antibiotics, Max expected the man would die, but they had done what they could. Sun-hee wrapped the stump, took the amputated leg out to dispose of it, and asked assistants to move the patient from the operating room. She dropped the leg into the bucket by the gate and watched as they threw it into the mass graveyard. As soon as it landed, two men picked up shovels, each threw in a couple of shovels of dirt. Then they continued to dig, using pickaxes to break up the frozen ground.

How big will the grave be? Is this my fate? To be added to the pit?

Sun-hee stopped to wash up and change out of her bloody clothes. She took her time strolling towards prisoners.

Hammer was there, cutting boards into two-meter lengths. He paused his sawing. She felt his eyes on her as she walked by.

Sgt. Kua directed her to enter the third concrete building.

Lt. Rim stood inside the door. There was a double row of Korean soldiers down the middle of the room, each with a rifle pointing toward the outside walls. Jin-taek grinned and nodded at her. Along each wall were six blindfolded American soldiers sitting with their legs and arms tied.

Four girls who usually worked in another barrack were there. Tsai Myung-hee and Ryom Kyuung-hwa were standing on the right side. Jo Yu-min and Shim Mi-kum were standing on the left. They had washbasins, soap, and bandages.

"Sun-hee, I need you to translate," said Lt. Rim. "Tell them there is to be no talking."

"Americans. Please be quiet and do not talk," Sun-hee said in English.

"You are prisoners of the DPRK."

Sun-hee translated, "You are prisoners of the Democratic People's Republic of Korea."

"We expect you to obey orders."

"Please obey our commands, and you will be treated fairly," Sun-hee improvised a little. "If you do not obey, you will be punished."

"First, we will treat your wounds. Then, you will be restrained for the night," continued the lieutenant.

Sun-hee translated.

"Sergeant Kua, take over," said Lt. Rim. He left the building.

"We will begin treating you two at a time. Please relax, we will be as gentle as possible," Sun-hee said to the Americans, taking charge of the situation.

"What did you just tell them, Sun-hee?" demanded Sgt Kua, a little anger in her voice.

Sun-hee realized she had over-stepped her authority and was very apologetic. "I'm sorry, Sergeant Kua. I told the Americans we would begin treating their wounds, and we would try to be gentle."

"Next time, let me know what you are going to tell them before speaking to them. I need to know what is going on."

"Tsai Myung-hee and Ryom Kyuung-hwa can start on this soldier. Jo Yu-min and Shim Mi-kum go ahead and treat that man," said Sgt. Kua, pointing to the first Americans on either side of the door.

"Sergeant Kua, removing the blindfold may take away some of the fear the Americans have right now. They are afraid of what they cannot see," Sun-hee said in Korean.

"Only remove the blindfold of those who are receiving treatment," Sgt. Kua said to keep some level of authority.

Four of the men had severe injuries, but none were life-threatening. Two had sustained minor gunshot wounds, one had shrapnel wounds in his arms and legs, and the fourth had a bayonet wound to his side. All of them had multiple bruises.

They have been beaten, observed Sun-hee.

For the next two hours, they performed minor surgery, cleaned, and bandaged the wounds of the Americans.

Sun-hee removed the shrapnel from one man and a bullet from another, continually giving instructions to the Americans and telling Sgt. Kua what she was saying and doing.

The other girls left. Sgt. Kua ordered in the planks. Sun-hee tried to give a calm explanation to the prisoners as Korean soldiers strapped each American to a board and laid them down on their backs. Sun-hee made sure blankets were wrapped around each prisoner.

When Sun-hee returned to the dorm, she saw only her belongings.

The rest of the room was bare.

"Whoopee," she said out loud.

Quickly, she thrust her things on the mat and rolled it up, then stuck it under her arm. As she headed out the door, she patted the wall where the calendar had hung. The entrance to the girl's side of the new dorm was only about ten meters from the boy's old dorm. But it was about ten times longer to run through the gates and around the fence. She raced on the packed snow as fast as she could, nearly slipping on the ice.

Joo-yun yelled at her as she entered the new dorm. "I saved you space next to me."

Sun-hee ran to the spot and put down her bundle. Joo-yun helped her unroll the mat and straighten out Sun-hee's things. The first thing Sun-hee noticed was it was warm. There was a stove in the middle of the room. She put her hands as close to it as she could without touching it. She heard laughter and Young-ja's non-stop talking. Eun-seong came up behind her and hugged her.

The new quarters consisted of five rooms and two privies. In the back were two sleeping quarters; one for boys and one for girls. Each was about eight meters wide and twenty meters long, giving each person a lot more space than the old dorm. Windows were on one side and across the back. There were three doors in the room. One was located at the outside corner next to the fence. One door—about a-fourth of the way down the wall—was the entrance to the privy. The third door, with a board nailed across it, led to an eight-meter square room exclusively for the girls. The boy's side was a mirror image. Between them was a great room measuring eight meters wide by twelve meters long.

The privy amazed Sun-hee. It had more space than the hut where she grew up. There was a shower area with three heads. Three stalls with half doors and three sinks meant no more waiting in line. Best of all, there was a rectangle cement basin on the floor, a tub where they could bathe. Windows were all around the high ceiling. Lightbulbs hung from the ceiling, but without electricity, candles had been placed strategically in the room.

After dinner, Sun-hee told them all about the new prisoners. The girls talked, giggled, and chatted late into the night. Having a new place to sleep was the first positive event since they had arrived at Yangseongso.

***

Sgt. Kua came to Sun-hee at breakfast. "We will be questioning the new prisoners today. Report to me when you are finished."

"You must tell us what you find out," said Young-ja. "I need to know all the juicy details."

"I will tell you what is permitted," said Sun-hee. "Some things General Park wants to keep to himself. I may not be able to tell you everything."

"I wish I knew how to speak English. Then I could get the inside scoop on the Americans. Will you teach me English?"

"I would be honored to teach you," Sun-hee said. "However, it may not be permitted under government regulations."

I wish someone else knew English. They could translate and deal with the Americans.

"Can we resume the language instruction at night and include English?" asked Young-ja.

"Yes. Then you can spend all your time talking to the Americans."

When Sun-hee arrived at the prisoner compound, Lt. Rim directed her to the same building where they had questioned Theodore.

She entered and noticed it was set up like before. One American was already in a chair, his back towards the door. She took her place opposite the American soldier, this time sitting back in the chair, and placed her hands in her lap. The American's eyes watched her the whole time. He was shaking slightly, his fingers tapping quickly on the arms of the chair.

Lt. Rim and a Chinese officer stood behind the American prisoner. The Chinese officer asked the first question. "How many Americans are in Korea?"

She struggled to translate the question from Chinese to English, not used to thinking in that manner.

The American gave his name, rank, and serial number. She translated into Korean and then Chinese.

"What were your orders?" asked Lieutenant Rim. "What was your objective?"

She translated and got name, rank, and serial number in reply.

He looks young and scared. I wonder how old he is.

The questioning went on for a few rounds with the same reply.

Sun-hee looked at the soldier and said in English, "Do privates in the American army know any more than their name, rank, and serial number?"

"I only know what my Sergeant tells me," said the American soldier.

"What did your Sergeant tell you?"

"To stay at my position and shoot any gooks that come."

"You were to shoot Americans? Please explain," said Sun-hee in a confused tone.

"We were told to shoot gooks. Koreans or Chinese. Like you," said the soldier.

"The word *migok* is the Korean word for American," explained Sun-hee.

"No, you are the gook," said the American.

"Sun-hee, what are you saying to him,?" asked Lt. Rim impatiently.

"I asked him if privates in the American army knew anything more than their name, rank, and serial number. His orders are to shoot Chinese and Koreans."

She felt Lt. Rim's glare at her. Then he turned and spoke to the Chinese officer quietly in the back of the room. She could not hear what they said.

"We are done with this man. Bring in the next," Lt. Rim said to the soldiers.

The next American soldier said the same thing. He also was a private. They got no additional information from him.

The third had an accent that was hard to understand. Sun-hee asked him why he spoke so differently from the others.

"I'm from Louisiana, ma'am. We do have an accent," he said.

Sun-hee thought, *I wonder where Louisiana is. I thought these were all Americans.* They exchanged him for another man.

Lt. Rim told the soldiers not to do all the restraints on the next one. Strapping and unstrapping the prisoners took longer than the questioning.

They are all scared. They are trained to not say anything other than their name, rank, and serial number. The questioning is getting us nowhere.

The interrogating went on through three other Americans until they got to John Peterson who gave his rank as a sergeant. Immediately, Lt. Rim had the full restraints put on.

This man's face is weathered, like Jin-taek's. He looks around more and is not nervous.

Lt. Rim focused on this soldier. He asked over and over, "What were your orders?" The American's answers were always John Peterson, sergeant, and serial number.

The American sergeant glared at Sun-hee, his eyes narrow, his words harsh. She could feel his hate.

The American will not answer anything Rim asks. Maybe if he was out of the room, I could get the American sergeant to talk. "Lieutenant Rim, maybe if you left, I could try to talk to him informally. He might say something to me."

Lt. Rim nodded, spoke briefly to the Chinese officer, and they stepped out of the building.

Sun-hee sighed, put her hands on the arms of the chair, and stood. "They are taking a break. The pause gives me a chance to stretch." She stole a glance at Jin-taek in the back of the room. He grinned at her.

She thought about what to say to get this man to open up. "My mother taught me English. She went to a school run by American missionaries. They were good people. Why do you hate me so much when the missionaries did not?"

"You are Commies!" John said.

"I am a fifteen-year-old girl. How can you hate me?"

"You are the enemy."

"Why am I your enemy?"

"You're Korean!"

"Are the South Koreans also your enemy?"

"You're North Korean."

"How is that different?"

"You're a Gook."

"You would kill a young girl just because she lives in North Korea?"

"My orders are to kill everyone in North Korea."

"You Americans are very good at killing."

Sun-hee motioned to a soldier by the door and sat down.

The soldier opened the door to allow Lt. Rim to enter. They untied the sergeant and escorted him out of the building. When they were alone, Lt. Rim asked, "What did you learn, Sun-hee?"

"John Peterson thinks North Koreans are bad and has orders to kill us all. He has been told incorrect information and believes we are all evil."

"If I didn't have orders to protect them, I would kill all the Americans," said Lt. Rim. "Does this make me like him?"

"I do not know how to answer your question, Lieutenant Rim."

The last American had very dark skin, darker than any person Sun-hee had ever seen.

Sun-hee asked, "What were your orders?"

"I make sure the men have a hot meal, Ma'am," he replied.

Sun-hee was puzzled for a moment before translating.

"What is his name?" asked Lt. Rim.

"I am Abraham Aldolphus Bryant," said the man.

"What is his rank?" asked Lt. Rim.

"Field cook, fifth-grade, Ma'am," replied Abraham.

"He has no information," said Lt. Rim, and he left with the Chinese officer.

She walked by Jin-taek and said, "He is the only American who showed respect. Treat him well."

***

Over the next week, wounded soldiers continued to arrive at the hospital. Ten to twenty injured a day, all Chinese. The wounded reported that they had stalled the American advance.

Medical supplies began to arrive across the mountains from the Chinese border carried on the backs of Chinese men or sometimes a mule. They sent only one mule at a time so it would not be a target for American planes. Woolen pants and coats, once worn by the Chinese soldiers, were mended and handed out to the students. They were much warmer than the clothes they had brought with them the previous summer.

By mid-December, new wounded reported that the Americans were in retreat along the coast. The Chinese told stories of a battle at Chosin Reservoir, where the Americans were defeated. Spirits of the students rose from the news. Sun-hee thought of her mother, and for the first time in months, took out the blue scarf. The road in front of their hut went from Yonggwang to the Chosin Reservoir.

***

One afternoon, near the end of December, Choe-me and Eun-seong helped a refugee. They put a new bandage on the woman's hand and arm. They got her something to eat and helped her wash up. As they worked with her, they listened to her story, which was similar to many other refugees. Weeks earlier she had ducked for cover when artillery shells began to fall. Shrapnel injured her hand and arm. American soldiers treated her wounds and let her go the next day. There was fighting along the south coast, so she fled north. For two weeks, she walked as far as she could travel each day. When they reached Sungam, the group she had been walking with chose to go into the mountains. Thus she ended up here.

Choe-me took her to the rehabilitation ward and found a mat where she could spend the night. The woman said, "You are so pleasant and pretty. What is your name?"

"Thank you. I am Moon Choe-me. I am pleased to be of help."

"You look to be about the same age as my daughter. She left for a boarding school last May."

Choe-me froze and said, "What was her name?"

"Lim Joo-yun. Do you know her?"

"Yes. Wait here." Choe-me ran from the room to the library where Joo-yun usually hid out.

"Joo-yun! Come with me. Your mother is at the hospital!" Choe-me called out as she entered the library.

"My mother?" Joo-yun ran with more energy than she had shown in months.

"Mother!" yelled Joo-yun as she dove down, firmly embracing her.

Sun-hee went over and put her arms around her friend, soon joined by Young-ja and an out of breath Choe-me. It brought everyone to tears. The joy of Joo-yun seeing her mother was an unexpected delight. But it brought to the surface the deep emotions of missing their mothers and families.

Mrs. Lim hugged her daughter with all the strength she had in one arm.

Joo-yun brought her mother, Lim Soo-kyung, to dinner. She introduced her to the other students, and so uncharacteristic of the past few months, talked on and on. Sun-hee saw Lt. Rim standing about thirty meters from where they were eating. A shudder ran down her spine.

After dinner, Joo-yun went arm-in-arm with her mother towards the student building, only to be met by Lt. Rim at the gate. He said to Joo-yun, "Your mother must remain in the hospital tonight." Then he stood there, making sure they obeyed his order.

Joo-yun moved her mouth to say something, stopped, glared, then took a deep breath and huffed.

Walking towards them, Sgt. Kua spoke up, "I will make sure your mother has a warm place tonight. Now you go get some rest." Sgt. Kua took Mrs. Lim by the shoulder, hardly breaking her stride, and led her away.

Sun-hee grabbed Joo-yun before she could complain and directed her to the dorm.

Joo-yun entered the girl's dorm and began yelling and throwing things. "How can they separate my mother from me? I hate this place!"

***

The door opened, and the candles in the room flickered in the invading breeze. The candle on the table blew out. "Sergeant Kua," said Lt. Rim as he stuck his head in the door.

"Yes, Lieutenant," Sgt. Kua said, while quickly standing and dropping her knitting.

"We need to decide what to do with the mother of Lim Joo-yun. Where is Joo-yun now?"

"She should be in the dorm."

"Get her."

"Right away, Lieutenant." She hurried out without grabbing a coat.

What are they going to do? They cannot let Mrs. Lim go. I doubt she will want to leave.

Sgt. Kua walked into the dorm. Most of the girls were sleeping except for two who were sitting by the stove. Joo-yun was one of them.

"Joo-yun, come with me," she said.

She put her arm firmly around Joo-yun and escorted her back to the guesthouse. "I will not tolerate the same attitude from your mother that you have shown," Sgt. Kua said as they walked.

As they entered, Joo-yun froze upon seeing Lt. Rim standing by the table.

"Come in," said Lt. Rim in a stern voice. He pulled out a chair. "Please sit down." After Joo-yun sat, Lt. Rim sat in a chair across from her. Sgt. Kua picked up a candle from the end table by the chair and moved to relight the candle on the table.

"We need to determine if your mother will fit in," Lt. Rim said in a gentle tone. "Where is your father?"

"My mother told me soldiers came, recruiting my father and brothers into the Korean People's Army. My mother has not heard from them since. She fears they are dead."

"If your mother were to stay here, what could she do for the program?"

"I don't know. She took care of our home."

"What line of work was your father in?"

"My father was the harbor-master in Kimchaek. He was away quite often."

Lt. Rim rubbed his chin for a moment and then stood. "Stay in this room until I dismiss you. Sergeant Kua, come with me."

Sgt. Kua grabbed her coat and rushed to follow. Lt. Rim gave a short blast on his whistle getting the attention of nearby soldiers. "You and you," he said, pointing to two of the men. "Go stand guard at the Sergeant's house. No one is to leave or enter. The rest of you go back to your posts."

Sgt. Kua followed the lieutenant into the command house. Gen. Park sat at the table in the main room with a few papers in front of him.

"Come in, Lieutenant, Sergeant."

"We need to decide about Mrs. Lim," said Lt. Rim who moved to stand by the table while Sgt. Kua remained by the door.

Gen. Park rose to his feet, took a couple of steps away from the table, and spoke, "What we do with Mrs. Lim does not matter. Max told me today the Soviets are reducing their support now that the Chinese are in control of the war. Our army is gone. Our country is in ruins." Gen. Park's voice wavered. "Either the Americans will regroup and defeat the Chinese or the Chinese will occupy the country."

"What will you do with the students?" questioned Sgt. Kua, stepping forward.

"This hospital is in a good place to survive the war. When the fighting stops, the students can return to their families," he said with a subdued, depressed voice. "Make sure we treat the American prisoners well. There may be fewer revenge killings by the Americans if they give a good report. Or we can offer them to the Chinese as a prize."

"What about the program?" asked Lt. Rim.

Gen. Park changed direction and walked as he spoke. "My plan to have a group of young people who would contribute to making Korea a great nation was going well. I don't believe the Americans or Chinese will give the North Koreans a chance to be great. Maybe we don't deserve to be respected," he said, staring at the floor. "For now, we will go on as planned. Very soon, there will come a day when we must leave. At that time, the students will have to survive on their own."

He turned. "Chun-ja. Glasses," he commanded while picking up a bottle of vodka. A petite woman in her late twenties came from the other room and held out two glasses. The general poured a generous amount into each glass, then refilled his own. Chun-ja bowed deeply, holding out the glasses to Lt. Rim and Sgt. Kua.

After downing half the glass, Gen. Park said flippantly, "Let Mrs. Lim stay with the students. She can be their mother and clean up after them."

Sgt. Kua sipped a little of the vodka and tried not to cough. The two men finished their shots in one gulp. Gen. Park poured himself another drink, sat at the table, and folded his hands under his chin.

Lt. Rim placed his glass on the table. Sgt. Kua followed his move, and then they left. When they were outside, Lt. Rim said, "Get Mrs. Lim and take her to your house. I will release the guards."

As soon as Mrs. Lim saw Sgt. Kua walk into the hospital ward, she said, "I don't understand why I can't be with my daughter."

"Come with me, Mrs. Lim. Bring your blanket, and I'll carry your mat," said Sgt. Kua.

The sergeant walked at a quick pace back to her house. Mrs. Lim struggled to keep up.

"Where are you taking me?" yelled Mrs. Lim as they passed the gate to the new dorms.

"To my house," replied Sgt. Kua without breaking stride. She waited on the porch for Mrs. Lim to catch up, then opened the door.

"Come in, Mrs. Lim," said Lt. Rim.

"There you are," Mrs. Lim said to her daughter. "This is a suitable place for us to stay together."

Joo-yun sat in silence, wringing her hands under the table.

Lt. Rim said in a stern voice, "General Park decided you can stay in the dorms with the students provided you do not cause any trouble. You will report to Sergeant Kua as long as we are in command of this camp."

"When do you expect a change of command?" asked Mrs. Lim.

"When the Chinese decide they want it or the Americans regroup and take over. Sergeant, take these two to the dorm."

"Yes, sir," responded Sgt. Kua. "Mrs. Lim, Joo-yun, let's go."

Joo-yun led her mother into the dorm. Mrs. Lim went to the back corner, arranged her mat, then pulled Joo-yun's things next to her.

20 — Sanshin - December 31st, 1951

Sun-hee and Eun-seong stopped by the hospital after breakfast. There were no new patients, and those who were in the hospital did not need surgery, so the two went to join their friends at the library. They sat at their usual table next to the stairs.

"What are we going to study today?" asked Young-ja.

"I don't feel like studying," said Choe-me.

"After yesterday, I don't want to study either," said Joo-yun.

"How is your mother?" asked Eun-seong.

"She will not talk to me. I couldn't sleep because I'm afraid she will say or do something to offend the general. I wish we could leave," said Joo-yun.

"You and your mother have to stay," said Choe-me.

"I should never have come here," said Joo-yun.

"You're one of us now," said Sun-hee.

"You're stuck with us," said Young-ja. "And all of you are stuck with me."

Eun-seong said, "You know Park will not let you leave. I will see what I can do to help your mother accept being here and accept the child you are going to have."

"My mother does not know I'm pregnant. How can I tell her?"

"I don't know how I would tell my mother. She would be so upset," said Choe-me.

"You'll find the right moment, Joo-yun. It will come up, and then we will help you deal with the situation," replied Eun-seong.

"I can't do what the rest of you do. Sgt. Kua picks on me," said Joo-yun.

"None of us can do everything," said Choe-me. "We do what we can, and that is all we expect of you."

"I hope you don't expect me to study today. I can do it, but I would rather do anything else," said Young-ja.

"I vote not to study today," added Choe-me.

"I sense we need a day off," said Eun-seong. "What do you think, Sun-hee?"

"Today is a relief from the stress of the past few months. I feel ten years older than I did when we arrived. I hope the next six months are not as stressful."

"We will have to deal with the Chinese or Americans," said Joo-yun.

"What do you mean?" asked Choe-me.

"Lieutenant Rim said last night that he expects a change in command depending on who wins the war."

Sun-hee added, "The last time I spoke to Strategist, he believed that one of them would control Korea in the future. The premier has fled to China. There is no army left, at least in this part of the country. If the Chinese want to take charge, they will."

"That will change everything," said Eun-seong. "I wonder if Park will stay or leave."

"If there is a change in command like Joo-yun said, then I think he would leave," said Young-ja. "Loyalty to our country was a positive motivator, but now the DPRK is almost non-existent. Our premier was an inspirational motivator, and he fled the country. General Park keeps us loyal by fear. If he leaves, what loyalties would we have left? We will have to be loyal to the Chinese and communism."

"I am loyal to the four of you and the other students. That has been my focus for months," said Eun-seong.

"I think Eun-seong is right. We commit to each other. Together we can face anything that happens in the future," said Sun-hee.

"Quiet. Sergeant Kua is here," whispered Joo-yun as she lowered her head.

"Sun-hee," Sgt. Kua called from across the room.

"Here, Sergeant," Sun-hee said while standing.

"Can you and the girls come and help with the prisoners?"

"Yes, Sergeant," replied Sun-hee. "Come on, girls. I'll introduce you to the Americans."

The girls bundled up and followed Sgt. Kua across the compound. They met Lt. Rim outside the gate to the prisoner area.

Lt. Rim said, "We need to make sure we take good care of the American prisoners. If the United States wins this war, they may treat us better if the prisoners are in good condition."

Lt. Rim and Jin-taek entered the building holding Theodore and Jeremy. The girls followed.

"Tell them we are here to check on their injuries," said Lt. Rim.

"Hello, Theodore and Jeremy," Sun-hee said in English. "We have come to check on your injuries."

"Hello, Sunny. We are still alive." He nodded his head at Young-ja. "I hope she is not going to sing again."

"She might. We are not here to cause you more pain. Hold out your hands, and let Young-ja and me look," said Sun-hee.

Eun-seong and Choe-me checked on Jeremy.

Young-ja began singing. Her improvised tune went through the names of the bones in the hand as she ran her fingers along each one.

Sun-hee smiled at Theodore. "She always talks while she works and sometimes makes it into a song. This hand is healing nicely."

"How is that hand, Young-ja?" Sun-hee asked in Korean.

"All bones in place. Should we take the splint off and see if the fingers bend?" said Young-ja.

"Leave the splints on. We shouldn't cause any pain today," replied Sun-hee.

"Can you wiggle your toes for Young-ja, Theodore?" asked Sun-hee in English.

He did.

"The toes look good. No circulation problems," said Young-ja.

"The cast and splints should remain on to make sure the bones heal," Sun-hee said to Theodore.

"How's Jeremy?" Sun-hee asked the other girls.

"The legs are okay. I am worried about his feet. They are cold, but I am not going to put them on my belly. Tell Theodore to keep them covered," said Eun-seong as she wrapped a blanket neatly around Jeremy's lower legs.

Choe-me rose from kneeling over Jeremy's head. "The wound is almost healed. The skull bones are fusing nicely."

"Jeremy, keep your feet warm. How does your head feel?" Sun-hee asked.

"I still get headaches, and I'm a little dizzy right now after having the prettiest girl I have ever seen so close to me," said Jeremy.

"I'm sorry, I can't help with the headaches. After we leave, your dizziness will go away," Sun-hee replied.

Theodore chuckled.

Lt. Rim led the girls into the building with the dozen American soldiers. Jin-taek checked that the prisoners were still bound tightly. The girls examined the men's wounds, which were healing nicely. They noted the bruises to the skin under the bindings on most of the men.

Sun-hee heard three of the men in the corner whispering to one another. She focused on what they were saying. They were talking about what they would like to do to her friends and mentioned the 'pretty girl' a few times.

"The three of you in the corner, be quiet," Sun-hee said in as stern of a voice as she could muster.

"She's the one who speaks English," said one of the men.

Sun-hee turned to Lt. Rim, "I told the men to be quiet. One spoke back."

"What did they say?" asked Lt. Rim.

"I will not repeat what they said, but they were impolite to the girls."

Lt. Rim walked over, pulled out his pistol, then hit each of the three men in the face with his other hand.

"Tell them that I would prefer to shoot them, but we are saving them for the Chinese."

Sun-hee translated. Then she said to her friends, "Finish up and let's get out of here."

As they returned to the library, Choe-me said, "I have never seen a person with green eyes before. He stared at me the whole time I examined him."

"You made him dizzy," replied Sun-hee. "The other prisoners made me mad."

Young-ja said, "I don't like being nice to them. As I examined Theodore's hand, all I could think of was the burnt arm of the child I held a couple of months ago."

"I think General Park wants to use them as trade with the Chinese," said Sun-hee.

They returned to the library where Choe-me read a Chinese novel, translating into Korean for them as she read.

***

"Please join me in a toast, Lieutenant," said Gen. Park, pointing to a chair by the stove as Lt. Rim walked into the main room of the camp's headquarters. Gen. Park put the papers he was reading on his lap.

"I will pass this time. I came by to inform you that the prisoners are healing from their injuries."

"That is good. Did any of the scouts return today?"

"No, sir. It has been over a week since we heard news from the front lines. Due to the recent snowstorms, only a few refugees have made it over the mountains. An elderly couple told me that the American planes are shooting at everything on the roads. They have not seen American soldiers in weeks."

"What do you think, Lieutenant?" asked the general.

"I think the Americans have retreated to the south and the Chinese are chasing them."

"Maybe the cold and snow have put a stop to the war. I do not remember it being this cold in my life. We will sit here and try to stay warm while we wait for news. Dismissed, Lieutenant."

"Yes, sir," replied Lt. Rim, and he retired to his room.

Gen. Park decided to stroll through the wards to check on the hospital before sunset. He found the two Soviet doctors sitting next to a stove, playing cards. Students were talking to patients and each other. *Lots of idle hands*, he thought.

The general liked what he saw. The students he brought here had done an excellent job, treating the most horrific injuries he had ever seen. They performed beyond his expectations, and it was time to give them some rest.

Gen. Park called the students in the hospital together and said, "It is time we ended the round-the-clock care. Civilians can watch the ward. Return to your new building after dinner."

***

A couple of the students in the hospital went to the library where they passed on the general's remarks. A few minutes later, the girls walked single file on the snow-packed path to the kitchen. They met the other students already eating.

Young-ja said, "What is on the menu tonight? Something new, I hope." She took her bowl. "The same great food we always have." She mingled through the students, talking while she ate.

Students milled about in their Chinese woolen garments, chatting, joking, and enjoying being together. Even though the temperature was about ten degrees below zero centigrade, the lack of wind and the presence of warm food caused them to linger around the kitchen.

After everyone finished their dinner, the students marched, following a snow-packed path in the moonlight back to the dorm.

As they approached their new home, Mr. Yun stood in the middle of the unfinished porch, a lantern in his hand. "Tonight, I have something special for you," he announced. "The common rooms are finished. Well, not completely, but you can use them tonight."

Sun-hee only caught the end of his speech since she was near the back of the line. She joined in the cheering.

Each student kicked the snow off their shoes before climbing the piles of wood that made up the steps to the porch. One by one, they removed their shoes and entered the great room.

The area measured eight-meters by twelve meters and had a vaulted ceiling starting about a meter higher than the side rooms. Windows at the top of the side walls allowed light to enter during the day. Two rows of posts supported the roof. A lamp hung from each post, providing ample light in the room. There were windows in the front on each side of the door that looked out to the porch. The all-important stove was by the back wall. The students gravitated to its warmth.

"Okay everyone, what are we going to call our new home?" yelled out Young-ja.

Names were yelled out such as "Prize Palace!", "Mr. Yun's Castle!", "Park Place!", "House of the four dozen!", and Numbers said, "House of the seven squared minus two!"

Sun-hee recalled Youj Mung-jo, who went missing almost six months ago.

"*Sanshin*!" said Kwong-ku.

"Did you say *Sammmshin* or *Sannnshin*?" Young-ja yelled back, emphasizing the difference between the 'm' and 'n.'

"*Samshin*, the mythical goddess of birth, would work!" Suk Jong-hui roared, putting her hand on her belly, revealing she was about six months along. Everyone laughed.

"I meant the 'n' version, 'Sanshin,'" Kwong-ku shouted back, his face turning a little red.

"Let's vote," said Young-ja. "Prize Palace," she yelled. "Raise your hand if you want the Prize Palace! That is zero. Mr. Yun's Castle." She paused to look around the room, seeing one hand. Yun Chul had put his hand up high even though he was not related to Mr. Yun. "One vote." She went through the other names getting no votes until she said, "Sanshin." Most of the hands in the room went up. "Voting over!" yelled Young-ja. "Our new home is now the House of Sanshin, the mythical mountain gods."

The gathering lasted another hour with everyone talking, looking around at the handiwork of Mr. Yun, and having a wonderful time. Young-ja yelled to get everyone's attention. "I want to give three cheers to Mr. Yun for doing such a wonderful job on the House of Sanshin!"

"Thank you," he said. "I still have work to do. Sergeant Kua wants a new house for herself, and she said it has to have two extra rooms for guests." Most everyone laughed, which brought a puzzled look to his face. "Goodnight," he said and left.

Sun-hee and her friends stood near the back corner. Sun-hee called Yong-gak over. Chulsoon and Kwang-ku came with him.

"We were talking today, Yong-gak. Lt. Rim mentioned that he expected the Chinese to take over this compound. We concluded that the students should declare our loyalty to each other now that the Premier and Republic of Korea are no longer prominent. What do you think?"

Strategist started talking with his hands before the words came out of his mouth. "We must never show disloyalty to Korea, our Premier, or General Park. The consequences are unthinkable." His fingertips were on the sides of his head. "To add our loyalty to each other is giving voice to the obvious. Our loyalty to the House of Sanshin must be used to support our other oaths. Young-ja, get everyone's attention."

"Attention everyone. Listen up."

Strategist said, "We are loyal to the Democratic People's Republic of Korea."

The students repeated Yong-gak's words.

"We are loyal to Kin-Il-sung."

In unison, the students replied.

"We are loyal to General Park."

The reply was weak.

"We are loyal to the House of Sanshin," he finished with his hands out wide.

Everyone responded in a loud voice. "We are loyal to the House of Sanshin."

The room buzzed with excitement at the added declaration.

Over the next half hour, the gathering began to disperse. Most of the students went to the dorms. Two couples headed off to the guesthouse to fulfill their duty.

As Sun-hee and her four friends walked out of the room, Mrs. Lim grabbed Joo-yun's arm and pulled her aside.

"How did that girl become pregnant?" Mrs. Lim demanded.

Joo-yun paused and took a deep breath and whispered, "She was with one of the boys."

"Raped?" Mrs. Lim inquired.

"No, mother." Joo-yun pulled on her pigtails. "It's not what you think."

"I know how girls become pregnant. Are you all under the influence of Samshin?"

"I don't know how to explain this to you, Mother. Seven of the girls are pregnant."

"What? Disgraceful!" blurted Mrs. Lim. "We are leaving now!" she said to her daughter in a quiet, determined voice.

Joo-yun froze, imagining the two of them running in the snow, Lt. Rim chasing them. "No. We can't leave right now. We would die in the snow and cold."

"I'll take our chances. Get your things."

"You are a good mother. You taught me well. I tried my best to avoid being with a boy, but…"

"You! Joo-yun?" Mrs. Lim yelled. "How could you shame me like this?"

"I won a prize mother. This place and situation is my prize. We cannot get away. We must stay. We are captive here."

"I did not pay the proctors to make you a whore," said Mrs. Lim.

"You bribed the proctors?" exclaimed Joo-yun.

"You were supposed to go to a high-class school. I would pay anything for you to be an elite."

"I can't believe all this suffering is because of you."

Mrs. Lim responded. "I do not understand this. Is the prize to be a whore? To get pregnant? I will never be able to show my face in public again."

"You were deceived, mother, like all the other families. The other girls earned their prize. They are also captive and have been forced to have children."

"Don't blame me for your indiscretion," said Mrs. Lim, and she raised her left hand to slap Joo-yun, but Eun-seong, who was standing behind Mrs. Lim, caught it in midair. Eun-seong immediately released Mrs. Lim's arm.

"Pardon me, Mrs. Lim," said Eun-seong with a bow.

Mrs. Lim turned quickly to glare at Eun-seong and Sun-hee. "Have you all become whores?" She turned to her daughter. "We will finish this later." She stomped into the dorm, went to her mat in the corner, and buried herself in a blanket.

Joo-yun started crying. Eun-seong, Sun-hee, Young-ja, and Choe-me cried with her. Mrs. Lim's words hit them hard. They knew their mothers would say the same thing.

"We must survive together," said Sun-hee.

"Let's get some rest and talk to her tomorrow," said Eun-seong through a sniffle. "Our emotions will have a chance to calm down."

***

The next morning, Mrs. Lim was still buried in her blanket. After the students left, she got up and began to clean up the room. There was not a lot to do, but her anger made her do something to keep herself busy. She would try to get Joo-yun to leave after lunch.

Mrs. Lim was startled when Sgt. Kua came into the dorm. "Mrs. Lim, we need to talk. Or maybe what I need to say is that you need to listen while I talk."

"Seven months ago, your daughter won a prize. The prize was not a wonderful gift from the government, but the opportunity to be a part of a secret program. This program has three requirements: loyalty to the Premier, loyalty to the Republic of Korea, and loyalty to the program. Now that you know that much information, your loyalty is also required. You may choose to leave if you cannot pledge these three loyalties. If you choose to leave, you will go and never be allowed back. You will never see your daughter again. Write a note saying goodbye, and I will walk you to the gate. Should you decide to stay, you must remain loyal, or I will walk you to the gate and say goodbye." She finished in a very stern voice, staring into the eyes of Mrs. Lim. "Stay or go, Mrs. Lim."

"You have forced my child to be a whore," cried Mrs. Lim angrily.

The words hit Sgt. Kua like a *bo staff* to the mid-section. She forced herself to inhale and choked out, "That is not a loyal statement, Mrs. Lim."

She took Mrs. Lim's arm and began to walk towards the door.

"No!" Mrs. Kim yelled, pulling her arm away. "I will not leave my daughter. We will leave together."

Sgt. Kua closed her eyes for a moment and swallowed. Then she said, "Outside these fences is a war. Inside the fences, there is food and a warm place to sleep. You know what is out there. Trust me. I know this is a better place."

"You forced my daughter with a boy."

Sgt. Kua reeled again at the accusation. It was true. She was responsible. Her eyes moistened. "You have a choice, as I had a choice. Be loyal or die. If you and Joo-yun try to leave, you will be killed. Your daughter resisted the program, more than any of the other girls. If I had resisted, I would have died. Choose, Mrs. Lim. Become a mother to these girls, or be buried in the mass grave outside of the compound."

Mrs. Lim trembled. "I am loyal to Korea and the Premier. A program that ruins my daughter will not have my loyalty."

There was a moment of silence while Sgt. Kua considered her options. Then she said, "As long as you do not openly oppose the program, you can stay." The sergeant put her nose about an inch from Mrs. Kim's face. "We must remain loyal."

Mrs. Lim cried, slumping to her haunches, hands over her face.

***

Sgt. Kua returned to her house. She entered, closed the door, and slumped to the floor.

What have I become? I told Mrs. Lim what was needed to save her and Joo-yun. For my whole life, I have kept people alive, hoping they find a better future. Mrs. Lim's hope for her daughter is destroyed. Park's desire for respect is destroyed. Korea's war for unification is destroyed. Does hope only amplify misery? What is my life without hope?

Part Two - The House of Sanshin

21 — Silent Winter - January & February, 1951

"I think we have run out of daylight," said Eun-seong as she closed her book.

Sun-hee and her friends closed their books, bundled up, and made the short trip from the library to the kitchen. They ate quickly to spend as little time as possible in the cold.

While eating Yong-gak said, "I spoke to a man who arrived at the hospital yesterday. He told me the Americans were loading their troops and supplies on ships in the port of Hamhung."

"Where are they going?" asked Choe-me.

"They are leaving North Korea," said Yong-gak. "I don't think we need to worry about the Americans. At least until the weather improves."

Sun-hee felt the ominous threat posed by the American army released out of her body. A smile extended into her cheeks.

Choe-me closed her eyes and sighed deeply.

Young-ja said, "One less thing to worry about. How many more worries do we have? I lost count."

Eun-seong smiled for the first time in weeks.

The camp was in total darkness by the time they arrived at the House of Sanshin. A couple of candles provided light in the dorm.

Joo-yun stopped abruptly when they entered. She took a couple of deep breaths, pulled on her pigtail, and shuffled her feet as she crossed the room.

"I'm not sure having Mrs. Lim here is good for Joo-yun. She was beginning to open up after her trauma in the guesthouse," said Eun-seong.

They looked at the mother and daughter whispering in the corner. The expressions revealed the tension between the two.

Joo-yun plopped onto her mat and turned away from her mother.

Mrs. Lim sat back in the corner, pulled her knees up, and stared at the floor beyond her feet.

The next morning, Mrs. Lim began to work to make the girl's lives easier. She took laundry to the wash, folded it properly, and placed the clean clothes on each mat. She kept the bathroom and dorm clean, sweeping and washing where needed, yet she would speak only with her daughter.

For the next few days, the girls went to the library during the day. They worked on languages or read. In the evenings, they tried to keep warm. The only thing to interrupt the boredom of a cold January winter was a summons to the guesthouse.

Sun-hee was scheduled for three nights starting on the eighth. Her relationship with Stone remained as cold as the Korean winter.

The night before she was to meet Stone, Mi-na and So-huy got into an argument. Soo-hy wanted the girls to join her in a revolt against the forced mating. Mi-na did not want to take the risk. Other girls joined in. Most of them supported a revolt.

Sun-hee sat on her mat, listening. Choe-me moved over and sat next to her. The big question in the discussion was, what would General Park do? How forceful would he be to continue the program?

"What do you think?" asked Choe-me quietly to Sun-hee.

"Yong-gak said we must not show disloyalty. What is more loyal to the House of Sanshin? To have children or not?"

"After I have this child I am carrying, my mother will find it difficult to find me a husband," said Choe-me. "And I could not bring a husband into the House of Sanshin."

"When this program started, I said we must consider the boys our husbands. Will they accept the risk of our revolt?"

"We are only getting pregnant because we fear General Park. Why must I have this child?"

"The general's plan is for us to have a new generation of children who will make Korea great. I fear we are committed to this path," replied Sun-hee.

"Do you agree with the general?"

"I agree with his goal. I do not like his plan or methods."

"He is using us to reach his goals. Will our rebellion change his plan?"

Sun-hee thought for a while. "The question Mi-na keeps asking, is what would General Park do?" She was silent for a moment. "To reestablish fear, he would make an example of someone. The persons most likely to suffer would be Mrs. Lim and Joo-yun. We can't let that happen."

Sun-hee stood up and walked to stand beside Mi-na and said, "I vote to not revolt."

Choe-me came to stand next to Sun-hee.

"Why?" yelled So-hy, putting her hands on her hips.

"Because Strategist said we must not be disloyal," said Choe-me.

"So, are you going to let General Park ruin your life?"

"My family life is already ruined," replied Choe-me.

"Since he will be gone soon, we are not going to let him force us to have children," said So-huy. "The majority rules. We will refuse the boys until the Chinese takeover, and then we will be free."

Mi-na dropped her hands to her side. Her lips quivered for a moment, then she went to her mat and pouted.

Sun-hee and Choe-me sat down. Sun-hee whispered to Choe-me, "I don't know what I dread more, tomorrow with Stone or the reaction of General Park if I refuse."

The next night, Sun-hee gritted her teeth and wished Stone would make her pregnant.

***

Every few days, Lt. Rim would ask Sun-hee to help with the prisoners.

One day, Theodore asked, "What is going on with the war? Being in this cement box with no news is torture."

Sun-hee thought for a moment before replying flippantly, "You tell us nothing, we tell you nothing."

"What do you want to know, Sunny?" he asked, seeming to open up for the first time.

Sun-hee again thought for a moment and turned to Lt. Rim who was standing by the door. "Lieutenant Rim, they wish to know how the war is going. Is there anything you want to know in exchange?"

Lt. Rim paused to think for a moment. "I can't think of anything I want to know. Tell him America is losing the war."

Sun-hee turned back to Theodore and said, "We require no information from you, Theodore. However, I'll answer your question about the war. The Americans are losing and have been retreating. You'll be staying with us for a while longer." She added the last part to see if she could get a reaction.

"I don't believe you, Sunny," he responded. "We had your army on the run. The only way you could be winning is if the Russians and Chinese were fighting for you."

She decided to play the game a little further. "You may believe what you wish, Theodore. For now, you will remain as guests in the Fargo fleabag motel."

Jeremy's head moved up, and his eyes widened. Sun-hee noticed her comment had hit where she thought.

Theodore observed her for a moment before replying, "When I get home, I will not be able to explain how we have been held captive by a little Korean girl. Just how old are you, Sunny?"

She thought for a moment, considering the change in Theodore's question. "I am fifteen," she said, while realizing her birthday would be in a couple of weeks, so she added, "Almost sixteen."

"Hear that Jeremy? Our host here at the Fargo fleabag motel is only fifteen. Everyone in the Air Force will be laughing at us when we get home."

"If we do get home, Theo., we will never live this one down."

The next day, Sun-hee looked through the maps in the library, trying to find Fargo. After an hour, she found a small town in the middle of North America. A fitting name for the compound where she was as much a prisoner, as Theodore and Jeremy.

***

Over a couple of days, at the end of January, Gen. Park met with each student to determine their condition. He met with the boys one day and the girls the next. It was late in the afternoon when Sun-hee's name was called.

The exams were in the room where Sun-hee spent many days with Max performing surgery.

General Park was sitting in a chair at the side of the room. "Come in, Sun-hee. Let me listen to your heart and breathing."

He placed a stethoscope on her back and moved it around, listening.

Sun-hee thought, *can he hear how nervous I am?*

He checked her eyes, ears, and throat. He sat back and looked her over. "You have gained weight, which is good. Are you pregnant?"

"No, sir," Sun-hee replied.

"When was your last menses?"

"December twenty-sixth."

"The records show you have not had regular menses. Many of the other girls are also irregular. From now on, you will have sex every day, starting thirteen days after your next period until you start another menses."

Sun-hee cringed.

"Ten pregnancies started in seven months is too slow," Gen. Park said in a frustrated tone.

"Send in the next girl."

Sun-hee left, wondering how the other girls would react.

That evening, Gen. Park addressed the students. "The plan to have children is not progressing at an acceptable rate. I have addressed the irregularity with the girls. I will give you one additional encouragement. The girl who remains after all the others are pregnant, I will consider disloyal and will remove her and her mate. Dismissed." He got a sour look on his face, then strode away from the House of Sanshin.

The next morning, Gen. Park and Alek left on foot for Chongjin.

***

The second of February was Sun-hee's birthday. She moped around, thinking of her mother all day. Six months had passed since the last letter. Her mother always made her birthday special. This day she was alone and cold. She wrapped her blue scarf around her neck and wore it all day.

A week later, the able-bodied soldiers were called together by Lt. Rim. He gave a motivating speech and asked for volunteers to form a unit to rejoin the fighting. Almost one hundred men stepped forward. He told them to be ready to leave the next morning. A dozen disabled men stayed at the camp. One of those who remained was Jin-taek.

Many of the men approached Sun-hee, expressing their gratitude for the treatment they had received. She recalled the horror of their wounds. She had believed Max when he said anyone who arrived at the hospital and survived their injuries were the lucky ones. She had struggled to save them. They should be free of the war, forever. Now, these men were on their way to fight again. All she could see was they were leaving to have a second chance to be wounded or die.

The students stood in a line, saluting as the men marched out of the gate to rejoin the fight.

Sun-hee let the tears flow, feeling empty that her efforts were in vain.

Over the next few days, they moved the remaining patients to two barracks. The move reduced the number of buildings needing to be heated. Remaining soldiers, disabled with missing legs or arms, maybe a missing eye or a plethora of other disabilities that kept them from rejoining the war, were asked to stay in one building to conserve fuel.

Sun-hee was happy Jin-taek remained in the camp.

Lt. Rim reduced the staff accordingly. He had sent the soldiers off, not for what they could do to influence the battle for Korea, but to help the survival of the camp.

***

On the last day of February, Sun-hee woke up, washed, and dressed like usual. She felt a little dizzy during the daily morning exercises but forced her way through them. After their loyalty chant, Joo-yun said, "Let's go get breakfast."

Sun-hee felt nausea overcome her. She ran to the privy while her stomach worked violently to empty itself. Joo-yun followed as did Mrs. Lim.

"You are pregnant," said Joo-yun as she helped to hold Sun-hee's hair back.

Mrs. Lim brought Sun-hee a wet towel and then went to get a clean shirt; a routine she had become familiar with the last few weeks.

Sun-hee heaved a couple more times with nothing to show for it. "Dry heaves hurts," she complained, wiping her mouth with the towel.

"You will be fine," said Joo-yun. "It is only morning sickness. It will pass."

"Still, it's not a pleasurable experience."

Mrs. Lim helped pull Sun-hee's shirt over her head, making sure the mess on her shirt did not get onto her hair. Joo-yun led Sun-hee to a sink to wash her hands and face. Mrs. Lim ran a brush through Sun-hee's hair and then helped her into a clean shirt. Sun-hee was again ready for the day.

22 — The Escape - March 1, 1951

"Sun-hee, there is no hurry, but when you are ready, we need your help tending to the prisoners," said Sgt. Kua who had stuck her head in the privy.

Sun-hee held her stomach as she heaved, spat then said, "I will come as soon as I can." Her gut wrenched, producing another mouthful of bile. Mrs. Lim held a moist towel. She took it and held it against her flushed face. After taking a couple of deep breaths, expecting more heaves, she paused, but that was the end, for now. She took off her nightshirt, put on a shirt, the Chinese woolens for warmth, and a smock, so she would look like a doctor.

Chou Sung-man, who was becoming an expert in chemistry, and Hung Young-jee, who asked journals on optics with every arrival from the Soviets, were already at the gate of the American prisoner enclosure when Sun-hee arrived. Four civilian women were there with a pot of food, bowls, and spoons. Two soldiers walked with canes, and one was on crutches but carried a rifle and a mean attitude. The fourth was missing most of the fingers on his left hand. Sun-hee looked for Jin-taek but did not see him.

They opened the door to Theodore and Jeremy's prison. Two soldiers went in, followed by two of the women. Sung-man, Young-jee, and Sun-hee followed to check on the condition of the Americans.

Sung-man was examining Jeremy when he said, "I am worried about circulation in these feet. It has been a long time without movement. They are cold but no signs of frostbite. We should change his cast next time we visit and see if he can put weight on his legs. His head has healed. Ask him if he has headaches."

"How is your head, Jeremy?" inquired Sun-hee in English.

"I get headaches every day," Jeremy replied.

"And he can't remember things which have occurred recently. Everything, before our capture, is fine," added Theodore.

"I understand," said Sun-hee. "Unfortunately, there is nothing we can do for his head."

Sun-hee turned to Sung-man and told him what the Americans said about Jeremy's head.

Young-jee looked at Theodore's hands, opening and closing them. "The bones in his hands seem to have healed, but not entirely straight," he said. "One of the Russian doctors could operate and reset the bones. Ask the American to stand to see if he can put weight on his leg."

"Theodore, can you stand and put weight on your foot?" Sun-hee asked in English.

"Yes," he said. With Young-jee's help, Theodore stood.

Young-jee knelt and examined the ankle and foot. "It has healed well. Tell him to use it, and it will grow stronger."

"As you use your foot, it will grow stronger, Theodore," Sun-hee said in English.

"Thank you, Sunny," Theodore said to Sun-hee as she walked out of the building.

Everyone moved to the next building to perform a similar service for the twelve American soldiers. Two soldiers went in, followed by Sun-hee and her two fellow students. Then two other soldiers and Lieutenant Rim entered the cement building. The Americans were unrestrained and standing around the walls of the room, as they had been the last few times Sun-hee had been there.

There was a shout, "Now!" The Americans all moved at once.

Sun-hee was grabbed and thrown violently into the front corner of the room. Her head and back slammed against the wall. She slid to a position, sitting in the corner. Her eyes fastened shut from the impact to her head and shooting pain in her back. Her ears told her of the fighting happening in the room. She forced her eyes open. The four Korean soldiers were lying on the floor, each with Americans standing over them. The Americans yanked away the rifles, and she watched in horror as rifle butts smashed into the heads of the Korean soldiers on the floor. An American knelt over Lt. Rim, holding him down while another one kicked him in the ribs. Young-jee was lying motionless in the corner on the opposite side of the door. Sung-man was picked up and thrown to the floor face first. He just lay there, holding his head. She watched in dismay as the Americans ran out the door.

Sun-hee focused on breathing. Each inhale and exhale triggered sharp pains in her back. One American ran in, grabbed some blankets, and hurried back out. While supporting herself with the wall, she stood, waited for her head to stop spinning, then staggered out of the door.

The four Korean women were huddled together in the snow. Sun-hee saw fresh footprints in the snow to her right, leading around the fourth building. A noise to her left caused her to quickly turn to see three Americans working on getting the lock open on Theodore's building. With a hard blow with the rifle butt, the lock broke. Still dazed, she wanted to see where the Americans were going and followed the tracks around the fourth building. She rounded the corner, finding the Americans at the west fence near the back of the building. Two were climbing the fence with blankets over their shoulders, one of them also held a rifle.

"Where are you Americans going," she yelled in English. All of them turned to look at her. Two Americans fell on the ground with rifles pointed at her. "That is not the way to the American army. They are two hundred kilometers that way," she pointed south with her left hand.

One soldier had reached the top of the fence and threw his blanket over to cover the barbed wire. The man with a rifle was now most of the way up.

Sun-hee felt anger towards the Americans trying to leave, and she let it show, "Are you going to shoot me? You Americans can beat up disabled soldiers, knock down the women who bring you food and take away your shit. Will you shoot an unarmed medical student? How Mongolic are you Americans?" She heard something behind her. With a glance over her shoulder, there was Theodore, and an American with a rifle. "Hurry up, Theodore, they are about to leave without you," she yelled with a wave of her hand. Then she saw Jeremy supported under the arms of two American soldiers. "Good to see you up on those legs, Jeremy. I hope they are good enough for you to get to South Korea, as that is where the American Army is now."

***

Sgt. Kua had heard the commotion in the prisoner compound from the guesthouse. She grabbed her rifle and ran out to see the Korean women in the snow and Sun-hee walk around the far building. She sprinted to the top of the garden area where she saw the Americans on the fence, one almost over. Dropping into a prone position, she aimed and fired. The man who had just gotten his legs over the barbed wire fell to the ground.

***

Sun-hee tensed at the sound of the shot and cringed as the American man fell off the fence, causing a twang of pain in her back. Theodore stepped up, putting himself between her and the Americans near the fence. The American next to her with a rifle, moved to Sun-hee's left looking to the southeast with the gun ready, looking for the shooter.

The two Americans at the fence with rifles also turned and were looking for who had shot their compatriot. The man near the top was trying to get the rifle off his shoulder and hold on at the same time. He dropped the blanket.

The American Sgt. was jerking around, pointing Rim's handgun in different directions, looking about for whoever had just shot one of his men. The rest of the men knelt or squatted down. The men carrying Jeremy had moved to flatten themselves against the wall.

Sun-hee overcame her shock at seeing someone shot, then yelled, "You can leave Americans. If you do, you might freeze to death in the snow. You might die of hunger. The Chinese might shoot you. Soviet planes may drop bombs on your head."

***

Sgt. Kua's rifle was a bolt-action, one shot and reload. She tried to hurry and get another shell from her pocket. She pulled them all out, dropping them in the snow.

"Over there," yelled the man on the fence, nodding behind the buildings. He hooked his left arm through the wires and brought his rifle up, aiming along the back of the buildings.

Sgt. Kua fumbled, and her hands shook. She got a bullet loaded and looked up. The man on the fence had his rifle pointed right at her. She got him in her sights, heard a gunshot, and pulled the trigger.

***

Sun-hee again tensed at the sound. The man on the fence slumped, his feet lost hold, the rifle dropped, his arm got caught in the wires, leaving him hanging. The American sergeant quickly turned and began to fire his handgun behind the building. The two men with rifles ran behind the buildings, out of sight.

***

Sgt. Kua was faster this time in getting her gun reloaded. She ignored the bullets flying over her head. She saw an American with a rifle running towards her, she fired. The American went down. But there was another with a gun, pointing right at her.

Gunfire rang out as Sgt. Kua reached for another bullet. She looked up and watched the American, who, a moment before was aiming at her, slump to the ground. Two guards ran past her to the fence and fired a couple more shots into the Americans. She swept her hand across the snow to gather bullets, jumped up, and dashed as fast as she could around the fence to the prisoner compound.

***

Theodore still stood about a meter in front of Sun-hee.

"Go back to your room, Theodore, or you will die here. Tell the others to go with you, or they will die. I am leaving," Sun-hee said to the back of Theodore's head before hobbling back to check on Lt. Rim and the soldiers.

The four women had crawled to the gate and were yelling for help, adding to the commotion.

As she entered the cement building previously housing the twelve Americans, she heard Theodore say, "Get back into our building. Out here we are sitting ducks."

Lt. Rim was trying to get up. He held his right arm close to his body. "Lay back down Lieutenant, there is nothing we can do out there now," Sun-hee said as more shots rang out. "The Americans will not get out of the compound."

"He's dead, Sun-hee!" yelled Sung-man. Sun-hee looked towards Sung-man. Blood covered one side of his face. He was kneeling next to Young-jee, who was half sitting in the corner of the room. His head hung awkwardly over on his chest. Sung-man looked at Sun-hee and cried, "They broke his neck."

For a couple of seconds, Sun-hee closed her eyes. Max's words came to mind.

Focus. Block feelings out. Do what you can for the next man.

She said to Sung-man, "Then help the soldiers." She unbuttoned Lt. Rim's shirt, noticed his collarbone was sticking up, almost through the skin. Then she felt his ribs where she saw bruising. He grunted a few times. "You have some broken ribs and a broken collarbone Lieutenant. None of it is dangerous unless you move and puncture a lung with a broken rib. The best thing to do is lay still."

Sun-hee went to the closest soldier. Her mind played out the rifle butt, being pounded into this soldier's face. "You have some broken bones around your eye. They will heal fine. Do you hurt anywhere else?" she asked.

"No, just my face and head," he replied.

"We will get you to the hospital in a few minutes. Lie still," Sun-hee said, patting his shoulder.

Sun-hee moved to the next soldier about the same time as Sung-man. "He has a head injury from the rifle butts," Sung-man said. "The first man I checked had his throat slit and has bled out."

"I will go get help," said Sung-man as he got up and took a step for the door.

Sun-hee grabbed his arm. "No, don't go out there. They will come when it is safe."

The American sergeant burst into the room, nearly stepping on Lt. Rim, followed by four Americans. Sun-hee stood, glaring at the sergeant. Sung-man scampered to the corner of the room next to Young-jee.

The American sergeant and Sun-hee faced off with one another for a moment. He was at least fifteen centimeters taller than Sun-hee and a lot bigger. He was breathing heavily and held the handgun in his right hand, pointing it at Sun-hee.

Sun-hee broke the silence. "Sergeant, if you are here to fight, you can shoot me or hit me. These men are beyond the ability to fight," she said, focused on his eyes. "If you and your men are here to surrender, then go lay down until I tell you something different. You decide how much blood you want on your hands today."

The American sergeant hesitated, glanced at the men behind him, then reached over with his left hand, took the end of the handgun, and held it out in front of Sun-hee. Sun-hee took the gun without taking her eyes from the sergeant. He walked to the back of the room and lay down on his face. The other four men did the same. Sun-hee dropped the gun from her shaking hand.

In relief, Sun-hee took a deep breath only to feel a sharp pain in her back.

"Lieutenant Rim. Are you in there?" came Sgt. Kua's voice from outside.

"Come in, Sergeant. It is safe," said Lt. Rim.

Jin-taek entered, ready to shoot and aimed at the men laying in the back of the room.

Sgt. Kua followed with her rifle pointed ahead of her. She was breathing heavily and covered in snow. She looked around for a moment before saying to Sun-hee, "Tell the Americans we will shoot the first one who moves."

"Americans," she half-choked on the word as her throat was dry, and she paused to get some moisture back. "You will be shot if you move," she said looking at the back of the room.

Lt. Rim struggled to retrieve his handgun from where Sun-hee had dropped it.

"Bring stretchers and restraints," yelled Lt. Rim, then he grimaced at the pain in his side.

Sun-hee felt herself becoming nauseous and pushed her way past Jo Jin-taek. As soon as she was outside, she threw up. The heaves sent shots of pain in her back and head. Dizzy, she leaned against the wall, trying to gain focus. "Theodore?" she muttered to herself.

She held the wall as she moved slowly to Theodore's building. A rifle lay in the snow next to the door. She opened the door a little before saying in English, "Theodore, may I come in?"

"It is safe to enter," Theodore said.

Sun-hee looked in and saw five men sitting along the right wall. "Good, Theodore. Stay there. I will lock you in," she said and closed the door.

She fumbled with the latch, trying to make it secure but did not know if she succeeded before becoming dizzy and dropping to her hands and knees in the snow. The pain in her back made her right arm numb, and it gave way. Falling into the snow, a hand reached under and held her up. Clenching her teeth and closing her eyes to the pain as she was lifted. She squinted to see Jin-taek carrying her. She lost consciousness.

Eun-seong and Mrs. Lim were kneeling over her. Her whole body was shaking, and her heartbeat throbbed in her head. Eun-seong asked, "What happened?"

The only thing on her mind was the vision of Young-jee slumped in the corner. She blurted out, "Young-jee is dead."

23 — Trials - Early March, 1950

Two of the Americans survived their gunshot wounds long enough to make it to the operating room where Kwang-ku assisted Max. That evening, they buried four American soldiers in an unmarked grave. Weeks later, Kwang-ku would brag about how Max painfully avenged the death of Young-jee.

The escape attempt was all everyone talked about, except Sun-hee. She had suffered a concussion and cracked ribs, which left a large purple bruise on the right side of her back. She rested on her mat, waited on continually by the other girls. Her constant fear was the piercing pain in her back and head during onslaughts of morning sickness.

Sgt. Kua downplayed the hero status the Korean soldiers gave her. She would smile and dismiss the praise by saying she had only done what she had to do.

Three days later, they held a ceremony for Hung Young-jee and a Korean soldier. For the first time since the escape attempt, Sun-hee went outside. The sorrow she felt strengthened the anger she had towards the Americans. She felt sorry for Youn Kum-ja, who was carrying Young-jee's baby and was extremely distraught. After a half-hour on her feet, she felt lightheaded. She asked Eun-seong to escort her back to the dorm.

Over the next couple of days, Sun-hee stayed on her mat, letting herself heal.

Late the next morning, Sgt. Kua came into the dorm after lunch and asked, "Sun-hee, how are you feeling today?"

"I no longer have a headache, and if I move slowly, my back does not hurt," replied Sun-hee.

"I am here to request your help with the Americans. If you are not up to it, I will tell Lieutenant Rim to wait."

Eun-seong, who had been sitting near Sun-hee, said, "She needs more rest, maybe a week before she is well."

"We must deal with the Americans," said Sun-hee. "Sitting in a chair will not be difficult. I can translate."

"Today, you only need to meet with Lieutenant Rim," said Sgt. Kua. "I am to bring you to him if you are able."

Sun-hee rolled over onto her hands and knees and was helped to her feet by Eun-seong. The three walked to the command house where Sgt. Kua knocked. A soldier opened the door. Sun-hee saw him and winced, recalling his screams when she was amputating his right arm. He motioned them in with his stub.

Eun-seong whispered, "I am with you." Sun-hee entered, leaving her escort on the porch.

Sun-hee had never been in the command house. A robust fire in the stove made the room the warmest one she had been in all winter. Lt. Rim stood by a cushioned chair in the corner, his right arm in a sling. Both eyes were reddish-purple.

"Please sit, Sun-hee," he said, motioning to a cushioned chair to his left. An end table separated the two chairs. An empty cup sat on the table edge.

"In respect, I should stand Lieutenant Rim," Sun-hee said while offering a slight bow.

"You are a medical student in the army, Sun-hee. Officially, you and the other students have the rank of lieutenant. We are of equal rank. I am requesting you sit as my equal," explained Lt. Rim, repeating the gesture.

"Yes, sir," she said awkwardly, realizing what she said did not fit with Rim's last comment. She moved to the chair, eased herself to sit on the edge, and placed her hands in her lap.

"Chun-ja," Lt. Rim spoke loudly.

"Yes, sir," came a voice from the other side of the room. Sun-hee looked to her left to see a woman in the doorway to the kitchen.

"Tea," commanded Lieutenant Rim with one word.

"Right away, sir," came the reply.

Lt. Rim sat down slowly, obviously in pain, and moved around a bit in his chair to try to get comfortable.

There was silence while Chung-ja poured tea for Sun-hee and then refilled the lieutenant's cup.

Chun-ja had been the housekeeper for many years. She was an orphan, raised in the comfort house with other children who had Japanese fathers. The Japanese commander brought her into headquarters to cook and clean. She had nowhere to go when the Japanese left, stayed to serve Capt. Kwang and now Lt. Rim and Gen. Park. The command house was her home, the officers who stayed here were her guests.

Lt. Rim lifted his cup. "First, I would like to thank you. Your English skills have been valuable in dealing with the American prisoners." He took a sip of tea.

Sun-hee took her cup and held it in her hands, absorbing the warmth.

Lt. Rim paused for a moment before saying, "When you are ready, we need to confront the Americans. To do that, I require your translation skills."

Sun-hee paused for a moment, fighting to keep herself from crying or yelling. Her mind was telling her to be obedient and say she was ready, but she knew she might not be able to control herself in front of the Americans.

"Tomorrow," she finally said. "Let's deal with them tomorrow." Then she took a big swallow of tea.

What is he going to do to the Americans? What will I have to see tomorrow?

Lt. Rim sensed her apprehension, and in a smooth tone said, "I need to let them know the bloodshed in the escape attempt is on their hands. They need to be held responsible for the deaths of Young-jee, my soldier, and their fellow soldiers. They will have a long time to think about their guilt." He finished while reaching for his teacup.

"Have you had lunch?" he asked.

"Yes, Lieutenant. With the double ration, I am more than full. Hopefully, I can keep it down as breakfast did not stay down."

"You are with child. Congratulations. General Park will be proud," he said, and his mouth formed a big grin. "That is one more thing we can use against the Americans."

Sun-hee, wishing an end to the conversation, took a big drink of tea, placed her cup down, and stood.

"Thank you for sharing a cup of tea with me, Sun-hee. It has been a long time since I have sat with a fellow lieutenant over a cup of tea." He started to get up out of his chair and grimaced at the pain.

"No, do not get up. It looks too painful. I will let myself out." When she opened the door, the soldier who had let her in saluted with his left hand.

As Sun-hee started to walk back to the dorm, Eun-seong came running up to walk with her. "Is everything all right?" she inquired.

"No. Nothing has been right since we arrived here."

"So true, Sun-hee. The only thing I like about this place is the girls I get to be with," said Eun-seong.

"I agree," said Sun-hee, taking Eun-seong's hand and giving it a firm squeeze.

When they got back to the House of Sanshin, Sun-hee laid down and tried to hold in lunch. The tea helped calm her stomach. Throwing up was so painful. Her mind was racing on what she could say to the Americans. It was late afternoon before her thoughts slowed enough for her to fall asleep. Her dreams about the Americans were very unpleasant.

The next morning, Sun-hee woke before the other girls began to stir and decided to be first in the shower. As always, the water was cold. She was letting it run on her head when Eun-seong said from behind her, "The bruises on your back are looking better. Are you still sore?"

"I am feeling better. Thank you for your support these past few days. You are the most loving person I know," she said, wanting to give her a big hug but not wanting to get her all wet.

"You are so kind, Sun-hee. And so strong. We all look up to you."

"When something strong breaks Eun-seong, it breaks with a loud sound. You must hope that you are not around when I break," Sun-hee said as she turned off the water.

"I will be here, so you do not break," she said, handing Sun-hee a towel. Then she grabbed another and reached up to dry Sun-hee's hair.

After dressing, Sun-hee waited in the now completed common room. The morning sunlight came in the front windows, shining against the back wall. One large, dark cloud hung in the sky, casting a shadow over the camp. Sgt. Kua came walking towards the House of Sanshin.

"Formation time," she yelled.

A few minutes later, they were doing exercises. Sun-hee moved gingerly, just enough to get her blood flowing, trying to keep warm in the cold, dry air.

About fifteen minutes into the exercises, Sun-hee felt nauseous and ran to the corner of the building to throw up. The pain in her side was less, and there was no pain in her head. She took a towel from the pile Mrs. Lim placed at the end of the porch and wiped her face, then dropped it into a basket for soiled ones. She glanced at the rake and shovel Mrs. Lim had placed there, knowing she would clean up after exercise.

At breakfast, Sun-hee ate little but drank extra tea.

Eun-seong gave her a little embrace before she walked to the prisoner compound. A few soldiers were there, including Jin-taek, moving in and out of the second building.

"Good morning, Sun-hee," came a male's voice from behind her.

She turned to see Lt. Rim and Sgt. Kua walking up to her.

"Good morning," Sun-hee replied.

"I will make sure everything is in order and call you when ready," Lt. Rim said as he walked into the building.

Sun-hee marched in place, partly because she was cold and partly because of being nervous. Sgt. Kua was doing the same.

"Come," said Lt. Rim from the doorway.

Sun-hee followed Sgt. Kua into the building. The setup was the same. Two chairs a couple of meters apart in the middle of the room faced each other.

Lt. Rim gave instructions. "I will ask questions, you translate to the Americans, then translate their responses. If you come up with something to ask, let me know, and then ask it," he added.

"Could I get a table next to my chair and some tea," Sun-hee requested. "It will help to keep my stomach calm. Oh, and a bucket just in case."

Lt. Rim gave the order to the soldiers next to him. Jin-taek motioned to the other soldier that he could not talk. The other soldier ran off.

They brought in the American sergeant first. His arms tied behind his back and his legs bound tightly. A cloth bag was over his head. He struggled as soldiers sat him roughly into the chair. It took a couple of minutes to apply the restraints.

Sun-hee wished she had asked for a few more days, maybe forever, before getting to this moment.

Three women came in with a table, a bucket, a cup, saucer, and a pot of tea.

"Ready?" questioned Lt. Rim, looking at Sun-hee.

"Ready," she replied.

Lt. Rim gave a signal. Jin-taek removed the American sergeant's hood. Sun-hee waited until the sergeant looked at her, then poured herself a cup of tea.

He had a black eye and a cut lip. His hair was dirty, and his thick black beard covered the bottom half of his face. His body odor made Sun-hee sit back as far as she could.

He does not look happy.

"I am going to say hello," Sun-hee said to Lt. Rim.

"Hello, Sergeant," she said politely in English.

"You, again," the American said.

"He recognizes me," she said in Korean.

"Ask him what military unit he is with," said Lt. Rim. "For the record, can you give me your name, rank, serial number, and military unit?" said Sun-hee in English.

"John Peterson, Sergeant, 723 48 75, 7th Infantry Division," he said.

Sun-hee translated.

"Good, we have recorded your name and can move on," Sun-hee said in English, implying he did not need to give the same answer again.

Rim: "Why did you try to escape?"

(Sun-hee translated between Rim and John.)

John: "It is our duty as soldiers."

Rim: "As the leader, is it your duty to lead your men to their death?"

John: "We tried. It did not work."

Rim: "Will you try again?"

John: "Why would I tell you?"

Rim: "Now you have tried, we will not trust you."

John: "You were too trusting."

Rim: "You were foolish."

John remained silent.

Rim: "Your foolishness killed two Koreans."

John: "This is war. People die."

Rim: "This is a hospital. We try to keep people from dying. We treat the wounded. No one should die here."

John: "This is a prison camp. How many prisoners do you have here?"

Sun-hee replied to John in English, "You must not ask questions."

Sun-hee in Korean said, "He asked, 'How many prisoners do we have?' I warned him not to ask questions."

Rim: "Tell me, step-by-step, what you did during the escape."

John: "We immobilized your men and tried to get over the fence. We failed and returned to our prison."

Rim: "I want every detail; every step you took."

John: "Why?"

Sun-hee then spoke in English, "I warned you." Then in Korean, "He asked, 'Why?'"

Rim made a gesture to Jin-taek, tapping his head with his left arm.

Jin-taek hit John in the back of the head and gave a big smile to Sun-hee.

Sun-hee took a sip of tea.

Rim: "You want to know why I ask? I must know which of the

Americans killed a soldier and a medical student. We will punish each for the specific crime they committed."

Sun-hee said to the American Sergeant, "Why do we ask? We want to know which of your men killed a soldier and a medical student. We will try those individuals for the murders and the rest for assault. I will decide the punishment for the person who threw me against the wall."

John: "This is war. We committed no war crimes. You cannot try us for crimes."

Rim was losing patience: "Who did you attack?"

John thought for a moment before responding, "There are five men left. One knocked down a male medical student, that student was alive when we returned to the building. The other three tackled soldiers, all were alive. I helped subdue your officer and took his gun. He was alive when we returned."

Sun-hee translated.

Rim angrily: "Who killed my soldier?"

John: "The last I saw him, he was hanging on the fence."

Rim: "Who helped him?"

John: "He was the strongest, so he attacked alone."

Rim: "He then took the rifle and was on the fence. Is that correct?"

John: "Yes."

Rim: "Who killed the medical student?"

John: "He was shot and fell over the fence. I do not know where he is at."

As she translated, Sun-hee thought, *The killers are dead. We can't punish them any further.* She took a deep breath and exhaled. *I will not have to face Young-Jee's murderer.*

Rim: "Four men took rifles. One ended up on the fence. Who were the other three?"

John: "I have not seen them."

Rim: "Two men with rifles shot at our men. Where are they?"

John: "I have not seen them."

Rim: "So the four men remaining under your command will be charged with assault. That leaves you." He was looking at Sun-hee, hoping she got his meaning.

Sun-hee looked back and nodded her head slightly. She sipped some tea.

Sun-hee said in English, "Only one person left."

John swallowed, staring at the girl in front of him. "I take the fifth," he blurted out.

Sun-hee translated and added, "What is meant by 'the fifth'?"

Rim: "Tell him, I do not understand."

John: "I have a right not to say anything that will incriminate me."

Sun-hee in English: "I do not understand the word, 'incremeight'."

John: "You dumb gook. Americans do not have to testify against themselves."

Sun-hee in Korean: "He will not testify against himself."

Rim: "Ask him if the escape was all his plan."

Sun-hee: "Was the escape your plan?"

John: "We all planned it."

Sun-hee: "Are you their commanding officer?"

John: "Yes."

Sun-hee: "Then, you are responsible."

Sun-hee explained their exchange in Korean.

Rim: "Enough, we will question the others and see if they say the same thing."

Sun-hee then said to Lt. Rim, "He is a fool. He testifies against his men but will not admit he attacked me. He is their leader but will not accept responsibility. May I tell him this?"

Rim: "We have accounted for all the attackers but yours, Sun-hee. He is the man who threw you against the wall. Speak your mind."

Sun-hee looked directly at the sergeant as she took a sip of tea. "Sergeant, you are a weak fool. You betrayed your men by telling me of the crimes of your men but refused to take responsibility for your actions. It was you who threw me against the wall. If you were wise, you would not have let your men rush outside to face a tall fence. You and your men had no chance to escape. Do you want to know what happened to your men? One died on the fence. You let him bleed to death while you ran back to your cell. One died from a gunshot as he tried to shoot a Korean soldier. We rushed the man who was shot and fell over the fence to the hospital where he later died of his wounds. A fourth man also died on the operating room table from wounds he received. These men bravely fought while you ran away. After your men killed a medical student, other students worked to save your soldiers' lives. You think you are a great American. I think you are an insect."

Sun-hee switched to Korean, "I told him off with the words I know."

Rim: "What do you think his punishment should be?"

Sun-hee paused for a moment before saying, "I do not know."

Rim: "I will remove him from command. He is too big a fool to lead. We will put him in a building by himself. His hands will be smashed one time for each person who died during the escape. He can figure out how to get his pants off to piss with the blood of six men on his hands."

"I will inform him of your punishment," Sun-hee said.

Sun-hee pushed herself up from her chair and looked down as she said to the American in English, "You are no longer a sergeant. You are the lowest of privates, a worker ant with no rank. You will be placed in a private room. The blood of six men is on your hands. We will help you remember the blood of these men."

John: "You're a fucking gook."

"Ready lieutenant," Sun-hee said.

The lieutenant gave instructions to Jin-taek and another soldier. They walked up and used wooden mallets to smash each of John's hands three times. With each smash, John yelled at Sun-hee, who walked into a back corner of the room and shut her eyes.

When the soldiers finished, Sun-hee turned to look John in the eye and said, "You are a pathetic human being." Then she walked over and slapped him across the face. "That is for throwing me against the wall. No respectable man would handle a pregnant fifteen-year-old girl in such a manner."

John yelled at Sun-hee, "I should have shot you when I had the chance!"

Sun-hee stepped back to her chair, sat down, picked up her cup, sloshing tea over the sides before she could grasp it with both hands.

They removed John's restraints. His feet and arms were tied, the hood placed over his head, and carried him out of the building.

"Take a short break before we question the rest. They will not take as long," said Lt. Rim.

Sun-hee walked back to the dorm. With shaking hands, she washed away her tears.

Stay calm was all she thought. *You can get through this.* Then Max's words rang in her head. *"Focus. Put feelings aside."* When she returned, another man was in the chair. His hood was still on.

Sun-hee started the same way, by looking the soldier in the eye, then pouring herself some tea.

The questions were the same. The answers fit with Sgt. Peterson's. This soldier tackled one of the Korean soldiers and held him down. He explained the plan: hit hard and run. They had not seen the fence when they arrived. They thought they could just run into the mountains.

Sun-hee found out he was nineteen and had enlisted in the Army in September. The unit had been in Korea only three weeks before their capture.

Rim: "Tell him the blood of the man he tackled is on his hands. He is also partly responsible for the blood of those who died."

Sun-hee translated then she told him about Sgt. Peterson. "Your sergeant is a fool and is now a private. He now has a room to himself. Four American soldiers died trying to escape. You left them to die and ran back to your cell. You are not brave. The blood of the Korean soldier you attacked is on your hands as well as the blood of two dead Koreans." Sun-hee nodded to Lt. Rim.

The American private received two swings of the mallet on his left hand.

The next three Americans went the same way. Each was a nineteen-year-old recruit, obeying orders. They all had their left hand smashed.

Lt. Rim called for another break, this time for lunch. Sun-hee took her time eating and visiting the privy.

When she returned, the black American, Abraham, was in the chair. She remembered him as one of the soldiers helping Jeremy during the escape attempt.

"Tell me what you did during the escape attempt," asked Sun-hee.

"I tackled the man with a scar on his face and held him down," said Abraham.

Sun-hee translated.

Rim: "Did you kick me in the ribs?"

Sun-hee asked, "Did you kick the man you tackled in the ribs?"

Abraham: "No, Ma'am. The sergeant kicked the man."

Rim: "Where did you go after you left the building?

Abraham: I went outside and helped break the lock on the door to the other building. I helped carry Jeremy. When Captain Reed ordered us back, I carried Jeremy back. I obeyed what I was told, Ma'am."

Rim: "Two hits on the left hand."

Sun-hee told him his punishment before she nodded. The soldiers smashed his left hand.

Abraham looked down and said, "I am truly sorry for what happened. I will not participate in another escape attempt."

The next soldier had been the man with the rifle near Sun-hee during the escape. He was very apologetic for his role. Sun-hee accepted his apology, so her message was shorter. His left hand took two hits from the mallet.

The last of the men from the 7th infantry was the man from Louisiana. Again, his accent was difficult to understand. He, too, had tackled Lt. Rim but said the kicks to the ribs were by the sergeant.

Next was Jeremy McLeod.

Rim: "Ask him to tell you exactly what he did and saw during the attempted prison escape."

Sun-hee translated the request.

Jeremy tried to explain what he saw happen. "I remember some loud banging and finally getting outside in the cold. I think you were there and…and it was sunny and really bright with the snow."

Sun-hee translated and explained his injury had affected his memory.

"Were you hurt during the escape, Jeremy?" she asked.

"My legs are broken. They are still in a cast," he said.

Rim: "We will not get any useful information from him. Take him back and get the last prisoner."

Theodore arrived in the same manner as the others. When his hood was removed, he stared at the blood on the arms of the chair. He looked up at Sun-hee. "Hello, Sunny. We must be here about the escape attempt."

Sun-hee sighed and tried to pour tea from an empty pot. She looked at Theodore and said, "From your point of view, what happened?"

Theodore began, "It happened so quick, Sunny. There was banging at the door, it opened, and these American boys told us to join them. 'We were getting out,' they said. I thought we were being rescued until I saw you standing there yelling at everyone. When I came around the building and saw the men on the fence, two pointing rifles at you, I felt I needed to stand in front of you, as they might shoot. When you left, I decided to do what you told me and go back to our cell. I pushed Jeremy and those two boys back into our building. I took the rifle and threw it in the snow. I made everyone sit down. We waited for what seemed to be a long time, with all the yelling and shooting going on. When you called my name, I was relieved. You probably saved my life again, Sunny."

Sun-hee then tried to translate all Theodore said. She stopped after the part where Theodore pushed them all back to their building and made them sit down.

Rim: "Theodore did not hurt anyone. No blood is on his hands. We must be fair."

Sun-hee said in Korean, "May I tell Theodore what has transpired today?"

Rim: "If he promises never to try to escape, you can tell him."

Sun-hee looked at Lt. Rim, then at Theodore. Instinctively, she picked up her cup, again saw there was no tea, and put the cup down. "What you already know, Theodore, is twelve foolish American prisoners tried to escape. Four Americans died in the attempt. Please understand, three of the Americans who died had rifles and were shooting at Koreans when they were shot. The fourth you saw shot when he was outside of the fence. He had escaped the compound. No unarmed American died or was injured. One Korean soldier died. One of my friends, a fellow medical student, Young-jee…" she began to choke up, tears formed in her eyes. She swallowed and continued, "…who had treated your wounds a few minutes earlier, died from the American assault." Sun-hee paused and took a deep breath. "Your compatriots injured six Koreans in this stupid escape attempt, including me." Sun-hee let her emotions get the better of her as she concluded, "All you Americans have brought to Korea is death and destruction!" She allowed her tears to flow. "Promise me this will never happen again in this camp, Theodore. I can't take it any longer. No more, please!" she pleaded, tears running down her cheeks.

Lt. Rim took a few steps towards Sun-hee.

Theodore said quietly, "The escape attempt was stupid. Until now, I did not know just how screwed up it was. I'm sorry for the deaths of the Koreans and Americans. I promise, Sunny, if I am in command of all the prisoners, they will not attempt to escape. If I had been put in command of these prisoners when they arrived, this would not have happened."

Sun-hee translated to Lt. Rim what Theodore had said, then added, "The little girl tears definitely worked on him."

They released Theodore from his restraints and allowed him to walk unbound to meet with the seven men from the 7th Infantry. Sun-hee stood outside the door to listen to Theodore.

"I am Captain Theodore Reed, U.S. Air Force. My partner, Captain Jeremy Mcleod and I were shot down about three months ago and have been here since. Except for the smashing of hands, we have been treated fairly. Your sergeant was a fool to have you try to escape. As the ranking officer, I am ordering that there will be no further escape attempts. Cooperate, and we might survive until this war is over. Any questions?" The room was silent. "I think we are lucky they did not kill us all."

As he walked out, he turned to Sun-hee and asked, "May I see Sergeant Peterson?"

Sun-hee translated to Lt. Rim.

Rim: "We have no American sergeant here."

Sun-hee said in English, "There is no longer an American sergeant prisoner here." And she paused to get Theodore's reaction. "I gave John Peterson the rank of insect," she said with a slight smile.

Theodore smiled and said, "May I see John Peterson, the insect?"

Sun-hee translated, "I told him I gave John Peterson the new rank of insect. He has requested to see the insect."

Lt. Rim smiled and gave the command to open building four and close building three. He motioned to Theodore to enter. Theodore limped in the snow to the next building.

"Mr. Peterson, we finally meet," said Theodore.

John stood next to the wall with two bandaged hands. "Who are you?" he demanded.

"I am Captain Reed, U.S. Air Force. As the ranking American in this prison camp, I am here to see you are treated fairly."

"Here's how those fucking gooks treated me," he yelled, holding up his hands. "I should have just shot them all, especially that fucking little bitch who speaks English. When she dared me to shoot her, I should have just blown her damn head off!"

"Then you would be dead right now," commented Theodore.

"Better than being in this damn icebox of a cell."

Theodore limped over to John, stood at attention in front of him, and looked him directly in the eye. "First, sergeant, I expect you to stand at attention when I am in the room and show me the respect deserving of an officer. Second, you are relieved of command and rank. Your men will now report directly to me. Third…" John tried to say something, "Shut up and listen, private!" Theodore said over John's voice. "Third, your orders are to survive, and that means to cooperate with our captors. Four of your men are dead because of your failed leadership. You will cooperate. Next time, I will be the one to court-martial you. Is this clear?" he yelled.

John scowled back at the Captain. "You stinking flyboys don't know what these gooks are like." he said in a detestable tone. "How can you cooperate with these bastards? Do you like that little bitch?"

"You're going to have some time to think about things in here, John. Hopefully, you can get your head on straight," Theodore said and walked out.

He did not even slow down, walking by Sun-hee and Lt. Rim saying, "He's just a ground-pounding asshole, Sunny." He went back to his cell.

The lieutenant motioned to soldiers to let Theodore in his cell, then turned to Sun-hee. "What did he say as he walked by?"

Sun-hee thought for a moment of the translation to Korean and replied, "Theodore said, 'John is a dirt hitting rectum.'" Then she added, "Their conversation did not go well. John Peterson showed Captain Reed no respect. John will not be cooperative."

"John has many lessons to learn, Sun-hee. I am afraid it will be like teaching mice to fly."

24 — Loyalty - Mid-March, 1951

The evening after, the girls were quizzing Sun-hee about the trials of the prisoners. She explained in detail the questioning and punishment of each man.

Most were satisfied that the punishment of the Americans was sufficient for their crimes with one exception, Youn Kum-ja.

She said, "My child will now never know his father. Young-jee was a wonderful man, and I fear we will forget who he was."

Eun-seong said, "I will draw a picture of Young-jee so you and your child can honor him.

The next day at the library, Eun-seong drew a couple of pictures of Young-jee. That evening she gave one to Kum-ja and hung the other in the joint common room.

Sun-hee commented to Eun-seong, "Your drawing is wonderful. I'm amazed how you caught an expression of Young-jee that is indicative of his personality just from your memory. Your drawing will be better to remember him by than the image I have in my mind of him slumped in the corner."

"Thank you, Sun-hee," said Eun-seong.

Then Sun-hee said, "We also need to remember Youj Mung-jo. Do you think you can draw a picture of her?"

A couple of days later, a drawing of Youj Mung-jo hung next to the one of Young-jee.

***

It was after lunch on March ninth when an older man with a cane walked into camp accompanied by two men and a mule. The other men looked like peasants arriving to beg for a handout. As he approached the main gate, he handed his cane to a guard and removed his tattered coat and hat, revealing Gen. Park. He strode directly to the command building.

Lt. Rim sat in a chair in the corner when the general entered. He tried to get up a little too quickly for his injuries. He grimaced and held his ribs.

Chun-ja came in and took the general's coat. As she did, she held his arm for a moment. "Welcome back, General," she said with a bow and a smile.

"What happened to you, Lieutenant?" exclaimed Gen. Park.

"The Americans tried to escape, sir," he said, trying to stand at attention. "My injuries are not important."

"Your arm is in a sling, your eyes are black and blue, and you move like you have broken ribs. If those are not important, then there is a lot more to the escape. I would like to hear the details after I clean up." And he walked to his room.

Lt. Rim had dreaded this moment. The death of Young-jee happened on his command. He had been too trusting of the Americans. He paced slowly back and forth across the room, practicing how to tell the general about the escape attempt.

Minutes went by before Gen. Park entered wearing a clean uniform. His hair was wet and combed back over his head. A small cut on his neck from shaving refused to stop bleeding. He sat at the table and looked at the cloth he had been holding to his neck. Seeing the fresh blood, he folded it and again applied pressure. Chun-ja placed food on the table, poured tea, and left. Lt. Rim eased himself into a chair at the table.

"Tell me about this escape attempt by the Americans," Gen. Park said, putting down the cloth and starting to eat.

"I offer you my resignation, General," he said, sitting at attention. "This camp and the American prisoners were my responsibility, and I failed to prevent the escape attempt and keep everyone safe."

Gen. Park looked at him with raised eyebrows and swallowed the food in his mouth before asking, "How many died?"

"Two Koreans," he said, getting right to the point. "One of the students, Hung Young-jee, and one soldier. Four Americans died trying to escape."

"Tell me everything, Lieutenant," he said, emphasizing 'lieutenant.'

Lt. Rim told the story of the escape attempt; how the Americans overpowered his men, the students, and himself. He emphasized the heroics of Sgt. Kua and the role of Sun-hee. He told the general of the memorial service held for his soldier and Hung Young-jee.

"What did you do to the Americans?" the general asked.

He told about the inquiry of the prisoners and the punishments he handed out. He finished with, "I have failed your orders to keep the students safe and take care of the Americans."

Gen. Park took his cup of tea, sat back in his chair, and said to Lt. Rim, "I was in Pyongyang ten days ago and had the honor of meeting with Kim Il-sung. He has no authority. As we suspected, Chinese Generals took control of our country."

"The Chinese have recaptured Seoul and are moving south, but the bombings and lack of supplies are slowing their advance. The capitol is in ruins. Our people are starving to death." He paused, looking past Rim and out the window.

"This camp is the best place in all of Korea right now. Mostly because of your efforts and leadership. There is no one else in all Korea I would want in charge of this camp," he said, placing his folded hands on the table and leaning forward. "The only other men of your rank alive are with the Premier. Every one of them would destroy this program. You will remain in your position."

"Yes, sir," replied Lt. Rim.

Gen. Park sat back in his chair and pulled out two cigarettes. He lit them both, handing one across the table. He took a long puff before he said, "The Soviets are going to start sending medical supplies, food, and aid to Chongjin. Half of the hospital is rubble, as is much of the city. When the weather improves, injured people will be coming here from all over the south. We are in a good location. Who knows why we have not been bombed like the rest of the country."

Lt. Rim bowed in acknowledgment, hiding the pain the movement caused.

"Carry on, Lieutenant. I will address the students tomorrow. Now, I need some rest," he said, standing and leaving the room.

***

The next morning brought a bright blue sky. The frigid night had returned the melting snow to ice. The students stood in formation, leaving an empty place in the front for Young-jee.

Sgt. Kua selected Hon-yong to lead the exercises, then she stood back and watched. The exertion brought clouds of cold breaths hanging over the students in the still air. Shim Mi-kum emptied her stomach at the side of the building.

Sgt. Kua noticed the students looking past her and Hon-yong. She turned to see Lt. Rim and Gen. Park walking towards them. "To the loyalty chant Hon-yong," she ordered.

Hon-yong looked surprised, then saw Gen. Park. At once, he barked, "Halt. We are loyal to Premier Kim Il-sung."

The students all chanted, "We are loyal to Premier Kim Il-sung."

"We are loyal to the DPRK!" yelled Hon-yong. The students repeated in unison. Then he said, "We are loyal to Gen. Park!" The response was not as loud.

Shim Mi-kum wiped her face, turning red in embarrassment, and ran back into line.

"I am pleased to see you again," Gen. Park said, then started pacing in front of them. "A year ago, I put into action a plan to bring you here with the hope you would be the foundation of great Korean people. I want you to know you have exceeded my expectations.

"What I did not plan for is how this war would be so horribly bad for our people. The Americans and Chinese are now fighting over Korea. The Korean people have been devastated by these two powers fighting for control of our land. When the fighting ends, I fear we will be pawns under the Chinese or the Americans. As cold as this camp has been this winter, you have been spared much of the horror occurring in the rest of the country." He stopped pacing in front of an empty place in the formation. He thought about what to say to earn the loyalty of these students. "We will miss Hung Young-jee like we miss our families."

He paused to study the expressions of the students, then walked back to stand next to Sgt. Kua and Lt. Rim. "We will try to locate each of your families and let them know you are well, and we will send Hung Young-jee's family condolences for their loss. Your families may have fled from the Americans or fled from the Chinese. They may be alive and well but not at home." He paused, putting his hands in his pockets, then taking them out and pacing again.

After walking back and forth in front of the students, he stopped. "In my travels I have seen too many children who are hungry, injured, and with no schooling. Korea will need strong, intelligent children in the next generation. I'm doing everything possible to keep you safe and fed in hope for the future. I made arrangements with the Soviets to get food and medical supplies. They should start arriving next week. We have been through a lot this winter, but we have survived and will begin to rebuild Korea." He turned and walked away.

***

As promised, mules arrived a few days later with medical supplies and food, though not nearly enough food. The students decided to refuse double rations, requesting the extra be given to the people outside the gates. Gen. Park allowed the boys to return to normal amounts, but he was stern with the girls. They were ordered to continue eating double, to nourish their babies. Prisoners received one meal a day. Water was added to thin out the leftovers before serving it to the hungry outside the gates.

Gen. Park asked students to write letters to their families. He did not have a plan to deliver them, but he wanted to have them write the letters, to show the students he cared. He asked Lt. Rim if he had a man who could travel around the country, read addresses, live off the land, and deliver letters without revealing anything about the camp.

On the evening of the eleventh, Lt. Rim came into the headquarters with Jin-taek. "Sir, Private Jo Jin-taek was a scout for the Korean People's Army. Shrapnel injured his neck, tearing his larynx and making it impossible to speak. He is the best man available."

Jin-taek stood at attention a step behind the lieutenant. Now that he had a second chance at life, he seemed eager to do what he could for the camp.

On the morning of the twelfth, Jin-taek was ready, dressed in civilian clothes, and wearing a backpack filled with food and forty-eight letters. Two of the letters were from Gen. Park, offering condolences to the families of Youj Mung-jo and Hung Young-jee. Jin-taek set out on his journey just after breakfast, where Gen. Park had told him to eat as much as he could.

25 — Attitude - March, 1951

On March seventeenth, Sgt. Kua informed Sun-hee she was needed to translate. They assembled after lunch. Lt. Rim brought along a dozen soldiers. It was the warmest day of the year so far. Clear skies and a slight breeze blew from the south. The camp was a sloppy, muddy mess from the melting snow. Gen. Park, wearing smocks to give him the appearance of a doctor, gave the command to open the building now holding all the prisoners, except John Peterson, who remained in solitary confinement.

"Sun-hee, tell the prisoners to come out," Gen. Park said.

Sun-hee moved towards the door. "Theodore, you and all the Americans must come out."

Theodore stood at the door for a moment, letting his eyesight adjust. It was the first time he had been out of the building since the questioning about the escape attempt.

"Will we be safe, Sunny?" he asked.

Sun-hee translated. Gen. Park stared at the door for a moment before saying, "Tell the American his actions and words will determine the level of harm."

Sun-hee translated.

Theodore studied the situation and turned, speaking into the building. "Line up behind me, men, and make no threatening movements." He walked out cautiously, the men following. Abraham helped Jeremy to walk. They lined up in front of the building with Theodore a couple of steps in front. "Nine present and accounted for."

Sun-hee translated.

"Tell them I come with a message, but do not use my name or rank," said Gen. Park.

"We come with a message, and you must listen," Sun-hee said.

The general began, pausing after each sentence for Sun-hee to translate. "Nine months ago, the Democratic People's Republic of Korea moved to unify Korea into one nation. The Americans came to the aid of their puppet government in the South. They have laid waste to both North and South Korea with their bombs, artillery, and tanks. Our land is now a country in which Koreans die, Americans die, Chinese die. The Chinese army has captured Seoul and continues to move south. The Americans must leave Korea, or they will die at the hands of the larger Chinese army. I have seen where the Chinese captured Americans and tied them up in a house, where they starved to death. I have seen ditches full of Korean, Chinese, and American dead, piled together. We are a people trampled under the feet of warmongering nations. What do you say to this, Captain?" he finished, letting his anger show.

Capt. Reed replied, also pausing after each sentence. "We are only soldiers, obeying the orders of our superiors. Our survival has been in your hands and will remain in your hands. We hope to remain alive and to return to our homes and families."

Gen. Park continued, "A year ago, Hung Young-jee came to this place as a student. He was my responsibility. His family entrusted his life to me. He did not deserve to die. He was only here to help others."

Theodore replied, "Hung Young-jee's blood is on American hands. We will remember him and honor him for the rest of our lives."

Sun-hee translated for Gen. Park.

"I have been told that the men directly responsible for Hung Young-jee's death, and the death of one of our soldiers, did not survive the escape attempt." He paused, watching the Americans, making sure they were nervous. "Each of you has paid for the blood of these men. As long as I am in command, if you are model prisoners, obedient, and maintain a good attitude, you will survive."

Sun-hee translated.

Gen. Park paced before the prisoners, pausing to stare into the eyes of each. When he returned to face Theodore, he said, "Your men are dismissed, Captain Reed."

Theodore sighed, turned around, and addressed the other Americans. "Men, return to the building." He watched them go, then he turned to face the doctor and soldiers.

Lt. Rim gave an order to lock the door. With a nod, he ordered the fourth building opened.

"Have Captain Reed bring the insect out," said Gen. Park to Sun-hee.

Sun-hee smiled at the words and translated in English. "Please have insect John Peterson come out, Captain Reed."

Theodore walked to the door and yelled, "Peterson, come out."

A gruff yell came from inside. "I can't fucking get up. If they want me, they will have to come to get me."

"Just a minute," said Capt. Reed. He went into the building.

"Come on. We are going to meet the doctor in charge of this place.

Stand still and be quiet!" Sun-hee heard Theodore say. A moment later, Theodore half-carried John Peterson out, standing him a meter in front of the door. He moved a couple of steps to the side and forward.

"Fuck, my feet hurt!" said John.

Sun-hee translated to Korean and added, "The prisoner has shown signs of frostbite on his feet."

"Prisoner John Peterson present," said Capt. Reed.

Sun-hee translated again.

The doctor took a couple of steps to stand in front of John Peterson and stared at him. Peterson's beard had grown long. He had a blanket over his head, holding it close around his body with his bandaged hands. John, being a few centimeters taller, looked down at Park's stare with one of his own. Sun-hee stepped up next to the doctor and stood a meter to his right, between Gen. Park and Capt. Reed.

Gen. Park addressed John. "You were in command of the escape attempt."

Sun-hee translated into English.

John: "They wanted to try to escape."

Park: "Who are they?"

John: "My men."

Park: "Did you lead the escape attempt?"

Theodore pleaded: "Sunny, let me answer for him."

John: "We were all in on it."

Sun-hee gave Theodore's response first, and then John's answer.

Park: "Tell Captain Reed we are evaluating John Peterson's attitude."

Sun-hee translated. Theodore shifted weight between his feet, squishing in the mud.

Park: "You injured Sun-hee and broke a lieutenant's ribs."

Theodore: "John, show a good attitude!"

John: "I was easy on them."

John turned to Theodore, "You have sold out to the enemy, Captain. I am not taking any orders from you!"

Sun-hee translated both men's statements.

Theodore: "John, turn around and go back inside."

Park: "Six men died because of your failed leadership, John Peterson."

Sun-hee translated Gen. Park's words to John while thinking about what Kwang-ku boasted.

John: "Not enough of them were gooks!"

Sun-hee hesitated before translating.

Park: "You have proven you are a dirt hitting rectum."

Sun-hee laughed internally at how the term had gotten from Lt. Rim to Gen. Park. She smiled, looked at Theodore, and translated. "You have proven you are a ground-pounding asshole." Theodore noticed the smile on her face and chuckled.

John: "And you are a fucking gook, Doctor!" he said, then he spit in the doctor's face.

Gen. Park reached his right hand to his left side under his smock and grabbed hold of a knife hidden in his belt. With one quick movement, he stepped forward and slashed John Peterson's throat.

"No!" Theodore yelled and reacted, trying to move towards John. The foot with his bad ankle slipped in the mud, causing him to fall into Sun-hee. He rolled, landing into the mire on his back with Sun-hee falling on top of him.

John Peterson dropped to the ground a half-meter from Sun-hee's face, blood spurting from the severed artery in his neck.

Theodore looked wide-eyed at John and then at Sun-hee lying on top of him. "Oh, my God. I am sorry, Sunny!" He held his hands out. "I'm sorry, Sunny. Tell them I am sorry. Are you hurt? I did not mean to touch you."

The guns were all pointed at the back of Sun-hee.

"The Captain is sorry!" Sun-hee yelled in Korean. "I am fine. He did not mean to touch me. Put your weapons down, and I will get up."

Gen. Park knelt beside the two. The bloody knife slowly moved towards Capt. Reed's neck. Sgt. Kua rushed in to help Sun-hee, grabbing her right arm to lift her.

"Don't kill him!" Sun-hee yelled as she was pulled to her feet.

Gen. Park slowly rose till he stood over Theodore. He said, "An insect has no value. Just a pest, eating food. A pilot is more valuable alive." Glaring into Sun-hee's face, he said, "Tell Captain Reed I have eliminated an insect with a bad attitude." He threw the bloody knife at the body of John Peterson. "I will not allow disrespect in my camp."

Sun-hee broke into tears as she said to Theodore, "He will not allow disrespect in this camp, Theodore. He killed an insect with a bad attitude. He wants a better world than this, Theodore. He just wants a better world. It must get better!" She wiped tears from her cheeks and ran towards the gate.

***

Capt. Reed lay on his back, hands out wide. He glanced around at the rifles pointed at him. John, an arm's length away, wheezed out a last bloody breath. The doctor was walking away towards the gate and Sunny hurried after him.

Theodore held up his hands, came to a sitting position, crossed his legs, and slowly rose with his hands high in the air. Stepping slowly, he backed to the door and went inside. The door closed, and he heard the lock click. He sighed heavily. As he lowered his arms, he clenched his fists to stop his shaking hands.

"What went on with the sergeant?" demanded one of the men.

Theodore took a couple of deep breaths before answering. "The doctor questioned Sergeant Peterson directly about the escape. The sergeant did not take responsibility. When he called the doctor a gook and spat in his face, the doctor slit his throat. Peterson is dead."

"Why didn't they kill us? We all had a hand in the escape," said another soldier.

"They did not like Peterson's attitude." He took a couple of deep breaths before continuing. "For that matter, neither did I. He was an asshole. If we respect the Koreans, they will allow us to live. We showed some respect out there, and they showed us some respect. If we build a little trust, maybe we can survive and return home someday." He paused for a moment before saying, "Sergeant Peterson was his own worst enemy."

Once he said that, his mind thought about what Sunny had said. *I am not your enemy.* He paced, letting his mind dwell on what she said to him today. *He wants a better world. It must get better!*

The doctor will not have a better life if the Communists control this country, he thought.

Then Theodore said to the men, "Life in Germany and Japan is getting better under the United States occupation. The Koreans need to understand and learn from that example. They would like us to go home and let them unify Korea, but they would not be free. China or the Soviets would control them. The Koreans would see how societies fair under Communism, just like Eastern Europe. They are screwed if America does not win. We must sit tight until we win."

26 — Manipulation - Late March - April, 1951

Temperatures varied greatly during March and April. Cold, dry winds from the west for a few days, then a day or two of warm winds from the south or east, usually bringing rain. As Dr. Park predicted, many people arrived at the camp needing medical care. Only a few were soldiers. Since Max decided to go to Russia to get supplies, mainly vodka, Sun-hee focused on studies. When needed, Kwang-ku, Chulsoon, and Alek performed the operations on the new arrivals.

Students spent their spare time at the library where Gen. Park told them again to focus on the sciences: geology, chemistry, math, physics, engineering, biology, and medicine.

Only three girls were not pregnant. San Sang-me had a miscarriage, Ri Hea-jung and Jo Yu-min had not become pregnant, even though they had nightly encounters in the guesthouse. Construction on the new guesthouse progressed as weather permitted.

Due to the concern about food supplies, they turned the unused areas of the compound into gardens. Even Chun-ja started a garden next to the headquarters. The only persons not working on gardens were the prisoners. Gen. Park wondered if he could trust them. He decided there was only one way to find out. He consulted with Lt. Rim who then rounded up a few soldiers and Sun-hee.

When they were standing in front of the prisoner building, Gen. Park realized he was wearing his uniform. He considered changing, but thought, *If I have their trust not to escape, then all will be fine. If not, I will kill them.*

"Get Captain Reed out," Gen. Park commanded. The general motioned for him to walk with him towards the old student compound where ten of the students were shoveling and raking. "Sun-hee, tell him about the garden the students are working on to help feed this camp through next winter."

Sun-hee explained to Capt. Reed what they were doing. She concluded, "We are going to plant potatoes, carrots, beets, peas, and maize."

Theodore remained silent.

"Ask Captain Reed if his men would grow their food," said Gen. Park to Sun-hee.

"Can your men grow their food, Captain Reed?" Sun-hee said in English.

Theodore thought for a moment at what was being presented to him, a chance to work and get out of the cell. He was uncertain of the details, but responded, "Yes, Sunny. We would be most grateful for the opportunity to work in your garden."

Sun-hee translated.

"Tell him he will turn this prisoner compound into his garden. At sunrise, we will open their door. They will work until sunset. Any attempt to escape will result in the execution of everyone. Make sure he understands." He finished with a stern voice.

Sun-hee turned to the captain and translated. She finished with, "Do you understand, Theodore?"

"Yes, Sunny. We will make this area a good garden and show our loyalty by not attempting to escape. Thank you for letting us do what we can to provide food for all."

"We will provide tools, and you can start today," said Gen. Park before walking away.

Sun-hee translated before following Gen. Park.

The prisoners had difficulty with the tools since their hands had not fully healed. Jeremy was unable to stand for very long. However, the men were glad to get out of the building and do something besides sit and try to keep warm.

***

On the evening of the fifth of April, Suk Jong-hui went into labor. All the girls stayed at the hospital during the night, wanting to be there when the birth occurred. They were so excited, stepping over each other to help. Dr. Park gave instructions to be woken up when she was five cm dilated, but not before.

An hour before sunrise on the sixth, Suk Jong-hui delivered a healthy baby boy. With every step, Dr. Park explained what was happening, demonstrating to the girls what to do during delivery. From then on, he would watch while the girls delivered each other's babies. His plan to have a generation of children, more magnificent than Korea had ever seen, had its first fruit.

After dawn, the girls returned to the House of Sanshin. They found all the boys waiting on the porch. "Chulsoon, you are the father of a baby boy," yelled out Young-ja. The boys congratulated him, slapping him on the back.

"We have a present for Jong-hui and the baby," said Hon-yong.

The boys separated, revealing a bassinet and a crib.

The girls made a big fuss, oohing and awing about how nice the Hammer was to make the gifts. "There are five more bassinets and two cribs complete outback," he bragged. "We have been making them in secret behind the dorm. You will all get one."

***

Alek knocked on the door of the camp headquarters. The one-armed soldier ushered him in.

"General Park, this is cause for celebration," he said in Russian, holding up a bottle of vodka.

Chun-ja peaked out of the kitchen.

"Celebrate what, Alek?" Gen. Park replied in Russian, looking up from the book he was reading.

"The first birth of your program."

Chun-ja brought out two glasses, placing them on the table before retreating to the kitchen.

"Max and I are observant. We have watched what is happening," Alek said, pouring vodka into the two glasses. "You brought these students here and have kept them in this camp. All those girls are getting pregnant. I think you are trying a positive eugenics experiment. Am I right?"

Gen. Park stood, took the glass Alek held out for him, and walked around the room. "You are correct, Alek." He took a sip of the vodka and glared at Alek.

"I am sure you know eugenics has been debunked in the science journals. The Americans tried it, one scientist, I cannot remember his name…"

"Charles Davenport," interrupted Gen. Park.

"Yes, him. He wrote a lot about keeping races pure, keeping the criminals, the feeble, the dumb, and the crazy people from producing offspring."

"I have read some of his work Alek. He seemed to be more of a religious bigot to me. Some of the genetics was sound, but his conclusions and methods are questionable. I know his work was discredited in America. His programs have ended."

"Were you in Moscow when Stalin had the geneticists beheaded? I think it was in 1933."

"Yes, I was at the University then. Have there been any follow-up studies to Mueller's insemination program?" General Park said, showing Alek he knew about the failed attempts of implementing eugenics under Stalin.

"No one would dare look at genetics in the Soviet Union, General," said Alek with a wave of his hand. "Stalin publicly denounced the writings of that Catholic Monk, what was his name?"

"Mendel," responded Park.

"Yes, him. You are having more success by using the behavioral modification teachings of Pavlov. Lead and control the people by making them behave the way you want. Isn't that what you are doing with these students?"

"They won a prize for the best students in Korea, the opportunity to become leaders. Here, as in the Soviet Union, I demand loyalty."

Alek continued, "Did you know Sweden has a national program defining who is unfit to have children. They sterilize all the people they find to be unfit. They have been at it for twenty-five years now. It does not seem to be working. Their society and culture are behind other European countries. Do you plan on such a program here in Korea?"

"I do not believe negative genetics works. A society needs unskilled labor. I started small with this program, with what I could manage. Without this war, I would be preparing to give another test to all the fifteen-year-old students. I do not want a super race, just enough individuals who can be leaders in science and technology, bringing Korea into the future."

Alek refilled both glasses, then said, "Some would say Kim Il-sung wants to have a pure Korea. But, he needed Soviet help to unify the country. Some people I have talked to have the impression that when there is one Korea, Soviets will no longer be welcome."

Gen. Park took a big gulp of vodka and said, "Who else have you told about this program, Alek?"

"Max and I have discussed what you are doing. We think it will be a good experiment to watch and see what results you get. Maybe in twenty years, we can publish a paper on your efforts. No one else has any knowledge of what you are doing. To everyone else, you are training medical students at this remote hospital. Do you think these students, and they are a very bright dedicated bunch, will have children who are significantly better than they are? The Soviet Union, with ten times as many people as Korea, will produce a hundred times more intelligent individuals than your forty-eight students. You will lose the numbers game."

"In a few generations, their numbers will be in the thousands," said Gen. Park.

"Do you think you can keep this program from the Chinese?" Alek said confidently and began to pace. "Or should the Americans win, which I do not think they will, would they let you continue? I think not. Only if the Soviets are in charge do you have a chance." He filled his glass.

"Max and I do not think the Korean race can be great under any circumstance. You may get a few hundred or a thousand who are superior to the Koreans here now, but Korea will never be a power in the world. These students are too meek. None of them have the backbone needed to rule a nation and do what is needed to eliminate opposition. They will be pawns of the strong or be eliminated." Then he added, "How did you manage to get such a meek bunch of students?"

"I did not start this program with the idea Korea would be a world military power. Part of the test I designed was to have them fight each other. None of the students here threw the first punch, yet every one of them ended up winning their fight. I eliminated the aggressive children. We need to build a nation without hostility, yet with the determination and ability to win should a fight occur. They are passive by design, which is one reason we have had so little conflict in this camp."

Alek went on. "Korea has been a puppet of other nations a long time. I believe it will always be attached to strings, at least during our lifetimes. Soon you will be bowing down to the Chinese or the Americans, or you will be reporting to me." Alek looked at Gen. Park with a grin on his face. "What you need is some genes from a different culture to enhance what you have here, give them some backbone. If your children are to grow up and get along with other nations, they need to be strong and equal. Take Max and me. We are each a few centimeters taller than any of your boys, and much stronger. What if we fathered a few of the children?"

"Out of the question! I will not allow these girls in your bed!"

"You forced them to sleep with the Korean boys. I am sure we are better lovers than they are," he said with a grin.

Gen. Park replied angrily, "That would not be acceptable."

"If you agree, we will not tell anyone else about your program. We become part of it, no longer outsiders."

"Unacceptable!" Gen. Park yelled. "I will find other girls for you, young girls, pretty and willing ones. As many as you want! Just leave my students alone."

"Then Soviet aid to you and this camp comes to an end. We will expose your plan and have you discredited."

"You will never leave here. I will not have my plans altered in this manner."

"If I do not report back to Max in the next week, he will expose you and bring some men to shut this program down. You will be executed for killing a Soviet officer. The students will be taken to Tumangang and placed in a hospital working for me. You have no options. Make us a part of the program, or it is over," he said sternly, placing his glass on the table.

Gen. Park glared at Alek his fists clenching and unclenching. He turned and gazed out the window. "OK, one girl each. No more!"

"Two girls each as a start. We will then have a sample size we can compare with the rest of the babies. Consider this part of your experiment, just another variable to study. And we want a better place to stay. The one-room hut we now have needs to be upgraded."

Gen. Park's eyes showed his rage. "You leave me no choice. You will each get a girl since only two are not with child." His heavy breaths whistled slightly through his gritted teeth. "I'll arrange to have a better place for you and Max to stay. We will have to build a new house." He grabbed the bottle from Alek's hand, filled his glass, then held onto the bottle.

"I want something in return," he added. "If you and Max are going to be part of this program, I want you here teaching the students. If I leave or get killed, I want you to promise to take care of these kids." His eyes rolled up to look at the ceiling. "And, I want you to arrange to deliver current scientific journals to the library."

Alek paused for a moment and smiled. "That, I can agree to, General. Our conversation has been a pleasure," he said, smiling and walking out the door.

Gen. Park sat down in the corner and drank vodka until he passed out. Chun-ja and the soldier who guarded the door got him to his room and into bed. Chun-ja dismissed the soldier and undressed the general so he would sleep comfortably. Then she undressed and climbed in as she had been doing most of her life. It did not matter who was in charge. This was her home. She shared the bed with whoever was in command. Plus, the mat in the storage room next to the kitchen was too hard and too cold.

The general awoke in the late morning with a headache and lots of questions.

Which of the girls can I give to the Russians? How will this alter my plan? Will the program still work? Should I end the whole thing? The offspring of the Russians will be rejected in the Soviet Union and Korea, no matter who rules.

***

That afternoon, Gen. Park sent an order to have Ri Hea-jung and Jo Yu-min meet him at headquarters.

Sgt. Kua led the two girls to headquarters and knocked on the door. The guard opened it, and Sgt Kua announced, "Ri Hea-jung and Jo Yu-min are here as requested."

"Come in, come in," said Gen. Park with a positive tone. "Please, take a seat at the table." He pulled out two chairs. "Chun-ja, some tea," he yelled towards the kitchen.

Ri Hea-jung and Jo Yu-min bowed low before taking a seat at the table. They folded their hands in their laps. Gen. Park sat. "I am concerned that you are the last two not pregnant." Chun-ja placed cups on the table and poured tea for everyone.

The general allowed the pause to let his words sink in. Then he said, "I am sure you know by now there may be many reasons why you have not conceived."

Ri Hea-jung held her head low and fought back a sob.

Jo Yu-min said meekly, "We have tried sir but have failed you. Jong-hui has already given birth, and all the others are with child. We apologize." Both girls began to cry.

"This may not be your fault, Yu-min. I do think a change is needed. I am considering different partners for you to help you conceive. If you accept this change, I will consider both of you as loyal and remove neither of you," he said with a caring voice.

Ri Hea-jung and Jo Yu-min both brought their heads up enough to look at Gen. Park.

"I planned for the next round of babies to have different fathers. The mixing of traits will deliver more variety and combinations of genes in the offspring. Now, after considerable thought, I asked Doctor Max and Doctor Alek if they would be willing to be the fathers of your children." He paused, watching the girls closely, letting his last comment set in.

The eyes of both Ri Hea-jung and Jo Yu-min opened wide in shock at what they had just heard. In pillow talk, the girls admired the Soviet doctors. Sometimes they flirted a little, but they had never thought of them as men who could father their children.

"I will have Sgt. Kua inform Chong-pil and Wa-dae, their services are no longer required. If you agree to have Max and Alek father your children, I will make arrangements for you to visit them."

Ri Hea-jung and Jo Yu-min peeked at each other.

"Do you want to join the rest of the girls in being mothers?" he asked to get some response.

"Yes, General Park," Yu-min replied in a quiet voice.

"And you, Hea-jung?"

She focused on her hands in her lap and finally said, "Yes, General Park."

"Yu-min, I will give you Doctor Alek. Hea-jung, I will give you Doctor Max. Doctor Max is in Chongjin and will not return for a while. Yu-min, I will let you know when Doctor Alek is ready."

Gen. Park went on reassuringly, "I know this is very hard, but it is best. We are all working for a better tomorrow, and we will have a great new generation of children to make our future. Thank you for being part of this program. I care deeply for each one of you." He stood, walked to the door, and held it open.

Later in the day, he found Alek. "I told Yu-min you would be her new partner. She is one of two that are not pregnant and available. Let me know when you are ready, and I will have her come to your cabin," he said in a disgusted tone.

"I am always ready, General," Alek said with a big smile. "I am looking forward to her visit!"

General Park stomped back to his command building.

***

That evening Ri Hea-jung and Jo Yu-min told the other girls that the doctors would father their children. The other important news that roused up a lot of conversation was that they would be changing partners for their next child.

27 — Sergeant Jo - April to June, 1951

Three more babies were born in April, two girls and a boy. The fathers presented a bassinet to each mother. Daily life for the mothers changed significantly. For the first few weeks, they cared for the children and then added in some study time as their children grew.

Gardening was left up to the boys. Mrs. Lim, her arm now healed, assisted with the childcare. She still rarely spoke, except to tell the girls what to do.

One day, near the end of April, a cart pulled by two men arrived at the main gate. The men begged for help for themselves and the woman lying in the back. Kwong-ku went out to check on their injuries.

"Bring a stretcher," he yelled into the camp.

The three were malnourished, and the woman was in the latter stages of pregnancy. The men received food and treatment for their injuries.

In the middle of the night, the woman went into labor. The civilian in charge of the ward sent for Alek who sent for female medical students. This night, it was Sun-hee and Choe-me's turn to get up. When they arrived, they found out they would soon be delivering a baby.

The woman was thin and weak. She screamed with each contraction. Alek had Sun-hee monitor the baby's heartbeat using a stethoscope. Choe-me monitored the woman's heartbeat and breathing. Alek focused on delivery.

After an intense contraction, the woman briefly shook. Choe-me moved her stethoscope around, then said in Russian, "Heart stopped."

Alek took the stethoscope off Choe-me's ears and listened for himself. "Baby?" he said towards Sun-hee.

Sun-hee said, "Still beating but weak."

Alek listened to the woman again. "We take the baby now," he said in Russian.

He grabbed a scalpel and cut across the woman's belly. He made a few more quick cuts, opened the placenta, and lifted the baby out.

Alek held the baby while Sun-hee tied a string on the cord and cut it.

"No bleeding," Alek said in Russian, pointing to where he had cut across the abdomen. "She is dead." He took the baby and left the room.

Sun-hee and Choe-me stared at each other. Together they folded the woman's arms, rearranged her clothes, and covered her with a sheet. As they walked out of the operating room, Alek was examining the baby.

"Baby good," he said in Russian. "Need breast milk," he said while cupping his hands under his chest.

The rising sun twinkled in their misty eyes as they returned to the dorm, sad and weary.

The woman was placed in the pit they used to bury the dead. When the men tending the camp's mass grave arrived later that morning, they shoveled dirt over the lifeless body.

Through her tears, Choe-me told the girls about the delivery. The baby was alive but had no one to care for her.

"We need to feed the baby," said Jong-hui, who was nursing her child. "The baby will need to be fed, or it will die. We could share in the feeding and give it a chance to live."

The other nursing girls voiced their agreement. Choe-me and Sun-hee jumped up and ran to the hospital to get the baby. They asked the men who arrived with the woman what her name was.

One man said, "Yi Yang-gae. Her husband died in the fighting, and her parents starved to death during the winter."

Sun-hee and Choe-me took the baby back to the House of Sanshin. The girls adopted the baby naming her Yi Si-ue.

***

May came and went. The students planted seeds in the garden. Babies were born. Max returned with cases of vodka and medical supplies.

Mr. Yun completed Sgt. Kua's new home with a bedroom for her and two guest rooms. He added a side room with a separate entrance for himself. Finally, he did not have to live in the woodshop. He started building a new residence for Max and Alek north of the command house.

***

On the afternoon of June second, Jo Jin-taek arrived. Gen. Park brought him to headquarters, sat him down at the table, and served him a bowl of potato soup and tea. Jin-taek wrote about his trip between bites.

"In Kilju found a family. Letter delivered," he wrote. Then laid a letter to the boy from his family on the table. "Kimchaek, house ruin.

Note from son there. I left the letter. Pukchong burned. Not find the street." He handed over an unread letter from one of the boys.

"Yonggwang, much American equipment. Find hut. Deliver the letter. Here letter for Sun-hee." Jin-taek gave a big smile as he laid the letter on the table. "Kosong, no people in town." He laid a letter on the table.

In this manner, Jin-taek wrote the story of his journey, one letter delivery at a time around North Korea in a clockwise direction. When he finished writing a description of the delivery, or the attempted delivery, he laid a letter on the table, then ate a bite of soup and went on to the next delivery. He delivered only a few letters in the far south, where the war had been worse, and none in the larger cities, which had been carpet-bombed. The last five letters along the north Hulu river and far north Korea were all delivered. He added letters from the families to the pile.

Gen. Park examined the letters on the table. A pile of twelve letters returned from the families of students. These families had survived a year of war and were still living in the same place. Fifteen letters lay in a second pile, where Jin-taek couldn't find the family or home. The other twenty-one letters he left at addresses where he hadn't located the family.

Gen. Park stood up and said, "You have performed a great service to us, Private Jo. First, I am promoting you to sergeant. Second, you may use my facilities to shower and shave. Then we will deliver the letters to the students."

"Chun-ja, assist Sgt. Jin-taek in cleaning up, and find him some clean clothes."

"Yes, sir," came a voice from the kitchen.

Gen. Park was pleased to hear that Sgt. Jo delivered his letter to Young-jee's family. He had told them the truth. Their son was a promising medical student and was treating American prisoners who made a foolish mistake and tried to escape. An American prisoner killed Young-jee. The American who killed their son died in the escape attempt. He had ended the letter with, "We will remember your son as a hero of the Democratic People's Republic of Korea."

Gen. Park read the twelve letters received from families.

Only twelve of forty-eight families found. Our country is in turmoil. Damn this war! Damn the Americans!

Jin-taek looked a lot better after cleaning up, except for the sergeants uniform Chun-ja found for him that hung loosely on his undernourished body.

Gen Park called towards the kitchen, "Chun-ja, bring another bowl of soup." Jin-taek nodded, smiled, and took the bowl from Chun-ja.

Gen. Park went into this room and opened a drawer where he kept a box of rank badges. He took out sergeant pins and returned. Jin-taek stood, swallowed the last bite, and saluted. Gen. Park fastened the pin on Jin-taek's lapel, saluted sharply, and said, "Let's go pass out some letters, Sergeant Jo."

The two marched to the House of Sanshin and called the students into formation. It took a couple of minutes to round up everyone from around the compound.

When everyone was present, the general began, "First, I would like everyone to meet Sergeant Jo Jin-taek, whom some of you remember as a wounded private arriving last fall. Over the last month, he traveled around our country to deliver your letters. Today he returned, and for his heroic effort, I have promoted him to sergeant. Please give him a warm welcome!" Gen. Park clapped, starting enthusiastic applause from the students.

"Let's go into the common room where we can be more comfortable," Gen. Park said, gesturing to the building behind the students.

Sgt. Kua led them, removed her sandals, and held the door open. The students funneled up and went in as a mob. Gen. Park and Jin-taek entered last.

"Please sit down and be comfortable," he said to the students who were milling around. Mrs. Kim was at the door to the left with a crying baby. She handed it to its mother who sat and began to nurse.

When it was quiet, Gen. Park began, "During a war, families are often displaced. They move to get away from the fighting. Now, I am glad you are here and have been spared from the direct fighting. You have been preserved to be able to make the future." He paused to let his point sink in, but seeing the anxious faces he continued, "If the letter you sent is returned to you, that only means your families were no longer at your home. Sergeant Jo left letters where he found evidence someone had been home recently but were not there when he visited."

Gen. Park began handing out letters, the ones receiving notes from their families first, then those who had their messages returned. Some of the letters revealed that everything was fine at home. Others read about the loss of family members or relatives. The ones who received their letters back were dejected. The room was a sobering scene full of tears and hugs.

Jin-taek stood at attention near the door and watched as the students received the letters. Their emotion brought him to tears.

***

Sun-hee took the paper she received and sat down between Young-ja and Eun-seong. Neither had received a return letter. Sun-hee began to read:

My Dearest Daughter,

I am so relieved to hear you are safe. I am well. When the Americans came, Mrs. Pae and I went north to Sinhung and hid in caves. Mrs. Pae's daughters and husband died when a shell hit their home. She is still in mourning, as am I. So many in the town were killed.

The Americans made a camp for their troops in Yonggwang. After the Chinese defeated their army, we returned. Most of the city was in ashes when they left. Somehow our home was spared. You are alive, and I am alive, which is all that matters.

Mrs. Pae lives with me. We are eating K-rations. The Americans left crates of them by the road. The man who brought your letter is eating a second one as I write. I wish I could see you, but the man gestures no when I ask. He showed me the letters he has yet to deliver and will not let me come with him.

I miss you! I am so happy you are alive and well.

You are my shining light, my little Empress!

Mom.

Sun-hee hugged her letter to her chest and cried. Young-ja placed her arm around Sun-hee as did Eun-seong. They cried together.

Choe-me came over and shared the news from her family. "They are all well, living in the countryside above the northern Yulu River, out of reach of the war."

Eun-seong was upset, knowing her family was not at home. Her abundantly giving heart was empty, and she left to be alone.

Young-ja looked at the positive, her letter was delivered, the house was there, but she received no note back.

The girl's dorm was full of a wide range of emotions that evening. Many were crying, some consoling, and most were sharing about their families. The solemn mood continued for days.

***

A couple of days later, Choe-me came to Sun-hee with an idea. "Do you think Gen. Park would allow our mothers to join us like Mrs. Lim? They are out there alone and would be better here. My mother taught elementary school and would be an immense help with the children. Would you go with me to ask?"

"Did anyone else get a letter back, and their mother is alone at home?" asked Sun-hee.

With few questions to the other students, they found three boys and two other girls, whose mothers were now alone.

Choe-me and Sun-hee approached Gen. Park. He listened to them present how the mothers would be very helpful, and they would be loyal to the program, as they were very loyal to Korea.

Gen. Park said he would consider it.

The next day, Gen. Park asked Sgt. Jo Jin-taek if he would be willing to go out to bring the single mothers to the camp. Having met them, remembering their pleading to take them to their children, Jin-taek nodded his head in agreement.

A couple of days later, Jin-taek was ready to set out. "One last thing, Sergeant Jo," said Gen. Park. "Take the women to the hospital in Chongjin. I will meet you there. I want to meet them before I bring them here."

Sgt. Jo nodded and set off.

Gen. Park found Choe-me in the library. "Choe-me, I sent Sergeant Jo out this morning to bring your mother to this camp. Please tell the others of my decision."

As soon as Gen. Park left, Choe-me ran as fast as she could in her pregnant state, to find Sun-hee. When she did, she screamed in excitement, "Our mothers are coming! Jin-taek is leaving to get our mothers." The two danced in circles until they were out of breath.

28 — Stalemate - June - August, 1951

The weeks of June passed slowly for Sun-hee, being six months pregnant in the summer heat drained her energy. She stayed in the library as much as she could during the day, avoiding doing anything strenuous and the smells of the operating room. Most of the arriving wounded needed rehabilitation, the task Joo-yun was assigned to do.

Lt. Rim had not requested her help with the prisoners for weeks. She focused on learning, teaching languages, and translating.

On a warmer day than most, Sun-hee blotted her forehead as she looked through the new science papers which had arrived from the Soviet Union the day before. She was separating them into piles by subjects when Strategist walked by.

"Yong-gak, here are a couple of political articles just in from the Soviet Union," she said, holding them out.

"Thank you, Sun-hee," he said with a slight bow, taking the papers. "Old news may be better than the latest news."

"What do you mean?" asked Sun-hee.

"I spoke to the new arrivals. The Americans have pushed into North Korea again. The Chinese are retreating. Fighting at the front is very intense. We get only a few casualties as there is no way to transport the wounded this far. Whether the Americans or Chinese wins depends on which country has the greater will to fight." He spoke with his usual hand gestures; only this time, one hand contained the articles.

"Do you think there is a chance an independent Korea will ever be a reality?" asked Sun-hee, just to be amused by his hands.

"A slight chance. If the war ends in a stalemate and the Chinese and Soviets pull out," he said, finishing with a hand gesture that looked like he was pulling the papers out of his pants.

Sun-hee held back her smile until Yong-gak left.

***

The monsoons roared in during July. Rainy days alternated with hot, muggy days. Everyone went about their tasks, slopping in the mud one day and simmering in sweat the next. Most of the girls were either pregnant or had recently given birth. The guesthouse was empty all month.

At times, formations of planes left contrails high in the sky, other times it was a few planes, and now and then one by itself. On the twenty-second of August, a single jet flew low over the camp while eight aircraft flew in formation high above. The only person who thought anything about this was Theodore. He hoped they got clear photos of his garden.

***

Garrett Stallings sat deep within the headquarters of the American Air Force in Tokyo, Japan. His job was to examine reconnaissance photos of the north half of North Korea, which was always dull. This morning, he was looking at photos taken of the north-east coast, trying to find Soviet military movements. He calculated there was a buildup of supplies in Rashin, less than twenty miles from the Soviet border. He delivered these photos and his interpretation of them to his superior.

He returned to focus on Chongjin, where photos showed camps of refugees and some rebuilding of the city's infrastructure. He switched to the Yalu River area, noting suspicious vehicles and boats that might be carrying supplies for the Chinese Army. He saw nothing of vital importance, but he sent the most likely photos showing potential targets to his commander.

Garrett then made a quick scan of the images taken of the mountainous regions where he had never seen anything of a military nature. One photo caught his eye. It looked like the number zero six in a garden plot. He used a magnifying glass to look closer. He made out a zero and the number six formed by using plants and paths in a garden in the grounds of a hospital. There had never been any weapons visible at this hospital, and the only activity was farming and medical personnel walking around. He turned the photo around. The letters were distinct, *9 OK.* He had found a message. There were nine Americans at this camp, and they were okay.

Garrett went to the file room and found the folder containing the photos of the camp. He examined each one. The first few, taken last fall, showed it nearly empty. Then he could see images of wounded arriving. A photo showing the capture of two pilots surprised him. He should have known about this. He looked through more photos, one taken each week, and could not see any evidence of prisoners or any action on this part of the compound until April. Gardens were emerging throughout the camp. Not unusual for North Korea in the spring. The recent photos showed men in this area of the hospital compound. He made out nine human shapes, looking up at the planes and always in the same area. He knew he had a POW camp. He gathered everything and ran to his commander.

"Thank you, Sergeant Stallings. We will take it from here," was all Garrett got for his work.

Garrett spent some of his spare time over the next few days in the darkroom, enhancing the faces of the Americans and Koreans he saw in the mountain camp. He wanted to be able to identify who was there and who might be in charge. The two pilots were easily identifiable from records as the two shot-down last December, Captains Reed and Mcleod. The other seven men he could not identify, but they must have been from the 7th Infantry who had ventured north along the coast last December. The one Korean face he got the clearest photo of was a woman in a doctor smock, looking up at the plane on the day the pilots were captured.

You are walking away while everyone else is with the American prisoners. Who are you?

He hung the photos of 9 OK and the girl on his wall.

The next day, he received more reconnaissance photos of the area. He saw the effects of three hundred tons of bombs dropped on Rashin. He smiled but knew he would have to wait for more photos of the POW camp.

29 — Mothers - September, 1951

Jo Jin-taek made his way to the southwestern part of Korea, to the city of Dandong, built on the mouth of the Yalu River where he found Ra Weon-kee's mother. She was the first to join him on his journey.

From there, he went to Pyongsong, just north of Pyongyang. He found the home where he had delivered a letter a few months earlier. Nobody was home. Neighbors said the woman had gone east a couple of days after receiving a letter from her son.

From there, Jin-taek then went east and failed to find any of the student's mothers at home. He ventured north, staying on mountain roads and paths to get to Yonggwang. Cha Sue-dae was excited to join him and pleaded with Jin-taek to have Mrs. Pae come with them. He showed them his orders to bring Mrs. Cha and the other mothers to the school, but he gave in to the pleas of the two women.

The party made their way northwest over the mountains, past the battlefield at Chosin Reservoir. Then keeping on mountain paths for a couple of weeks as they crossed to the upper Yalu River. The second week, Mrs. Pae came down with dysentery and became very weak. They were forced to travel slower, which extended their journey by a couple of days. Finally, they reached Moon Choe-me's home in Manpo.

They stayed, tending to Mrs. Pae, hoping she would overcome her illness. Her condition did not improve. Three days after arriving at Manpo, Mrs. Pae died. They held a hasty ceremony for her the next morning, then left for the trip to Chongjin in the afternoon.

The next morning, they boarded a boat, offering to help row, which took them upriver to Hyesan. They hiked over a mountain pass, two days up and two more down, where they came to another river. They were able to talk their way onto a barge and rode it to Musan. There they turned east and crossed the mountains to Chongjin. His trip took two-and-a-half-months.

Jin-taek's ability to trap rabbits and squirrels, knowing which roots and leaves were edible, and a knack of staying away from bandits, kept them fed and safe.

After showing his orders to officials at the hospital, Jin-taek and the women were provided food and a place to stay nearby. The shared room was a palace, considering what they, and the multitude of refugees crowding the town of Chongjin, had been through.

Having received notice of their arrival, Gen. Park made his way to the hospital, arriving two days after Jin-taek and the three women.

He congratulated Jin-taek, who led him to the room where the women were staying. He took the last drag from his cigarette, straightened his smock, and walked in to meet the three women. "Hello, I am Doctor Park." He looked around first, seeing Mrs. Moon was the prettiest and had features he saw in Moon Choe-me. "Let me guess. You are Mrs. Moon, Choe-me's mother."

"Yes, Doctor. How is she? When can I see her?" replied Mrs. Moon with a deep bow.

"Choe-me is fine, as are all your children. We will see them in a couple of days." He looked at the other women, trying to figure out who belonged to whom. "Are you Ra Weon-kee's mother?" he said, pointing to Cha Sue-dae.

"I'm Weon-kee's mother," interrupted the woman next to Cha Sue-dae. "Why will it take days before I can see my son?"

"I need to make some arrangements. I want you refreshed before we continue your travels." He turned to the next woman, "And you must be…"

"I am Cha Su-dae, Sun-hee's mother," said Mrs. Cha bowing.

"I am honored to meet all of you." He gazed at each woman before continuing. "About eighteen months ago, before the war started, I implemented a plan to bring the best young students in Korea together to study and grow into adults who could define the future of our country. This was the prize your children won. They are amazing children, and I compliment you on raising them.

"Our Premier, Kim Il-sung, appointed me to lead the building of our country's hospitals and medical facilities. Your children are now at a medical facility close to here. I chose an isolated location, so they would not be distracted by city life and could focus on their studies. This isolation has also been very advantageous in keeping them removed from the war. They have become proficient in medicine, and by treating the wounded, they have performed a great service to our country."

He began to walk around the room, fidgeting with things in his pockets and looking the women over. Then he continued, "There are a few things I demand of everyone in this remote medical facility. First, you must be loyal to Kim Il-sung. Second, you must be loyal to the Democratic People's Republic of Korea. And third, you must be loyal to me. You must commit to these loyalties before I allow you to see your children." He studied their anxious faces. "You must remain loyal. If you cannot pledge your loyalty, you may leave. However, you will never have another chance to be with your children." He said sternly and paused again. "Do I have your complete loyalty?"

The mothers bowed.

The General concluded by saying, "It has been a pleasure to meet all of you. I am glad you are safe. Take tomorrow to recover from your journey. We will leave the day after tomorrow. Get some rest."

***

They traveled the fifteen kilometers from Chongjin to the compound in a donkey-drawn cart, arriving in time for dinner.

He took the women to the headquarters building and had them take a seat at the table in the main room. Chun-ja stood at the opening to the kitchen, her belly revealing she was pregnant. "We have three guests for dinner Chun-ja," Gen. Park said.

"Yes, sir," Chun-ja said with a slight bow, rushing off to get food from the camp kitchen.

Gen. Park turned to the three women. "I must attend to a few things. The privy is to the left at the end of the hall," he pointed. "Please make yourselves comfortable and enjoy dinner."

The women sat, fidgeting, eager to see their children after such a long journey. Chun-ja returned to serve each woman a large bowl of vegetable soup and tea. She bowed before returning to the kitchen.

Cha Su-dae broke the silence, "This is the best meal I have eaten in a year. If this is what Sun-hee has been eating, I am very pleased."

Mrs. Moon choked back tears as she ate. Mrs. Ra put her spoon down. "I am too excited to eat. So many delays."

***

Gen. Park went to the student compound to find the children of the mothers who were eating dinner at his table. He found Sgt Kua. "We need to bring Sun-hee, Choe-me, and Weon-Kee to the guesthouse immediately. Help me locate them."

Moon Choe-me was in the dorm nursing her child. Sun-hee was found in the library by Gen. Park. "Go meet with Sergeant Kua in the guest house," he said to her.

She stood, using a table for support as her round belly made it hard to balance, and she waddled out of the library. Gen. Park headed for the hospital.

Weon-Kee was repairing irrigation pipes when Sgt. Kua found him. She ordered him to clean up and report to the guesthouse.

***

Sun-hee held her hands around her belly as she carefully ambled to the guesthouse, not wanting to slip in the mud. She entered to find Moon Choe-me sitting at the table with her baby boy. "How are the two of you doing today?" she asked.

"We are very well. He just finished eating," Choe-me said with an endearing glance down at the child she carried in a sling. "How are you feeling?"

"Enormous. Carrying a child is so uncomfortable."

"It will be over soon."

The door opened, and Ra Weon-kee stepped in and closed the door behind him, saying, "Sergeant Kua told me to report here."

Sun-hee's eyes got wide. "Our mothers! There must be news of our mothers."

"Every day I have been dreaming my mother would arrive," said Choe-me. "I was afraid that after so long that Jin-taek had not made it."

Just then they heard Sgt. Kua's voice outside the door. "The three students you requested are present."

"Thank you, Sergeant," came Gen. Park's voice outside the door. "Tell the students that Jin-taek was not able to find the other mothers."

Sun-hee's feet started prancing. She grabbed her stomach to keep it from jiggling.

Choe-me lept to her feet, holding her baby close.

Weon-kee went to the window and looked out.

The door opened, Gen. Park walked in.

"Can we see our mothers, General?" blurted out Weon-kee.

"Your mothers are enjoying dinner at my house," he said with a smile. He stepped aside and held the door open as the three rushed out.

Sun-hee grabbed Choe-me's arm to steady herself as they trudged across the slippery compound. Weon-kee ran ahead then stopped to let them catch up. Choe-me's tears raced down her smooth cheeks and lept off her chin onto her cooing baby.

They trembled when they got to the porch and waited for Gen. Park to open the door. Weon-kee took a step to enter before stepping back politely to let the girls in first.

Choe-me entered first. "Chooe-meee!" exclaimed Mrs. Moon as she rushed to her daughter.

Sun-hee stepped around Choe-me, bounding into her mother's

arms, grasping her with all her strength. Sun-hee felt the bones of her mother's back through her thin shirt and realized how difficult the past year had been for her mother. The baby she was carrying kicked as if it wanted to be a part of the embrace. The emotional dams of both mother and daughter broke in a flood of tears and wailing.

Mrs. Ra, her hands clasp in front of her, eyes fixed on her son, said through her sobs, "You are bigger and taller, so much stronger than when you left." She turned to Gen. Park. "Thank you. Thank you so much for taking care of my son." She bowed over and over towards the general. "I am deeply indebted to you."

Mrs. Moon took her grandbaby, holding it while crying. Choe-me wept on her shoulder.

"You look so good, Sun-hee," cried Mrs. Cha. "You are so grown up, and soon, you will have a baby for me to take care of." Then she turned to Gen. Park and bowed deeply. "Thank you so much for taking care of my little girl. Thank you!"

Chun-ja brought sweet rice cakes and tea. They ate. They ogled over Choe-me's baby. They cried.

Gen. Park put his empty bowl on the side table and stood, saying, "I am pleased you could join us. There is room in the girls dorm for all of you. I only ask you to help with the students and their babies. Girls, show them where they will be staying."

"Thank you again, Doctor," said Mrs. Cha with a deep bow.

"Thank you for everything, Doctor," said Mrs. Ra, bowing lowly again.

"I am so pleased with how you have taken care of Choe-me, Doctor. Thank you!" said Mrs. Moon, bowing.

Weon-Kee, Choe-me, and Sun-hee bowed.

"Burp," went the baby.

Sun-hee held her mother's arm, talking as they walked through the compound. "Here are the hospital wards, where we have treated many injured."

Someday, I may tell her of the horror.

"Over there is the library, where I spend most of my time. The languages you taught me have been of immense help. Here is the kitchen where we eat. As you can tell, we have been well fed."

Only so our babies are healthy.

"Over there is the woodshop, metal shop, and garage. Storage buildings are in the buildings on down the road."

They turned, passing through the gate leading to the student housing. "This building is Sergeant Kua's house. I will introduce you to her later."

But I will not tell you what else happens there.

"This is our dorm. The boys have the right side, and the girls are on the left."

They stepped up on to the porch and entered the common room where she saw Mrs. Lim. "Mother, this is Mrs. Lim. Her daughter is one of the students. She arrived injured a few months ago and is helping with the children.

Mrs. Lim bowed. "I will get some mats and blankets." And she scurried off.

They tiptoed through the room full of bassinets and napping babies, into the girls sleeping area. Sun-hee moved her mat to make space for her mother. Then she carefully sat down on her mat and asked, "How was it at home, Mother?"

Mrs. Cha arranged her mat and blanket before speaking softly. "The day the Americans arrived, I fled into the hills with many others. They bombed and shelled the town. A few days later, I went home and found Mrs. Pae in our hut. She was in shock. Her husband and children died in the shelling. I helped her bury them while American trucks and tanks drove by. So many people died.

"We went north to Sinhung and lived in a cave until the Chinese came. The fighting went on for days, or I should say, the fighting went on for many nights."

Mrs. Cha stared at the floor. "The Americans were defeated. They burned what was left of the town as they left. Our hut, being outside of town, was spared. Mrs. Pae and I stayed there through the winter and spring. We gathered boxes of American K-rations and survived by sharing one a day. Mrs. Pae went through so much. She came with me on the journey to be with you. But she fell ill and died at Mrs. Moon's home."

She looked up at her daughter. "I am so glad you won the prize and were spared the misery I have seen. I am so happy to be here. We are together. That is all that matters."

Sun-hee embraced her mother as tears flowed.

After a few minutes, Mrs. Cha said, "Show me more of this place. Tell me what you have done."

Sun-hee led her mother to the front porch and waited a moment to let their eyes adjust to the bright sun. "We can see most of the camp from here. We lived in those two buildings," she pointed south, "while this building was erected. We moved into this building in December. That is Sergeant Kua's old house." She pointed out each place as she mentioned them. "Beyond there are the buildings where we keep the American prisoners. I am the only one who knows English, so when needed, I translate to the Americans.

"When we were receiving lots of wounded, I assisted a Soviet surgeon at the hospital. General Park chose me because I can speak Russian. The Soviet doctors live in a building in the far corner of the compound.

"The library is to the north. General Park brought books from the library in Pyongyang. I go there when I am not at the hospital.

"As you can see, there are gardens all around the compound. We work in the gardens trying to grow as much food as possible."

Mrs. Cha took hold of a support post, looking over the camp and said, "This is a wonderful place, Sun-hee. I am so proud of you. When did you get married? Why did you not tell me about this in your letters?"

Sun-hee paused, wondering how to tell her mother about Stone and the program. "I am not married, Mother. None of the students are married. Gen. Park arranged our mates. Each of the girls has a baby from one of the boys. Han Young-soo and I made this baby." She rubbed her hands lightly over her large tummy. "The students are all one family. The boys care for all of us, and we care for them. Han Young-soo is a fine man, better than any I knew before I came here. Your grandbaby will be the most amazing child, and we will raise it to be a leader in our country's future. This is part of the prize, Mother. The next generation will be the offspring of the best students in Korea." She tried to be positive. She wanted her mother to accept her and her baby.

"Were you forced to have this baby?"

"Mother, I accepted, and all the girls here accepted this as the best choice. We had to be loyal to General Park, or we had to leave."

Should I tell her about Mung-jo? No, not now.

"I could have walked out and suffered with you. Those were my choices. I chose to stay here. Now, you are here. I will have a healthy baby. We can build a future. The students are the best people my age in all of Korea. I will be loyal to them forever. Please accept my baby as a hope for the future."

"You have grown in so many ways," said Sue-dae, looking directly into her daughter's eyes. "I have listened to how you explained this place and yourself. You are no longer a little girl. You have become a confident woman in the last fifteen months. In looking at you and all this," she gestured with her hand, "I believe you made the right choices given the circumstances."

Sue-dae looked out over the camp. Her breath slowed, and she said, "The boy I was arranging for your husband was recruited into the army. His parents fled into the mountains when the Americans came. I have not seen them since. My dream of planning your wedding day was already in ruins." She choked up, her eyes watering. "This war has shattered so many dreams. So many lives. Now here I am, blessed with a daughter who stands before me as a confident young woman who is greater than my dreams." She reached out, pulling Sun-hee into a long hug.

They chatted on the porch for the rest of the evening. Sun-hee pointed out Han Young-soo to her mother and how Young-ja nicknamed him Stone. She explained how he fit his nickname very well.

***

The next day, Lt. Rim asked Sun-hee to explain to the Americans that they needed to place the harvest of their garden into baskets by their gate.

Sun-hee went to the gate of the prisoner area and yelled, "Theodore, I need to pass on instructions."

Capt. Reed came to the gate. "Hello, Sunny. What instructions do you have for me today?"

"The harvest from your garden needs to be placed in the baskets we provide. We will store it with the rest of the food."

"So, this is how communism works. All the food we grow is collected, and then a little is given back to us. In capitalism, we would sell you our excess food to buy other things we need. You could then resell our food at a profit." Theodore finished with a smug expression on his face.

"Our communal food supply has fed you for almost a year. The food you have grown will not pay for what you have eaten thus far. If this were a capitalist system, you would be in debt. The food from your garden is combined with food from all the farmers in the area. Some will be sent to the coast for the fishermen who will give us some of their fish. This camp will exchange kim-chi for lamb and chicken to put in your meals. In this manner, everyone has enough to eat. There is no need for money. Nobody gets rich."

"Where is the incentive?"

"The incentive is for people to stay alive. To get rich or have more during the war is wrong. Give us your food, Theodore. Your share will be delivered daily." Sun-hee turned and walked in the opposite direction from the dorms. She entered the area of storage buildings. There were linens laid out to dry fruit. Grains were being ground into flour in a building. Two women were shelling nuts. Her heart grew heavy.

So many people are laboring to feed the other students and me. What am I giving in return?

A man was unloading coal from the backs of mules, adding to the pile by one of the buildings. "Where are you from?" asked Sun-hee.

"The mines at Musan," he replied.

"Are they still in operation?"

"No. But there are still a few piles that did not catch fire in the bombing. This camp is the only place where I can exchange coal for food."

"Thank you," Sun-hee replied. She walked back to the House of Sanshin to get her mother before going to the library.

They entered the two-story building where Sue-dae stopped and took it all in. "I have not seen such a collection of books since I was in college." She strolled around the room, browsing through the books. Then she sat beside her daughter. "Are you translating that article?" she asked Sun-hee.

"Yes. Stinky wanted me to translate any article related to agriculture for him. This one discusses the chemical properties of fertilizers."

"Stinky?"

"Young-ja's nickname for the boy who controls the garden," replied Sun-hee.

"I see. Is there anything else to translate?"

"Yes. That pile on the end of the table are articles for Gears, or I should say, Chou Sung-man. He wants to be a chemical engineer."

"How do you get current Soviet technical journals during a time of war?"

"The two doctors from Russia have arranged to have them shipped here," Sun-hee said. Then her head quickly lifted as two bits of information collided together in her mind.

I wonder if Max and Alek made a deal with General Park? Two girls are pregnant in exchange for the technical publications. I can't prove it so I mustn't tell anyone. Disgusting.

Cha Sue-dae took the pile of articles and began to translate. She helped to teach languages and was delighted at how bright Sun-hee's classmates were and how fast they learned.

When she wasn't helping with her grandson, Mrs. Moon could be found teaching the orphans how to read and write.

Ra Weon-kee's mother seemed out of place for a few days. She worked up the nerve to enter the boy's dorm, something no woman had done for almost nine months. She immediately began to scold the boys concerning their filthy room and bathroom. Over the next day, Mrs. Ra directed the cleanup. When a boy complained, Mrs. Ra said that children shouldn't protest to adults and men would not live like children.

A week after her mother arrived, Sun-hee went into labor. Sue-dae remained at her side the entire ten hours, as her coach and comforter, until a girl was born. Dr. Park looked in a couple of times, while a couple of fellow students oversaw the delivery. Mrs. Cha became the proudest person in camp, showing off her new daughter to everyone.

The next day, Sun-hee nursed her baby, her mother coaching her.

Mrs. Cha said, "I was thinking, it would be a good gesture to name your baby after Mrs. Pae's daughter who loaned you the dress. It would be nice to honor her."

"That would be a good name, Mother," said Sun-hee. "However, I want to name my baby after you." She looked down at the baby she held. "This is Cha Su-dae. Only we can change the character a bit to make it Su-dae instead of Sue-dae. I will name my next girl after Mrs. Pae's daughter."

"I am humbly honored," said Mrs. Cha bowing deeply.

30 — Harvest - October - November, 1951

Fall set in, and life at Yangseongso slowed to a boring routine. Injured people arrived sporadically. The students now had the medical knowledge needed to attend to most of the injuries. Kwang-ku and Chulsoon performed the surgeries when required. Max and Alek spent most of their time in Chongjin, where there were other Soviet doctors.

The harvest of the gardens was completed by the middle of October. The plants were turned over into the soil to become nutrients for next year.

The first snow arrived the last week of October, blanketing a compound that was well prepared for winter.

Chun-ja gave birth to a baby boy in early November. For the next week, Gen. Park was seen smoking cigars.

Yangseongso settled down into a quiet community for the upcoming winter.

***

It was a bright cold day on the twenty-seventh of November. Most of the students were eating lunch, the women with their babies squatted together. The boys sat in a group to themselves. A few planes flew over the camp, then more at different altitudes, interrupting conversations, but no one seemed concerned. The roar abated for a moment, then the shrill sound of a lone plane flying low caused everyone to pause. Later, those who looked for it said they could not see it until it was right above the camp.

"Bombs!" someone yelled.

The rumble of the jet mixed with screams of fright and yelling sent the students into chaos. Everyone reacted, diving in different directions to find cover. The bombs fell, fluffy white parachutes opened over each one, slowing the descent of the shiny metal objects onto the camp.

Sgt. Kua ran, waving her arms wildly, yelling, "Get away from the bombs. Take cover!" Then she dove behind her house. Soldiers pulled civilians behind buildings, crouched, and covered their heads. Sun-hee ran into the back of the kitchen with Eun-seong, both holding their babies tight.

The first cans landed in the American prisoner compound where

Americans were grabbing them and frolicking. More landed near the old student dorms and some on and around the House of Sanshin.

Mrs. Cha was in the common room of the House of Sanshin, and upon hearing the commotion, dropped to the floor. No explosions occurred, so she sneaked a peek out the window. There was a shiny can, attached to a fluttering parachute, a few meters in front of the steps. Having seen hundreds of cans like this among the garbage left by the American army, she walked out onto the porch. An American prisoner was yelling in English. "Don't be afraid. It is only food. The cans contain food." The man yelling had his arms tightly wrapped around one of the cans.

There was an awkward silence across the camp. The white parachutes fluttered in the light breeze attached to chest-size metal cans. Mrs. Cha took a few steps down the stairs and noticed Sgt. Kua sticking her head out from behind her house.

She yelled, "The American says the cans are food."

Sgt. Kua went into her house then came back out, holding her rifle. She looked across the camp at Capt. Reed, who was trying to open one of the cans. "Mrs. Cha, since you speak English. Come with me," she commanded and started running towards the prisoner compound.

As Sgt. Kua arrived at the prison gate, the guards came crawling out of a ditch, wet and muddy. Mrs. Cha, not used to running, arrived a moment later, panting. Each one of the prisoners held a can. Most were trying to open them. "Mrs. Cha, tell the prisoners to put the cans down," Sgt. Kua said as she pointed her rifle in their direction.

Mrs. Cha turned to the Americans and said in English, "Sergeant Kua says, put the cans down."

Capt. Reed stopped and looked at Mrs. Cha with a shocked expression on his face. Then he bent halfway over and placed the can on the ground in front of him. But the rest held their prize tightly.

"Mrs. Cha, tell Captain Reed the rest of the men need to put down the cans."

Mrs. Cha was a little more formal this time. "Sergeant Kua requests your men put down the cans."

"Men put down the cans. We need to reassure the Koreans the cans are food, not bombs," Capt. Reed commanded.

The men hesitated. "Put them down. Now!" he yelled. The men reluctantly dropped the cans.

"Ask him what is in the cans," said Sgt. Kua.

"What do the cans contain?" asked Mrs. Cha in English.

"They are a package of food and other items for prisoners of war. The American Air Force drops these to prisoners on holidays. If this is the last Thursday in November, then today is Thanksgiving, an American holiday."

Mrs. Cha translated to Sgt. Kua. Just then Lt. Rim ran up with more soldiers. Sgt. Kua explained the situation.

"Mrs. Cha, ask Captain Reed to bring his men over near him," said Lt. Rim.

"The Lieutenant would like you to gather your men," she said in English.

"Everyone over here, pronto," commanded Capt. Reed. The men hustled over.

"Mrs. Cha, tell the captain to open the can. You and Sergeant Kua take cover over there. If it explodes, they all die."

"Please open the can, Captain," she said and hurried to join Sgt Kua at the edge of a ditch where they laid down.

Capt. Reed knelt by the can. Using the twist can opener he had pried off the top, he took the wrapping off the edge. He lifted the lid and poured the contents into a pile on the ground.

"Not a bomb, Sergeant," said Lt. Rim. "Open the gate," he said to his men. "Mrs. Cha, can you read the labels and determine what is in those packages?" he asked over his shoulder.

"I may be able to, Lt. Rim," she said, taking small steps, her eyes watching the Americans standing over the items.

"Tell the prisoners to back up while you look over the packages."

She swallowed and glanced warily around at the prisoners. "I have been asked to read what is on the packages and would like you to step away."

The prisoners took a couple of steps back. Mrs. Cha knelt beside the pile. "Socks and underwear," she said in Korean, holding up two bundles and then dropping them. She started on a new pile. "K-rations which are food," she said, holding up two tins. She looked up at the Americans, saying in English, "Do Americans like this K-ration? I found them to be barely edible." She added the K-rations to the pile.

Capt. Reed replied, "They are the worst food, but they will keep a person alive."

"Yes, they kept me alive last winter," she said in English. Then she said in Korean, "Crackers, fruit preserves, a small brush, and another small brush." She held each item up and then dropped them on the new pile.

Mrs. Cha held up a thin, rectangle slab with a wrapper that said Hershey on it. "I do not know what this is, Lieutenant Rim."

"That is for you," said Capt. Reed. "You take the chocolate."

In Korean, Mrs. Cha said, "The captain says this is chocolate." And she dropped it on the new pile.

"Enough, Mrs. Cha," said Lt. Rim. "Is there anything looking like a weapon?"

She sorted through the remaining pile. "Maybe this?" she said, holding up a table knife, fork and spoon wrapped together with tape. The Lieutenant took the utensils and examined them. He glared at Capt. Reed for a moment, then he threw them on the new pile.

"Tell the American captain that each of his men may keep one can. Tell him to place the rest by the gate."

"Lieutenant Rim says each man can have one can. The rest are to be placed by the gate," Mrs. Cha said in English. She stood and began to walk away.

"Don't forget your chocolate," said Captain Reed.

Mrs. Cha turned to look at Capt. Reed and then at Lt. Rim. "He wants me to take the chocolate," she said to the lieutenant.

Capt. Reed turned to the men. "Get the chocolate out. Let us give it to the students who have taken such good care of us." Capt. Reed held the chocolate out to Mrs. Cha. The men ran to get the cans open.

"They want to give all the chocolate to the students," she said in Korean.

Lt. Rim had considered keeping all the extra cans for his men, but he was now reconsidering based on the actions of the prisoners. "You may take the chocolate, Mrs. Cha. Take it and give it to the students."

Mrs. Cha took the candy bar, saying, "Thank you, Captain Reed."

The Captain responded. "You know my name, but I have not had the pleasure of your introduction."

Mrs. Cha paused before saying, "I am Cha Sue-dae."

The men were handing chocolate bars to Capt. Reed. A couple of men brought extra cans and placed them by the gate.

"It is a pleasure to meet you, Cha Su-dae. Please call me Theodore."

"Theodore," she repeated and turned to walk out the gate.

"Wait, the rest of the chocolate." He grabbed the last couple of bars from his men. He took a couple of steps towards Mrs. Cha and held them out. "And promise me Sunny will get one of these. Tell her it is from Theodore."

"Sun-hee?" Mrs. Cha asked.

"Yes, Sunny. I have seen her across the camp, but I have not talked to her recently. I hope she is doing well," said Theodore. "Please give her one of these chocolates." He held out a stack of eight more bars.

Mrs. Cha, tongue-tied for a moment, looked over Theodore, then said, "Sun-hee is well." She took the candy, bowing slightly.

"How is her baby? Was it a boy or girl?" asked Theodore.

Mrs. Cha looked up at Theodore with a puzzled expression, then said, "Sun-hee had a baby girl. I have a lovely, healthy granddaughter." Then she turned and walked out the gate.

Theodore's eyes got wide as he watched Mrs. Cha walk away.

That evening, twenty-three girls shared the nine chocolate bars. For some, this was the first milk chocolate they had ever eaten. It was a real treat.

31 — Relationships - December, 1951 - January, 1952

On December fifteenth, a little over eighteen months after they had arrived, the last of the twenty-three girls gave birth. Max was the father of a baby boy.

The babies born during the year were all healthy. The orphan baby adopted by the girls, Yi Si-Ue, was doing well but still was the smallest baby her age.

Jung-hui handmade a calendar for 1952 and hung it in a place visible to Sgt. Kua, then she wrote her name on it.

That evening, Sgt. Kua gathered the students. "I noticed a new calendar. As before, I will add the boys on the days they are needed. You will find the rooms are much nicer in my new home."

"I am not ready," Jung-hui whispered to Choe-me, as she dipped her forehead on her arms which were wrapped around her knees. She was the first to give birth, and now the first for the next round.

"None of us will ever be ready," Choe-me whispered back. "We have talked about this day. We knew it was coming, which only makes it worse. I am glad he reverted to three days together unless we are irregular." She squeezed Jung-hui's shoulder.

Sgt. Kua walked over and wrote the name of Han Young-soo next to Suk Jung-hui's name on the calendar.

"Stone gets a new mate," said Young-ja to Sun-hee.

"I think he will do better this time," Sun-hee replied. "Still, he has not come to see or hold his daughter."

"He is taller and has developed some muscles. If you didn't tell me he spoke to you, I would believe that he couldn't talk," said Young-ja.

"The only time he has spoken to me since our daughter was born was to ask for help in translating Soviet journals on geology and mining," said Sun-hee.

"I'm lucky. Skinny Beast comes by to hold his son almost every day. But as soon as the baby fusses, even a little, he hands him back," said Young-ja.

***

The morning of December twenty-fifth was partly cloudy and bitterly cold. Two days of falling snow had left a white layer over thirty cm deep, covering the camp. The winds had shifted overnight, blowing out of Siberia and whipping the snow into drifts around the buildings. The students bundled up in Chinese woolens and began to line up for morning exercises. They heard a plane approach and everyone scanned the sky but did not see it until it blotted out the rising sun. By then, it was directly overhead. Cans attached to parachutes blew across the compound, catching on the fences.

Sgt. Kua commanded, "Back in line. Young-ja, it is your turn to lead exercises."

Young-ja, in her enthusiastic style, took over and made the exercises fun.

Sgt. Kua walked to where she could look through the fences and see the prisoner area.

The Americans came out of their hut, running to the two cans blown to the near fence by the wind. The men began to open them vigorously. Sgt. Kua stood watching the prisoners as Theodore yelled something that was half-drowned out by Young-ja and half by the wind.

Lt. Rim strolled along the fence, counting the cans on the other side. "More cans, Sergeant," he said, pointing towards the prisoner compound.

"The prisoners have opened two and are going through the contents."

With a quick motion to the soldiers with him, they began collecting the cans that the wind had blown into the fences. Gen. Park came up, bent over against the wind, and plowed his way through the snow. Lt. Rim leaned towards him, saying, "I estimate thirty-five cans, the same number as before."

"Do we need anything in these cans?" Gen. Park asked.

"We have no immediate use for the contents, sir."

"Open one," he said to a soldier. The soldier took a couple of minutes to open the can and dump out the contents into the snow. Gen. Park used his foot to move the items around. "Nothing we need or want lieutenant. Give two cans to each prisoner, store the rest. The cans may come in useful. Tell the prisoners to return the cans after they take the contents."

"Yes, sir," said Lt. Rim. He turned to the soldiers. "Place sixteen cans inside the prison gate." To Sgt. Kua, he said, "Bring Mrs. Cha." Then he leaned into the wind and plodded through the snow to the prison compound, his hands deep in his pockets.

The soldiers opened the gate and placed the cans a couple of meters inside. The American prisoners huddled in front of their hut, observing the Koreans soldiers. Mrs. Cha, wrapped up in a Chinese woolen suit, hands in her armpits, fought the wind to join the lieutenant.

Lt. Rim spoke loudly over the wind. "Tell the Americans they may keep the contents, then leave the empty cans by the gate."

Mrs. Cha yelled in English, "Captain Reed, when you have removed the contents, place all the empty cans by the gate."

Capt. Reed looked at Mrs. Cha with a broad smile while the other Americans slapped backs and shouted for joy. Capt. Reed's voice boomed out, "Thank you very much. This is a wonderful Christmas present. I will leave chocolate with the cans for you. Consider it a gift to my friends."

Mrs. Cha replied in a sharp voice. "We are not your friends. I will never be your friend. Do not give me a gift thinking you or any American will ever be my friend. I do not want your chocolate." She stomped away.

The lieutenant, hearing the tone in Mrs. Cha's voice asked, "What was just said?"

Sue-dae said as she walked away, "Captain Reed said he would leave chocolate with the cans for his friends. I told him we would never be his friends. I refused his gift."

***

A few days later, Sun-hee wrote her name on the calendar. Her mother watched, then asked, "Why did you put your name on the calendar two weeks from now?"

"My time has come to make another baby, Mother. Sgt. Kua will put the name of a boy next to mine as she has done here," Sun-hee said, pointing to the names on the calendar.

"You are going to allow Sgt. Kua to determine who you mate with?"

"General Park chooses the partners. Sergeant Kua is only the messenger."

"I do not like how you are forced to have children with different partners."

"I pledged to be loyal to the program. You pledged to be loyal. This is the price of our loyalty. I have a wonderful daughter. A year from now, I will have another child. We do not have options mother."

Sue-dae stood, frowning and glaring at the calendar. "I do not like it. But I have not liked many things. Life does not always provide good options." She took Sun-hee's hands and peered into her eyes. "Together, we will get through this."

The frigid days of early January went by slowly for Sun-hee. Each day, she took her child to the library, hiding herself in books. In the back of her mind, she thought about each of the boys. The only one she thought would be a problem was the skinny beast. The thought of him made her chuckle.

The day before Sun-hee was scheduled for the guesthouse, Sgt. Kua wrote Seok Yong-gak by her name on the calendar.

That evening her mother asked, "Do you know this boy?"

"His nickname is, Strategist. He has an excellent understanding of politics and what is happening in the world. He is tall and gangly and has a habit of talking with his hands. Having his child will be bearable."

***

While eating dinner the next day, Sue-dae said to Sun-hee, "I spoke with Seok Yong-gak."

Sun-hee's heart rate jumped, and she choked on the food in her mouth. She turned to scowl at her mother.

"We had a good discussion. We talked for over an hour," said Sue-dae, who then paused to take another bite.

Sun-hee forced a swallow, continuing her scowl while holding her chopsticks in midair.

Sue-dae swallowed and continued. "As you said, he is a very knowledgeable young man with an excellent grasp on politics. I am pleased with the choice. He is a nice boy and will make a good father for my next grandchild."

Sun-hee took a deep breath and sighed, letting her eyes close momentarily. She did not know what to say and did not want to continue talking about Yong-gak. They finished eating in silence.

That evening, as Sun-hee cleaned up, preparing herself for the guesthouse, Sue-dae, in tears, wrapped her arms around her saying, "If I thought we could survive, I would take you away."

Sun-hee, without tears, said, "If I thought I could survive, I would have left a long time ago." She held her mother tight. "Don't think about what is happening. We do what we must do to survive." Then she pushed her mother away and walked out of the dorm.

A minute after she entered the guesthouse, Yong-gak arrived. Sgt. Kua pointed to a door and bowed slightly. The rooms in the new guesthouse were larger, a mattress stuffed with wool lay against the far wall. Two candles on a table across from the mattress dimly lit the room.

Sun-hee's stomach was full of butterflies, unlike being with Stone when she was so exhausted and stressed. This time, she was more prepared. She backed up to a wall and crossed her arms over her chest.

Strategist broke the silence. "I am very honored to be paired with you, Sun-hee." One hand pointing to himself and one towards Sun-hee in typical Yong-gak fashion. "I feel this is like an alliance between two countries, benefiting neither in the short term, but producing long-lasting unity in the future." He bowed until his head was below his waist.

"You always speak in strategic terms, Yong-gak," Sun-hee said as a smile broke out. "I, too, am honored. What we produce will bind us together for the rest of our lives." She forced herself to take a couple of steps and blew out the candles.

After Yong-gak left, she stared at the dark.

I should feel more than anger. This place should not exist. But it is the best place. Mom is here. We are safe. Someday. Someway. I will change this.

She jumped up, dressed, and returned to the dorm.

The next two nights were similar. Yong-gak was polite and efficient. Sun-hee did what she had to do. Her mother cried enough for both.

32 — Ancestry - February, 1952 - June, 1953

In late February of 1952, almost twenty months after they arrived, Max and Alek received orders to return to the Soviet Union. The two took a bottle of vodka to Gen. Park. They gave a short toast, then Alek said, "You have a great experiment going here, General. I will look in on you in a few years to see how the children are progressing."

"We will keep your program secret," Max said as he shook Gen. Park's hand. "If Korea is to rebuild, it will begin here. The students are smart and committed. I am not sure they have enough fight in them to survive in the real world. If you can keep them safe, they have a chance."

The two Soviet doctors then said their goodbyes to the students. They gave gifts to the mothers of their children. "Teach him Russian," Alek said to his son's mother.

Max sought out Sun-hee. "You are a good doctor, and I was honored to work with you. I am amazed by how well you learned what to do in the operating room. Adversity is always a good teacher. I wish good fortune in your future."

"I will miss you, Max. Thank you for being a wonderful doctor," Sun-hee said, taking a deep bow.

The two Soviet doctors left, trudging through the snow, pulling a sled with their belongings towards Chongjin.

***

In March, after the weather began to warm, Gen. Park left to work near the front lines of the war. The demands of being the head of medicine kept him away until late spring.

Mrs. Cha and Mrs. Moon expanded the school, teaching Korean to everyone in the camp and many in the surrounding community.

With Lt. Rim's capable organizational skills, Yangseongso ran with high efficiency.

Sgt. Kua watched over the guesthouse. Other than that, she had little to do except knit booties and sweaters for the children. The boys, now developing more into men, took on doing exercises on their own. The girls were too busy with their children to participate.

Four times a year, Easter, Fourth of July, Thanksgiving and Christmas, an American plane dropped cans on the camp. Only a few times over the year was Mrs. Cha asked to translate.

Mr. Yun started a new complex of buildings where the original dorms were turning them into rooms for a school. A playground was added and the fence between the old dorms and the House of Sanshin was torn down.

***

Sun-hee's second child, a boy, was born in October of 1952. She named him Cha Hong-do after her father. Her mother was pleased. She breastfed Hong-do for two months before handing off the feeding to a wet nurse.

Within a month, she placed her name on the calendar. Two weeks later, she saw Kwang-ku's name next to hers.

"What do you think of this boy?" asked Sue-dae of her daughter.

"Kwang-ku is the best doctor in the camp. General Park has been absent so much, Kwang-ku, along with Chulsoon, has taken charge of the hospital."

"Do you like this boy?" asked Sue-dae.

"He is just another one of the boys, Mother. He will make a great father. Both of his children are healthy. He does have a pointy-head and a large nose. That is why Young-ja nicknamed him Unicorn."

"Someday, I must get to know this boy," said Sue-dae.

That afternoon, Young-ja came over to Sun-hee and said, "I see you get the Unicorn."

"Yes, I feel like I am looking forward to being with him," said Sun-hee. "He is a very nice man. Who do you think you will be paired up with next?"

"I hope anyone but Stone or Numbers. The Unicorn was the third I would not want," Young-ja said, smiling. "I cannot stand pointy heads."

That night, when Sun-hee entered the guest room, the Unicorn was lying on his side under a blanket, his head held up under his arm.

"Welcome, Sun-hee," he said with a nod. "I will try to make this easy for you. Tell me what would be best."

"Close your eyes while I get undressed," said Sun-hee. She watched him put his head into the mattress. She undressed and put on a robe before lifting the blanket and lying down beside him. "You can look now."

They stared at each other for a moment before the Unicorn broke the silence. "I find this very awkward. I admire you, Sun-hee. You're confident, and you have shown tremendous ability to work with patients. You have earned my respect. So here we are, two of the best doctors in this camp together, and I am hesitant to operate."

Sun-hee let the kind words sink in. They permeated the walls she had built up. She felt emotions rising and wanted to express her feelings, but they were too strong. She slammed her emotional doors shut.

"We are here to make a baby," she murmured rolling onto her back and closing her eyes.

The Unicorn held her gently for a few moments before acting. He was gentle and smooth, slipping out of the blanket when finished, then exiting quickly, leaving her alone.

She choked back her emotions, taking deep breathes. Unwilling to release her repressed feelings, she dressed and ran back to the dorm.

After her third night with the Unicorn, she realized how sensitive he was to her feelings. As he dressed, she said, "Thank you for understanding how difficult this is for me."

He bowed, saying, "It is I who is blessed to be with such a wonderful person." He opened the door and left.

Sun-hee laid still and closed her eyes.

I hope I am pregnant. My walls will not hold if we are together again.

A month later, her period did not arrive. Sun-hee believed she was now carrying the Unicorn's child.

***

With so many babies being born to different parents, the students felt there was a need to build pedigree charts to record the ancestry of each child back three generations. In this manner, they documented the parents, grandparents, and great-grandparents of each child born into the program. Many of the students knew their ancestry for more than three generations. When the project was complete, the students concluded that the newborn children were pure Koreans, except for the two boys fathered by the Russians. Yi Si-ue's pedigree was unknown.

Some of the girls studied the pedigree charts, looking for patterns, and arrived at another conclusion. The original forty-eight prizewinners were already the result of good breeding. All the students came from families who were, each in their own way, successful. Before the war, the parents owned businesses, large farms, or had university degrees. None of the students had parents who were unskilled laborers or in the military. When they shared this conclusion, it triggered a debate.

"From the pedigree charts, it is obvious that our family lines are superior," said Han Soo-hy.

"My parents raised me to be in the ruling class. I am here because I have the proper manners of a noble person," said Joo-yun.

"When I think of each of the boys, I see them by their specialty as a result of education. Numbers, Strategist, Hammer, and even Stinky have mastered a subject," added Eun-seong. "The general chose them because of their ability to learn."

"The ability to learn is hereditary," stated Soo-hy.

"Hereditary only plays a role when your parents are noble. They pass on honorable behavior to their children. My parents raised me to be who I am," said Joo-yun.

Young-ja went to a blackboard and divided it into three parts. She labeled one Heredity, a second Behavior Modification, and the third Education.

"Put your references on the board in the right category so we can refer to them as we talk," she instructed.

Over the next week, the students perused the literature in the library and found many examples of all three being influential in the lives of talented people.

Eun-seong wrote a heading on another blackboard*: tteusbakk-ui il.* She said, "The fact that serendipity has brought us here together, and the chance occurrence of events that are shaping our lives, is also an influence."

After days of discussion, there was no consensus on whether they won the prize as a result of heredity, their education, their upbringing, or just by chance.

Sun-hee avoided participating in the debate until Choe-me sat down beside her and asked, "What do you think?"

"Probably all four," replied Sun-hee. "Heredity makes a capable person, education gives them a specialty, and behavior guides them in how to use it. Serendipity brings the opportunity to utilize your talents."

"My parents were uneducated farmers and not noble. Am I here only by chance?" questioned Choe-me.

"You're here because you are the prettiest girl in the world. And also the nicest," said Sun-hee with a broad smile.

***

One day, during the second week of April 1953, a bundle of journals and papers arrived from the Soviet Union. Strategist went through them, grabbing the newspapers and heading to a room on the second floor where he studied. A few minutes later, he came out and shouted to everyone, "Joseph Stalin has died."

At lunch, Sun-hee asked Strategist, "Do you think anything will change in the Soviet Union now that Stalin is dead?"

"One editorial I read speculates that there will be less support for the war in Korea as Stalin was firmly behind keeping the United States out."

"What affect will that have on the war?"

"The Chinese and the Americans are discussing the terms of a cease-fire. I fear that the unification of Korea is impossible. There will be two Koreas, one controlled by the United States and one controlled by China," Strategist concluded with his hands outstretched.

On the way back to the dorm after lunch, Eun-seong asked, "Do you think the Chinese will ever come to the camp?"

"We are out of the way. They may never arrive and put a stop to Park's plan."

A month later, the last girl gave birth to her second child. The total number of children was now forty-eight, including Yi Se-ue and one set of identical twins. Babies and toddlers were everywhere in the House of Sanshin.

***

The discussion of genetics came to the forefront again by a journal received in late May of 1953. An article, translated into Russian from a British science journal, was on the structure of a molecule called deoxyribonucleic acid. James Watson and Francis Crick, the authors, claimed this molecule contained the code for all the human traits. Most of the students read it, trying to understand how one molecule could determine their heredity.

33 — Return - August, 1953

One day, near the end of July, Sun-hee was at her regular table in the library when a shout rang out. "General Park is here and wants to meet with us."

Sun-hee, about eight months pregnant, gathered up her son while her mother picked up her daughter. They covered themselves and walked as quickly as they could on the rocky paths, avoiding the mud. When they arrived at the House of Sanshin, Sue-dae took the children inside. Sun-hee took a position in the formation next to Joo-yun, who was holding her newborn.

"How are you and your new baby?" asked Sun-hee.

"My baby is fine," said Joo-yun. "I have not had enough sleep. I feel fat and cannot seem to stop crying. Young-ja thinks I am afflicted with the melancholy that comes after childbirth."

"What do you think, Joo-yun?"

"I am so angry about being here," she said, gritting her teeth. "I just want to leave and live my own life."

Eun-seong turned and gave a, "Shhhh," to Joo-yun.

"Not so loud. Here comes General Park," said Sun-hee as she stood at attention.

Gen. Park strode up with a smile on his face. He stood at attention and said, "The Americans and Chinese have agreed to a cease-fire. The Chinese have given up on defeating the Americans. The Americans are happy to have the fighting end."

Sun-hee shot her arms up over her head. Others cheered and hugged. She looked at Joo-yun, who had her hands over her face, crying. She wrapped her arms around her while Eun-seong did the same.

Sun-hee closed her own eyes.

The war is over. There will be no more wounded soldiers. There will be no more women and children arriving with damaged bodies.

Images of the dead, who she had carried to the burial pit, sped through her mind.

"Attention!" commanded Sgt. Kua. Sun-hee and the others lept back in line.

Gen. Park held his hands up towards the students. When they were quiet, he brought his hands down and said, "I need to leave for

Pyongyang. The city is in ruins, and the hospital needs to be rebuilt. I will be helping to restore a functioning government."

"Keep on doing what you have been doing. Lieutenant Rim provides me updates on the status here at Yangseongso. I am extremely pleased with the reports he sends. I will return as soon as I can. You are very important to the country." Then he turned and left.

Everyone was in a festive mood. The stress of the war vanished. Laughter and smiling faces filled the House of Sanshin. For the first time since Park's program started, Sun-hee enjoyed being at the camp. Even the monsoon rains did not dampen spirits.

***

One evening, in mid-August, Sun-hee asked her mother, "Have you been asked to tell the American prisoners the war is over?"

"No. I do not think the Americans know," said Mrs. Cha. "I have been wondering what will happen to them. They have been no trouble at all."

"Some tried to escape soon after they were captured," said Sun-hee. "Five of them were killed."

"You have never told me the story of the escape. What happened?"

Sun-hee proceeded to tell her mother about the escape. She included all the details but left out how serious her injuries were.

Mrs. Cha listened intently, commenting now and then. When Sun-hee finished, Mrs. Cha said, "Maybe we should let them go. They can find their way home from here."

***

Gen. Park returned near the end of August. He called together Lt. Rim, Sgt. Kua and Sgt. Jo. "We have been ordered to transport the prisoners to the border and hand them over to the Americans. Lieutenant, we need transportation and supplies. Sergeants, you will go along to be in charge. I think six soldiers will be able to guard the prisoners for a few days. Mrs. Cha will go along as an interpreter."

That evening, Sgt. Kua explained to Mrs. Cha that she would help return the prisoners to the border. It would be a long trip, but nothing like the trip she took to get to the camp.

After they put the children to bed, Mrs. Cha said to Sun-hee, "Sgt, Kua told me that I will be part of a group taking the prisoners to the border."

"They are the lucky ones, Mother. Too many were unlucky. There always needs to be some survivors to remember those who died."

"I will see them safely to the border and return. Jin-taek will be coming. He will not let anything happen to me." They laid down and held hands as they fell asleep.

***

Two days later, at the break of dawn, a bus arrived at the camp. Sgt. Kua came to get Mrs. Cha. They walked to the prisoner compound, enjoying the chill of the morning air. The brisk walk was refreshing. Mrs.

Cha thought, *I must make sure I drink lots of water; It will be hot today.* They arrived at the prisoner compound, and Lt. Rim had soldiers open the gate.

"Tell them to line up," said Lt. Rim to Mrs. Cha.

Mrs. Cha yelled out, "Captain Reed, please come out and have your men line up."

"Get lined up men," Capt. Reed said to the other prisoners. He stood in front of them, eyes fixed on Mrs. Cha. "I am pleased to see you again, Mrs. Cha. It has been a long time since we talked." Mrs. Cha stayed silent.

The American uniforms were in tatters. Capt. Reed always made sure they were cleanly shaven and groomed

The lieutenant began, "Tell the Americans it is time to leave. We will bind their hands and legs for our safety and their safety. If they look like they are free, they may be shot."

Mrs. Cha translated into English, "The time has come for you Americans to leave. We must bind your legs and hands for the safety of yourselves and others. Any American seen in Korea might be shot. Please cooperate. You are going home."

The American prisoners cheered, gave each other hugs, and a couple of them had tears in their eyes. They lined up and cooperated while soldiers bound the hands together in front of each prisoner. The feet were bound loosely, allowing them to walk with short strides.

Once completed, Lt. Rim said, "Have them follow me single file." Mrs. Cha passed on the instruction.

They walked out of the fences which had held them prisoner for thirty-three months. No chance to harvest the crops they had worked on all summer. This year, the garden was looking better than ever.

Captain Reed wondered, *Will the Koreans discover my message, 9 OK?. It doesn't matter. We are getting out of here.*

Sgt. Jo stood by the door of the bus with a clipboard. Mrs. Cha stopped near the back and stared. The paint on the bus was faded, there were many dents on the sides, one front fender was missing, and the tires were bald. A few of the windows were missing and others were cracked.

Sue-dae realized, *This is the same bus Sun-hee boarded to take the test so long ago.*

The remains of the five Americans killed at the camp had been dug up, placed in body bags supplied by the red cross, and stacked carefully next to the last row of seats. Food and supplies took up the next two rows of seats from the back.

Two men rolled a fifty-gallon barrels of fuel up a ramp and into the rear of the bus. As the barrel was almost in the door, one of the bags of remains shifted, landing on the arm of the man moving the barrel. He jerked. His grip slipped. The barrel fell. The man on the outside tried to hold the barrel, but it was too heavy, and he lost his grip, jumping aside. The barrel of fuel rolled down the side of the ramp and into the legs of Mrs. Cha. She shrieked as she fell. The barrel came to rest on top of her.

Theodore was moving before the barrel hit Mrs. Cha. "Look out!" he yelled as he shuffled over and grabbed the barrel. Two other Americans seized the other end of the barrel, and the three of them lifted it off Mrs. Cha, setting it on end. Mrs. Cha, the wind knocked out of her initially, caught a breath and let out a blood-curdling scream.

Sgt. Kua dropped to her knees beside Mrs. Cha and held her head as she screamed.

Lt. Rim yelled, "Someone, run and get a doctor."

Jin-taek ran to kneel next to Mrs. Cha and held her oddly bent leg.

Lt. Rim yelled, "Get on the bus." To Capt. Reed, while pointing towards the bus.

Theodore got the idea and told his men, "Get on the bus and be still!" He followed them on then hung his head out a window to watch the commotion.

A couple of minutes later, Kwang-ku came running up in a full sprint. He quickly checked the breathing and pulse of Mrs. Cha. Then he examined her leg. Choe-me arrived followed by Gen. Park. "A dislocated knee and ligament damage, General," Kwang-ku said. "It can be repaired but will take a long time to heal."

By the time they got Mrs. Cha on a stretcher, she had caught her breath and calmed down. Word had gotten to the dorm, and most of the students had raced over to see if they could help. Sun-hee, waddling as fast as she could, was one of the last to arrive. She pushed her way through to get to her mother. "Oh, Mother," Sun-hee cried as she held her mother in her arms.

"Get her to the hospital," said Gen. Park. Four of the boys grabbed the handles of the stretcher and walked carefully to the hospital. Sun-hee took her mother's hand, comforting her as they went.

At the hospital, Kwang-ku gave Mrs. Cha a shot of morphine and went to work on her leg. Eun-seong and Choe-me held Sun-hee, easing her away to let the doctors work. Gen. Park paced around the room.

A few minutes later, the morphine had taken effect, and Mrs. Cha said, "I will be fine, Sun-hee. Kwang-ku will take care of me."

Gen. Park stomped out of the hospital in a rage and tramped to the gate. By the time he arrived, the soldiers had maneuvered the wayward barrel into the back of the bus.

Sgt. Jo was standing in the bus, guarding the Americans.

Lt. Rim had the two men responsible for the accident sitting on the ground. He had chewed them out in all the ways he could think of and was now repeating the insults.

Sgt. Kua was standing alongside the bus with her hands on her hips.

"Explain to me how this could happen," Gen. Park yelled.

Sgt Kua stood at attention and replied, "Those two men were loading the barrel onto the bus and it got away from them. It rolled off the ramp into Mrs. Cha. Once they lost it, there was nothing anyone could do. She was standing in the wrong place."

Gen. Park paused for a moment before saying, "Sergeant, go get Sun-hee. Have her say goodbye to her mother and help her get what she needs for the trip."

"Yes, sir!" she replied, starting into a trot.

"Lieutenant! Those two men will be cleaning privies until Mrs. Cha's leg heals."

"Yes, sir! Gladly, sir," he said. Then he turned to the two men and barked, "You heard the General, move!" The two men jumped up and sprinted away.

Gen. Park started pacing along the bus. He went to the driver who was smoking a cigarette. "Do you have more of those smokes?" he asked.

"Yes, sir," the driver said as he pulled one out, handing it and his butt to the general.

The general resumed pacing. He was on his third cigarette by the time Sgt. Kua and Sun-hee walked up.

"Sun-hee, this will be a long trip. Are you up for it?" he asked.

"Yes, sir," she said, wondering if she truly was up for the trip and what the journey would entail.

"Keep her safe, Sergeant.," he yelled at Sgt. Jo, who saluted.

The seven American privates occupied four seats in the middle of the bus. Jeremy and Theodore had seats to themselves. Jin-taek took the seat in front of Jeremy. Kua and the other soldiers were behind the driver. This left the seat in front of Theodore open.

Sun-hee sat, looked out through a cracked window, put her hands around her belly, and looked straight ahead.

The door closed, the bus roared to life with a cloud of smoke out of the exhaust, causing Gen. Park to take a few steps back. With a loud grinding of the gears and a lurch, the bus moved off. The warmth of the morning sun poured through the windows as the bus headed over the mountain pass.

"How is your mother?" asked Theodore as the bus began to climb towards the pass. "I feel so bad about what happened."

"She has a dislocated knee, Theodore," said Sun-hee. "She received some morphine and is having it treated. Her knee will take months to heal."

"I'm sorry she was injured," said Theodore.

"Are you finally sorry a Korean person is injured? How many injured Koreans does it take for you to feel sorry?" asked Sun-hee.

"I'm just trying to offer my condolences to you…for your mother Sunny," said Theodore in an appeasing tone. "Except for Sergeant Peterson, excuse me, Insect Peterson, I have not personally seen anyone killed or injured in this war. I won't count Jeremy and myself."

"I have seen too many of the injured and dead. Insect Peterson is just one of many faces I see before falling asleep each night."

"I guess this camp isolated me from the war," said Theodore.

"From the stories I have heard, Theodore, I also have been isolated. As a Russian doctor said, 'Only the fortunate return from war.'"

"I must count myself as one of the fortunate," said Theodore as he stared at the floor.

***

The drive to the southern border was slow and rough. The bus often took detours around destroyed bridges and bombed-out portions of roads, hindering their journey. It was dusty on the dry days and sloppy on the rainy ones. But always a bumpy, rough ride. For Sun-hee, the movement became more miserable with the passing of every hour.

She spent her time looking out the window, watching the ruined and bombed countryside pass by.

She thought, *What a terrible waste. For what? Korea gained nothing.*

The American privates continuously talked about what they would do when they got home. Mostly it was about the food they were going to eat or the girls they wanted to see. Theodore, Jeremy, and Abraham sat quietly.

Every few hours, the bus would stop. The driver would open the hood to add oil, fuel, and water. This gave them all a chance to stretch and take care of bodily functions. There was no way to cook. Only prepared foods were available. The contents in the extra cans from the holiday drops were on the bus for the prisoners. They ate the K-rations.

On the third day, they passed through Hamhung. Not a single building was standing. People stood around makeshift tents and lean-tos erected in the ruins. Every person looked dirty and hungry. It had been over three years since she had come here to take a test. Now the town was rubble.

Sun-hee felt blessed to have been at the camp. Now her friends, her children, her mother, her whole life was there. She had eaten well and had a safe place to live while her country was mangled beyond recognition. Yangseongso was an isolated place in a ruined nation, a haven, but only for the students and now their children. Viewing the devastation soured her stomach. She could not eat and wanted to curl up in a ball and hide.

On the afternoon of the sixth day, the bus arrived at Pyonggang, a city near the southern border. Fierce winds blew threatening clouds across the sky. They checked in at a North Korean military camp at the south edge of town. Red Cross workers came aboard the bus. They checked off the names, and then one asked in broken Korean, "Five American soldiers. Deceased. Where are they?"

Sgt. Kua pointed to the back row of the bus. "Those men are in the body bags."

The Red Cross worker checked the five names off and flipped to the next page and pointed, "Forty-three South Korean Army Prisoners. Where are they?"

"We have never had a South Korean Prisoner," replied Sgt. Kua.

"These papers say that there were South Koreans," he said, pointing at the paper.

Sgt. Kua looked perplexed. She turned to Sun-hee, "Can you tell me what the list says?"

Sun-hee looked at the Red Cross worker and said in English, "May I read what is on the list?"

"You can speak and read English?" the man said in surprise.

"Yes."

The man held the clipboard so that Sun-hee could read the second page. There was a list of Korean men. She took the clipboard and released the paper so she could read the top. It said that the following men were held in a prison camp in Chongjin.

"We were at a hospital a few kilometers outside of Chongjin. I have no knowledge of the South Koreans in the city," Sun-hee said.

"We cannot check off the South Korean men." He took the clipboard back and wrote missing on the pages with the South Korean names. The man walked down the aisle and handed the clipboard to Sgt. Kua and said, "Give this to the Americans at the checkpoint."

The bus continued another couple of kilometers, coming to a line scratched across the road. Sgt. Kua told the driver to stop before the bus reached the border. About twenty meters on the other side of the line were two American tanks. American and South Korean soldiers manned gun emplacements, and a truck was about fifty meters beyond the heavy armor.

Sgt. Kua stepped out of the bus, motioning for Sun-hee to join her. Sgt. Jo stepped off and stayed by the door.

Sgt Kua put her face close to Sun-hee. "I do not like this. There are no North Koreans here. I want you to listen and make sure what I say is translated properly. Let me know if it is not."

Then she approached a South Korean soldier who seemed to be waiting for her on the south side of the line. She handed him the clipboard with a polite bow, saying, "I am Sergeant Kua."

"I am Lieutenant Loo. Where are you from?" he asked while examining the papers.

"A hospital in the north, near Chongjin," replied Sgt. Kua.

"Where are the South Korean Prisoners?" demanded Lt. Loo.

"We have brought fourteen American prisoners, nine alive."

"How many South Korean Prisoners?" Lt. Loo said strongly.

"We do not have any South Korean Prisoners."

"How many remains of prisoners did you bring?"

"We have brought remains of five Americans."

"What did you do with the South Korean soldiers?"

"We have never held prisoners from South Korea."

Lt. Loo held up the clipboard. "This says you had forty-three of my countrymen. What did you do with them?"

"I have no knowledge of those soldiers."

Lieutenant Loo turned to the American commander and said in English, "Major Johnson, they killed five Americans on the way here, nine remain alive. They killed all South Koreans and left them along the road. These are war criminals! We must arrest them."

Sun-hee brushed her blowing hair off her face, watching the reactions of the American in charge.

The American Major was glaring in her direction. "Have the bus come over, and we will unload the Americans. With our men safe, we will arrest the others."

"He lies, Sgt. Kua," whispered Sun-hee. "We must stay here. Do not move."

Lt. Loo began waving his arm and yelling, "Move the bus ahead and unload the Americans. Move. Go! Go!"

Sun-hee walked back to the bus and leaned over to whisper in Jin-taek's ear, "Do not move the bus. They want to arrest us."

Jin-taek climbed into the bus, reached for the keys, and shut off the engine. The bus driver struggled with him for a moment before Jin-taek threw the keys to the back of the bus.

Lt. Loo ran to the bus, yelling in the door at the bus driver to move the bus to the south.

"We will not move the bus," Sgt. Kua said, as she took up a stance between the bus and the border and put her hands on her hips.

Lt. Loo fast-walked to Sgt. Kua, grabbed her, and threw her to the ground. All the rifles went up, and the South Korean soldiers ran to surround the bus. The North Korean soldiers pointed their weapons out the windows. Lt. Loo yelled louder, "We will open fire if you do not move the bus."

Sun-hee could hear Theodore and the almost free prisoners yelling, "Don't shoot! Don't shoot."

Sun-hee stood near the door of the bus, turning around to look at the uproar. Then she turned and started to walk, well more of a pregnant waddle, towards the American Major. Two American soldiers moved in front of the commander and pointed their rifles at Sun-hee. Sun-hee walked up to them and said calmly in English, "I must speak with you, Major Johnson." Then she looked at the rifles pointed at her chest, "Will you shoot a pregnant girl? Americans are supposed to be better than that."

"How do you know my name and rank?" Major Johnson asked.

"Lieutenant Loo called you Major Johnson a moment ago," she replied.

The American Major said, "Back away men, she poses no threat."

She looked up at the Major and said, "We have brought you nine Americans. They are in good condition. They were treated well at our hospital in the north. Two-and-a-half-years ago, five men died trying to escape. They were doing their duty by trying to escape. Their remains are on the bus. There were never any South Korean prisoners at our hospital. Captain Reed will verify what I say when you talk to him." She paused, looking for a reaction.

Getting none, she said, "The bus will not move. I will go get the Americans." She turned and walked by Sgt. Kua, held on the ground by Lt. Loo's foot and rifle. She got on the bus, told the driver not to move as he sat with his hands in the air.

As she untied Capt. Reed's hands, she said, "The South Koreans want to arrest us and charge us with war crimes. Will you come and tell Major Johnson we are not criminals?"

"I will be honest with the Major," replied Theodore.

Sun-hee led him off the bus. Guns still held ready by both sides. Lt. Loo continued to yell for the driver to move the bus but took his foot off Sgt. Kua to follow Sun-hee and Theodore.

As Sun-hee approached the Major, American soldiers again aimed their rifles at Sun-hee. She ignored them and stopped a meter from the major.

Capt. Reed stepped up to her left and saluted. "I am Captain Reed, U.S Air force. Have your men stand down. These North Koreans have treated us well. There is no crime here."

"Welcome, Captain Reed," said Maj. Johnson. "Were there any South Korean soldiers at your POW camp?"

"I have not seen a South Korean soldier before today, sir. I was shot down thirty-three months ago and have been treated fairly by this…" he looks at Sun-hee, "…this doctor and the North Koreans."

"What about the five dead, Captain?"

"They died in a foolish escape attempt. I hold Sergeant Peterson, who is one of the dead, responsible for their deaths."

"Stand down, men!" Maj. Johnson yelled. The Americans lowered their rifles, but the South Korean soldiers did not. He yelled again, "Lt. Loo! Have your men lower their weapons."

Lt. Loo pushed Sun-hee aside, almost knocking her down, while saying, "These people are criminals. We must arrest them for war crimes."

Capt. Reed, seeing Lt. Loo shove Sun-hee, turned and decked Lt. Loo with a quick left hand to the jaw. "I will not tolerate any disrespect to Sunny. She has shown me respect and deserves respect herself," he said, standing over the Korean soldier.

Sun-hee turned and yelled forcefully in Korean, "Everyone put your guns down. There will be no bloodshed today." Everyone looked at her and slowly lowered their guns.

"Get Lieutenant Loo out of here," Maj. Johnson said to his men. The two Americans who had been holding their rifles on Sun-hee grabbed the unconscious soldier and dragged him away.

"Get your men off the bus, Captain," said Major Johnson. Then to Sun-hee, he said, "That is the bravest thing I have seen anyone do in this whole goddamn war. You have earned my respect, Sunny. That is your name, Sunny?"

"I am Lieutenant Cha Sun-hee," she replied, emphasizing each syllable. "Captain Reed calls me Sunny." She turned and walked back to the bus.

Sgt Kua and Jin-taek untied the Americans, releasing them from captivity.

Capt. Reed stood outside the bus shaking the men's hands as they exited. Sun-hee noticed he was holding his left arm in front of him. "Are you injured, Theodore?" she said. "Let me look at it." She took his arm in her hand. "You have broken your hand again. Thank you for standing up for me." Then she called into the bus, "Hand out the first aid kit."

"Lieutenant Loo was an ass-hole Sunny. He got what he asked for."

"Is he a dirt-hitting rectum?" Sun-hee asked.

Theodore laughed as he held out his hand to Sun-hee.

Jin-taek stepped out with the first aid kit and held it open.

Sun-hee chuckled as she wrapped a bandage around Theodore's hand. She picked up a stick and wrapped it in the dressing. "This will keep the hand still until you get to an American hospital."

The American soldiers respectfully took the remains of their comrades off the bus and carried them across the border. A photographer, standing behind Maj. Johnson, took pictures of each man as they walked across. Capt. Reed was last.

Maj. Johnson asked the photographer, "Did you get a photo of the pregnant girl?"

"Yes, sir, when she was next to the bus with the Captain."

"Make a note. Her name is Sun-hee."

"Yes, sir." The Photographer took a notepad from his pocket and wrote down, Sunny by the bus.

Jin-taek helped Sun-hee climb onto the bus. He gave her a big smile. Sun-hee checked on Sgt. Kua, who was holding her shoulder.

"Just a bruise, Lieutenant Cha. I am fine."

Sun-hee went to sit down in her seat. It was covered with chocolate bars. She pushed them onto the floor and sat down. She looked out the cracked window and put her hands on her belly, feeling her baby kick. The bus driver ground the gears into reverse, and with a lurch, the bus began to back up and turn around. They started the trip home.

They stopped again at the North Korean camp. Sgt. Kua filed her report, warning about the South Koreans trying to accuse North Koreans of war crimes. They filled the bus and the fifty-gallon barrels with fuel, restocked the food supplies, and drove off into the night.

Sun-hee had Jin-taek spread out blankets on the floor. She laid down and stayed there for the return trip. Jin-taek was always there to help her up when they stopped to refuel.

***

The sunset was full of oranges and reds on the seventh day of the return trip. The bus came to a stop at the gates of Yangseongso. Sun-hee rose from the floor to see all her fellow students, Lt. Rim, and Gen. Park there to greet the bus.

Sun-hee walked with Eun-seong and Young-ja at her side to the hospital. Young-ja was full of questions.

"Where was the prisoner exchange? Why did it take so long? How are you feeling? Did you see the capital? Are you happy or sad the prisoners are gone? You got to go out of the camp. Did you feel free?"

Sun-hee was glad to be free of all the questions and ecstatic to see her mother. They exchanged a warm hug. Sun-hee was relieved that her mother was in good spirits, and Mrs. Cha was thankful that her daughter returned safely. Mrs. Cha could see the exhaustion in her daughter's face and insisted that Sun-hee get some rest.

Eun-seong escorted her to the dorm. Sun-hee gathered some clean clothes and headed for the shower. When she entered the privy, she saw that her friends had filled the bath with hot water.

Sun-hee stepped into the tub, and with help, sat down. She leaned back and let the warmth wash over her body. She looked at her large, round tummy protruding out of the water and felt a kick. She absorbed the love of her friends hovering over her, inquiring about the trip.

"We survived," she said. "We survived." She closed her eyes.

We survived.

Eun-seong knelt beside the tub and washed the dust out of Sun-hee's hair, turning the water brown.

Choe-me came bounding in with a bag and announced, "Jin-Taek brought us chocolate. Enough for everyone!"

Sun-hee took a bite of the milk chocolate, laid her head back as it melted in her mouth, and allowed her dam to break. The emotions of the last three years flooded out in a stream of tears.

34 — Photos - Late August, 1953

"This way, Captain," said a corporal. "We have a truck to take you and your men to the airstrip. You'll be in Japan in a couple of hours."

Capt. Reed turned to look at the bus—in which he had ridden across Korea—drive away.

Long ride home for a girl in her condition. I hope she makes it back to the camp before she delivers.

He joined the men who had been captive with him for over two-and-a-half-years. They stood at attention and saluted as the remains of five men were placed carefully inside the canvas-covered bed of the truck.

The nine survivors climbed into another truck. Before Theodore sat, he said, "Men, it has been an honor to have you as companions during this ordeal. You are good men. I am glad you are safe and can return home."

"Sit down, Theo, and enjoy the ride," said Jeremy. "I am glad to be going back to what I remember. I will easily forget this place, especially since I can't remember shit!" The truck spun its tires in the mud before pitching ahead.

"You get some more blood on your hands, Theo?" asked one of the soldiers.

"I hit the South Korean asshole who almost got everyone shot," said Theodore as he examined his bandaged hand.

Within an hour, the former prisoners were on a transport plane and out of Korea.

Theodore slept on the plane ride to Yokota Air Base outside of Tokyo. Then he sat quietly on the short trip to the hospital to be examined. The long bus trip across Korea had drained him. The responsibility of being the officer in charge and keeping the men's morale up was a never-ending challenge. The only things he had returned with were the clothes on his back, his honor, and his fellow prisoners. Now, with the weight of command off his shoulders, he felt tired and wanted to find a soft bed and sleep for days.

Theodore let his eyes close while the doctors examined him head to foot. His hand would need to be operated on to reset the broken bones. For now, they put it into a cast. The doctors said his ankle had healed and would be fine. When they finished checking him out, he got some new clothes.

He walked out of the examination room and encountered Jeremy sitting in a wheelchair. "Jeremy, what's the good word?"

"They are going to keep me here to check out my head," said Jeremy. "Otherwise, the doctor said I was in the best condition of any returning POW he had seen."

"Great to hear that," said Theodore. "I bet they are saying that to make us feel good."

"No, it is true," said a voice behind him. He turned to see a man in a white coat, gray hair, and an expression conveying, I am in charge. "I have the reports on the enlisted men under your command right here, Captain Reed," he said, holding up a fist full of folders. "Except for the hand injuries, they are all in excellent condition. Whatever you did to keep these men so well treated, is to be commended."

"Nothing I did. We were lucky to have a hospital as a host."

"Considering the poor condition most returning POWs are in, you and your men were well-off. All the men that came in with you, except for Captain McLeod here, have walked out already. They are the first men I released the day they arrived. They are on their way to catch a boat back home. Jeremy's legs were treated as well as we could have treated them here. The specialists will check out his head tomorrow."

"Captain Reed, a driver is here for you," said a male orderly who had walked towards them from the front door.

Captain Reed looked past the orderly and saw a man down the corridor by the front door, standing patiently. He turned to Jeremy and stuck out his hand. "I'll be back soon to check up on you, partner. I won't leave without you."

"Go home to your wife. She's probably not as tired of your ugly mug as I am," said Jeremy squeezing Theodore's hand.

Theodore fought back his tears, let go of Jeremy's hand, and walked to the door. "I'm Captain Reed. Where are we going?" he said to the driver.

"Headquarters, sir," he said as he held the door and motioned to a jeep outside.

The trip took a few minutes, but it gave Theodore a moment to reflect. He had been lucky. The Fargo Fleabag motel was not the best place to spend three years, but it was the best place in Korea to survive and keep the men with him safe.

The driver escorted him inside headquarters, introduced him to a clerk who looked at a clipboard, then said, "Take him to the basement, room nine."

Room nine was a small room, maybe ten feet square, containing a single table and two chairs. Captain Reed stopped in the doorway. A voice behind him and said, "Captain Reed, I am Walter Anderson. Please take a seat."

Mr. Anderson sat across from him, placing a pad of paper on the table. "Captain Reed, I am tasked with learning as much as we can about North Korea. What I must ask is that you tell me as much about your captivity as you can remember."

Over the next hour, Theodore recounted everything he could about the camp and the people stationed there. He told of the escape attempt and interrogations. Mr. Anderson seemed to be most interested in the doctor in charge, who had killed Sergeant Peterson, and the lieutenant who ran the camp. When Theodore mentioned Sunny and her mother, he noticed Mr. Anderson did not even write down their names.

"If you should remember anything further about the doctor or the Lieutenant, please write them down and forward the information to me." He handed Capt. Reed a card with his contact information, and he left.

Theodore got up and started down the hall, not knowing where he was going. A man he recognized approached and passed him.

"Hi George," Theodore said as the man went by.

The man stopped. "Do I know you?"

"You used to, unless my memory has faded over the last three years," said Theodore.

The man paused for a moment, his face contorted. "You look like someone, but he is...did you just get back from North Korea?"

"Yes," said Theodore.

"Theo?" George said, grabbing Theodore by the shoulders. "Theo. Theo! My God, it is good to see you! You were one of the first pilots we lost. Damn, I am glad you're back!"

They were shaking hands when a head peeked out of a room down the hall. "Did I hear Theodore is back?" said Garrett Stallings.

"Yeah, Garrett, Theo is back," said George.

"Man, I'm glad you made it back, Theodore. You are looking well," said Garrett. "I knew you were okay. Did all nine of you get out?"

"Yes, we are all here," said Theodore.

"Let me shake your hand. I process the photos for the far north and have been watching you since you were shot down. Hey, I have a photograph you might be interested in," said Garrett. "Come on in, and I will pull it out."

Theodore and George walked into Garrett's workplace, a sizeable room with file cabinets along the walls, and a large table in the center. Pictures hung from the walls and covered the table. Garrett looked through a file drawer.

"Here it is." He pulled out a folder and opened it. "The first one is just after you were shot down." He handed Theodore a photo, showing the outline of two men in flight suits lying among rocks. Korean soldiers were pointing rifles at them.

What caught Theodore's eye was the next photograph in the folder. It was a picture of Sunny looking straight at the camera.

"Sunny!" he said, reaching for the image. "This is the girl who captured me. She stood on a rock over me and said, 'shoot me or surrender.'"

"Sunny…Sunny. That name came up today," Garrett said while sorting through the images on his table. "Here it is. Is that you with your back to the camera?" He held up a photo of Captain Reed and Sunny standing next to a bus.

Theodore took the photo and looked it over. "She diffused a real nasty situation and then took the time to bandage my hand. An amazing kid," he said, then paused, swallowing hard. "Garrett, can I have these photos of Sunny?"

"Yah sure," said Garrett. "Here is another one you might want." He took the thumbtacks holding a photo to the wall and handed it to Theo. It showed a garden laid out with the message, 9-OK.

"You got the message?" said Theodore.

"Loud and clear! Your garden was an inspiration to all of us," said Garrett.

Theodore took the photos and stepped out of the room. Mr. Anderson was walking towards him.

"Captain Reed," said Mr. Anderson. "If you leave right away, you can catch a plane that will get you to Hawaii. From there, you can catch a plane back to the states. You will be home in a couple of days if you hurry."

"Thank you, Mr. Anderson. Thank you for the photos, Garrett. George, take care," Theodore said as he bounded for the stairs, climbing them two at a time. "Can you get me to the airbase?" he asked the driver in the lobby.

"Right away, Captain."

He was heading home. His possessions totaled four eight-by-ten black & white photographs.

35 — Family - September, 1953

A week after returning the American prisoners, a storm battered the region. The rain poured out of the sky like Kuryong Falls. Sun-hee had taken it easy since returning from the south, staying around the dorm, spending time with her children. She felt contractions and sent Choe-me to find her mother.

Just two days previously, Mrs. Cha had returned to teaching reading and writing to the staff.

Choe-me interrupted the class. "It is time. Mrs. Cha. Sun-hee is on her way to the hospital."

Mrs. Cha reached for her crutches and said, "Class is dismissed."

Choe-me, being eight months pregnant herself, and Mrs. Cha struggled to make their way across the camp in the driving rain.

"Couldn't she have picked a better day?" Sue-dae said as her stick slipped in the mud. Choe-me caught her and kept her from landing in a puddle. Jin-taek came running over, lifted Mrs. Cha, and carried her to the hospital.

Jin-taek sat Sue-dae on a bed and pulled it next to the other bed in the birthing room before bowing and leaving. Sun-hee was removing her wet clothes and climbing onto the bed next to her mother.

"Have you decided on the name?" asked Sue-dae.

"If it is a boy, I will name him Cha Seo-Woo, after your father.

"He would be proud."

"If it is a girl, I will name her Cha So-min." She grimaced with the start of a contraction.

"You would honor Mrs. Pae."

Eun-seong and Choe-me came in and began to prepare for the delivery. Kwong-ku entered an hour later to watch and aid in the birth of his child. Four hours later, Cha So-min entered the world with all her toes and fingers. Eun-seong handed the child to Mrs. Cha as Choe-me cut the cord.

"I'm so blessed to have such a cute granddaughter," said Mrs. Cha.

The number of babies in the camp was now up to sixty-five. Sixty-six if the count included General Park's son. This didn't count the orphanage set up by Chulsoon and some of the girls.

Widows, hired by Lt. Rim, were helping with nursing, the laundry, and tending to the needs of the children. The fathers came around now and then to see their children, but they avoided the rooms full of babies. They were, however, continuing to make wooden toys, bassinets, and other useful items. Sun-hee found out that Strategist could not hold his son and talk at the same time.

A week after So-min's birth, Sun-hee needed some quiet. She decided to take her three children to the library for the day. With a lot of help, Sun-hee made her way to the library with her three children and mother.

Mrs. Cha made herself comfortable in a chair and held So-min. Cha Hong-do, now one year old, and Cha Su-dae, now two, sat on a mat playing with blocks. Mrs. Cha watched her grandkids while Sun-hee made flashcards.

The door to the library flew open, a cold blast of air blew across her back.

"Sun-hee," she heard her name booming from Gen. Park.

She stopped mid-stroke on the character she was writing, stood, turned, and bowed deeply.

"Yes, General Park," she said, looking at his shiny shoes.

At least he could say hello. What can he want from me now?

"Have you seen Ahn Ching-ying, Ra Weon-kee, I Kwong-ku, or Chou Sung-man?" asked Gen. Park.

"Ching-ying is usually in the corner room upstairs," she said, pointing over General Park's head. "Sung-man reads his engineering books in the room over there," she said, indicating a room on the second floor behind her mother. "Kwong-ku is usually at the hospital. And Weon-kee has been helping Mr. Yun with the new buildings."

General Park climbed the stairs and found the two men. As the three were walking down the stairs, Gen. Park was saying, "You will be leaving tomorrow for the Academy of Science recently established in Pyongyang. Remember, you are part of this program, and should we be revealed to the government, the lives of everyone will be in jeopardy. I will require each of you to return to father more children. Ching-ying, you will come back when Sun-hee there is ready. Otherwise, I ask you to learn and serve the Democratic People's Republic of Korea to the best of your ability." The door opened, and the three of them stepped out. The chill of the September morning air again rushed in.

Numbers? I will have a child with Numbers, Sun-hee thought.

Sue-dae looked around the library to make sure no one would hear her before saying quietly, "It's too soon. I will not allow you to be forced to have another child so soon."

"It is part of the plan, Mother."

"This plan does not treat you as you deserve. I cannot stand for this any longer. We must leave."

"Where would we go?"

"Anywhere. He can't dictate our lives like this!"

"Where could we go? If we do get away from this camp with three children, we must leave Korea to live as refugees in another country. We give up on making Korea better and will struggle to survive in a foreign land. You would have to leave the school you have started here."

"You will be free of General Park's hideous plan to mate you with every young male in this camp. We can make our lives like it was before you left home. We were happy."

"Mother, you are not thinking straight. I will not leave my friends. We must make this our place and endure the pains confronting us. There is greater hope for the future here than in the unknown out there. We can be happy here."

"This is hardly a place where we can make a home for you and the children. I would be much happier if our family had our own house."

"Our family is much larger than the five of us. We have our own house. We call it the House of Sanshin."

"Do you think this is the home of the mountain gods? No one would treat gods like breeding stock."

Sun-hee stared at the table for a moment. She took a deep breath. "If we are gods, what will our children become?" She took a fussy So-min from her mother and offered the child her breast. So-min began to suckle.

"How many children does General Park need?"

"How many great citizens does our country need?" replied Sun-hee.

Mrs. Cha pursed her lips, looked away, and stared at the wall.

During dinner, the conversation among the girls was about the boys who were departing. Numbers, Wires, Unicorn, and Gears were leaving for the Academy of Science. Yeo Wa-dae, nicknamed Waves because of his wavy hair, would be going to Nampo to work in the shipyards. Skinny Beast would be leaving to study economics in Bejing. Sketcher, the name given to Yun Chul, was going to Pyongyang to work with a leading builder, rebuilding the city. Stone would join a mining survey team from the Soviet Union. And Stinky was going to help restore the irrigation systems in the central farmlands.

Later in the evening, the boys invited the girls to a going-away party in honor of those who were leaving. Most of the children were asleep, and the mothers and hired staff took care of those still awake.

The forty-six eighteen-year-old students milled about chatting and saying their goodbyes.

Sun-hee said goodbye to the fathers of her three children, Stone, Strategist, and Unicorn.

Then Numbers came over to her and said, "I'll see you after the first of the year. Send me a letter to let me know you are ready." Sun-hee smiled and nodded slightly in his direction.

Young-ja stood in the middle of the room and said loudly, "Everyone, quiet down. I have something to say."

"We know, you always have something to say," said Skinny Beast, which got everyone laughing.

Young-ja said, "Over the last three years, we have been through a lot. Our country has been through much more. Tomorrow, we begin to reach outside of the house of Sanshin to help our country. Each of us has found our strengths and interests. We must use those strengths to make our country better. As we leave the confines of these fences, let us remember we are family."

Strategist stepped forward. "We leave here to serve our Premier, to rebuild the Democratic People's Republic of Korea and honor General Park who brought us together. Our strength will be in working with each other." He grasped the hands of the boy next to him and raised them in the air. "To the House of Sanshin," he yelled.

And everyone hailed, "To the House of Sanshin."

36 — Assignments - Late September, 1953

Sun-hee held her two-week-old daughter So-min with one arm, as she waved goodbye to eight young men, who she had spent the last three years with. She bore children with three of them. With their leaving, a part of her left. The men were freed from the camp like birds from a cage. The barbed wire fences they had once longed to escape from were no longer relevant. For the rest of the morning, she tended to her children, picked beans, and pulled up carrots. There did not seem to be a need for any of the young women outside of Yangseongso.

It was just after lunch when Sgt. Kua came to them and said, "General Park wants to see both of you. Mrs. Cha, Lieutenant Cha, please come with me."

Mrs. Cha picked up her crutches, two sticks with a crosspiece, and struggled to stand. Sun-hee handed her newborn daughter to Mrs. Moon to watch until they returned. They walked out of the house of Sanshin into a rain threatening sky. Mrs. Cha took a deep breath and started down the stairs. Sgt. Kua held one arm and Sun-hee the other.

Hon-Yong walked by and asked, "May I offer my assistance?"

"That would be very nice," replied Mrs. Cha.

Hon-yong gently lifted Mrs. Cha, carried her down the steps, and steadied her as Sun-hee handed her mother the crutches.

"Thank you, young man," said Mrs. Cha.

Hon-yong bowed and went on his way.

Mrs. Cha turned to Sgt. Kua and said, "Why didn't General Park choose that strong, handsome, man to father my daughter's children?"

"Mother!" said Sun-hee as her face turned red.

Sgt. Kua took a step back and said, "I only follow orders, Mrs. Cha. You should ask General Park that question when you meet with him."

"Maybe I will," she said with a big smile.

Sgt Kua strode off towards her house.

Sun-hee stewed at her mother as they slowly made their way to the camp headquarters.

Chun-ja brought in tea as they were taking seats at the table. Then she went to the corner of the room and picked up her two-year-old son, Duk-bae.

"What do you think General Park wants with us?" Sun-hee asked her mother.

"I am wondering who the other person is." said Mrs. Cha, pointing to the two extra cups.

They did not have to wait long to find out. Gen. Park walked in, followed by another man in a general's uniform. Gen. Park said, "This is Cha Sue-dae and her daughter Cha Sun-hee. They have taken on the leadership of the education here at this camp."

"Ladies, this is General Ma. He is the newly appointed leader of the National Education Program."

Sun-hee stood and bowed. Mrs. Cha started to get up.

"Please do not get up, Mrs. Cha," said Gen. Park, holding out his hand. "No need to struggle with your injured knee. I have added how to repair knees on my research list. Ligament damage is so difficult to repair."

"Now, if you will excuse me," said Gen. Park. "I must attend to other business. Call Chun-ja if you need more tea." Gen. Park left as Chun-ja came and poured tea for Gen. Ma.

Gen. Ma cleared his throat and began. "I'm pleased to meet you. General Park has said good things about the education program you have implemented. Under my new position, it's my responsibility to rebuild the education system of the Democratic People's Republic of Korea.

"The Japanese tried to convert us to their culture by forcing Koreans to learn their language. In the process, they destroyed most of the books and teaching materials in the Korean language. During the fighting, American bombs and troops destroyed eighty-eight percent of our schoolrooms and all the libraries except one, the one here at this camp. I have put out a call for teachers but have had a far less than expected response. All that to say, we need teachers, schools, and teaching materials."

He took a sip of tea. "General Park had great insight to bring books from the Pyongyang library to this location. He told me you are currently teaching adults from this area how to read and write, and you have started a school for the local children. This is excellent since the government has decreed all Koreans are to be educated in our language."

Sun-hee looked to see her mother's reaction. It was unreadable.

He is setting up something he wants from us, she thought.

General Ma continued, "The overwhelming task before me is getting the educational materials we are receiving from the Soviets, translated into Korean. I understand both of you are fluent in Russian. I must get Korean teaching materials updated with current information. Once available, they can be replicated and provided to teachers." General Ma paused and took another sip of tea. "Sorry for my nerves. I feel I am talking in circles."

Sun-hee again checked to see if her mother was reacting. Her mother was expressionless, eyes focused on General Ma with hands in her lap.

"I need citizens like you who can translate and write. My attention needs to be on recruiting teachers and building schools. But what good are teachers without books and teaching materials? Your experience, your knowledge of languages, and being the only place where there is a library, makes this the best place to produce teaching materials in the whole country."

"We are most honored," said Sue-dae, bowing in her seat.

Sun-hee, surprised by her mother's quick response, followed her mother's lead and bowed her head.

"Now, a few details. First, as you know, the military is in control of everything, including education. I understand Sun-hee has been trained as a doctor and has the rank of lieutenant."

Sue-dae glanced over at her daughter.

"What we need to do, Mrs. Cha, is to have you join the military under the education branch. Being an officer will provide you with the authority to request materials and command others. You will need to have the rank of at least a lieutenant. I have the authority to promote you right now, but I must ask a few questions."

Sue-dae bowed again in acknowledgment.

"Are you, Cha Sue-dae, completely loyal to Kim Il-sung?" General Ma asked.

"Yes, I am," said Sue-dae.

"Are you completely loyal to the Democratic People's Republic of Korea?"

"Yes, I am."

"Do you have any ancestors who are not Korean?" the General asked with a stern look.

"I can trace my father's ancestry back a thousand years to the Yeonan Cha clan founded by Cha Hyo-jeon. There have been many marriages with other clans, and there are some questionable lines during the time of the Mogul empire. My husband was also of the Cha clan, coming from a line separated from my father's line eight generations ago."

"And where is your husband?"

"Ten years ago, he died from a lung infection."

"Do you have any family in South Korea?" the General asked.

"No immediate family. I was an only child, and my parents have passed. I'm sure there are extended family members all over Korea. To my knowledge, none are in South Korea. I haven't seen any of my family since my mother's funeral fifteen years ago."

"Are you willing to do what I ask to help structure the education of our people?"

"It would be a great honor, General Ma," she said, lowering her head towards the table.

"I will have the paperwork drawn up to promote you to the position of lieutenant in the National Education Division, reporting directly to me." He paused as he wrote on the paper in front of him.

Sun-hee now saw a wide grin on her mother's face.

"Let's talk about how to begin. I have materials provided by our friends in the Soviet Union. We'll model our education system after theirs and must have these materials translated as soon as possible. I trust Lieutenant Cha will be willing to assist," he said, looking at Sun-hee.

"I'm also honored, General Ma," said Sun-hee while bowing.

How could I object?

"The next step is for me to deliver the materials from the Soviets with plenty of paper, ink, and pens. When you have some lessons complete, forward them to my office in Pyongyang for review." He paused again, writing something on the paper in front of him. "Thank you for taking on this important task." He stood.

Sun-hee stood and bowed. She helped her mother to her feet and steadied her while she respectfully bowed.

They started their journey back to the dorm, and Sun-hee asked, "What do you think about what General Ma said?"

"I'm thrilled," said Sue-dae who stopped and took her daughter's hand. "We have a chance to do something wonderful for our country. For my whole life I've longed for the opportunity to educate people. This is beyond my dreams." She looked deep into her daughter's eyes. "You won the prize and were made to sacrifice, yet I get what I have always wanted. You made all this possible."

The sun peaked through the thinning afternoon clouds, basking them in warm light. Sun-hee held her mother's arm as they made their way to the House of Sanshin. Tears of joy streaming from her mother's eyes.

The fates had come together. My mother's dream to educate the Korean people is fulfilled.

Part Three - Core Songbun

37 — Demands - Late September - Early November, 1953

Sue-dae was in the main room of the library, teaching her afternoon class. Sgt. Kua walked in and saluted. "Can I help you, Sergeant?" Sue-dae said, looking around the room, wondering who Sgt. Kua was saluting.

"Lieutenant Cha, a truck full of boxes has arrived for you at the main gate. Where would you like them placed?" she said, holding the salute.

The soldiers in the room stood at attention and saluted.

"I…I am uncertain of the formalities, Sergeant. Please relax. And all of you sit down as you were," she said as her face got a little red. "Here in the library will be the best place for the materials. And there is no need to be formal. Refer to me as before. I am in the education division and not the army."

"Yes, Lieutenant," said Sgt. Kua with a slight smile while releasing her salute.

"Class, please assist Sergeant Kua," said Sue-dae. The soldiers in her class took this as a command from an officer and went to work. Boxes and more boxes were brought in, piled all over the main room.

Over the next week, Sue-dae and Sun-hee worked to get the material organized. They recruited the other girls and assigned each of them to a grade level. The amount of material needing translation was daunting. Childcare took up a significant amount of each day, limiting how much time the women worked on the curriculum.

They sorted the materials and assigned one room on the bottom floor of the library for each of the first seven grades. Sue-dae and Sun-hee moved into the left front corner room and made it their office. The upper eight rooms were assigned subjects: mathematics, history/geography, politics, literature, natural science, engineering/manufacturing, economics, and psychology/social science. Medical books remained in the main room. Sun-hee and her mother paired up the girls and assigned them to grade levels. Boys selected subjects according to their interests.

Sun-hee and her mother went to work, translating the teaching materials while the others finalized the lesson plans.

Initially, Sue-dae felt overwhelmed at the task but was pleasantly surprised how competent everyone was at getting things done. In a few days, she had more material to review than she could get through.

By the first of November, a month's worth of teaching material for the younger grades was ready. Two boxes were sent off to Pyongyang for Gen. Ma's approval. Sue-dae was proud of what they had accomplished. Collectively, she felt they had done an excellent job.

***

A week later, Sue-dae was working in her office when a booming voice bellowed in the main room, "Lieutenant Cha."

She jumped up, putting too much weight on her bad leg. She gasped from the pain and caught herself on the desk. After taking a couple of deep breaths, she grabbed her crutches and limped out.

"Yes, General," she said, bowing the best she could and hesitating before wondering if she should stand at attention and salute. Gen. Ma stood near the door, hands on his hips, glaring at her. Some of the girls came out of their rooms, looking curious. Sgt. Kua walked in and stood behind the general.

"Stand at attention for General Ma," Sgt. Kua blurted out.

Sue-dae saluted, the others quickly realizing they should be at attention and changing their posture. Young-ja saluted with a fountain pen in her hand, placing a black mark on her forehead.

"I need to speak with you, Lieutenant Cha," barked Gen. Ma. "The materials you sent were all wrong!" and he returned the salute.

"Yes, General," said Sue-dae. "I would be most pleased to hear your review." She shuddered.

What had they done wrong?

She backed up as Gen. Ma nearly ran her over as he marched into her office. She hobbled to her desk and stood behind it, an angry man standing on the other side.

"The Premier was not pleased with the materials. Thus, I am not pleased. The Premier is the father of Korea and must be given honor in all materials," he said, pointing to a poster on the wall.

"All illustrations must show that hard work is expected and rewarded. You must emphasize loyalty to the Democratic People's Republic of Korea in all teaching. Eliminate references to materialism and personal ownership. Any concept of individualism must not be present. Kim Il-sung is the father of our country and our only hero." He pointed at the poster again. "Remove all references to Russians. We honor only the Premier. We are educating the masses to be loyal citizens. They do not need to think. They need to learn to obey."

"Yes, General. I understand and will begin to revise our material," said Sue-dae with a bow.

"Good. Revise the first two weeks of what you sent me. I'll expect the revision in a week."

"Yes, sir," she said with a deep bow.

Gen. Ma marched out.

Lt. Rim saluted as Gen. Ma passed then let himself into the room. "Mrs. Cha, can we speak privately?" said Lt. Rim while closing the door.

"Yes," she said.

Do I have a choice?

Rim closed the door, sat in a chair, and motioned to Sue-dae. "Please sit," he said.

She sat, hands shaking in her lap, her heart pounding.

"We are both lieutenants, Mrs. Cha. I speak to you as an equal," he said in a calm voice, leaning forward in his chair, his hands on his knees. "We are in a special place. We have an opportunity to make a difference. My father was a street businessman. I learned from him how to barter, trade, and manage transactions. He taught me how to give people what they want and extract what I want in return." He paused, removed his hat, and brushed back his hair before replacing the cap and adjusting it on his head.

"I can't help you with the preparation of the educational materials. That is your expertise. What I can offer is my skills in negotiating and dealing. Let me take the completed materials to Pyongyang where I can request things we need and get a sense of what they expect. Maybe, I can prevent General Ma from showing up in anger in the future. He must have been humiliated in Pyongyang when he presented your materials. He took it out on you today. I offer myself as a go-between to avoid situations like this in the future. However, your materials must be of the highest standards."

Sue-dae paused for a moment, digesting Lt. Rim's words. "I am not used to such responsibility, Lieutenant Rim," she said, choosing her words carefully. "You are such an important person in this camp, and I am only a teacher."

I cannot refuse his offer, but what are his real motives? Everyone fears him.

How can I trust him?

"Your expertise is needed and will be appreciated," she bowed.

"I will do all I can to see General Park's vision to its end. You are now an important part of his vision. Thank you, Lieutenant Cha." He stood and marched out.

What is this vision he mentioned? How am I a part of it? I'll ask Sun-hee tonight.

Sue-dae wrote down what she remembered of Gen. Ma's demands. Then she walked from room-to-room, reviewing what they needed to revise. She was uncertain about how to make all the materials acceptable to the Premier. She encouraged everyone to try their best to comply with Gen. Ma's words. He had said a lot but did not give examples. The task became significantly more difficult.

38 — Truth - Mid-November, 1953

The week after General Ma stormed into the library was hectic. Sue-dae found it easier to sleep in her library office than crutch-commute across the compound. She thought she understood the changes mandated in the teaching materials and needed every moment to get them done correctly.

This morning, she was up before dawn reviewing papers that had been submitted for her review last night. She marked up a third-grade lesson, then sent it to Eun-seong to be revised, for the second time.

Sitting in the corner of her mother's office, her children at her feet, and a grade list of Russian vocabulary in her hand, Sun-hee said, "There are some words that do not translate. Like 'morozhenoye,' which translates 'ice cream.' Why would anyone leave their milk out in the cold and let it freeze?"

"We cannot translate the Russian material directly to Korean as initially instructed. Make a list of Korean words to learn in each grade, then use Russian methods to develop our materials. That is the best plan for the moment."

A knock on the open door drew their attention.

"Come in, Eun-seong," Sue-dae said.

"Please excuse my lack of understanding, Mrs. Cha," said Eun-seong while bowing. "I need help to understand what you mean when you say these materials are not acceptable?" She offered the materials in her hand. "I changed the Russian story to a familiar parable. Was I not to do that?"

"The story you included is about children who make decisions on their own," said Sue-dae in a soothing tone. "What I believe the government wants, are stories of children who make decisions, but only decisions the state has taught them."

"This parable has been taught for centuries," said Eun-seong. "It is rooted in the teachings of Confucius. I learned it from my grandmother, who learned it before the Japanese occupation."

"You told me that story years ago, Mother. How can it be wrong?" said Sun-hee.

There was another knock at her open door. Sue-dae said, "Come in."

"Pardon me for interrupting, Mrs. Cha," said Yong-gak, bowing at the door.

"Welcome, Yong-gak. What is on your mind?"

What does Strategist want? thought Sun-hee.

He took a couple of steps into the room. "I have been talking to others and have come to realize we need a written framework for all our materials." He made a square with hand gestures in front of his thin body. "I have taken from what General Ma said. I have evaluated the statements coming from Kim Il-sung, and I have spent days studying Soviet doctrines. I now believe I have an idea of what is needed." He finished with his hands open, palms up.

"How would your political ideas affect a children's story, Yong-gak?" said Sun-hee, leading him into the discussion they had been having.

"We are to produce education materials for the masses. Materials for teaching the people who they are, within the framework of the Korean nation. Their past," he pointed to the right with his right thumb, "their present," his fingers pointing down, "and their future," he pointed with his left thumb, "need to be defined, giving them an orientation to perform their role in society. We need to give them a foundation as to where they are in relation to the past, the rest of society, and the world." His fingers made a ball. "The present needs to be defined in a manner which will make them productive citizens, adding to the wealth of the nation. The future must be defined as what positive results will occur if they do what is asked of them. The teachings must reflect national self-reliance and group identity, resulting in a congruent move into our future." He finished, pointing left.

"The teachings of Confucius were taught for centuries to our people and have served us well," said Eun-seong. "Am I just to cast them away?"

Yong-gak had intertwined his fingers across his upper stomach as he always did while listening. Then his hands went into motion. "What we need, more than anything, is a sense that we are a self-reliant people. We need our own identity apart from Chinese teachings and apart from Soviet doctrine. We need to redefine everything to be a Korean story and stress our own identity. We must learn that we are reliant on our abilities. Make the story about us," all fingers pointing to his chest, "not about a Chinese philosopher. Rewrite the parable to be a Korean story," he said, making a writing gesture.

"What about the education material we got from the Soviets?

Switching to a communist society makes everything different. Nothing in Korea is as it was before Japan attacked us. Who are we? What of the past do we include?" asked Sun-hee.

He started with a point of the right finger. "The Soviets have given us a framework for what we must do to be a Communist/Marxist society. Politically, we must not vary. The Premier can't allow it. Modify the story to tell Koreans how to act in a Communist/Marxist society. Include what we as Koreans are. Leave out or revise what the other nations have done to us." He made small circles with his hands. "The common person outside these fences needs a national identity, something to believe in. Not the Soviets or the Chinese. We must become a nation unto ourselves, and if we are to do this, Kim Il-sung," pointing with both hands to the poster on the wall, "will be our leader. Anything else, and we are again only pawns of another culture. Anything not in line with what Kim Il-sung says will result in our death," and he gestured with a finger across his neck.

"Yong-gak," started Sue-dae, folding her own hands on the desk. Her eyes looked up as she paused. "For the sake of clarification, let me state a different point of view. All my life, there have been men in power, telling the people what to think. They all want to control people through education. Wouldn't it be better to tell the people everything and then explain that what their leaders are doing is best? I don't feel we are educating people. We are only making them think the way the government wants them to think."

"We are in the midst of an ideological war," Yong-gak said, hitting his fists together. "A war for the loyalty of the people. Many are being imprisoned and killed for stating an ideology different from the government. Presently, we do not have the freedom to think or act differently. The freedom we seek is freedom for the Korean people. I believe once we are free as a nation, we can move to have freedom of thought. Right now, dissent will result in chaos," he wiggled his fingers outwardly, never moving his elbows, "and ultimately lose us our freedom as a nation."

"We will need your help in getting all the education materials in line with this ideology," said Sue-dae.

"I am completely committed to this path," Yong-gak said, holding his hands flat to his chest. "I will do what I can."

"How soon will you have a policy statement we can use as a guideline?" asked Sue-dae.

"I will get it to you tomorrow," replied Yong-gak.

"Do you have an idea of what you need to do, Eun-seong?" Sue-dae asked.

"I think so. The materials I write for the third-grade level are to educate and teach how to behave according to the direction the Premier is taking us. We do not have any influence on the heredity of the people or the opportunities they will have in the future." she said, before walking out.

Sun-hee sat for a moment after Eun-seong left. "Mother," she said in a quiet voice. "Do you feel this education path is the right one for our nation to take?"

Sue-dae leaned forward, her hands still folded on the desk, and looked directly at her daughter. "I was very fortunate to get a good education and have the talent to learn languages. This allowed me to read books from many cultures and see the world through the eyes of others. Every civilization has an ideology or religion which provides morals and guides to the common man. The dynasties of the past, the caste system in India, Islam in the middle east, Christianity in Europe, the Emperors in China, the Czars in Russia, and the Emperor in Japan all have a base teaching for how to live. Now Kim Il-sung is setting up a similar society. When there are no leaders, tradition is passed from the elders to the next generation. This has been done throughout history. When the old does not work, a leader emerges and implements change. Kim Il-sung is now such a leader. He is defining the future for our people. Since we are in an ideological war, our teaching must be narrowly defined. His edict, demanding that all people be educated, is a new concept for a culture. I think it is wonderful. We are in a unique place to guide this education, and I want to do what is best for the country. The best path is to educate the people and define their behavior in a manner acceptable to our leaders. As Yong-gak said, 'in a few years, we will see the results.'"

"You are right, Mother. Let's build the vision of Kim Il-sung into the materials," said Sun-hee.

Sue-dae stood and limped around the desk without crutches, taking her daughter's hands. "I am most proud to be in this position to assist our nation. That is minuscule to how proud I am of the young woman you have become," she said as she teared up.

Sun-hee bowed her head, holding her mother's hands tightly. "I'm the one who is honored, Mother," she said as drops fell from her cheeks onto her arms.

Their grip tightened and held for a moment. "There is much to do.

We must get busy," said Sue-dae. She released her grip, turned to her desk for support, and moved around to sit in her chair. She looked up to see her daughter attending to her children while wiping tears from her face.

Sue-dae blotted her eyes and tried to focus on the characters on the paper before her. She glanced at the poster of Kim-Il-sung on the wall.

You are the father of Korea. I hope you are pleased with what I do.

Four days later, she placed the last of a month of teaching materials in a box. Then she added a folder, the one containing Yong-gak's education guidelines, on top. She held her shaking hands against her stomach, which fluttered like a flock of swallowtail butterflies on a blossoming cherry tree.

What will happen if the Premier does not like these materials?

She sealed the box, sent word to Lt. Rim, and cleaned off her desk. Then she put on her coat and headed out the door.

With only one crutch, more for balance than taking the weight off her leg, she forced herself to fight through the pain. She carefully picked her steps through the ice and snow, the gusty wind, piercing her coat, trying to knock her off balance. She made her way across the compound as the vapor of her heavy breath whipped away.

She walked by a car as her boxes were loaded.

Our future rides to Pyongyang in that car.

She passed by the kitchen, wanting sleep more than food. As she stepped through the rooms of children, she took a few moments to hug each of her grandchildren.

They seem so happy. How will they feel when they learn their education is tailored to make them loyal citizens? I'm molding the lives of all Koreans.

She limped to her mat, carefully laid down and fell asleep in one move. Her dreams were filled with Gen. Ma yelling, "This is not acceptable!"

She thought she was awake as she wiggled her fingers in front of her face, but she saw nothing. She felt around for her crutch, slowly making her way, feeling the ends of mats with her feet as she stepped carefully in the darkness. She pushed opened the door to the privy and closed the door behind her before increasing the light on the lamp. She limped to the sink and looked at herself in the mirror. The bags under her eyes looked like hammocks, and her hair needed to be trimmed and combed.

Who is this person? I taught what the Japanese wanted. I did what I could to survive until Sun-hee brought me here. I have conformed to Kim Il-sung's government and set forth the education of the people to follow him. What would happen if I taught truth and only truth?

Her mind scanned through books she had read, so many views of the world, so many thoughts.

Which is right? Which author has an insight into life? Who is right? Is anyone right? Why do people fight over the truth? Maybe life is better when it is simple. Knowing more only leads to uncertainty.

She made her way to the front room, where her grandchildren slept. She changed diapers and helped with the children until dawn, enjoying every minute of it.

39 — Moves - November Sixteenth, 1953

For Sun-hee, the morning started like the rest of the mornings that month. She looked for her mother, who was not on her mat, then went to check on her children. Her mother held Hong-do as the others slept next to her.

The room was full of children, and Sun-hee knew at least eight girls were pregnant. Sun-hee was amazed at how Mrs. Kim kept everything in order and how she maintained the schedule for local workers to help with laundry, feeding, and changing.

"Good morning, Mother. How are my little darlings this morning?" Sun-hee whispered.

"They are wonderful," said Sue-dae.

"You look so tired, Mother. Why don't you rest today? I'll make sure everyone is working, and I'll teach your class this afternoon."

"I think everyone needs a day off from writing and translating. Teaching is a nice break. I enjoy it and find it refreshing. So, you get the day off, too. My orders. What are your plans?"

"If I have a day off, I will spend it with my children and say goodbye to some of the boys who are leaving today," said Sun-hee.

"Where are they going?" asked Sue-dae.

"Noh Ki-young is going to Tumangang where he will be a liaison with the Soviets. He will make sure materials are transferred to our library. Chong Gil-hyung is going to study finance in the capital. The postal service needs rebuilding, and San Hien-jin is going to work there. Chou Sung-man, we call him 'Gears,' was sent to a military weapons facility. Chweh Han-gyong is going to work with the railroads. The only men left are Strategist, Hammer, and Doc Chulsoon."

"I need Strategist around to make sure we are getting the political philosophy correct. Hammer makes such nice furniture. We can't let him go. And we still need someone to oversee the hospital. Only three men in so much space?" said Sue-dae, pointing to the other side of the House of Sanshin.

"I know what you are thinking. I will talk to the remaining men to see if they will let us expand into their quarters," said Sun-hee.

Sue-dae smiled. "We will need the space when more babies are born."

So-min woke up. Sun-hee lifted her off the mat and held her for a moment before changing the diaper. A woman brought over a bucket to collect the soiled cloth and bowed as Sun-hee placed it in the bucket. Sun-hee looked carefully at the skin that covered the area where the woman's left eye should have been. It had healed well. Three years ago, Sun-hee had worked with Max to repair a shrapnel wound that had damaged the woman's eye. The elderly woman had gone to the laundry area the day after surgery and started helping.

"Thank you," Sun-hee said to the woman, placing her hand lightly on her shoulder. The woman returned a smile.

How many have stayed to serve this camp? Thirty? Forty? They work for their meals and a mat.

Another woman delivered breakfast, pulling a small cart with pots of food, and began to hand it out. More girls came out of the sleeping area, changed diapers, nursed, spoon-fed, and dressed their children. They were chatting and stepping over each other while tending to children.

Sue-dae spoon-fed Hong-do while Sun-hee breastfed So-min. Together, they encouraged Sun-hee's oldest daughter, Su-dae, to eat on her own. After everyone ate, Sun-hee wrapped So-min in a blanket and set out on a mission to convince the remaining men to give up their half of the building.

She found Chulsoon tending to patients at the hospital. He was now the primary doctor as Gen. Park was seldom around.

"Good morning, Chulsoon. How are our patients today?"

"Nothing serious this morning. It has been a while since you were here to help out," Chulsoon said.

"I am not here to help. I need to make a request. Our side of the dorm is getting quite crowded. Since most of the boys have left, I am requesting Yong-gak, Hon-yong, and yourself move to another building, allowing us to move into your half of the House of Sanshin."

"If I have a suitable place to move to, I would be happy to let you have our half of the dorm," Chulsoon asked.

"Good. I will speak to the others."

She went to the library where Yong-gak spent most of his time. He was in the upstairs room reading. She knocked on the open door.

"Sun-hee, good to see you," said Yong-gak, his hands illustrating his words. "I was hoping you might be around soon. I was going over these books of Chinese history. There are a few characters I do not understand. Could you help me?"

She spent the next few minutes translating some characters and listening to Yong-gak discuss what he had been reading.

"Now I need to ask your help," Sun-hee said.

"Anything!"

She explained her request to have him move out of the House of Sanshin.

"I suppose that is the correct thing to do. Since I spend most of my time here, I only need a quiet place to sleep. Let me know when you find me a new home."

"I will let you know. Thank you." She turned and left.

He is always thinking about the big picture but not about the little things of life.

The Hammer was harder to find. She asked around and found him in the camp woodshop where he was using a plane to shape some wood.

"Hon-yong, I need to ask a favor," she said.

Hon-yong looked up from his work and stood up straight to face her. He was quite a bit taller than her, his broad shoulders and muscular arms stretched tight on his shirt. "What can I make for you today, Sun-hee?" he said, stepping towards her.

A whiff of his sweating body caught her nose.

I like the way he smells.

"I…I…" she stuttered for a moment, "…no, we need more space for the children. We want to move into the boys' half of the House of Sanshin, allowing the children more room."

"I noticed it was getting crowded in your half, and since most of the guys have gone on to other things, you have a reasonable request." He thought for a moment. "Maybe we can move into the house built for Max and Alek. It has three rooms and beds. I'll confirm it with Lt. Rim and talk to Yong-gak and Chulsoon. If they all agree, we will have our things out by the end of the day."

"I have already spoken to Chulsoon and Yong-gak. They both agreed if there is a suitable place to move. The house built for the Russians sounds like the right place, but Lieutenant Rim is out of town. He will not return for a few days."

"Then, we will move today and find someplace else if Lt. Rim objects."

Thank you for cooperating, Hon-yong. I admire the work you are doing to improve the camp." She bowed before walking out.

Mother was right. Why couldn't I be paired with him? He is so decisive and handsome.

Her mind flashed to a vision of her wrapped in Hon-yong's strong arms. She blushed and hurried back to the dorms.

Sun-hee spent the rest of the morning with her mother and children, playing games, teaching them new things. They were so much fun.

She was laying her son down for an afternoon nap when she heard her name being spoken in a whispering voice.

"Sun-hee. Sun-hee."

She looked up. Hon-yong was at the door, motioning to her. When she got outside, Yong-gak and Chulsoon were standing with Hon-yong with three rolled-up mats on the porch.

"We have our things," said Hon-yong. "The House of Sanshin is now a place for children to grow-up. Let me know if you need anything. You know where to find me."

"I'm going to miss this place," said Chulsoon. "It is not the same with most of the guys gone."

"I will see you at the library," said Yong-gak as he picked up his rolled mat.

Ra Weon-kee walked up. "Where are you guys going?"

"We are moving out and letting our children have more room," said Yong-gak. "Are you moving back in?"

"Just here for the day," said Weon-kee. "You are going to miss out. Once I insert the fuses," he flipped one into the air and caught it, "you will have electricity."

"Fantastic!" said Hon-yong. "How soon will the rest of the camp be powered up?"

"If there are no problems, I should have every light shining by sundown."

Sun-hee bowed slightly. "Wonderful news, Weon-kee. Thank you. And thank all of you for giving up your space."

She walked back into the girl's common room and looked around.

How will we divide up this space? First, the announcement.

"Hey, everyone. I have an announcement. Get everyone in here," she said while picking up Hong-do.

A moment later, the girls were all gathered in the room. Sun-hee said, "Most of the boys have left, and the others have taken their things to where Max and Alek use to stay. We can move into the boy's side and have more room for the children. And…" she paused to get everyone's attention again, "and Weon-kee is restoring electricity as I speak. We will have lights tonight."

The girls cheered. After a lot of discussion, they decided to split up equally between the four rooms, leaving the middle room for everyone. Sun-hee and her mother would go into what had been the boy's area. With them would be Young-ja, Eun-seong, Choe-me, Mrs. Moon, Joo-yun, Mrs. Lim, and their sixteen children.

Mrs. Lim placed her mat, Joo-yun's, and her grandchildren's mats in a corner, isolating the family from the rest of the room.

Sun-hee was arranging her things when Weon-kee entered and flipped the light switch. Five of the six lights around the room shone brightly. He changed the bulb in the sixth, and it lit up.

"Wow, we have as much room as we did when we first moved into the House of Sanshin," said Young-ja. "The boys leaving is indeed a blessing."

"I am going to miss them being around all the time," said Eun-seong. "I know they will do a lot to rebuild our country. I wish I could go and do something to help. But I am stuck here with my children and writing third-grade lessons."

"I agree, Eun-seong," said Choe-me. "We remain captive in this camp, unable to leave and do anything to help our nation rebuild."

"We are important!" said Sun-hee. "We are responsible for the education of the next generation of Koreans. If General Park's plan to have a generation of children who can make a difference in the future is going to work, we need to educate our children. Consider it our responsibility to train the second wave of nation builders."

"Great," said Mrs. Lim from the corner. "You think we are important. But we are still prisoners. Since the boys are leaving, do you think we could get up and leave without being killed?"

Sue-dae looked at Mrs. Lim and said, "Going or staying is not the issue. General Park demands our loyalty. If disloyalty influences a person to leave, then I believe that person will put their life in jeopardy. Furthermore, it will put everyone's life in jeopardy. I, for one, will remain loyal, trying to accomplish what I can for our country and these children."

"You have an education. The only reason I am important is I tell the laundry women when the diaper pail is full."

"Mrs. Lim, you are important to all of us and our children," said Eun-seong. "The girls view you as the mother of the House of Sanshin. Mrs. Moon and Mrs. Cha are teachers. Mrs. Ra only takes care of her grandchildren while you have looked over all of us. You are showing all of us how to be mothers, and you cannot continue to do that by leaving this camp."

"You have taught me a lot, Mrs. Lim," said Young-ja. "I greatly appreciate you."

Mrs. Lim started to cry. "We had such a good life, even under Japanese rule. My husband was respected. A harbormaster is an important person. I was invited to all the social events in town. Someday, I hope I can return home."

40 — Fourth Child - 1954

"Sorry I am late, Mother," Sun-hee said as she walked into the corner office of the library. "I was trying to give So-min solid food this morning. She made such a mess."

"She is growing so fast," replied Sue-dae. "Your oldest was running all over, and with my bad leg, I could not catch him. He is such a handful. Mrs. Lim took over as I need to get the next shipment of teaching materials ready. It has been two months and no word from Lt. Rim about the last shipment. I'm worried they will be rejected."

Four days later, Sue-dae's fears were put to rest. Lt. Rim returned, conveying a message of praise from Gen. Ma and bringing a car full of supplies. Lt. Rim had bartered for items needed in the camp. A truckload of food and clothes arrived a few days later.

Sun-hee saw her mother become more positive, taking more time to be with the children. But it made her wonder, *Am I just a slave laborer in Park's prison? I'm treated well, lots of food, clothes washed, an adequate home with electricity. Compared to the rest of the country, I live in a palace. Still, except for the clothes I wear and the mat I sleep on, I have no possessions. Lt. Rim provides everything. My work goes to the nation. This is socialism.*

***

Spring brought more flowers than usual. The camp was full of joy and laughter with first-born children now old enough to play outside, running, jumping, and laughing.

At the end of April, Sun-hee wrote her name on the calendar. Sgt. Kua sent a letter to Ching-ying requesting he return to camp.

Numbers arrived on May thirteenth, and after dinner, Sun-hee met him at the guesthouse. Sun-hee was a bundle of nerves and asked him many questions.

Numbers filled her in on the efforts to rebuild Pyongyang using the assistance from the Soviet Union and China. He told her of how Kim Il-sung was back in control and how his party was bullying or eliminating the opposition. He talked about the classes he was teaching at the university and how he enjoyed working with the other mathematicians at the Science Academy.

Sun-hee sensed how happy he was in his new role. He could apply the mathematics he had been studying so relentlessly in the past few years. She filled him in on the camp and what she knew of the other boys.

Sun-hee yawned. "We must have been talking for hours. We should get on with making a baby."

"It is getting late. I apologize. I get very nervous," said Ching-ying. "There is no logic to the emotion of making babies. I don't know what to do. I mean I do, but how to get to doing…"

"Just stop talking and get undressed," said Sun-hee as she got up and turned out the lights. She undressed and led him through the motions. She sensed when he finished and rolled over with him, laying her head on his shoulder.

"You are a good man, Ching-ying. I hope our child is as smart as you," she said as she rubbed his chest slowly.

"I hope our child has your confidence," Ching-ying said as he tried to get up.

Sun-hee pushed him back down. "Lay still." And she pressed her hand on his chest. "Bring your arm up and hold my shoulder." He obeyed, taking her shoulder. "Your heart is beating so fast. Try to relax. Take some deep breaths. Enjoy the moment." Sun-hee felt him tense up more.

After a couple of minutes, Sun-hee kissed Numbers on the cheek, rolled away, and started to dress. Ching-ying grabbed his clothes, dressing in a blur, before leaving the room with the door open. She chuckled to herself as she closed the door and turned on the light to finish dressing.

The next night Numbers seemed to be even more nervous. He entered the room, turned off the light, and began to undress. As he moved towards the mat, he bumped into Sun-hee in the dark and fell to the floor. Sun-hee removed her pants and knelt beside him.

"Lay down and put your hands behind your head. On your back, silly," said Sun-hee. She felt him turn over and she climbed on top, taking charge of the situation. Feeling his release, she sat still for a moment before rising and dressing. As she left, she turned on the lights and closed the door.

***

Sun-hee wondered what the third night would bring. She entered the guesthouse. Sgt. Kua pointed to a door and said, "Ching-ying is already here."

Sun-hee entered to see Numbers on his back, a blanket over his body, his hands behind his head. "Looks like you are ready," Sun-hee said.

"I...I'm trying not to be nervous. I thought..."

"Quit thinking," said Sun-hee as she turned off the lights and took control. She went through the motions quickly, dressed, and left.

By the end of June, Sun-hee knew she was pregnant. Three nights with Numbers was enough.

In early February of 1955, Sun-hee gave birth to a fourth child, her second son. She named him Cha Eun-mi.

41 — Fifth Father - February, 1955 to May, 1956

"Why?" Sun-hee muttered as she fell back against the cold cement of the hospital. The energy drained out of her, and she slid down, coming to rest on her heels. Her bloody hands crossed over her knees. She lay her head on her arms, tears dripping onto her bloodstained smock.

"What did I do wrong?" said Chulsoon as he squatted next to her. "I did everything I knew."

"You did all you could," she said into her lap. "Max said, 'sometimes, our skills are not enough.' She was unlucky."

"Hea-jung is family," he replied through his sobs.

No one expected the birth of Ri Hea-jung's fourth child to be any different. She pushed out a healthy baby girl, and then the blood began to flow. Chulsoon and Sun-hee worked frantically through the night but couldn't overcome fate.

They sat until shivers forced Sun-hee to stand. She put an arm around Chulsoon, and together they trudged through the snow back to the hospital room. They found Eun-seong and Choe-me tending to the baby. After washing and changing, the three girls took the baby to the dorms.

Four young children no longer had a mother. Mrs. Ra, the grandmother to one of the children, adopted the orphans. Sun-hee took a turn nursing the newborn every day for the next three months.

Hammer made a beautiful casket for Ri Hea-jung. Five days after her death, they buried her next to Hung Young-jee. Eun-seong drew her picture and placed it next to the other drawings on the wall in the common room.

Chulsoon took the loss personally. He could have saved her life if he had the capability to type and store blood. He complained loudly to Lt. Rim, demanding better equipment and a freezer to store blood. In the next few months, new medical equipment began to arrive at the camp.

***

General Park came back to the compound in late spring. He gathered the students together, and his voice boomed out. "I'm pleased with the progress you are making. Those of you who remain here and those who have gone out into the country are making a huge impact. You have vastly exceeded my expectations. I'm pleased to see so many healthy and happy children who, with education and training, will bring a new generation of exceptional men and women to help shape our nation's future."

"He looks funny, patting himself on the back with both hands," whispered Young-ja to Sun-hee as the general continued to talk.

"After one more round of births, the total children in the program should be about one hundred and twenty. I hope we can complete this within a year."

"Like he has anything to do with giving birth to children," whispered Young-ja.

"Then, we can focus on raising the next generation to make them great," Gen. Park said.

"When he says 'we' he means us," whispered Sun-hee to Young-ja.

"Kim Il-sung is doing everything possible to rebuild this country," said Gen. Park.

"To the House of Sanshin," Young-ja said so quietly only Sun-hee could hear.

Sun-hee nodded as a wide grin grew on her face.

"We will have a great nation under Kim Il-sung," said Gen. Park.

"We probably will have to do that, too," whispered Sun-hee.

"Do not think I'm unaware of what occurs here. In every city I travel to, I visit the schools. In each one I find the educational materials you produced."

"He does give us credit for that," quipped Young-ja.

"To the glory of Kim Il-sung!" Gen. Park said, raising his arms.

Sun-hee and Young-ja repeated, "To the glory of Kim Il-sung."

"To the glory of the Democratic People's Republic of Korea," said Gen. Park loudly.

Sun-hee and Young-ja joined in the chant.

Gen. Park paused for a moment. "You make me proud." He turned and started towards the gate.

Yong-gak said, "Excuse me, General Park. May I speak to you for a moment?"

"What's on your mind, Yong-gak?" replied Gen. Park as he turned to face Strategist.

"I compiled my research and wrote a document that I feel outlines our countries political direction. I would appreciate it if you would review it and provide me some feedback."

"I'm interested in reviewing your document. Before you hand it to me, are you sure what you have written shows complete loyalty to our Premier and the DPRK?"

"Yes, General Park," said Yong-gak, and he hesitated. "I request that you tell me if I'm incorrect in any way. What I have written I have done to the best of my ability. I apologize in advance if my thinking is in error."

"Bring it to headquarters, and I will read it tonight."

"Yes, General Park. Right away, sir." Yong-gak took off at a run.

***

The next morning, Gen. Park approached while everyone was eating breakfast. "Yong-gak, I read over your document a few times last night. You have written an excellent statement defining the path and ideology our country needs to take. I found nothing to improve in your document. With your permission, I would like to give it to some friends in Pyongyang to review."

"I would be honored for your friends review what I wrote," said Yong-gak with hand gestures that ended with all his fingers pointing to himself.

"Remarkable writing young man. Very impressive," Gen. Park said, and he patted Yong-gak on the shoulder.

Two weeks later, Lt. Rim informed Yong-gak that he was wanted in Pyongyang. The next morning, Yong-gak said goodbye to everyone before leaving.

***

Sun-hee and the rest of the girls breastfed their infants as long as they could with the hope of increasing the time between having children. It worked for most of the girls. However, during Gen. Park's visit, he enlisted as many local women as he could find around the area to serve as wet nurses. He wanted the women to stop nursing and immediately get on with their last pregnancy.

On the fifteenth of August, Sun-hee wrote her name on the calendar. She hoped this would be the last time.

"Don't take up all the space on those dates, Sun-hee," said the familiar voice of Young-ja behind her. "I need to fit my name in there, too."

"We can visit the guesthouse together again," said Sun-hee.

"Your support was important to me during those days," Young-ja said while giving Sun-hee a little hug.

"You and the Skinny Beast made me laugh, which relieved some tension," Sun-hee said, returning the hug. "I hope I don't get paired with him."

"Only nineteen possibilities left. I'm happy that Park only wants five children from each of us and not one with each of the boys. Of the four men you have been with, who should I hope for?" asked Young-ja.

"Kwang-ku is the only one I would recommend."

"Unicorn? If he was your best, the rest must have been awful," said Young-ja, chuckling.

"Then choose between Stone, Strategist, or Numbers."

"Hmm, I hope it will be one of the others? Especially Waves. I want a girl with wavy hair."

"She would be too cute," laughed Sun-hee. "I have a class to teach. See you tonight."

A week later, Sergeant Kua wrote Yeo Wa-dae next to Young-ja's name. Young-ja's wish had come true. Her next baby would have Waves as a father. Space next to Sun-hee's name on the calendar remained blank.

On the twenty-ninth, Sun-hee again checked the calendar. Still, a blank space beside her name. She sat facing the window in the library, watching to see which of the boys were in camp. She saw Waves and one other boy, who was already partnered. She began to hope for a reprieve, another month to evade mating.

After dinner, she showered and went to the guesthouse with Young-ja, who was in a glee mood. "I'm so excited, Sun-hee. I'm going to have a girl with wavy hair!"

"She will be the star of all the children," said Sun-hee.

"I didn't see a name next to yours. Who's your mate tonight?" asked Young-ja.

"I don't know. Nobody showed up at camp today. Maybe I get the night off."

"You would be so lucky. He will probably show up tomorrow," said Young-ja. "Let me think, who is always late? I know, the Skinny Beast is always late! He has to come all the way from Bejing."

Sun-hee hit Young-ja's arm. They laughed as they entered the guesthouse.

Wa-Dae sat waiting at the table. Young-ja said, "Come on, Waves. I want a girl." And she sauntered into an empty room.

Sun-hee laughed. Wa-dae gave her a funny look as he followed Young-ja and shut the door.

Sun-hee said to Sgt. Kua. "I'm here."

"Please have a seat. I will go check on the delay."

Sun-hee sat in a chair in the corner, waiting patiently as the minutes passed. Wa-dae came out of the room and left. A couple of minutes later, Young-ja came out.

"Are you still here? It looks like you have been stood up," said Young-ja.

Sun-hee stood and gave Young-ja a hug saying, "Sergeant Kua went to investigate. I will wait until she returns. How was Waves?"

"He's a nice man. But I will only like him if I get a wavy haired girl. I need to get my children to bed. Wake me and tell me everything when you get back."

"I will," said Sun-hee, and she sat back down.

Sun-hee waited. She fidgeted, then she paced and looked out the windows.

Maybe I should go back to my room.

The door opened, and Sgt. Kua walked in. "Sun-hee, your partner was delayed. Go get ready," she said, pointing to a room. "He will arrive shortly."

Sun-hee went in, removed her clothes, lay on the bed, and pulled the blanket over her. She shivered, pulled the blanket tight, and closed her eyes.

The door opened. Sun-hee tried to keep her eyes closed, shuddering at who had walked in. She heard movement like clothes being removed. She opened her eyes, and there stood the Hammer in all his glory. He combed his wet hair back over his head with his fingers. A broad smile terminated with small dimples stood above his square chin.

"Hello, Sun-hee," he said.

Sun-hee's heart soared to her throat. "Hi…" came out at a high pitch. She coughed lightly. "Hon-yong," she said in a more normal tone while pulling the blanket up to her chin.

"I'm sorry I'm late," he said, closing the door." I delivered some furniture to Chongjin today. It took me a while to get back." He reached up and pulled the string sending the room into darkness.

Sun-hee tensed, every muscle tightened. She tried to see or hear Hon-yong but sensed only his smell. Then a hand moved under her head. The blanket lifted. She raised her arm to receive his body next to hers. It arrived. She rubbed her hand along his back, feeling the muscles, then up to his neck, where she rubbed lightly. Her hand moved higher to slide her fingers through his wet hair.

She felt his hand on her waist, pulling her close, the warmth of his body next to hers sent a shiver down her spine. His aroma, like the smell of a spring rain, enticing one to frolic in the grass, filled her nostrils. She could feel his breathing, slow steady, smooth. Her diaphragm froze.

She felt his leg. She lifted her leg. He shifted, his hand caressing the back of her head. She grasped his hair, pulling his head beside hers. She inhaled deeply. He shuddered, muscles tensed, drawing her head tightly to his shoulder. She clenched his hair tighter. He grunted and relaxed. She exhaled.

He rolled to his back, pulling her head to his chest. She listened to his heart. It beat once while hers beat twice. They lay there, Sun-hee catching her breath and calming her heart. He stroked her shoulder a couple of times before lifting his arms around her head and rolling away. A moment later, the door opened. His broad silhouette filled the doorframe as he exited the room.

What just happened. Hon-yong is nothing like the others. What makes him different? Why do I feel so good tonight? I have never felt like this.

She dressed and returned to the dorm. A hand grabbed her in the dark, and Young-ja said, "Who showed up?"

"Hammer," said Sun-hee in a quiet voice.

"Really?" said Young-ja, Choe-me, and Eun-seong at the same time.

"How was he? Tell us," said Young-ja.

A jumble of thoughts flew through Sun-hee's head, "I…I…don't know how to describe it. We accomplished our task and will try again tomorrow."

"Indescribable? Sun-hee? Sounds like a good time to me," said Young-ja.

"I'm sure you had a better time with Waves," said Sun-hee.

"Waves was not great when I was with him," said Choe-me. "I do have a lovely daughter. But I wish she had inherited his wavy hair."

Young-ja and Sun-hee laughed while Choe-me had a puzzled look on her face.

Sun-hee went to her mat and lay down. Her mother reached a hand out from her blanket. "How are you, Sun-hee. Did things go well tonight?" she asked.

"You have gotten your wish, Mother," said Sun-hee. "I laid with Hon-yong tonight."

"Wonderful. Now, I'm anxious to see my next grandchild. I hope you have a boy and he's as strong as his father," said Sue-dae.

Sun-hee turned over. Dreams of Hammer soon filled her slumber.

The next day went by like most, tending to her children, teaching, and translating. But each free moment, her mind sneaked back to thinking about what would happen that night.

Sgt. Kua came up to her that afternoon as she was walking back to the dorms from the library. "Sun-hee. Ho Hon-yong was called away to do some cabinetry in Hyesan. He will be gone for a few days, maybe a week. You are relieved of your duty."

Sun-hee felt a wave of sadness come over her. She would not get to spend another evening with Hammer.

***

In Mid-September, Lt. Rim called everyone at the camp to the area outside headquarters. He brought a radio onto the porch. Together, they listened to Kim Il-sung speak on to the nation about his political ideology and the guiding principles of action for the people.

After the broadcast, Sue-dae grabbed Sun-hee's arm. "Come with me. I need to show you something." She walked as quickly as she could—with her stiff left knee—to her office in the library. She pulled out a folder from the bottom drawer in her desk, opened it, and handed it to Sun-hee. "Read what this document says."

Sun-hee began to read the pages in the folder. She looked up at her mother and said, "This is what Kim Il-sung said in his speech."

"Yes. Do you know who wrote the paper you're holding?" asked Sue-dae.

"Yong-gak wrote them," said Sun-hee. "Kim Il-sung liked Strategist's thoughts so much he made them our country's policy."

"You see the problem, don't you?" asked Mrs. Cha. "The Premier claimed this writing as his ideas for the country. They were Yong-gak's words."

"I think it is wonderful," said Sun-hee. "Yong-gak took all of the ideas he learned and put them into a coherent message. I have read most of these ideas in other documents from the Soviet Union and China. The rest I saw in statements and publications received from the Workers Party."

"Yong-gak wrote this message. His writing, Sun-hee, not Kim-Il-sung's."

"I'm sure Yong-gak gave the documents to the Premier with the expectation they would help our country. Quit worrying about credit for Yong-gak. Remember, he is the father of your oldest grandson."

"I wish we would get more credit for what we do around here.

General Park and Kim Il-sung control everything."

"They are the brain and nerves. We are the major organs of the body. We must work together in unity for the country to survive," said Sun-hee. "Speaking of working together, I think our children may need some attention."

***

In October, Sgt. Kua assembled the students. All the girls showed up along with Chulsoon and Hon-yong. "I received a message today from General Park. One of our friends has passed away. Chweh Han-gyong died in an accident while working in a train yard."

Two days later, Eun-seong hung a drawing of Chweh Han-gyong on the wall in the communal room of the House of Sanshin.

The next morning, the camp held memorial ceremony for Han-gyong with a special breakfast made by the cooks. As they started serving food, Sun-hee ran out.

"Leaving so soon," said Hon-yong turning to watch her go by.

"Your fault," Sun-hee said, putting her hand over her mouth to catch a bout of morning sickness.

***

Sun-hee delivered a boy at the end of May 1956. She named him Cha Hon-yong after the boy's father. The relief she felt for fulfilling her duty lifted her spirits. Now she faced the task of raising five children.

By the end of the year, all the remaining girls had given birth to at least five children. Three women gave birth to twins giving them six children.

42 — The Next Generation – April, 1966

Yi Si-ue ran as hard as she could during the children's morning run, and, as always, she finished last. She raised her hands as she reached other students who were yelling encouragements. Yi Si-ue amazed Sun-hee with the joy she exhibited in everything she did. She was the smallest, least athletic, had the poorest ability to learn of all the children, and still was the happiest.

What made this girl, the daughter of a starving peasant woman, so different? Sun-hee wondered.

Did the girl's heredity influence her traits or the mother's lack of nourishment during pregnancy?

Yi Si-ue hopped to the first position on the girl's side and yelled, "Formation."

The one hundred and nineteen students, now aged ten to fifteen, got into formation, facing Jin-taek. Jin-taek pointed to a boy to lead, then walked around, encouraging students with hand gestures and his ever-present smile.

Sun-hee stood on the porch of the House of Sanshin, enjoying the warmth of the rising sun and watching the exercises.

Jin-taek enjoys working with the children, thought Sun-hee. She looked for her five children in the sea of moving bodies. Su-dae, who got her petite size from Stone but, thankfully, was the opposite of his personality. Hong-do had inherited Strategist's analytical mind and love of politics. There was So-min, who was obsessed with how the human body worked, exercising with her close friends. In the back of the line of boys was Eun-mi, but everyone called him Little Numbers after his father and because he knew more about mathematics than anyone in camp. In the front stood Hon-yong Jr., taller and stronger than the rest of the boys his age, and just as handsome. His two older half-brothers also took after their father. The rest she knew by name, by their parents, by their abilities, strengths, and weaknesses. Collectively, they were way ahead of their parents.

What will they be like in a few more years?

Her mother came out of the door behind her, and they made their way to breakfast. As Sun-hee finished eating, the students ran and queued up in line for their morning meal.

"Come, Mother, time to prepare for another day of teaching," she said, and the two went to their classrooms.

It was nearly lunchtime when Gen. Park walked in and interrupted the class. Sun-hee saluted.

The students stood and bowed in respect except for one, Duk-bae, Gen. Park's son, who said, "Hello, Father."

Sun-hee resented Duk-bae's non-conforming attitude when his father was around. But there was nothing she could do.

Gen. Park returned the salute to Sun-hee and said, "Finish your lesson."

Sun-hee wrapped up what she was teaching and dismissed the class.

"Cha Sun-hee, I have drawn up a plan for the next generation," began Gen. Park in a matter of fact tone. As usual, he gave no greeting, just got to the point. "I asked Sergeant Kua to look it over. She suggested I have you review it."

"Is the plan similar to how you mated the original forty-eight?" Sun-hee asked.

"The same. I have the first set of partners defined," he said, holding out some folded papers. "Review them this afternoon, then come to headquarters and share your findings."

"Yes, Sir," said Sun-hee with a bow.

Sun-hee found substitutes for her afternoon classes and went to the library. She located the pedigrees diagramed out years ago and began to read Gen. Park's mating plan.

Immediately, she felt the old emotions rise.

I cannot cooperate with this. The girls cannot be subjected to what I went through.

She decided to present Gen. Park with marriage partners for the second generation. She began to write out the pairings with comments on her justification as to why this would be better for the offspring.

Just then, her daughter, So-min, bounded into the library.

"Hello, Mother. What are you doing?"

"I'm looking over some research. Shouldn't you be in class?"

"I was and am. Mrs. Moon allowed me to come to the library to prepare a report on DNA based on the articles that came in last month. Are those pedigree charts?"

"Yes. But the charts are not for your eyes. What is new about DNA?"

"The new research explains how the sequence of nucleotides in DNA is a code to make proteins. What was known until now is that proteins are made up of twenty amino acids, and DNA is made up of four nucleic acids. If DNA is the holder of the information to make proteins, what is the translation? In other words, how can DNA be read to understand the protein it makes? What I started reading yesterday was a paper showing some of the three-letter codes of nucleic acids that translate into an amino acid. This is the best thing ever, Mother. If I understood it all, I could tell you from these pedigrees who would be my ideal husband and what my children would be like."

"So, do you think they discovered the key to life?"

"It's a piece of the puzzle to heredity. Hopefully, I will understand it someday. Tomorrow, I need to present a report on what I read today. Have fun with those charts. I am available to help after tomorrow," So-min said, skipping up the stairs and disappearing into the natural sciences room.

Sun-hee sighed.

Only thirteen and she knows so much. I need to concentrate on what to present to the general.

It was dark when she left the library and made her way to headquarters. Along the way, she rehearsed her presentation on why the children should marry. She knocked on the door.

"I expected you hours ago," said Chun-ja in a disrespectful tone while holding the door open.

Sun-hee bowed. "I apologize for the time I have taken to be thorough."

"Let her in, Chun-ja. She has kept me waiting long enough," came Park's voice from the other room. Chun-ja motioned to Sun-hee to enter. Gen. Park stood, reached over to a television, and turned it off.

"I was watching that!" exclaimed Duk-bae.

"I need to meet with Lieutenant Cha. Please go to your room."

"She's my teacher. I'll sit here quietly and watch television."

Sun-hee, in embarrassment, bowed, and said, "I can come back tomorrow when your son is in school."

"No. We need to discuss this now," Gen. Park said firmly. He pointed to his son. "You, to your room." His son stood, arms crossed, and did not move. "One day of extra exercises from Sergeant Jo."

"Father!" said his son.

"Two days. Shall I make it a week?"

Duk-bae stomped out of the room, followed by a slamming door.

"I'm away too much," said Gen. Park, straightening his uniform. "You have a lot more paperwork than I gave you this morning. Sit and tell me what you have come up with." He moved to the table and yelled towards the kitchen. "Chun-ja, some tea."

Chun-ja rushed out with tea and poured two cups. "Lieutenant Cha, have you eaten?" she asked.

"I am not hungry, thank you," said Sun-hee.

Gen. Park's eyes squinted like they were drilling into her mind. Her prepared speech was a jumble in her head. She arranged the papers and took a deep breath. "The plan you gave me this morning is here. I have made a couple of changes."

"Tell me what you have on the rest of the papers.

She took a deep breath and swallowed. "I took the liberty to set up what I feel would make good marriages. I paired the children according to complementary abilities and strengths. The pedigree of the two individuals is with each couple. Let me explain the first couple."

Sun-hee went into detail on the first proposed marriage and the couples extended backgrounds. She concluded, "As you see, this couple would have similar interests yet would have sufficient variability in their family history to produce unique offspring. Each child would have a chance of having talents beyond their parents."

"You have more information than I do on the family history of these individuals. Do you feel each couple in this pile is equally qualified?"

"Yes, sir. I could explain my reasoning for each proposed marriage."

"Who do you propose marries my son?" Gen. Park said, looking at Sun-hee intensely.

"Your son shows great interest in medicine, taking after you. I propose a wife whose father is I Kwang-ku and myself, my daughter Cha So-min." Sun-hee finished with an honorable bow.

"What would be the benefit of having these children marry instead of the mating plan I proposed?"

"The main benefit, General Park, is the family can have a father. As our country has a father to lead our nation, each family has a mother and father to instruct the next generation. Mothers will always care for their children. When a man fathers many children by many wives, he has no family to care for." She shuddered to realize how her words may have spoken directly to the relationship Gen. Park had with his son.

Gen. Park pulled the pile of papers on the table towards himself. He folded his hands over them and said, "Get out, Sun-hee."

Sun-hee stood and bowed, "I apologize…"

"Out!" Gen. Park yelled.

Sun-hee exited as fast as she could and ran back to the House of Sanshin.

What have I done? I hope General Park does not think I am disloyal.

She sat down on her mat, pulled her knees up around her ears, and cried.

"What is wrong?" asked her Sue-dae.

"I cannot talk about it," said Sun-hee into her lap.

Eun-seong and Choe-me came over to offer comfort, but Sun-hee remained silent.

The next morning, Sun-hee asked others to teach her classes. She told her mother she would be at the library. She came out onto the porch as the students were doing morning exercises. The first thing she noticed was Jin-taek running behind Duk-bae. When Duk-bae did not run fast enough, Jin-taek would give him a little shove.

She knew her marriage plan for the next generations was correct and proper. The offspring would be as good as if they were conceived individually. Each child would have a stable family, to help them grow and mature. She looked through books and journals, searching for information on arranged marriages, primarily marriages arranged by the state. A couple of journal articles spoke of the science of eugenics, but always in the context of not letting the weak, the feeble, or those with mental illness reproduce. She put a hand over her mouth.

I have done this by not selecting a mate for Yi Si-ue.

Throughout the day, she investigated the concept of eugenics. A journal article from the Soviet Union discredited eugenics completely. Another article referenced the Hitler Youth Program and discussed how children were educated and trained to be soldiers in Germany before World War II. She wondered if Japan had something similar early in the century. *What did Gen. Park want to do with his program when he started it? What would it be like if there was no war? Have we fulfilled his plan?*

"Sun-hee, what is troubling you?" Sun-hee jumped, startled by her mother's voice.

"I really cannot talk about it, Mother. It is probably better you do not know."

"I know you talked to General Park. What did he tell you?"

"Mother, if you do not know, you are not responsible. Only I am accountable."

"At least you must eat. It is time for dinner, and I know you have not eaten all day."

"It's that late already?"

"Yes, come to eat with your children. They are wondering what is going on. You have not spoken to them in almost two days."

Sun-hee went to dinner and spent the evening with her children. They needed her. Children needed parents. Both parents. She would have to figure out a way for her children to get to know their fathers.

The next morning, Sgt. Kua approached and said, "Sun-hee, General Park would like to see you."

Sun-hee hugged her mother. "Tell my children I love them." Then she hugged her close friends, Young-ja, Choe-me, Joo-yun, and Eun-seong.

The door opened as she stepped onto the porch. Gen. Park sat in a corner chair, sipping tea. "Come in, Lieutenant Cha. Please take a seat."

"I would prefer standing," she said with a deep bow.

General Park picked up a cigarette, lit it, and took a long drag. He looked directly at Sun-hee, compressing his eyebrows while blowing out the smoke slowly through one side of his lips.

Sun-hee shook and found it difficult to breathe.

"Sit, Lieutenant," Gen. Park said in a commanding voice while gesturing with the hand holding the cigarette.

Sun-hee pulled out a chair and sat on the edge. She wrung her hands together on her lap to keep them from shaking.

"I reviewed the changes you made to the plan. The couples will make strong marriages. I could not find a way to arrange them better. However, this will negate the desired genetic diversity in the next generation." He took a long drag from his cigarette then a sip of his tea. "You realize having this generation marry is a crucial change in the program."

Sun-hee bowed in acknowledgment.

"You are bold, Sun-hee. You risk your life for what you feel is right, an amazing quality." He took another long pull on his cigarette and blew it out slowly. "And you do it without disrespect." He took another puff. "One question: you did not have time to draw up all the pedigrees of the children. Where did you get those?"

"All the students got together and drew up the pedigrees years ago, so our children would know their heritage."

Gen. Park stroked his chin while staring at the floor. His head slowly raised, looked at Sun-hee with squinted eyes, and he said, "You and your classmates were to be the first of a yearly group in the program. If I could have brought fifty students every year, there would now be over seven hundred prize winners and over two thousand children. With that many children in Korea, all well-educated, we could improve this country and get out from under the influence of the Soviets. The men who came here when you did are making a tremendous difference. But Kim Il-sung and our country need more individuals like your generation. Do you think marriages will have more of an impact on the future of our country, or will a greater diversity of children be better?"

Sun-hee's eyes stared into her teacup as if the floating bits of leaves could tell the future. "I don't know how the future will turn out," she said without looking up.

"You want your daughters to avoid the sacrifices you made. We all sacrifice for the good of Korea."

Sun-hee sat up straighter as a shiver ran down her spine.

Gen. Park stood and stepped to a window to stare out. He said into the window, "We will have marriages per the traditions of our people. The pairings will be as you drew up. You are the architect of the next generation, which must be born as soon as possible. The children will marry at age fifteen."

Sun-hee stood and bowed. The pent-up anxiety overwhelmed her. She trembled and began to cry. The pain she had suffered rushed out.

Gen. Park turned and pounded out his cigarette in an ashtray. "I can't stand women crying. You're dismissed."

Sun-hee bowed again, trying to control herself.

"Thank you, General Park," she said through her blubbering, shuffling out as fast as she could. She got to the bottom step, sat, put her head in her hands, and bawled.

The door opened behind her. She jumped up.

General Park said in a loud voice, "You are not to speak to anyone, including your mother, about this. I'm deciding to have marriages. As far as anyone else will know, you only made sure there were no errors. Am I making myself clear?"

"Yes, General Park," Sun-hee said with a deep bow.

"And go cry somewhere else!" he bellowed, slamming the door behind him.

43 — Marriages - Summer & Fall, 1966

On a warm August evening, Sun-hee sat chatting with her mother on the porch of the House of Sanshin.

Young-ja hurried towards them from the gate. As she approached, she said, "Sun-hee, you won't believe what General Park told Chulsoon and me." She paused to catch her breath. "He wants to have a marriage ceremony on the first of October for the older children. Isn't that grand?"

"Weddings?" Sue-dae said in an excited tone. "This is wonderful. Who arranged the couples?"

"General Park will announce the couples on the day of the weddings."

Sun-hee tuned Young-ja out and looked towards her oldest daughter, Su-dae, sitting at the end of the porch with a few other girls. Then she glanced over to the playground where the boys relaxed in the evenings. She located Young-ja's oldest son talking with other boys.

I put them together. They will make a good couple.

"Sun-hee, are you listening to me?" said her mother as she received a tap on the shoulder.

"Sorry, Mother. I was lost in my thoughts."

"Which boy do you want for a son-in-law?"

"I'm not going to speculate, Mother."

"Let's see, how many possibilities are there? There is …"

Sun-hee cut her off. "Mother, as girls, we played this game. I did not like it then, and I will not play it now?"

"You still feel the pain of how General Park mated you? You must be overjoyed. Your daughter is getting married."

Sun-hee swallowed and submerged herself in her thoughts.

I must not talk about it. Secrets are impossible to keep.

She stood and went for a walk by herself.

***

The wedding day was the topic of discussion all summer. Lt. Rim brought in bolts of fine cloth and arranged with dressmakers in the nearby village to make Joseon-ots for the brides.

From around the country, the fathers sent money or supplies to contribute to building eleven, four-by-four-meter square rooms — one for each couple. Extended plans would turn the former prisoner area into a sixty-unit housing complex in the next few years.

Lt. Rim had the last of the internal fences within the compound torn down. He insisted the perimeter fence stay in place as it kept beggars and thieves out.

Eleven boys and twelve girls would turn fifteen by the end of the year. One girl would prepare for her wedding day and not have a mate. Sun-hee knew which girl it was but remained silent. The mothers secretly hoped their daughter would have another year to mature before marrying.

As the momentous day approached, activity in the camp increased. Many of the men returned, spending most of their time catching up with each other rather than interacting with the women.

Two days before the wedding, Su-dae came bounding up and proudly said, "Mother, did you know my father oversees the mining in North Korea?"

"I knew Young-soo worked on mines. I didn't know he is in a high leadership position."

"He told me the exporting of raw materials is of great economic benefit to the country. Mining is one of, if not the biggest, source of income for North Korea. Why didn't you tell me he was so important?"

Sun-hee saw how her daughter radiated joy and pride about her father. "I couldn't tell you because your father has not talked to me in over twelve years. Other men rarely speak about him. I'm glad you had the chance to talk to him."

"Did you want to marry him?"

"No. Young-soo is too quiet of a man for my liking. And with his career, I do not think we would have spent much time together."

"He said almost the same thing when I asked if he wanted to marry you. He said he was too busy to have a wife. I have more questions to ask him about the economics of exports. If I can find him." So-min ran off.

Sun-hee watched her go.

What bundle of energy. She has a keen financial mind. She would make a good capitalist.

Sun-hee ran into Yong-gak the next afternoon in the library.

She asked, "What's your opinion about the condition of the country and politics in the capital?"

"North Korea is doing very well compared to our neighbors," he said, beginning his usual hand gestures. "China has lost millions of people to starvation and rebellion. They are a country in turmoil. South Korea is struggling. They have little in the way of natural resources. Their economy survives by stealing technology and providing cheap labor to American companies. They are slaves to capitalism."

"Japan is recovering from the war and continues to rebuild, mostly with trade from the United States. They are also a source of cheap labor for products exported to the United States. Japan does have more resources and education. Their culture gives them an advantage over South Korea.

"The Soviet Union is now one of the world's most powerful countries, and we benefit greatly from our relationship with them. Today, North Korea is more advanced than China, Japan, or South Korea due to the technology and assistance we receive from the Soviets. I'm encouraged by our progress.

"I'm giving you only the positives, Sun-hee," he said with index fingers crossed. "Officially, I can tell you nothing else. However, there is much more to do. The Premier's plan is acceptable for now. Your work here, raising our son Hong-do and the other children, is remarkable. I must say my son's knowledge is equal to my students at the university. You and your mother are excellent teachers.

"This little program of General Park's has worked well in its limited capacity. Someday I will take you and show you the rest of the country." Yong-gak finished with an unusual gesture, his arms out wide.

"Thank you for the update. I look forward to visiting the rest of the country someday," Sun-hee said with a smile while taking his hands and squeezing them. "And I look forward to getting out of this compound."

At dinner, Sun-hee saw Kwang-ku sitting with their daughter, Cha So-min. She took her meal and walked over to them. "May I join you?"

Kwang-ku stood and bowed deeply towards Sun-hee, saying, "I would be delighted to have you join us. Our little thirteen-year-old was showing off how much she knows about human anatomy, physiology, and this molecule called DNA. She knows a lot more than I did at thirteen."

"I think she was born with your medical knowledge. She absorbs new information like a sponge. I wonder how much she would learn if we sent her home with you for the next couple of years."

"Can I, Mom? It would be so much fun!" Cha So-min said. "Being stuck in this prison camp is driving me insane."

"With my schedule, I would not have time to spend with you," said Kwang-ku.

"I'm sure there are lots of things to do in the city. I will be fine," said So-min.

"I think it best you stay here for the next few years," he said, winking at Sun-hee.

The conversation continued, and Sun-hee felt the loneliness of not having a husband like Kwang-ku, Yong-gak, or even Young-soo to share meals and childrearing. Hon-yong does spend a lot of time with his son, but is too busy making furniture to spend time with me. She had her mother and friends, yet there was something more to having dinner with her children's fathers.

Later in the evening, Eun-mi, who had just turned ten-years-old, came to her. "When will my father arrive?"

"I do not know, Eun-mi. He is an important man and may be unable to get away from his responsibilities."

"My father will be the only one not here," Eun-mi said with disappointment, and he hung his head down.

The next day as she was eating lunch, Sun-hee heard shouts announcing the arrival of Ching-ying. Numbers had arrived. He greeted everyone at lunch, including Sun-hee, with a quick bow, saying, "Hello, Sun-hee", before moving on.

Sun-hee saw Eun-mi walking with Ching-ying to the library after lunch. Eun-mi was carrying a new abacus.

That evening, Eun-mi could not stop talking about how much his father knew about mathematics, showing off how to work his abacus.

As Eun-mi explained how his father solved a math problem, Hon-yong Jr. came and squeezed himself between Sun-hee and Sue-dae. He began to irritate his mother and grandmother while Eun-mi energetically talked about his abacus.

Hon-yong Jr. interrupted his older brother. "That thing isn't so neat. I bet my father could make a better one."

"Shhh…let your brother talk," said Sun-hee to Hon-yong Jr.

"Why is he so excited about seeing his father? My dad is always around and has made everyone many toys."

"Quiet, while I show mother one more trick with this," said Eun-mi loudly.

"I don't have to be quiet," said Hon-yong Jr.

"Hon-yong, what's bothering you?" asked Sun-hee.

"Everyone is happy. Their fathers come to visit, and everyone is excited. Today is not special for me," he said with a pouted lip.

Eun-mi retorted, "You are lucky to have your father close by all the time. After the nuptials, your father will still be here, and mine will leave for a long time." And his lips began to quiver.

"I'm sorry, brother," said Hon-yong Jr.

Just then, Choe-me came into their room and called her son over. "Get your things and go to the new apartments. Your father is waiting for you there." Then she stood and said to Young-ja's and Joo-yun's sons, "Boys get your things and go to the apartments. It's time for you to leave this home and prepare your new one."

The next morning, the women rose early, wanting to shower, fix their hair, dress, and make their children look their best for the wedding. Sun-hee and her mother spent hours making sure Su-dae looked beautiful. Sun-hee escorted Su-dae to the main room and allowed her to wait with the rest of the brides.

An hour before the wedding, Sun-hee went out onto the porch. The scene took her breath away. Twelve archways made by Hon-yong stood towards the south, each covered with a variety of flowers. The colors enthralled Sun-hee.

The kitchen staff prepared tables for a feast after the ceremony. White tablecloths and a flower centerpiece adorned each table.

Sun-hee looked past the archways, trying to detect activity around the new apartments. She could not see any of the men, nor could she determine which of the flats belonged to Young-ja's son and soon her daughter.

Today, my daughter is marrying the son of the Skinny Beast.

She chuckled to herself.

Sgt. Kua came out of her home and stood on the porch. The building was no longer a guesthouse and, hopefully, would never be used for that purpose again. Her dress uniform made her look years younger, or maybe the bowl hat sitting neatly over her greying hair took a few years off her appearance.

The day was perfect. Fluffy white clouds, the type one could stare at for hours, making out shapes of animals and monsters, adorned the blue sky. A light, cooling breeze fluttered the flowers and ribbons.

Choe-me strolled up and took Sun-hee's hand. "You look wonderful in your light blue Joseon-ot. My stomach is turning like I'm the one getting married. I'm so anxious about who will marry my son."

Sun-hee felt the clamminess of Choe-me's hand in hers. She looked at her friend. "You are stunning. Now that I see you in lavender silk, I wish I had gotten in line ahead of you."

"How can you remain calm? Don't you wonder who Su-dae is marrying?"

"I know who she will marry. I determined the pairings," Sun-hee said. Then she turned and grabbed Choe-me's other hand and looked her straight in the eye. "Never tell anyone. It just slipped out. Keep it a secret, or I will be viewed disloyal," Sun-hee said in an urgent voice.

"Yes, Sun-hee," said Choe-me, chuckling. Then she whispered in Sun-hee's ear, "I have waited this long, I guess I can wait a little longer to see who my new daughter-in-law will be."

Sue-dae came out to stand by Sun-hee.

"You look prettier than ever, Mother," said Sun-hee.

"Thank you, dear," said Sue-dae. "Next to you and Choe-me, I feel like a wilted rose."

Sun-hee jerked back. "I forgot something. I'll return in a minute." She walked quickly into the sleeping room and then to her mat. She dug to the bottom of her bag and pulled out the blue silk scarf. She smoothed out the wrinkles and wrapped it around her shoulders. It matched the color of her dress quite nicely. A horn sounded. The wedding ceremony had begun. Sun-hee hurried to the common room.

Sgt. Kua ordered the rest of the children to get into formation, leaving an aisle between them.

The mothers accompanied their daughters out of the House of Sanshin and down the steps. The fathers of the brides each stood in an archway.

Lt. Rim, Sgt. Jo, and five remaining soldiers stood at attention in front of the tables.

The fathers marched the young men to the ceremony. They looked so attractive, dressed up in traditional wedding clothes.

Each bride located their father and strolled with their mother to a flowered archway. Su-dae and Sun-hee joined Young-soo near the middle. A man with a camera took a photograph of each bride with her parents.

The horn sounded again, signaling the arrival of the grooms. Gen. Park marched out of Sgt. Kua's home accompanied by Max. They proceeded down the line of grooms, handing each one an envelope.

When he reached the end of the line, Gen. Park turned and said in a booming voice, "Men, open your envelopes." He paused as the grooms opened and read the names on the cards inside. Then he commanded, "March to your brides."

The young men shuffled, rearranging themselves to align with their appointed mates, and walked forward.

Sun-hee watched the man she had chosen for her first daughter be the last to get in front of his bride. She chuckled as he came up and bowed deeply to Su-dae.

The photographer moved from arch to arch, taking photographs of the newly married couples.

The celebrating began with a cheer for the new brides and grooms. Young-ja ran up to Sun-hee, grabbing her in a hug. "We are family! I could not be happier for my son. They know each other way too well to be married. Our grandchildren will be something. I cannot wait. Oh, Sun-hee, what a wonderful day."

The Skinny Beast came over and shook the Stone's hand. Then the two men approached Young-ja and Sun-hee. The four of them held each other's hands for a moment in a circle, parents of the new couple. Sun-hee felt a void. No union between the men and women except the two children now joined together. The men released their grasps, bowing slightly, before walking away, joining other fathers showing little emotional attachment to the mothers of their children.

The rest of the afternoon the crowd milled about talking, eating, laughing, and celebrating. Sun-hee tried to chat with the twenty-two men who came to the camp as prize winners sixteen years ago. She could sense a strong bond in the men to the House of Sanshin. Each man had taken on significant responsibilities in Korea, but their hearts were still loyal.

Max made his way to Sun-hee. His hair had greyed some, and the lines on his face stood out more distinctly. "Hello, Sun. What a lovely day for a wedding feast. I was surprised when I received an invitation from my son to come to his wedding. Wild bears could not keep me away," he said in Russian.

"How have you been, Max?"

"Life is good. I'm a surgeon at a hospital in Volgograd. My life is effortless as I mostly treat the minor ailments of peacetime. You look like you have not aged since I saw you last."

"Except for the weddings today, nothing has changed in the fifteen years since you left. I guess that includes me."

Max chuckled and looked off at the hills. "A little birdy told me that you're the one who convinced the general to let the kids marry."

Sun-hee turned abruptly and said in a low voice, "Where did you hear that?"

"Like I said, a little birdy."

"If that ever gets back to General Park, I will be in trouble."

"He told me he wanted the information to remain between him and I. Now, it is the secret of the three of us. I do admire the person who was able to convince Park to change his program. It takes a lot of leverage to do that. Someday, maybe you will be in charge."

"I can't even get outside these fences. And how could a woman take charge of this paternalistic society?"

"I know it's not in your nature to be aggressive. General Park selected non-aggressive children for his students. He wanted a group of talented wimps to support the real men leading this country."

Sun-hee took a step back. "I accept that we are leaders, but we will not rule."

"Come, Sun. There is some vodka waiting on ice. We can drown out our memories together."

"You go ahead, Max. I need to talk to some other people who I have not seen in a long time." She strolled around, chatting and enjoying the celebration.

Late in the afternoon, the clouds gathered together, blotting out the sun. Gusts of wind whipped at the centerpieces, knocking them to the ground. Sprinkles of rain chased the celebrants inside. Workers rushed to remove dishes and decorations before the heavy rain fell. By dusk, pouring rain washed fallen flower petals down stone-lined channels to the river.

44 — Cancer - April, 1967

Sue-dae gathered up a pile of graded assignments and walked around the classroom, returning them to the students. Everyone had written an excellent essay except Duk-bae. She placed his paper on his desk last and walked towards the front of the room.

"Why did I get a low grade?" came a loud voice behind her. "I don't deserve this."

Sue-dae turned to face the class, nodding her head with furrowed eyebrows to stifle the chuckles and murmuring. "I grade essays rigorously so that you may perfect your skills."

"My father will hear about this!" yelled out Duk-bae.

"Jjok-bari," came a muffled voice from the back of the room.

"I'm not Japanese, you Russian half-breed," replied Duk-bae as he stood and glared at his accuser.

Max's son stood, saying, "Your mother is half Japanese."

Duk-bae lunged at Max's son. They fell to the floor in the back of the room, wrestling and throwing punches. The girls moved away while the boys circled the fighters.

Sue-dae pushed her way past the boys and yelled, "STOP!"

When they did not stop, she tried to grab Duk-bae. Other boys reached in to help separate the combatants.

Duk-bae scrambled to his feet, lashing out, flinging his arms at everyone. A wild swinging fist caught Sue-dae solidly in her stomach. She groaned and bent over. Hon-yong's oldest son interceded and placed a palm strike onto Duk-bae's nose. A piercing scream followed the loud crack of a breaking bone. Duk-bae fell to the floor, his hands over his face.

Unable to breathe, Sue-dae leaned against a desk. Girls took her arms, helping her to her chair in the front of the room. As she sat back, she took a little breath, then another. Her face was flushed, heart racing. Then her stomach spasmed. She bent over, threw up, and fell forward. The girls caught her and lowered her gently to the floor, where she continued to heave.

"Get the doctor!" someone yelled.

***

A few minutes later at the hospital, Sun-hee stood nervously next to Chulsoon as he examined her mother. "There is internal bleeding somewhere," said Chulsoon. "The only way to stop it is to do surgery." He motioned to others to move Sue-dae into the operating room. "Don't worry, Sun-hee, she'll be fine," he said while placing a comforting hand on Sun-hee's shoulder.

Sun-hee stayed near the door to the operating room, anxiously waiting. Eun-seong sat next to her holding her hand. The minutes passed into hours.

The door opened, and Chulsoon came out. "Your mother is resting," he said, sitting down next to her. "We found the bleeding in her stomach and easily repaired the injury. The blow to her stomach revealed another problem. Your mother has cancer."

Sun-hee looked at Chulsoon with wide eyes. "Can you remove the tumor?"

"There is not just one tumor. The cancer is in all the organs of her abdomen," said Chulsoon in a quiet, sympathetic voice.

"Can I see her?" asked Sun-hee.

"Yes. For a few moments," said Chulsoon. "She is sedated. I'll be here if you need anything."

Sun-hee held her mother's hand, watching her inhale and exhale, wishing she could do something to help. Eun-seong remained by her side.

"Come, we should get some dinner and rest," said Eun-seong, putting a hand around Sun-hee's shoulder to guide her away. "We'll come back in the morning."

At dinner, Sun-hee tried to force herself to eat, but the knots in her gut strangled her appetite. Many of the girls came to offer their sympathy. Sun-hee slightly bowed to acknowledge each person, barely registering who was there.

"What happened to my son?" shattered the mournful silence. Gen. Park stood with his hands on his hips, eyes glaring under his wide-brimmed hat.

The cold voice froze everyone. Nothing moved except the birds, who took flight and fluttered away.

Hon-yong's oldest son stood, cleared his throat, and said, "General Park, I broke Duk-bae's nose."

A girl impulsively jumped up and blurted, "He deserved it."

"I did it to stop the fight. Mrs. Cha needed help," said Hon-yong's oldest son.

"Who started the fight?" demanded Gen. Park. He looked around at the women and children too frightened to speak up. He pointed at the girl who had blurted out before. "You! Tell me who was fighting."

The girl froze for a moment, then pointed at Max's son.

Gen. Park took a step toward Max's son. "I should have known it was one of the Russians." He stared intently at Max's son for a few seconds. "I'll figure out what to do with you later. As for you," Gen. Park said as he stepped towards Hon-yong's oldest son. "Why didn't you break his nose?" He pointed to Max's son.

"He is not the one who hit Mrs. Cha."

"So, Mrs. Cha can tell me all about this little fight," said Gen. Park.

Eun-seong stood and bowed deeply. "Respectively, General Park, Mrs. Cha is in the hospital. Chulsoon operated on her this afternoon."

Gen. Park glared in her direction. His mouth started to move, then he turned sharply and marched away.

That evening, Jin-taek forced Max's son to exercise and run until the boy was in tears.

The next morning, Sun-hee went to see her mother. Chulsoon stopped her before she went in. "General Park came last night. I explained what I knew. He returned this morning and yelled at her for not controlling the class."

"I called Kwang-ku last night. I hoped he might have more experience with this type of cancer. We will treat her with herbs and acupuncture for her symptoms. Unfortunately, we concluded that your mother has about six months to live."

Sun-hee's lips quivered, her eyes closed momentarily. "Thank you, Chulsoon," she said, turning to enter the room where her mother lay.

"Sun-hee."

"Mother." She leaned over to bestow an embrace, tears in her eyes, fighting the lump in her throat.

"Chulsoon explained to me what he found yesterday. My time has come to an end," Sue-dae said softly.

"You have a lot more time, Mother. Don't give up," Sun-hee pleaded.

"I'm not giving up, dear. I realize my condition is poor. Chulsoon said I would be able to get up in a few days. I will teach until cancer takes me."

"You do not have to teach any longer. Others can take your classes."

"Allow me to do what I love to do."

"You have done so much, Mother. You can take a break now."

"My dream was to teach children so that they would have a chance at a better life. By teaching, I gave all of Korea a better life. The prize you won made my life a winner. There was no way we could have foreseen what has occurred. Fate has been kind to us."

"I cannot accept how it ends. Kwang-ku is searching for an answer with the Soviet doctors. Someone will know how to cure you."

"You're ready to go on without me. Keep working to educate our people. Life for everyone is improving. It's up to you to continue what we have started."

"I don't even know what to do now, Mother."

"Go get some books from the library. Find some new fiction to read to me."

Sun-hee spent the next few days reading to her mother. Slowly, Sue-dae healed from her surgery and, within a week, returned to the House of Sanshin. She checked in with Chulsoon daily. Three weeks after he revealed her cancer, she resumed teaching.

Over the next few months, Sue-dae grew weaker. She could not keep food down. Chulsoon finally kept her in the hospital. Sun-hee and others read to her when she was awake.

On October first, they held a second wedding celebration similar to the year before for the second-born children of the prize winners.

Sue-dae attended, propped up in a bed. She thoroughly enjoyed seeing Hong-do and his new bride.

A week after the wedding, Sue-dae passed with Sun-hee and her five grandchildren at her bedside.

Sun-hee, overcome with grief, went to her mat, curled up with her blue scarf, and stared at the place where her mother had slept. Eun-seong sat all night by her side.

The next morning, Choe-me and Young-ja placed chairs on the porch of the House of Sanshin for Sun-hee. All-day, a procession of comforters came by to offer their sympathy. Each person would sit with Sun-hee for a while, telling stories of how Sue-dae influenced their lives. There were many shared memories, tears, love, and laughter.

Jin-taek came up late in the afternoon and bowed deeply. With tears in his eyes, he took a worn piece of paper from his pocket and showed it to Sun-hee.

Sergeant Jo-Jin-taek,
You're my hero.
Sincerely, Cha Sue-dae.

***

Sue-dae was laid to rest in a lovely ceremony six days later. The cooks made sweets and a splendid banquet for everyone.

Sun-hee was talking and reminiscing with a couple of girls when Mrs. Lim came over and said, "I'm sorry about your mother. She was a great woman. Did you notice the only people not at the ceremony were General Park, his son, and Chun-ja? He is so disrespectful."

Sun-hee opened her mouth to respond when Eun-seong interrupted, "You have to try these sweets the cooks made. Come, Sun-hee. I'll show you which ones are the best." As Sun-hee turned, with Eun-seong's arm around her, she saw Lt. Rim. His eyes fixated on Mrs. Lim. Sun-hee tried to turn back, but Eun-seong held her firmly, walking her towards the table full of sweets.

"I think we should avoid Mrs. Lim," said Eun-seong while picking up an orange square candy. "She has been quite negative this week. Try this. It tastes like baeksalgu."

Sun-hee bit into the candy, chewing slowly. "This is wonderful. I'm going to take another piece for later," said Sun-hee as she picked up a piece and wrapped it in a paper.

The sun started to set, and the crowd dispersed. Sun-hee made her way to her mother's grave. She laid the candy on the grave and said, "I saved you one, Mother. You always loved baeksalgu."

45 — Butterfly - Mid-April, 1972

"This is a butterfly," Sun-hee said to a group of four-year-old children, as she pointed to the insect fluttering on the blossoms of a cherry tree. "They eat the nectar the flowers make, and they pollinate the flower."

The children started to run around, trying to catch butterflies, jumping and running through the grass around the trees. The butterflies were too quick, eluding the small hands chasing them. Sun-hee giggled at the joy of the frolicking children.

"Cha Sun-hee!" yelled a man's voice. She turned to see a soldier walking towards her. He wore the uniform of a captain and had a stern, rugged face. He was not tall but carried himself with authority.

What can he want with me?

She noticed three soldiers following him, their rifles ready.

What is going on?

"I'm Cha Sun-hee," she said, bowing in respect.

"Take her," said the captain, waving his arm and pointing to Sun-hee.

She froze in place and held her arms out as soldiers grabbed them.

"How may I be of assistance, Captain?" she said as the soldiers jerked her towards the officer. She noticed Jin-taek running towards her, his face stern like a wild dog about to attack. "Jin-taek. Stop," she shouted. "We need to see what these men want."

The soldier with the rifle turned, aimed at Jin-taek, and fired. Jin-taek dove to his right, avoiding the bullet which flew by him and whizzed into the grass.

"Everyone, calm down!" Sun-hee said sternly. "We will not resist these men, Jin-taek."

The captain held out his hand to the soldier and said, "Hold your fire." The gun remained pointed at Jin-taek, crouching in the tall grass.

"Drop your gun and stand up," said the captain.

Sun-hee nodded positively. Jin-taek stood with his hands out, leaving his gun in the grass.

"Now, Captain, please explain why I'm being treated in this manner."

"You are under arrest. I'm taking you in for questioning."

She bowed as deeply as she could with her arms held to show her submission and said calmly, "Let's get the children back to the orphanage. Once we are there, we can discuss this further."

"Children, get in line and follow us," Sun-hee said. The children quickly lined up behind her. "Jin-taek, follow, and make sure the children do not stray."

Jin-taek kept a few meters distance as he moved around to the end of the line. His eyes glued to the soldier with the rifle pointed in his direction.

Sun-hee asked the captain, "Why are we waiting? Proceed, and we will follow."

After an awkward moment, the captain motioned to his men and began walking towards the compound. Sun-hee, held firmly in the hands of two soldiers, followed. Then came a line of children, Jin-taek, and another soldier.

Sgt. Kua and a few of the children's mothers came out as they approached the camp. Sgt. Kua held her rifle in front of her. Her shoulder-length gray hair whisked in the light breeze, her eyes studying the situation. "Pardon me, Captain," she said as they approached. "May I inquire what this is about?"

"Who are you?" said the captain.

"Sergeant Kua Eun-young. I have known this woman for twenty years. She has done nothing to warrant treatment like this."

The captain took a notebook from his breast pocket and wrote in it. "Is there a Cha Sue-dae at this facility, Sergeant?"

"She died five years ago, Captain."

"What do you want with my mother?" asked Sun-hee.

"You are to remain silent," yelled the captain, pointing the finger at Sun-hee.

Jin-taek ushered the children towards the camp and into the arms of their mothers, who whisked them back to camp.

"Is there a Lieutenant Rim Seung-Gin at this camp, Sergeant?" inquired the captain.

"He left a few days ago," replied Sgt. Kua.

"Where is he?"

"He did not tell me where he was going," said Sgt. Kua.

"You are to stay in this camp, Sergeant. We will come back should we need you for questioning."

"You have not answered my question, Captain," said Sgt. Kua. "Why are you taking Lieutenant Cha?"

"My orders are to bring this woman in for questioning. I never ask why." An army truck rumbled down the road, the back covered with canvas. The captain motioned. His men took shackles and bound Sun-hee's hands and legs. They placed a black cloth bag over her head.

Sun-hee heard Sgt. Kua, "Gently! You must not handle her like a criminal."

A shot rang out. Sun-hee heard screams. She could not see. She struggled.

Who was shot?

Hands picked her up and cast her into the back of the truck. Someone pulled her to the front of the truck bed, where she lay on her side, back to the cab. She felt the truck move.

Why are they taking me?

She reviewed everything she had done over the years.

Why would they want me, my mother, or Lt. Rim?

Eventually, the truck stopped, and the men removed her hood. The soldiers offered her water and allowed Sun-hee a moment to relieve herself. She noted the position of the sun. It was near the horizon. Then the hood went back on.

Time seemed to drag on forever before the truck stopped again. The moon was up. She acted as polite as she could, but the soldiers still handled her roughly, bruising her arms and legs. The soldiers did not put on the hood, which reduced Sun-hee's anxiety.

The next time the truck stopped, the sun was up. She drank from a metal cup and looked at the flat land around them.

We must be going to Pyongyang. Where else would we be going?

The men forcefully lifted her back into the truck and shoved her to the front.

She was awoken by the hood sliding over her head. Hands grabbed her legs, arms, and clothes, pulling her out of the truck and standing her upright. Someone pulled her by the shackles around her wrists. She shuffled her feet as fast as she could to keep up.

The floor is solid. I'm in a building.

Her nose turned as a musty smell mixed with body odor, and urine penetrated her hood. They pulled her sideways. Then all was still for a few seconds. The shackles came off. Then the hood yanked away.

She blinked her eyes and caught sight of the backs of the soldiers going through the door before it banged shut. The sound of sliding metal and clanging keys, amplified by the small room, told her she was in a cell.

She turned all the way around, viewing the cement walls. The only things in the room were a worn mat and a bucket. A cockroach scurried across the floor in front of her. With a quick movement of her foot, she squashed the bug. The light went out. Pitch black. As her eyes adjusted, a few slivers of light snuck in under the door. She moved to the mat and sat down against the wall.

I'm a prisoner. Why?

The sound of clanking keys woke her. She could make out the sounds of doors unlocking, opening, closing, and locking, one after another. The lock on her door turned. The door opened. Hands held out a bowl of rice and a cup of water. She took them and bowed in thanks. She ate, savoring each morsel to pass the time.

My life has been active reading, studying, writing, caring for children or patients. I don't like doing nothing. When there is nothing to do, time passes like a snail on a thousand-kilometer journey.

Sun-hee stood and began to pace. Her pacing became circles. She began to go through the morning exercises they did at camp, slowly, methodically, feeling her muscles work and stretch. She examined her bruises. Multiple handprints were evident on her arms.

She exercised again, at a faster speed, exhausting her strength. She paused, felt her heart pound in her chest, and the sweat trickle down her face. The only sound was her deep breaths and blood pumping past her ears. She repeated her loyalty chant in a quiet voice as she had done for so many years with her companions. Then she sang the national anthem.

She paced the cell to cool down and thought of each of the remaining forty-four prizewinners.

What are they doing? Are they under investigation?

She paced, thinking of the children of the first generation and over one hundred fifty grandchildren who lived at Yangseongso. She saw their faces, their names, and their personalities. She stopped and sat facing the door.

I'm ready for questioning. Tell me why I'm here.

The day passed, and she exercised again but felt faint.

I'm dehydrated.

The quiet, with no interaction and no children, unraveled her nerves.

I cannot stand the waiting, the uncertainty, the silence, the loneliness.

The lights went out. Sun-hee laid down and slept.

The lights came on. As the day before, she heard doors being unlocked, opened, closed, and locked. Her door opened. She bowed and took the food. The hands remained.

"Give me your empties," said a voice.

Sun-hee quickly sat her food down and handed over the empties from the day before. An empty bucket was pushed in, and Sun-hee handed out the other. The door closed and locked.

Again alone. The silence was maddening. After twenty years around friends, her children and grandchildren, there was nothing, no one. She limited her exercise to avoid sweating and to conserve water. She sat, stood, laid on the mat, never finding a position she wanted to stay in for long.

She heard heavy footsteps in the hall and her lock turned. She faced the door. The door opened. Two large men in khaki brown uniforms entered. They wore no insignias or markings.

They grabbed her and pushed her out of the cell, down the corridor. The men forced her into a room and strapped her to a chair.

I am strapped down like the American soldiers. Who will question me? I will tell them what I know. I have nothing to hide except for the program. I must protect the others. I cannot tell them about Gen. Park's plan. If I do, everyone will be in danger.

The men left.

Another silent room, only I cannot move.

One bare light bulb hung directly overhead. The barren cement wall in front of her offered no clues as to why they had taken her prisoner. Time passed, how long?

How far had the snail moved on its journey?

She was alone with her thoughts and fears.

Talk to me! I will tell you anything.

Her heart pounded, her head hurt, and her bladder began to scream.

Faint footsteps grew louder.

Is this someone to talk to? There must be many men coming into the room. Who is this man who walks before me? He is in the same brown khaki clothes without markings as the men who brought me here.

"Are you Cha Sun-hee," the man said.

"Yes, I'm Lieutenant Cha Sun-hee."

"What was your relationship with Gen. Ma?" he asked.

"At General Ma's direction, we wrote educational materials for the Democratic People's Republic of Korea."

"Who are the 'weee'?" he said, drawing out the last word with a grin.

"My mother and I. Many others helped."

"What did you receive in return?"

"The satisfaction of knowing we served our country."

"How much money did you receive?"

"I was never given money for my work."

"How much money did your mother receive?" He lit a cigarette.

"She received no money, sir."

"Cha Sun-hee," the man paused, taking a puff of his cigarette. "I know General Ma paid his workers. He paid them well. He demanded more funds over the years. All to pay the workers who he said demanded more money from him. Now, how much did you receive?" His voice increased in intensity as he spoke.

"I received no payment from General Ma for my services. There was a man who took the teaching materials to General Ma. He requested things for the camp."

"Are you referring to Lieutenant Rim?"

"Yes, sir."

I hope I have not gotten him into trouble.

"General Ma told us about Lieutenant Rim."

The man took her left hand and grabbed two fingers in each of his hands. "Now let me ask again, over the years, how much money did you receive from General Ma?"

What is he doing?

"I received no payment, sir."

The man pulled her fingers apart, sideways, and jammed his thumb between the knuckles. "Ahhhhhhh," she screamed, trying to jerk her arm back. The straps held firm while the man's thumb separated her knuckles, causing extreme pain.

Her hair was pulled back by an unseen hand, forcing her to look up at the lights. Again, the man's thumb jammed between her knuckles. She screamed.

"Tell me about the money!" the man yelled at her. He pressed his thumb harder.

She could feel her heart pounding in her chest. "I know of no money," she cried.

"How did you live without money?" the man demanded.

"We lived in a compound with a hospital and school. There was food to eat. Lieutenant Rim saw to the needs of the camp over the years. I did not receive any money. Never."

"How did you pay for what you needed, like clothes and medicine?"

"Seamstresses in the town near the camp make our clothes. Lieutenant Rim arranges the payment. The camp is a hospital. We have all the medicine we need. General Park saw to that."

"What goes on at the camp?"

"It's a hospital, orphanage, and school."

"How do you think the camp gets everything it needs?"

"The military provided supplies."

"So, you just wrote all the educational materials and did all this work for no payment?"

"My mother's dream was to teach so that her students have a better life. Isn't our country better off because of the materials we have written for teachers?"

"I ask the questions!" he said as he slapped her. Then he put his cigarette out on the back of Sun-hee's hand. "What do you gain by withholding the truth, woman?" She grimaced. The smell of her burnt flesh resurfaced memories of the children she had treated long ago.

The man stepped back and said to the men behind Sun-hee, "Bring the other one in."

Sun-hee heard shuffling behind her, and then two men dragged a beaten and bloody Lt. Rim in front of her. He hung in their arms, and his head settled forward towards his chest.

"Is this Lieutenant Rim?" the interrogator asked Sun-hee.

"Yes, sir."

The interrogator pulled up Lt. Rim's head by his hair. "Is this Cha Sun-hee?"

Lt. Rim's eyes opened, and without expression, Lt. Rim said, "Yes."

"Did you give her money for her work?"

"No."

"Did you keep all the money General Ma paid you for Sun-hee's work?"

"I bought supplies for the hospital and orphanage," said Lt. Rim in a barely audible voice.

"What you bought did not cost as much as General Ma says he paid you. Where is the money?" the interrogator yelled.

"I gave you my ledger, which accounts for all the payments," Lt. Rim forced out.

"Your ledger shows what you spent. General Ma's books show you received much more money. Should I believe a lowly lieutenant? Or a general?"

The man moved to Sun-hee and put his face a few centimeters from hers. His smoky bad breath blew over her face as he said, "Who is telling the truth. Do you support Lieutenant Rim or General Ma?"

The question brought the years of fearing Lt. Rim into her heart. She saw the face of Mung-jo, who left in the night, and Lt. Rim as he walked up with the bundle of her things. The image of the man Lt. Rim shot for stealing food, who she frantically tried to save, flashed before her. Then the times of reasonably questioning the American prisoners came to mind. The time he brought bolts of cloth for the weddings, and how the camp always seemed to have enough. She shuddered.

"Answer me," said the man.

"I don't know anything about the financial arrangements between General Ma and Lieutenant Rim," said Sun-hee in a confident voice.

"You know nothing about what is going on around you. Lieutenant Rim feeds you in exchange for taking care of children. You are a waste to Korea. I label you hostile Songbun and sentence you to the gulag. You do not know what the truth is."

"What I know as truth is this. Many years ago, I held babies burnt beyond recognition by American bombs and performed surgeries on soldiers who were lucky enough to return from the front lines. In those days, I dedicated myself to serve our Premier and make our country better to the best of my ability. My mother and I wrote the teaching materials because we wanted everyone to have a good education. My reward is in serving and seeing our people become great. While sitting in a cell waiting for you to ask me questions, I realized these are the first days of my adult life wherein I have done nothing to serve our country. If I knew something which would help make our country better, I would tell you."

The man hit her with all his might. The crack of her jaw-bone was the loudest sound she had ever heard.

She faintly heard the man's next words. "If you do not talk, then you will not talk."

She felt dizzy and struggled not to vomit, while the agonizing pain in the side of her face blocked out everything else. She inhaled, spat out a tooth, and forced herself to breathe. Her head throbbed with each heartbeat.

Focus on breathing.

The walls became dizzy. She closed her eyes, and the world went dark.

***

"Sun-hee. Sun-hee. Can you hear me? Sun-hee?" She felt fumbling at her wrists and tried to open her eyes. Only the right eye opened. The light forced her to squint.

"I…" The pain shot through her face, Sun-hee moaned.

"Be still," whispered the voice in front of her.

"Who are you? What are you doing?" She heard the voice of the man who had interrogated her.

"I work for the finance minister and am here investigating the allegations against General Ma. I came to ask Cha Sun-hee some questions. It looks like I'm too late. This doctor has methods to get people to talk."

The voice sounds familiar. Who is he?

Sun-he forced her eye open. Unicorn was looking at her from a close distance.

"What did you find out from Sun-hee about the funds General Ma embezzled?" asked the familiar voice behind her back.

"She said she received nothing," said the man who questioned her.

Kwong-ku started undoing the straps on her legs.

"After examining Lieutenant Rim's financial records, which were in good order," said the familiar voice. "I would say Sun-hee received a lot. Food, housing, clothes, and all her other needs were met. But I found no records of money given directly to her or her mother."

"Under interrogation, General Ma said that this woman received payments," said the man who interrogated her.

"Lieutenant Rim kept good books. There is a great discrepancy between what Lieutenant Rim received, and what General Ma said he gave them," replied the familiar voice.

"The difference must have been given to this woman and her mother."

"I'm now considering another option. We have uncovered information that shows the relatives of General Ma have spent lavishly over the years. Far beyond what their jobs would have paid. I think Cha Sun-hee is a person he used as a diversion. She has no accounts, no money, no possessions."

"Yet, you came to question her?"

"There are other matters of which she may have information. Things that do not pertain to General Ma or the missing money." He turned to Kwang-ku. "How is the prisoner doctor?"

"She has a broken jaw and a concussion. We will need a stretcher," said Kwong-ku as he released the strap across her chest.

"With the injury, may I assume you have completed your questioning of Cha Sun-hee?"

"She insulted me and the Premier."

The familiar voice interrupted, "We will transport her to a facility where we may continue our investigation."

Sun-hee felt arms from both sides lift her and place her on a stretcher. She fought the pain, stabbing at her face and head. The person attached to the voice became visible. It was Bear.

The two men from House of Sanshin helped her into the back seat of a car. Unicorn held her as Bear drove to the hospital.

How did they know I was there? Why did they risk coming to get me?

She fought to stay conscious as they carried her into the hospital and laid her on a bed. She looked up at Unicorn and reached out a hand to him. She felt a prick in her arm. The room grew dark.

She dreamed she was a butterfly, captured by little children.

46 — The Cave - Late April, 1972

I feel so warm and comfortable.

She snuggled down a little and cracked her eye open.

Where am I? Oh, I remember. I am in the hospital. How did I get this headache? My jaw. I can't move my jaw. A tooth is missing.

She lifted her left hand and touched her face.

"OW," came out muffled. "OW!" She closed her eyes and grimaced until the jolt of pain subsided.

Speaking hurts.

She looked around the room. She focused on her right hand. There was a bruise between the middle knuckles. A tube ran into her arm.

The questioning came back to her.

What now? Where do I go from here? I am comfortable.

She closed her eye and fell back asleep. She dreamed she was a cloud floating over Korea. She watched children play, running through the grass, laughing, chasing butterflies.

"Sun-hee. How are you feeling?" a voice said, bringing her out of her dream.

She opened an eye to see Kwong-ku a few centimeters from her face.

Why do you ask questions when I cannot talk?

"Your interrogator really walloped you," he said, examining the bruising around her left eye. "I had to wire your broken jaw together. It may take a couple of months for it to heal."

A couple of months!

"You also have a concussion. You will experience some headaches."

Yes, I know.

"Other than that, you are in good health. Make yourself comfortable. You will be here for a few days. In fact, I will keep you here as long as I can. Just between you and me, I have written on your chart that you have a serious concussion and need time to recover before transport. Don't tell anyone I overstated your injury."

She caught his smile. *As if I could talk.*

"According to the government, you are a prisoner. I have your leg attached to the bed," he said as he grabbed a toe and wiggled it. "I do not want anyone to take you without my permission."

Wait until I tell our daughter that you chained me to a bed.

"For now, get some rest. I'll check up on you a couple of times a day. Don't worry about anything. You're safe."

She moved her legs to test the chain attaching her to the bed.

I am still a prisoner, always a prisoner. This hospital bed is better than a cell. I hope the food is better! Can I eat? Nothing to do, I feel useless.

***

A-day-and-a-half later, Kwong-ku walked down the quiet corridor of the hospital, half asleep. He had spent most of the night operating on a couple of accident victims and was going to get some rest. He noticed a small man dressed in an overcoat come out of a room. "Excuse me. What are you doing here at this hour?"

The man looked up and down the hall like he was figuring out how to escape. Then the small man looked directly at him and smiled.

"Jin-taek," exclaimed Kwong-ku.

Jin-taek's smile increased, and he bowed to Kwong-ku.

"What are you doing here?

Jin-taek pointed to his throat.

"I know you cannot speak. And I know what your answer would be. Come with me," he said motioning for Jin-taek to follow him down the corridor.

He led Jin-taek to Sun-hee's room and said in a whisper, "Sun-hee is here. She is asleep. Wait in the corner. I'll be back." Jin-taek nodded with a big smile then watched Sun-hee.

A few minutes later, Kwong-ku came in and gave some papers to Jin-taek. "These are orders for you to watch Sun-hee. She is a special prisoner of the government. You are now her guard." Jin-taek removed his coat, revealing his dirty, unkempt uniform and stood at attention. "I'm glad you are here," Kwong-ku said before leaving.

Jin-taek stood for a while then sat and fell asleep.

When Sun-hee woke, light was coming in through the closed curtains. She could smell someone in the room, so she listened carefully. She could hear breathing. She looked around but could see no one. She sat up and closed her eyes until the dizziness faded. A soldier was sleeping in the corner. She lay back down, wondering why the soldier was there.

A few minutes passed. The door opened.

"Good morning," said a nurse as she entered and whipped open the curtains. The nurse turned back to Sun-hee as Jin-taek got to his feet.

"Who are you?" the nurse exclaimed.

Sun-hee stared at Jin-taek. Her heart fluttered. She wanted to say something. The nurse put her hands on her hips. "Start talking, soldier. No one is to be in this room."

Sun-hee grabbed a pencil and paper and wrote. "He is my guard. He should be here."

Jin-Taek pulled out the papers Kwong-ku gave him and held them out with one hand while pointing to his throat with the other.

Sun-hee frantically waved her note at the nurse. The nurse took Sun-hee's paper. The nurse approached Jin-taek slowly, taking his papers. The nurse read them, she paused for a moment, looked at them both, then handed the papers back.

"Well, you now have a guard," said the nurse to Sun-hee. "It is up to you if he stays in the room." And she handed Sun-hee a bedpan. Jin-taek turned his face into the corner and stood at attention.

After the nurse left with the bedpan, Jin-taek slowly turned around. Sun-hee motioned for him to come to the bed. She wrote, "I am so glad to see you. How did you get here?"

Jin-taek wrote, "I follow you. Kwang-ku showed me your room. He made me your guard." He gave Sun-hee the paper and then his guard papers. As Sun-hee read them, her eyes lit up.

I am glad Kwong-ku and I think alike.

Jin-taek looked closely at Sun-hee's face and frowned. Then he wrote, "I am here. No one else will hurt you." He submitted the note with a bow.

Tears formed in Sun-hee's eyes as she read the message. She lay back, feeling secure. A smile formed until it hurt.

***

Two days later, Kwong-ku entered and said, "Time to leave, Sun-hee." He dropped some clothes at the end of the bed and unlocked the restraints. Then he handed a new uniform to Jin-taek. "We have taken care of everything. Your trip has been planned out."

He removed the bandage on her hand and then held it saying, "It has been great to see you again, Sun-hee. I am not going to stay around to see you off. Jin-taek will remain as your guard. Remember, the House of Sanshin lives on." She saw his eyes were blinking fast, holding back tears. "I will keep in touch." He let her hand slip out of his and left the room.

A couple of nurses came in and helped her to dress. Jin-taek changed in the corner while Sun-hee sucked up her lunch through a straw. A few minutes later, two soldiers came in the room. Jin-taek helped her up and motioned to the soldiers to lead the way. They walked to a truck outside the hospital. She clambered aboard and sat still while her feet were chained to the bed. Jin-Taek mounted and sat across from her.

Five other prisoners were lifted, shoved, or ordered into the truck. Their bruises were evident, and their beaten, defeated spirits, cried out at Sun-hee. The tarp was tied, and the journey started. The other prisoners rode with their heads down, conquered, lifeless.

What had they done?

The truck hit a bump. A jolt of pain shot through her head. She closed her eyes. Each successive bump resulted in a blast of pain in her head. She drew inward, focused on breathing, getting through the moment. The rough ride, the roar of the engine, and the smell of diesel exhaust overwhelmed everything else.

When they stopped, Jin-taek was there, helping her down, secretly giving her his water and food. He helped her back in the truck. With the other guards, he could do no more. She lost count of the stops. The day followed by night and another day. She focused on surviving the pain.

Another stop. A guard told the prisoners to stand in line. Jin-taek took hold of her arm. He led her into a privy. There was another woman, dressed like her, and with a similar hairstyle. Jin-taek motioned for her to stay, then took the other woman away. A few minutes later, she heard the truck leave.

"Sun-hee. Follow me," came a voice.

She turned to see Stone motioning to her. She hurried to follow him. He led her to a truck where he pulled back a tarp and lifted her in.

He climbed in behind her, unlocked a big crate, and lifted a false bottom saying, "Lay down and remain quiet."

Sun-hee got in. There were cushions and enough room for her to lay down if she curled her legs. A board came down over her. She heard something hefty being loaded in the box over her. A lock was latched, some shuffling, the motor started, and she sensed movement. The cushions made the ride a lot better than sitting on the hard bench.

Where is he taking me? Why do I have to be crated up? What is going on?

The exhaustion of two days of travel caught up with her. She fell asleep.

There was complete silence and darkness when Sun-hee woke.

We have stopped.

She began to panic, pushing on the board above her. Then she pounded on it. She heard shuffling. Someone was unlocking the crate. Finally, the board trapping her into her little space was raised. Stone reached in to lift her out.

"That space is a little cramped. My apologies for the ride," said Stone. He held her as she stepped to the end and pulled back the tarp. He jumped down then reached up to lift Sun-hee off the truck.

She heard footsteps. A familiar face walked out from behind some crates. A hand reached out to take hers. Her eyes widened. It was Strategist.

"Sun-hee. I am so glad to see you are safe," said Yong-gak.

She choked up, grabbed Strategist with one hand and Stone with the other. Tears formed in her eyes. She broke down into a hearty cry, emotions flooded out.

"I needed to make sure you were safe," said Strategist. "Come, we will get you situated. There is much we need to talk about."

She looked around. They were underground. A few bare light bulbs hung along a wire on the rock ceiling. The men escorted Sun-hee through the piles of crates and mining equipment to a large wrought iron gate fixed into a cement archway. Stone unlocked the gate. They walked through, and he locked the gate behind them.

Stone turned on a flashlight and led them into another large, damp room also full of crates and mining equipment. He made many turns, the narrow beam of light from the flashlight offering only glimpses of the items in the room. In places, small puddles shined brightly on the uneven rock floor. He stopped at a large crate, about two meters tall and at least a meter wide. He took out a key and unlocked it.

She backed away shaking her head.

I am not hiding in a box.

"This leads to where you will be staying," said Strategist. "This box hides a door. You'll see." He held out his hand and guided her steps into the box.

Stone led her down some steps while the strategist locked the crate behind them. At the bottom was a large door made from support beams. Young-Soo unlocked this door and pushed hard, swinging it inward. As she stepped through, bare bulbs hanging from the ceiling flickered on.

They proceeded down a mineshaft carved out of the solid rock, deeper into the mountain. Tunnels branched off to the left and right. They turned right, left, right, soon Sun-hee lost track. She followed, trusting where two of her children's fathers were taking her.

Stone opened another door into a large room containing four chairs, a table, and a bookshelf full of books. There were rugs on the floor.

The fresh warm air hit her face. Sun-hee took a deep breath, then another. Her apprehension began to subside.

"This is the place, Sun-hee," Strategist said while gesturing with his hands in front of him. "The door to your left is a bedroom." He pointed. "To your right is a bedroom and a privy. Ahead is a kitchen and, well, let me show you the view." He strode to the door on the far side of the room as he opened it, bright light cast into the room along with a blast of fresh air.

Sun-hee walked through the door into the light.

"This is your kitchen," Stone said, stepping through the door behind her.

The sunlight blinded her for a moment. The entire far wall was open.

"What do you think of this view," Stone said as he walked forward.

She took a few steps and looked on a mountain valley filled with infinite shades of green. Traces of snow slithered down from the peaks on the other side. A river tumbled through the valley below, fed from the bowl of mountains to her right. It trailed away down the curving valley to her left. She felt a twinge of pain in her jaw as it tried to drop open in amazement.

What a wonderful view. This must be the prettiest place in the world.

"Careful, it's a long way down," said Stone. "This opening is in a large cliff and can't be seen from the air. The valley narrows downriver and is impassable. The only way to get into the valley is over the mountain passes or the mines. No one comes here. In this place, you will be safe."

Why are they so concerned about my safety?

She smiled at them, wishing she could express her feelings verbally. She just squeezed their arms.

"There are a few things I need to tell you," said Strategist. "You know all of the men, with two exceptions, left camp and went to work throughout the country. We have kept in touch and worked together to the best of our ability. We need to be able to communicate better and faster. We would like you to be the communication center of the House of Sanshin. We plan to have our sons join us in various roles. The original twenty-three will expand with the addition of our sons, which is too many for any of us to organize. We need you to coordinate our efforts."

How? Why do I need to be here and not back home? What is it they want me to do? What are they coordinating? Damn it! I wish I could talk!

She made a writing motion with her hand on her palm.

"Yes, let's go back in the other room," said Strategist, motioning with his hand.

They sat at the table. Sun-hee started writing down questions. *Why was I arrested? Why can't I go home?*

Strategist said, "A professor at the university accused General Ma of charging too much for education materials. The professor claimed he could do it much cheaper and requested less than the money General Ma was getting. The authorities questioned General Ma about his rise in expenses over the years. And he accused your mother and you of demanding more funds. Diverting the blame from himself to you."

"Gil-hyung, what did Young-ja name him?" asked Strategist.

Sun-hee wrote, *gom,* the Bear, because of his hairy chest and back.

"Bear and his finance department reviewed General Ma's records. He then compared them to the records Lieutenant Rim kept of what the compound received from General Ma. They did not match. After some further investigation, Bear found that General Ma took most of the money he received from the government and gave it to his family. We made up new books for General Ma, showing his embezzlement of funds," Strategist concluded by dropping his hands to his side.

"With the new decree by Kim Il-sung, all enemies of the state are eliminated through three generations. General Ma and his family are being rounded up."

When can I go home? wrote Sun-hee.

"You can't," said Strategist.

Where is Jin-taek? Sun-hee wrote.

Young-soo smiled and said, "He is accompanying your double to the gulag. Once he makes the delivery, he will come here."

Strategist added, "That amazing man followed you to Pyongyang. By chance, Kwang-ku recognized him and made him a guard. He would have tried to rescue you from the hospital by himself. I don't think anyone will be able to harm you again without killing him first. He is like a cat. He has nine lives and is very loyal. I wonder how many lives he has left?"

What are you working on? she wrote.

"I'm working with Huang Jang-yop to write out the details of Juche for the Premier. I know a little of what you feel like, as I do most of the writing and Jang-yop gets the credit. I hope he never accuses me of demanding more money like General Ma accused you."

Sun-hee wrote questions until she could not keep her eyes open for the answers. The men showed her to her new bedroom. There was a bed with a mattress and down pillow. Sleep arrived as soon as her head settled into the pillow.

47 — New fate - Spring, 1972

Sun-hee woke.

What time is it? How long have I been asleep? This bed is so soft. I feel so warm.

She snuggled down a little.

Where am I? It's so dark. Oh, I am in a cave. My tooth is still missing. My jaw is wired shut.

The events of the past week all came back to her.

For now, I am safe and comfortable.

She rolled over and went back to sleep. She dreamed she was a cloud floating over Korea. She watched the men of the House of Sanshin work, live, and change Korea.

Her eyes opened. The room was pitch dark. She got up and felt for the light switch. She found the door handle and opened the door.

Light!

She turned.

That box by the door was not here last night.

She opened it. It was full of clothes.

How nice!

She changed clothes. She went into the main room and found more boxes which were not there last night. She went to the room with a view.

From the position of the sun, it must be about midday.

She took some deep breaths and felt refreshed by the air and majesty of the valley. She heard the door open, and she went back to the main room. Jin-taek was setting two boxes down by the others. He looked up and smiled at her. She smiled back until her jaw hurt.

Jin-taek opened the boxes, showing off food, utensils, and everything else they might need to live in this hole in the rock. Together, they unpacked, putting things where they thought they should go, neither able to talk and discuss the arrangement. Jin-taek put the empty boxes back into the passageway while Sun-hee went into the kitchen to prepare something to eat. She looked at the food, the pots, and the stove.

Where do I begin? I have never made a meal for myself.

Jin-taek came and took over. He made rice and boiled vegetables then mashed them, creating a soup that Sun-hee could suck through a straw.

She helped clean up, picked up a chair, brought it to the kitchen, and sat it a couple of meters away from the ledge. The choice of books was not great, but there was plenty she had not read. After selecting one, she sat in the kitchen and read. Now and then she looked out, watching the shadows move over the valley. The sunset over the mountain ridge across the valley was followed by a magnificent orange display in the clouds.

What an incredible place!

The next morning, she finished cleaning up after breakfast and was about to sit down to read when the door to the shaft opened. Stone walked in carrying bags and went into one of the bedrooms. He came out just as her sons Hong-do and Hon-yong Jr. came into the room, holding boxes.

"In there," said Stone, pointing to the bedroom. Chulsoon then walked in and followed them into the bedroom.

My sons! Chulsoon! Sun-hee followed them into the bedroom.

Hong-do said, "Here are some things you might need, more books for you to read and technical journals to translate. You did not think you could avoid your responsibilities."

As Hong-do and Hon-yong Jr. put down their boxes, they each took one of Sun-hee's hands. They were huffing and puffing. Sweat was dripping down their foreheads after carrying the boxes through the mine. "I am so glad you are okay," said Hong-do.

"We were so worried," said Hon-yong Jr. "We did not hear anything for four days. Chulsoon got a message you were alive."

"How is your jaw?" asked Hong-do.

Sun-hee shook her head up and down a little. Frustrated, she could not talk.

Hon-yong Jr. hit Hong-do lightly with his fist, and said, "You dummy. Her jaw is wired. She can't answer questions."

"Young-soo said he hid you in a mountain. I never imagined it was this far inside," said Hong-do.

"If Young-soo didn't lead the way, I would be lost forever in those shafts," said Hon-yong Jr.

Sun-hee gave her sons' hands a little squeeze as they went into the main room. She sat and wrote out, *How are things in the camp? Is everyone alright?* She pulled Chulsoon's sleeve and handed him her note.

"When the soldiers arrested you, Sergeant Kua was shot in the lower abdomen, shattering her pelvis," said Chulsoon. He cleared his throat. "I did the best I could, but the trauma was too great. She passed away that night. We were all shaken up because some trigger-happy soldier shot Sergeant Kua."

Sun-hee lowered her head, placing her palms on her forehead for support as tears streamed down her cheek.

Chulsoon continued, "The camp was a little chaotic for a while. Sergeant Kua was dead, you were taken away, Jin-taek had taken off after you, and Lieutenant Rim was gone."

Sun-hee wrote, *I saw Rim at prison.*

"He was with you?"

They beat him. I don't know if he is alive or dead.

"I'll find out. You also should know, Mrs. Lim decided it was her chance to leave. She took Joo-yun and her unmarried granddaughter with her. Mrs. Lim believed her husband and sons were alive and went to find them. Hon-yong and I took charge until General Park showed up. He ranted and raved around for a while. Then I told him about Mrs. Lim. He went off on a tirade worse than I have ever seen. If General Park ever finds the Lims, I think he will kill them."

"Sergeant Kua was buried two days ago. Yesterday, Young-soo showed up to let everyone know about your rescue. We are keeping everyone inside and locking the gates. No one can arrest anyone without everyone knowing," concluded Chulsoon.

"Your bruising is beginning to fade. Let me check your jaw," he said as he started to examine Sun-hee's face. "Everything looks like it is healing. No infection. You will be good as new soon."

"Wow, Mother. You have the best view in the world," said Hong-do as he came out of the kitchen with Jin-taek and Hon-yong Jr.

"This is a nice hole in the mountain, Mother," said Hon-yong Jr. "I like the open-air kitchen and dining area, just like camp." He laughed at his attempt at a joke. "We will need to make a window for the opening before winter."

"We need to get back to the camp," said Chulsoon. "We left before dawn and need to be back as soon as we can. We wanted to see you and used the excuse of bringing you some boxes. I see Young-soo has already left." He gave Sun-hee's hands a firm squeeze and started towards the door.

"I am so glad to see you after worrying about you for so many days," said Hong-do, placing his hand on her shoulder.

"Take care of yourself, Mother. If you need anything, tell Jin-taek, and he will get us a message," said Hon-yong Jr.

"Jin-taek, can you show us the way out?" asked Chulsoon.

Jin-taek nodded his head and opened the door to the mineshaft.

Sun-hee waved goodbye, watching them walk to the first turn. Once she lost sight of them, she closed the door.

Sun-hee went to the bedroom and looked through the books.

This one appears interesting.

She went to the kitchen and began to read.

For the next week, Sun-hee waited for word from anyone on what was going on in the rest of the world. Jin-taek showed her how to cook food that could be mashed and made into soup. The best thing about the cave: the view was amazing. Sun-hee enjoyed looking out at the valley and listening to the rush of the river below.

Late in the afternoon of the next day, Stone arrived. "I do not have much time, Sun-hee. Word has gotten out to all the men. We need to relocate our children and their families. Only a few of the men have gotten back to me on how many positions they have." He placed some papers on the table. "Here are the positions and locations I have at this time. More will come as we get word back from others. Since you know all our children, you need to make the assignments."

What about the women? she wrote and pushed the paper towards Stone.

"I don't know," he said, shaking his head. "Do you need anything? I have provided the supplies I thought you might need."

She shook her head to communicate no.

"I wish I could stay longer, but I have lots to do." He rushed out the door and down the mineshaft.

She sat down and made a list of everyone in the program and their descendants.

I wish I had the genealogy we made up years ago. I wonder what Gen. Park did with it.

For all the second-generation boys, she listed their strengths.

Most of these children are as smart as their parents. Maybe it was their education? I did teach them well. They always had plenty of food and a positive environment. Now I am to separate them. How will their children fair? What will be their fate?

After making a separate list of her children and grandchildren, Sun-hee needed to decide where they should go. *My oldest daughter, Su-dae, and her husband, the son of the Skinny Beast, must go to Beijing to be with the Skinny Beast. They will do well at the Economics Institute.*

Hong-do. The thought of him made her remember her father.

What would he think of me now? He must be with his father, Strategist, in Pyongyang. He doesn't have the political mind of his father, but his diplomatic skills will be excellent support for Yong-gak. His wife, the daughter of Joo-yun, has the moodiness of her grandmother. I hope she will be happy in the capital.

I wonder if Park Duk-bae would do well at the research hospital in Hoeryong. So-min will not like being so out of the way, but it is a place where she can learn and keep some control over her husband. It is near the Gulag, which may be a strategic place if someone from the House of Sanshin is sent there.

Eun-mi needs to be with his father at the University of Pyongyang. Eun-mi inherited his father's math skills.

She smiled, recalling how Young-ja had nicknamed him Numbers Jr.

They will support each other. Choe-me's daughter will be happy to be in the capitol where she can experience the culture and the arts.

Hon-yong Jr. takes after his father and should be with him doing woodworking. His wife, the daughter of Eun-seong, has a good business sense.

A smile started before her jaw hurt as she recalled how Eun-seong was so pleased her youngest daughter was married to Hon-yong Jr.

If she ever knew I arranged the marriage, she would be so overwhelming with her praise, it would be embarrassing.

Sun-hee made notes about the rest. Many of the boys in the second generation would go to positions in construction and designing infrastructure.

Then she stewed for a day about the women of her generation. There was no place for them in the male-dominated society.

***

Two days later, Jin-taek led Strategist into their cave.

"Sun-hee, I hope you are doing well," said Strategist.

She bowed and smiled. Her jaw did not hurt quite as much. She tried to talk, but her grunts were not understandable. She sat down to write.

Have you heard anything from my children? She passed the paper across the table. *Any news from the camp?* She pushed another note towards him.

"Could we get some tea, Jin-taek?"

Jin-taek bowed in acknowledgment then went into the other room.

"I wanted a little privacy for a moment," Strategist said as he sat down and read her questions. "Your children are fine. Everyone is preparing to move. Do you have your suggestions for the moves?" He talked quickly with rapid hand gestures.

She retrieved her list of the boys and their wives of the second-generation and gave them to him to show them.

He spoke as he reviewed. "Engineering, design, electricity, medicine, mining, teaching, and finance, all positions where they can make a difference. I like this, Sun-hee. I already told Hong-do I wanted him with me," he said, pointing to his chest.

Strategist leaned towards Sun-hee and said, "There is a new designation for the class who are leaders in the Democratic People's Republic of Korea. The survivors of the war who are in good standing are the Core Songbun. This class has special privileges. The men of the House of Sanshin have all been accepted as Core Songbun. Thus, our recommendations for these appointments will not be questioned."

Jin-taek brought them tea and went back to the kitchen.

"Even as Core Songbun, we must be careful with the lists we are making. Should it get out, there would be an investigation. Destroy them if you are found." Strategist wrung his hands. "We are not doing anything against the government. There is so much distrust."

"One thing I do need to tell you. Officially, you died when you arrived at the gulag. Your death certificate says a blood clot formed in your brain," he said, pointing to the side of his head. "This was done to prevent anyone from taking you in for questioning again. The Bear and I considered trying to get you reinstated as core Songbun but it is too risky for us to be seen meddling in the security files. There are no Sanshin in the Security Service to help us."

She looked at him with concerned eyes.

"General Ma's relatives were investigated. They executed General Ma and sent his family to the gulag. And I am sorry to inform you, Lieutenant Rim succumbed to the injuries he received during his interrogation."

She paused, tapped the pencil on the paper, then wrote, *I'm sorry about Rim.*

"Me too. He was loyal to Park and took care of us. For what we need to do in the future, he was a liability because he knew too much."

Rim only loyal to Park. Not to Sanshin, she wrote.

Strategist nodded his head in the affirmative.

Will I be stuck here in this mine for the rest of my life? she wrote and pushed the paper at him.

"No. In a while, we will figure out a new identity for you, and you will be free to do what you want. However, I have some other ideas on how you can be useful. First, I need to get some things confirmed."

She looked passionately at him with misty eyes.

"Now, I must continue my journey," he said as he stood. "I am meeting with some Chinese officials tomorrow in Musan. That is my cover to come to meet with you." He put his hand on her shoulder.

Jin-taek brought out a plate of steaming rice, mutton, and vegetables and sat it in front of Strategist. Then he sat a soup mixture in front of Sun-hee.

Another meal through a straw.

"I do have time to eat. Jin-taek is feeding you well," Strategist said, gazing into Sun-hee's cup as he took a bite of his meal.

Sun-hee looked at him and then wrote, *What are you boys really up to?*

Yong-gak took a couple of bites before putting down his chopsticks. "We committed years ago to making Korea great. We do what we can to shape the country and make it better. We are always behind the scenes, never in the open. Our coordinated efforts are making a difference. I do research and advise the government. Once a month, I meet with Kim Il-sung privately to update him on politics. Mostly, I tell him what he wants to hear while inserting a statement or two to shape policy. I believe he trusts what I say. Hopefully, I can keep him from making a serious mistake. Information from the other men helps me know what is going on throughout the rest of the country. I pass on information to them that is helpful to their work. We have concluded we need a way to communicate better. We identified this location where we could have a communication center. Some of us have met here in the past. We were looking for the right person to stay here and coordinate our communication. Now that you are here. I hoped you would be the person in charge of this place." He picked up his chopsticks and took another bite.

Sun-hee sat back in her chair.

I'm going to miss my children and grandchildren.

"You do not have to make any decisions now," he said, pointing at her with the chopsticks. "As I said, I have many things to confirm. Right now, you need to heal and rest."

She bent forward and quickly wrote, *I want to be with my children and grandchildren.*

"Your children and grandchildren will be moving to other parts of the country. From here, you will know what each one is doing. I am sure we can work things out. You can visit them often."

He finished his meal, stood, and bowed slightly. "I'll be in touch soon. Take care, Sun-hee." He walked out at a quick pace.

She picked up the plate and her cup and walked into the kitchen.

Jin-taek was sitting on the ledge, looking out over the valley. She placed the plate on the counter and finished the soup in her cup. The sun had set, offering up another stunning orange sky over the valley.

What has fate led me to now?

48 — Communication - Mid-May, 1972

Sun-hee was halfway through her third book that week when Stone walked in carrying a couple of boxes.

"More food and supplies, Sun-hee. Anything else you need?"

She shook her head in the negative and picked up a pencil. *Just lonely*, she wrote. *Can you cut these wires in my mouth?*

The quiet and boredom are driving me insane. If it weren't for the books, I would go crazy, she thought.

"I wish I could help you, Sun-hee," he said. "Cutting wires is beyond my ability. Kwang-ku told me he would try to get up here as soon as he can. We will be doing some work in this mine tomorrow. Ignore the sounds and blasting. Keep the door closed and locked. I have a key and can let myself in. See you tomorrow."

***

Sun-hee woke to rumblings and little pebbles hitting her in the face. She turned on the light. Dust filled the room.

How can I ignore this?

She walked out and into the kitchen. Jin-taek had a hard hat on his head and handed her one. Then he gave her a glass of ground-up fruit covered by paper. Paper and cloth covered everything else.

Each time there was a rumble, dust fell from the ceiling. It was unnerving. She could not concentrate enough to read. She paced around the cave. Another blast sounded, and she squeaked.

I can't even scream!

She pounded her fist against the wall. Jin-taek tried to calm her by getting her to look at the valley. Having a wall-size view was the only thing keeping her from running out. If it hadn't been so far, she would have tried to climb down.

Stone stuck his head in the door. Sun-hee ran to him and tried to yell at him, but what came out were unintelligible squeaks and grunts. She stomped her foot and flailed her arms.

He grabbed her arms. "Sun-hee, we are done blasting for the day. I did not know it would upset you so," he said. "We will not blast with you in here again. I'll get you out tomorrow." He looked around, held up his hand's palm out, and looked at Jin-Taek.

Jin-taek held his palms out and shrugged his shoulders.

"I'll be back in the morning and take you someplace for the day," he said, reaching to hug Sun-hee. She hit his arms away and pointed towards the door. "It's all fine. No more blasting today. Never again while you're here." He went out the door, shaking his head.

When she came out of her bedroom the next morning, Stone was eating breakfast with Jin-taek. Her cup of liquid fruit mixed with yogurt was on the table.

"As soon as you finish eating, I will get you out of here while we blast," said Stone.

We are leaving this cave.

Sun-hee rushed to get ready, changing clothes. In a few minutes, she returned.

Stone led Sun-hee and Jin-taek down shafts of the mine, making many turns. They entered a larger tunnel with rails down the middle. They followed this tunnel and came to an elevator. Stone walked onto the wooden platform surrounded by a wire fence and motioned for Sun-hee to follow. She stepped slowly on. Jin-taek followed with his typical smile.

"Are you ready?" said the Stone.

Jin-taek secured the gate and nodded.

Stone pushed a button. The basket lurched downward.

Sun-hee grabbed the men's sleeves. She held on as she watched them pass light bulb after light bulb. Light and shadows moved down the basket as they descended. The elevator came to a stop.

"Bottom floor, everyone out."

The group proceeded through a tunnel, coming to an opening to the outside. A board path led through mine tailings to the valley floor. They walked among the pine trees and down the hillside.

Stone stopped and motioned to Sun-hee to walk on. She walked through a path between shrubs twice as tall as she stood. The river appeared before her, and she rushed towards it. Then she saw a table, chairs, and an awning.

She turned to see Jin-taek smiling while walking towards the river. Stone entered the bushes.

He is leaving. I wanted to show him some appreciation.

Jin-taek held up books and a basket of food. Sun-hee accepted a book, sat by the table in the shade, and watched the water flow on its merry way.

After sitting, watching, and getting in some reading, she went exploring. She ventured up and down the river, enjoying the scenery. Never in her life had she been in such a delightful place.

My new home has the best yard in the world.

She took in deep breaths of the clear mountain air, letting her hands glide over leaves and tree trunks. The water sparkled as it cascaded over the rocks. The sound soothed her emotions. She could not recall being in a place so relaxing with no demands on her time.

***

The two spent the next four days by the river, while Stone and his men worked in the mine. No matter how far she went up or down the river, Jin-taek kept her in view. She loved being in the valley. It was so much better than what it looked like from the kitchen. At the end of each day, they took the elevator back up into the mountain. Then they went to work cleaning dust off everything.

On the afternoon of the fourth day, Stone met her as they entered the cave. Strategist was there as well as Kwang-ku. Then her heart fluttered a bit when she saw the Hammer. She gave a formal bow to them, and her eyes watered.

"Time to see how your jaw is healing," said Kwang-ku. "Let's step into the kitchen where the light is better."

Sun-hee let out a squeak as she ran into the kitchen. She turned to face Kwang-ku who sat a black bag on the sink.

"Hold still while I look at your jaw."

She froze with her chin up and eyes closed. Kwang-ku felt along the jawline, pressing as he went. "No movement and no pain. If the bone had not healed, you would have reacted to my touch. Let us get those wires off. This will hurt a little." He used thin cutters to sever the wires and pull them out of Sun-hee's mouth. "Now your jaw is free to move. Open wide so I can take a look at your gums."

She forced herself to open her mouth. The muscles ached as she used them for the first time in six weeks. Kwang-ku put his fingers in and pushed her mouth open wider.

"Ow!" she grunted.

He put a piece of wood between her teeth. "I don't want you to react and bite off one of my fingers." Then he checked her gums.

The pain was less than she had prepared herself for.

He pried out the wood and stood back. "Now close your mouth. Open. Move your jaw right to left."

I am free again!

"Han ou Kwn-gu!"

"You will need a few days to get the movement back," said Kwong-ku with a smile on his face. "In a week, you won't know your jaw was broken."

She took his hand and bowed.

"Now bite down. Let me make sure the teeth properly aligned."

She opened and closed a few times, testing her bite and feeling the space of her missing tooth.

"Good," she said, working on saying the word. She smiled ear-to-ear.

Kwang-ku reached into his bag and handed her a toothbrush and a box of salt. "Brush lightly and rinse with saltwater."

She smiled and pointed to a box of salt by the sink next to a cup and a straw. Then she picked up the straw and threw it into the trash with all her might.

"I forgot you are a doctor. If the role Young-gak has for you does not work out, I will take you on as my assistant surgeon," he said and left her alone.

She looked at herself in the mirror.

Kwang-ku has become a great surgeon. I raise children. Now he gets to live in Pyongyang, and I get to live in a cave. Life is not fair.

She washed the blood from her lips and mouth. She looked in the mirror, moving her mouth around, feeling the stiffness in her jaws. Then she went out to the room full of men and said, "Hel-yoo. I ca tal again. Tallk a..gain."

The men laughed and applauded. She bowed and smiled. When she looked at Jin-taek, she saw his eyes were watery.

Poor Jin-taek, he will never be able to talk again. I wish I could fix that.

Jin-taek served dinner. Sun-hee got an actual plate of food. Chewing was difficult, but she ate slowly, savoring every bite.

Weon-kee entered and walked over to a desk which had not been there earlier that morning. He picked up a telephone and dialed.

What is Wires doing? What are these electronic devices? Sun-hee thought.

Weon-kee put down the phone and said, "I called Wonsan and got a clear connection. The phone and radio work. Everything is in place."

"Good work," said Strategist. "Now we can talk to Sun-hee anytime. Here is a list of numbers for each of the men." He held out a paper for Sun-hee. "Memorize them. Then destroy the list. The number for this phone is on the list. We know it, and you can give it to others to call you. Only use the radio to listen. Weon-kee, what do you expect Sun-hee to hear?"

Wires replied, "The radio is connected to the latest surveillance equipment on top of the mountain. Depending on the power of the transmitter and the band, she can pick up broadcast stations throughout eastern China, South Korea, Japan, and maybe some from the Soviet Union. If we could break American codes, we could listen to their military transmissions in the Sea of Japan."

"The next week will be a busy one," said Strategist. "All of our children will be moving out of the camp. Sun-hee, your list was perfect," he said, pointing fingers at her again. "Chulsoon talked to General Park, and he agreed. He was insistent on being able to track our grandchildren and have them mated together when they get older. I am excited about the future."

"We are far ahead of South Korea. Political unrest has kept them poor. They are behind us economically and technologically. If it were not for the Americans, they would crumble in a few months. North Korea is the second strongest economy in Asia after the Soviet Union. We have been a significant part of our countries progress. Having our children with us will enhance our work for a better Korea," Strategist concluded, holding his hands out.

Wires stayed for a few hours after the others had left. He showed Sun-hee how to operate the radio and find transmissions on the various bands.

"If you have any questions, call me," he said before he walked out.

"I will. It has been so good to see you again. Goodnight, Wires," Sun-hee said, slowly working on saying each word. She closed the door behind him and locked it.

She went into her bedroom and found a new wardrobe and dresser with a large mirror along the wall. The handiwork of Hammer.

They must have moved them in while my wires were removed.

The boxes she had been keeping her things in were gone. She opened the wardrobe to see the clothes she had left at the camp. She opened the top drawer of the dresser and found the blue silk scarf her mother had given her. Tears flowed.

I miss you so much, Mother. I wish you were here.

49 — Giving of the Goose - July, 1972

Sun-hee rummaged through their food supplies to see what would be good to take on a picnic.

Jin-taek came over, pulled items from the cupboard, elbowed her gently out of the way, and in a couple of minutes, he had made them a picnic lunch.

He will never let me do it myself.

Her hands shook as she cleaned the counter. They had been shaking since Chulsoon's phone call last evening to announce that Young-ja was going to be dropping by. The last time she had seen any of her girlfriends was the morning she had been trucked off to Pyongyang for questioning. There was so much to discuss after three months apart.

Young-ja could be heard before the door opened. "This is a really long tunnel. Another door? I cannot believe Sun-hee lives way down here."

"Just behind this door," she heard Stone's voice say, as the door unlocked.

Sun-hee couldn't wait for the door to open.

"Young-ja!" she yelled.

"Sun-hee!" came the voice from the other side of the door.

The door swung open, and Young-ja jumped into her arms. They hugged, shedding tears.

"I was so worried when they took you away," said Young-ja. "You must tell me everything."

"We have all day," said Sun-hee. "Jin-taek and I have planned a picnic in my yard. You have never seen a place so wonderful. Come, I'll show you the view from my new home." Sun-hee grabbed Young-ja's arm and took her to the kitchen.

"Oh my, Sun-hee. This is incredible. I am in love with the towering mountains. Look at all those trees, and there is a river snaking down the valley. I can hear the water rushing over the rocks. Ahh! It's such a long way down." She took a couple of steps back from the opening.

"If you are ready, we will go down there and spend the day," said Sun-hee.

"First, I have something for you. Let me show you what I brought."

Young-ja grabbed Sun-hee's arm and pulled her back into the main room. Stone stood by the table where he had sat a box. Young-ja opened the box and pulled out a light blue dress with blue and yellow flowers. Then she pulled out a pink dress with red and yellow flowers. "One for you and one for me. Which do you like?"

"Oh! Young-ja. These are so beautiful!" Sun-hee held the blue one up to her bosom and flowed around the room. She swapped for the pink dress and flowed the other way. "I like the blue dress."

Stone shut the door on his way out without saying a word.

"Come, let's change for our picnic," said Young-ja.

"These dresses are too nice to wear down in the valley," said Sun-hee.

"Let's wear them down, and if we want to change, we can send Jin-taek to get our clothes," said Young-ja.

"Good idea. I have not dressed up since last year's weddings."

They changed into the dresses and made up each other's hair. Sun-hee shared her ordeal in Pyongyang.

Young-ja talked about the camp, how quiet it was now that the children had left. The death of Sgt. Kua, and the leaving of Joo-yun and her mother were explained in detail. She filled Sun-hee in on the remaining twenty girls and that there was nothing to do now that they had no more teaching materials to revise. She discussed anything that came to her mind.

Sun-hee enjoyed Young-ja's voice as it had been so quiet in the cave the last month. They took their time to make each other look pretty. The last thing for Sun-hee to do was to take her blue scarf out of the wardrobe and put it around her neck.

"I am ready," she said.

"You look absolutely gorgeous!" said Young-ja.

"You always look delightful," said Sun-hee.

When they came out of the bedroom, Jin-taek was waiting with his hand on the box containing the picnic lunch. He had on his dress uniform. He bowed, with his typical big grin across his face, and opened the door.

"Jin-taek, you look so handsome today. I am glad you dressed up for our little picnic," said Young-ja.

"I feel like a little girl, Sun-hee. Getting dressed up for a picnic by a river all by ourselves. This mine is so confusing. I know I would get lost in here without Jin-taek guiding us." Young-ja went on in her usual talkative manner.

Jin-taek turned his head to look at them, smiling and nodding his head up and down, leading them to the elevator.

"Oh, I hate heights, Sun-hee," said Young-ja. "Hold me while we go down." And she grabbed onto Sun-hee. "The light and shadows going over your face are making me dizzy. How far down do we go?"

"I am not sure how far down we go, but it gets us to the valley," replied Sun-hee.

The elevator jerked to a stop. "Oh, good, we are on solid ground again," Young-ja said with a sigh.

Jin-taek opened the gate, picked up the food, and led the way.

"More tunnels to walk through," Young-ja said as she followed. "I hope we are not getting these dresses dirty in the tunnel. I do not want to wash them tonight." They came to the opening in the rock. "We see the light again. Oh, these boards are precarious. We must be careful walking down, no twisted ankles allowed today. I must be careful through the bushes, they are so pretty, and we must not snag the silk. Where is this river Sun-hee? How far do we have to walk?"

Sun-hee followed, enjoying Young-ja's chatter.

As Sun-hee cleared the bushes, she noticed Young-ja jump to the side. She looked at Young-ja and said, "Just a few steps further, and we will come to the river."

Young-ja gestured with her arm towards the river, and her gaze followed her hand. For once, she said nothing.

Sun-hee's eyes followed Young-ja's gesture to see a crowd of people.

"Ahhhh!" she screamed. There stood four of her five children and many of her grandchildren. She ran to greet them. Tears flowed, and her heart was in her throat, making her speechless.

It was minutes before she realized there were many others present. Strategist, Unicorn, Stone, Eun-seong, and Choe-me were near the center of the crowd. She circled among her friends and family, hugging each, exchanging greetings. Finally, she came to Young-ja, who had a smug smile on her face.

"You knew all along this was planned. You are so sneaky." She hugged Young-ja.

There were tables piled with a feast. Sun-hee had never seen so much food for so few people in her life. A whole goat roasted over an open pit. Then she noticed everyone looking upriver. Some of the children were pointing. She followed their stares to a man on a mule holding a goose. More people walked behind the mule. She looked around at who might be the bride.

The hat cast a shadow on the face of the man riding the mule, keeping his identity a mystery. She looked around again to see everyone looking at her. Her hands flew to cover her mouth.

"Oh my, this is my wedding proposal," she gushed.

Hammer, rode up to the crowd and hopped off the mule. His children and grandchildren came up and stood around. He knelt and offered the goose to Sun-hee.

She had the option to refuse the offer, but there was no way she would. She reached out and clasped the goose in her hands. It squawked and tried to get away, flapping its wings and making itself a challenge to hold. After getting a firm grip, she held it to her bosom. The goose quieted and buried its head under her scarf. Her gaze moved to Hammer, staring directly into his eyes. His eyes showed longing and desire, his face steady. She heard the river and a bird singing.

Don't look at the bird. Don't look at the people. That would convey doubt. I want to marry Hammer. I do want to marry him. I do.

The corners of her mouth curved up slightly, and her eyes open a little wider. Then she closed her eyes and bowed deeply. She sensed Hammer standing up. She stood and opened her eyes to the applauding crowd.

Tears streamed from her daughter's and his daughter's eyes. Young-ja dabbed her face with a hanky.

Her three-year-old grandson finally broke the silence, looking up at his mother, he said, "Now can we eat?"

Sun-hee took the Hammer's hand and led him to the tables of food. "The children are hungry. You must go first."

"You are always thinking about others, Sun-hee," said the Hammer. "Today is your day."

And a pleasant day it was. No imagination could come up with a more fantastic setting. The sky was clear, and a very light breeze brought the fresh mountain air through the valley. Leaves fluttered overhead, causing light and shadows to dance over the bride, groom, and guests. They ate, they chatted, and they laughed.

Sun-hee and Hon-yong stood as everyone strolled by to offer their congratulations. Su-dae and Stone walked by together.

"Congratulations," said Young-soo to Hon-yong, shaking his hand.

"Congratulations, Mother. I wish the two of you all the happiness in the world," said Su-dae as she gave her mother a firm hug.

Sun-hee asked, "Are the two of you becoming reacquainted?"

"Now that I am working in Bejing, my father and I are going into business together. I think I can become a marketer of the coal China imports. Wouldn't that be great?" said Su-dae.

"That would be wonderful. Has your father told you how he became the person in charge of all mining?" asked Sun-hee.

"No." Su-dae turned to Stone. "How did you end up in charge?"

"There was no one else. The Japanese didn't train Koreans to operate the mines. Then so many men my age died in the war."

"I thought your success was because you were talented and were the best person for the job," said Sun-hee.

"I was the only person available with any talent or interest. It is the same with many of my peers. There is a void of men our age in the country. The success of the men in the House of Sanshin is because of a lack of competition for the jobs, plus we had some talent," replied Stone.

"And now that I am working with Skinny Beast, and he is still skinny, I get to work with my father," said Su-dae.

"That sounds wonderful. We should talk about this further," Sun-hee said as she turned to receive the next person in line.

Sun-hee relished seeing all her friends and family after her ordeal. They were all so happy for her.

The line of well-wishers came to an end, and she surveyed the crowd.

I wish mother were here. She would be so pleased.

Sun-hee looked up at a lone, fluffy white cloud and stroked her scarf.

Maybe, she is.

The day seemed to fly by. The sun dropped behind the mountains to the west, casting the wedding into shadow. The women began to pack up the food and take it to the elevator. Since only five people could fit onto the elevator at a time, the guests took a long time to leave.

Sun-hee Joined her three lifelong friends, Choe-me, Eun-seong, and Young-ja, on the trip up the elevator. They huddled together as the elevator crept up the mine shaft. Sun-hee thought she remembered the way, but somehow managed to take a wrong turn, and the five of them became lost in the mines. Choe-me panicked and screamed. A few seconds later, Jin-taek rounded a corner, motioning them to follow and leading them to the cave.

Sun-hee showed her friends around her new home. They were admiring the view in the kitchen and the brilliant colors of the sunset, when Stone stuck his head in and interrupted.

"Time to leave."

"He always has such a way with words," said Young-ja.

They all laughed. Sun-hee gave each friend a final hug and saw them into the mineshaft. After one last wave from Young-ja, she closed the door.

"Oh, what a delightful day. But here I am again, alone in this cave," she said out loud.

She felt exhausted after such a grand time with her family and friends. She started to change her clothes and heard the door to the cave open and close.

It must be Jin-taek. I must thank him for all he has done. She opened the door to her bedroom, saying, "Jin-taek. Thank you so much for…Hon-yong!" Her jaw froze wide open, her breathing stopped, and her eyes grew large.

"Sorry to startle you Sun-hee," said Hon-yong. "You look more surprised now than you did when I rode up on the donkey." He chuckled, standing before her with a wide grin.

"I…I…I should have expected you," stammered Sun-hee all flustered, her face turning red.

"Jin-taek will make himself a camp by the river tonight," said Hammer.

"I…I have not had time to prepare…to think…to…" she stuttered.

"You have all the time you need. I will sleep in the other bedroom until…"

"No…no…I want…a few moments..." She started to turn back into the bedroom, stopped, then turned and leaped into Hammer's chest, grabbing him around the neck, and planting her lips on his.

I want this.

Hammer caught Sun-hee and effortlessly lifted her in his arms. Her feet fluttered in the air, bouncing off his shins. Sun-hee slid her head onto his shoulder. Joyous tears flowed onto his neck. His aroma sent her heart into a frenzy. She had never felt so excited as she did at this moment. He took a few steps forward then kicked the bedroom door closed with his heal. Sun-hee reached over and turned out the lights.

The next morning, Sun-hee fumbled at making them breakfast. As they ate, Sun-hee said, "After breakfast, I will pack my things, and we can go back to camp. If all our children are moving away, we can choose our apartment."

"We are staying here," he said. "There is an old house at the entrance to this mine. It is a little run down, but I can easily fix it up for our son, his family, and us. I have some plans for this mine as well. This is a better location for the woodshop. There is more space, we are closer to lumber, and you will be able to handle communications for everyone. I will make this our home."

50 — Home - July, 1972 to 1982

"I plan to get the mine area cleaned up. Then I can begin to transfer the woodshop at the compound to the front area of the mine. As soon as I have the woodshop set up, I can start refurbishing this cave and the house," said Hon-yong.

"That is great. Let me change. I will come help."

"Jin-taek and our son will be with me," said Hon-yong. "Junior and his family stayed in the house last night. I am sure Tae-seon would appreciate your help with the children."

Sun-hee grabbed the dishes, placed them in the kitchen for later, and changed her clothes. As she came out of the bedroom, Hon-yong opened the door. Jin-taek was leaning against the rock wall of the mineshaft. Seeing them, he turned and led them out of the mine.

Her new husband and son got into a truck with Jin-taek and drove away.

Sun-hee walked up to Tae-seon, who held her youngest child, a boy now five months old, while the twenty-month-old girl held on to her mother's dress. "Good morning, Tae-seon. How are you and the children?" said Sun-hee.

"We had a restless night. This one wanted to be fed twice last night," she said, looking at the child in her arms. She looked at her daughter. "She ate too many new things at the wedding, upsetting her stomach."

"Did you get any sleep?" asked Sun-hee.

"I was able to doze off a few times," Tae-seon said in a tired voice.

"Show me this house we are to be living in," Sun-hee said as she picked up the young girl and motioned for Tae-seon to lead the way.

Tae-seon walked through the crates of mining supplies and rusting machines to an opening. The sun was up, showing off another clear summer day. They walked down a crushed rock path among overgrown birch and sycamore trees, arriving at the door of a cabin. All the windows were broken, the door stuck.

"Hon-yong had to lift and push hard to open it," said Tae-seon as she struggled to get it open.

Sun-hee tried the door once, then she put her granddaughter down to grab the door with both hands and pushed. It opened with a creak. The main room was empty except for the mats where Tae-seon and her family had slept. A sink was on the far wall, and next to it stood a table with a cutting block top. Bare shelves adorned the wall behind the sink. On the right were two empty rooms with broken glass on the floor and tree limbs growing into the broken windows. The back door hung limply on one hinge, leading to the privy.

"This house will need a lot of work if we are to make it into a proper home," said Sun-hee.

"It is larger than the apartment we had at the camp. My husband assured me he would work as hard as he can to make this a proper home," said Tae-seon.

"His father said the same thing," said Sun-hee. "We might as well do what we can today. First, we will clean up a bedroom, and you can get some rest while I watch the children."

They proceeded to sweep out one of the bedrooms and clean the cobwebs from the walls and ceilings. Sun-hee moved a mat into the room. Tae-seon went in to lay down with the baby while Sun-hee played games with the young girl.

At midday, Hon-yong Jr. arrived with food. He looked in on Tae-seon sleeping in the bedroom.

"I am glad you are here, mother. She got no sleep at all last night," he whispered. "Jin-taek and dad are unloading the trucks. We will get two more loads today. Tomorrow, we will be able to start working on this place," he said with a wave of his arm.

By the time the sun was setting, Sun-hee had cleaned the rest of the house and hung pieces of old tarp above the windows. They had running water, and the sink drained. Where there was a light bulb, it worked, which gave Sun-hee some hope. The men arrived with food, and they all went up to the cave to cook and eat. Sun-hee convinced the family to sleep in the cave until the house was in shape. No need for Tae-sun to suffer in a home with no windows.

Over the next week, the men tore the house apart, and then the rebuilding began.

On Friday, Hon-yong told everyone they would take a break and go back to the camp. There were to be more weddings.

***

They left mid-morning for the hour-and-a-half drive through the mountains to the camp. Being able to see the countryside as they drove gave Sun-hee mixed emotions. She had ridden to the compound twenty-two years ago during the night. Then four months ago she had left the area of the compound with a hood over her head. Her trip to the cave was in a covered truck and a box. All her prior journeys were associated with traumatic experiences. She tried to put her memories out of her mind and take in the scenes of the mountain roads.

When they arrived, the camp was set up as it had been for the other weddings. Sun-hee admired the seven arches with flowers arranged on them as she walked with Tae-seon.

"Seven weddings, Tae-seon. I wonder who is getting married. Everyone in your generation is married." Then it dawned on her. "It must be some of the women of my generation."

She hurried into the House of Sanshin to find out who was getting married. She arrived to find Moon-Choe and Eun-seong all dressed up.

"Mother, why didn't you tell me you were getting married?" said Tae-seon as she ran up to Eun-seong.

"I wanted to surprise you," said Eun-seong with a big smile. "After Sun-hee's wedding, Kwang-ku did not know how to go about arranging a wedding ceremony, so he asked Young-ja who had organized yours. It took Young-ja less than a minute to figure out that Kwang-ku wanted to marry her."

"Then Wires and Gears asked Young-ja to arrange their ceremony. And you know that if you want the world to know something, you tell it to Young-ja. Choe-me and I soon knew we were to be married. In a few days, the number of weddings was up to seven. And I hear the disease is spreading. Other men have caught the bug and are looking for brides."

"After today, you will not be the only woman of the House of Sanshin who is married," said Choe-me to Sun-hee.

Sun-hee gave each of her friends a hug. Eun-seong told them about the other women who were getting married today and which men she thought would ask certain women soon.

"Then there is Stone and Strategist. I doubt they will ever marry," Eun-seong concluded.

"Time for the ceremony," said Choe-me's daughter.

Sun-hee went over to take Choe-me's daughter's hand. "My daughter-in-law looks as beautiful as her mother. Are you excited to see your mother married?" she said as they began to walk out.

"Oh, yes. Then tomorrow we are going to Musan where we will all live in grandmother's home. I am so excited that we can get out of here and live a normal life."

Sun-hee went to stand with Hon-yong Jr. and her husband.

"See what you started," she said to Hon-yong.

"That way I could choose the best," he said with a smile.

The ceremony proceeded with Young-ja directing everything. Then the feast began.

Sun-hee spent the day catching up with the other women, especially those who did not attend her wedding.

Mrs. Ra was depressed that her son was not among the men getting married. Young-ja said she was so excited to move to Pyongyang with Kwang-ku. Chulsoon would stay at the camp headquarters with his bride now that Gen. Park and Chun-ja had moved to Pyongyang. Together they would run the hospital and orphanage.

On the ride home, Tae-seon said Eun-seong would be moving to Paekam-rodongjagu.

"Where is that, Tae-seon?" asked Sun-hee.

"My mother did not know exactly. She thinks it is somewhere south of the camp in the mountains. Gears is working on engineering projects for the government there. My mother said he couldn't talk about the projects."

Over the next month, Hammer and his son tore the house apart and put it back together. They added two large bedrooms, each with a private privy. They constructed a separate kitchen with new appliances in the kitchen: a refrigerator, an electric stove, and an oven. There was hot and cold running water and electric heat from baseboards.

Wires came to redo the electrical wiring in the house. Jin-taek built a rock facing around the entire outside. They paneled the inside with white ash and installed new windows with double-pane glass in every room.

Hon-yong also did what he knew best and built cabinets, tables, and chairs made of hardwoods from the Korean forest. He declared he was finished the day of the first snow in October.

To celebrate, Tae-seon hung the wedding photo of her and Hong-yong Jr. in the living room. She then announced she was pregnant again. The extended family was comfortable and cozy in their grand home.

For the first time, Sun-hee felt she had a place of her own. She was the matriarch of a family. Living with her husband, her son, his wife, and her grandchildren made her very content. She could not believe how much she looked forward to every evening when the family would eat together. She had tried to cook until Hon-yong brought in a maid. She was a woman who had arrived at the camp hospital during the war and had stayed all those years helping in the kitchen. Now she took over the cooking and cleaning for the family in exchange for a place to stay.

Relieved of kitchen duties, Sun-hee played with the children and helped get them ready for bed each night. As soon as the children were quiet, Sun-hee and Hon-yong would retire to their bedroom. After all the trauma of being forced to make babies years ago, she found relations with Hon-yong to be the highlight of her life. She creatively came up with new ways to pleasure him and to be pleasured. Their relationship filled them both with immense joy.

While Hon-yong worked during the day making furniture, Sun-hee went to the cave to read, translate, and listen to the radio. She enjoyed looking at the valley while waiting for water to boil for a pot of tea. It always boiled too fast.

In October, the colors of the leaves were amazing. The reds, yellows, and oranges mixed in with the remaining greens against a patchwork of newly fallen snow created an awe-inspiring image in the valley. As the beauty changed with the season, the cave, on the other hand, became colder and less hospitable. In November, the kitchen became uninhabitable. The blowing snow drifted across the floor, making it slippery. Sun-hee refused to go in.

With a little request, Hon-yong went to work on the cave. By the end of November, he had installed a wall of double pane windows across the opening to the valley. The windows interfered with the view, but they kept out the snow and cold. He redid the kitchen with new appliances and furniture. As winter progressed, Hon-yong finished out the entire cave with walls of wood paneling and furniture. He installed an electric furnace, making the cave warm all the time. Sun-hee was so pleased, she would have moved back into the cave permanently if she hadn't enjoyed her grandchildren and spending nights cuddling with Hammer.

Jin-taek worked with Hammer, building furniture during the day and guarding the place at night. He adopted a couple of stray dogs and trained them to watch the workshop. Soon the dogs became companions to the children, adding their playfulness to the household.

As the snow began to melt in the spring, Jin-taek spent more time in the valley. Hon-yong never asked him to work but allowed Jin-taek to keep himself busy when he wanted to. Over the summer, Jin-taek built himself a one-room cabin near the stream and started a garden. Increasingly, he would spend his days in the valley and nights guarding the workshop.

Sun-hee felt very content during the summer of 1973. The Korean economy was doing well. The members of the House of Sanshin were contributing in a significant way. Many grandchildren were born, including another boy to Hon-yong Jr. and Tae-Seon. By Sun-hee's record-keeping, her new grandchild was the 225th child in the second generation.

Sun-hee now had nineteen grandchildren. Five from Su-dae who was in China with her husband at the School of Economics in Bejing. Four from Hang-do who was with Strategist in Pyongyang. So-min now had four children and was living at the rehabilitation center near the gulag with Duk-bae. A second son had been born to Eun-mi and his wife last winter in Pyongyang, giving them three children. And now she had a third grandchild from her youngest son.

For Sun-hee, life was as good as it could get. She received Soviet journals from the children of Max and Alek, who had settled in Khasan just across the Soviet border from Korea. Since Jung-sip now oversaw the postal system, nobody could question the transfer of materials. She would read the journals, translate those she thought were essential, and send them on to those who would benefit from the knowledge. Daily, she would listen to reports and news over the radio, gleaning information from Chinese, Japanese, South Korean, North Korean, and at times Russian broadcasts. To her surprise, she heard Young-ja reporting the news on the radio.

Yong-gak completed the ten principles of Juche ideology in 1974, establishing the guidance for the life of all Koreans. Kim Il-sung took all the credit for the thoughts, but the Sanshin knew it was the work of Strategist.

***

For the next ten years, Sun-hee enjoyed living with her grandchildren and loving her husband, isolated in the mountains but very well informed, loving life as much as anyone could, anywhere in the world.

51 — The Birthday - May, 1982

"Mother, your oldest grandchild will be fifteen in a few weeks. Can you come to Beijing for the party?" Su-dae said through the phone.

"It is so difficult to get across the border. I do not want to take the risk," replied Sun-hee.

"We do it all the time. With the proper papers, I am sure it will be no trouble for you."

"I am not sure I can get the papers."

"It is easy. I'll have my contacts in Pyongyang make them out. You just have to pick them up."

"Do you remember when they took me in for questioning?"

"How could I forget? But what does your arrest have to do with your grandson's birthday?"

"I was supposed to be taken to the gulag. Your father and others rescued me. They made me officially disappear by faking my death. To the government, I have been dead for over ten years."

"Mother, I am sure we can work around that issue."

"No, Yong-gak told me to stay here and be sure not to be picked up by the police. Why don't you come here for a few days after his birthday? We will have another celebration."

"It will not be the same. I want you to come to Beijing and see what is happening."

"You can tell me all about it when you arrive. I may know most of it already as I watch the Beijing news on my new television. If you have access to a video camera, you can take movies at the party, and we can play them on my new video recorder."

"You have a video recorder? They are so hard to get here, and if you can find one they are expensive."

"Yong-gak gave one to Hon-yong the last time he was in Pyongyang. Bring movies with you to watch. We have plenty of room in the cave for your family."

"You win, Mother. I'll call you back with our travel plans. I miss you."

"I miss you, too. I am excited to see you and your family."

Sun-hee hung up the phone and blotted her eyes. She wished she were closer to her other children and grandchildren. Strategist had warned her repeatedly not to expose herself to the authorities, as she did not officially exist. She shuddered with the memories of her questioning.

A few days later, Su-dae called back with the date they would arrive. Since Su-dae was married to the son of Young-ja, she called her to invite her to the birthday party. After Young-ja accepted, Sun-hee thought it would be an excellent time to get her closest friends together. She asked Choe-me and Eun-seong as well. The four of them had not been together since the joint wedding. Finally, as a courtesy, she invited Stone, thinking his grandson would want to see his grandfather.

Three weeks later, Su-dae arrived with her family, including Skinny Beast.

Late in the morning of the next day, others began to arrive: Young-ja and Kwang-ku, Choe-me and Weon-kee, and Eun-seong and Sung-man.

They played games, watched movies, and caught up on each other's lives. Jin-taek roasted a pig. He seemed to enjoy cutting out large portions for everyone. Sun-hee so enjoyed being with her family and wished all her grandchildren were close enough to celebrate birthdays.

In the late afternoon, Stone arrived. He presented small leather bags as presents for his grandson and his daughter.

His grandson opened the leather bag and poured some of the contents onto his hand. "Sand? You gave me sand for my birthday, Grandfather?" he said disappointedly.

"It's not sand. It's gold dust," said Stone.

Su-dae opened her bag and poured out polished garnets, amethysts, and other precious stones. Her eyes widened and sparkled like the gems as she exclaimed, "Oh my."

"The government takes these and sells them to China," said Stone. "I thought you could take them and trade for something you want. There is no market for gems in North Korea."

"There is a fortune in this bag," said Su-dae. "Maybe worth the value of an automobile."

"Then get my grandson a new automobile. He will have something I cannot get here, not that I need one."

The birthday boy bowed deeply. "You honor me, Grandfather. I have not known you my whole life, yet you offer such an expensive gift."

"The bag is just a collection of the dust from one mine. Now you and your mother can exchange it for something of value to you."

While the commotion over the gems and gold was going on, Sun-hee watched Stone walk to the table of food and fill a bowl. She recalled the times they were forced together, resulting in her daughter, and now, this moment. The connection of events and the flow of life passed through her mind. His emotions had briefly broken through when they were together. She had shut them down, and now feelings of guilt grasped at her for rejecting his feelings. She wondered if he would ever be able to open to someone. She knew, deep within his soul, Stone was a very caring person. His emotional walls were like the mountains in which he worked. It would take a lot of digging to get to what was valuable.

Choe-me interrupted her introspection, saying, "Sun-hee, will you show me what you have done to the cave?"

"Us, too," said Young-ja as she grabbed Eun-seong's hand. "We want to see all the changes."

Sun-hee took her girlfriends through the rooms, showing them how cozy her cave had become. Their husbands remained near the food table, grazing and sharing stories. As usual, Young-ja carried on eighty to ninety percent of the conversation, commenting on everything from the placemats to the doilies on the end tables to the view of the twilight over the valley through the new windows.

As the women came back to the main room from the kitchen, Sun-hee heard In-Jung ask, "Sung-Man, what are you working on these days?"

"Officially, I am not supposed to talk about it," replied Sung-man. "In this unofficial gathering, I am working on nuclear energy and nuclear bombs. The premier has become obsessed with them in the last few years. That is where your gold money is going, Young-soo. Equipment to enrich uranium."

"I presume you also get most of the uranium I mine," said Young-soo.

Sun-hee noticed Young-ja had stopped talking and was listening intently.

"Most likely, we now have large stockpiles of it."

"What about selling some of the uranium to China? I could arrange it," said In-jung.

"The Soviets will not allow us to sell uranium to China. And the Soviets have plenty, so we have no market for it," said Young-soo. "It is useless unless we can build reactors to make electricity to sell to China."

"There is something I can buy more of," stated In-jung.

Weon-kee broke into the conversation. "We already have an agreement with China to give them more electricity than we can spare. They pay us for thousands of kilowatts every day. I am under constant pressure to get more electricity out of the dams. The appliances we are making in the factories are useless to families because most of the electricity goes to China."

"Am I correct in saying, the money coming from China goes to pay for the military and improved weaponry?" says In-jung.

"For the most part," said Sung-man. "My superiors have a long list of weaponry they want to have. All of it costs lots of money which we pay to the Soviets."

Sun-hee finally spoke up. "What I hear is that all our extra efforts in mining, producing electricity, and engineering are going to the military."

"There are many needs," said Young-soo. "All the mining equipment in the country needs to be improved. But we can neither buy nor devote any resources to building better equipment. Korea's refining is now so out of date, we get more money from China for the raw materials than our net after processing."

"All of our manufacturing facilities need upgrades," said Sung-man. "Government restrictions and quotas do not allow us to change anything, and the military people in charge do not have the brains to understand how things can be improved. They only tell the workers to work harder."

"I think we have summarized a real problem," said Weon-kee. "We are all working for the government, and the military controls the government. There have been many advances over the years, most at the direction of the Soviet Union. The quality of life for people needs to improve, but our military establishment is only concerned with themselves."

"Without appearing to be disloyal to our premier or the DPRK, there is nothing we can do to change the situation," said Sung-man.

"Sun-hee, you and your mother were too efficient with the materials to educate the people to follow the state," said Weon-kee. "The new generation is compliant. They do not know any different."

"The Sanshin are all very good at what we do," said Sun-hee. "Our children are also beginning to make a significant impact on society throughout the country. But I hear things. The country is becoming stagnant. Less aid is coming from the Soviets. Our neighbors are progressing rapidly. Japan is flourishing, and South Korea is making significant economic advances. There is nothing we can do to influence the government. I wish Yong-gak were here to add his insight."

"When the discussion comes to politics, we are at a loss. Yong-gak makes us all look ignorant," said Kwang-ku.

"The next time I talk to him, I will bring up our discussion and see how he responds," said Sun-hee.

"I am sure he will explain everything with minute gestures with his hands," said Young-ja while wiggling her fingers in front of her chest. This set off a round of laughs, releasing the tension of the conversation.

"I think it is time to get some rest," said Choe-me while taking Weon-kee's hand and leading him to their room. "Goodnight all."

After a quick round of "Goodnight" from everyone, they made their way to rooms.

Sun-hee changed and lay down next to Hon-yong, saying "We are truly blessed, dear. We have good friends, a wonderful family, and a great place to live. Everything we need is here. I feel I need to do more for the Korean People. I do not know how to help them any more than I already have."

"You have too much idle time on your hands," said Hon-yong. "I need to find some real work for you to do." He reached under Sun-hee and, with his strong arms, lifted her onto his chest. "Tonight, you do all the work." He kissed her passionately.

52 — New plans - Fall, 1983

The list of three hundred grandchildren was now complete. They ranged in ages from nine to sixteen. Sun-hee had spent weeks compiling their names, ages, their parents, and grandparents. She remembered many of them as small children. From talking with their parents and grandparents, she added their strengths and weaknesses. Now she knew a little of how they had grown up. The remaining original women had agreed, she was the best person to arrange the marriages of the next generation.

Her priority was to have unions where there were no common parent or grandparent. With the mixture of offspring in the first generation, the task was daunting. She recreated the pedigree chart for the children and began to match them according to strengths, avoiding common weaknesses. It took her over a month before she was satisfied with the pairings. Now all she had to do was tell everyone the marriage pairings. She had become the matchmaker for another generation.

The only problem was there were four more males than females. The males with the least abilities did not have partners. For some reason, she felt guilty about this even though it was the only logical choice.

She wanted a second opinion and called her daughter, So-min, inviting her to come down to review her list.

So-min arrived on the third of October.

"So-min, you are looking well. It has been too long since we have been together," said Sun-hee.

"I miss you and everyone I grew up with," said So-min.

"How are your children?"

"They are great," said So-min. Then she told Sun-hee about each one, spending the rest of the day catching up on family and discussing what was happening in their lives.

Together they spent a week reviewing the list of marriages. So-min and her husband, Duk-bae, had been studying genetics, especially genetic diseases. She was very intent on making sure there were no weaknesses brought together by marriage and combined in the offspring. So-min's understanding of the genetics of strengths and abilities led to numerous changes in the pairings. By the end of their week together, Sun-hee was convinced the proposed marriages would result in an even greater generation of children than anyone had seen before.

What Sun-hee found valuable from this time more than anything was the bonding with her daughter. She was so knowledgeable about genetics and understanding human beings from their traits and upbringing. She could sense who a person was deep down. Her time at the gulag working with prisoners had given her the sense of who could be rehabilitated into Korean society and who should be kept there until they died. So-min dedicated herself to finding the decent people sent to the gulag and returning them to their families. Her primary battle was against the government officials who sent good people to the gulag to get rid of them.

The morning So-min was to leave, Sun-hee said during breakfast, "I have enjoyed our time together, So-min. I have learned so much over the past week, and I am so proud of the person you have become."

"I had great parents," said So-min, "and a wonderful education from the best teachers in all the land. I must commend whoever arranged for us to get all the latest research. The material has been vital."

"A parent can only do so much, and then it is up to the person to define their life," said Sun-hee. "General Park gets credit for bringing the first generation together. The fates also have a lot to do with what happens, as it has with my life. You have taken what was given to you and done well. You are an incredibly strong person."

"Is this why you paired me up with Duk-bae?"

"You are the only person I knew of your generation who could cope with his temper and strengths. I knew it would not be easy. But everyone else would have warped under his dominating personality. Only you could keep him under control. Any lesser man, you would have dominated."

"We achieved a balance, Mother. The balance grew into respect. You were wise in putting us together. I know how to handle him and keep our children from his wrath." So-min said, giving her mother a big hug.

Sun-hee cherished the embrace for a moment. Then said, "Your brother will drive you back as soon as you are ready."

"Half-brother, Mother. Let him know I'm packed. Just show me the way out of this hole in the mountain."

So-min got into the truck with Hon-yong Jr. and left.

Sun-hee returned to the cave. The message light was blinking on the recorder. She pressed the record button. "This is Sung-man. I have an idea. Call me."

Sun-hee dialed Sung-man's number. Eun-seong answered.

"Eun-seong, this is Sun-hee. How are you?"

"I am very well. How are you?"

"I just spent a week with So-min. We had a great time going over the arranged marriages of our grandchildren."

"I so want to know who will marry my grandchildren. However, my husband is excited about the idea that he has. He wants to talk to you and is trying to grab the phone from my hand."

"I'll talk to you later. Let Gears have the phone."

"Sun-hee, I need to get together with Young-soo, Weon-kee, and In-jung about what we discussed the last time we were there. Can you arrange a meeting at your cave?"

"I can set up a meeting. What dates are you available?"

"As soon as you can. I will be there. Just tell me when."

"OK. You must bring your wife as we also have important matters to discuss."

"Not as important as what I need to discuss. Get the meeting arranged as soon as you can."

"I will call the others today," replied Sun-hee. The phone went dead.

Sun-hee needed her tea, so she made a pot before making the calls. By midafternoon, she had arranged a meeting for the fifteenth of October.

Skinny Beast was not able to get away. In his place, he sent Su-dae. Sun-hee was more than happy to see her daughter. Su-dae arrived the evening before the meeting, wanting to spend time with her mother and Tae-seon. Mid-morning of the next day, Stone and Wires showed up. Gears and Eun-seong arrived about an hour later.

Eun-seong immediately embraced her daughter, Tae-seon, and her grandchildren.

Sun-hee led the men to the cave, where Su-dae had spent the night. The five of them sat down in the main room. Sun-hee served tea and rice cakes.

Sung-man began, "In my research of nuclear reactors, there is a type which can be used to produce electricity using thorium. The officials overseeing my projects don't want to use thorium because uranium reactors produce plutonium as well as electricity. Thorium reactions do not result in materials that can be used for weapons. What I propose is making thorium reactors and selling the electricity to China, creating a huge profit."

"If thorium reactors are not approved, how can you make them?" asked Weon-kee.

"I do not make them. You do," Sung-man said, pointing at Weon-kee. "We build them near dams and add their electric output to the hydroelectric energy you are now making."

"How can I hide a nuclear reactor at a dam?"

"A thorium reactor is much smaller than a uranium reactor and isn't dangerous. The Soviets, China, and the United States all want the byproducts of a uranium reactor to make bombs. Thus, they have not invested in thorium-based molten-salt-reactors."

"Where do we get thorium?" asked Weon-kee.

"Thorium is a waste product of most mines. I can get an unlimited supply of thorium," said Young-soo.

Sung-man's eyes widened. "You mean thorium will be easy to get? I wanted you here to tell me where it is and how hard it would be to mine."

"How much do you need, and where do you want it?" said Young-soo. "I could deliver hundreds of kilograms anywhere in North Korea in a couple of weeks."

Sung-man took a deep breath. "This may be easier than I thought. What we need are a few items to make the first reactor." He pulled out a list from his pocket. "This is what I currently do not have. How can we get the rest?"

Weon-kee looked at Su-dae. "We have put in orders before to get parts direct. Can you see if you can get these items and ship them directly to me?"

"If it results in increased electricity for China, I can do anything," said Su-dae.

"We can't build the thorium reactor near the uranium reactors. I am under too much scrutiny by the government," said Sung-man.

"The men overseeing my operations at the dams have no clue what is going on and, for the most part, do not care," said Weon-kee. "We can build it near a dam without being questioned."

"I can move equipment via railroad or truck at any time," said Young-soo. "Just label it as 'mining tools,' and I can get the transportation arranged."

"You are sure thorium molten-salt-reactors work?" asked Su-dae. "The items will be sent on credit. If there is no increased production, the risk is a significant debt."

"The literature I have read lays out the reactor," said Sung-man. "I do need to make one to prove it works. There is a risk. I believe it to be a small one. I will write up the specifications on how to refine the thorium to put into the reactor and redo the blueprints on the reactor to change all the names to disguise it as a coolant pool."

"After the inadequate blueprints and instructions we receive from the Soviets on the transformers and generators they send us, I am sure this will be easy," said Weon-kee. "Let me see the list. I will put in requests for various parts, and then you can ship items from this list with the descriptions in my requests. If the paperwork matches, the officials are not educated enough to know what's in a crate."

"I can repackage and re-label the parts and send them separately. No one will know," said Su-dae. "And, just a thought, what about coal-generated electricity?"

"We are already shipping a train of coal to China every day," said Young-soo.

"If I can get financing for a coal generation facility, can I get the coal directly from you? I can also cover the equipment needed for the thorium reactor in my budget for the coal plant."

"We may need to redirect the coal from our current buyers. I'll have to let you work that out."

The five of them glanced at each other to see if there was more to say about the building of a Molten Salt Reactor. Everyone was silent.

Sun-hee had been listening to the discussion and decided this pause was a chance to speak up. "If this works, more electricity will be produced. It will be sold to China, and more revenue will be available to the Korean government. How do we know they will spend the money to improve the lives of the people and not just buy more military equipment?"

"It increases revenue and the amount of electricity available," said Sung-man. "We need to talk to Gil-hyung to see what he can do to redirect some of the funds."

"Is this idea worth the risk?" asked Sun-hee.

"I think it is," said Weon-kee.

"I am for it," said Young-soo.

"I must try," said Sung-man.

"I will do my part from China," said Su-dae.

"Then we keep this between ourselves and make it work," said Sun-hee.

"One last need is for Ching-ying to look over the calculations for the reactor and confirm the numbers," said Sung-man. "A few days ago, I left him a message but have not heard back."

"I will call him or get in touch with our son, Eun-mi, and have them contact you," said Sun-hee.

"Working within the House of Sanshin is so much more efficient than working with the government. I am in awe of who we have become," said Weon-kee.

"Agreed," said Sung-man.

"I need to get going," said Young-soo as he got up and quickly left.

"Always the man of many words," said Weon-kee as he stood. "Sun-hee, thank you for hosting us."

"This meeting was shorter than I had planned. Lunch will be ready soon. I hope you can all stay," said Sun-hee.

"Eun-seong will not let us leave without eating first," said Sung-man.

Sun-hee led them through the mineshafts, gates, and doors to the house where the maid had already set the table. The talk over lunch was about the marriages Sun-hee had arranged for the children. She avoided Tae-seon's inquiries as her children were in the room, and she did not want to give anything away. Eun-seong wisely asked only about her other grandchildren.

With lunch finished, Sun-hee bowed to Weon-kee. "Give my love to Choe-me."

"I will," he said, reciprocating the bow before leaving.

She hugged Eun-seong, and as they separated, Eun-seong grasped her shoulders with her hands and said, "I wish I could be here more with Tae-seon and her children. I see they have been raised well with you around."

"I wish we could spend more time together," said Sun-hee.

"Being married to men has pulled us apart," said Eun-seong. "But I would not want to go back to being single."

"Me, either," Sun-hee said with a smile. They released their hold on one another, and Eun-seong proceeded to say goodbye to Tae-seon and family.

After lunch, the guests had left, and Sun-hee proceeded to the cave to call Numbers. Sun-hee left a message for him to call. Then she tried Eun-mi's number, and his wife answered. They talked for a while about the family before she asked her to have Eun-mi call her back.

Late in the afternoon, the phone rang.

"Eun-mi. How are you?"

"We are fine, Mother," said Eun-mi. "I was told you called and needed to talk to me. What can I do for you?"

"Sung-man has an important project he needs you to review. Would you or your father have time to visit Sung-Man at the nuclear facility?"

"The nuclear projects are of high priority. I think I could get my overseers to let me go to see him for a day or so? There are so many military requests for our math assistance, my dad and I are buried. We never get to work on projects of our choosing. Being the smartest has its disadvantages."

"Let me know if there is anything I can do." said Sun-hee.

In a quiet voice, Eun-mi said, "Get me out of North Korea."

"Your request is beyond my abilities, Son. And never let anyone hear you say that. Never hint at leaving to anyone else."

"Only to you, Mother. I will call Sung-man. Goodbye, Mother. I miss you."

"I miss you and your family. We will need to get together someday."

Sun-hee hung up the phone.

The government constrains us. The House of Sanshin could do much more without the restrictions. I must talk to Strategist on how we can have more influence.

53 — Park's New Plan - April, 1984

The message light was blinking on the answering machine when Sun-hee arrived in the cave. Anything anyone felt was important was transferred to her number. Thus, two to five messages were waiting for her every morning. As always, she made a pot of tea, taking the time to stare at the canyon. The snow was starting to recede up the mountain slope across the valley, adding to the torrent of the river below. The trees on this side of the river were beginning to leaf out, providing an incredible mixture of all shades of green.

Her kettle whistled. She made herself a pot of tea and carried it to her desk in the other room. She pressed the "play message" button on the answering machine and listened.

Click, click.

"Sun-hee, this is Choe-me. I am not happy with the canceled marriage plan. We need to talk. Call me."

No pleasantries at all. She must be extremely upset.

Sun-hee wrote a note: *Call Choe-me.*

"Mom, General Park changed the marriage plan. Help! Love you."

What is General Park doing now?

She wrote, *Call So-min first.*

"Good morning, Sun-hee, this is Eun-seong. I hope you are doing well. Everything is great here. Sung-man has never been so excited. I called to give you a warning. General Park was here yesterday, and he is reverting to the old way. I spoke to Choe-me and tried to break the news as gently as I could. She became overly emotional. I am worried about her. Call me when you get the chance."

Sun-hee quickly scribbled, *Eun-seong.*

After canceling the messages, Sun-hee dialed her daughter.

We spent months arranging one hundred and fifty marriages. Now Gen. Park is changing them. He thinks he still controls us!

"Hello."

"So-min. Good morning. How are you doing?" said Sun-hee in a cheerful voice.

"Mom," So-min said in an agitated voice. "General Park threw out the marriage arrangements. He wants to go back to individual mating to emphasize traits. He said we need more variety."

"He knows our society is too structured on the traditional family for individual mating to work. I convinced him that marriages were best for your generation."

He needs convincing again!

"General Park said he is not happy with the results. He insisted on selecting individual mating. He said, 'Anyone who refuses will end up in the gulag.' Mom, what are we going to do?"

How can I get General Park out of our lives?

"What does your husband say about this?" asked Sun-hee.

"He suggested we harvest eggs and sperm and do in-vitro fertilization with surrogate mothers."

"Where would we find the mothers?"

"My husband would use women at the prison camp," So-min said in a matter-of-fact manner.

"How confident are you with in-vitro fertilization?" asked Sun-hee.

"We are getting about thirty percent healthy births right now. We are working on the procedures to improve the success rate," replied So-min.

"That rate is not very good. I cannot support in-vitro fertilization with that low rate. How many children does General Park think we need for the next generation?" asked Sun-hee.

"He has used the multiplier of two-and-a-half. The original forty-eight became one hundred and twenty, who became three hundred," replied So-min.

"So now Park wants seven hundred fifty children with different sets of parents. That is impossible. Where is General Park? Do you know?"

"He was here yesterday. He left in the afternoon to visit all the families and give them his orders. Eun-seong was first on his list."

"I have received messages from Eun-seong and Choe-me this morning."

"Choe-me was third on his list. He will not be there until this afternoon."

"I need to call her," said Sun-hee. "I'll call you later. I love you, So-min."

"I love you too, Mother," said So-min before she hung up.

Sun-hee dialed Choe-me's number. A female voice answered, "Hello. Yung-li speaking."

"Good morning, Yung-li. This is Sun-hee. How are you today?"

"I am doing well. My grandmother is a little emotional this morning."

"I understand. Is your grandmother able to talk?"

"She is in the garden. I will go get her."

"Thank you. I will hold."

Choe-me will tell her whole family and get them involved before I have a chance to talk to her. She never could hold her emotions in.

Choe-me's excited voice came over the phone. "Sun-hee. General Park does not want our grandchildren to marry."

"I know. Can I come over today?"

"Yes. Please. I need you to be here when General Park arrives."

"I will leave as soon as I can. If General Park arrives before I do, keep him there until I get there. See you soon."

"We have to do something. Hurry!"

Sun-hee hung up the phone, gathered a few things, and ran down the passageways to the storage room. She ran to the shop and yelled at Hon-yong. "I need to go to Choe-me's right now!"

"Is something wrong?"

"Terribly! I will tell you about it on the way."

"The truck over there is empty. Let me grab my papers, and I will be right back."

Sun-hee walked over to the truck and climbed in the passenger seat, pursing her lips.

Not my grandchildren. I will not allow my grandchildren to go through what I was subjected to. I must change Park's mind. He cannot be allowed to mate children without marriages.

Tears started to flow as she remembered the nights in the camp with the girls returning from the guesthouse.

We had no way out. What is our way out now?

Hon-yong opened the door and climbed in. Seeing his wife's tears, he said, "What is wrong?"

"Just drive!"

Hon-yong turned the ignition, and the diesel truck rumbled to life. He backed out and started down the road to Hyesan.

Sun-hee took out a handkerchief, wiped her eyes, and blew her nose. "General Park wants to mate our grandchildren as he did us," she blurted. "He wants more variety in the next generation. He will be at Choe-me's this afternoon. We need to change his mind. I will not allow our grandchildren to be treated as we were."

"If there are no problems along the road, we will be there by midafternoon." Hon-yong coaxed all the speed he could get from the truck along the winding mountain road. "Being forced to mate with all of us must have been very difficult for you," said Hon-yong in a calm voice.

"We had no other option. We were captive of General Park. We were young and did not know we could resist."

"I am sorry for being part of your trauma," he said.

"My eye was on you from the time we arrived at Yangseongso. The moment we had in the guesthouse was the highlight of my life until you came riding towards me on a mule."

"I felt cheated getting only one night with you. Something in me said I want more. When you were taken away, I told myself to marry you if you survived."

"I am glad I survived, and our relationship blossomed. Now we must stand up for our grandchildren as I did for our children. There has to be a better way," she said.

"You always find a way to bring peace to a situation, Sun-hee. It is one of the reasons I fell in love with you. You always find a better way."

"I'll need your support. I fear General Park will not be easily convinced." Words she could say raced through her mind. She shivered at her thoughts of the confrontation she was about to have. "How can I change Park's mind? I wonder if he knows I am alive."

"I never thought about that. You may give the general a big surprise," he said with a chuckle.

Sun-hee looked out the side window, watching the flowing river beside the road, the sheepherders on the hillside, and now and then the small farms. The road was bumpy, full of potholes and areas partly washed out from the spring runoff. She wanted to take Hon-yong's hand, but he was busy with the steering wheel and gearshift.

***

Knock knock

"Hello. Can I help you?" said Yung-li.

"This is General Park, Tae-song. I would like to talk to you. Open the door."

Yung-li opened the door and bowed. "Welcome, General Park. My grandmother is expecting you. She is in the garden. Please follow me." She led Gen. Park into the garden behind the house.

The fenced garden of the Moon farm contained a variety of fruit trees, flowers, spices, and vegetables. Choe-me had worked off her nervous energy all day by planting seeds and pruning. She was on her knees, planting radish seeds using a Hori Hori garden knife when Yung-li and Gen. Park approached.

"Grandmother, General Park has arrived."

Choe-me stood and bowed respectively.

"Moon Choe-me, you're still as pretty as the cherry blossoms behind you," said Gen. Park.

"Thank you. I know why you have come."

"The program must continue. The work your generation is doing amazes me. When I visit the men and their families, I wonder what this country would have been like if my plan of bringing fifty children to Yangseongso each year had been implemented."

"We are doing most of the significant work in the country. My husband and his sons are in charge of all the electricity in the country. How will forcing my granddaughters to mate with multiple men do more than we are doing now?"

"The families are staying together. Sons are taking after their fathers. Like you said, Weon-ke's sons are working with him. There are segments of our society where there is a lack of leadership. Diversity is needed to accomplish more. Korea is not great enough."

"Your plan to greatness for Korea should not rely on forcing girls to mate with whomever you decide."

"You will agree to have Yung-li mate with who I choose, or I will turn in everyone to the security forces."

"You will expose yourself."

"Will you let Yung-li and the rest of your grandchildren be sent to the gulag?"

"You are despicable," yelled Choe-me.

Gen. Park slapped Choe-me hard across the side of her face, turning her half-way around.

She put her left hand on her cheek and rotated her head towards the general. "Long ago, I made a promise." From her bent over position, Choe-me swung her right hand with all her strength, still holding the garden knife, into the left side of Gen. Park's chest.

Gen. Park's eyes got wide as he looked down at the spade buried in his chest. Choe-me's hand was still attached. His breath froze. His eyes turned to Choe-me.

"What did you promise?" he wheezed.

"I promised myself to kill you for what you did to me," she said, then she let her hand go limp, falling back to her side.

Park mumbled out, "Between fourth and fifth ribs. Perfectly placed. You learned anatomy well."

He fell forward into Choe-me who stepped aside while pushing the falling general away.

Choe-me stood over the body, her own body shaking. Yung-li stood wild-eyed with her hands over her mouth. The birds chirped in the trees. A stiff breeze rustled the blossoms in the cherry trees. Choe-me panicked, dropped to her knees, pulled out the spade, and tried to apply pressure to the wound. Blood oozed around her fingers. For a few minutes, she tried to stop the blood and bring the general back to life.

Yung-li pulled her grandmother away and led her into the house.

***

Hon-yong asked for directions when they arrived in Hyesan. The Moon family home was outside of town, a farmhouse overlooking the Yalu River. As they drove north from the heart of the city, the view of the meandering river rivaled the one looking out of the valley from the cave. Blossoms were on most trees, making this one of the most colorful scenes Sun-hee had ever seen. She might have enjoyed it if her mind and heart had not been so consumed with the problem at hand. Her stomach turned. She resisted throwing up.

When they pulled up at the farmhouse, there was a black sedan in front. A young man dressed smartly in a private's uniform stood next to the car, smoking a cigarette. He became alert when they drove up. Sun-hee jumped from the truck, ignored the driver, and went to the gate. It was closed but not locked. She rang the bell and waited a few seconds before she pushed the gate open and let herself in. She strode to the door and knocked.

Yung-li spoke from the other side of the door. "We are busy now and cannot accept visitors."

"Yung-li, this is Sun-hee. We spoke earlier. Can I come in?"

"It would be better if you went away."

"Yung-li, I must speak with your grandmother and General Park. I can help you."

"Is anyone with you?"

"My husband is with me. Please, let me speak to General Park."

The door opened a crack, and Sun-hee pushed it open. Yung-li stood there shaking, a rag in her hands and tears running down her face. After Hon-yong entered, Yung-li quickly closed the door, locked it, and put her forehead against the door.

Sun-hee put her arm around Yung-li. "We are here to make things right. Do not be upset. Everything will be fine."

"No. You are too late."

"Where is your grandmother?"

"She is in her room. Second door." She pointed down the hallway.

Sun-hee went to the door and knocked, getting no response, she opened it. Choe-me was kneeling in the corner with her head down.

"Choe-me, I'm here. What happened?"

Choe-me did not move. "You must leave, Sun-hee."

"I will not leave until this is resolved."

"It's resolved. See!" Choe-me held up her bloody hands. "I killed him."

"Choe-me!" Sun-hee fell to her knees, wrapped her arms around her, and held her close. "Oh, Choe-me. I told you I was coming. I came as fast as I could. I'm so sorry."

For the next few minutes, they stayed in the corner weeping together.

Sun-hee finally said, "Where is he?"

"In the garden," replied Choe-me.

"I will be right back."

Sun-hee walked out of the room and motioned to her husband. "Come with me." She walked through the kitchen and out the back door into the fenced-in garden. Cherry and apricot trees were in blossom, and newly planted vegetables were sprouting in neatly planted rows. She saw two feet behind some irises near the cherry trees. She walked over to see Gen. Park lying on the ground. Blood soaked his shirt. She put her hands to her mouth and gagged.

Hon-yong put his arm around his wife. "We have a bigger problem."

Sun-hee knelt beside the body and felt for a pulse. "No heartbeat. He's dead." She looked up at Hon-yong.

"Choe-me?" he asked.

Sun-hee acknowledged with a shake of her head. "She put the spade through the ribs, directly into the heart."

He knelt and put his arms around Sun-hee. "I'm sorry. I wish I could have gotten us here sooner."

"No. Only I am guilty," said Choe-me behind them. She stood there with her bloody hands clasped in front of her. Blood smeared on her garden apron. The left side of her face was red and bruising. Tears flowed through a streak of blood running across her bruised cheek and under a swelling eye. Her hair, though tied back in a bun, was uneven with clumps protruding out, a strand of hair crossing her face. Still, the beauty of her lips and chin made her attractive.

"Choe-me, did he hit you?" asked Hon-yong.

She bowed her head and shook it up and down in minute fashion.

"She defended herself and her honor. She was justified in killing the general," he said.

"When a general is killed, no one is innocent," said Sun-hee.

Yung-li came up behind Choe-me. "The driver is knocking at the door. What should I do?"

"Let me answer the door," said Hon-yong. He walked into the house.

Sun-hee held Choe-me. She looked at her face and said, "Yung-li. Get a cold compress we can put on her eye. Ice if you have it."

Yung-li went into the house.

"They will put me to death for this," cried Choe-me.

Hon-yong walked into the garden with the driver. "This is Chweh, Chong-pil's son. He has been General Park's driver for the past few years."

"My father has told me stories of the forty-eight prize winners. I am honored to meet three of you today." He bowed low. Then he walked over to the body of Gen. Park. "My father told me someone would kill the general one day. Today is that day." He looked at Choe-me. "I am sorry it fell on you to end his life." He bowed towards her.

Yung-li approached and placed a cloth wrapped around the ice on Choe-me's face. With her other hand, she held a rag. "Here, wipe your hands."

"Let's go inside, and we can discuss what to do," said Sun-hee. She took the ice pack from Yung-li, holding it on Choe-me's face as she led her inside. "Yung-li, would you be so kind and brew some tea?"

"I would be pleased to," said Yung-li.

Sun-hee took her friend to wash up and change. After a few minutes, they entered the main room and knelt on silk pillows around a low table.

"How is Chong-pil?" said Sun-hee. "I have not heard from him in a while."

"He is well. He is now in Sinuiju. He coordinates grain trade with China."

She turned to Choe-me. "Choe-me, where are Wires and your sons?"

"They are working on installing new hydroelectric generators at the dam. He'll be home after nightfall."

The thorium reactor, thought Sun-hee.

Yung-li brought in tea and poured everyone a cup. When she finished, she bowed and went to her room.

"I will go into town and buy some lumber to build a crate. We can take the body and bury it somewhere," said Hon-yong.

"If he goes missing, there will be an investigation," said Chweh.

"Who knows where General Park is at?" said Sun-hee.

"Only those here in this house and maybe those we have visited recently," said Chweh.

"Can you think of anyone who is not part of the program who knows where he is?" asked Sun-hee.

"Only his son. But they were arguing before we left. He felt there were better ways to get the same results. General Park insisted natural conception was the only way."

"Then we prepare the body for burial and take it to his son," said Sun-hee. "We can traditionally wrap the body for burial. We can say he had a heart attack. To unwrap the body would be against tradition. Duk-bae will never know."

Hon-yong took his wife's hand and squeezed it. "You always come up with a great solution."

Sun-hee said to her husband, "Go buy the burial cloth and supplies." She turned to the Chweh. "Is there a clean uniform in the car?"

"Yes, I will get his bags." He walked out with Hon-yong.

"You did everyone a favor today," said Sun-hee, taking Choe-me's hands. "I was prepared to kill him. I am in your debt." She bowed low.

"I swore I would kill General Park for what he forced me to do," she said through her sobs. "I did it."

Preparation of the body for burial took the rest of the afternoon. Choe-me stood watching Hon-yong and Sun-hee clean Park's body and put on a new uniform. They moved the body to the truck and cleaned up the house and garden.

Weon-kee and his sons arrived late in the evening. Hon-yong took them to the garden and described the events of the day.

Chweh was the only one who spoke at dinner. "The general talked to himself a lot during our drives around the country, usually in Russian or Mandarin, sometimes in Japanese. I knew his thoughts, all because of your insistence on learning the languages, Mrs. Cha. He thought I only knew Korean. I never let him know I understood. He raged a lot. He hated the poor and common man for not doing enough. He hated disloyalty."

"Five years ago, he insisted we go to Kimchaek. He had been ranting on about a person who bribed their way into his program. He killed Mrs. Lim, Joo-yun, and her daughter."

"Why didn't you stop him?" said Weon-kee.

"I stayed in the car. At the time, I didn't think a doctor could be a murderer."

"He killed people with bad attitudes before," said Sun-hee, remembering Sgt. Peterson. "I wasn't there to keep Joo-yun out of trouble."

"Don't blame yourself for Joo-yun's death," said Hon-yong. "If Mrs. Lim would have stayed for a few months, she could have left without being disloyal."

Chweh went on, "The general wanted everyone to do what he wanted. Nobody was good enough for him. He even complained about the inadequacy of our rulers. I could have turned him in for being disloyal."

Yung-li began to gather dishes. Sun-hee helped her clean up. Choe-me retired to her bedroom with her husband. Weon-kee's sons brought mats to the living room for Sun-hee and Hon-yong.

Sun-hee and Hon-yong laid down. He put his arm around Sun-hee. "How are you feeling?"

"I am so sorry for Choe-me. She will hold onto this day for the rest of her life. I wish it were anyone but her," said Sun-hee. "Yet I am relieved. General Park's influence on our lives is now over."

"You are right about Choe-me," said Hon-yong quietly. "I hope she can put this day behind her."

They laid quietly, sleeping restlessly through the night.

54 — Loss of hope - April, 1984 to October, 1987

Moon Choe-me's dress matched the vivid cherry tree blossoms under which she sat. Her head held low, her lengthy hair flowing over her shoulders. The morning sun rising from behind the tree lit up the blossoms. Sun-hee approached and sat next to her, placing an arm around her.

"How are you this morning?" Sun-hee asked quietly.

"The fates allowed me to release a pain of my past while adding a new trauma," Choe-me said without lifting her head. "I have a new burden to bear, yet a great relief. Ying-li will have the joy of a husband, as will many others. Maybe this will also allow soothing of your pain and the pain of the others."

"I wish anyone but you had killed General Park. If only I could take your burden and see you happy and vibrant again."

"I am very content here with my family, Sun-hee. We will see much joy in the future. Wires is proud of me for standing up for myself. He is a wonderful companion. You are a wonderful friend."

Sun-hee held her tight. The birds sang, and bees made their morning rounds above their heads.

"We will take General Park's body to his son. Everything will be fine. Only those of us here will know what happened."

"Thank you," said Choe-me.

"I will return soon," said Sun-hee. She rose and stroked Choe-me's head, feeling the silky softness of her hair.

***

Sun-hee and Hon-yong drove to the home of So-min and Duk-bae with the remains of Gen. Park. Chweh followed. Arriving mid-afternoon, they moved the casket to a room in the house.

Duk-bae bowed low in gratitude for properly preparing his father for burial. They returned the respectful bow and left.

Duk-bae issued a death certificate from the hospital. The cause of death read, "Heart Attack." He signed it and gave it to Chweh, who left to deliver it to the officials in Pyongyang. Duk-bae sat with the body of his father until the burial plot was prepared.

***

A week after returning to the cave, Sun-hee spent a few days contacting the second-generation families to inform them of her matchmaking efforts. She let everyone know of Gen Park's passing and that the timing of the marriages was up to the parents. There were a few who objected to remaining part of the program now that the general was no longer in charge. However, when Sun-hee asked them if they wanted a different marriage arrangement, none offered alternate choices. Out of courtesy, Sun-hee also asked the objectors if they would like to resign from being a part of the House of Sanshin. Each was adamant that they remain.

After the last call, Sun-hee went down to the valley and sat by the river. She watched Jin-taek fish in the lake he made by throwing rocks in the river until he had a small dam. She contemplated whether Park had succeeded in accomplishing anything.

Is the House of Sanshin accomplishing his plan? The remaining prize winners were Songbun and have integrated themselves into the economy of Korea.

In speaking with them over the past few days, they were all contributing significantly but expressed frustration with the lack of overall progress in the country.

Sun-hee wondered if the Sanshin were not there, if it would have made any difference? Probably not, she concluded. When they did more, the government confiscated the additional product.

Can anything more be done? Are we the ones to do it?

The only one she could ask those questions of and get answers from was Strategist. She rose, went up to the cave, and left a message for Yong-gak.

The next day, Hong-do called back, "Hello, Mother. How are you?"

"I am fine, Son. Do you return all of your father's calls now?" asked Sun-hee.

"Only the ones he wants me to return," said Hong-do. "My father has become somewhat of a recluse. He only speaks to the Premier, Huang Jang-yop, and me. Everyone else must communicate in writing. He allows government security to screen all written messages. Mostly, he sends out questions and requests for materials and gets what he requests. At his insistence, all communication goes through me. He is one of only a few people to receive time alone with the Premier. In this manner, he keeps himself far above suspicion. Kim Il-sung listens to him as he knows my father is objective and untainted in what he has to say."

"Is there a way you and I could talk privately?"

"Let me see what I can arrange. I'll call you soon," said Hong-do.

A week later, Sun-hee received a voice message from Hong-do. "Eun-mi and I are going on a fishing trip with our sons on the second weekend of May. See you then."

Sun-hee knew where they could fish. Jin-taek had a continual supply of fish when his lake was not frozen over. The next time she was at the river, she let him know that her sons and grandsons were coming and wanted to fish in his lake. He lifted his fishing poles as if he was showing them off, nodded, and smiled.

Hong-do, Eun-mi and their four sons arrived on a Friday night. They brought a gift, a new videotape recorder with a couple of American movies. They were part of a shipment of recorders and movies brought into the country for the political elite. The Premier had given a couple to Yong-gak. Yong-gak told Hong-do to deliver one to Sun-hee.

After dinner with the family, they connected the recorder to their small black and white television and watched *Superman*. The children were thrilled with the movie and wanted to watch it again. To settle the confrontation, Sun-hee had to command her sons to take the recorder to the cave so that everyone could retire for the night.

Early the next morning, they went down to the valley. Jin-taek took the boys to the lake to fish. Sun-hee and her sons walked upriver and sat on rocks in the morning sun.

"I am very concerned about our country," said Sun-hee. "From talking to the others of your generation around the country, they are very frustrated. They cannot make progress with the current level of control by the government. All the money coming into the country is devoted to the military and the entertainment of the political elite. Is there anything we can do?"

Hong-do hung his head low. "No, Mother. There is nothing that can be done."

Eun-Mi leaned in towards his mother. "My father and I have gone through every scenario logically. The chances of any event changing the current state of affairs are minimal."

"Let me go over the possibilities," interrupted Hong-do. "First, the Premier does not want to change. He is in a very secure position. His focus is to unify Korea. Any change from this position will weaken the military hold he has on the nation. Second, any attempt at a military coup d'état will either be put down violently or be done by a group so ruthless the nation will be in a worse situation. Third, a revolution by the people will result in thousands of deaths and possibly a total collapse of order. With the military offering rewards for turning in people who voice dissent, a revolution cannot gain a foothold. If a revolution were successful, the winners would need to purge the existing political elite, which will result in even more deaths."

"Our scenarios all determine chaos is the result. If this happens, we will return to a puppet state of another country. The Soviet Union, China, and the United States may go to war over control. They would destroy our nation. Fourth, should the Premier die and his son succeeds him, we get more of the same, maybe worse. Last, if we initiate an all-out war with South Korea, we are also doomed. America will destroy us. Right now, we have stability, and our families can live according to government rules in peace. It is not anywhere near the best, but it is our only option."

"Isn't there anything we can do?" pleaded Sun-hee.

"This is why I want to leave," said Eun-mi. "I would like to work on many things, but the pressure is on my father and me to come up with a way to defeat the Americans. While the American military is ready to take on the Soviet Union, we would be like a fly on the wall to be swatted aside."

"I will not leave my father," said Hong-do. "He is committed to offering advice on directing Korea to a better future. However, he has told me, there are no good options for removing Kim Il-sung."

"We need to come up with something," said Sun-hee. "In my lifetime, I hope to see the Korean people having more hope at a better life. Maybe we need a Superman."

Hong-do replied, "If the Mountain Gods themselves were to come out of hiding and take up the fight, it would still result in much bloodshed. They would need to remove the Supreme People's Assembly who has the backing of the military."

"The House of Sanshin does not influence the Supreme People's Assembly," said Sun-hee.

"The members are all suspicious of each other as they maneuver for power and influence. Anyone in the assembly would need to be extremely careful," said Hong-do. "A presence there would put all of us in danger."

Sun-hee felt all hope for the future advancement of Korea melt from her body like the snow melting off the mountains in the spring sun. She felt as useless as the lichen covering the rock she sat on.

"I am going to see if our sons are having any luck catching fish," said Hong-do as he stood. "Maybe I can catch one myself." He disappeared through the trees, walking down to the lake.

"I hope you can get to the United States someday," Sun-hee said to Eun-mi. "When you do, try to find a peaceful way to keep the Americans from conquering us."

"I will, Mother. I have to get there with my family first," said Eun-mi as he took his mother's hand to reassure her.

Together, they stood and slowly made their way to where the others were fishing. When they arrived, Hong-do hooked a fish. A move of the fish pulled him off balance. He fell into the lake. The boys got a big laugh at his expense.

Sun-hee chuckled, watching her son clamber out of the lake with the assistance of Jin-taek. It was a pleasant moment with family in a beautiful place.

We can live happily. Why must I worry about the fate of others?

Sun-hee's grandsons each proudly held up three or four fish.

Jin-taek seemed to enjoy the moment most of all. He took the fish and showed the boys how to clean them. They made their way to the elevator and, in a couple of trips up the shaft, returned to the cave. Jin-taek prepared a few fish for a feast, wrapping the rest for them to take home.

After they ate, Sun-hee's sons and grandsons left for Hyesan. Weon-kee was going to take them fishing at the reservoir.

Sun-hee retired to the cave to watch the other movie her son had brought. *The Godfather*. The horse head scene made her sick, and she turned it off.

***

Summer went by quickly. Sun-hee kept track of the marriages and stayed in contact with the women of her generation. She encouraged them to teach their grandchildren about loyalty to the House of Sanshin. She noted the roles the grandchildren were taking in Korean society. Most were moving into positions of technical or scientific endeavors. Monitoring world events took an hour or two a day. The rest of her time, she spent thinking about how the rest of the world might influence Korea for the better. Revelation on how to affect change continued to escape her. She realized that she would have to accept the plight of the people and herself. As fall approached, she spent more time with her family, appreciating her life with Hon-yong more and more.

Hong-do sent another box of American videos. She used these to improve her English-speaking skills and teach English to her grandchildren. The next box of videos were copies dubbed into Korean. She recognized Young-ja's voice in many of the female roles, sometimes all the female characters in a movie. Each of these videos produced lots of chuckles.

***

Over the next three years, Sun-hee monitored the House of Sanshin. The men were all in essential positions. Stone ran the mining operations for the country. Strategist was a political advisor to Kim Il-sung. Unicorn was the lead surgeon at the hospital in Pyongyang. Numbers was head of the mathematics department at Pyongyang University. Chulsoon ran their old camp and the hospital there. Waves built submarines. Skinny Beast was part of the finance ministry in Bejing. Stinky headed up the Department of Agriculture. Ki-young was now in charge of all the railroads. Hein-jin headed up the mail systems. Chong-pil oversaw shipping with China. Sung-man was involved in building nuclear reactors. Wires was head of the hydro-electric dams and the generation of electricity. A few others were doctors at major hospitals. One ran the printing facilities in Chongjin, and another was an engineer for radio and television for the country. Her husband made the best furniture in Korea, and Young-ja was active in the media. Despite all this influence, Sun-hee still had no hope for the future of the country.

When she talked to the women, they were all happy and satisfied with their lives, relishing in the marriages of their grandchildren and the births of great-grandchildren. The second generation was progressing into positions of influence, following their fathers or developing their careers. What her peers conveyed in every conversation was a lack of hope that the life of the people would be better.

One success in 1986 did give her a little hope. It was a short phone message from Choe-me. Weon-kee had a thorium reactor up and running. It was producing electricity, adding to sales to China. Sanshin had accomplished something without the authorization of the government.

***

On the morning of the third of October of 1987, So-min called. "Good morning, Mother. How are you today?"

"I am doing well. No change here. How are you and the grandchildren?" replied Sun-hee.

"We are all doing great," said So-min. "I'd like you to know, Duk-bae and I have perfected in-vitro fertilization. We are ready to begin making a generation of children for the program. Our last twenty tests have all come out with healthy children. When can we harvest eggs and sperm?"

Sun-hee paused, trying to understand what this would entail before asking, "How do you harvest the eggs and sperm?"

"The sperm is easy," replied So-min. "To get the eggs, we need to perform a simple operation to remove them from the ovary. We try to take about twenty eggs from each female."

"Does this affect the woman for the future? Can she still have more children?" asked Sun-hee.

"There is no long-term problem. After a couple of weeks to recover, the woman is fine," explained So-min. "We would like your approval to proceed. However, I must tell you, Duk-bae is committed to doing this. He will make it happen."

The last statement aroused Sun-hee's suspicion. "How will he make it happen if I do not approve?" asked Sun-hee.

"He will have girls in the second generation picked up and brought to the gulag for questioning. I would rather they all volunteer. It would be so much easier. Mother, you must agree, or Duk-bae will take eggs by force."

"He is just like his father," said Sun-hee.

"He is," said So-min as her voice cracked and she began to cry over the phone. "I have argued with him and…"

"Are you alright? Did he hurt you?" Sun-hee demanded.

"I cannot oppose him any further," So-min blurted over the phone. "I do not see a way to stop this. There is no long-term harm to women."

Sun-hee read through her daughter's words. If I say no, my daughter will suffer. Sun-hee paused for a moment before replying, "I will call the other women and let them know the egg harvesting may begin. But only after the girls have given birth to as many children as they desire. Do you think Duk-bae will wait?"

"I will tell him," said So-min.

Sun-hee scanned her list of marriages and children born. "There are two girls who have not had a first child after three years of marriage. They may have fertility problems. Maybe we can start with them and provide children. It will make it easier for the rest to give us some eggs."

"I will work with this plan mother. You always come up with the right solution."

"I wish I could solve everything," said Sun-hee. "Some problems do not have a solution."

"I know, Mother. We do what we can and hope the fates will act in our favor. I need to go. I will call you soon. I love you."

Sun-hee put her head in her hands.

The fates have provided us a hopeless and uncertain future. Where will this decision lead? What future will the children I agree to give life to have? Will their biological mothers accept them? Or will they be children with surrogate mothers, orphans in a gulag hospital, no one to care and raise them? What have I agreed to?

55 — Cha Eun-mi Leaves - Spring, 1988

Sun-hee pushed her food around her plate, eating very little.

After the rest of the family retired for the evening, Hon-yong said, "Something is bothering you. When you do not eat, I know you are troubled."

She picked up both plates and took them to the kitchen, ignoring her husband's comment. She washed the dishes slowly.

Would this plan work? If it fails, we will all be thrown into prison.

She reviewed her plan in her mind while she cleaned up. She then prepared for bed, putting on her silk nightgown and laying down. She stared at the ceiling, thinking of possible pitfalls.

Hon-yong came in and changed into his nightclothes in the near darkness. He lay down, rolled on his side, and looked at Sun-hee. "You have been deep in thought today. Tell me what is consuming you." He paused, expecting an answer. "I can't help if you don't talk. Have I done something to offend you?"

Sun-hee sighed, eyes focused on the ceiling and said, "I am worried about the new submarine Waves has designed. The military thinks his stealth sub will allow them to sink American ships. Whenever they think we have a way to hurt the Americans, they want to go to war."

"You think the military can't win a war? Our anti-aircraft guns are greatly improved, and our artillery far exceeds what they have in the South."

"The Americans already hate us. Their strategy would be to bomb our country to rubble like last time. Too many people will die, and all the progress we have made will be lost. We must prevent actions which might provoke America into an all-out war. I have been working on some ideas."

"Tell me about these ideas that consume your thoughts." said Hon-yong as he adjusted his pillow to draw closer to her.

"The military wants to use the new submarine Waves designed to blow up American ships. Yesterday, he told me that he would destroy the submarine to keep it from being used as a weapon." She adjusted herself to look at her husband. "I think we can use it to get Eun-mi and his family out of the country. He has been very frustrated lately. Everything he has been working on is being solved much faster and easier with computers."

"Eun-mi will defect? What about Ching-ying? The authorities would arrest him."

"Numbers would go with Eun-mi."

"You're risking all of our lives. Tell me about your plan."

"Here is what I have been thinking. If the submarine can get Eun-mi and his family to an American ship, he can request asylum. He must escape without suspicion. How to do that is something I have not figured out." She rolled onto her back, staring at the ceiling. "I keep thinking the risk is worth the benefit. Convince me the risk is too great or show me how it can work with less risk."

They spent the rest of the night discussing her plan.

***

Sun-hee looked again at the food she had prepared for her family, trying to think of anything they might need. She added a few more hard candies to the bags, containing rice cakes and dried fruit.

Is this the third or fourth time I have added candies to these bags? Maybe I should take them out? No, leave them. They only need enough for twelve hours and have no room to relieve themselves. Two equal bags, one for each crate, and a few diapers for the children. Jugs of water should already be in the crates.

Waiting patiently for the events to unfold had made her a nervous wreck. She had lost weight and grown bags under her eyes from lack of sleep.

Did I hear a car? She looked at the clock — *three minutes since I looked last time. I did hear a car door closing.* She stood still, straining to listen.

Definitely a car door. She grabbed the bags and walked to the warehouse.

She rushed past the completed tables, desks, and other wooden furnishings her husband was so good at making. The new piles of rough lumber and shipping crates cluttering the workshop frustrated her as she made her way to the loading area.

"*Jeungjo halmeoni,*" said her great-grandson who ran up to her. She set the bags down and lifted him and kissed him on the cheek. He smiled and gave her a slobbery kiss.

Eun-mi's oldest son, now eighteen and a hand taller than his father, came over with his wife and said their goodbyes. She gave her great-grandson one last hug and handed him to his mother while giving her a firm embrace.

"Take care of my great-grandson," she said and wiped her eyes with a silk hanky as she watched them climb into the back of a truck.

She stepped over to Eun-mi's other son and his wife. Both had just turned seventeen. She took their hands and wished them well. She hugged and kissed their infant daughter before her father handed her into the truck. She watched as each family climbed into large wooden crates.

Numbers came over and took Sun-hee's hands. "Sun-hee. I wish we had more time to talk and say a proper goodbye. It must be difficult for you to have them leave."

"I let my son go to be taken care of by you a long time ago. You have done well raising him. I am very proud of the result. Thank you for going with them to America."

"I will be in touch. Watch the communications on the frequency I provided. Just remember, it may take me a while before I can send word."

"You have done so many great things, Numbers. Don't worry about us. Go live life as you want. Have a safe journey." She released his hands and blotted her eyes.

"Just one question before I leave. Was it you who gave me the nickname, Numbers?" asked Ching-ying.

"Young-ja was the assigner of nicknames to the boys," said Sun-hee with a grin.

Eun-mi came over and took hold of her hands while Ching-ying climbed into the truck. His wife, the daughter of Waves and Choe-me, came over to stand next to him. She had inherited her mothers' perfect facial form and smooth skin. Her radiant smile and gracefulness had not diminished with the passing of years and raising four children. Sun-hee tried to speak, but the words would not come. She grasped Eun-mi's hands tightly, tears flowing down her cheeks, and then reached for his wife's hands and squeezed them.

"We will be fine, Mother. Everything will go as planned. We have calculated everything over and over. I will find a way to help you." Eun-mi clasped her hands tighter and shook them lightly.

Their hands slipped slowly apart. She watched through blurry eyes as Eun-mi took his wife's hand, climbed into the truck, and vanished inside a crate.

Hon-yong positioned the lids on the crates and nailed them shut. He jumped down, tied the canvas down, and gave Sun-hee a quick kiss on the cheek. "I'll be back before sunrise. Don't worry." He climbed in the driver seat, and a minute later, the truck vanished into the twilight.

Sun-hee marched directly over to the car Eun-mi and his family had arrived in and got into the passenger seat. She did not need to participate in this part of the plan, but she could not sit at home.

Jin-taek sat down in the drivers' seat. She read his stare and returned with a positive look, saying, "Yes, I am going with you."

He smiled at her and nodded as he always did when he agreed. He started the car and drove away.

The headlights gave just enough light to glimpse the sides of the mountains along the winding road. It seemed like they drove forever before they saw a small truck parked at a wide spot. They stopped behind it. Jin-taek left the lights on.

Kwang-ku got out of the truck and opened the back. Human bodies illuminated by the headlights lay in a heap. She gagged and got out, walking back along the rushing river.

They told me to stay home. Maybe I should have. Kwang-ku said he could get research cadavers. Nameless people are taking the place of my family.

In her mind, she saw the gravestones of Eun-mi, Numbers, and their family with faceless people in their graves.

She could not look at what they were doing. She stared up at the stars as Jin-taek and Kwang-ku moved the bodies, positioning them into the car.

"The car is ready," said Kwong-ku as he climbed into the truck. Sun-hee turned to look at her son's car, now filled with nine dead people, two of them infants. Jin-taek soaked their coats in gasoline and then poured methanol inside. He looked up at her. She shook her head in approval. Kwong-ku had turned the truck around and was driving back towards them.

Jin-taek reached in the driver's window and placed the car in neutral. He kicked a rock out from under the front tire and pushed. The car started to roll down the road towards a turn. Jin-taek pulled out a flare gun, firing it into the open window. The inside burst into flames as the car gathered speed. It went off the cliff at the turn, tumbling over and over onto rocks about thirty meters below.

Sun-hee stared at the burning car, lighting up the narrow valley and river. She felt a hand on her shoulder and looked to see Jin-taek. He moved his head, signaling they should go. She walked to the truck, got in, and scooted to the middle of the seat. Soon they were driving back through the mountains on this moonless night. Sun-hee sat, contemplating all the possible things which could go wrong.

When they arrived at the woodshop, Kwang-ku squeezed her hand as she started to get out. "Let me know when you hear something."

"I will," said Sun-hee. Then she made her way to the cave. She turned on the radio, listening to the communications of the North Korean police and the American Navy.

***

Cha Eun-mi stroked his wife's hair and felt her body relax against his. He played hand games with his grandson in the dark. He gave the child candy when he got too fidgety. They faced a three-hour drive huddled in crates.

The truck stopped. Sounds revealed Hon-yong had manned a forklift. He felt the crate lifted. As they were sat down on the dock, the forklift rocked them violently. He urged his family to be quiet while helping everyone readjust their positions. Then there was silence.

Time crawled. Eun-mi's son and daughter-in-law played with their son. His wife rested her head on his shoulder. Her heartbeat throbbed against his chest. His foot was asleep, his bladder screamed for attention. Footsteps came from a distance and got louder. Something hit the top of the crate. Nails squeaked as they were pried out. The lid lifted a little, and he saw Wa-dae peek in and say, "How is everyone?"

"Get us out of here, Father!" said Eun-mi's wife while lifting her grandson towards Wa-dae. "I was beginning to wonder if you were going to make it."

Wa-dae reached out and lifted his great-grandson. "How is my little tiger?" he said, placing the boy on the dock who ran to the edge to pee in the water.

Eun-mi pushed his wife up, helping her stand. His step-daughter was assisted out of the crate by Wa-dae, who then assisted his wife.

"I was waiting for the perfect time. I hope your trip was good so far?" said Wa-dae.

"Too much time in this crate," Eun-mi's wife said as he heard her walk away with his daughter-in-law.

Eun-mi helped his son pry open the other crate and lift the rest of his family out onto the dock. He walked quickly to the end of the dock, working out the cramps, getting blood back into his legs, and found a place to relieve his bladder.

They were in a covered dock, perpendicular to the sea with lots of machinery, shipbuilding parts scattered everywhere. The door was down, almost to the water's edge, separating the dock from the bay. Small waves rippled under the door and dissipated as they moved into the dock.

Eun-mi jumped at a loud bang and turned. It was Wa-dae nailing the crates shut. He felt his heart thumping in his chest. He walked back to meet Wa-dae, who stood above his creation floating in the water.

Wa-dae designed the submarine in the shape of a humpback whale, about sixteen meters in length. It had a finlike propulsion system designed to mimic a whale's movement. A second mini-submarine, the size of a whale calf, floated behind the larger one. Three men were required to operate the large submarine while one person could run the calf.

Wa-dae's trial runs demonstrated the incredible design. The submarines had been able to swim together and join up with a pod of humpback whales near shore. Wa-dae loved the whales and had hoped to use his invention for research. His descriptions of swimming with the whale pod, becoming one with them in their environment, was a fantastic story. Wa-dae had built these to study life in the ocean. The military wanted a weapon. It's potential to sink ships made it a threat to initiate conflict. Today had to be the submarine's last voyage.

Two days ago, Wa-dae had sabotaged a component to make the submarine officially unavailable. It took him a couple of minutes to fix the problem.

Wa-dae had read reports of a pod of whales feeding offshore today. He would try to pass through them first. Then he would swim to the area where American navy ships routinely patrolled, just outside of Korean territory in the Sea of Japan.

Ching-ying walked up to greet Wa-dae. "Are you sure you are up to this?" Wa-dae said. "We could put you back into one of those crates. Hon-yong will pick you up in a few hours."

"There is nothing in Korea for me any longer," said Ching-ying. "Time to go on an adventure and see the world."

Wa-dae looked at his watch. "Eleven-thirty," he said. "I told the guards I would be working to find and fix the problem with the submarine. The evening watch will be getting ready to go home soon and will not be very attentive. Nothing happens on the docks at night."

Eun-mi looked over his family, thinking through their places in the submarine. The wives of his two sons got in first and crammed themselves into the back where they would hold the children. He handed Ching-ying the candies in his pocket and helped him climb in to curl up in front of the women and children. His sons took their places in the communication and navigator seats. He seized his wife's hand and held it for a moment before helping her into the submarine. She was Wa-dae's third child, first of his two daughters. She sat on her son's lap, unthinkable in Korean culture, but they would not be in

Korea for long.

Eun-mi walked over and got into the calf, settling himself into the pilot seat.

Wa-dae stuck his head in the hatch. "Remember, hit the side of the hull once for yes and twice for no. We will be able to hear you. You cannot transmit on the radio, but you will be able to hear what we transmit." Wa-dae closed the hatch and latched it shut.

Eun-mi put on the headphones connected to the craft's hydrophones. He felt the boat rock as the lines holding the calf were released. He looked out of the middle of the five port windows and watched Wa-dae release the ropes of the bigger submarine and climb in. A few moments later, the craft in front of him dipped silently under the water. He took hold of the controls, submerging the calf, and slipped under the door into the bay.

***

A light storm pelted the Sea of Japan with rain. The waves and rain helped to mask any sound they might make.

Wa-dae was confident that they could swim right up and bump an American destroyer before they knew he was not a whale. His only concern was transferring the passengers to the American ship in the choppy seas; the submarine was not designed to float on the surface.

Eun-mi found piloting the calf was as easy as riding a bike. The hydraulics moved the flippers, and the submarine slipped through the water. He only needed to follow the row of lights on the bottom of the other submarine. He kept close, finding the others in the dark would require communication, which might alert the Americans.

He tried to relax, focusing on staying a couple of meters to the side and back.

So free and easy, swimming in the ocean as a small whale. Amazingly quiet. Only the irregular hum of the windblown rain falling on the surface.

An hour, maybe two, passed. Eun-mi did not have a watch and probably could not have seen it in the darkness. He heard whale song, a faint melody coming in over the sound of the rain. Over the next hour, the intermittent whale songs grew louder and more distinct. He strained through the darkness, hoping to see a whale through the portals.

Suddenly the submarine in front of him dove downward. A whale stared at him directly ahead. He jerked on the levers, turning right and down, yet the whale bumped his little craft, pushing him over sideways. He lost balance in the seat and released the controls to put his hands out to catch himself on the side of the sub.

The submarine turned nose down in the water. Eun-mi fell forward, landing on his side against the portals. He panicked and grabbed at the levers, moving one or another without having control of all of them, which caused more random shifting. He had no bearing except the submarine going down.

I'm sinking!

"Eun-mi. Let go of all controls. The submarine will right itself in a moment." Wa-dae's voice said through his headphones. "Let the submarine balance itself." He looked through the portals, seeing only a luminescent jellyfish floating by his face.

He waited, balancing himself in his awkward position, rolling and moving as the submarine righted itself. He felt the submarine shift every few seconds.

Soon, he could get to the chair and sit. He tried to catch his breath and calm himself. He studied the portals, looking for the larger submarine.

Finally, he saw the lights above, coming slowly towards him.

"Eun-mi. Are you all right? Rap your knuckles on the hull once if you are well." He hit the side of the hull next to him with his left hand.

"Can you see us?" said Wa-dae. Eun-mi hit the hull once. "Hit once again when you are ready." Eun-mi adjusted himself and looked up at the other submarine. He struck his knuckles on the wall and sighed.

His nerves had almost returned to normal when he heard a faint ping. A minute later, another ping came through his headphones.

I must stay close. I must not lose contact.

The pings grew louder. Eun-mi counted each one. When he was at fifty-seven, he started to hear ship propellers. The propellers got louder and louder over the next eighteen pings, then they slowed and stopped.

He looked out of the left portal to see the bow of a ship approaching. He gave a quick flip of the controls to make the small submarine move ahead and felt the push of the ship's wake rock the boat.

Morse code rang in his ears: . SOS ASYLUM over and over. He listened for a moment before raising the calf to the surface.

"Time to get out," he said out loud.

The waves rolled up and down over the portals, rocking the calf back and forth. Eun-mi shut down the systems and, as instructed, flipped the arming device before opening the hatch. The rain and wind pelted him as he peered into the night.

Spotlights from the American ship focused on the submarine about thirty meters away. The hatch opened, and his wife rose out of the opening.

So beautiful is her pose in the light. I am such a lucky man.

An inflatable with three men aboard roared between him and the American ship, speeding towards his family.

His wife clambered to get on top. Eun-mi watched her struggled to keep her balance. His heart stopped as a wave rocked the submarine and she fell into the water.

He reached down and grabbed a life vest, hurrying to put it on. He was fumbling with the tie strings while men in diving suits jumped from the American ship.

Get her!

Another inflatable sped into the light from the other direction and stopped next to the submarine. His oldest son appeared in the hatch and dove into the water towards his wife. His other son appeared and handed out a child to the men in the boat, then another child.

The lights from the ship blinded him as he got the straps to his life vest tied. He jumped into the water and swam towards his wife.

Eun-mi was a good swimmer, or he thought he was. But he had never swum in the open ocean with waves carrying him up and down. The light from the ship was all he could see.

A wave caught him as he took a breath, and he inhaled some water. He coughed, floundered, and another wave caught him, rolling him over.

Someone grabbed him around the chest and turned him towards the sky. The man gave him a firm squeeze, and he coughed up seawater.

"Relax. I've got ya," said a deep, booming voice in English. The strength of the man allowed him to do nothing else but breath and feel the rain against his face.

A wave crashed over him, and he struggled to turn, pushing the American's arm away. Immediately, he was below water, disoriented, being pushed and grabbed by the American diver. He felt a strong arm grab him again around the chest. Water gave way to air. He heard a commanding voice accompanying a mighty squeeze.

"Hold still!"

Eun-mi relaxed and let the American pull him through the water.

Two hands grabbed his life vest. He met the eyes of an American sailor who, in one smooth move, lifted him into an inflatable boat and dumped him on the bottom. He turned his head and saw his wife lying at his side looking at him.

She smiled and said, "You are here."

"What about the others?" said Eun-mi as he got to his knees. He saw one son sitting in the front of the inflatable. Ching-ying lay at his son's feet.

He looked over to the submarine. Wa-dae was partly out of the hatch. The inflatable next to it had two women holding children, and his son, amongst three Americans. Eun-mi breathed a sigh of relief.

A diver was trying to hand a rope to Wa-dae who pushed it aside. Another American diver was tying a line to the submarine. Wa-dae waved him off. Yelling in English, "Move away. Move away!"

Another diver attached a rope to the submarine behind Wa-dae. He pulled a knife and cut it, then motioned for them to move back. Wa-dae looked up at the American ship. He saluted, then reached down with his other hand.

A loud explosion caught all their attention. Parts of the calf were falling into the water.

Wa-dae waved his arms at the Americans, yelling, "Move Away!"

The Inflatables backed off from the submarine. A small explosion ripped the back off the whale submarine.

"Father, NO!" yelled Eun-mi's wife next to him as he watched the submarine slip into the water. Wa-dae slumped over in the hatch.

His wife moved to jump into the water. Eun-mi grabbed her at the same time as one of the American sailors.

"No, no!" she said, slumping to the bottom of the boat. Eun-mi fell on top of her in a comforting grasp. The shock of a more massive explosion came from under the water.

Moments passed, then he heard his wife mutter, "No, my father did not have to die. He could have lived with us."

Eun-mi felt her sobs under his body.

A hand touched Eun-mi's shoulder. "Sir, time to get out of the boat. Please, let me help you," came a voice in English.

He got to his knees. "Come, dear, we need to get into the American ship." He lifted his wife with the help of his son. Then with the assistance of American sailors, they got her onto a platform on the side of the ship.

American sailors took hold of him, pulling him out of the inflatable, and his son followed. Hands rubbed down his body. His sons were searched. He started to grab his wife when, to his relief, a female sailor stepped forward and gently patted down her clothing.

He accepted a blanket and wrapped his wife, then he held her as they made their way into a hatch and down a long gray corridor. He felt his wife shaking. He did not know if she was sobbing or shivering.

Sailors escorted them to a room which looked like a clinic. Eun-mi quickly counted: nine members of his family were there. Waves had gone down in his whale.

Why didn't he tell me he was going to go down with the submarines? He did not have to die.

They completed the second part of their journey. Eun-mi and his father had not been able to calculate what would happen once they were aboard an American ship.

An American doctor was telling everyone in English to get out of his or her wet clothes.

Eun-mi took charge and directed his wife and his son's wives to go by the beds in the corner with the children. He took up some of the clothes and towels and handed them to his wife, saying, "Change into these dry clothes." When they were all in the corner, a man pulled a curtain around them.

His sons accepted clothes and towels and moved to another corner. Eun-mi took two more sets and stood by a third bed as they were curtained off.

"We made it, Father. We will get to America," he said in Korean as he began to take off his wet clothes.

"At the loss of a good friend," said Ching-ying in a whisper. "He told me he would not be joining us. The submarine was too valuable. The Americans either would question him until he told them how the submarine worked, or he died. Going down with his creation was the only way. We will remember him as a Korean hero."

"Yes, Father," said Eun-mi. He finished changing in silence, putting on the loose white pants and shirt before pulling back the curtain. He looked up to see a man in a white uniform with graying hair staring at him.

"I'm Captain Atwood," said the man with authority.

Ching-ying quickly spoke in English. "I am Numbers," pointing to his chest. "This is my son." He gestured to Eun-mi. "My grandsons are behind the curtain. Their wives and my grandchildren are in the corner."

One of Eun-mi's sons pulled back their curtain. He thought they looked funny standing in white gowns. The curtains pulled back in the corner, revealing the women and children. The white garments hung loosely on the women. Their hair was wet and straight. His wife had wrapped a towel around her head, giving Eun-mi a contrasting image to her natural black hair framing her gorgeous face. The children were wrapped in blankets and held by their mothers.

"I want to talk to her," said the captain, pointing to Eun-mi's wife. She was still shaking. Her eyes were red, and she held her arms crossed in front of her.

"Captain Atwood," said Eun-mi in near-perfect English. "It is not polite for a Korean woman to talk directly to a man who is not her husband. May I answer for my family?"

The captain glared at him with piercing hazel eyes under bushy eyebrows. "Why would you speak and not your father?"

"We speak with the same mind," said Eun-mi. "Please pardon me, Captain Atwood. I should introduce myself. My name is Cha Eun-mi."

"Let me get your name again," said the captain. "It sounded like 'The enemy'"

Eun-mi smiled slightly at the confusion, "In English, my surname is Cha. 'c' 'h' 'a.' My given name is Eun-mi. 'e' 'u' 'n' hyphen 'm' 'i.' In western format, it is 'Eun-mi Cha.'"

"May I call you Mister Cha?"

"Yes, Mister Cha is acceptable, Captain Atwood."

"Who was the man who blew himself up in the submarine?"

"He was my father-in-law. Will you offer us asylum in the United States?"

"Asylum is not mine to offer," said Capt. Atwood with a flipping gesture of his right hand. "Tell me about the submarine you came in. How did it move? How did it avoid detection?"

"Respectfully, sir, may I request to answer further questions in private?" Eun-mi said with a slight bow. "Also, may my family be given food and a place to rest?"

Captain Atwood paused a moment, stroked his chin, then furrowed his eyebrows at Eun-mi. "Lieutenant, take these people to the galley. Make up the guest quarters to fit a family of nine. Set a course for Sasebo. When we get a response to my message, bring it to my ready room."

"Yes, sir," came the reply from a sailor moving for the door.

"Mr. Cha, follow me," said Capt. Atwood as he marched out of the infirmary.

Eun-mi hurried to follow along the narrow passageway, climbing up a flight of steep stairs and then another passage. He looked around.

Two sailors were following him. The captain reached a door. A sailor opened it. They stepped into a small room containing a table with four chairs on each side.

Capt. Atwood motioned to the chairs. "Please have a seat. Can I get you something to eat or drink?"

"Hot tea would be very appreciated," said Eun-mi while pulling out the first chair.

"Bring me coffee and some tea for our guest. And bring breakfast," Capt. Atwood said to one of the sailors who hastened out of the room. The other stood at attention by the door.

As the soldier left, a man with Korean features wearing a tan uniform burst into the room. He said in poor English, "I heard we have *talbugja,* Captain."

We are already defined as defectors. Thought Eun-mi.

Capt. Atwood turned and said, "Captain Sin, I would like you to meet Mister Cha. He arrived with his family tonight. Mister Cha, this is Captain Sin of the Korean Navy. He works with us to coordinate with the South Korean government." He pulled a chair around to the end of the table.

Capt. Sin sat in a chair opposite Eun-mi. Eun-mi bowed politely towards the South Korean captain.

Capt. Atwood folded his hands on the table and stared directly at Cha Eun-mi. "Now, Mr. Cha, tell me why you are here?"

"I am here to ask for asylum in the United States of America."

"Why are you here to request asylum?" said Capt. Atwood.

"We receive *talbugja* from North Korea," interrupted Capt. Sin with a smile on his face. "You move the family to the South. We help you start a new life."

Eun-mi bowed slightly towards Capt. Sin. "I am grateful for your offer to settle in South Korea, Captain Sin. However, I must request immigration to the United States."

"Today, everything in the United States is found in South Korea," said Capt. Sin.

"We are not looking for things, Captain Sin. What we can offer would be more suited to the United States," said Eun-mi.

"What can you offer the United States?" said Capt. Sin with a slight chuckle as he sat back in his chair.

"With all due respect, the answer to your question must be for me to discuss with a person who has the authority to offer my family and I asylum."

"I have authority, Mister Cha," said Capt. Sin with an attitude of importance. "I suggest you start talking! Or you will go back home as a *talbugja*. You know what happens to *talbugjas* in the North. Don't you, Mister Cha?" He finished with a wicked-looking grin on his face, turning Eun-mi's stomach.

The plan was to go directly to the Americans and avoid the South Koreans. Capt. Sin is messing things up.

Eun-mi bowed slightly to show respect. "My family and I are of no value to South Korea. I must request that there is no mention of our defection on any transmission within South Korea," said Eun-mi.

Capt. Sin sat forward in his chair and said in a menacing tone, "What are you running from, Mister Cha? What you afraid of?"

Eun-mi smiled. "I am not afraid, Captain Sin. We are not running from North Korea. We are running to America."

"You are hiding something. You stink of secrets," said Capt. Sin, standing up and leaning forward on his fists.

Eun-mi paused for a moment and took a deep breath. He looked directly at the American. "Captain Atwood, may we speak alone?" said Eun-mi calmly while wringing his hands under the table.

"I would like you to answer Captain Sin's questions," said Cap. Atwood.

Eun-mi bowed towards the American captain. "Please forgive my reluctance, Captain Atwood. The North monitors all communications in South Korea. I will not discuss anything of substance in the presence of a South Korean, or with the knowledge that what I say will be given to South Korea."

"I take him to the interrogation center. I will get answers," said Capt. Sin.

The door opened, and a sailor brought in pots of coffee and tea. Capt. Atwood sat back in his chair, looking at Eun-mi while rubbing his chin. Capt. Sin remained standing with his fists on the table, glaring at Eun-mi. The three men remained still, staring at one another as the sailor poured coffee and tea.

Capt. Atwood broke the silence. "Captain Sin, let me speak for a few moments with Mr. Cha. Let me hear what he has to say."

Capt. Sin stood up straight and pointed at Eun-mi. "This man up to no good. I sense it. He is like all North Koreans. He is trouble!" Capt. Sin strode toward the door. Then he stopped and turned. "How did he get out here in the Sea of Japan?"

"Thank you, Captain Sin. I will give you a copy of my report," said

Capt. Atwood while keeping his eyes focused on Eun-mi. The sailor held the door open until Capt. Sin exited.

"Now, Mister Cha, you have until breakfast arrives to convince me to not hand you and your family to Captain Sin, which is my normal operating procedure."

"Thank you, Captain Atwood. What I can tell you is my father, my sons, and I are all mathematicians. We wish to be in a place where we can study math freely and contribute positively to the world."

"We have mathematicians in the United States. What makes you so special?"

"We may not be special in the United States. We were the best mathematicians in North Korea. Some of the projects we were working on would give our government the belief they could fight America equally. For example, the submarine in which we arrived. With us gone, there is less chance of war. We only want to work freely on new, peaceful projects in the United States."

"Where did you learn English?"

"My Grandmother and mother are fluent in English. American missionaries taught my grandmother. Understanding languages was her gift. I have also watched many American movies and television shows."

"Tell me, how did the submarine work?" said Capt. Atwood.

"It is designed to mimic a humpback whale. The man who designed and built it went down to the ocean bottom. He loved the ocean and used the submarine to study whales. The government viewed the submarine as a weapon which could change the balance of power. The designer and I considered it too dangerous. If the calf that I came in was full of explosives, I could have moved it next to this ship and blown it up."

"Yes," repeated Captain Atwood stroking his chin. "A whale submarine and the calf have the potential to damage a lot of ships. How many of them are there?"

"We arrived in the only ones. The prototypes. There are no more."

A sailor walked in and handed some papers to the captain and left. He glanced at them, folded them in half, and laid them on the table.

"How did you fool our sonar?"

"The submarines are the size and shape of a whale. The shell was designed to mimic the sonar reflection of a humpback whale."

"The outer shell was not made of metal. What was it made of?"

"I am sorry, Captain Atwood, the person with the answer to your question went down to the bottom of the sea."

"What was his name?"

"I am sorry, sir. I will not give you his name. If his name was ever known, or it was known he helped us get out of Korea, the rest of his family would be tortured and killed. I hope you understand."

Captain Atwood grabbed the papers, flipped to the second page, and held it so Eun-mi could see. He pointed at the paper as he spoke sternly. "On the top is the sonar reflection of a humpback whale. On the bottom is your submarine. The reflection is identical. You need to assure me there are no more of these, or the American Navy will be killing a lot of whales."

"We do not want war with America. My mother and father survived the last one. We are doing this to prevent death and destruction," Eun-mi said, trying to keep himself calm.

Captain Atwood picked up his coffee cup, sipped, and sat back in his chair.

"So, you brought out your family. What happens when they notice you are missing?"

Eun-mi looked at his teacup as he spoke. "We told our friends we were going on a picnic. Our automobile should be found today at the bottom of a cliff. There will be nine bodies burned beyond recognition in the automobile. Those people were medical cadavers, already dead."

Captain Atwood shook his head. "You thought of everything."

"As I mentioned, we are mathematicians. We considered all the variables we could control."

"What variables can you not control?"

"I have no control over what happened from the moment we arrived next to your ship." Eun-mi noticed Captain had a little smile on his face after his answer.

"Tell me, Mr. Cha, how advanced is your mathematics?"

"My family is as advanced as anyone without computers. What makes America more advanced is the use of computers to do calculations. There are many problems I would like to work on when I have access to them."

"How do you know you are as advanced as the rest of the world?"

"We have worked closely with mathematicians from the Soviet Union."

"Do the Soviets know about the submarine?"

Eun-mi thought for a moment before responding. "Not to my knowledge, sir."

"How thorough is your knowledge?" Capt. Atwood said. He sat

forward, placing his arms on the table while still holding his coffee cup.

Cha Eun-mi took a sip of his tea. "I see the logic in your questioning, sir. If my response reveals my knowledge is not extensive, then you will doubt I am knowledgeable enough to have value to the United States. If I say I am certain the Soviets do not know about the submarine, then you will suspect I am withholding information about the submarine from you. Either way, I leave myself as less credible. May I respectfully refuse to answer your question directly?"

The door opened, and two sailors brought in trays with breakfast. Eun-mi watched as they set down a bowl of scrambled eggs, a bowl of hash browns, a plate with toast, a platter with fried bacon, and a dish of pastries.

Eun-mi watched Capt. Atwood's face, knowing his time to make a convincing argument for asylum was up. A table setting was placed before each man. He sipped his tea, then held his cup with both hands while dishes were arranged. His fate and the fate of his family lay on what he said to the American captain. He pressed his lips together, swallowed, and ground his teeth.

Capt. Atwood reached over to spoon eggs onto his plate, casually taking the tongs and selected strips of bacon and a piece of toast. He then spooned some of the roasted potatoes onto his plate, like nothing was urgent. He shook salt and pepper onto his eggs and placed a spoonful of strawberry jelly on his toast. Eun-mi watched all this and started to shake.

The American picked up the toast and knife then began to spread the jelly. "We will need to verify your claim to be mathematicians," he said before he took a bite of toast and chewed. Eun-mi watched him swallow. "I wish I knew more about your submarine. The sonar signature was so identical to a humpback whale and calf, Japanese fishing boats were moving our way at full speed." He watched the captain take a big scoop of eggs on his fork then stabbed a potato. "I am glad the calf you were in was not next to my boat when it exploded." He stuffed his fork in his mouth, then spoke with his mouth full. "For now, I think we should keep you away from Capt. Sin." He gestured to the table. "Please, have some breakfast and tell me about your children and grandchildren."

Eun-mi bowed, his head almost touching his plate. "I am most grateful, Captain." He took a spoonful of eggs and placed them on his plate, selecting a piece of toast. "My two sons are nineteen and seventeen years old. They were married when they were fifteen." He took one small bite of his eggs.

"Very young to be married. At least by our standards," said Capt. Atwood as he continued to shovel food into his mouth at many times Eun-mi's pace.

"Yes, sir. My grandchildren were born within a year after marriage. I am very blessed."

A sailor came in and handed the captain a piece of paper folded in half. He opened it and read. Eun-mi held his toast in his hand, waiting for some response.

"Please excuse me, Mister Cha," said Capt. Atwood as he stood and walked towards the door. "Enjoy your breakfast." The sailor closed the door then stood at attention in front of it.

Cha Eun-mi ate his eggs and toast.

What happens next? He said we would not be given to the South Koreans. What is happening? His mind raced through all the possible scenarios.

He sat quietly for a minute after finishing his meal. He patted his lips with his napkin and turned to look at the sailor by the door. "May I be taken to my family?"

"Yes, sir." The sailor opened and held the door.

Why was I left waiting?

Two armed men escorted him to a room. There were two more sailors standing at attention outside the door. He was ushered in.

***

Sun-hee heard her husband enter the bedroom.

He is home. Everything is well.

The light of the new day coming in through the garden window allowed her to watch him change into his nightshirt. She let him pull back the covers, attempting to be quiet.

"I am glad you are home," Sun-hee said.

"I was hoping you were finally getting some sleep."

"I could not sleep until you are safe beside me."

"What did you hear?" said Hon-yong as he rolled over to look at his wife.

Sun-hee looked to her husband. "No news from the police. An American destroyer communicated they had nine refugees in good health."

Hon-yong sat up on his elbow. "Nine? Ten boarded the submarines."

Sun-hee reached out her hand to her husband, touching him lightly on the shoulder, "Wa-dae told me he would not allow the Americans to get his submarines or his knowledge. The communication mentioned the transport vessel sank with one casualty. The rest are on their way to the American Naval base at Sasebo. It will take most of the day to get there."

Hon-yong lay back down and pulled the blanket over himself and Sun-hee. He drew her close. They held each other for a few moments before Hon-yong choked out, "He was a good man. I will miss him."

Sun-hee leaned over and kissed her husband's cheek. She felt the wetness of his tears. "He made an amazing submarine," she said. "Things are not right when a person has to destroy his creation out of fear of how it will be used."

She put her head on his shoulder and cuddled close. "Eun-mi will be safe and happy in the United States. He has hope for the future of his family. I do not know how to restore hope for us."

Hon-yong squeezed her tightly. "We have each other, which is enough for me."

56 — Prisoners - Spring, 1988

Sun-hee sat up quickly.

I'm in bed. What day…what time is it? The garden is already in shadow.

"Oh, my!" She was alone and dressed as fast as she could. Then she went to look for Hon-yong, finding him in the furniture shop as usual.

"Hon, any word?" she blurted out.

"No visitors. You know, we may not hear about the automobile accident directly. We have no connection to the car. It may take days before the government lists your family as dead. I hope the government never makes a connection. Kwang-ku told me he would keep an eye out for any report on the accident. Have you been listening?"

"No. I just got up. I wish you had woken me up by lunch. The destroyer may be to Sasebo by now. I am going to the cave." She hurried into the mine.

"I'll bring up dinner later," Hon-yong yelled as she left his sight.

When she got to the cave, she began to listen to the recordings of the American Navy communications. There was only one message which mattered: a destroyer would be arriving in Sasebo within the hour.

***

Eun-mi couldn't sleep. His family lay before him, sleeping lightly or not at all. It was hard to tell in the dark. The guest quarters were small, designed for one person. The bed and floor were not big enough for them to all lay flat. The men were leaning against the walls, hoping others could sleep. As soon as one of the children moved, a hand reached to still the child. He sensed how nervous they were, even though he assured them his conversation with the American captain had gone well.

Taking a seat in a corner by the door, Eun-mi wrapped his arms around his knees and considered the questions they would ask him. He had to avoid ending up in the hands of the South Koreans. His thoughts kept him awake while the others, exhausted from the trip, slept into the afternoon.

The door opened into the room, hitting his legs and shining light from the passageway on his family. His grandson, startled awake by the intrusion, cried out.

"So, these are the defectors from North Korea," said Capt. Sin in Korean.

Eun-mi pressed himself to a standing position. The door swung wider, trapping him. He gently tried to push the door to meet Capt. Sin, but it was held open.

His sons and father all seemed to speak at once but were drowned out by the wails of the startled children and the complaints of their mothers.

"Quiet!" Eun-mi yelled from behind the door. His family slowly became silent. "Captain Sin, if you would be so kind as to let me out from behind the door, I will be glad to continue our conversation."

He felt the pressure on the door lessen, and he pushed lightly. He had enough room to step over his wife and get around the door. He took a deep breath, reminding himself to be polite. He bowed deeply and said, "It is good to see you again, Captain Sin. Is there a place we can talk while my family gets some rest?"

"This is your family?" said Capt. Sin. "Please, introduce them."

"I will be very pleased to make proper introductions after they have rested and have a chance to make themselves presentable," said Eun-mi. He gestured in a sweeping motion with his right hand. "These sleeping quarters are very ah…limited, and not a suitable place for conversation." He tried to avoid showing his offense at the invasion.

"This is an outrage!" said one of his sons in Korean. "How dare you enter our sleeping quarters like this."

Eun-mi held his open hand behind him, signaling he wanted them to remain silent while holding out his left hand towards the passageway. "Might we find a more suitable place to talk, honorable captain?"

Capt. Sin moved his head to look around Eun-mi at the young man who had spoken. "Some men have no respect for authority," he said. His eyebrows squinted together, creating rows of flesh between them. He licked his lips. "Come, Mr. Cha."

Eun-mi stepped out into the corridor, pulling the door shut behind him.

Capt. Sin turned and walked down the passageway at a brisk pace.

Eun-mi followed. The metal floor felt cold on his bare feet. He walked at a leisurely pace, letting Cap. Sin distance himself. He wanted time to think where the conversation would lead. After a couple of turns and down a flight of stairs, he caught up to the captain by an open door. A hand was held out, directing him into the room.

He stepped in and heard a voice behind him say, "Captain Sin. Mr. Cha. I was on my way to lunch. Would you both like to join me?"

Eun-mi stepped halfway out the door to address Capt. Atwood. "My appetite has returned, Captain Atwood. I would be most honored to join you for lunch." Capt. Sin glared at Capt. Atwood.

"The galley has a fine assortment of food available this time of day. We will not have to wait at this time of the afternoon." He faced Capt. Sin. "I am almost done with my report, Captain Sin. You will have it before dinnertime." Capt. Atwood walked on down the corridor. Eun-mi stepped between two armed sailors and hurried to follow, leaving Capt. Sin to bring up the rear.

Sin is frustrated. What angers him so much? I must work out a way to allow him to save face while gaining asylum in America.

Capt. Atwood led the way down the buffet line. "Point to what you want. Eat as much as you like. One thing we have plenty of on this ship is food."

Eun-mi pointed to rice, steamed vegetables, baked fish, and fruit. He noticed the sailors in the room were watching him. He tried to listen to their conversations, but there were too many conflicting noises. Capt. Atwood ushered the way to the only table with a cloth covering. A sailor came over and handed chopsticks to Capt. Sin and offered him a set.

"Thank you," he said in English.

Capt. Atwood said, "I apologize for the cramped sleeping quarters, Mr. Cha. The guest room is for a single person. When we reach port, your family will have more suitable accommodations."

"Thank you, Captain," replied Eun-mi.

Sitting forward in his chair, Capt. Sin said, "I demand you place Mister Cha and his family in my custody."

"Your request is noted, Captain Sin. Mister Cha has some questions to answer to the U.S. Navy before I let him go. I need to know a lot more."

"There are two other items regarding my father I did not mention last night, Captain Atwood," said Eun-mi. "He has cancer and hopes treatment in America might prolong his life. Also, he would like to renew a friendship he made with an American prisoner during the Korean War."

There's the bait which will allow Capt. Sin to save face. Will they accept it?

"How far along is your father's cancer?" asked Capt. Atwood.

"Doctors in Pyongyang said they have no further treatment for him.

Men with his type of cancer have an average of a year to live."

Capt. Atwood held his fork, glaring directly at Eun-mi.

Does he see the game I am playing? Will he accept it or call me out?

"I am sorry your father is ill. I will have the doctors at the base examine him this afternoon. Did you know the American Pilot?" said Capt. Atwood.

"No, sir. I was born after Captain Reed returned to America."

"His name was Captain Reed?"

"Theodore Reed, a captain in the U.S. Air Force. His serial number is 493 72 82. My father used it as a passcode."

Capt. Atwood wrote on a paper napkin, *Reed 493 72 82*. "I will need to verify this Mr. Cha. If Reed vouches for your father, we may be able to get him to America."

"This is unacceptable. All North Koreans are to be settled in South Korea," said Capt. Sin.

Cap. Atwood put down his fork, cleared his throat, and said, "If Mr. Cha's father befriended and aided an American prisoner of war, then I believe we must grant him his request to visit America. If his claim proves to be false, I will deliver Mister Cha and his family to South Korea personally. Would this be acceptable to you, Captain Sin?"

Capt. Sin put down his chopsticks, pushed his plate towards the middle of the table, and stood. "I look forward to the day when Mr. Cha and his family arrive in South Korea." He threw his napkin on his chair and left.

Capt. Atwood took a couple of bites, seeming to ignore everything else. He sipped his coffee and said, "You are putting me in a difficult situation, Mister Cha. I have no reason to disbelieve you. However, if anything you have told me is a lie, I will consider everything you have said to be a lie."

Eun-mi had been placing only tiny bites of food in his mouth, not wanting to be caught with a mouthful when something needed to be said. "I understand, Captain Atwood. I deeply appreciate your trust. My hope is you understand, should my family and I end up in South Korea, there is high probability blood will be shed. I seek only a peaceful existence. My comments over this meal have been made to allow Captain Sin to save face with his superiors."

Capt. Atwood leaned forward, adjusting his fork, holding it in a closed fist and pointing it at Eun-mi. "This is what worries me the most, Mister Cha. You can calculate ahead of me and tell me only what will gain you favor towards the decision you want." Then he scooped up a fork full of mashed potatoes and shoved them in his mouth.

"You are correct, Captain Atwood. Considering your suspicion, please allow me to correct one item of information. It was my mother and grandmother who spoke English and were interpreters for Captain Reed. Korean tradition does not allow a woman to speak to a man who is not her husband. Captain Sin would not have believed my mother befriended an American Pilot. My father knows who Captain Reed is, but Captain Reed will not know my father. He will know my mother and grandmother."

"Where are your mother and grandmother? Why did they not come with you?"

"It has been twenty years since my grandmother passed away. My mother chose to remain. When you communicate with Captain Reed, please let him know, the son of Cha Sun-hee wishes to meet with him."

"The one thing I do not doubt, Mr. Cha, is your intelligence. You have all the answers. I will deliver you to the American base at Sasebo and let them get to the bottom of who you are. My main concern is how you were able to sneak up on this destroyer. I worry that there are more submarines like the one you arrived in. They will put my crew and ship in danger."

"If I were not here now, the future would hold more danger. You may rest assured, there are no more whale submarines in North Korea," Eun-mi said and took a large bite of the fried fish.

Capt. Atwood finished a bite and said, "From your perspective, Mr. Cha, what do the North Koreans have I should be afraid of?"

Eun-mi took a drink of water to collect his thoughts before saying, "From a technology standpoint, North Korea has or is working on technology equal to the Soviets. What is lacking is the funding and the ability to make many of the parts required for missiles, ships, and planes. The political situation is where we should worry. The leadership is only interested in maintaining their power. They will imprison or kill anyone who opposes them. When they arrive at a point where they believe there is an advantage, they will initiate conflict with the South."

"Why don't the Korean people revolt and overthrow their oppressive government?" said Capt. Atwood.

"Political revolution requires many people and much coordination. The North Korean people do not know who they can trust. One wrong word may result in death. My father and I have calculated all the possible scenarios for the future. All result in massive bloodshed. For the time being, maintaining Kim Il-Sung in a position of power is the best option. Also, North Koreans believe Kim Il-sung is the father of the country. An outside force removing the Premier will not change the views of the people. His death will only strengthen them. Kim Il-sung has done well to lead North Korea from ruin to a strong country today."

Capt. Atwood leaned forward again. "Did you consider overthrowing the government?"

His body language now gives him away as he leans forward to ask trapping questions.

Eun-mi could not suppress his smile. "My mother and I spoke of options for the future. We asked ourselves how we could make North Korea a better place for the people. Replacing the government is impossible. The only way would be for a new leader to change the country's path. Kim Il-sung's son, Kim Jong-il, will most likely take over leadership when his father steps down. I am afraid it will be a long time before a leader of North Korea changes the power structure. Thus, I am here, willing to risk everything to pursue a better life."

"But your mother was not willing to leave with you?"

Eun-mi looked at his plate for a moment before replying, "She wanted to stay with her husband, other children, and grandchildren. Everyone could not come. She saw a way for me to have a better life and insisted I take my family and leave."

"Your mother insisted you leave?" he said as his head lifted and his eyebrows rose. "Who thought up this plan?"

"This is my mother's plan. I think only a mother who wants the best for her family would devise such a risky plan."

Shaking his head in acknowledgment Capt. Atwood said, "What is next in your mother's plan?"

"Only one thing in her plan is left. She hopes Captain Reed is still alive and will remember her."

Capt. Atwood smiled as he stood. "We should be near Sasebo. Get your family ready to disembark." He motioned to a sailor by the door who rushed over. "See Mr. Cha back to the guest quarters." He walked out.

Armed sailors escorted Eun-mi back to the guestroom. The clothes they arrived in had been laundered and placed by the door. He picked them up and entered.

"Time to change and get ready to disembark."

"Are we in good standing with the American Captain?" asked Numbers.

"Captain Atwood is very intelligent. I have been able to appeal to him on this basis. We will not be taken to South Korea if the Americans do not catch us in a lie. Speak only the truth, no deception."

"How have you dealt with the rude South Korean captain?"

"He only needs to save face. We must allow him to look good," said Eun-mi.

He changed and stepped into the hall. His father and sons followed, leaving the room for the women to change. Sailors handcuffed the four men.

"Why the restraints?" asked a son in Mandarin.

"I don't know," replied Eun-mi in the same language.

Five minutes later, sailors escorted Eun-mi and his family at gunpoint off the American destroyer. Capt. Sin stepped in front of Eun-mi and scowled.

Eun-mi stopped and bowed to Capt. Sin saying, "It has been my pleasure to meet you, Captain Sin. I wish you well."

Capt. Atwood said from behind Capt. Sin, "Let's go, Mr. Cha. I do not have time for you to chat."

Eun-mi moved around Capt. Sin to see Capt. Atwood with his hand out. He took the hand and felt the squeeze. Capt. Atwood said, "The intelligence officers down there will not be as easy on you as I have. Goodbye, Mr. Cha."

"Thank you for your hospitality, Captain Atwood. Our discussion has encouraged me. Good people can maintain peace in this world if we work together. I am most grateful." Eun-mi added his last statement, hoping the captain would convey his message of peace to the Americans he now approached as he filed down the gangway.

A few minutes later, Eun-mi and his family stood in cells at the Sasebo naval base.

"You did not tell us we are prisoners," said his son.

"How the Americans treat asylum seekers is one of the unknown aspects of our journey," replied Eun-mi. "We have more questions to answer."

Soon, they came for Eun-mi. He was escorted alone to another building and into a room. A metal table with three metal chairs sat in the center of the bare, windowless walls. One of the fluorescent lights flickered constantly.

"Please sit," said a voice behind him. Eun-mi turned to see a tall man in a white uniform and white navy officer hat walk to the table. Another sailor entered with a phone, knelt to plug a wire into a socket, and then placed the phone on the table.

"We need to verify your story, Mr. Cha. A few questions will be asked to verify what you told Captain Atwood. In the meantime, here are a few questions we would like you to write out the answers to." The man nodded to a sailor by the door. The sailor placed a clipboard on the table with a pencil and stepped back.

"My name is Cha Eun-mi," he said with a slight bow. Getting no response, he looked at the clipboard. At the top of the page was, 'SOLVE THE EQUATION.' The equation on the paper was one he recognized as a simple calculus formula he taught at the University in Pyongyang. He looked up, expecting the American to introduce himself but got a hard stare.

He picked up the pencil and began to write the solution while staring back at the man before him. As soon as he finished, the American said, "Next page." He turned the page to see another familiar equation. He wrote out the solution. Then he turned the page.

He wondered how difficult this was going to be, so he read ahead. The mathematical questions were progressively more difficult. The next to last equation he knew had never been solved. He wrote, *There is no known solution.* The final page contained an equation he had never seen. He quickly filled out the solutions he knew and then proceeded to evaluate the last page.

"Time is up," said the man before him.

He reviewed his work on the last page for a moment before looking up and saying, "All of the problems, except for the last one, I cover in my advanced mathematics classes at the university. This last problem is one I am not familiar with and would require more time to examine it for a solution."

The American picked up the clipboard and handed it to the sailor by the door who then withdrew.

The phone rang. The man picked it up after the first ring. "Yes, sir. Right here, sir. Yes, sir."

"I am putting you on speakerphone, Mister Cha," said the man.

Eun-mi said towards the phone, "Hello. This is Cha Eun-mi."

"Hello. I'm Theodore Reed. I was told you wanted to speak to me."

"Yes. My family and I were able to leave North Korea yesterday. My mother, Cha Sun-hee, asked me to call you.

"Sunny? Your Sunny's son? How is your mother?" said Capt. Reed with an excited voice.

"My mother is very well."

"And Sunny's mother, Sue-dae. How is she?"

"She passed away from stomach cancer."

"I'm very sorry to hear that, Eun-mi."

"My mother spoke highly of you, Captain Reed. She said you are a man with honor. I am seeking asylum in American with my family."

"Are you truly Sunny's son? And will you and your family be a benefit to the United States? Those are the questions the authorities are asking."

"What may I say to convince you I am Sun-hee's son?" said Eun-mi.

"Did she eat what we left for her on the bus when we were released from North Korea?" asked Capt. Reed.

"As she told the story, she was very depressed about the condition of the country after the war. She said she swept all the chocolate bars onto the floor of the bus. Jin-taek collected the bars and gave them to my mother after returning to camp. She shared them with all the other women."

"Who was Jin-taek?"

"He was a sergeant who could not speak."

"I remember him. A little guy who I would not have wanted to meet in a fight."

"Yes, sir. He was a rugged soldier."

"Sunny was pregnant during the trip. Are you the child she was carrying?"

"No. I was her next child, born in 1955."

"Did your mother ever tell you what happened to the American Sargent, John Peterson?"

"She said he died for having a bad attitude. She said you called him a 'dirt hitting rectum.'"

Theodore laughed loudly over the phone. "In English, that would be a 'ground pounding asshole.' Who killed Sargent Peterson?"

"General Park."

"Is the General still alive?"

"No. Mother said he died of a heart attack. The rumors say Moon Choe-me stabbed him to death. He, too, died for having a bad attitude."

"Moon Choe-me? Was she the talkative one?"

"No, the talkative one is Seo Young-ja. Moon Choe-me is very beautiful. I married her daughter, who is just as pretty."

"I remember Moon Choe-me. I agree she is one of the prettiest girls I have ever seen. If your wife looks like her, you are a lucky man. I look forward to meeting you. Let me talk to Captain Johnson."

"It has been a pleasure talking to you, Captain Reed. I look forward to more conversations," concluded Eun-mi, and he sat back in his chair.

Capt. Johnson picked up the receiver and turned off the speaker.

"Johnson here…Yes. Good. OK."

Capt. Johnson hung up the phone and started asking questions. The questioning went on for hours. He tried to relax and answer each question openly and honestly.

The sun had set by the time guards escorted Eun-mi back to the cells. When he arrived, his family told him of their questioning. Numbers reviewed the mathematical questions posed to him and the inquiry about their family, and Sun-hee. Most of all, the Americans demanded to know about the whale submarines. His sons and wife shared their story of questioning.

Eun-mi asked them only one thing. "Did they tell the truth?"

Everyone replied, "Yes."

"Then we can sleep well, knowing we have done what we can. The rest is out of our control."

They spent an uncomfortable night in the cells. Everyone worried that they would not receive asylum. Eun-mi hoped that his conversation with Capt. Reed went well enough to convince the authorities.

The next afternoon, they were released from the cells and taken to Okinawa by plane. They spent two weeks in a two-bedroom house with round o'clock guards. There was no more questioning and no information. All they could do was wait and worry. Their nerves were on end.

Capt. Johnson arrived at the end of the two weeks. "Your story checks out, Mr. Cha," he said. "After some digging through intelligence reports, we found that you and your family were declared deceased in an automobile accident. There is some concern about your loss in Pyongyang. Get yourselves packed. You are going to Washington."

"We get to see the United States capital," exclaimed Eun-mi's son.

"Not that Washington. You are flying to the Naval Air Station on Whidbey Island in the state of Washington," said Capt. Johnson.

"Thank you, Capt. Johnson," said Eun-mi.

"Johnson is not my real name. It is a common name used when questioning prisoners. My name is not essential. I'll be back in half an hour to see you and your family on their way."

***

Once in the United States, they were offered asylum and ferried to Seattle. There, Eun-Mi and Ching-ying met Theodore Reed.

Theodore welcomed them to the United States, told them stories of his captivity, and how Sunny had saved his life multiple times. He showed them the aerial photos of Sun-hee and his garden with 9OK.

Eun-Mi had not heard most of the details of Theodore's capture, the escape attempt, and none of his mother's heroics at the border until now. He had a new appreciation of how wonderful his mother was.

He told Theodore about their escape from North Korea. Theodore was impressed with the submarines and how they were designed to look like whales.

Theodore expressed his respect for Sunny. He wished she had come with the family to America.

The families' relocation to Princeton, New Jersey occurred the next day. Numbers and Numbers Jr. began to teach in the mathematics department at Princeton University the fall semester.

***

Ching-ying went to work on radio frequencies and proved he was an expert. It took him almost a year before he had access to the communication equipment he needed to get a coded message to Sun-hee. "All safe in the US. No cure for my cancer, but I will live a little longer. Your family sends their love, as do I."

Before another month passed, lung cancer took Ching-ying's life. Cha Eun-mi and his sons taught math and studied computer science at Princeton. Three years later, they were all awarded Doctorate degrees in Mathematics. Eun-mi got his wish. He and his sons went to work for IBM at their research facility in Poughkeepsie, New York.

57 — A Wonderful Life - April, 1989

Spring arrived early in 1989. The tree blossoms, wildflowers, and perfect weather made Sun-hee feel like she was living in paradise. Every day after breakfast, she would go to the cave to listen to recordings of what was happening in the world.

On this morning, she received messages of the last of the marriage ceremonies of the third generation. If the rest of the country looked as lovely as the family gardens and the valley below the cave, the weddings must have been gorgeous. Sun-hee looked over her papers, where years ago she had made the arrangements. She regretted not being able to attend the weddings, preferring not to decide which to appear at and which to stay home, she went to none. Besides, gasoline was rationed and requesting extra would raise some red flags.

She skimmed through recordings from the Korean Government, she heard nothing new. Then she scanned news from China, the Soviet Union, Japan, and what they could decode from the American military. Only the continuing reports of revolutions in the Soviet Union were of concern. Nothing new to initiate a message to a member of the House of Sanshin.

She packed a lunch and took it down to the valley for a picnic by the creek. Before eating, she helped Jin-taek plant vegetables in his garden. The physical labor in this majestic mountain setting blocked out her worries of the world.

After lunch, she sat by the roaring stream and read. The fresh smells of the tree blossoms whiffed by on the cooling breeze. She returned to the cave in the late afternoon to watch a video. Hong-do sent her a box every month, containing movies from Russia, China, and America. He usually placed the Korean translated versions on top, the ones with Young-ja as the female voices. She watched the movies, looking for ideas on how to change the situation in Korea. Even the greatest of heroes did not overthrow a government without war.

How does a government change without war, turmoil, and bloodshed?

A movie about Gandhi gave her some encouragement until she saw that part where soldiers beat the marchers and threw Gandhi in prison. Civil disobedience in Korea would result in shooting and the gulag. She could find no examples in movies that would work in North Korea.

It was dark by the time she returned to the house to spend time with her great-grandchildren. Dinner was on the table, but Hon-yong had not returned from delivering furniture to the capital. For the children to get to bed on time, they ate without him.

It was well after midnight before Hon-yong returned. "I was delayed until I could get more gasoline. I have a big pile of fuel credits, but there is no petrol. I was finally able to get an agreement with an official to make him a special table, then he would give me gas," he said in a frustrated tone.

"I hear about all kinds of shortages across the country," said Sun-hee as she reached out and stroked his arm. "I'm glad you're home. I was worried about you."

Hon-yong began to rant. "I can't get the parts I need for the saws. The last shipment of nails and fasteners was short. People are willing to trade almost anything for food. The only ones who have things are the officials and the military, and they are demanding more. My quotas have increased over and over. I haven't met them in over a year even though we are producing fifty percent more than we were just five years ago. The system is broken, Sun-hee. Just between us, the decisions of our government are not working." His voice increased in volume with each statement until he was yelling.

Sun-hee put her finger to his lips and said quietly, "The children are asleep. Let's not wake them. You can tell me the details after you eat."

She stepped into the kitchen and retrieved Hon-yong's dinner then went to prepare herself for bed. When Hon-yong entered, she listened to all the details of what he saw while making deliveries. Then she made love to him to calm him down, allowing him to get a good night's rest. For the first time, she did not enjoy the union.

After he was asleep, she sat by the garden window and watched the tree blossoms frolic to the beat of the breeze in the moonlight.

All this spectacular beauty. A loving family. My life is wonderful. What have I done to deserve this? My mother was the leader of education. The men in my life protected me and have provided everything. I arranged the marriages of two generations. Anyone could have done it.

Choe-me killed Park. I should have been there. Hon-yong works tirelessly every day while I picnic by the river. There is nothing to do but pass messages. Tae-seon could do it. I must start teaching her tomorrow. I could go somewhere...but officially, I died. I have no papers. I'm only Hon-yong's wife. I can't leave this place without him. Why do I feel so depressed?

58 — Transition - April, 1989

Sun-hee called Young-ja. Talking to her always cheered her up.

"Sun-hee! Good to hear your voice. Sorry, you could not make it to the wedding of my youngest grandchild. I know travel is difficult, but you could have come down with Hon-yong and stayed a few days."

"I didn't go to any of the weddings since I couldn't make them all," said Sun-hee. "And you would not have enjoyed my company. I have been in a poor mood lately."

Young-ja chuckled. "A little depressed at times, happy others? Feel cold, then hot? Sweat at night? Join the club. Kwang-ku told me I was going through menopause. We'll get over it in a few years."

Sun-hee was startled by Young-ja's quick diagnosis. "Are you saying my feelings that the world is going to end are just hormone changes?"

"No, the world is in a mess. Your emotions are magnified. Try not to overstress. Dress in layers and get some petroleum jelly for you know what. We'll get through this together."

Sun-hee began to laugh, and Young-ja laughed on the other end of the line.

"Sorry to cut this short, but I'm about to be late, or later than I usually am. I always love to talk to you. I can let my words flow freely. Around everyone else, I must be careful. Tell everyone you talk to that I say hello. I am sure they are all tired of listening to me on radio and television." There was a click from the other end.

Sun-hee sat back in her chair. Comforting warmth swept over her.

Young-ja always has a way of cheering me up.

A few minutes later, she got up and made a pot of tea before listening to the recorded messages. Only one needed her attention, a call from her daughter, So-min.

"Mom, it is urgent we talk. Call me."

Sun-hee dialed her daughter. "So-min, it is good to hear from you. What is so urgent?"

"Can you come up here tomorrow? If so, I will have our son pick you up early in the morning."

"Do you have the extra gasoline to drive down here?" she asked.

"There is always fuel for transporting prisoners to the gulag," her daughter said smugly. Then she changed to a cheerful voice. "I'll have an early lunch ready for you and make sure you get home by dinner."

"I will be ready after breakfast," said Sun-hee. "I am looking forward to seeing you and the family."

A few moments later, Tae-seon came into the cave, prepared to learn how to listen and forward messages. It would be difficult to teach her what was important and what was not. Sun-hee knew Tae-seon would learn how to use the equipment, but the wisdom to know what to do with all the information would be a long learning process.

The next morning, her grandson arrived driving a military transport truck. He helped her into the passenger seat and drove through the mountain roads a couple of hours north to see So-min. The sun was bright except when the big fluffy, ever-changing, monster clouds got in the way. As promised, lunch was ready when she arrived. She ate with her six grandchildren and twelve great-grandchildren.

After lunch, So-min took Sun-hee on a tour of the medical research facility Gen. Park had set up for his son. They went through wards full of patients, the emergency treatment area, and the operating rooms. Sun-hee strolled, while So-min explained everything.

The suppressed memories of when she was operating on men, women, and children with Max so many years ago brought her to a stop.

"I wish we had such a facility during the war. Maybe we could have saved more lives," she said. A bead of sweat trickled down the side of her face.

"Are you alright, Mother?" asked So-min with concern.

Sun-hee wiped the sweat away with the palm of her hand. "Just a hot flash." Max's words flared, *Stay focused.*

"Where is your office?" she asked to get out of the operating room.

"This way. We can take the elevator," said So-min as she took her mother's elbow and walked with her down the hall.

So-min sat behind her desk and motioned for her mother to sit across from her. "We have already received a hundred and ten egg samples and one hundred and thirty semen samples," So-mi said. "I need your help to make sure I match eggs and sperm together, avoiding fertilizing first cousins. Putting together the pedigree for each sample and then looking for new unique combinations is a daunting task. You did well with arranging marriages. I hope you will help."

"Since we are not dealing with marriages and families, why do we need to worry if they are first cousins?" asked Sun-hee.

"There are many rare recessive diseases which may be present in the genes," said So-min. "Fertilizing an egg with a close relative will increase the chance of a genetic disease occurring up to twenty-five percent."

"Can you screen the specimens for these genes?" asked Sun-hee.

"We only know the genetic abnormality when a baby is born expressing the traits. The technology does not exist to allow me to examine a sperm or egg for a genetic disease."

Sun-hee paused for a moment. "I do not know of any child in the program born with a genetic disease. If there is no history in any of the families, what is the chance of both an egg and a sperm having a disease?"

"Not just a disease, Mother, they must have the same genetic disease. We all carry abnormal genes. When a baby gets two copies of the same abnormal gene, there is a problem. If we can eliminate the chance by making the right fertilizing choices, then all the children should be healthy."

Sun-hee stood and stepped to the window, gazing out. She turned and said, "Maybe it is time to take a few risks. The problems facing our country are different from the problems of previous generations. We need children who will be able to solve the issues the country will face in twenty to thirty years. I suggest we fertilize to get strong, intelligent leaders. Men and women who can rise in leadership and give direction to the country."

"I can do this easily from the information on the notes for each specimen," said So-min.

"Good. Let's get to work," Sun-hee said and sat back down.

A few minutes later, Sun-hee asked, "What will you do with the fertilized eggs?"

"The fertilized eggs are placed into surrogate mothers. There is a dorm next to the hospital for the mothers. They will each have a room, and we can monitor their food and activity. We selected the mothers from the prisoners. They are all healthy single females who have previously borne children. Once the implantation step is complete, we will have births in nine months."

"Do you foresee any problems?"

"Other than normal pregnancy issues, none."

"This all sounds so easy," said Sun-hee. "Maybe we should have done this with your children."

"The procedure was not very robust twenty years ago," said So-min. "Artificial insemination would have worked, but in-vitro fertilization was something new. We have perfected this procedure in preparation for this effort."

"How soon will you start?"

"We will start as soon as you tell me to," So-min said, looking at her mother for approval.

Sun-hee paused.

Why am I the person to make this decision?

She looked again out the window and said, "A hundred babies at a time will be a lot of work. Do you have the staff available?"

"We will do one implantation a day starting this week. The surrogate mothers will take care of their babies."

"You have thought of everything. I approve," Sun-hee said as she picked up the lists of egg and sperm donors and began to review the pairings. They worked on this for the next couple of hours, finalizing the matches.

They walked back to where So-min's son was waiting to take Sun-hee home.

"Keep in touch. Let me know if you encounter any problems," said Sun-hee.

"I will, Mother. Planning a generation is so exciting. Something like this has never been done with humans before."

Sun-hee took her daughter's hand and squeezed them. "These children are a long-term hope for our country. I feel they are in capable hands. I love you, So-min."

"Your vision inspires us all, Mother," said So-min with a sincere stare into her mother's eyes.

On the ride home, So-min's last words ran through her mind.

What vision is she referring to? That I want a better Korea? I do not know what a better Korea would look like. I only know what I don't want.

Sun-hee arrived home after dark. She went to the cave and sent a quick message to Yong-gak and Hong-do. *So-min starts this week. One hundred within a year.* Then she went to bed.

Hon-yong arrived soon after she got comfortable and snuggled up beside her. "I could see your mind was on something else at dinner. Do you want to talk about it?"

"I made the decision today to proceed with the fertilization of a hundred new lives. Not the normal way. So-min will combine eggs and sperm in a test tube and implant the fertilized egg in a woman. I wonder if we are doing something wrong. We do not have to do it. We can let the program end right now."

Hon-yong did not respond. Sun-hee turned on her elbow and

looked at him. "Don't you have anything to say?" Her voice was louder and sharper than usual.

"You approved the start of additional children today," said Hon-yong. "Why you?"

"I asked myself that same question. Why me? Do you agree with my decision?"

"Hundreds have already been born in their generation."

"Are you saying we don't need more?"

"Let me think through this. The mothers will raise the children as siblings. They will not have fathers, much like our children."

"Correct. Do you think that is good or bad?"

"Part of the success of the House of Sanshin is our commitment to each other. The same has occurred with our children. They treat each other like brothers and sisters. There is no union among our grandchildren."

"So, you approve?" she said.

"Our families are so scattered. I have not seen some of my children and grandchildren in years. Some of my great-grandchildren I have never met. These children will never have fathers. Their mothers may not treat them as their own. They will have no family." He sighed.

"You are not telling me if that is good or bad. Maybe this is something we should not do. It is such a distant hope for the future."

"Our children were Doctor Park's hope. They are making a tremendous influence in the country."

"We have done so much. If Park did not bring us together, would Korea be any different? Have we been able to change the inevitable path of our country?"

"If the new children are fighters, they may initiate change. It may not be pretty."

"I'll call So-min tomorrow and have her stop."

"No, the one-hundred may be a needed refresh to the program," he said and put his arm around Sun-hee. "What is the best thing from Park's program?"

"The House of Sanshin?" she replied.

"I met you. You make my life worth living." He pulled her gently on his chest.

"Hon," was all Sun-hee got out before her lips pressed against his. Together they moved as one, making each other's lives worth living.

59 — Hope then Floods - Spring, 1989 to Fall, 1990

As summer approached, Tae-seon and Sun-hee would go to the valley early in the day to avoid the heat. They worked in the garden, read, and had lunch with Jin-taek, before returning to the cave to catch up on the news.

The second week of June, So-min called to report she had implanted the first fifty women with embryos. All of them were doing well. So-min spoke matter-of-factly like this was not exciting news. They agreed to talk monthly to keep Sun-hee up to date on the progress.

At the call in mid-March, So-min said, "We delivered the first child on March fourth, a healthy girl. Since then, seven more."

"Have there been any complications?"

"The births went smoothly. Since the surrogates have all given birth before, they knew what to do."

"Are the mothers getting enough to eat? Are the babies nursing?"

"I am monitoring the feedings and each infants' weight. Don't worry, I'll let you know if there is anything wrong," said So-min.

From then on, Sun-hee called every week to get updates. By the first week of June, one hundred test tube children had been born. So-min reassured her mother that the surrogate mothers nursed and cared for their children.

It would take time to discover what these children would grow up to be. Were they family? She had just turned fifty-five years old. Could she call test tube babies her great-grandchildren?

The only question So-min asked about the program was, "When should we start the next hundred children?"

The only response Sun-hee came up with was, "When we have a plan to educate the children, we can consider it." This idea weighed on her mind, along with her husband's words.

We built unity among ourselves.

How could she set up an environment to raise these children, so they were loyal to each other, as well as Korea?

***

The summer of 1990 was perfect. News reports predicted good

crops in Korea, and the expectation of a record harvest gave everyone hope the food shortages would end. For a nation short on food, and a lack of money to pay for imports, this was great news. Their gardens were doing better than ever, and Jin-taek had filled their storehouse with deer and goat jerky.

The monsoon rains arrived in late August and September as usual. Only this year, there was more rainfall than ever recorded. Flooding demolished the anticipated harvest. Crops were ruined all over the country.

For days, Sun-hee listened to reports of the flooding: Roads and bridges were washed out by raging rivers. High water destroyed towns and cities.

The roads to their home were washed out, leaving them isolated. Then the phone lines went dead, and the electricity they had taken for granted all these years stopped. Sun-hee was at a loss, disconnected from the world for the first time in years. She did not go to the cave as the mineshafts were dark. Hon-yong could not make furniture without the electric saws. They had no news of what was happening in the rest of the country.

For Sun-hee and her family, this was a good time. Their garden did not flood, and they had a good supply of dried fish and meat. Their harvest was good. They canned food for the months ahead. Their supplies of coal and wood were more than enough to make it through the winter.

***

By the first of October, Hon-yong was concerned about Jin-taek. They had not been able to use the elevator for a month. But everyone was sure if anyone could survive the monsoons, it was Jin-taek.

Hon-yong found some oil lamps that had not been used in years and got them working. He checked the elevator shaft but saw no signs of Jin-taek. Over the next few days, he devised a pulley system to operate the elevator manually. They tested it by lowering the elevator one day and raising it the next.

Since it took all the men to work the pulley, they decided Sun-hee would go down to get Jin-taek. A rope was rigged for Sun-hee to pull when she was ready to come up or if there was a problem. They lowered her down slowly. The trip usually took a few minutes. Now it took over an hour. Sun-hee sat with a lantern in the darkness of the elevator shaft, wondering when she would reach the bottom. When it finally settled to the ground, she found stacks of harvested vegetables, dried meat and fish in the mineshaft. Jin-taek had protected his harvest from the rains.

Sun-hee walked to the river. It had breached its banks, so she had to bushwhack her way to Jin-Taek's home. What she found was a pile of rocks. A massive rockslide had buried Jin-taek's wooden hut. Boulders, much bigger than she, lay on top of the rubble which had once Jin-Taek's home.

"JIN-TAEK!" she yelled at the top of her lungs. Her voice echoed in the valley, *TAEK…taek…taek…ek*. She shuddered and shouted again. "JIN-TAEK." *TAEK…taek…taek…ek*. Her heart jumped to her throat, and her eyes formed tears.

She ran around the pile of boulders, looking for signs of life, but she found only splintered wood amongst the rocks. She checked his drying shed, only jerky, no indications that Jin-taek was alive. No new footprints in the wet soil or around the garden.

She clambered back to the mineshaft and pulled hard on the rope. As the elevator jerked, starting the trip upwards, she slid to her knees and sat, holding her head between her knees, crying as the elevator slowly crept upwards.

After an eternity, where she thought of all the things Jin-taek had done for her, she felt Hon-yong's strong hands lifting her and carrying her out of the elevator.

"What did you find, dear?" he asked.

Sun-hee took in a stuttered breath and cried out, "A pile of rocks. His hut is buried under a rockslide."

"Any sign of Jin-taek?"

"No footprints. Vegetables are rotting in the garden. I fear he is under the rocks," Sun-hee said through sobs.

"I'll go down tomorrow and look," said Hon-yong as he picked Sun-hee up and carried her back to the house.

The next day, Hon-yong was lowered down to the valley. He climbed back up the elevator shaft using the supports.

After he caught his breath from the climb, he said, "I think Jin-taek was in his house when the rockslide came down. There is no way to remove the boulders to confirm he is there. If he survived, I would expect he would have moved into the mineshaft near the elevator."

For weeks, Sun-hee mourned Jin-taek. She would stay in her room until late in the morning and come out only to eat. Then in the afternoon, she would sit in the garden wrapped in a shawl. Hon-yong brought out a blanket when it was cold, set up an umbrella when it was sunny or raining. One windy day he picked her up, chair and all, and brought her inside.

She stood looking out the window in the middle of the night.

Hon-yong said, "How long are you going to stand there? Come to bed."

Sun-hee did not move.

"How long are you going to mourn?"

"Until my shame of not telling him how much he meant to me is gone," she said in a low voice. "He was always there for me, my mother, and us. He never asked for anything."

"You gave him a second chance at life," said Hon-yong as he moved beside her and put his arm around her.

"My mother called him a hero. He is what I wished when I chose him to get the last of the antibiotics. Two other men died from infections, and Jo Jin-taek lived. I will mourn the loss of my hero for as long as I live."

The next afternoon, there was a knock on the door, startling everyone. When Hon-yong opened the door, there stood Weon-kee. A surprised Hon-yong gave him a big hug.

"It is great to see you. How did you get here?"

"One of the government priorities is getting the spy antennas on top of the mountain operational. I am getting the electricity restored. Just wanted to tell you to turn everything off before we connect the lines. There may be a surge," said Weon-kee.

"Is the road repaired?" asked Hon-yong.

"We had to put up three makeshift bridges to get here."

Within the hour the electricity was restored. Sun-hee came out of the bedroom. "I am pleased to see you, Wires. And very happy to have electricity," she said.

"I see you and your family have managed just fine through the storm," said Weon-kee.

Sun-hee dropped her head and looked at the floor.

"Jin-taek did not make it. A rockslide buried his home," said Hon-yong as he moved and put an arm around Sun-hee. "She has been in mourning since we found out."

"I am terribly sorry. He was a great man and so loyal to you, Sun-hee. We will miss him."

"How are Choe-me and your family?" asked Sun-hee quietly.

"They are all fine. I have not been able to see them, I have been in

Pyongyang restoring power. The first task was to get lines to the capitol repaired, and then they sent me here."

"With electricity, we will be fine," interjected Hon-yong. "Better than fine, as no one will be expecting furniture deliveries until the roads are repaired."

"You will get the winter off," said Weon-kee. "There are only a few bridges left and at least three washouts on the road from the west to repair. I have no idea about what is east of here." Then Wires cleared his throat. "I have one more item of bad news. The Premier blamed Stinky for the crop failures. He was executed last week."

The next day, they tested the elevator before going down to the valley. Sun-hee had Hon-yong make a plaque reading, HERE LIES SERGEANT JO JIN-TAEK, OUR HERO.

They brought up the unspoiled fruits of Jin-taek's garden: corn, peas, potatoes, sweet potatoes, onions, garlic, ginger, and carrots. The drying shed and mineshaft contained over fifty kilograms of jerky and numerous bags of pine nuts. There was enough food to feed the family for a year.

60 — Famine - January to September, 1992

Throughout the winter, Sun-hee monitored reports of famine throughout North Korea. Daily, she made attempts to contact the members of the original House of Sanshin.

In early January, she was able to get ahold of Choe-me. "I am so happy to hear your voice, Sun-hee."

"How are you and the family?" asked Sun-hee.

"I have not heard anything from Wires in two months. He left to restore electrical connections in the south. I am worried that the government blamed him for the outages like they blamed Stinky for the crop failures," Choe-me said.

"I didn't think of that possibility," said Sun-hee. "There are reports on the restoration of electricity on the radio every day. This morning, I think the news was about Wonsan. I'm sure that is the work of Wires and his sons."

"That is what I needed to hear to give me hope that Wires is still alive. We are so isolated here."

"What else is happening?" asked Sun-hee.

"A couple of weeks ago, the army came and took all the food from the regional storage warehouse. There is no food in the market. We have plenty hidden in our pantry, but most of the workers didn't. When the river froze over during last week's cold spell, thousands of the working class fled to China across the ice. The next night, soldiers killed dozens as they tried to cross the river. There are not enough workers for the factories, and the army recruited all able-bodied people to work, including my daughter and granddaughters. I'm home alone with my great-grandchildren and feel so vulnerable by myself."

"I can't imagine what you are going through. The official news doesn't reveal what is really happening.

"My great-grandson needs some attention. Can you call again tomorrow?"

"I will," said Sun-hee. "Call me if you need anything."

Sun-hee turned on the news. The voice was not Young-ja. Sun-hee reinterpreted the reports of food supplies given to the capital, the need for more workers because factories were expanding, generous aid coming from China, and peace along the border allowing for soldiers to return home, as distortions of the truth.

The next day, Sun-hee called Young-ja. They talked for hours as, for once, Young-ja had nothing else to do. Some high government official had complained about her being too old, and they needed a younger face on state television.

Kwang-ku and the family were well. Being part of the core class in Songbun gave them many privileges that the lower levels did not have. Young-ja was confident they would survive the winter.

Sun-hee was able to contact Eun-seong in the second week of January. Eun-seong told her of their isolation in the nuclear facility for months, but they had electricity as the local hydroelectric dam continued to operate. Food was a problem. The military cut off food for all but essential staff, causing a riot. Many workers died. The status of Sung-man protected Eun-seong and her family.

Over the next couple of months, communication continued to be re-established around the country. The House of Sanshin, with their core class status, were provided food before the common man.

By April, she renewed contact with all but fifteen of the remaining forty-two prizewinners. Then she received news of two deaths. San Hien-jin and Youj Kum-ja had died in food riots. Hien-jin was a doctor in Kaesong and had married Kum-ja. Their whole family perished, including one of Sun-hee's granddaughters who married into their family.

When she was able to contact Sue-dae in China, she learned that Chong-Pil and most of his family had made their way to Beijing and were staying there.

Sue-dae's main concern was the interruption of power from North Korea. The disconnect was causing severe economic repercussions and a rethinking of the reliance on North Korean electricity.

She got a call from So-min in late April. "Mother, I'm so glad to be able to talk to the outside world. We finally have electricity. We are starving. The prisoners were all denied food. We fed the mothers half rations so that they could feed the babies."

Sun-hee felt like a hand had reached out of the phone, grabbed her, and shook her. She swiped her arm over her cheeks. "Oh, So-min. I'm so glad to hear you are safe."

"We are fine right now, but we will not be for long. We need food."

"How can I get food for all of you? We cannot travel. I will ask around to see if anyone can help. I will call you tomorrow. I love you, So-min."

"We need a miracle or the hundred children will be starving to death, Mother."

Sun-hee hung up and dialed. She spoke to anyone and everyone she could to see if she could get food to So-min. There was no food, and no way to get it to So-min.

The next morning, she made her tea and sat by the phone. Eyes fixed on the dial, what would she say? The phone rang. She picked up the receiver.

"Oh, Mother, thank you! Thank you!" said her daughter sobbing. "A helicopter landed this morning and gave us enough rice for weeks. And thank Young-soo who the pilot said ordered the delivery."

Sun-hee closed her eyes, pushing out a tear from each and said, "He did not tell me he was sending food. I will honor him with my praises."

"Give him my praise as well, Mother. He is a good man. Food will still be short, so Duk-bae is ordering the remaining staff to leave. They must walk out of here with two meals worth of rice. For the long term, we need to feed our family and fifty mothers who are each nursing two children. We are the only ones left, except for the inmates who have been living off the carcasses of the dead in the gulag. Can you find us somewhere to go?"

Sun-hee sat still, stunned by her daughter's request. With the level of starvation in the country, where could she find a place for So-min's family, the one-hundred children, and their mothers?

"I…I…do not know," she stammered. "People are starving all over the country. There is nowhere for all of you," she said softly. "Your family can come here. But we cannot feed the mothers and children."

"You have to come up with something, Mother. Put the word out. Someone in the House of Sanshin has a place for us. You have to find a place."

Sun-hee's mind raced through all the conversations she had the day before and over the last few months. "I will call everyone. Hopefully, there is a place for one hundred children."

"I love you, Mother," So-min said before hanging up.

Sun-hee went to get more tea. While waiting for the pot to boil, she stood looking over the valley. She had never felt so hopeless. She bent over and put her hands on her knees, hope fleeing from her heart.

During the next two weeks, she heard more grim news as spring allowed workers to reestablish communication. The fifteen members of the House of Sanshin she was unable to contact previously were confirmed dead from riots, bandits, or starvation. The southern rural areas of the country were the worst.

She had nightmares of the road being repaired, allowing bandits to attack her home. Hon-yong only laughed at her when she told him of her fears. He did realize they would need to be self-sufficient over the next winter, so he expanded the gardens and made everyone work to get them planted. The one staple they would not have was rice.

May came and went. The roads to the east and west were passible on foot. The government priority was to get the main roads repaired. This remote mountain road they were on was only a shortcut and not a vital artery. Hon-yong walked to the nearest village every other week. The trip took him two days. When he was not working in the gardens, he made toys for his great-grandchildren.

The situation for So-min continued to have no solution. Young-Soo continued to divert food to So-min every few weeks. But he was never available when she called. She so wanted to thank him for taking care of everyone. The reports Sun-hee gleaned news from told her Young-soo had reestablished much of the mining exports to China. The government had money to buy food on the international market. Young-soo brought it in on returning trains.

There were no official figures of deaths over the winter, but Sun-hee estimated over a million people had died from starvation or the riots.

***

The first week of July, Eun-seong called. "Sun-hee. They are forcing families to leave the nuclear research facility. I have spoken to Chulsoon. My family and I will return to yangseongso."

"How can they force you to leave your husband? That is not right!" Sun-hee said in an agitated voice.

"Somehow, information leaked out on the projects. They are trying to make this area more secure. I must also tell you, Sung-man is not well. The doctors have diagnosed him with leukemia. He says it is probably from being exposed to too much radiation over the years. They will not let him leave. He knows too much."

"Oh no, Eun-seong. I'm so sorry. Are you sure there is no treatment?"

"Many of the men working at the facility have already passed from cancer and other illnesses," she said, whimpering. "It is the way things are here. For the sake of my family, I'm happy to leave."

"Stay safe, Eun-seong. When they repair the roads, I will come to visit."

"I need to finish packing. When I get to Yangseongso, I will call."

Sun-hee slowly placed the receiver on the phone.

Emptiness came over Sun-hee. She was so helpless to do anything for anyone. She knew things happened because she was in her cave, talking to others. She wanted to do much more. But what?

A week later, Chulsoon called to inform her that Eun-seong and her family had arrived safely. She was under strict orders not to speak to anyone about her previous residence. She could not use the phone. He did say the orphanage was doing well through all the turmoil in the country. Some food from Russia had made it down to them, and the farms around the area received only a little damage from the monsoons last fall. Since most of the farmers in the area were either a patient at the hospital or former orphans, the local support was excellent. They also had a good supply of fish from the coast as the road south was still impassible.

An idea flashed into Sun-hee's mind. She asked, "Is there room and food for a hundred children, fifty mothers, and So-min's family?"

She heard a pause on the other end. "That many would stretch our resources," Chulsoon said hesitantly. "We have over three hundred orphans now." The line was silent for a moment. Sun-hee craved a positive response and held her breath. "We take orphans. That is what we do here. The mothers would be an issue with the officials, but we would need additional staff to care for the children. I do not think I could bring in the fifty mothers."

"What if they came a few at a time? Not all at once," pleaded Sun-hee.

"A few at a time would be best. Start with six children and their mothers, and we will work to get the rest here before winter."

"Oh, thank you, Chulsoon. I will make this up to you somehow."

"Consider it payment on what I owe you," he said and disconnected.

Sun-hee immediately called So-min and relayed the basics of the plan.

Within a week, the first six children and three mothers traveled to the old camp. So-min was able to have a truck take the mothers and children to where the road was washed out. Then they walked for a day to another washout, and Chulsoon provided transport the rest of the way. By the end of July, twenty of the children were at the old camp.

The second week of August, Hon-yong was able to deliver furniture again. The morning he was leaving on his first trip, Sun-hee received a call from Young-ja.

"Sun-hee, I need to have Hon-yong pick me up. When is he coming to Pyongyang?" she said urgently.

"Today," replied Sun-hee.

Young-ja hung up. She had never spoken so few words. Something was wrong.

She waited by the road for Hon-yong. It was after dark when she heard the truck coming up the valley. Young-ja jumped out and grabbed Sun-hee in a blubbering embrace.

Hon-yong put his arms around both and whispered in Sun-hee's ear, "Kwang-ku is dead."

"No!" exclaimed Sun-hee.

"They killed him," said Young-ja. "Shot him in front of the hospital," she wailed. "They threw him into a mass grave with others."

Sun-hee cried with her friend for a while before they slowly walked to the house. For most of the night, Sun-hee sat with her friend in silence, mourning Kwang-ku. Sometime in the early morning, Young-ja fell asleep. Sun-hee slept beside her.

After a silent breakfast, Sun-hee led Young-ja to the cave, away from the children, where they could talk. "Kwang-ku had come out of the hospital to help some people injured by the military," said Yong-ja. "The soldiers told him to leave them alone. But he picked up an injured girl and started walking into the hospital. They ordered him to stop. He refused. A soldier came up and shot the girl with his pistol. My dear husband yelled at the soldier. He yelled at all the soldiers, telling them that they were as bad as the Americans, killing defenseless children. Then they shot him in the head. They took him, the injured, and the others they killed and dumped them in a mass grave."

Young-ja stayed in the cave for the next week. She looked thin and admitted she had not eaten enough since the monsoons last fall. Sun-hee brought her meals and made sure she ate. After a week, Sun-hee finally got Young-ja to go down to the river. They worked in the garden and talked.

Sun-hee was glad to have her friend around, but not under these circumstances. Tae-seon listened to the reports and messages. Occasionally, Sun-hee read Tae-seon's notes. The only thing to worry about was the food supply. Many farmers had died over the winter, the farms looted. Too much of the country's farmland was left unplanted in the spring. There was no livestock to replenish herds. Hungry people had killed the farm animals.

The harvest this fall would be plentiful, but without Jin-taek, they did not have as much deer and goat jerky. Her grandsons fished in Jin-taek's lake, hoping they did not take too many to replenish the stock. The family put themselves on a strict ration, hoping their food supply would last.

***

On the seventh of September, one of the grandson's ran up to Sun-hee as Young-ja and her were digging potatoes in the garden. "Grandma, there is a beggar at the house who wants to talk to you."

Sun-hee and Young-ja looked at each other dumbfounded. "Who would know to come here to find me?" Sun-hee said to Young-ja.

"I don't know. It has to be someone we are friends with," said Young-ja. "Let's go find out. Any friend of yours will be a friend of mine."

They picked up their sacks of potatoes, and Sun-hee handed hers to her grandson. Together, they proceeded up the elevator and through the mineshafts to the house. Outside, they saw a woman sitting in ragged, dirty clothes with a scarf over her head.

"Can I help you?" Sun-hee asked.

"Oh, Sun-hee!" the woman said as she jumped up and ran towards them. Her scarf fell from her head.

"Choe-me!" Sun-hee and Young-ja yelled together.

"What are you doing here?" said Sun-hee

"I am so glad to see you!" said Young-ja at the same time.

Choe-me just grabbed them and began to bawl.

After a few moments, Young-ja said, "You can tell us all about it after we get you cleaned up and fed. The bathtub is better in the cave. Come."

Sun-hee said to her grandson, "Bring some food to the cave." Then she guided Choe-me through the mineshaft.

After a bath, they sat down before a meal. Choe-me ate while Young-ja rambled on about lots of unimportant things.

Choe-me stared at Young-ja for a moment, letting her finish her sentence, then she said, "The farm was looted. Weon-kee took the family to China. I drove until some bandits stopped me. I gave them everything and walked the rest of the way."

"Slow down Choe-me," said Young-ja. Tell us everything from the beginning.

She told them about soldiers looting all the farms around Hyesan, how they took food and everything of value from the farm. She said, "When Weon-kee came home, he wanted to leave. I argued with him. He called Young-soo, who got everyone onto a train to China. I could not leave my country. I had to stay. Things were not well between Weon-kee and me. I have not been a good wife since…"

"…since the incident with General Park," Sun-hee filled in.

Choe-me nodded. "The only place I knew to come was here. I hope you will allow me to stay," she said sheepishly.

"I get a roommate! Yeah!" said Young-ja.

"Why are you here?" asked Choe-me to Young-ja.

Young-ja proceeded to tell Choe-me about Kwang-ku and needing to flee the capital. The trio cried, shared, and comforted one another until late into the evening.

61 — Choe-me's Plan - Fall, 1992

The three friends talked about everything in their lives. Young-ja carried most of the conversation. Sun-hee got in a word now and then, and Choe-me listened. They discussed in detail the problems with the country and wondered what they could do.

Choe-me came up with an idea. "What if Wires were to build molten salt reactors in China. Would this increase the money coming into Korea?"

"How would electricity generated in China bring us revenue?" asked Young-ja.

The room was silent for a moment. Sun-hee then said, "The money would not have to come to Korea. Skinny Beast and Su-dae could accumulate the funds and use it to invest. At least they would be richer."

"I like it," said Young-ja. "Someone wealthy in the House of Sanshin."

"I can't remember ever having money in my hands," said Sun-hee. "Let's call Su-dae to see if she thinks it is possible," said Sun-hee.

A few minutes later, Su-dae was on board with the plan. Sun-hee left a message for Stone who called back in the middle of the night saying he would come by in two days.

***

The three women tried to make a detailed plan for how it could work. When Stone arrived, they called Su-dae, who had invited Wires to her place. After an exchange of greetings over the speakerphone, Sun-hee laid out their plan for reactors in China.

Stone said, "Su-dae, can you add thorium to your refined materials list?"

"By writing it on the request form," she replied.

"How much do you need, Weon-kee?" asked Stone. He wrote down the reply and said, "I will expand my equipment requests. Pay me in equipment, and the revenue stream will remain the same."

Su-dae followed with, "Skinny Beast is always asking if we need funds for development. I'll get you the equipment so you can get the materials flowing in less time and then pay back the loan from the profit from the electricity we sell."

"We can place the reactor at the coal generating plant Su-dae has built, increasing the electrical output," said Wires.

"Can you keep this hidden from the Chinese government?" asked Sun-hee.

"All of our workers are Korean," replied Su-dae. "The refugees here are more than happy to work for us."

"Are we sure we can get this by the officials in Pyongyang?" asked Choe-me.

"Gil-hyung reviews my transactions at the finance department," replied Stone.

"I'll coordinate with Bear to make sure he gets the documentation he needs," said Su-dae.

There was a pause. Sun-hee looked around the room, getting nods from her friends. She said, "And all this was Choe-me's idea."

"I miss you, Choe-me," said Wires for everyone to hear. "I wish you had come with us."

"I felt if I left, I would be abandoning my friends," said Choe-me softly. "I needed to be with them."

Sun-hee turned off the speaker and handed the receiver to Choe-me so she could talk in private.

She turned to Stone. "I cannot thank you enough for what you are doing for everyone. Providing food to my family and being so helpful. You are truly a great man."

Stone stood, gave a slight bow, and said, "I have things to do." Then he strode out of the cave.

Choe-me put down the receiver while Young-ja, having been silent through the whole meeting said, "In all my days in the Capitol, I never saw decisions made so quickly and easily. Officials would talk over something for months and wait for the Premier to decide what to do. They would haggle forever on the details until they all agreed. Working with Sanshin is so refreshing. I'm thrilled to witness such a great plan put together…" On and on she went.

Sun-hee handed a handkerchief to Choe-me, helped her from her chair, and said, "We have some harvesting to do. Let's go down to the garden." All while Young-ja continued to talk in an excited voice.

***

Three weeks later, while Sun-hee and Hon-yong were getting ready for bed, there was a knock at the door. Hon-yong answered. It was Stone.

"Hon-yong, I need some things made. Can we talk about them in your shop?"

Hon-yong grabbed a jacket and left with Stone. Sun-hee anxiously waited for Hon-yong to return, wondering what Stone needed.

It was a couple of hours before Hon-yong returned. "What did Stone need at this hour of the night?" Sun-hee asked.

"He has a long list of needs. What is important is what he is providing to meet those needs. He came with two trucks full of new equipment I have desperately needed. New modern saws, a jointer, a plainer, and a new drill press. He said more equipment would be coming in the next few weeks."

"He was able to get all those items? How?" urged Sun-hee.

"He said it was part of the plan to build thorium reactors in China, thanks to you three," he said with a big smile. "Then there is the bad news. Young-soo also had another big request. He has orders to rebuild a lumber mill and woodworking shop which was destroyed in the flooding last year. The site is near Kanggye where there is lots of wood and a railroad. I will go there and take charge of the site while Junior and his sons manage things here."

"I guess we get to move to Kanggye and see some more of the country," Sun-hee said gleefully.

Hon-yong replied, "I can't take you right now. After the mill is operational, you can join me. You need to stay here until I build a house."

That night, Sun-hee passionately made love to her husband before she fell asleep. She dreamt of what it would be like without her loving husband sleeping next to her. The next night, she found out. Tossing and turning, she lay awake, feeling abandoned. Then she shuddered as she thought of her two friends, sleeping alone in the cave, with no hope of being reunited with their husbands.

62 — Children - Winter - Spring, 1993

Large flakes fell leisurely past the window on their way to the valley below. Sun-hee stood at the window, warming her hands around a fresh cup of tea. The phone rang, and she knew Tae-seon would answer it.

"Sun-hee, So-min is on the phone," Tae-seon shouted from the other room. "She says it is urgent."

Sun-hee took the phone from Tae-seon. "Good morning, So-min.

"Good morning, Mother. All of the babies and their mothers made it safely to their new home."

"Wonderful. Are they comfortable in the camp?" asked Sun-hee.

"There is a problem," replied So-min. "Some of the mothers left."

"How many?"

"Eight last night and four the night before. We have locked up the camp, and Chulsoon has posted guards at night."

"Did they take the children?"

"No. The women who left are trying to get back to their families. The rest also want to leave. Many are refusing to help with the children as we have constantly told them the children are not theirs. We promised that after they weaned the children, they were free. We do not have enough people to take care of one hundred children. It is too soon to have all the mothers leave. I need help!" So-min pleaded.

"I will come over. Can you have someone pick me up?"

"I will call Duk-bae and arrange transportation. Thank you so much, Mother."

Sun-hee approached Choe-me and Young-ja. "So-min needs me to help with the hundred children in the camp. Would you like to join me?"

"How is it So-min needs help with one hundred two-year-old children? What happened to the mothers?" asked Young-ja.

"We promised them freedom, and now they are demanding it. I need to go oversee the raising of these children."

"I'll go with you," said Choe-me.

"I am not going to stay here alone. When do we go?" asked Young-ja.

The phone rang. Sun-hee put the call on speaker. It was So-min. "A truck will be by tomorrow morning, Mother."

"We will be ready. Young-ja and Choe-me will be coming with me."

***

The next morning, the three climbed into the back of a truck, each with a bundle of clothes and personal items. By lunch, they were at the camp. Eun-seong met them. After a short and joyous reunion, Eun-seong filled them in on the situation.

"The mothers of the children tried to leave again last night and were kept in by the guards. The twenty women who regularly help at the orphanage are helping with the children the best they can. Chulsoon put up a notice in town asking for workers," said Eun-seong.

Then she got a serene look on her face. "Sun-hee, I need to be very honest about something. So-min is treating the surrogate mothers poorly. She walks around with a stick and beats the women when they are not doing what she wants. They are rebelling against So-min, not abandoning the children. I tried to talk to her, but she just yelled at me. She scares me." Tears formed in Eun-seong's eyes. "Chulsoon and I do not know what to do."

"Oh, my. I did not know she was beating the women. Where is So-min?"

"She has the women and children in the House of Sanshin."

Sun-hee walked quickly to the House of Sanshin, climbed the stairs, and located So-min. She grabbed the stick out of her hand and said sternly, "Follow me." She led her outside and in an angry voice asked, "Have you been using this stick on those women?"

"I have to maintain control, Mother," yelled So-min back at her.

"Then you are done here. Beatings are unacceptable. Go get in the truck I came in and go back to your husband," Sun-hee snarled. "I will handle things here."

"But, Mother," So-min pleaded.

Sun-hee turned and walked back into the House of Sanshin, followed by Choe-me, Eun-seong, and Young-ja. She stood in what was the large shared room for a moment, looking over the mothers and children. She spoke in a commanding voice.

"Get the women from the other rooms. I need to talk to you."

The room was in confusion for a few moments as the women assembled. They became silent as Sun-hee glowered at all of them. In an authoritative voice, Sun-hee said, "I am Cha Sun-hee, mother of So-min and great-grandmother of many of these children. With me are Moon Choe-me, Seo Young-ja, and Ryoo Eun-seong. They are also great-grandmothers of your children. I regret how So-min has been treating you. This stick will no longer be needed." And she tossed it to the floor behind her.

"My daughter is no longer in charge. I understand you wish to leave and resume your lives. These children need care and to be brought up in the right manner. I need women who will provide care. Consider yourselves employed as of this moment. What I will provide is a place to live, food, and payment. When we hire replacements, I will allow you to leave."

"Why can't we leave right now?" asked a voice from the back of the room.

"These children need you or other women who will raise them properly. If all of you leave, the needs of these children go unmet. The four of us are not a replacement for all of you, but we will be supportive. Should you stay, I will help you get back to your families. Leaving on your own and trying to walk home in the winter puts your lives at risk. However, I will have the gates opened, and no one will force you to stay. Right now, I need you, and these children need you." Sun-hee stood, looking over the women before her with their despondent eyes and hollow cheeks, hoping that her pleading had affected their motherly instinct.

"How can you help us get back to our families?" asked another woman.

"Let me say these children have many great-grandparents and grandparents who I can contact to find your families. When we do, and you decide to return to them, I will provide transportation home. If you walk out now, you are on your own."

"Why should we believe you?" yelled another voice.

Young-ja spoke up, "We all believe Sun-hee. She does not know how to lie. She keeps lots of secrets but never lies. I assure you, you will be treated well from this point on."

"I know your voice," said a woman right in front of Young-ja. "You're the voice on the radio and television."

"Yes, you are correct. I was employed as a voice of the government, but no longer. Presently, I am a person here to help you be great mothers and see these children become productive adults."

Murmuring came from the women. Some looked fearful.

Choe-me smiled, bringing out her mesmerizing charismatic personality, and she spoke soothingly. "I see your fears and apprehension. A group was assembled many years ago to make Korea a better place. Some of them we now honor with pictures on the wall."

She pointed to the wall behind them. "As a group, we have done many things to improve our country. There is much more to do. We are loyal to the Premier, the Democratic People's Republic of Korea, and each other. We take roles, doing things correctly, improving the lives of all Koreans. In many ways, we have not done enough, yet we will always work to do the best we can. If Young-ja had not been the voice on the radio someone else would have. She has a gift of communication and put it to use as well as she could. I only wish I had some of her talents."

Sun-hee stared at the pictures on the wall. Eun-seong had kept up with the drawings, placing them on the wall as their friends had passed. A lump grew in her throat, the last picture was of Eun-seong's husband, Chou Sung-man.

"Are you saying that forcing us to have children is part of your plan?" said the woman in front of Choe-me.

"No. It was my decision," said Sun-hee. "I was assured you were treated well and would benefit. I regret you were not treated well by my daughter and son-in-law. I'm here now and will treat you with respect. Let me start by helping to change some of these diapers." She picked up a child. "Will you assist me?" she said to the closest woman. "What is your name?" she asked as they walked to the privy where Sun-hee changed children for much of the afternoon.

Thirty-five mothers remained. A few women were hired from the nearby town, and over the next week, routines were put in place to care for the children round the clock. Sun-hee met with each surrogate to inquire about their family and their home. She sent the information to Tae-seon who sent out inquiries to find the families. As she received information back, she passed it on. She arranged transportation for those who chose to leave. Classes were started for the remaining women, instructing them on how to be teachers.

It was January before she heard from Hon-yong. He had built a small one-room cabin. The mill and woodshop would not be ready until early summer. If all went well, he would start building a house.

As winter progressed, the constant care of the children demanded most of Sun-hee's time. The four women took up residence in Sgt. Kua's house. They found they enjoyed living and working together, as they had many years ago.

Winter gave way to spring, and the growing children loved running around the camp. So many two-year-old children and only forty women to care for them. They grew fast and learned even faster. They all seemed so advanced compared to the other children in the orphanage. Best of all, they were healthy. The coughs and colds afflicting the other children did not seem to affect the new generation of children.

Sun-hee and the others knew these children were special and needed to be brought up and educated in the right way. She focused on teaching the staff on how to educate the children and brought in some soldiers to work with the children in games and exercise. Some of the surrogate mothers commented to Sun-hee at how advanced these children were. From what Sun-hee heard from others and saw for herself, she realized they had brought forth a new generation, without family ties, which could be trained to do something great in the country.

In late May, a letter came from Hon-yong:

> *I miss you so much, my darling. I long to see you and be with you. However, this lumber mill is still not a place I want you to be. The army has taken over. My lieutenant rank allows me some respect and spares me the fate of a worker.*
>
> *Requests from China for wood are being filled at a more than acceptable rate. The military does not question my authority.*
>
> *There would be no life for you here. You would be the only woman for miles and stuck in my hut on the side of a hill. Until I can make this more livable, I cannot ask you to live here.*
>
> *I miss you.*
>
> *Love, Hon-yong.*

Sun-hee read between the lines and muttered to herself. "The lumber camp is full of slave labor. Su-dae is getting the materials China needs at the expense of the Korean people." She wrote back:

> *I miss you so much. The children, all now at the orphanage, need me. I cannot leave them. We must do what fate has destined for us.*
>
> *I hate that we are separated. Soon we will be together. Come see me when you can get away.*
>
> *Love, Sun-hee.*

63 — Change in Authority - Summer, 1994

The children grew fast, but not quickly enough for Sun-hee. She wanted them to grow up, learn everything, and change Korea. On the eighth of July, the news of the death of Kim Il-sung arrived at the camp. Sun-hee's heart bounded with the hope that a change in leadership would end the class system.

She made a call to Tae-seon to get any inside news. Tae-seon informed her of a short call from Hong-do, where he told her he did not anticipate change in policy. Those who held power in the Workers Party were not going to alter the plan. If anything, their controlling grip on the nation would increase.

***

Sun-hee was on the porch of the House of Sanshin when she first noticed a general wandering around the camp. He was short and thin, but he carried himself like he was in command of everything. His pursed lips and beady eyes seemed to look through walls, taking note of all the hidden secrets.

She watched the officer walk in and out of buildings and finally towards the house of Sanshin. Sun-hee slipped inside as he approached, then she held and talked to children while keeping an eye on the general's movements. The general never looked down as he walked through the house, avoiding the energetic five-year-old children. Sun-hee remained inconspicuous, wondering what he was doing at the camp. He walked out and proceeded into the apartment area. Sun-hee went out to the porch of the House of Sanshin. Young-ja, then Eun-seong, and finally Choe-me joined her. Together, they watched as this man moved about the camp.

"Who is this general? What do you think he is looking for?" asked Eun-seong.

"I have not seen him before," said Young-ja.

"He is making me nervous," said Choe-me.

Finally, the general stopped in the middle of the camp and yelled in a loud, authoritative voice, "Who is in charge here?"

They watched a teenage orphan run over and bow deeply while saying something. "Bring him to me," the general bellowed.

The orphan ran to the hospital. A few moments later, Chulsoon came out with the teenager close behind. They watched Chulsoon walk confidently to the general. After a brief exchange, Chulsoon pointed to the command building and escorted the general there. The two disappeared inside.

The four women grasped hands in their nervousness. "I get a terrible vibe from this general," said Eun-seong.

"Me, too," said Sun-hee. "Nothing good can come from a general arriving at the camp. Where is his staff? Why is he alone?"

"Well, I have a strong urge to walk into the command house and talk to this general," said Young-ja. "He could be an imposter, here by himself. Or he could be inspecting us for some reason."

"We must wait," said Sun-hee, turning to go back inside. "Chulsoon will fill us in as soon as he can. Let's get back to the children."

The sun had set by the time Chulsoon made his way to the guesthouse. Together they sat down to talk.

Chulsoon said, "General Baik Hae-sup has decided to retire after forty-five years of service. He is looking for a place where he can get away from the front lines. He wants a place that would keep him away from any future war. He likes it here and will be moving in, taking command of the camp. Be ready. Tomorrow, he wants to address all the officers."

"What did you talk about all afternoon?" questioned Young-ja.

"He wanted to know about all the logistics of the area. How we maintained food and supplies. How many children there are. The history of the camp. Everything about how I run this camp. I filled him in, except for the eugenics. I emphasized this is a school, hospital, and a place for orphans."

"Is he going to stay here?" blurted Choe-me.

"Yes," Chulsoon replied. "I think he has found in this camp a place to get away from the political tension. I do not like him coming in and taking over. The camp is running smoothly. We don't need anyone to make changes or tell us what to do."

The next morning after breakfast, the message was circulated for all officers to report to the library at ten. The four women walked over together and sat at a table. Chulsoon and three disabled sergeants who worked at the camp arrived and took seats. It was precisely at ten when General Baik entered. Everyone stood and saluted.

The general glared at the four women for a few seconds before returning the salute. He looked over at the sergeants with a satisfied smile. One was missing a foot and stood with a crutch. The other two were each missing an arm as well as showing scars from injuries. Then he turned to Chulsoon. "Introduce your staff."

Chulsoon proceeded to introduce the others in the room.

"How did four women attain the rank of lieutenant?" Gen. Baik asked in a commanding voice.

Young-ja spoke up, "We were all medical staff at this facility and were awarded the rank during the war."

"You look familiar," said Gen. Baik, pointing to Young-ja.

"For many years, I was a voice on radio and television. When my husband died, I decided to come here to take care of orphans."

"You were a great voice of the party, much better than the women who now fulfill that role. I'm honored to be in this camp with you."

Sun-hee told him of how the four wrote the education materials for the country after the war.

"You have been valuable servants to the Democratic People's Republic of Korea. Your continued devotion to the youth of our country is commendable," said Gen. Baik.

He questioned each of them about their husbands. Choe-me fibbed, saying her husband was dead, not wanting to reveal his fleeing to China. Eun-seong mentioned her husband died of cancer. Sun-hee mentioned Hon-yong was running a lumber mill.

"Continue your work," Gen. Baik said. He glanced at each of them briefly before turning and walking out.

Within a week, Gen. Baik's wife, two sons, and their families arrived. Both sons were army captains. At first, they stayed to themselves. Soon, the sons began to lead exercises, and the women helped with the orphans.

In the fall, Gen. Baik emphasized physical training and being ready to fight when war broke out. He staunchly believed war with South Korea and America would occur.

Gen. Baik's sons oversaw games, Tae Kwon Do, and the physical training of the orphans. The goal was to prepare them for fighting.

***

As for the rest of Korea, the death of Kim Il-sung brought no change. His son, Kim Jong-il took command, the Workers Party leaders maintained the policies and rule of Kim Il-sung.

This gave Sun-hee little hope for the near future of Korea. Her only concern was the one hundred children she was teaching and training, preparing them for a day where they might direct change in a nation of over twenty million and a government who maintained tight control of everything.

Sun-hee was always contemplating what it would take to overcome a culture built on power and greed while keeping it from the chaos of revolution.

64 — The 100 - Fall, 1998 to 1999

Knock, Knock.

The five a.m. wakeup startled Sun-hee from her deep sleep. The schedule demanded by Gen. Baik made her appreciate Sgt. Kua. With endless teaching and training of the children, she could not remember the last time she'd had a day to rest. The ninety-minute morning exercises would start in fifteen minutes.

She pulled her legs up and rubbed her sore, swollen knee. She rolled over on her good side and used that leg to stand. Her shoulders ached, her hips were painful when she walked, but the exercise demanded of her, and everyone else, had brought her to the best physical condition since the war. If only her sixty-three-year-old joints would hold up. She put on the fatigues Gen. Baik insisted all officers wear. The jacket hung loosely, and the pants were baggy but had been hemmed to the right length. She tied her hair back, made sure her lieutenant bars were straight, and limped out to join the rest.

She went through the motions at the back of the lines of children, standing with Choe-me, Young-ja, and Eun-seong. The movement kept her warm in the crisp autumn air while the breeze soon brought her cheeks to a bright red. As soon as the exercise was over, she gobbled her breakfast as fast as she could and then faced five hours of teaching. She taught Korean, Mandarin, Cantonese, Russian, and recently, English.

Gen. Baik had the revelation that if these children knew English, they could better infiltrate South Korea, and the rest of the world, as assassins.

Young-ja taught Korean doctrine and policy. Choe-me taught math. Eun-seong covered the sciences. The fifth class was in military tactics taught by Gen. Baik's sons.

After an hour break for lunch, there was another round of classes followed by intensive physical training for the children. Sun-hee used the evenings to prepare for the next day of teaching and instructed the teachers who taught the other orphans in the camp. Most orphans arrived malnourished and weak. They were years behind the hundred children in their development and abilities, and they struggled to keep up. That evening, she made her way to Chulsoon to see if he could help with her knee.

"Have a seat on the table," instructed Chulsoon. She pushed herself up on the table and pulled up her pant leg, exposing her knee. Chulsoon poked and prodded a few times. Sun-hee winced at the pain.

"Some tendonitis and inflammation," said Chulsoon. "I suspect the meniscus is about gone, causing the bone to rub against bone. What I would like to prescribe is rest and no exercise for a while. I doubt General Baik will allow you to stop the morning exercise. I will send you an ice pack for the knee after exercise and a hot pack for the evenings. Also, take one of these anti-inflammatory pills in the morning and after dinner."

"Thank you, Chulsoon," said Sun-hee.

"On a more important note, Tae-seon called today. She said you needed to call her. You can use the phone in my office."

Sun-hee dialed the cave phone number.

"Hello," came Tae-seon's voice.

"Tae-seon, how are you and your family doing?"

"We are all very well. I have two items of news. First, Su-dae called from China this morning. She wants you to come to China. She has the funds to buy your passage along with anyone you wish to bring. The electric generation business is very profitable. Second, So-min called and wanted to talk to you."

Sun-hee paused for a moment, closing her eyes and sighing.

I am so tired. I could retire in China and live well. Maybe Hon-yong could join me? I have grandchildren there and great-grandchildren I have never met. She paused and groaned. *No, I cannot leave these children. They are the hope for the future.*

"Tell Su-dae I cannot leave right now. I love her and miss her. My work here is important. Promise her I will visit when I can. On our next holiday, I will come to see you. Have you heard any news from Hon-yong?"

"My husband was at the lumber mill last month. Your husband is doing fine. He misses you."

"I miss him dearly," Sun-hee said as her voice cracked and tears trickled down her cheeks. "I miss all of you. Take care, Tae-seon. Goodnight." She hung up the phone and sobbed. In her emotion, she forgot the message from So-min.

Chulsoon sent a note to Gen. Baik informing him of Sun-hee's injury and requested a release from exercise for Sun-hee and the other women. The next day, the knocks on the her door came at six a.m.

On New Year's Day, the camp was set up for games among the

orphans. Foot races and a soccer tournament in the snow was fun to watch. Sun-hee was observing the games with Eun-seong when a car pulled up nearby. So-min stepped out. Sun-hee recognized her and ran through the snow to her daughter, taking her in a hug.

So-min pulled back from her mother's embrace and bowed low saying, "I am so sorry I was mean to those women. I have come to apologize to you and any of the women who are still here. I submit myself to any punishment you may wish to inflict."

Sun-hee reached out and lifted her daughter from her bow. "Being apart and silent towards each other these last seven years has been enough punishment for the both of us." Sun-hee again took her daughter in a warm embrace.

"Thank you for being so forgiving, Mother," she said through tears. "I missed our talks and your wisdom," So-min said tearfully.

"Come," said Sun-hee, putting her arm around So-min. "Let's get something to eat. You can tell me all about your family, and what wonderful things my grandchildren are doing." They ate, talked about family, and what was happening with the hundred children. They went into Sun-hee's home and sat by the stove, continuing their conversation into the afternoon.

"I also wish to tell you about what is happening in genetics research," So-min said, her voice changing to reflect her excitement. "So many new things are going on in America. I wish I had gone with Eun-mi and could do research there. I have also thought about going to China as they are participating in a worldwide project to sequence the human genome. We have been able to replicate much of the research, but we are many years behind. We need better facilities and more people capable of doing research. Can you put the word out to the descendants of Sanshin that we need smart people to assist us in medical research?"

"I can do that," said Sun-hee. "When there is hope for a better future, you know I will support you fully. Tell me more about the new research you are reading about."

For the rest of the afternoon, So-min explained some of the new technologies: the transformation of bacteria, DNA sequencing, genetic engineering of crops, and medical research. Sun-hee listened and questioned how to apply the techniques in Korea. By dinnertime, her daughter had convinced her that genetic manipulation had the potential to meet some essential needs of the people.

After dinner, So-min left. Sun-hee told Young-ja, Choe-me, and

Eun-seong about the research So-min was doing. She knew the country was still in turmoil with the food shortages and emphasis on military preparedness. If the children they were training could get into positions of authority in the military, there might be a chance to influence the government. She would increase her efforts to create a bond between the children and loyalty to her in changing the future.

Two days later, Sun-hee and the other teachers were in the library reviewing the next day's lessons. Gen. Baik walked in and commanded, "Everyone out except the four lieutenants."

When the other women had left, Gen. Baik said, "I need you to tell me the truth as to how one hundred of these children are so special. They are all the same age, and their abilities are far above the other orphans. What do I not know?"

Sun-hee glanced at her friends. They were all looking at her. She raised her head with a guilty look on her face.

"Lieutenant Cha," he barked, "Tell me about these orphans."

Sun-hee stood and cleared her throat before saying, "Yes, General Baik. There are one hundred children here who are part of an experiment. They were conceived by a method called In-Vitro Fertilization. In simpler terms, they are test-tube babies. Eggs and sperm were collected from high-performing individuals across the country and mixed to produce higher-performing children. The four of us, having been involved in writing much of the teaching materials used by our school system, took on the role of raising and educating these children to be leaders for the glory of the Democratic People's Republic of Korea."

Gen. Baik scowled while she spoke. He roared, "Why did I not hear of this before? Who oversees this experiment? What will you do with these children?" His eyes narrowed, and the wrinkles on his forehead stood out.

Sun-hee shook.

Young-ja stood and spoke in soft words, "Respectfully, this experiment carries a need-to-know restriction. Presently, the four of us oversee this program. It was initiated by Doctor General Park Tae-song, who is now deceased, on the authority of the Premier. Our role is to raise the children as loyal subjects of the Democratic People's Republic of Korea. We appreciate your assistance, especially in the physical training of the children. It has enhanced their development."

"Who else knows about these children?" demanded Gen. Baik.

Sun-hee responded, "Doctor Chulsoon, General Park's son, and his staff. My husband and our son. Others only have orders to meet our needs."

"One hundred is not enough. Why isn't there more?"

"The famine had a lot to do with limiting it to one hundred children, sir. Resources were too short to continue producing more children," replied Sun-hee.

Gen. Baik breathed deeply while his eyes darted between the four women. "Who do you report to in Pyongyang?"

"I am not privileged to provide you with that information, General Baik. Soon after you arrived, I made it known to our superior that you were here."

He removed his hat and scratched his nearly bald head, then said, "There is no respect in the capital for retired generals." He readjusted his hat and stood tall. "We will see what these children accomplish. I commend your devotion to raising one hundred children at your age." He turned sharply and marched out of the library. The four women let out a collective sigh.

65 — The New Sanshin - Fall, 2004

The children's soccer games were highly competitive and gave them a chance to show off their physical skills. Standing on the porch of the House of Sanshin allowed a great view of the action. Today, the boys were playing as hard as Sun-hee had ever seen. The referees, some of the older guards, were not calling thrown elbows and hard trips today. The girls had been equal or better players than the boys a couple of years ago. Now at fourteen, the boys were more mature and had increased in physical maturity. They were dominating the girls. A broken jaw suffered by one of the girls convinced Sun-hee to approach Gen. Baik about splitting the genders in physical games.

"You are saying I must separate the genders during games from now on. You think the boys are too strong," said Gen. Baik.

"Yes, sir," Sun-hee said with a bow. "A girl suffered a broken jaw today."

"And I heard a boy broke an arm. Maybe it is time for a change," said Gen. Baik, rubbing his clean-shaven chin. "These kids of yours are more advanced than any recruits I have ever known. You are dismissed, Lieutenant."

What did he mean by time for a change? Sun-hee thought as she left.

A few days later, Sun-hee noticed Young-ja walking towards her across the compound, taking long quick strides.

Something is up.

She made her way down the steps to meet Young-ja.

"General Baik has had a stroke," Young-ja said in a hurried concerned manner. "Chulsoon is with him but did not give the General much hope for recovery."

"Oh my!" exclaimed Sun-hee.

The next day, Gen. Baik died. His sons went into a week of mourning.

The day after his burial, Chulsoon met with Sun-hee and the other women. "I overheard General Baik's sons. They want to make a name for themselves by taking command of our children as an elite unit."

Young-ja went into a long dialogue explaining the reasons why she felt Gen. Baik's sons would intrude. Sun-hee agreed with them all. A change was in the air.

***

A month after General Baik's funeral. They received an order:

> *From this day forward, the Lieutenants will cease classes with the special children and focus their teaching and training on the other orphans.*
>
> *Captain Baik*

***

A few days later, Capt. Baik ordered the children to make themselves ready to leave.

Sun-hee felt nauseous as she lay in bed. She got up, wrapped her blue silk scarf around her neck, went out to the main room, and put the kettle on the stove. She turned and jumped, giving out a slight yell.

"Oh, I did not mean to startle you so," said Eun-seong, taking hold of Sun-hee's arm lightly. "I could not sleep and came out to make some tea. I see you are, as usual, a few steps ahead of me."

"Your company is most welcome," said Sun-hee. "I am so concerned about the future of the children. They are too intelligent to end up on some battlefield where they cannot get away from bombs."

"I was dreaming some of them defied some ridiculous command and were shot," said Eun-seong. "They can reason for themselves and are a little defiant in their youthfulness. They have been challenging me quite often lately, and most of the time, they are right. They have lived only in this camp and have no real-world experience. I fear they will not be accepted and will test authority."

"We taught them all we know," said Sun-hee as she watched the teapot. "I have worked hard these past few years, giving them problems to solve involving human and ethical dilemmas, but I fear I have fallen far short in teaching them how to deal with the real emotions of people. I have been sheltered all these years. What is the real world like?"

"The men did just fine fifty years ago when they went out to their jobs," said Eun-seong reassuringly.

"There was little structure and authority to challenge them after the war. The next generation had the experiences of their fathers to rely on to show them the way. These children will have only themselves as they enter the army."

The kettle whistled. Sun-hee poured the water into a pot and added tea leaves. Eun-seong took two cups, and they sat at the table.

"We knew this day was coming," said Eun-seong. "I can't stand to see them go."

"This must be the feeling all mothers have when their sons and daughters are recruited into the army," said Sun-hee.

"Men should not have the right to make us feel this way," said Sun-hee with anger in her voice. "This is something I will change when I am in charge."

"You are going to take charge of the government?" said Eun-seong.

"If I could change it without bloodshed, I would do it now. Everything I think of leads to chaos and people dying. I'm convinced it can't be done. We are stuck with the fate of being controlled by men with power."

"What are our options?" said Eun-seong. "We can stay here. We could walk into Pyongyang and say we are taking over. We can go to China. Maybe we can lead a revolution from there."

"Maybe we just do what all women do as they approach their seventies. We spend as much time as we can with our grandchildren."

"I thought I was just dreaming when I heard some talking," said Choe-me, walking into the room. "Is there any tea left?"

"Plenty," replied Eun-seong. "All you need is a cup."

"Get two. Young-ja is behind you," said Sun-hee.

"Oh, I would love some tea," said Young-ja. "I got up to make some for myself as I could not sleep. My mind was wandering all night thinking, do I want to stay here and teach the orphans in this camp or go back to Pyongyang?"

"Sun-hee just told me that was an option she was thinking about," said Eun-seong.

Choe-me returned and poured tea for Young-ja and herself, topping off the other cups while she was at it.

"Do you want to go back to Pyongyang with me?" said Young-ja. "We could have such a grand time walking around the city with the other old folks."

"You know Sun-hee better than that. She wants to go to the capital and rule the country," said Eun-seong.

"I'd support her," said Choe-me.

"Wonderful," said Young-ja. "The four of us could attempt a revolution and be shot together. I like this, only because we would all die at once. I do not want you to mourn my death, nor do I look forward to mourning your passing."

"No, no, NO!" Sun-hee exclaimed. "There is no option for a change in our government which does not result in a bloody revolution. I will never be a part of a plan which does. Stop talking about it." The women were silent for a moment.

"I do miss my family," said Choe-me, staring into her cup. "I think it is time for me to make my way to China and spend the rest of my time with my children and grandchildren."

"I have not seen my children in many years, and there are grandchildren I have never met. It is time to go south and visit them. Someone will have space for me, I hope," said Eun-seong softly.

"Maybe I can convince Hon-yong to retire, and we can return to the cave," said Sun-hee. "There is nothing more we can do to make Korea better. We have done all we could. We can only hope our offspring will have better lives and make life in this country better for all."

There was silence for a few moments before Young-ja spoke, "I do not want to leave the three of you. We have been so close all these years. After we say goodbye to the children, can we have a few days here together before we head off?"

Eun-seong reached out and took Young-ja's hand. Then she took Sun-hee's hand. The rest of the hands clasped. "We will always be together in spirit. Our work here has ended. We have a lot to do to build up our families with hope for the future."

"There are phases in life. We are starting a new one," said Choe-me.

***

They met with the children, now mature teenagers, in the afternoon, where they said goodbye to each one. The children thanked them for their education and training. Sun-hee cried most of the day, tearfully accepting the children's gratitude while wishing them well. By the end of the day, she was emotionally exhausted.

Sun-hee retired to the guesthouse and made a pot of tea. She took four cups to the table and sat, staring into her cup of tea and wondering what would happen to the children. Soon Choe-me, Eun-seong, and Young-ja joined her, sitting in silence and sipping tea.

A knock at the door startled all four women. They stood in unison. Sun-hee opened the door to see one of the girls standing at attention. She was taller than Sun-hee by a few centimeters and filled her uniform to where it looked a size or two too small.

"I am here to request the presence of our honorable teachers in the dorm. Will you allow me to escort you?" said the young girl calmly.

Sun-hee replied, "Yes, I would…" she looked at the others before correcting herself, "We would be pleased to be escorted to the dorm."

They followed the young girl as she marched like a soldier ahead of them. When they entered the House of Sanshin, all the children were dressed sharply in uniform. The girl who had led them turned to face the four women and saluted. The rest saluted in unison. Sun-hee stood for a moment before realizing she needed to return the salute.

As she put her hand down, one boy, Gan Li-sam, stepped forward. "We do not have much to give to you to show our thanks for the many hours you spent in guiding our education. As your great-grandchildren we wish to offer you something to remember us. We tried to find a camera so we could offer you photographs, instead, we have drawn our portraits and put them in notebooks." Four of them stepped forward and handed each a notebook.

Sun-hee took hers and looked through some of the pages, recalling each name. "Thank you. Thank you so much." She sniffled and glanced over her shoulder to see Eun-seong wiping away tears with a hanky and tears in Young-ja's eyes. She wiped the moisture from her own eyes as she turned to the children.

"We will always be loyal to you and what you have taught us," said the girl who had led them to the dorm.

Sun-hee looked at them and felt it was time to give one last bit of instruction, but her mind raced around her life, wondering where to begin. She swallowed deeply and began speaking, "Life often goes in stages. Tomorrow, you start a new phase, one full of trials and danger. I do not know anything about army training camps. What I do know is the men and women I have met who are soldiers are strong.

"You are some of the best people in Korea. You may wonder how I know. It is because you were designed to be the best. Let me tell you a little history."

"Fifty-four years ago, General Park brought forty-eight children to this camp. We were only fifteen, a year older than you. He brought us here in a deception. We thought we were attending a superior school. General Park's plan was to have us make babies who would be better physically and mentally than the rest of the people in Korea. Our children would then be able to make Korea a great nation. Part of his plan worked. The forty-eight of us and our offspring have taken positions of leadership across the country. North Korea is better off because of the efforts and sacrifices of the forty-eight. We remember those who have passed with the images on the wall behind you." She pointed, then paused as the soldiers turned to look.

"You are the fourth generation born in this program, designed to be more advanced than any generation before you. The Premier approved the program, yet after all these years, I believe our existence is now unknown to the government."

"You," she said, pointing to the girl in front of her, "have just confessed your loyalty to me. First, we must be loyal to our Supreme Leader and loyal to the Democratic People's Republic of Korea. Then you must be loyal to each other and finally to me. Only be loyal to me if it does not conflict with your loyalty to the nation. Finally, do not harm people unless they are showing harm to others."

"You have the ability to be a positive change in the country. Be careful, as our biggest fear is that we have not been able to expose you to the real world. What you will see and experience is very different from life in this camp. Humble yourselves to those in power. If you do, they will take you in and help you succeed. I don't know what the future holds nor what you will do in the future. I do know that you are better prepared to do something greater than any other children...I should say, young soldiers, in the history of Korea.

"Fifty-four years ago, we assembled in this room and named it the House of Sanshin. Today, I appoint you as new members of the House of Sanshin." She reached out to take Choe-me and Eun-seong's hands. Choe-me took Young-ja's hand, and she reached out and took a hand in the crowd. "We are loyal to Kim Jong-il," Sun-hee said in a loud voice.

The soldiers echoed the chant.

"We are loyal to the Democratic People's Republic of Korea!" Sun-hee said firmly.

The soldiers followed.

"We are loyal to the House of Sanshin!"

They all yelled in unison, "We are loyal to the House of Sanshin."

Sun-hee considered the eyes of the children staring at her. "You have given me hope for the future. Thank you." She turned and walked out, trembling, nearly stumbling down the steps.

What will become of these children?

66 — Departures, Fall, 2004 - Winter, 2005

Eun-seong, Young-ja, Choe-me, and Sun-hee stood outside their home nervously waiting for the new soldiers. Gen. Baik's sons had walked by moments before and entered the House of Sanshin. Chulsoon walked up, followed by his sons.

"Good morning," said Chulsoon with a polite bow.

"Good morning, Chulsoon," said Young-ja. "Nice to see you and your sons so early on this fine fall morning."

Sun-hee looked up at the wispy clouds, orange from the rising sun blowing in the brisk fall wind. She tucked in her scarf and pulled her jacket around her.

"I'm sad to see these children leaving at this young age," said Chulsoon. "They need to grow up a little more before being exposed to the world."

"We cannot protect them forever," said Young-ja. "They are the new Sanshin."

The door to the dorms opened. The two captains led the recruits. Two-by-two, they filed out, a line of young women and a line of young men. The four women and Chulsoon saluted the captains who returned the salute. The recruits saluted as they passed. They were all tall, lean, and muscular. In their uniforms, they were a good-looking team of soldiers. A minute later, the lines ended, and the women released their salute.

The rumble of diesel truck engines coming to life thundered through the morning air.

Chulsoon turned to the women and said, "Now we only have the orphans to teach. They will not be such good learners."

"We have some bad news for you, Chulsoon," said Young-ja. "We have decided to return to our families and spend time with our grandchildren. We will not be here to help you with the orphans. I hope you can survive without us."

"I am sure my sons can run this place without us," replied Chulsoon. "I must also confess to some bad news. I have prostate cancer. My prognosis is that I will be dead within a year, maybe within a few months."

"Oh, no, Chulsoon!" cried out, Young-ja. "You can't be dying."

Eun-seong reached out and put her arms around Chulsoon even though it was not an acceptable thing to do. "I am so sorry," she said in his ear and started to weep on his shoulder.

Choe-me and Sun-hee reached out and joined the embrace. Chulsoon's sons stood awkwardly nearby.

"It's my time and my way to depart. Please do not mourn for me," pleaded Chulsoon as he released himself from their embrace. "My sons will take good care of me and this camp. I am happy to hear you have decided to leave and return to your families. Those children have given me some hope for the country." Chulsoon stood, blinking his moist eyes, wringing his hands, and said, "There are some children in the hospital who need looking after. I'll see you before you leave." He bowed, as did his sons, before walking away.

Sun-hee walked quickly into the house and slammed her fists onto the table. "All Chulsoon has done for others in this life, and his end is to die from cancer. The fates are so unfair," she spat out loudly.

"Sun-hee, Chulsoon has accepted his fate and, thus, so should we," said Choe-me.

"We have not accepted our fate since we became part of the House of Sanshin," said Sun-hee, looking at Choe-me. "We have spent our lives making the lives of other people better. To what end? To watch the army take our children while our bodies are killing us from the inside."

Eun-seong stepped up to Sun-hee. "What would we be if we did not try? Many of the orphans would have starved or been enslaved by others without Chulsoon. They have a life because he worked so hard. We cannot live forever. We leave behind a better world."

"Is Korea a better place?" said Sun-hee forcefully to Eun-seong's face. "Take a good look at what the forty-eight prize-winners have done. All the technology and resources we have worked on has provided a better place for the government to maintain their life of greed and power. Too many of us have died, many of our families have left. For what? I have no hope anymore."

Young-ja stepped between Eun-seong and Sun-hee and took hold of Sun-hee's upper arms. "I will commit to investigating ways to change the government when I get to Pyongyang. If I must start a revolution, I will. Something must change…"

"…or we will die trying. Is that what you want to say," interrupted Sun-hee. "So many have tried, and so many have died. For years, I monitored the reports. You knew men and women who opposed the

Worker's Party. Where are they now? What has changed?"

Eun-seong interrupted. "I will work with my grandchildren and great-grandchildren to install our spirit in them. Our hope lies in our descendants now."

"I feel like I am abandoning you by going to my family in China," said Choe-me in a soft meek voice. "The years have allowed my heart to mend. Now I long to be with my husband and grandchildren."

"Going to the cave seems like retreating. How can I do anything there?"

"Be our communication center again," said Young-ja. "Something will happen. We need you there."

Sun-hee looked at Young-ja for a moment, turned, and went to her room.

The next day the four women were packed and ready to depart. Eun-seong said, "I am going to take down the drawings of those who have passed. They will have no meaning hanging on the walls of the empty House of Sanshin."

"What will you do with them?" asked Choe-me.

"I will keep them with the rest. Many years ago, I finished all of the drawings in case I passed before they were complete."

"May I hang them in the cave? I can make a memorial wall along the tunnel," said Sun-hee.

"I think the cave would be a great place for them," said Young-ja.

Choe-me left to get Chulsoon. Then the five of them solemnly took down the drawings of those who had already passed. Eun-seong put them with the others in a folder, holding back her tears, she handed it to Sun-hee saying, "I hope that all of you will not mourn my passing. I have cried while drawing each picture, and that is enough."

"We have all had a fulfilling life," said Chulsoon. "I am sorry I must leave you and my family. I wish you all well." He turned while wiping his sleeve across his face.

Sun-hee held the folder against her breast as they walked back to their house.

Eun-seong and Young-ja took a car to Chongjin where they would catch a train south. Choe-me and Sun-hee departed for the cave. When they arrived, they put up the pictures of the thirty deceased prize-winners. The next day, Choe-me left for China.

***

Sun-hee tried to spend time with her grandchildren and great-grandchildren, but they were more interested in things other than learning. She watched American movies with the children.

Hong-do continued to forward movies when he could get them. Most of the voiceovers were in Mandarin. She tried to assist the children with their language skills using the films to learn.

Sun-hee wrote to Hon-yong asking him to join her. In his reply, he said he would come home for good within a month. She was so excited.

Tae-seon spent only a little time each day reviewing messages and had not kept up with world affairs. Sun-hee wondered if knowing what was going on in the world was important. Hon-yong brought home new communication equipment to upgrade what was in the cave.

Since she had little else to do, she began to play with the computer and the internet. North Korean intelligence was using internet access, acquired from China, to spy on the world. She began to see what she could find and was not impressed. She passed the time reading novels, waiting for her husband to return.

Hon-yong walked into the cave on the first of December. Sun-hee jumped up and ran to leap into his arms. Then she forced herself to stop and gently put her arms around her husband. He was so thin, Sun-hee could feel his ribs as she held him tight. His once stout body was frail and weak. His cheekbones stuck out from his hollow face, and his jaw jutted out. What was left of his hair was white and hung over his ears.

"Oh, Hon-yong," said Sun-hee. She started to cry.

He coughed violently and released his hug to cover his mouth.

"My husband, you are ill. Come, and we will get you some food. Have you not had enough to eat?"

"My dear Sun-hee. I did not want to come to you like this," said Hon-yong softly. "But I had to see you again. There were no antibiotics at the mill. I fear my tuberculosis has progressed too far."

"Come, I will take care of you. Best we go to the cave and not expose others." She put his arm around his shoulder, helped him to the cave, and laid him in bed. Then she frantically sent messages to everyone to send her antibiotics.

The medicine was received too late. Hon-yong died in Sun-hee's arms a week after he arrived. Sun-hee went into mourning. Hon-yong was buried a week later in the valley near the pile of rocks which was once Jin-taek's home.

I always loved you, Hon. You were so handsome, Sun-hee thought as she hung Hon-yong's picture, drawn by Eun-seong on the cave wall next to

Chulsoon. *He was strong, confident, and capable.* She beat her fists against the paneling, wailing at the fates of life.

She moved into the cave and spent the winter holed up, eating little, seldom bathing. Her hair was unkempt, and her fingernails grew long. She refused to see her grandchildren. Tae-Seon became afraid of her. Hon-yong Jr. brought her food. His presence reminded her of her husband, so she hid when she heard him coming. She spent her days sitting in the kitchen by the stove, staring at the frozen, snow-covered valley.

***

In late February, Sun-hee heard the phone ring. It had not rung in months. She picked up the receiver. "Mother. Help!" cried a voice over the phone. "I need you. Can you come right away?"

"What do you need me for, So-min?" Sun-hee replied tersely.

"I'll explain when you get here," replied So-min's urgent voice over the phone. "Please, come quickly," she pleaded. "I cannot talk now." The other end went silent.

Sun-hee stood with the receiver in her hand for a moment before putting it down.

Why am I needed and not wanted?

Part Four - San Yeosin

67 — Rats - Late Winter to Spring, 2005

After tossing and turning for unknown hours, Sun-hee sat up. Sleep would not be her escape this night.

What does So-min need of me after five years of not talking? Seven years before then? She was all worked up about modifying bacteria the last time we spoke. What is she up to now?

She turned on the lights and took a hot bath. Then she made up her hair, trimmed her nails, and put on a clean dress. The clock said, three am. It would be hours before Hon-yong Jr. brought breakfast. She made some tea, fidgeted, cleaned up the kitchen, and wiped the condensation from the windows, hoping to see the falling snow. It was another hour before there was enough light to see the white valley.

She heard the door latch and ran to meet Hon-yong Jr. "I need to go see So-min today. When can you take me?"

"Good to see you are up and about, Mother," replied Hon-yong Jr. in a calm voice as he sat a steaming bowl on the table. "What is so urgent that you need to risk the icy roads?"

"I don't know. So-min called last night saying she needed me to come right away. Then she hung up."

"I have things that need my attention today. Would it be okay with you if someone else drove you to the gulag?" he asked.

"Yes. Anyone," she urgently replied and began to eat breakfast like a hungry dog.

"Come down when you finish eating. Dress warmly, the heater in the truck does not work, and it is bitter cold out this morning."

Sun-hee finished breakfast and realized she hadn't eaten a full meal in months. She put on her coat, grabbed a blanket and the empty bowl, then headed down the mineshaft.

The ride was cold and slow on the icy road. Sun-hee watched the white mountainside go by, her mind lost in all the possible reasons So-min needed her so badly.

After a four-hour ride, she climbed out of the truck, telling her grandson she would call when she was ready to return home. She walked into the gulag medical facility and asked for Cha So-min.

The receptionist hesitated, finally saying, "I'm sorry, Cha So-min is not able to see anyone right now."

"Is Doctor Park Duk-bae available?" Sun-hee demanded.

"He is…I…I am..." she stuttered.

"I must see my daughter," Sun-hee insisted. "If you do not point the way, I will go find her."

The woman gave a slight nod of her head, directing her down the hall, saying meekly, "The last door."

Something is not right. That woman is afraid.

Sun-hee strode quickly away. When she opened the door, Duk-bae was there with his back to her. He was in a white gown and pants, holding a stethoscope on the chest of what Sun-hee concluded was a young unclothed woman. Her face did not look feminine, and there wasn't a hair on her head. What gave the gender away was the budding breasts.

"Duk-bae, I am here to see So-min," said Sun-hee as she caught a glimpse of three other men in the room.

Duk-Bae turned quickly to face Sun-hee and walked towards her.

"You are not wanted here," he said with a wave of his arm. "Go back to the camp and take care of the orphans."

"I am not leaving until I see So-min," Sun-hee said in a stern voice.

"You cannot see her. Leave, or I will have you thrown out in the snow," Duk-bae said a couple of centimeters from his mother-in-law's face.

"You will not lay a hand on me. Take me to So-min or I will go find her myself," Sun-hee said without moving.

Duk-bae motioned with his right hand to one of the men. "Take her to So-min's room and leave her there."

The man took Sun-hee's arm. Sun-hee pulled it away. "I can walk by myself. Thank you."

Duk-bae nodded. The man led Sun-hee out of the room and to a flight of stairs. Sun-hee seized a firm hold of the rail and stepped slowly, using her right leg on each step to lift her. The man waited at the top, tapping his foot and glancing between Sun-hee and the hallway.

Sun-hee ascended the last step and said, "Don't be such an impatient young man. Someday you will have old knees."

The man moved three doors down the hall and removed a latch. When Sun-hee caught up, the man cautiously opened the door. The room was dark.

"Mother!" yelled So-min's voice.

Then So-min rushed out of the room, tackling the young man, knocking him to the floor. She sat atop the man and clasped her hands around his neck.

"So-min, stop!" yelled Sun-hee, grabbing her daughter and pulling. She was too weak to remove her daughter's hands, which were firmly pressed into the man's neck.

The man struggled as Sun-hee pleaded for So-min to release him. The man's eyes closed. His breath stopped.

So-min released her grasp, and he wheezed in a breath then coughed. She stood, grabbing the man's legs and lugged him into the room where she was captive, latching the door.

"What is going on?" asked Sun-hee.

So-min looked up and down the corridor and said, "Come on, we need to get somewhere safer." She grabbed Sun-hee's hand and pulled her down the hall, coercing her up a flight of stairs. Then she strong-armed Sun-hee into a storeroom and stopped.

"I knew you would come and rescue me. Is Hon-yong with you?"

Sun-hee paused to catch her breath. "Hon-yong is dead. Why were you a captive?"

"Who is with you?" asked So-min.

"Just me. Now talk."

So-min took a couple of deep breaths. "Duk-bae started doing experiments on people." The words flew out of her mouth. "I did the research and let him do the experiments. When I found out he had started working on people, I opposed him. He locked me up."

"The young woman I saw who had masculine features, was she one of his experiments?" asked Sun-hee.

"Testosterone and growth hormones. At high doses it turns a woman into a man," blurted So-min. "There are worse, much worse cases."

So-min turned towards the door at the sound of footsteps. "Check every room," came a voice from the hallway.

"Duk-bae," whispered So-min as she looked for a place to hide in the little room.

The door opened. A man in a white coat stood in the doorway. "Here they are," he yelled over his shoulder.

Duk-bae strode into the room, a long knife in his hand. "I should have done this earlier. Then your mother would not have been included." He lunged at So-min.

So-min dodged, deflecting the knife with her forearm while incurring a deep gash. She grabbed Duk-Bae around the head with her right arm.

Sun-hee interlaced her fingers over her head and struck Duk-bae's arm with all her might, knocking the knife from his hand.

So-min and Duk-bae struggled. He seized her round the waist, lifted her, and threw her to the floor. So-min held on, pulling Duk-Bae on top of her, but lost her grip when she crashed onto the concrete. Duk-bae sat up and pounded her face with his fists over and over.

Sun-hee picked up the knife at her feet, grabbed Duk-bae's hair in her left hand, pulled back and swiped the knife across his throat. Blood spurted across the room onto the wall and floor.

Duk-bae grabbed at his throat. Sun-hee released his hair, and he fell on his side, looking up at her as his blood drained from his neck. So-min lay unconscious next to her husband.

Sun-hee stood up straight to see the men in the doorway start to move towards her.

So, this will be how I die.

She looked again at her daughter, lying lifeless in a pool of Duk-bae's blood. She tossed the knife at the feet of the approaching men. Then she knelt beside So-min, checking to see if she was breathing.

Two men grabbed Sun-hee's arms and hauled her to the room where she found So-min. They closed and latched the door, casting her into darkness.

She sat on the edge of the bed.

So-min is dead. I killed Duk-Bae. I am a murderer. What will happen next?

She felt sick to her stomach. Her head began to spin. She laid down and fell asleep.

"Mrs. Cha. Mrs. Cha," said a voice, startling her awake. She sat up abruptly and beheld a man in the doorway. "Mrs. Cha. Please come with me."

Sun-hee shook her head to clear the cobwebs. She shivered as events of the day came back to her. She made her way to her feet and followed the man to a conference room.

So-min sat at one end of a long table, her eyes nearly swollen shut. Bandages wrapped around her head and left arm. Sun-hee stepped quickly to her side to embrace her daughter. "So-min, you're alive. I thought you were dead."

"The doctors say I will be fine in a few days. For now, my head hurts, and my arm throbs."

"Please sit-down, Mrs. Cha," said a man, pulling out a chair next to So-min.

Sun-hee sat and looked at the men in the room. Four stood by the far wall, their hands clasped in front of them, their chins held low, mouths pursed. Their eyes darted away from her glance. One stood mid-table, his hands at his side, staring at the middle of the table. The man who held her chair walked to the other side of the table and stood against the wall.

"What are you going to do with us?" asked the man staring at the table.

Sun-hee looked up quickly at the man. Then she turned her head slowly to gape at So-min.

So-min spoke, "I am not going to punish any of you. You were only following the commands of Duk-bae. There are some experiments…no! There are some people you need to care for in the lab. Then we need to terminate all further experiments."

So-min stood. "Come with me, Mother. Let's get something to eat."

Over dinner, So-min explained, "The experiments you saw were with growth hormones and steroids. For a few years now, Duk-bae has been modifying the doses on young men and women to determine the best combination. At first, the testing did little to hurt the patients. As Duk-bae used larger doses, the subjects developed issues such as sterility, sex changes, and then cancers."

She took a bite before continuing. "A few years ago, Duk-bae started adding or altering chromosomes on rats. Last year, without my knowledge, he started to modify chromosomes in fertilized human eggs and implanting them in women. Most of the fetuses were miscarriages or stillborn. Many of the live births revealed severe deformities. Only a few were healthy enough to survive. When I found out about these experiments, I tried to stop him. He beat me and locked me up."

"Now, can you get away from here? Come live with me. Enough of this gulag and this hospital."

"No, Mother. I want to stay here. There is a possibility of curing many genetic diseases and improving humans. A lot of research needs to be done to perfect the processes of genetic manipulation. There can be no mistakes with humans. But there is some hope."

"What could a perfect human accomplish? The one hundred IVF children I raised are wonderful. We could produce more."

"Where are they? What are they doing?" So-min asked anxiously.

"I don't know. The army found out about them and sent them to training camps in the south. They are on their own."

"All that effort and you lose influence over them? What a waste! Currently, I can make a quicker and healthier rat. I think I can make a smarter rat. There is also the possibility of extending life, maybe doubling it. In America, the whole human genome is now online available to everyone. Incredible amounts of information are being added every day." So-min's voice got more and more excited with each statement she spoke. "What if we could make people resistant to viruses and bacteria. Cholera, colds and flu, pneumonia and tuberculosis all conquered by changing our genetics."

"Tuberculosis? It killed him," Sun-hee said quietly looking down at the floor.

"Killed who?" asked So-min.

"Hon-yong."

"I am so sorry mother," said So-min, putting her hand on her mother's arm. "You didn't tell me how he died."

Her chest grew heavy as she thought about her husband. "I…I have not told anyone. I have been hiding since he passed. Your call brought me out of the cave." Sun-hee looked up at her daughter. "Wait, you're not mourning your husband. I killed Duk-bae, and you are not the least bit sad."

"Our relationship was over years ago. We have lived at opposite ends of this facility for a long time. I could never bring myself to harm Duk-bae, but now that he is gone, I feel like a mountain has been lifted off me. I ordered his body put in the gulag grave. There will be no funeral ceremony. I will not mourn the person who was trying to beat me to death," So-min ended, staring at her empty plate.

"I am sorry Duk-bae was not good to you," Sun-hee said in an empathetic voice. "I take the blame for putting the two of you together. Now, I regret my decision. But there was no other person I was willing to have him marry."

"What are you going to do now?" asked So-min.

"I don't know."

"Stay here with me and help me with my genetic research."

"For a while. Maybe you can show me how you access the genetic information in America," said Sun-hee.

"Access is easy. I connect through an anonymous server in China, which routes my requests for information through a couple of other servers, and then a hub in Hanoi. To the Americans, I look like a university student. I can set you up an account."

**

Sun-hee learned how to search for information from all over the world.

The two of them spent a lot of time defining what research would be relevant. Finding the genetic makeup which makes a Korean person Korean, was of high importance. Then understanding what the optimum genetic composition for a Korean person was and what made a person smart, healthy, and wise. The Americans were working hard on curing diseases. Their research was easy to access. By the end of the second week, So-min felt she had a good plan. All Sun-hee could do to help was check in on her periodically to encourage her in her work.

Sun-hee went back to the cave and started to research how genetics could be used to improve Korea.

68 — Blame - Spring, 2010

The last five years went by slowly for Sun-hee. She kept communication open with her remaining peers by contacting them every month. She investigated the use of GMOs but felt the expertise was not available to make the seeds required every year. She did pass on information about growing better crops to the few descendants of the Sanshin who were in farming areas. Transforming bacteria to make drugs was a possibility, but building the infrastructure required too much investment and involvement by the government, and she was concerned about the possibility of weaponizing bacteria.

There was nothing she could change and nothing changing on its own in North Korea to improve the lives of the people. She tried to help with Hon-yong Jr's grandchildren, but they were more interested in things other than learning from great-grandma. She was tired of reading books and thought about writing one. But if she were to write down her real thoughts, they would get her, and everyone associated with her, thrown in the gulag.

So-min continued her genetic work on rats. She told Sun-hee on one of their calls that she needed a DNA sequencer. Sun-hee mentioned the request to Su-dae who sent one via Young-soo. So-min also acquired something called CRISPR, which reportedly would allow her to edit chromosomes. She was having fun making better rats in the lab but assured her mother she was staying away from any experiments on humans. Sun-hee made sure to talk to her every week to keep her spirits up.

She received a call from Su-dae in early March. "Guess what, Mother. I found Eun-mi through an internet search and sent him a message. I got a long e-mail back."

"You got ahold of my son! How is he?"

"He is very well. The entire family is living in upstate New York." She went on to read the e-mail, bringing joy to Sun-hee's heart.

"I am so happy he is in America and doing what he loves," said Sun-hee.

"You can go to America, Mother. I'll contact Young-soo, and he can transport you here. We can fly to New York. Then you can remain here in China. We have space for you and would love to have you."

"That is something I will keep in mind. I do not feel I am ready to leave yet."

"Mother, you will not believe the home I have here."

"No one believes how nice a home I already have."

"Oh, Mother. Whenever you are ready, our house is yours. I need to go. Bye."

***

On Sunday, April fifteenth, Sun-hee was enjoying the Day of the Sun holiday with Hon-yong Jr's family. There was a knock at the door. It was Ok-myung, daughter of Hong-do.

They talked for a while, catching up on family before Ok-myung asked, "May we speak privately?"

"Yes, we can talk in the garden," replied Sun-hee, ushering the way with her hand.

"I want to visit the valley while I am here. May we go there?" Ok-myung asked.

"Yes," replied Sun-hee. "Let me get a wrap as it may be chilly."

Sun-hee grabbed a shawl then led the woman through the mine to the elevator and down to the valley. They walked through the leaf-covered rocks and shrubs to the river.

Ok-myung said, "I remember your wedding in this valley. It is more spectacular in the springtime. I am in awe at the lush foliage and the river."

Sun-hee led her to the river where the sound of rushing water over the rocks would almost drown out their voices when spoken directly to each other. She turned to face the woman. "This is a place where we speak privately. What do you wish to discuss?"

"The reason I have come," said Ok-myung as she repositioned herself and looked Sun-hee directly in the eye. "First, Yong-gak and Hong-do are in good health. Since Huang Jang-yop defected, Yong-gak went into seclusion. He isolated himself to do research and give advice to our leaders. He got a coded message to Hong-do that they need to correct a crucial error of the House of Sanshin."

"What did we do wrong?" asked Sun-hee.

"We did nothing wrong. Yong-gak believes our error was that we were too good. He feels that if he did not give such good advice to the Premier, the Premier might have been less of a leader. The efforts of Young-soo, Weon-kee, and Chong-pil supported the economy. Gil-hyung and his sons expertly ran the finances of the country. You and your mother wrote the materials that educated the masses to follow and be loyal to Korea. If the House of Sanshin were not so competent at the roles we play in our society, the Kim's dynasty would not have survived this long."

Sun-hee sat on a rock and buried her head in her hands. Ok-myung sat and put her arm around Sun-hee.

"Strategist is right. We have propped up a family of madmen to rule Korea," said Sun-hee as she lifted her head.

"Hong-do sent me to ask for your help to devise a way to change our government. To change our country, we need new leaders with a new vision and less corruption. My grandfather needs a person who could lead our nation."

"Your grandfather would be a great leader as would your father," said Sun-hee.

"They say they are too old, and officials would notice any attempt by them to organize change. The new leader must be someone outside the current government. They were hoping one of the hundred children would be a capable leader."

"There are two who became leaders of the rest. However, I have lost contact with them," Sun-hee said, looking down at the ground. "They were taken into the army six years ago, they are twenty years old now. I have not heard anything about them. Before they left, they committed their loyalty to the House of Sanshin and each other." She paused, gazing around at the valley, collecting her thoughts. "I do not know of a person who could run our country. I have spent countless hours considering how to change our government without bloodshed. How would this be done?"

"Hong-do believes a revolution can occur without great bloodshed," Ok-myung said. "What is needed is a strong young leader to rise and be the face of a revolution. Someone with charisma who the people would follow."

"If they are planning a bloody revolution, tell Hong-do I will not help him," said Sun-hee sternly.

"So many are dying at the hands of the government. A bloody revolution would be less painful than what we have now."

"I will look for a new leader, only if there is a plan for a change in leadership without bloodshed or at least limited casualties. I have devoted my life to improving Korea. I will not contribute to anything that tears it down. Your task is to convince your father and grandfather to make a revolution occur without death and destruction."

"What you are proposing has rarely occurred in the history of the world. Especially in a country where power is held so absolutely, like this one," her granddaughter claimed. "I will convey your position to my father. He is without hope."

"As am I. As am I…" said Sun-hee with sadness in her voice. "I do thank you for coming. I felt as if I were the only person who was considering these things seriously. But what have we to gain if thousands or more are killed in the attempt? All that blood would be on our hands."

"The Worker's Party sheds the blood of suspected dissenters every day," said Ok-myung. "Our inaction increases bloodshed. Where is the balance?"

Sun-hee's lips pressed together. Her granddaughter's words sliced to her heart. Ok-myung spoke precisely what Sun-hee had felt for a long time. Without a proper leader, there was no hope.

The two of them went back to the house and enjoyed the holiday meal. Ok-myung left long after the sun had gone behind the mountains. Sun-hee hugged everyone before retiring to the cave where she spent the night reviewing all the descendants of Sanshin, hoping to discover someone who could be the leader of the country. She lamented, having lost contact with the hundred children she ordered and then raised.

The sun was coming up as she made her third pot of tea. An idea came to her. She called So-min. "I need to talk to you. I am coming up today."

"It will be good to see you, Mother," said So-min.

Sun-hee hung up and went to find Hon-yong Jr. to arrange a ride.

This day, Hon-yong Jr. drove to the gulag himself. When he inquired about what was happening, Sun-hee told him it was better he did not know and implored him to drive faster. Upon arriving, Sun-hee sent her son home and would call when she could return.

She found So-min and demanded a private place to talk. They went to the conference room and closed the door. Sun-hee took her daughter's shoulders and said, "I am going to tell you to do something that I asked you not to do. Make a modified human."

"What? Mother? Why? What changed your mind?" So-min stumbled out the questions.

"It became clear to me," Sun-hee said. "If we are to change Korea, we need a change in leadership. Since I have not been able to come up with a person alive who is capable of leading Korea properly, I think we should make one."

"Make one?" exclaimed So-min. "A new leader? I can make a new person who has the best of human abilities, but I cannot make them a leader."

"Make me a person who could lead with intellect, wisdom, strength, and most of all, charisma, and I will teach them how to lead." The words came forcefully from Sun-hee's mouth.

"The…the processes are there," So-min stammered. "We have almost perfected them. I guess I know what to include. But there are so many variables. I don't know if I can make one person who will have all the abilities you need."

"How many would you need to make to cover all the variables?" demanded Sun-hee.

"I…I have never seen you like this, Mother," implored So-min.

"There is no hope of making a change in our government unless we have a leader who can take over. We need such a person!" Sun-hee demanded. "You need to make me that person! Can you do it?" Sun-hee said, hitting her fist on the table.

"I…I will try. It's just …"

Sun-hee cut her off. "Try your best." Then she paused for a moment and put her hand on So-min's arm. "If you cannot, then we will go to China and live out our lives with Su-dae. We will give up on Korea."

"It is possible," said So-min while brushing hair back. "Help me define what this person needs to be like, and I will attempt to rearrange genes to make this person."

Over the next week, the two of them defined the traits needed for a person who could lead the country. Then Sun-hee went home. When she arrived, she called Ok-myung and gave her a simple message. "There is no one alive who can do what you asked. We will make someone who can."

69 — Bees - Early July, 2011

Sun-hee swatted at a bee on the sliced fruit before her. They were so pesky in the warmth of the summer sun. Her swing missed but had the desired effect of getting the bee away from her food. She watched as two bees tried to enter a wild iris a meter in front of her. She took a bite of apricot. The insects seemed to be more numerous along the river this year. There were many flowers, yet the bees would compete to pollinate them.

She went back to her thoughts on how to get one of the six designed males who would be born next month, into a position of power. She had put together a complete education plan in case she passed before they reached maturity. Her days over the past year had focused on revising a daily instruction plan from birth to the age of eighteen. Today, she considered how to keep the genetically engineered boys from fighting with each other for power as they got older.

She wanted to be able to select whom she thought as best when they were around the age of twelve, maybe as old as fourteen. She plopped another baeksalbu slice in her mouth.

How can I make the other boys loyal to the man I choose? They are designed to be leaders. Will they be like male mountain goats who fight to see who is toughest? The strongest may not be the best leader. How will I make a choice? Can I write down how to choose so someone else can make the decision? Who can I designate as my successor in this decision, should I die?

She reached for another slice of baeksalbu. Three bees labored to get a morsel of the fruit. *Why do you bees work so hard?*

Sun-hee jumped up, shook her leg with the bad knee, and made her way over the rocky path as fast as she could to the elevator. For the first time in a long time, she was impatient at how long the elevator took to raise her to the level of the mines. Once in the mineshaft, she strode as her heart raced with excitement. When she got to the cave, she grabbed the phone and called So-min.

Hurry answer, pick up your phone!

So-min said, "Hello, Mother."

"We need a queen!" Sun-hee blurted out. "So-min, we need a QUEEN, not a king!"

"I...I thought...we have six boys," stammered So-min. "What do you mean we need a queen?"

"We need a beautiful, smart, talented, perfect woman to lead. Not a man," Sun-hee said. "It is the only way we can take power without a bloody revolution. We need a queen everyone can love, someone for whom everyone will sacrifice. Can you make a perfect woman?"

"Of course, yes. But you wanted a man. Why now a woman?"

"Men fight with one another for power yet will become emotionally attached to a woman and die for them out of love. Men must be forced to follow another man. They must be made submissive. That is the variable in a revolution which leads to bloodshed. Get me the perfect woman," Sun-hee implored.

"Alright…umm…what do I need?" So-min conveyed her thoughts out loud. "I need fresh eggs from someone you would consider beautiful. Is there a descendant of Choe-me who is in their early teens?"

"Yes," replied Sun-hee. "Tae-seon's great-granddaughter has Choe-me's looks and can supply the eggs."

"I can make modifications and get them implanted in a month or two," replied So-min.

"I will bring my great-granddaughter up tomorrow," Sun-hee said.

"Mother, I also want your genes," said So-min.

Sun-hee paused for a moment before saying, "Whatever you need, I will provide." There was silence on the phone.

"I like your idea, Mother," said So-min. "I will make you the perfect Korean woman."

"Thank you. I will talk to you soon," Sun-hee said before ending the call.

A bee landed on her arm. She moved her hand to brush it away. "Ouch," she yelled and smiled.

70 — Raising kids - August, 2011-September, 2027

On August thirteenth, 2011, the first genetically engineered boy was born. Sun-hee immediately went to the hospital at the gulag to take command. She made sure the child was continuously held, often rocking the infant herself while he slept. The second boy was born a week later, and by the end of August, Sun-hee and So-min had six healthy boys.

The nursery was filled with classical music while Sun-hee read books to them in various languages. She ensured the newborns and their surrogate mothers had adequate nourishment. The mothers were healthy and happy yet remained ignorant of the strategic importance of the children they ushered into the world.

Sun-hee had a plan, specifying what to do for each child each moment of each day. She fretted as if each minute was critical to making sure their minds and bodies developed flawlessly. She slept in the same room, held them, talked to them, changed their diapers. She immersed herself in the children. They were her last hope.

The six mothers carrying girls were included in the nursey to expose the developing fetuses to the music and pleasant environment.

One boy concerned Sun-hee. He was not developing as fast as the rest.

So-min ran some tests and determined there was a developmental flaw in one of the boy's chromosomes.

Sun-hee decided to have him removed and sent him and his mother to Yangseongso. Chulsoon's grandsons would raise him as a robust child, but he was not up to the standards of being the Premier.

Six girls were born in June of 2012. Sun-hee attended each birth with So-min, examining each newborn to ensure they were perfect. One was not. A red birthmark stood out on the side of her nose. Sun-hee sent the girl and her mother to the orphan camp.

Sun-hee asked Hon-yong Jr. and his sons to remodel the mineshaft to accommodate ten children. A dorm room for each sex was built and furnished with modern toilets. Rooms for play, study, and eating were constructed. Hon-yong modernized the elevator, making the trip to the valley more convenient.

A year after the last birth, Sun-hee moved the ten children to the caves where she could raise them in a controlled environment. So-min joined her, and she enlisted her great-grandchildren to help with childcare, teach games, and work on the children's physical abilities.

She taught them proper Korean, Mandarin, Cantonese, Russian, Japanese, and English. They learned math, science, and history all per her view of the world. The children were quick, both physically and intellectually. Everyone had an eidetic memory, allowing them to learn at a tremendous pace.

***

One day, a three-year-old girl asked Sun-hee about a butterfly she had seen in the valley. Sun-hee explained the lifecycle of the insect and how they pollinated plants. The next day, to her amazement, Sun-hee discovered all the children knew about butterflies. The children taught each other. Sun-hee tested this ability by giving each child a different word to learn. The next day all the children knew all the words. The children absorbed knowledge at a faster rate than Sun-hee's aggressive teaching plan.

***

When the last girl turned five, So-min sat down in front of Sun-hee. "I don't feel I am needed here any longer. You have a plan for teaching, and I have nothing to do. There are some things I want to work on, so I am going back to the gulag hospital."

"You have been a tremendous help, and I would like you to stay," replied Sun-hee.

"My home is at the gulag. In talking to my research team, my grandsons want to do genetic experiments on humans. I need to monitor what they are doing. I'll research what I can do should these children not work out," So-min said. "I arranged for transportation in the morning. Now I need to pack."

"I am going to miss you," said Sun-hee with moist eyes. She stood and hugged her daughter. "You have been the source of most of my hope over the years."

"I love you, Mother. You have always been my inspiration," she said and went to pack.

The next morning, So-min left for her home at the gulag.

***

By the time the boys were eight years old, they had exceeded Sun-hee's plan by a year. The girls were more advanced, maturing faster, and learning from the boys. Sun-hee would give them the lesson for the day each morning. The children mastered the knowledge by lunchtime.

***

One morning in July of 2023, Young-ja showed up unannounced.

"Sun-hee, I am sorry I had to do this," said Young-ja as she walked into the cave. "My great-granddaughter was convicted and sentenced to the gulag. I am so grateful Gan Li-sam pulled her aside and let me take her. Can you keep her here? You must, for me. You have some great looking children running around here."

"Where is she now? And can she go to the camp?"

"In the car, and no. If she left the camp and the police found her, she would be shot."

"What if she walks away from here?"

"I am hoping she cannot find her way out until you talk some sense into her."

"But…"

"I will accept no excuses. She will help you with these children. How many are there?"

"I do not need any help with these ten children."

"Come with me to get Young-loo out of the car. Is there anyone around who can help me carry her in?"

"Carry her?"

"We had to drug her to get her here."

Sun-hee said to the boy who was reading at the table, "Chun, can you help us."

"Yes, Mrs. Cha."

They walked out to where Chweh stood by a car. Young-ja said as she approached, "Open the trunk." The lid rose to reveal a woman dressed in a blue t-shirt, jeans, and sandals. "Can the two of you men carry her into the cave?"

"I think so," said Chweh.

"No problem," said Chun as he seized Young-loo under her arms and lifted her gently over his shoulder.

"Stay with the car, Chweh. And forget you saw Chun," said Sun-hee as she led Young-ja and Chun back into the cave.

"That is a strong boy for someone who looks to be about twelve," said Young-ja.

"He is eleven," said Sun-hee.

"What have you been feeding him to grow so big and strong?"

"Everything, just about everything."

Chun laid Young-loo in a bedroom. Sun-hee dismissed Chun and went into the kitchen. She put a pot on the stove and turned to Young-ja. "Explain to me how your great-granddaughter got in so much trouble."

"I'll start with a family secret. My granddaughter had a fling with her music teacher at the university twenty years ago. Young-loo is the result. She composed some songs the Worker's Party deemed as disrespectful. The first time she was reprimanded. The second she spent a month in prison. This time she was sentenced to the gulag. Li-sam brought her to me. We drugged her and sneaked her out of town," said Young-ja as she took down two cups and placed them on the counter.

"She can't stay here," said Sun-hee with her hands on her hips.

"The cave is the only place I could bring her where she would be safe. Hopefully, you can send her to the valley every day where she can play her music and not get in any more trouble. She is a brilliant musician," said Young-ja.

Sun-hee was about to yell at her friend for bringing someone here and jeopardizing everything, but the pot whistled first. Sun-hee turned and filled the teapot. "I can't take her, and I can't tell you why. By being here, she may endanger more than just herself. If she sees what is here and tells the world, we are all doomed."

"What is here beside you and the children?"

"Is one life worth all of Korea?"

"Are you still the Sun-hee I used to know? What is going on? Are you keeping secrets from me?"

"Yes, I have secrets to keep. After ten years, do you think you can show up and dump your problems on me? Now go and take Young-loo with you."

"I can't take her back. She will die, and I will lose the trust of Li-sam."

"Are you referring to Gan Li-Sam? One of the hundred?"

"Yes. Li-sam is now in State Security. We do not want to be on his bad side. He knows everyone in the House of Sanshin. If we offend him, we will have a family reunion in the gulag."

"Does he know about this cave?"

"I don't know. He told me to take Young-loo away."

"You have brought me two new things to worry about. State Security can't know about this place. Please leave and do not mention the children you see here to anyone."

"Will you pour my tea, and we can talk about it?"

Sun-hee filled a cup and handed it to Young-ja. "You can take the cup with you. I won't talk about anything. You're making Young-loo a prisoner."

"That is what I wanted, along with having some time to catch up on our lives."

"I can't talk about what is going on in my life. Someday, I will tell you all about what I am doing. But not today."

Young-ja pouted as she stomped out, taking her tea with her.

Chun entered with Young-loo's clothes and her *kayagŭm* and put them in the room with Young-loo.

***

That evening, Sun-hee was helping two of the girls at the table when Young-loo came out of the bedroom.

"Where am I? And who are you?" demanded Young-loo.

"This is my home. I am Cha Sun-hee, and these are two of my students. Girls, this is Young-loo."

"This isn't the gulag? We stopped to see my great-grandmother. Where is she? And how did I get here."

"Young-ja drugged you and brought you here. She thought this place would be much nicer than the gulag."

"Good. I'll get my things and be on my way."

"I saved you some dinner if you would like to eat before you go. The food is in the kitchen through that door." Sun-hee pointed.

Young-loo opened the door and went into the kitchen. "Wow, what a view! We are not near Pyongyang, are we?" she yelled.

"We are not near the capital," replied Sun-hee.

Young-loo stood in the doorway, held a bowl up to her face, and shoveled food into her mouth. Sun-hee continued with her instruction.

A few minutes later, Young-loo picked up her clothes and *kayagum.* "Thank you for the food. I'll let myself out."

"Goodbye, Young-loo," said Sun-hee without looking up.

About an hour later, the door to the mines opened. Young-loo took a step in. "What? I can't believe I am back where I started. How do I get out of here?"

"You don't," said Sun-hee. The girls snickered.

***

Young-loo was in a horrible mood about everything the next day. Then one of the girls asked, "Can you show us how to play the *kayagŭm?*" Thus, over the next year, the young girls and boys learned how to play and sing. Young-loo could play the music she wanted and debate with the students but found they did not disagree with her revolutionary ideas. Just the opposite, they expanded upon the ideas and took the discussion into methods of implementation which soon made Young-loo dizzy.

***

Changes occurred during the following year that surprised Sun-hee. The boys in their eleventh year, the girls in their tenth all reached puberty. The boys became violent with each other, fighting and arguing. The girls undermined one other. They formed and broke alliances many times a day. She had seen the competitiveness of the hundred IVF children who had the cooperative genes of her peers, but these had been designed to lead.

On several occasions, Sun-hee became a doctor again. There were broken arms, hands, and ribs. One concussion and numerous cuts and bruises required her to recall her medical training. Then she taught the children what she knew about first aid and let them treat each other.

After a few months, Chun Jang-yop, who So-min modified for total strength, dominated the other boys physically. He looked like a larger version of her late husband, eight centimeters taller, broader shoulders and muscular arms. He was quick as a mongoose and strong as a bear.

About the same time, Sun-hee noticed that Cloe Moon-ja could overcome the manipulation of the other girls. Sun-hee could see how she could subtlety manipulate the others and resolve disputes.

Cloe Moon-ja began to use her charm with the boys, gaining their allegiance. The other four girls soon fell into place, allowing Moon-ja to lead. The decision of who to present to Strategist was clear. Cloe Moon-ja was Korea's future.

***

When the first boy turned fourteen, Sun-hee called Ok-myung and left a message. "The person who can lead is nearly ready."

A week later, Ok-myung called. After the usual small talk, she told Sun-hee that they would be coming to the cave in two days. She was anxious to see the man Sun-hee had raised to lead the country. Sun-hee did not let on that her choice was a female.

A fall monsoon was pelting the area in heavy rain. The snow was falling on the peaks the day a group arrived from the capital. Sun-hee had the students prepare for visitors. Ok-myung was the first to enter the cave. Sun-hee welcomed her. Then her son, Hong-do, now with graying hair and wrinkling around the eyes and mouth.

Then Young-ja limped in, stood with her hands on her hips, and eyed Sun-hee. "My dear old friend, I knew you were up to no good when you kicked me out and have not called."

Sun-hee felt her lips quiver, and she moved to embrace Young-ja. "I'm sorry I cut you out of my life…"

"Oh, I have heard that it was all for a good reason. I also got the message from Ok-myung to leave you alone. They tell me the children I saw are now grown up. I'll bet they are super."

"They are," said Young-loo, who came bounding out of her room.

"My great-granddaughter! You are looking well."

"I am well. And I must tell you that I have been happy to be here. I have been able to teach some music and compose some songs."

"I'd love to hear you play and sing."

Another man, wearing the uniform of a captain, entered and bowed deeply. "I am extremely honored to see my teacher again." Then it dawned on Sun-hee. This was Gan Li-sam. One of the hundred IVF children.

Sun-hee bowed and took his hands. "I am honored to see you. You must tell me the stories of your last twenty years."

"First," he stood tall and said, "I must see this man whom you believe is worthier than I to lead."

A shiver went down Sun-hee's back as she glanced around the room.

Have they developed other plans for taking over the country? Have I raised Moon-ja for nothing?

She motioned and said, "Let me introduce you to some remarkable young men and women."

She led the procession through the mineshafts to the student study area where she made introductions. When she got to the last girl, she said, "This is Cloe Moon-ja. I believe she is the person you are looking for."

Sun-hee looked at her guests. Hong-do's jaw hung low, revealing his tongue. Young-ja's eyes were wide, a startled look on her face. Gan Li-sam looked like a million things were running through his mind. Ok-myung, with her eyebrows pursed, appeared confused.

Sun-hee broke the silence. "If you young men and women would excuse us, we have things to discuss." The ten teenagers exited down the mineshaft.

Gan Li-sam looked around the room and unplugged all the electronic devices. "Has anyone you do not know been in this cave?"

"No, only my family has been here in the last twenty years," replied

Sun-hee with an unsteady voice. "You are the only person new here since Young-loo and Ok-myung."

"None of this equipment is new," he said. "I think we are free to speak without being overheard. Now Sun-hee, what is your plan?"

Sun-hee cringed at the forcefulness of Gan Li-sam's words.

Who has he become? Can he be trusted?

Young-ja read Sun-hee's thoughts and spoke first. "I ran into Captain Gan many years ago, or should I say he recognized me and followed me around for a while. You remember he brought me Young-loo when she was in trouble. He is an officer in the State Security, as are most of the hundred we trained at the camp. Captain Gan and I have talked a lot over the years, and I know he can be trusted. I have taken him on as my son, and he considers me his mother. The man we raised is extremely good at his job. Years ago, he confronted me, not wanting us to do anything foolish. I agreed to let him know if we were planning something. When Ok-myung told me you have a person who could lead North Korea, I had to inform him."

Hong-do said, "Captain Gan and I meet periodically in an official capacity. He watches over my father and me. Having a member of the House of Sanshin watch over us the last few years is very comforting. He keeps us away from suspicion, and he has thwarted a few plots by men who would try to take power. Each would have resulted in the chaos we have long feared."

"How can I know your presence here is not to arrest us and end our plotting to put a different person in the leadership of the country? There, I said it," claimed Sun-hee. "I have spent the last fifteen years with one thought in my mind, overthrowing our government."

Capt. Gan smiled. "You taught me very well, Sun-hee. The plots I put an end to would have put an even more evil person in charge. I hope your choice is not a violent person. And let me say, I have spent many a sleepless night trying to figure out how to overthrow our government. My only answer has been to lead an armed rebellion and take charge. If you have a better plan, I want to hear it."

Sun-hee sat at the table, motioned to the others to relax, and then folded her hands in front of her. "Soon after you, Captain Gan, were marched out of our lives, Ok-myung came to me to ask if there was anyone I knew of who could lead the country. At the time, I said no, however, now I must say yes. Right now, there are eleven persons who could lead North Korea, any of the ten children you have just met and yourself. The best person would be Choe Moon-ja. She has become the leader of the students you have just met and is qualified to lead the Democratic People's Republic of Korea."

"Why a woman?" asked Ok-myung.

"First, I think our new leader needs to be someone who will elicit loyalty because of who they are. Choe Moon-ja's beauty, charisma, and personality will attract the masses. My hope is they will instantly fall in love with her. Intellectually, she is equal to anyone in the world, and she has all the wisdom I could give her."

"What does she lack?" asked Hong-do.

Sun-hee thought for a moment. "She lacks firsthand knowledge of the country. She has been isolated in this cave, knowing only her siblings and me. Yes, she has seen videos and read many books about the rest of the world, but she has not been exposed to it."

"I think this is a wonderful idea," Young-ja cheerfully said. "A woman in charge. But how can we put her in that position? How do we get rid of the existing government and put her in place?"

"Do you also believe one of the boys could lead?" asked Hong-do.

"They have the abilities, much of the same genetics as she does. If we need someone who exhibits power, then Chun is my choice. The other boys and girls are also talented. I would not object to any of them."

"So," said Capt. Gan, "we have the same question. How to get Cloe Moon-ja or anyone else into the leadership position in this country."

"Without tremendous bloodshed," added Sun-hee. There were nods of heads around the table.

"What we can do, Sun-hee," spoke up Young-ja, "is to take Cloe Moon-ja around the country as our great-granddaughter. She can get to know the people she will be leading. We will have a grand time."

Ok-myung added, "Can I have my son accompany you? He is educated in the economy and politics. He can update her on the present state of affairs."

"One issue to take care of," interrupted Capt. Gan. "I hope Moon-ja and the others were issued papers when they were born. If not, we can get them issued. I will check the national database and make sure everything is correct. This was an issue for me and my siblings. We are classified as orphans and without heredity confirmation, rising in rank has been difficult."

"My daughter, So-min, issued all of the children papers when they were born. I think she put my name down as their mother," said Sun-hee. "I will remain here, as my knees make it difficult to walk far."

I wish I could see the country. Someday I will.

"What about the others?" asked Hong-do.

"Put them in a training camp run by two of my peers. They are loyal to the House of Sanshin and will watch over them," said Capt. Gan.

"And we will focus our thoughts on how to get this girl into power," said Ok-myung.

"I will go home and pack," said Young-ja. "This will be so much fun traveling around, seeing the country again."

"I will be back in a day or so with transportation for the others," said Capt. Gan.

Sun-hee said goodbye to each. Such a monumental day, getting to see her son, Young-ja, and what an exceptional person Capt. Gan had become. She made herself a pot of tea and watched the rain pelt against the window over a valley obscured by fog.

The next morning, she informed the students they would be leaving.

For the last time, I will feel the pain of releasing children into the world. They are the last hope I have in this lifetime.

She told them the story of the House of Sanshin, showing them the pictures of her peers who had come together seventy-four years ago, to make Korea a great nation. She told of the generations and their accomplishments throughout the country. How one hundred children were born, and now they were doing their part.

Then she sat forward and said, "Tomorrow, all but one of you will be joining Captain Gan for further training. Cloe Moon-ja will tour around the country with Young-ja. My heart will be leaving with you while I stay here. Please pack your things."

Moon-ja let her peers leave the room. She turned to Sun-hee and said, "Thank you for preparing me to enter society. I know you designed me to lead the nation. After reviewing what I know of our country, I have not seen a way to get me into power unless you have an army hidden somewhere or an agreement with China's military. What is your plan?"

"I have no plan to get you in power. My role was to prepare you. The fates are in control from here on. Remember, you will always have the House of Sanshin working with you."

"North Korea has prepared for seventy years to wage war against the United States with the hope of winning. You have prepared me to lead North Korea with the hope of overcoming the government. Is it possible our hopes are misguided?" said Moon-ja, who then strode out of the room.

Sun-hee went to the kitchen and sat by the window for the rest of the day.

71 — The Premier's Wife - October, 2027 - April, 2028

After the last sixteen years of raising ten children, even if they were exceptional, Sun-hee was a tired ninety-two-year-old woman. She welcomed the quiet and time to relax. In the three weeks since the children had left, Sun-hee had caught up on world events and read a few novels. In the back of her mind was Moon-ja's last question.

Then came a secure text message from OK-myung. "Grandfather says he has a solution. He is not telling it to anyone."

Sun-hee added to her thoughts: *What is Strategist planning? What solution does he have?*

Days turned into a week, then two weeks with no news.

Young-ja sent a message. "We have returned home after a wonderful time touring the country. Our girl is amazing! Did you know how many instruments she can play? You didn't tell me she could sing! She's a natural!"

The next day, news of the death of the Supreme Leader's wife dominated the airwaves. The country went into a period of mourning.

Sun-hee heard no news about the ten children until New Year's Day. A message from one of the engineered girls came through.

"Happy New Year from all of us! We are doing great. The military camp is a lot of fun. Thanks to you, we know more than our teachers except for hand-to-hand combat training. We hope you are doing well."

Sun-hee messaged back. "I love you all. I hope you have a great year!" Then she sat with Hon-yong Jr.'s family and watched American movies over the internet. Today, they were all about Marvel Superheroes.

The winter was mild. Warmer than any winter she could remember. The day after her ninety-third birthday, she received the news of Eun-seong's passing from pneumonia. A week later, Su-dae called with bad news. Wires died in his sleep. Sun-hee hung their pictures with the rest, mourned their passing. Only five of the original forty-eight were still alive. Beside Young-soo, who she had not heard from in many years, there was Young-ja, Yong-gak, Choe-me, and her.

Spring came early. It was mid-April when Ok-myung came to see her.

"Sun-hee, you must come to the capital with me. Cloe Moon-ja wants you to attend her wedding."

Sun-hee looked at her and smiled. "This is Yong-gak's plan. Moon-ja is marrying the Supreme Leader."

"How did you know?" Ok-myung said with a surprised look.

"When I heard of the first lady's death, I figured it out," replied Sun-hee. "At least Moon-ja will be close to the leader. She may have some influence over him."

"You set it all up, Sun-hee," Ok-myung said, taking Sun-hee's hands in hers. "All you have done over the years is now resulting in hope for us all."

"When is the wedding?" asked Sun-hee.

"In two days."

***

Sun-hee arrived in Pyongyang in the middle of the night. She tried to view the buildings along the poorly lit streets through the car window. Having seen only the cave, the gulag, and Yangseongso, she was amazed at the tall buildings and spacious streets.

Her grandson took her to a hotel near the center of the city. She asked her grandson, "Can you give me some money to pay for my room?"

He replied, "You don't need money. The family of Gil-hyung owns the hotel."

"Bear's family has a hotel? Hon-yong must have stayed here when he could not return home the same day," she said.

The staff directed her to a nicely furnished room and her grandson to another. Sun-hee slept until late the next morning in the soft bed. She dressed and went to the lobby.

A young woman came up to her. "Mrs. Cha, a table is reserved for you in the dining room. Please follow me."

"Did you know I was coming to the hotel and would be here for breakfast?" she asked the woman.

"Yes, Mrs. Cha. A reservation was made for you weeks ago. You are on our top priority roll for bookings, the only person on my great-great-grandfather's roster who has never visited. Here is your table."

Sun-hee sat at the table and ate a splendid brunch alone. She sought out the young girl and asked if there was anyone to meet her. "My instructions are to meet all of your needs. I have no other messages. Is there someone you were expecting or would like to contact?"

Sun-hee replied, "No. They will contact me." She was unsure about who she could trust with names, so she retired to her room. In the early evening, Ok-myung came to join her for dinner.

Sun-hee asked, "Will I be able to see the bride before the wedding?"

"No. Cloe Moon-ja is under heavy guard," explained Ok-myung. "Only a few secret police are allowed near her. Rest assured, those who can see her are members of your hundred children. Captain Gan has made sure she is in good hands."

"I was hoping to assist in the planning. I guess I am just an outsider now."

"We are all outsiders now. If you need anything, ask the staff." Then she whispered, "They are all House of Sanshin. They take all guests, yet we always have a place in the city where we can meet."

"Yes, the girl I met this morning said Bear's family owns the hotel."

They talked about family over dinner. Sun-hee was surprised at how distant she had become from the fourth and fifth generations of the original forty-eight. She knew all the names of the third generation, having arranged their marriages over thirty years ago, but she did not know their children and now their grandchildren.

As they were about to leave, Sun-hee noticed Ok-myung looking behind her. A voice spoke over her shoulder.

"May I join you?"

Sun-hee turned to see Young-soo, bent over, leaning on a cane. His hair, or the hair around the sides of his head, was white, and he wore thick glasses which, from Sun-hee's view below him, magnified his bushy grey eyebrows.

"Young-soo," Sun-hee blurted out. "Please, please join us."

He maneuvered slowly into a chair at the table. "I am thrilled…to see you again…Sun-hee," he said, taking short breaths between words. "You look well."

"After all these years. Are you still in charge of the mining operations?" asked Sun-hee.

"Only as an overseer," he said, taking a deep breath. "I have not been in a mine in years. I keep the shipments running. Young-ja told me I needed to be here. She did not tell me I would meet you." He coughed lightly and cleared his throat.

"I am here for the wedding tomorrow," said Sun-hee. "I would not miss it."

"I heard our leader…found another pretty girl to marry," he said in short bursts. "Too soon after the passing of the last one."

"You do not know? She is one of us," Sun-hee whispered.

"Sanshin?" Young-soo exclaimed, looking wide-eyed at Sun-hee through his glasses.

"Yes," said Sun-hee. "A girl I raised from birth for this moment."

He coughed, sat back in his chair, and smiled. "We now have a place in the palace." He looked content. Then his eyes brightened, and he sat forward. "Don't they have any food in this place?"

Ok-myung got up and went to the kitchen to order food.

Young-soo ate and periodically acknowledged Sun-hee as she told the stories of the other forty-eight prize-winners and how she had raised the new generation to lead the country.

***

The wedding was a grand affair in the gardens of the royal palace. Sun-hee attended with Young-soo, and together they were given seats in the back of the auditorium. Officials of the Worker's Party were seated with their wives according to their status. A few men nodded to Young-soo, who returned their silent greeting.

Sun-hee recognized a few of the guards, including Capt. Gan, but she was never acknowledged. The state did everything possible to make the affair a national celebration. The flower arrangements around the altar extended for meters on either side. Sun-hee was in awe of the beauty.

The national orchestra and choir were superb. Sun-hee felt her heart race and tears welled up in her eyes. Another daughter was getting married. She was ecstatic.

Cloe Moon-ja wore a silk cherry blossom colored hanbok and a white veil over her face. She moved with grace throughout the ceremony and festivities. Sun-hee wished she could personally congratulate her, but she knew she must watch from a distance. Soon the extravagance of the festivities made her feel uneasy, the drinking by the officials and loud, boisterous talk from the men brought shivers to her spine.

She was relieved when Young-soo began coughing and politely said, "I must go." She took his arm, and together they strode out of the palace.

In the car, Young-soo continued to cough and wheeze. "I am sorry I made you leave early," he said at a moment he had some breath.

"I saw as much as I needed," Sun-hee said with a squeeze of his hand.

At the hotel, Young-soo said, "I am retiring to my room." And he walked away.

She took a few steps towards her room when Young-ja caught up to her.

"Sun-hee," said Young-ja in an excited voice. "Tell me about Moon-ja's wedding."

They spent the evening talking over a dessert about the wedding. Sun-hee felt so good, having the chance to spend time with Young-ja. It was late when Young-ja left to go home.

The next day, she said good-bye to Young-soo. Chweh drove her home. She arrived late in the evening and retired to the cave. As she lay down to sleep, she wondered, *How will Moon-ja deal with the excesses of the party members?*

72 — The Embryo - Summer, 2028

The month after Moon-ja's wedding was quiet but unsettling for Sun-hee. There was nothing about the Premier's new wife in the official communications or unofficial. Her mind was always wondering, *What is happening with my girl?*

Ok-myung arrived in late May. She had a package and a request.

"We need a genetically designed embryo for Moon-ja to carry. A boy. He must look like a Kim, but with an improved temperament and leadership qualities to our liking. Here is a sample of the Premier's DNA and a sperm specimen. Can you get So-min to make a male?"

"Yes, I can go see her today," Sun-hee replied.

"Sorry I am in such a hurry. Let me know when this is ready," said Ok-myung as she hurried back to her waiting car.

Sun-hee sent a message to So-min, letting her know she was on the way and got her grandson to drive her to the gulag. She met So-min and explained what was needed. With the current technology, it would only take a couple of days to engineer an heir. Sun-hee stayed until the package was ready.

When So-min handed her the thermos with a male embryo frozen in liquid nitrogen, she messaged Ok-myung, *It is ready.*

So-min drove Sun-hee back to the cave the next morning. They arrived moments before Ok-myung. Sun-hee handed her the thermos. "Instructions for insertion are inside," Sun-hee said.

"Thank you," said Ok-myung. "We now have the next generation. I must get back to Pyongyang." She quickly got into the waiting car and left.

We have designed the next leader. Moon-ja now has a plan for the future of the country.

***

Sun-hee spent her summer days picnicking in the valley with her family, reading books, and watching movies. She listened to the news each day, looking for information on Moon-ja, but the world was silent on the Premier's wife.

73 — Yong-gak - September, 2028

On a cloudless day in the first week of September, Strategist showed up at the cave. "Yong-gak!" Sun-hee could not hold her excitement. "What are you doing here? I thought you kept to yourself."

"I am retiring at the end of the month," said Strategist with his characteristic hand gestures. "I will meet with the premier one more time. How are you, Sun-hee?"

"I am well," Sun-hee said. "It is so good to see you again. How is your health?"

"This is the reason I have come," said Yong-gak as he started to pace. "About twenty years ago, I was treated for lung cancer. Doctors said they cured me. Now cancer has returned and metastasized. I have only a few months to live. Hopefully, that is enough time to correct my mistake."

"What mistake are you referring to?" she asked.

"I enabled this corrupt government," he said, placing his hands over his heart. "I advised the Premier on running the country and staying in power."

Sun-hee reached out her hand. "You did not tell the Premier to oppress people, be greedy, and seek military might over providing the necessities of life to the people. What would have happened if you were not there?" she implored.

Strategist's hand began to move, and he said, "We would have had a different government years ago. There would have been turmoil, war, and revolution. The current regimen would not be in power. I don't know who would have taken charge or if they would be as evil. What I do know in hindsight is the risk fifty years ago would have been worth the attempt."

"You can't blame yourself," Sun-hee said, taking hold of Yong-gak's hands and staring into his eyes. "Moon-ja is now in a position to influence the premier. We may not be around to see the change, but I believe Moon-ja will find a way to invoke changes."

Yong-gak stammered until he could pull his hands from Sun-hee's grasp. "I…I have a plan. You will know when it happens. Moon-ja will need you when it occurs." He looked at Sun-hee for a moment. She wiped the tears from her eyes as his gaze went around the room. He looked at each picture on the wall.

"Forty-three," he said. "I am sad to convey, Young-soo passed a few days ago. Do you have his picture?"

"I have it here in the drawer. Eun-seong drew them all years ago," she said as she pulled out a folder. "Here is Young-soo." She handed the picture to Yong-gak, who then walked over and attached it to the wall.

"Hand me my picture," he said. "I might as well put it up."

Sun-hee hesitated as she looked through blurry eyes at Yong-gak's picture. He looked so regal in Eun-seong's drawing. She handed the drawing to her longtime friend.

Yong-gak put his picture up on the wall next to Young-soo. "Just as it should be, you, Young-ja, and Choe-me are left. The three of you were the best of us."

"We always looked to you for direction," said Sun-hee.

"All I did was keep the country from making big mistakes. I had little impact on the lives of the people," said Strategist. "I must not keep Captain Gan waiting. He was kind enough to bring me here to say good-bye. Pack and be ready to support Moon-ja." Yong-gak turned and walked down the mineshaft.

Sun-hee looked over the valley and cried for the fathers of two of her children. She packed a bag with all she might need to support Moon-ja. Then she went to the valley to enjoy the break in the weather.

***

It was September fifteenth, the trees were starting to turn color throughout the North Korean capital. Billowy white clouds broke up the bright blue sky. It was a perfect fall day.

Seok Yong-gak arrived at the Premier's palace. He looked up at the majesty of the building, reflecting on how many times he had been here with his wisdom to keep Korea from harm. Now he was going to deliver something different.

The bodyguards, assigned by Capt. Gan, assisted him out of the car and up the steps. He took a moment at the top of the steps to catch his breath. Then he entered the palace and shuffled down the hall, his cane echoing in the marble passage. He bowed to General Ngai Se-jin, head of State Security and a leader in the Worker's Party, who sentineled the door for the Premier. The entrance to the office opened.

He thought as he stepped in, *Each month for the last seventy-four years, I have come to offer advice. One final meeting with a chance to make a difference.*

With his cane in his left hand, he ambled into the office of the Premier. "Thank you. You may leave now," he said to the guards. He moved to the oak desk, lightly ran his hand along the edge and muttered, "Hon-yong, you made great furniture."

A couple of minutes later, the Premier entered and sat behind the desk. Cloe Moon-ja followed him in. She wore a light crimson dress that flowed around her like a waterfall. She brightened up the room like a vase of sunflowers. A more luminous red veil hung over her head and face. She took a position by the Premier's side.

"Your report, Mr. Seok," said the Premier.

Yong-gak offered a minimal bow, leaning heavily on his cane and said, "I feel it is time, Honored Premier, to offer a change. Due to health, I cannot fulfill this role any longer." He took out a letter from his breast pocket and handed it to the Premier. "Here is my resignation, and I am providing you a list of men who I believe are plotting your assassination."

The Premier took the letter and began to read. "General Ngai Se-jin," the Premier yelled towards the door.

Gen. Nagi, a tall, middle-aged man who had let himself get a bit overweight, entered and hustled towards the desk.

"General Ngai, Seok Yong-gak has your name on the top of a list of men who wish to assassinate me."

General Ngai reached out, took the list, and began to read.

Moon-ja silently moved behind the Premier as the general reviewed the paper. Then, with incredible quickness, Moon-ja slid behind Gen. Nagi, grabbed his gun from his holster and fired off one shot into the head of the Premier. Then she turned the gun and shot Gen. Ngai three times in the chest.

She looked at Yong-gak and said, "I did it."

"Finish my plan," said Yong-gak, pointing at his heart.

As instructed, she raised the pistol and shot Yong-gak where he pointed. He fell to the floor in a heap.

Moon-ja placed the gun on the desk and took the Premier's bloody head, holding it against her bosom. She took a deep breath to ready herself for the guards and began to cry as they rushed into the room.

"He killed my beloved husband," she wailed, holding the Premier to her chest.

The guards stopped, surveyed the situation and beheld Moon-ja, holding the Premier in her arms.

"I killed Nagi with his own gun," she confessed, pointing to the desk. Her enhanced mind raced with possibilities which might endanger her and the plan. She knew she had to sell the moment to the guards and officials who would soon investigate the scene. The plot had worked as Yong-gak had told her a month ago. Now she had to take charge of the situation and the country.

Capt. Gan was the fifth person to rush into the room. "Madam Premier, what happened?"

Moon-ja and the captain had rehearsed this moment. She recounted the shooting with the right emotions. "I can't believe he shot my beloved husband," she cried, pointing at Gen. Nagi, lying on the floor. Mr. Seok had given our leader his resignation and a list of possible assassins." She directed the men's attention to the papers lying near the general. "My dear husband called for General Nagi and gave him the list. Then the general…he…" she sniffled, "…he killed my beloved and shot Mr. Seok." She overemphasized her crying under the veil, sniffing and taking a breath before she said, "I grabbed his gun…and I shot him."

Capt. Man turned to the guards in the room.

"Secure the palace!" he commanded. Then he examined the Premier and the gunshot in his head. He checked the body of Gen. Nagi, picking up the papers from the floor. Then he moved to kneel by Yong-gak, lying on the floor in a pool of blood. He stood and strode to Cloe Moon-ja's side. "I am truly sorry, Madam Premier. We will find out who conspired with the general in this execution. They will pay with their lives."

The guards led Cloe Moon-ja to her room where she met with her State Security attendants, all members of the one hundred. "We must take control and make sure there is no more violence. Put out the word." Then she removed her clothes and commanded an attendant to burn them. She bathed to remove any gunshot residue.

Cloe Moon-ja gave the order to have the individuals named on Yong-gak's list arrested and held for investigation. Gen. Nagi had been the first person named on the list. Other power-hungry officials followed down the page. Yong-gak had told her to isolate the people on the list until she was firmly in control.

Her next command was to declare a period of mourning for the country and prepare for a state funeral.

74 — Aftermath - September, 2028

After her picnic lunch, Sun-hee sat by the river, reading a book. The sky was clear, and the air had a slight chill, yet sitting in the sun warmed her. Hon-yong Jr. came running up.

"The Premier has been assassinated!" he said, breathing heavily.

Sun-hee looked up from her book and calmly said, "I need to go to the capital today. Can you drive me?"

"Why do you need to be there now? Don't you realize how dangerous the city will be?"

"Yong-gak told me to be ready to support Moon-ja," she said, standing and collecting her things. "My bags are already packed. Drive me, or I will drive myself."

"Is this Strategist's doing? Were you…"

Sun-hee interrupted. "He told me nothing, but to be ready." She walked quickly through the rockfall to the mineshafts.

"I will drive you," said Hon-Yong Jr. as they stood in the elevator.

During the long drive, they listened to radio reports of the assassination of the Premier by the head of State Security.

Sun-hee sat in silence as she tried to determine if the assassination was the plan of Yong-gak or if this had occurred without his influence.

How would Yong-gak have known to tell me to be ready if he had not planned this? What is he doing? Can Moon-ja succeed in becoming the countries leader? She is only fifteen.

Hon-yong and Sun-hee arrived in the early morning hours at Bear's family hotel in the Munsu-Dong district. The elderly man at the desk took keys from a board behind the front desk and said, "Let me show you to your room, Mrs. Cha. Good to see you again, Hon-yong."

Sun-hee entered her room and thought, *Yong-gak planned the final step. How else would they have a room ready for me?* She smiled, feeling a great weight lift off her chest. She prepared for bed and fell fast asleep.

It was mid-morning when she woke. She dressed and went to the dining room, where she found Hon-yong. As she sat, he said, "The city has gone into lockdown. No one is getting in or out. We were lucky to get here last night." He took a bite of the meal before him. "Seo Young-ja!" he exclaimed as he looked up.

Sun-hee turned quickly to see her friend.

Young-ja bent over and hugged Sun-hee. Sun-hee returned the

embrace.

"I did not expect to see you here this morning," said Young-ja. "I got an anonymous note a few weeks ago to be here at ten in the morning if there was a national emergency. Did you have anything to do with this?"

"No. I got the same message, only personally from Yong-gak," said Sun-hee. "Any idea what he is up to?"

"I have not seen him. His son, as well as the rest of his family, avoid me. Then again, they avoid everyone," commented Young-ja as she sat at the table. "I wonder how Moon-ja is doing. The assassination must have been quite a shock to her. There has been no news except General Nagi was also killed. Officially, the nation went into mourning today, and the army is making sure no one moves. I am amazed and glad you are here. I have some wonderful company to eat with." She went on in her usual joyful tone.

They chatted over breakfast, and as usual, enjoyed their time together. Then the hostess approached them and said, "Your car is here, Madam Seo and Madam Cha."

They looked at each other in surprise. They left Hon-yong at the table and strolled out the front door. Sun-hee and Young-ja immediately recognized the driver as one of the hundred children they had spent years teaching.

As he drove them through the city, they inquired about his time at the military camps and learned he, too, was part of State Security. He could not tell them anything about the events of the previous day. He had received orders this morning to pick up his former teachers. They crossed the river and, after several turns, stopped in front of a large house guarded by soldiers.

Soldiers assisted Sun-hee and Young-ja out of the car. Four soldiers in a diamond formation bracketed each as they approached the door. The two women were carefully examined top to bottom by a gruff-looking old soldier with deep dark eyes. The door opened, and they entered to see soldiers standing at attention along the hallway. A metal gate barred the stairway from floor to ceiling.

Two women soldiers stepped smartly towards them. Sun-hee caught their smile, and she nodded a twitch to them. They were two of the one hundred. Sun-hee smiled at Young-ja as the soldiers searched them by hand and metal detectors.

They finished the search and stood at attention. A lieutenant approached them, unlocked the gate to the stairs, and held it open.

Sun-hee climbed the stairs one slow step at a time. Young-ja followed. When they got to the top, another woman Sun-hee recognized bowed and motioned to her left. Sun-hee turned, and there stood Cloe Moon-ja in a long black dress and gloves with a black shawl draped over her head. Only her face was visible.

Moon-ja reached out, saying, "Please come in."

The three went into a room, and Moon-ja shut the door. "I am so scared someone will find out what happened," Moon-ja said with a shaky voice. "Everything has worked like Yong-gak said it would. But there is so much that could go wrong. I am so glad you are here. He gave me a message to send a car for you at eleven this morning. I was worried you would not be there."

"I am happy you were not hurt in the shooting," said Sun-hee. "I was shocked to hear about the assassination. I do not know how Yong-gak knew what was going to happen and how he gave us messages to coordinate this meeting…"

"He planned it all," blurted out Moon-ja. Then her voice went to a whisper, "General Nagi did not pull the trigger, I did."

"What?" said Young-ja loudly before turning her voice into a whisper. "Where is Yong-gak? I will…"

"He is dead. I shot him too. And General Nagi." Moon-ja said.

"There is a lot we do not know. Tell me what happened, the whole story," said Sun-hee.

Moon-ja went over the story of how Yong-gak planned the shooting and how it had to be her who took General Nagi's gun, to make sure everyone was dead. She then said, "Shooting the Premier was a joy. He was horrible to be around, and General Nagi was a pervert. He arrested families so he could use the young girls for sex. I took pleasure in ending his life."

Tears began to stroll down her creamy cheeks as she told of shooting Yong-gak. "He was a good man and in a lot of pain. He demanded I shoot him out of mercy, and it would close up the loose ends."

"Strategist is dead," exclaimed Young-ja.

"Yes," Moon-ja said with a sob. "I know I was designed to be decisive and able to do the hard things a leader needs to do. But you never told me how emotional it is to end the life of a friend. My stomach has turned over, and I can't get it turned back around."

Young-ja was speechless. Her mouth just hung open as she listened.

"I'm sorry Strategist made you shoot him. With his death, nobody will suspect that you are the one who shot the three men," Sun-hee said. Then she got a stern look on her face. "This story must remain our secret. We will tell only the story of how General Nagi shot the Premier and Yong-gak, and how you took the general's gun and shot him. Yong-gak had cancer and was dying. He knew being shot was better than suffering. Listen carefully, you did what I have wanted to do for many years. I raised you for this day, this purpose. Yong-gak strategized the steps, and you executed his plan. The country is now yours."

75 — The Big Day - September 23, 2028

To look anonymous, Sun-hee donned a lieutenant uniform. She would dress as an army officer for the funeral even though she had not been in uniform since she last left Yangseongso and detested the idea that she was part of the army.

She held her blue scarf. *Should I or not? It will help with the autumn chill.* Then she proceeded to wrap it around her neck. *Mother must join me for this day.*

I can do no more, she thought, looking at herself in the mirror. *I decided to create Moon-ja. Today is her day, if she succeeds.*

The ushers guided Sun-hee to a seat in the south side of the large crescent-shaped stands. The chair was in the middle of the back row. She observed other party officials file in and take their seats. The men around her were all majors, colonels, and generals. Heads of state and dignitaries from countries around the world sat in the front rows.

A circular stage, protruding from the stands over the edge of the street, would be where Moon-ja presented herself. Being directly behind the platform, and fifteen rows up, gave Sun-hee a perfect view. A similar crescent of seats was on the other side of the road, only without the stage.

High ranking military men were seated across the street, as well as an orchestra and choir. She recognized some of the one hundred children she raised, now secret police in their late twenties, acting as ushers.

A huge double-sided screen hanging over the street came to life. A closeup of men loading the coffin of the deceased premier onto a horse-drawn cart filled the view. Draped over the coffin was a Korean flag and red-flowered wreaths. The procession began, and many kilometers away, the horse-drawn carriage moved with Moon-ja walking behind. She wore a long black cape, a black shawl, and a black veil hiding her face. She always covered her face in public.

How will the people react when they see her for the first time?

For over two hours, the procession moved down the main highway. Soldiers lined the sides of the boulevard, holding back thousands of people, maybe a million who had come to mourn their fallen leader. She watched the screen, focusing on Moon-ja as she was shown amongst images of people weeping and throwing flowers into the street. A show of military force followed. Tanks, rocket launchers, missiles, and other military equipment trailed the coffin and Moon-ja.

Sun-hee was tired of sitting by the time the display showed the horses approaching the Arch of Triumph. She stood, with everyone else, and craned her neck to see the procession entering the arena. The horses brought the coffin to the midpoint of the two crescents of onlookers. Handlers unhitched the horses and led them away. Moon-ja entered the stands in front of her.

Sun-hee felt her heart beating like hummingbird wings. Her breath was quick and shallow. This was the moment she had longed for most of her life. She lost focus, and her knees grew weak. She sat, adjusted her scarf, leaned back, and closed her eyes.

The orchestra began to play, Sun-hee forced herself to her feet, peered between the heads in front of her, and saw the veiled figure of her design, Moon-ja, on the giant screen above the street. She felt satisfied.

76 — Theodore Reed III - September 23-24, 2028

Theodore Reed III reached for his smartphone on the table by the bed. The alarm was just as he programmed it, annoying. He had been up late, confirming the list of heads of state and dignitaries in Pyongyang for today's ceremony. He hit the screen, turning off the alarm, and turned to see his wife was not in bed. As usual, she had gotten up early to make sure he had a hot breakfast. She was a delightful companion.

He showered, dressed, and as he walked into the kitchen, his wife poured him a cup of coffee, adding the right amount of artificial creamer. Breakfast was on the table. He scrolled through his messages, looking for reports on new arrivals in Pyongyang. The information came from the air traffic controllers monitoring flights over South Korea and satellite data. They revealed a couple of planes which had come in over northern China during the night.

Those must be delegates from Eastern Europe or Turkey.

"It will be quite a show in Pyongyang today," he said to his wife.

"Who will not be there, dear?" said his wife. "Me and you. Why didn't you get us tickets?"

"I'm an analyst, honey. The ambassador and his staff are going. CIA analysts like me were not invited."

"I think it would be grand to see the ceremony. My family will celebrate this day, the day there is no Kim to rule the north."

"The ceremony will be broadcast. Will you be with your family all day?"

"Yes. What time will you be home?"

"I don't know. I will message you when I can get away."

"Last night, it was one o'clock when I got your message, and it took you almost two hours to get home."

"Reports kept arriving, and I am responsible for keeping a list of who will be at the funeral," said Theodore without apology. "Thanks for the breakfast, honey! I love you."

"I love you, too," she said as they gave each other a gentle hug and a kiss.

***

Theodore entered a four-story office building near Bukhansan

National Park and walked to the elevator, taking it to the fourth floor. He passed through security, proceeded to the end of the hallway, turned left, and a man in uniform pressed a button next to another elevator. Theodore examined the cheap paintings on the wall as he waited. He heard a ding, stepped in the elevator, and pressed the down button. He didn't know how far down this elevator went underground. What he did know was the bunker was made to withstand a nuclear attack. The doors opened to a passageway where he got into the back of an electric cart. The driver took him to where he worked, the North Korean Surveillance Center. It was almost nine. He was the last of the staff to enter.

"Mr. Reed, you are earlier than I expected. Thank you for getting the attendee list up to date before you left this morning," said Mr. Watson. "We should be able to identify the people on your list as they are revealed on the broadcasts. The seating chart should tell us who is important and, maybe, who is now running the evil empire. In the meantime, we get to watch the bullshit documentaries of the life and times of the late Premier." He looked over his shoulder at a screen replaying a video of the Premier's wedding.

"I wish we could get a look at his wife's face," Theodore said under his breath. "She's always veiled. What do you look like?"

Theodore sat at his monitor and drank coffee to get his mind in gear. He was anxious to find out who was ruling the nation he had devoted his life to studying. He glanced at the clock on the wall as the funeral procession started, ten a.m. The video feed they were getting from the North Koreans showed Sungri Boulevard lined with soldiers at attention, rifles on their shoulders.

As the camera focused in, he noted the cart carrying the deceased Premier drawn by six horses, draped in a Korean flag. The slight breeze caused the corners of the flag to flap. The premier's widow walked about ten yards behind the coffin, dressed all in black. A single soldier held the horse reigns and marched—way too slowly for Theodore's over caffeinated attention span—towards the Arch of Triumph. Periodically, the camera would pan over to crowds of people lining the street crying, bowing, and paying their respects to their fallen leader.

"They do put on an emotional show," Theo commented barely loud enough for anyone to hear. He sat back in his chair. "I should start on the task of providing an analysis of the weapons in the parade." And he began a list on his computer.

A text from an aide to the Ambassador came in. *We are in the back row of dignitaries on the entrance side. The ambassador is not happy as we will be amongst the last to see the casket.*

Theodore brought up a satellite photo. The funeral arena was constructed to the east of the Arch of Triumph: two half circles of stands with the road going down the middle. He noted where the ambassador was sitting, the last row on the southwest—the worst seats in the stadium.

More messages came in telling where other dignitaries were seated.

He texted back, *Can you see any of the North Koreans?*

No, we cannot see above us or over the platform.

Theodore did not worry. The facial recognition software would tell him who was who, as soon as they received a video feed of the crowd. The list he had completed last night was used to set up the software and would put a name to every face.

He picked up his tablet and went to the break room to get another cup of coffee. He took a pastry, something he rarely did, but today his mind was more on what was happening a couple of hundred miles to the north than his weight.

He pulled out a chair and played a game while munching on the pastry. When he finished, he refilled his coffee mug and went back to work. Video feeds were now showing views from the Arch of Triumph, an imposing scene with the crowds of people lining the street.

"The ambassador just went dark," said one analyst.

"I am reading electronic suppression over the whole area," said another.

"We will only have the video feeds they want us to see," said Mr. Watson. "Let's see if we can figure out who is in command."

Theodore paid attention to the large screen on the wall across the room, currently focused on the horse-drawn cart entering the arena. The crowd stood, and those with hats removed them. A soldier unhitched the horses from the cart and led them away. Some Korean official randomly switched the video feed between six cameras placed around the arena. A computer built a composite image for the American analysts, showing attendees and their names. The center camera panned up to the walkway, projecting out from the upper level to a circular stage. A figure walked out, her black veil fluttering in the slight breeze.

"There is Choe Moon-ja," said Mr. Watson.

Cloe Moon-ja took a position in the center of the stage and bowed deeply to the casket before her. The only movement was the breeze jostling the flag on the casket and Moon-ja's cape. A *kayagŭm* was wheeled out by two men and set in place in front of Moon-ja. She shook her hands out of the flowing gown, revealing matching long black gloves. The orchestra began to play. Moon-ja stroked a harmony on the *kayagŭm* and began to sing the North Korean national anthem.

"What a voice," said the female analyst who sat next to Theodore.

"One of the best vocal renditions of their national anthem I have heard," replied Theodore.

"Probably dubbed in," said Mr. Watson. "The veil covers her mouth."

When the anthem finished, the orchestra took up another tune. Moon-ja began to play and sing a moving tribute to her fallen husband.

The singing was as emotionally powerful as anything Theodore had ever heard. He was fluent in Korean and found the words Moon-ja sang to be angelic, tender, and loving. Theodore noticed tears in the eyes of some of his fellow analysts and then magnified his monitor to scan what he could see of the crowd. Korean generals were wiping their eyes, the only dry eyes were in old white men. The music was mesmerizing. Everyone in the arena, and in the room where he sat, focused on Moon-ja.

He studied his monitor, adjusting to get a close-up of the figure in black, trying to see if she was actually singing. He watched her pause, take her veil in both hands, and lift it over her head, revealing a stunningly beautiful face and a small microphone in front of her mouth. Theodore blew a little "wow" out of his lips. The cameras focused in as she continued playing and singing.

Theodore's eyes were glued to the screen before him. She was a gorgeous woman, singing a sweet, powerful, tender, love song to her fallen husband. As she tilted her head back, a tear crawled out of the corner of her left eye and crept its way down her creamy cheek. She closed her eyes, held a note, and a tear snuck out to stroll down her right cheek.

The song continued for a few more minutes. Then the stunning figure in black stepped back from the *kayagŭm*. She bowed deeply towards the casket on the street below her and tapped her face with a silk handkerchief.

Moon-ja stepped to the *kayagŭm* and strummed a chord. The orchestra across the street matched the harmony.

Theodore focused on her face and how well she could sing.

She is incredible, he thought.

The song she sang was upbeat, one of encouragement for the Korean people.

Theodore looked around at the other analysts in the room, noticing how they focused on Moon-ja.

She can captivate an audience.

"Who is in charge of the North?" barked Mr. Watson.

"I'm checking, sir." Theo scanned the names on the screen. No one jumped out at him as a person who could take over leadership. He brought up a list of ten names, identified as primary candidates to be the next premier. He noted only five of these names in the crowd, including the nineteen-year-old daughter of the late Premier, Kim Ju-ae. He put a line through General Nagi's name and four others, wondering what had happened to them. The other four were standing off to the right of the platform among Worker's Party officials and Kim Jong-un's daughter.

He studied the names in the front and center. None were on his list with strong enough position to take charge. "I do not know," Theo said in an apologetic tone. "If I had to guess, I would say Kim Ju-ae who is in the midst of the top officials of the Worker's Party."

"If she takes the lead, who controls her?"

The song Moon-ja sang called for a continuing of a great Korea, declaring the future for the male child she carried, the new Supreme Leader.

"Come on, folks. The music is over. What have you discovered?" yelled Mr. Watson.

"We discovered Cloe Moon-ja can sing," said the woman to his right with a sniffle while wiping a tissue carefully under her eyes, trying not to smear her mascara.

"And she is really hot," said the analyst to his left.

"I want clues on leadership!" said Mr. Watson.

"She is pregnant," said another analyst.

"I think Moon-ja has declared her child as the new Premier. But for now, the leader must be one of the following," said Theodore, and he ran off five names, highlighting them on the screen. "The other names on my shortlist are not near the stage."

"What do we know about these five?" said Mr. Watson.

"Except for Kim Ju-ae, all have been part of the government for many years, and as far as I know, are loyal to the former Premier," said another analyst. "Any could take over. I do not see any difference in policy."

"Who is that old woman?" said a female analyst on Theodore's right. She took control of the main screen and zeroed in on a woman who was near the middle of the upper stage. "We have names for everyone else. The computer has not identified her."

Theodore looked up at the big monitor to stare at the older woman. *There is something familiar about her.* "The scarf," he said quietly.

"What, Mr. Reed," said Mr. Watson.

"Sun-hee," Theo said, thinking out loud.

"Yes, it is a sunny day, Mr. Reed," Mr. Watson barked. "What the hell does the weather have to do with this old lady?

"Hold on a minute," said Theodore as he logged into a personal account where he kept photos of his family. He pulled up a picture of his great-grandfather in his study. He transferred it to the large monitor and magnified a photo on the mantle. It was a picture of his great-grandfather next to a bus and a woman wearing a blue scarf.

"It looks like the same blue scarf," he said. He launched the facial recognition program and ran the compare photo application with seventy years of aging. A timer whirled for a couple of seconds before a window appeared. *70% MATCH: an unknown person.* Theodore quickly typed in, *Cha Sun-hee.*

"Who is Cha Sun-hee, Mr. Reed?" demanded Mr. Watson. "And why should we care?"

"My great-grandfather was a prisoner during the Korean War. Sun-hee was one of the medical students at the hospital in the camp where he was held captive. He gave her credit for saving his life."

"Why is she in attendance, Mr. Reed?"

"She was last seen in 1953. In 1988 her son defected and met my great-grandfather. She must be in her 90's now."

"Do you think she could be the one taking charge, Mr. Reed?"

"From the stories my great-grandfather told me about her, she was a very confident and intelligent person. At her age, I do not think she would be in charge. I have no idea what she would be doing at the ceremony unless she is related to someone."

"Anything more current on Cha Sun-hee? She is our only unknown. Get me more information on her!" boomed Mr. Watson.

The room was silent for a moment before Mr. Watson continued, "Mr. Reed, I want a full report on your great-grandfather's stories!"

"Yes, sir." Theodore stared at the image he had frozen on his screen.

What are you doing there, Sun-hee?

"The rest of you get busy on the other five names. I need to know, before you leave today, who the new Premier is, or why they would not be the new Premier?" barked Mr. Watson.

Lunch was brought in as Theodore began to search the archives to see if there was a record of Cha Sun-hee, the hospital in the mountains near Chongjin, or anything else related to his great-grandfather's time as a prisoner. The great thing was every bit of information in the world was available to him, and the horrible thing was every bit of information in the world was available to him.

Dinner arrived as Theodore ran another search to find anyone who was born in North Korea in 1934 to 1936. The records were scarce. He couldn't connect any of the people he found to Sun-hee. He spent the afternoon finding and reading what he could of the other men who were prisoners with his great-grandfather and researching Gen. Park. Nothing on Gen. Park related to Cha Sun-hee except his great-grandfather had mentioned both. What he hoped to find was a death announcement or biographical reference to anyone born the same year as Cha Sun-hee. His long list included Seo Young-ja, Status unknown; Han Young-soo, deceased; Ahn Ching-ying, died in Princeton; he was the defector's father; Shon In-jung, teacher of finance in Bejing, deceased. The one name he came up with that sparked his interest was Seok Yong-gak, Political analyst and recluse. No death record. He refocused his research on Yong-gak, of which there was little information. His only role was a political researcher for the Worker's Party.

A text came from his wife, *What time will you be home, honey?*

I'll be working late. I will let you know, Theodore texted back.

The widow of the Premier has a fantastic voice. What did you think?

I can't tell you what I think.

Did you cry? My mother and I cried. For hours.

Nice try. See you later. Love!

Theodore went back to focus on the connections of Seok Yong-gak. Then he thought about the children his father had mentioned who were born while he was a prisoner. He did searches on North Koreans born in 1951 -1954 to see if he could find Cha Sun-hee's children. What he found was thousands of puzzle pieces and maybe a few which might fit into the picture of Sun-hee. He focused on putting the puzzle together.

His smartphone chimed with a text from Mr. Watson. *Pack a bag.*

You are going to Pyongyang.

"Shit! It's six am already," he said with no one to hear. He transferred all his information to his tablet. Then he sent a text to his wife. *On my way home. Pack my bag. I have to leave.*

***

Theodore caught a bullet train to the DMZ where he went through extensive security both by the Americans, who made sure he took nothing into North Korea which could be used by the North Koreans, and then searched by the North Koreans as they looked for items which would be useful. He watched them go through the bag his wife had packed, a couple of changes of clothes, toiletries, pajamas, and a love note. Security agents chuckled over it before taking photos so they could analyze it for secret messages.

That note will keep some Korean analysts busy for a few hours.

The electric train on the North Korean side took him into the country he had studied all his life. The North Korean soldiers accompanying his journey sat in seats in front and back of him. He slept between stops, when people moving in and out of the train would wake him. The trip was slow, taking most of the day.

He arrived at a hotel late in the afternoon with a plan to find and talk to Sun-hee. He met with the U. S. Ambassador who said the Secretary of State was to arrive later in the night. The North Koreans had given a message to the Ambassador after the funeral, stating they wanted to negotiate on sanctions on their country, immediately.

Theodore asked, "Who in North Korea sent the request?"

"It was signed, DPRK. We still do not know who is in charge. Have you found out anything?" said the ambassador.

"I have five potential candidates. Nothing definite. Lots of leads I need to research. I'll be in my room if you need me," said Theodore.

Theodore took a shower.

The water pressure is excellent.

He remembered what one of his professors in college had told him. *One of the signs of a civilized nation is water pressure.* At the end of the shower, he turned on the cold water to shock the cobwebs out of his head.

He dressed modestly in a polo shirt and a light jacket. He made sure his American diplomatic pin was visible on the lapel of his coat. He did not want to be perceived as being covert. His six-foot frame and white skin would make him stand out anywhere he went, but the pin would immediately identify him. Then he went to find the Korean officer in charge at the hotel.

He asked a couple of guards, who directed him to a soldier who looked to be in his thirties. He had a very stern look on his face.

"What do you want?" the man said in English with a tone indicating he did not want to be bothered.

"I would like to meet someone here in North Korea. My great-grandfather was a prisoner many years ago, and this woman was an interpreter. She would be very old now, and I would like to tell her how much she helped my great-grandfather to survive. Could you send a message to Cha Sun-hee? Tell her Theodore Reed III would like to talk for a moment. I would be most grateful."

The soldier's eyes lit up. "What room are you in?"

"Room 432."

"Return there. I will send up a response if I get one."

"Thank you very much," said Theodore with a polite bow.

Theodore returned to his room and laid down, wondering if he would get a message back. He sent a text to his wife and tried to do more research on the children born in the 1950s. He fell asleep to be awoken by a knock on the door. He jumped up to answer it.

The soldier he had spoken to earlier stood at the door. "Mr. Reed?" he said.

"Yes, I'm Mr. Reed."

"A message for you," said the man while holding out a small envelope.

Theodore opened the note and read, *I would be very pleased to meet you, Mr. Reed. If you are available for dinner, the bearer of this note will provide transportation. Sincerely, Cha Sun-hee.*

Theodore's adrenaline rushed. He grabbed his jacket, retrieved his tablet from the bed, and placed it in his pocket. "I am ready."

"Follow me," said the soldier, who led him to a car waiting outside of the entrance of the hotel.

Theodore knew the city from aerial photos but was glad to be able to see it from ground level. The streets were clean, no litter, no areas overgrown or barren, and no traffic. He knew extra care had been taken to clean up for yesterday's memorial, but this was one of the loveliest cities he had ever been in.

They arrived at a hotel Theodore guessed was built in the late 1950s. A soldier directed him towards the entrance. "This way, sir."

Theodore walked into the lobby, and two uniformed men approach.

"Mr. Reed, we request this conversation not be recorded in any manner and must make sure you have no weapons," one of the men said in English.

Theodore undid the buttons on his jacket and held it open. He pointed to his pocket, took out his tablet, and turned it off before handing it to the man before him. He knew the security on the phone was unbreakable. They scanned him with a hand-held wand which beeped at his lapel button, room key, and belt buckle.

"Thank you for your patience, Mr. Reed. Dinner is being served through that door," the man said, pointing towards the back of the lobby.

"Thank you, gentlemen," said Theodore as he started to walk to the restaurant. He tried to calm his rapidly beating heart by taking slow deep breaths.

A waiter greeted Theodore and spoke in English. "Theodore Reed, this way." Then the waiter led him towards the back of the room. There were many tables all set with fine china ready for dinner, but there was only one person seated against the back wall, Cha Sun-hee.

"Mr. Reed, thank you for joining me for dinner," Sun-hee said in English.

"Thank you for finding the time to meet with me," said Theodore in English as he bowed deeply. "I am most honored!" he said in Korean, letting her know he knew her language.

Theodore sat. The waiter refilled Sun-hee's water glass and then his.

"Are you here as an official of the U.S. delegation for the memorial service?" Sun-hee asked, returning to English.

"I arrived today at the request of the Secretary of State. He wants me available during talks on sanctions. My role as an intelligence officer may be helpful." Theodore did not want to hide anything from his role or status from Sun-hee.

Dinner consisted of roasted lamb chops, rice, vegetables, and kimchi.

"How did you know I was in Pyongyang?" asked Sun-hee as she started to eat.

Theodore swallowed his first bite. "The video feed of the funeral. I saw you in the back row. I recognized the blue scarf from the photos my great-grandfather had on his mantle."

"Captain Reed has photos of me?" she said with a surprised look on her face.

"He has three photos of you," explained Theodore Reed. "The first was on the day of his capture. The photo shows my grandfather on the ground surrounded by soldiers. You were looking up at the plane with another soldier on the ground beside you."

"The soldier beside me was Sergeant Kua."

"The second was a poor photo of you with your arms around two children."

"Were these babies?"

"No, probably three to six years old. They had bandages on their heads, and one had bandaged arms."

"Wounded children from American bombs. I will never forgive America for firebombing cities during the war," she said and took a bite of lamb.

"My great-grandfather told me the camp where you were located was never bombed, largely due to that photo. They knew it was a hospital which took care of children." He took a drink of water before continuing. "The third photo was taken during the prisoner exchange. You were bandaging my great-grandfather's arm.

"As a child, I asked him over and over to tell me the story of his release from Prison. He always ended the story by telling me the only reason he survived three years in North Korea was because of you. Therefore, I had to meet you to say thank you. Without you, I would not exist. I owe my existence on this planet to you."

"Now, the whole world knows who I am. I presume you have labeled my face on your recordings of the memorial."

"Our information is still highly classified. Only those who need to know have seen your name," said Theodore.

Am I being too open? Theodore questioned himself.

"I would enjoy hearing your life story between 1953 and now. And, to be honest, the big question I have is why you were at the funeral of the Premier? You must have a role, some importance to be sitting in the center of the back row during the memorial."

"What has your intelligence gathering concluded?"

"Only the one thing my great-grandfather told me. Your son defected in 1988 and insisted on giving the U.S. a message. 'Cha Sun-hee is not your enemy. Do not interfere.' There is a half-page of information about their meeting on file in Washington."

"Does the United States plan on interfering?" asked Sun-hee, folding her hands on the table in front of her.

The puzzle instantly became clearer to Theodore. In some way, Sun-hee was involved in the government. "We do not know enough to interfere. As far as I know, there is nothing to interfere with,"

Theodore said, trying to show honesty.

"Do you know everything your government knows?" inquired Sun-hee.

"My job is to know everything about North Korea," he said with a little pride. "Which is why your presence at the memorial is such a mystery to me. You were the only person in attendance I didn't know ahead of time. Although I know almost nothing about Cloe Moon-ja."

"You do not know much, Mr. Reed, which is good. Now what I want you to tell me is what you suspect," she said, continuing to eat.

"Speculation should only lead to research. While I am here, I am away from the tools I use to do research."

"I am here, Mr. Reed. What questions do you have? Maybe I can be of help and end your speculation."

Theodore paused, deciding to be direct. "Who will be the next premier? I have narrowed it down to five persons." He went through the list, watching Sun-hee's expression with each name.

Sun-hee cleared her palate with a sip of tea. "An outstanding list, Mr. Reed. I am impressed with your research. None of those men would change North Korea. Some would make it worse. I would not allow them to be Premier." She took another bite, waiting for Theodore's response.

"You would allow?" he questioned in a surprised tone. "Are you in a position to influence the decision?"

Sun-hee swallowed and said chuckling, "I am way too old to be in a position for anything. There is one person who was prepared for the position from before her birth." She knew she was letting the cat out of the bag. "I will tell you if you promise to tell no one until the announcement, which will be soon."

Theodore's mind raced to put more pieces into the puzzle. "You said 'she was prepared for the position.' So, Cloe Moon-ja is the new Premier. Does this mean you were part of the assassination of the Premier?"

"Korea needed a change a long time ago," Sun-hee said, and stared off in the distance for a moment, her eyes watered. "Forgive me, Mr. Reed. I lost a close friend that day."

"Did you know General Nagi?"

"I didn't know General Nagi. A man I called Strategist, since the day I met him also died. Young-ja gave him the nickname."

Mr. Reed paused for a moment. "Is the person you called Strategist, Seok Yong-gak?"

"I am impressed Mr. Reed. You are correct."

"I studied Yong-gak at the academy. We learned a lot about him when Huang Jang-yop defected in 1997. So, Seok Yong-gak and Seo Young-ja are your friends. Were they at the hospital when my father was there?"

"Yes. Did your grandfather ever tell the story of his capture and the setting of his broken ankle?"

"He told the story about a girl who sang while she yanked off his boot and put his foot into a cast. That was Young-ja. Oh, my God," Theodore exclaimed, plopping his head back and laughing. "I listened to her for hundreds of hours when I was a new agent."

Sun-hee smiled at the vision of Theodore, like everyone else, listening to Young-ja talk.

He sat forward. "Let me go back to the question. Were you involved in the change in leadership?"

"I prepared a person. Fate, as is usually the case, determined the events before us. The world will be pleased with the change in leadership. Hopefully, America will not interfere." She motioned for her plate to be removed. The waiter came and cleared her place.

"Again, I do not know how the United States would interfere with Korea. You are raising more questions than have been answered," Theodore said.

"Each question you ask provides you with more information so that you can ask more questions," Sun-hee said with a smile.

"How has Cloe Moon-ja been prepared to be the premier?" Theo asked while pushing his plate aside. The waiter quickly cleared it.

Sun-hee sipped her tea, pausing until they were alone again. "I taught her everything I know."

The waiter placed a raspberry tart with whipped cream before each of them. Theodore sat wide-eyed.

"You taught her?" he said, leaning forward.

"That was my primary occupation since the war. Teaching and raising children."

Theodore shook his head, trying to get the baffled look off his face. "What does North Korea want in the negotiations with the U.S. tomorrow?" he asked and took a bite, getting cream on his upper lip.

Sun-hee cleared her mouth with a sip of tea. "We will ask for an end of sanctions. That is all, nothing more." She took another dainty bite of her tart. "The food here is so good. A pity I had to cancel the other reservations tonight."

"This has been an excellent meal. One of the best I have eaten in years," said Theodore. "But don't let my wife know I said that."

Sun-hee smiled and patted her lips with her napkin before continuing. "Your great-grandfather left the prison camp in a hurry, or I should say, he was made to leave with no notice. He left a few things behind, a couple of which I have. I think it is time I returned them. Will you accompany me to my room so that I can get them for you?"

Theodore's heart leaped at the thought of some artifacts of his great-grandfather he would receive. "Yes, of course. I would be greatly honored."

"Please, come with me." Sun-hee stood and slowly walked out of the restaurant and down a hallway to a room. She put in a key, opened the door, and walked in. Theodore followed.

Sun-hee turned and closed the door. "I am sorry, Mr. Reed. I believe you know too much, which may place our plans in jeopardy. Please accept this room as your new home for a few days. I will personally keep your tablet. No one will tamper with it."

"Shit," Theodore said and made a fist.

"That is what your great-grandfather said when he surrendered to me. He could not bring himself to shoot me then, and I do not think you would hit me now. Relax, you will be safe. All will be fine."

Theodore unclenched his fist and held out his hands. "I am your prisoner."

With a big smile on her face, Sun-hee said, "This room will be more comfortable than the place we held Captain Reed," she said, moving to open the drapes, revealing a garden area with maple trees in their majestic fall colors and roses still in bloom. A small fountain flowed in the middle where a couple of birds were splashing and bathing. "The leaves are so beautiful this time of year. And you will not need to tend to this garden."

"Did you know about nine-okay?"

"I have never heard the term nine-okay."

"The paths in the garden my great-grandfather kept spelled out nine-okay. It was a message that planes took photos of from the air. The air force knew there were nine prisoners in your camp and that they were okay."

"You will be better than okay here, Mr. Reed. Again, I am sorry for taking you captive." She walked towards the door. "Should you need anything, there are paper and pen on the nightstand. Slip the note under the door. The television works. You may find channels twenty to twenty-five very informative. Thank you again for meeting me for dinner."

"What will you tell the American delegation?" Theodore asked with a nervous twinge in his voice.

"They will be told you are now an honored guest. Please make yourself comfortable. If you would hand me your key, I will have your things transferred from the hotel."

Theodore handed over his room key. Sun-hee smiled and opened the door.

"One last question Sun-hee, if I may?" Theodore said, while stroking his chin, "How have you done all this and remained hidden for all these years?"

Sun-hee paused for a moment. "Officially, I died fifty years ago. Since then, I have lived in a cave."

77 — Worker's Party - September 24, 2028

The morning after the Premier's funeral, Cloe Moon-ja received a request to meet with the assembly of the Worker's Party. She pulled together her four sisters to prepare for the meeting.

"We must reassure the assembly that their positions are secure. I don't expect a challenge to me as the acting premier. Is there anyone we need to be concerned about?" asked Moon-ja.

"The men Yong-gak thought would be a problem are locked up. Captain Gan and the security force is keeping a close eye on everyone. I don't see any obstacle currently," said one of the sisters.

"I will inform our brothers of the meeting and have them join us," said another.

"Let's get dressed and go meet the assembly," said Moon-ja.

An hour later, Moon-ja entered the back door of the assembly hall. Her sisters and brothers followed her in. The collection of generals took their seats.

Moon-ja, dressed in white silk, walked confidently to the center of the stage. "Thank you for inviting me to speak to you this morning. The Democratic People's Republic of Korea is strong, and as the acting Premier, I am committed to making our nation stronger."

Out of the corner of her eye, she saw Kim Ju-ae walking towards her. "Ju-ae, I am pleased you can join me to honor your father." She bowed slightly in respect.

Ju-ae, also dressed in white silk, returned the polite bow.

A major walked onto stage and stood next to Kim Ju-ae. The major looked young for a man of his rank and looked to be in top physical condition. He said, "Assembly delegates. I am here to announce a continuation of the Kim bloodline as our Supreme Leader. Kim Ju-ae is gracious in her willingness to fill her father's shoes until her son is born. Is it not more fitting that a direct descendant of the Kim line, assume the position of premier until her son is ready to lead?"

Moon-ja's enhanced mind quickly ran through the possible scenarios. The only one that made sense told her that many men put Ju-ae into this position to take power. Which men did not support her? Why didn't Capt. Gan discover this plot?

I can't let Ju-ae take over, or Yong-gak's plans will fail. They will purge the entire House of Sanshin. I can strongly oppose Ju-ae and the men who put her up to this and risk a battle. Chaos will ensue. I can suggest we rule together. That will only delay the confrontation as the men supporting Ju-ae will plot to secure power.

She gave Ju-ae a broad smile. "My dear step-daughter, I'm confident you will maintain the government as it was under your father." She spoke loud enough for all to hear. "There is so much more to do to make our country great. In our private moments, your father and my husband shared dreams of what he wanted Korea to become. He wanted other nations around the world to respect the Democratic People's Republic of Korea. A land where the people prosper. I know Kim Jong-un would want me to guide our people until our son is old enough to rule."

Ju-ae glanced into the crowd. Her hands shook.

The major said, "Ju-ae must take command. The country cannot be given over to a girl from the mountains. We know too little of your family and their loyalty to the nation. You are not even old enough to make it into the Ministry of Public Securities database. You once said your mother's name was Cha Sun-hee. The person in the records with this name was born in 1935 and has an address on a remote mountain road. She gave birth to one child in 1956."

"Major, you should know that to protect my family, your father ordered the removal of my ancestors' data from the database. You can't use them to influence me."

I must draw out the men who put Ju-ae up to this. Moon-ja turned to the assembly. "Patriots, men of honor, I ask you to decide. Those of you who chose Kim Ju-ae for the next premier, please stand. Those who remain seated cast their vote to me."

Moon-ja waited for men to stand. Heads turned side to side, but no one moved.

"This is the problem with our assembly. You are all full of fear. If you stand and are in the minority, you fear for your lives. If you remain seated and are in the minority, you fear for your lives." She took a couple of steps forward and offered a smile." As the next premier, no one in this assembly will fear for their lives by standing in opposition to me. You have my word. Your position and status are not in jeopardy. I do fear, should Kim Ju-ae and the men who support her take power, the son of Kim Jong-un no in my womb, will die. Who stands for Ju-ae?"

The large room remained as silent as a graveyard on a cold winter night. Then footsteps came from Moon-ja's right. Capt. Gan walked in front of the stage and looked up at Moon-ja. Five more of the one-hundred, also in state-security, came from different directions to stand with Capt. Gan. A general in the front row slowly stood, followed by nearly a dozen more.

Ju-ae cracked a weak smile towards the general in the front row. More men rose to their feet.

Capt. Gan climbed onto the stage and approached Moon-ja.

Moon-ja slipped her right foot back a couple of foot lengths under her dress. "I didn't suspect you," Moon-ja whispered.

He whispered back. "I needed to get Ju-ae's supporters to stand."

"They are sheep. Look, they are all standing," said Moon-ja.

Then Capt. Gan turned and addressed the assembly. "As the current head of state security, I am in total support of Cloe Moon-ja as premier of North Korea. The security forces will protect Kim Ju-ae and each one of you in honor of the Premier's words."

Moon-ja interrupted. "My great late husband ruled by fear. All of you were afraid to stand for Ju-ae until Captain Gan stepped forward. Then many of you were scared to remain seated to show your support of me. I see your terror because you are standing. Fear has conditioned you to be followers. The only reason any of you need to be scared of me, is if you seek power for yourself. If you oppose me with your words, I will respect you. If you resist me by acting against my authority, you will lose my respect. If you attempt physical harm, you will put your life in danger."

"Those of you who initially stood with Captain Gan have my respect. The rest of you are pathetic followers who need to prove to me that you deserve to be part of this assembly."

At the urging of the major, Ju-ae took a step towards Moon-ja.

"Do you have something to say, Ju-ae?" asked Moon-ja in a commanding voice.

"I…I am Kim's daughter and…"

Moon-ja interrupted. "You are the daughter of our late Premier. If I stepped aside and allowed you to be the next premier, you would be a puppet of these powerful men." She swept her hand towards the crowd. "You merit the honor of your heritage, but you do not deserve to be manipulated by others."

Ju-ae glanced at the generals in the front row and stepped back towards the side of the stage.

Moon-ja took a moment to gaze at the assembly. "Today is the beginning of a new chapter in the history of North Korea. It starts with meetings with the delegates who have come to convey their respect to our fallen leader. Diplomats, please coordinate with my assistants to set up meetings. Over the next few weeks, I plan on meeting with each one of you to review your departments." She walked briskly off the stage, passing her sisters and brothers, and headed for the exit.

She pulled the door open and walked into the sunlight and an ambush.

Soldiers with bayonets attached to their guns stood on both sides of the walkway. They lunged at Moon-ja. She dropped and rolled to her left and grabbed the nearest soldier, pulling him down on top of her. The momentum of the soldiers from the other side of the walkway drove their bayonets into the man on top of Moon-ja.

A sister attacked the soldier closest to the door, and a second sister followed closely behind, engaging another man. Then Chun barged out and plowed into the men around Moon-ja like a wrecking ball. Capt. Gan followed and emptied his pistol into attackers. The rest of the brothers and sisters streamed out, and in seconds, the attempted ambush was over.

Capt. Gan yelled commands into a hand radio as he helped Moon-ja to her feet while the sisters gathered around her. Chun stood with his back to the women, looking for any possible attackers. Three brothers were busy disarming the soldiers. One lay on the ground with blood spreading across his midsection.

"Get back to the presidential palace and stay there until I get this sorted out," said Capt. Gan.

"Find out who is behind this and bring them to me," demanded Moon-ja.

Chun led the group away. One of the brothers picked up his injured sibling and followed.

78 — Confrontation - September 25-26, 2028

Please sit here, Mrs. Cha," said Capt. Gan, pulling out a chair at a small desk in the back of the room. "You will be able to view the meeting on the screens." He pointed to the far wall. "The monitor on the desk in front of you is a live video feed of Mr. Reed."

"Thank you," said Sun-hee as she sat down.

The other five people in the room got up from their monitors to greet their mother. Moon-ja's siblings greeted her: three males and two females of the ten engineered children.

"How have the meetings been going?" asked Sun-hee.

"Very well," said one of the men. "The twenty-three delegations Moon-ja has met with have all agreed to recognize her as the premier."

"Moon-ja will meet with the United States next," said one of the girls. "We are monitoring the meetings and preparing background information for Moon-ja."

"Where are your two sisters and brother?" inquired Sun-hee.

"Our sisters are with Moon-ja. We are forwarding information to them, and they pass on the data to Moon-ja as she prepares for each meeting," said another sister. She glanced at her siblings. "Our brother was injured yesterday in an assassination attempt and is in the hospital.

Sun-hee turned to Capt. Gan. "What do you know about this attempt on Moon-ja's life?"

"Arrests have been made. A faction of the military thought that if they killed Moon-ja they could take control."

"You must allow Moon-ja to win them over without violence."

"I have the situation under control."

Sun-hee looked at the six large screens across the room. "What am I seeing on the monitors?"

"There are six cameras in the conference room. One in each corner and two above the doors that allow us to see Moon-ja and the delegation she is meeting."

The four corner views all looked alike, and Sun-hee could not determine the orientation. After some evaluation, she counted seven chairs on each side. Still, she could not figure out which side Moon-ja would be sitting and which would be the Americans. She decided it would not matter.

She studied Mr. Reed, who sat on his bed, flipping channels regularly. She hoped he would click on the channel showing the negotiations.

The screens showed a door to the conference room open. The U.S. Secretary of State entered, followed by six men and two women. The American Secretary was a heavy-set man with broad shoulders and receding gray hair. He had on a charcoal gray suit and red tie with an American flag lapel pin. The other men wore charcoal grey or black suits and red ties. The two women were dressed in navy blue pantsuits. Grey hair was the norm among the men, while the women were blonde. Sun-hee studied the monitors to see if she could gain any insight on the Americans. The only thing she concluded was that blonde was not the women's natural color.

The opposite door opened. Sun-hee watched Moon-ja, and six Koreans enter and spread themselves out along the table. Two of Moon-ja's siblings, outfitted in cream-colored silk dresses, moved to the ends of the table, and four older Korean generals stood behind seats on either side of the center.

Moon-ja looked elegant in a crimson red silk dress that flowed over her slender figure. She admired Moon-ja's long black hair flowing down her back, nearly to her waist. She was a stunning contrast to the men in khaki Korean military uniforms flanking her at the table.

Sun-hee flipped her attention from screen to screen, listening to every word, and studying body movements.

"Welcome, Mr. Secretary and honored delegates. I am Cloe Moon-ja, acting Premier of the Democratic People's Republic of Korea," she said in English.

Excellent diction with the right amount of accent, Sun-hee thought. *She learned everything perfectly.*

Moon-ja gestured gracefully with her right hand. "On my right are the heads of commerce, education, and an assistant."

"On my left are the heads of foreign relations, the military, and an assistant."

"I am very honored to meet you, Madam Cloe," the Secretary of State said as he sat. "These are members of my staff who will assist me in our negotiations. Let me begin…"

"I will begin, Mr. Secretary," Moon-ja interrupted. She took a paper from the man on her left. "Here is an agreement we wish you to approve. It terminates the conflict between our two countries." She handed a single page document to the Secretary, which he read:

September 25, 2028

On this day, the United States of America and the Democratic People's Republic of Korea agree to terminate all conflict and sanctions.

Signed ____________ U.S. Secretary of State Date: _________

Signed Cloe Moon-ja Premier of DPRK Date: 25 - 9 – 2028

The Secretary sat back. His eyes focused intensely on Cloe Moon-ja.

Sun-hee felt he was letting the silence create tension.

The Secretary folded his hands over his waist and said, "There is a little more to ending an eighty-year-old conflict than this simple statement. We have drafted the Korean & American Partnership Agreement, outlining a plan which will ensure peace between our nations in the future." He motioned to his left. An aide pulled out a bound document about an inch thick from his case and handed it to the Secretary. "I understand you may be new to how governments and countries work with each other on a friendly basis. The policies put in place in this document will ensure North Korea's acceptance as a complying nation in the future."

Moon-ja reached out her hand, pushing her one-page document before the U.S. Secretary of State. "Sign this document ending the conflict between our peoples, and I will read your proposal."

"Unfortunately, I cannot sign your document as long as North Korea has nuclear weapons," he said.

"We are seeking peace with our neighbors and seeking a new start with all nations. Why does America, so far away, want North Korea to disarm and become an economic puppet."

The Secretary sat forward in his chair, interlocked his fingers together on the table. "We want North Korea to join the rest of the world in free economic enterprise. What is it you want for North Korea?"

Cloe Moon-ja sat back, took her hands off the table, and placed them in her lap. "We do not want America to interfere. All I ask of America is to leave us alone," she finished with a slight turn of her head.

"How can we leave you alone when you have weapons of mass destruction and intercontinental ballistic missiles. The United Nations determined Korea is a threat to the stability of the region and the interests of the United States of America." he said, eyes firmly locked on the girl before him.

"Are we a threat, Mr. Secretary?" said Moon-ja with an enticing voice. "You have many more weapons of mass destruction than all other countries combined. I do not view the United States as a threat." She gave him a little smile and paused. Then she sat forward and placed her palms on the table. "We are requesting the United Nations vote to free North Korea of the sanctions. By signing our simple peace treaty, we will show the UN we are no longer a threat."

"There is much more to peace than this document."

"Why does America feel threatened, Mr. Secretary?"

Sun-hee was amazed at the capability to capture the sound. Every word was clear. She concentrated on the U.S. Secretary of State as he sat considering his options. "Take the next move, Moon-ja," she said quietly to herself.

She glanced at the monitor in front of her to see Theodore Reed standing, staring at his television screen. "Good, you are watching," she mouthed silently.

"You need some time to think and talk to your Congress and President," Cloe Moon-ja said. "We will resume at nine a.m. tomorrow."

"One additional item. I have reason to believe you are holding a United States diplomat," said the Secretary of State.

Moon-ja nodded to her left.

The general in charge of the military said, "A member of the American delegation was found last night outside of the boundaries set for foreign delegates. We are holding him in a comfortable hotel." He typed in a password on his tablet and handed it across the table to the secretary. "This is a real-time video feed of a Mr. Reed."

The Secretary looked at the tablet screen and scowled. "I demand you return Mr. Reed to the hotel where we are staying."

"After our document is signed," said Moon-ja.

Sun-hee laughed as Theodore jumped up and down with clenched fists in his hotel room. She looked at the video feed from behind the secretary to see Theodore on the tablet.

Moon-ja left the room before the U.S. Secretary had a chance to react further. The finance minister grabbed the American proposal and followed Moon-ja. The general retrieved his tablet and followed the rest of the Korean delegation from the room.

As the Korean delegation left, the U.S. Secretary of State stood, paused, then pointed to the one-page treaty on the table while nodding to another man. Then he left the room, leaving his aides to gather their things.

A man from the American delegation used a handkerchief to place the Korean document into a plastic bag then seal it.

Why are they putting the paper into a container? Sun-hee wondered.

She had longed for this day. Decades of planning in her mind had gone into these events.

Moon-ja is not the old Korean government that stalled and played negotiations like an untimed game of GO. Nor are they dealing with a naive girl who can't make decisions. Hopefully, she could maintain the advantage. She must continue to keep them off guard.

She looked to another screen in the room showing the American delegation outside the conference room. She watched the Secretary of State turn to the aide who had picked up the peace treaty document, and said, "Get her DNA analyzed immediately." Then he turned to the rest of his aides. "Let's get back to the hotel and analyze what just occurred. I was not prepared to lock horns with that young girl."

Why do they want Moon-ja's DNA?

Sun-hee returned her attention to the monitor before her. Theodore paced back and forth. She asked one of the other people in the room, "How can I replay the view of this room in the hotel?" After they brought up the video to the point the negotiations began, she watched the actions and listened to what Theodore had to say.

After the video replayed, two statements of Mr. Reed stuck in her mind. "You came to play the old game Secretary. This girl does not see you as an enemy, just a hindrance." And, "Damn, I wish I were there. For once I could change the outcome."

***

"The edited video of yesterday's meeting was uploaded onto social media last night," said Young-ja. "Reports this morning showed that hundreds of millions of people around the world viewed it."

"That many? So fast?" said Sun-hee with her mouth full of breakfast.

"That does not count the times it aired on news programs. All the television news stations in the U.S. have shown the meeting. And what is even better, videos of her singing at the funeral are the most-watched videos on the internet."

"I designed her, hoping for a person like you. Somehow we got a lot more."

Young-ja put her fingers to her cheeks, forcing up a smile as she said, "What you got was my sparkling personality in Choe-me's body with Eun-seong's empathy and your confidence. Plus, you threw in Hon-yong's strength, Strategist's wisdom, and the best possible intelligence. I am so glad you did not include Strategist's hand gestures." She finished with a chuckle that turned into a hearty laugh by both.

"Too bad we are the only ones left of our generation. The original Sanshin would be happy to see what we accomplished," said Sun-hee, holding her teacup in her hands.

"The fates kept alive those who needed to be here and spared the others the pain of mourning each death."

They finished their breakfast and reviewed the plan for today. Young-ja would again oversee getting the video of the negotiations uploaded and coordinating news releases about agreements with other nations.

Sun-hee wrote out a message to be delivered to Mr. Reed, informing him of the time of today's meeting and the channel to watch. She hoped he had not seen himself on the tablet.

Young-ja typed into her tablet as Sun-hee gave the waiter the message to deliver to Mr. Reed. She waited until Sun-hee finished before saying, "I have a surprise for you."

"What could surprise me now?" Sun-hee said.

Young-ja paused with a smile on her face and then said, "Your daughter, Su-dae, is flying in from China. She will be here later this morning."

"Su-dae! Great! It will be so good to see her," said Sun-hee. "I wish I could meet her at the airport, but I need to be at the meeting."

"Your car is waiting," said the waiter.

They stood, and on the way out, Young-ja said, "I am so excited to see how Moon-ja handles herself. The meeting will be grand!" Together, they exited the hotel to the waiting car.

***

At precisely nine o'clock, Sun-hee watched Moon-ja and her delegation enter the same conference room as the day before. She peeked at Mr. Reed, who sat directly in front of his television.

Nine minutes after the hour, the American delegation entered the room. The U.S. Secretary was the last person to take a seat. Moon-ja sat silently, as did the rest of the North Korean delegation, waiting for the Secretary to make the first move. One of the men in the U.S. delegation placed another copy of the Korea & America Partnership Agreement (K&APA) on the table.

"Good Morning, Cloe Moon-ja. You are looking lovely today," said the U.S. Secretary of State with a big smile.

A sister at the end of the table said, "Please address her as Madam Premier."

"We do not recognize her as the Premier. Now, after conferring with the President of the United States, his staff, and our allies across the world, I must inform you, if North Korea wishes to join in an open exchange with the rest of the world, you must agree to the tenants of the K&APA."

"Korea will not be subjected to the tenants of your document. We wish no partnership," said Moon-ja, folding her hands before her on the table. "Please sign the agreement we have proposed." The Minister of Economics produced a new copy and placed it on the table.

The U.S. Secretary said, "Being a nation on the world stage requires so much more than a one-page document can define. I realize that you have been isolated, you are young, and there are so many new things to learn and comprehend to become part of the international community. I assure you, we will assist your country in many ways, education, products, loans, and generally bring your citizens up to speed with the rest of the nations of the world. North Koreans will enjoy everything all other people enjoy."

"America has nothing, nor does any other nation have anything the Democratic People's Republic of Korea needs," said Moon-ja in a calm voice.

"Isolation will only keep your people hungry and ignorant," said the U.S. Secretary. "Do you want the people of North Korea to continue to live a meager, backward life? The former Premiers have been comfortable with letting their citizens starve and live without freedom. They have run up billions of dollars in debt on the international market. America is offering you the opportunity to join the rest of the world as a free nation with all the benefits of being a sovereign nation, participating in the world economy and world affairs. Agree to this document, and we will assist in paying off your debts, and you will see your nation and people thrive."

Sun-hee could sense the confidence of the U. S. Secretary. She studied Moon-ja's expression on the monitor.

"Do you understand what is in your agreement and what it means to the North Korean people?" asked Moon-ja.

"I do, Madam Premier," replied the U.S. Secretary.

"Then turn to a random page, and we can discuss it," said Moon-ja in a confident tone.

The U.S. Secretary turned to his left and gave a slight nod. A man reached out and flipped open the document.

"What page did you open to?" asked Moon-ja.

"Page 137," said the man.

"Page 137 reads," said Moon-ja and she rattled off, "…adopt and maintain consumer protection laws related to fraudulent and deceptive commercial activities online. It also includes commitments ensuring that privacy and other consumer protections can be enforced in K&APA markets. Governments have different ways of implementing privacy protections, and K&APA recognizes that diversity and promotes interoperability between diverse legal regimes. The chapter also includes provisions requiring Parties to have measures to stop unsolicited commercial electronic messages or spam."

Moon-ja paused and glared at the U.S. Secretary. "We have none of these problems and require none of the protections this passage provides. Why would I want to worry about stopping spam, when we currently have no spam?" She held her hands out wide. "We need none of this agreement, Mr. Secretary." She delicately flipped her hand at the document.

The U.S. Secretary sat forward in his chair. "I have not wanted to mention the consequences of not signing this agreement. The United States will continue to enforce the resolutions of the United Nations and increase sanctions against North Korea. We will enforce the U.N. sanctions against nations who trade with you and isolate you further from the rest of the world. Your people will wither and blow away, leaving the land for anyone who wishes to take it. Sign the agreement!" he said emphatically.

"Please sign our one-page agreement, Mr. Secretary," said Moon-ja calmly, returning his stare.

The Secretary, his eyes narrow, brows pursed together, said, "Sign the K&APA, and the United States will recommend to the U.N. Security Council to terminate sanctions. North Korea can join the rest of the world. Refuse to sign, and you will remain in the stone age." He pointed at her with his large right hand.

Moon-ja met his stare with a slight cute smile. She pulled the thick document towards her and thumbed through the pages, ending up on the last page, the one she could sign. She stared at it, then flipped the pages over and closed the document. Her eyes rose slowly to look at the U.S. Secretary. She calmly picked up the three-centimeter thick stack of paper, and with no visible strain, tore it in half, saying, "If America wants to continue to oppress us, Mr. Secretary, to suppress what I can accomplish with my people, then I will push back. My only goal is to make peace after eighty years." She leaned forward, scattering the paper on the table. "We will take our message to the United Nations."

The U.S. Secretary stood and said, "So be it! We are done here. The United States of America will have nothing to do with a nation that has violated all moral decency by genetically engineering humans. We condemn the Democratic People's Republic of Korea for making you!" He thrust his arm out, pointing his index finger at Moon-ja. "We condemn you as an abomination to the human race." He stood, grabbed the door handle, jerked the door open, and stormed out.

Sun-hee rose to her feet in her excitement at seeing the U.S. Secretary lose his cool.

Moon-ja held her hands out sideways towards her staff in a gesture to have them remain calm. They did not. The men yelled Korean insults as the Americans left the room.

After the Americans exited, Moon-ja chastised her staff for their reactions. "We must present ourselves as the more advanced race."

Sun-hee quickly went out of the surveillance room to meet Moon-ja. "Bravo! You were perfect," she said, taking Moon-ja's hand.

Moon-ja looked Sun-hee in the eye and said without emotion, "That's how you made me." She released herself from Sun-hee's grasp and walked away.

Sun-hee felt a little dizzy. She looked for a chair. The closest was through the door to the conference room. She sat in the chair Moon-ja had just occupied, put her elbows on the table, placed her head in her hands, and considered what she had done.

I made the perfect person to rule Korea. She is now in charge. Did I do enough to train her? Will she now make her path? She is smart enough, strong enough, but will she be wise enough? Will she withstand the rejection of who she is? What have I done?

She got up and returned to the surveillance room to replay the video of Mr. Reed's reaction. She watched as he sat still, engrossed in the interaction. He mouthed something as Moon-ja recited the document from memory and moved his head side to side slightly when she ripped it in half.

Young-ja entered the conference room. "Sun-hee, you have to see this." She took Sun-hee by the arm and led her back to the surveillance room. She loaded the recording of the U.S. delegation outside the conference room. They watched for a moment, then one of the American aides said, "Who do these fucking gooks think they are?"

Sun-hee sat back, recalling the time an American sergeant said that to Gen. Park and what had happened.

How should I react? How will Moon-ja react?

She looked up at the monitor to see Mr. Reed watching her hold her head in her hands. She pounded her fist onto the desk.

79 — To America - September 26, 2028

"The video is ready, Sun-hee," said one of the men in the room, breaking her out of thinking about Mr. Reed.

"So quickly?" she said as the door opened.

Young-ja answered, "So quickly because I can narrate real-time now that there are not innumerable men," she rolled her eyes, "who feel they need to approve what I say."

"Only a little in the video was changed," said the man in the room. "I left out the statements the U.S. Secretary of State said about the Premier being engineered."

"Did you include the words of the aide?" asked Sun-hee.

"Yes," he said with a bow of his head.

"I added statements about how Americans think of people who stand up to them," said Young-ja. "It will be great! We can get something to eat and watch the views total up."

Capt. Gan entered the room, interrupting. "Every news organization in the world is requesting an interview. What should we tell them?"

"How soon can we schedule the interviews?" asked Sun-hee.

Young-ja said, "If we do the interviews from here, anytime. I am sure Moon-ja is ready."

"If Moon-ja were to interview in person? When and where?" inquired Sun-hee.

"When we get to a news studio, I am sure they would go live," said Young-ja.

"The greatest impact would be to go to New York," said Capt. Gan. "We will need a plane."

Young-ja started pounding away with two fingers on her tablet while talking. "I wish there were an easy way to type Korean characters on this tablet. Stinking Americans design everything for themselves and expect the rest of the world to adapt. There, I sent a message to Su-dae."

Sun-hee pushed herself up from her chair. "Do we have a plane capable of getting us to New York?"

Young-ja looked at her tablet, strumming her fingers on the table. "I have a reply. Su-dae has landed in Pyongyang. She says her plane can get us there," said Young-ja, showing the text message on her tablet to Sun-hee.

"My daughter owns a plane?"

"That is what she wrote."

"I need a dress. Captain, can you have someone get a dress from my room at the hotel? On second thought, have them grab everything, there are only a few bags. And get Mr. Reed. He must join us."

"Yes, Mother," he said with a big smile.

"I'll take care of things here," said Young-ja, giving Sun-hee a quick hug. "Enjoy America."

A blank look came over Sun-hee's eyes as she thought, *America? I am going to America.*

***

A few minutes later, a man assisted Sun-hee out of a car. Su-dae ran up and gave her mother a big hug.

"Moon-ja arrived a couple of minutes ago and is already on the plane with her assistants and Chun," Su-dae said in an excited tone. "We were waiting for you."

"We need to wait for Mr. Reed. He may be useful," she said, looking around to see a black Mercedes speeding up. Capt. Gan stepped out, followed by Mr. Reed. A soldier grabbed bags from the trunk and ran to throw them to a man at the top of the steps leading to the plane.

"Hello, Mr. Reed. Thank you for joining me on such short notice. It's time for you to go home," said Sun-hee. "Let me introduce my daughter, Su-dae. We will be traveling on her plane today."

"I am very pleased to meet you," said Mr. Reed with an overly polite bow.

"Please board. I understand we are short of time," said Su-dae.

Theodore took a step to Sun-hee and asked, "Sun-hee, what are you setting up to do?"

"Get on the plane, Mr. Reed. We can talk there," she said as she turned and was assisted up the steps by her daughter.

Theodore paused for a moment, shook his head, and followed Sun-hee onto the rear of the plane.

Sun-hee took the seat on the right, then motioned. "Please sit across from me, Mr. Reed."

Theodore took the left seat. Su-dae helped her mother buckle in, saying, "Make yourself comfortable. We will be in the air in a few minutes." The plane began to move. "I need to get to my seat up front. I will be back later."

"This is a new experience for me, Mr. Reed. I have never flown on an airplane before. Forgive me as I feel a bit nervous," she said as she grasped the armrests firmly.

"Modern planes are very safe, Sun-hee. It is a short hop to my home in Seoul, but I do not think that is where we are going.

"We are going to New York, Mr. Reed." The plane went into full acceleration, forcing Sun-hee's head back into the cushion. "Oh, my!" she said and closed her eyes. Her fingers curled around the ends of the armrest, her knuckles turning white.

Theodore kept his eyes on Sun-hee as they lifted off and climbed quickly into the sky. He looked up the aisle, no faces to see. Then he returned his attention to Sun-hee. "Look out the window." The plane circled to the right to gain altitude. "You can see the capital. We are making a circle over your grand city. It is an amazing place from the air."

Sun-hee looked at the city sprawled beneath the plane. She noticed the rivers and main streets, the buildings. "I feel like I am going to be sick," she said and closed her eyes, putting her head back against the seat.

"Focus on breathing normally. Try to relax," Theodore said while searching the pocket of the seat in front of him. He found what he was looking for, a barf bag, and blew into it, releasing his seatbelt. He readied himself to move at the first sign Sun-hee would be sick. "Focus on something pleasant, something other than the plane motion. Tell me about your children, grandchildren, or great-grandchildren. What are they doing today?"

"I had five children, Mr. Reed. One you just met. I have twenty-five grandchildren, over one hundred great-grandchildren, and many more who consider me their ancestor."

She paused, so Theodore pried a little more. "How many great-great-grandchildren do you have, Sun-hee?"

"As I think about it, Mr. Reed, everyone on this aircraft except for the pilots—I do not know about them—are, in a way, my children." She sighed and released her tight grip on the armrests. "The rest are out there." She pointed to the window.

"I am impressed. Maybe I should refer to you as the mother of Korea."

"There are others who should have that title, Mr. Reed. I am only here as the fates have dictated. Do you have any children, Mr. Reed?"

"No. I married six months ago. We plan to have children in a couple of years," he said, placing the barf bag back into the pouch in the seat ahead of him.

"Your wife must be worried." She turned and said in Mandarin, "Bring me my blue bag, please."

The attendant arrived a moment later with her bag. "Help me find Mr. Reed's tablet," she said to the attendant continuing in Mandarin. The attendant removed Mr. Reed's tablet from a metal mesh bag and handed it to her.

She addressed Mr. Reed. "You may send a message to your wife. Let her know you are well. Please do not mention where you are going or message anyone else. You would not want to complicate things, and they are complicated enough right now."

"Thank you, Sun-hee. You are a kind and thoughtful person," he said.

Theodore entered a text message. *Honey, I'm fine. It will be a few days before I get home. Don't worry*. He held out the tablet, showing the message to Sun-hee before he hit send. He confirmed the message was sent and turned the tablet off. He handed the tablet back to Sun-hee.

She held her hand up, shaking it side to side. "Keep it in the bag. No need to drive the surveillance people crazy."

Theodore turned the tablet off and slid it into the mesh bag, placing it in the seat pocket. An attendant asked Sun-hee, "Can I get you anything to drink?"

"Hot tea, please."

"For you, Mr. Reed?"

"Do you have coffee?"

"We have a Tanzanian dark roast, a medium roast from Luckin Coffee, and Starbucks Blonde roast."

"The Tanzanian sounds wonderful. A little cream and sugar, please."

The attendant bowed and left.

The plane leveled out, and Theodore looked out the window at the mountains of North Korea. They were heading northeast and would go across Alaska and Canada. It would be a beautiful trip, he thought, and then realized it would be dark most of the way.

The attendant came and set up the table from the aisle arm for Sun-hee. Having done these many times, Theodore pulled out his table and adjusted himself in his seat.

Tea and coffee arrived. Theodore turned to Sun-hee. "I can see the area where my great-grandfather was a prisoner. Was this your home?"

"I lived in a mine shaft in the side of a mountain not far from the camp. Windows in the cave looked over a secluded valley, a lovely place, and a wonderful home. Someday, I will take you there."

"I would like that, Sun-hee. It would be a great honor. One thing I would like to ask…"

The chair in front of Sun-hee pivoted around, revealing Moon-ja holding a glass of iced tea. "We are scheduled to address the United Nations the day after tomorrow." She held a tablet out to Sun-hee, saying, "I have reviewed the speech written by my sisters. Would you like to go over it?" She turned her head and politely said, "Hello, Mr. Reed. I am glad you could join us on this trip. What is New York like?"

Theodore bowed, and before he could respond, Sun-hee said, "I am sure you know our new Premier, Mr. Reed."

Theodore said in Korean, "Premier, I am honored to meet you in person. New York is an amazing city…" Theodore went on for a few minutes, talking about the cosmopolitan city with the lights, the foods, and entertainment. He tried to sell the positive aspects and leave out the negative.

"You speak Korean very well. What is your occupation?" asked Moon-ja.

"I am employed by the government as an analyst."

"Are you with the Central Intelligence Agency?" she asked.

"Yes. The stories my grandfather told me when I was a boy sparked an interest in North Korea. I am lucky to study your country as a profession."

"What is your analysis of me?" Moon-ja asked.

"With the little information I have seen, I am delighted that you are the new Premier. You are charismatic, have a delightful singing voice, and are very intelligent. After being taken prisoner, I hope I can remain as an analyst and…" Theodore paused.

"Study me in the future," Moon-ja finished his thought for him. "Do you speak Mandarin?" she asked in Mandarin.

"Only a little," Theodore replied in Mandarin.

"What other languages do you speak?" Moon-ja asked.

"A little Cantonese and some Russian," replied Theodore.

"Do you know how to speak *Nihon*?" Moon-ja asked in Japanese.

"I'm sorry. I didn't understand you," Theodore said in Korean.

"I need to review for our meetings tomorrow," Moon-ja said as she turned around.

Theodore began to ask a question, and the chair in front of him pivoted around.

Sun-hee said, "Let me introduce Mr. Chun. He is an assistant to the Premier. Should you think you can initiate conflict on this plane, let me inform you, Mr. Chun is an expert in martial arts."

Theodore looked Mr. Chun over. He was dressed in a tight black polo shirt revealing his broad shoulders and muscular chest. His thick neck held his large head topped with a crew cut. What caught Theodore's eyes were Mr. Chun's hands, about twice the size of his, attached to forearms resembling rocket engines.

"I have not thought of conflict," said Theodore. "Mr. Chun, I'm pleased to meet you." He held out his hand. Mr. Chun took it and squeezed. Theodore pulled back his hand and wiggled his fingers.

Su-dae approached and said, "How are you doing, Mother?"

"I am well. Just a little tired."

"I want you and Moon-ja to know that I have ordered all of the treasury securities we own to be dumped onto the market tomorrow morning."

"What is the total value of the treasury securities at this time?" asked Moon-ja as she turned her seat around.

"Nearly one trillion dollars," answered Su-dae.

"What will that do?" Sun-hee asked.

Moon-ja spoke, "The release of this volume of securities onto the open market will weaken the value of the dollar. Interest rates in the United States may rise temporarily. Also, the United States will find it more difficult to find buyers of new securities which are issued to cover their deficit." She turned to Su-dae. "You may lose more value than we gain in influence. I do like the show of force we portray to the United States and the rest of the world."

Theodore interrupted. "May I ask how you acquired the securities?"

"Our power generation facilities, especially from thorium reactors, have been quite profitable. We have taken American Treasury Securities as payment from the Chinese government."

"That should raise a few eyebrows," said Sun-hee as she laid her head back.

"May I ask what you are attempting to accomplish?" said Mr. Reed.

Moon-ja looked at Theodore and said, "I want to define our relationships with other countries on my terms. The United States is the only obstacle."

Theodore responded, "The United States is only enforcing the decisions of the United Nations. All of the resolutions in the last twenty-five-years were made to force North Korea to halt their development of nuclear weapons and missiles that could deliver them anywhere in the world."

"Our presentation to the United Nations will ask for a removal of all resolutions against North Korea. The influence of the United States and its allies, England and France, on the Security Council is our challenge. How do we change their vote?" Moon-ja asked, looking directly at Theodore.

"If you were to convince everyone that you will terminate the development of nuclear weapons, and allow inspectors to verify you are dismantling them, then there is a chance they will vote to end sanctions."

"America always interferes and seeks control," said Moon-ja and turned her seat forward.

Su-dae turned to Sun-hee. "Get some rest, Mother. Our time in New York may be busy." Then she walked forward down the aisle.

Sun-hee adjusted herself and requested a blanket. She was soon tucked in with a pillow and eye-covers.

Mr. Chun said to Theodore, "I thought we were going to New York to be interviewed by some of your news organizations. I see they added a meeting at the United Nations to our agenda. I am looking forward to seeing America firsthand." Then he pivoted his seat around.

***

Theodore sat back and reviewed the conversation.

Moon-ja and Su-dae both called Sun-hee mother. How can that be?

The coffee had kicked in, and his mind was abuzz. He looked out at the setting sun over the Aleutian Islands.

Sun-hee is the architect of the revolution. Her descendants and the descendants of the others who were at the camp my great-grandfather was a captive at are now in charge of North Korea.

He now understood what his great-grandfather had said in his stories.

We are not your enemy, do not interfere. They are carving out their future. The U.S. continues to dictate terms and interfere with Sun-hee. Is Moon-ja a roaring mouse or the crouching lion?

He took out his tablet and powered it up. He felt he needed to get a message out to tell his superiors to sign the peace treaty offered, and all would be well. Mr. Chun's chair pivoted quickly. A big hand was extended out towards him. Theodore handed his tablet to Mr. Chun. "I…"

Mr. Chun held his other hand to his mouth, finger extended. "Shish.

She needs rest," he whispered. He took the tablet and turned around.

Sun-hee heard a whisper from Mr. Chun.

Foolish American, always trying to interfere. All will be well soon.

She slept.

***

Moon-ja took Sun-hee's hand and rubbed it lightly. "We are close to New York. I hope you have rested."

Sun-hee lifted off her eye-covers and looked around. Moon-ja was radiant. Out of the corner of her eye she saw Theodore staring at her. She did not feel rested, and her right leg had fallen asleep. She shook it, but it did not seem to want to wake up.

"How long until we land?" Sun-hee asked.

"About an hour," said Moon-ja.

"I must make myself presentable."

With the help of Moon-ja and the attendant, Sun-hee made her way to the back of the plane. When she returned to her seat, she had on a clean dress and her blue scarf around her neck.

The attendant served breakfast consisting of rice cakes, fruit, and tea. There was nothing Sun-hee could do now. Just be ready to follow events as they occurred. She noticed Theodore eating his breakfast of eggs and pancakes. He asked for more coffee.

Americans do run on caffeine.

Sun-hee handed the attendant her dishes. Another stowed her table and made sure Sun-hee's seat belt was fastened. A moment later, the plane touched down. Before she had a chance to be nervous, the flight was over.

"Your first plane ride has ended safely," said Theodore.

"I am too old for this, Mr. Reed. I should have stayed home."

"Where is your sense of adventure, Sun-hee? There is a lot of this world to discover."

"That is one quality of life I have not had the liberty to enjoy, Mr. Reed. Perhaps I can do more traveling after your government decides to end sanctions on our people."

The plane came to a halt. Mr. Chun followed Theodore off the plane. The rest of the occupants followed. Su-dae assisted her mother down the steps. One of Moon-ja's sisters ran to the customs agent and handed over documents for everyone except Mr. Reed. The customs agent reviewed the diplomatic papers and expressed surprise that the Premier of North Korea was among the passengers. He quickly radioed for the assistance of a security detail to accompany a visiting head of state.

Theodore handed the customs agent his passport. The agent placed it under the scanner and studied the screen.

Sun-hee and Mr. Chun stopped and stood nearby, listening.

"I must ask you to come with me, Mr. Reed," said the agent.

"I am here at the request of the government of North Korea."

"You are listed as detained, sir. Are you sure you're okay?"

"I have come to the realization I have been placed into a special place right now, sir. I am not in any danger. Please let everyone know I am in excellent condition. For the good of our nations, I request you not interfere."

The customs agent paused for a moment before saying, "Very well, Mr. Reed. I will forward your status to Homeland Security. Proceed."

As Theodore turned, Sun-hee took his arm and walked silently with him through the terminal, followed by Mr. Chun. Two SUV's waited to take them to the studio of MSNBC.

Sun-hee got into one SUV with Mr. Reed. Mr. Chun rode shot-gun. Moon-ja rode in the other SUV with Su-dae and Moon-ja's sisters. They sped off. A police escort joined them shortly after they left the airport.

Mr. Reed rambled on about the city, telling Sun-hee about buildings they passed and pointing out the landmarks.

Sun-hee looked at the place she had hated all her life. Just people. It was the government and their policies she needed to hate, not the people. She was surprised that most of the vehicles had no drivers, and they pulled over to let their convoy pass without obstruction. "Without drivers, how do the cars know to pull over?" she asked.

Mr. Reed explained, "Computers control most cars and trucks in the city. The vehicles can communicate with one another. They automatically pull over for our police escort. Thus, our official vehicles have a clear right of way."

The convoy stopped in front of a tall skyscraper, a group of men and women escorted them to elevators and up into the heart of the building. Moon-ja and two of her sisters went off to a makeup room. Sun-hee and the rest of the assembly took seats in front of the news set, where they watched the flurry of events preparing for a broadcast. Two reporters took their positions and made last moment preparations for their special guest. Then it started.

"At this time, we have an exclusive interview of an extraordinary guest," said a female reporter. "The new Premier of the Democratic People's Republic of Korea is with us today. Welcome, Premier."

Cameras panned over to follow Moon-ja as she strode into the set and sat down at the high-backed chair. She smiled into the camera, radiating her loveliness to the viewers.

"Premier, thank you for joining us here in New York. First, I would like you to tell us in your own words, what happened in the office of Kim Jong-un, resulting in his assassination."

"Ladies and Gentlemen of the nations of our beloved planet," she began holding out her arms. "Thank you so much for allowing me to speak to you today. A few days ago, at a meeting with a long-time advisor, a plot to overthrow the Premier was revealed. My beloved husband called in one of the alleged perpetrators." She paused, pursed her lips, tears formed in her eyes, and then she took a deep breath. "He shot my husband in the head." She paused again, cleared her throat as tears trickled out. "Then he turned the gun on the advisor. I wrestled the gun from his hand and shot him." She shuddered, closed her eyes, and lowered her head.

The reporter held out a tissue while Moon-ja raised a silk handkerchief and blotted her face.

Moon-ja looked up, saying, "The moment was a very traumatic experience that will haunt me for the rest of my days."

"You killed the man who murdered your husband."

"Yes."

"You have now become Premier. Why you?"

"For the sake of my son. He will take over when he is ready."

"So, you are pregnant."

"Yes," she said, evoking a little smile. "Doctors have confirmed I am carrying a male heir."

"Your English is excellent. How have you come to speak English so well?"

"Education in Korea is essential. I was fortunate to have an excellent teacher who is fluent in many languages."

"The Secretary of State issued a statement saying you are genetically engineered. How do you respond to that statement?"

"I am here. I am a real person. There is nothing inhuman about me."

"Why do you think the Secretary would say you are genetically engineered?"

"The American government needed to find a way to make me a

villain. I assure you and all Americans, I am not a villain."

The lights went out on the cameras. "This interview is over," came a booming voice. "These people are here without authorization," said a man in a black suit, walking onto the set.

Sun-hee looked behind her to see a row of men with guns pointed at them. Mr. Chun jumped to his feet. Sun-hee reached out and took his hand.

"No," she shouted.

Moon-ja stood and faced the man in the black suit. "Who are you?"

"Homeland Security," he said, holding out a badge.

Mr. Reed blurted out, "They have diplomatic immunity."

"We do not recognize the government of North Korea," the man said.

***

Homeland Security agents escorted the Korean delegation out of the tall building. Moon-ja walked next to Sun-hee, holding her arm, followed by the two sisters. Mr. Chun and Mr. Reed followed.

Once outside, a crowd of protesters yelling, "Communists," "Genetic engineered gooks," "GMOuk," and other obscenities stood between them and the SUVs.

The men who stopped the interview tried to hold back the crowd. A brick flew out towards Moon-ja. Mr. Chun lept forward and reached up like a cat, caught the brick, and directed it to the ground. Moon-ja gently pulled Sun-hee aside. Mr. Reed stepped around to stand beside Mr. Chun as the security men pushed the protesters, trying to make a path through the crowd. Another rock flew in only to be grabbed by Mr. Chun, then another and another.

"Freaks."

"Monsters," yelled the mob.

"Back inside," yelled Moon-ja, carrying Sun-hee. The sisters were guarding them both by deflecting rocks and bricks.

Once inside, Sun-hee found herself shaking uncontrollably. Glass shattered as a brick smashed a door to her right. She could hear rocks hitting the building around her. Uniformed men were running around them as they moved further from the doors. Once they were a few meters inside, Sun-hee turned to look at the scene.

Mr. Chun carried a uniformed man over his left shoulder while deflecting projectiles with his right hand and backing into the building. Mr. Reed ran with his hands on his head through the broken door. The Homeland Security agents retreated to the lobby, and the man who had interrupted the interview lay on the sidewalk.

Su-dae pulled Sun-hee further into the lobby. Mr. Chun gently lay the wounded policeman on the floor.

A female Homeland Security officer came up to them and said, "Come with me. We will take you out through a different entrance to a secure location. Is anyone hurt?"

"We are unharmed," said Moon-ja.

"Just a scratch," said Mr. Reed.

Sun-hee looked to see a cut over Mr. Reed's left eye. Blood streamed down the side of his face.

"You moved into that one, Mr. Reed," said Mr. Chun. "You should have gone to your right."

"Without your quickness, Mr. Chun, I think we would have been stoned to death," replied Mr. Reed.

They followed the female officer who took them to three police SUVs. The motorcade then sped out a rear entrance. A few minutes later, they entered a parking garage under a large building. The security people escorted them to an area with four holding cells.

Mr. Reed spoke up. "This is not an appropriate place for an official delegation from North Korea."

"I have my orders, Mr. Reed," said a man walking up to the group. "They are to be kept here until a decision is made on where they are to go. You need to follow agent Johnson there," he pointed to a man standing by an elevator, "to be debriefed."

Theodore stepped up to the officer, "I will stay here with the Koreans."

"I am sorry, Mr. Reed. You will go with Mr. Johnson," he said sternly and grabbed Theodore, pulling him off balance into the waiting arms of two other men.

"No!" said Mr. Chun forcefully as he stepped forward.

Guards in the room drew their guns while Moon-ja moved in a flash, stepping in front of Mr. Chun and holding him back.

She chuckled and said to the American officer, "This is all so dramatic, and I must applaud you for your willingness to escalate this situation." She was smiling cutely, almost flirting with the officer. She motioned behind her back to Mr. Chun. "Let me de-escalate this situation as I am sure you do not want to shoot the pregnant Premier of North Korea." She looked into the eyes of the officer who stared back at her. Mr. Chun took a big sigh and backed up. "Now, can you show me to a lady's room? I need to pee," said Moon-ja.

"When he is in a cell," said the man in front of Moon-ja, pointing to Mr. Chun.

Sun-hee watched the elevator closing on Mr. Reed.

I hope he can rejoin us.

"Sir, I do not think we are a threat to you, so if you could direct us to a privy, I would very much appreciate it. It has been a long day, and I am tired."

"Are there better accommodations than a cell?" asked Su-dae.

"We are working on finding a suitable secure location for your party. At this time, this is the best I can do. A restroom is down the hall." He motioned to two female officers who accompanied the women.

***

They spent most of the night in cells before Mr. Reed, wearing a bandage over his right eye, approached with a group of men. "The Secretary of the United Nations confirmed your meeting today. Homeland Security will move everyone to a local hotel where you can rest and freshen up."

The trip to a hotel took a few minutes. The delegation was directed to suites on the same floor. Mr. Chun decided to remain in the hall as a guard.

Sun-hee looked at the clock in the room. It was four o'clock in the morning. She tried to rest, but the commotion of the day and the time change was too much to allow her to relax.

***

It was mid-morning when Chun knocked on Sun-hee's door. "Time to get ready," he roared.

They were soon in SUVs.

Mr. Reed looked at Sun-hee and said, "I was able to do a little digging this morning. Su-dae's plan to dump nearly a trillion dollars in Treasury Securities affected the markets. When they opened in Europe, more notes were dumped, and the markets opened substantially lower. The tactic shows you have some influence. I must say, I greatly underestimated what you were capable of doing."

"I also requested a meeting with the President. He refused to meet with you."

"What did you recommend to your President?" asked Sun-hee.

"Only what you have wanted all along. Leave North Korea alone."

Sun-hee asked, "Do you think this will be enough to convince your President to leave us alone?"

"There are many other players in the decision. I do not know how they will react. I can hope they realize that it is not worth the effort to maintain sanctions against North Korea. A month ago, North Korea was discredited as a country ruled by a madman. Moon-ja changed everything. Videos of her have gone viral. The meetings with the Secretary of State, and her interview, even though interrupted, are the most viewed news stories worldwide. They are the headlines of all the news programs. Then there is Seo Young-ja, who I watched for so long as the voice of North Korea. She has been interviewed remotely by most of the news organizations and has driven home the message of a new Korea."

"Do you think this is enough to sway your government?" asked Sun-hee.

Mr. Reed paused for a moment. "I do not believe they will allow North Korea to be free. The real power behind the government will not be swayed."

"Why were there so many protestors outside the news building? Do Americans hate Moon-ja?"

"That was an organized flash mob. Someone opposed to genetic engineering and North Korea called out the protestors. My speculation is that they were paid."

"I think they took your policy giving freedom of speech too far. How is your head?"

"I will be fine."

Sun-hee turned to look at the flags flying outside the United Nations building. She could not find North Korea's.

***

As they walked towards the building, Moon-ja asked Mr. Reed, "How do your people view me?"

"Many are very impressed with your poise and beauty. However, some news organizations are focusing on your genetics. They say you are engineered. Our government is suspicious of you, saying you are not human."

"I am real, Mr. Reed," she said as she reached out, taking his hand. She looked him in the eye. "Thank you for being honest and doing what you can for me and North Korea. Hopefully, the United States will see how I can lead North Korea to a peaceful and prosperous future."

"Unfortunately," said Mr. Reed. "I think that is what they are afraid of."

80 — The Prize - September 26, 2028

An official-looking man greeted them as they entered the United Nations building.

"This way, Madam Premier." He led them through a side door and down a long hallway. They entered a large room where the Secretary of State and another older man in a black suit stood. Eight security guards stood around the room.

The Security of State stepped forward. "I see that you have made it to America. For generations, the leaders of North Korea held a state of war with America and made it impossible to negotiate peace. You replaced your husband and wished to make a change in North Korea's relations with the United States. A few days ago, we made a proposal in good faith which would mutually benefit the interests of both our nations. I am at a loss to understand why you completely refuse our proposal."

Moon-ja said in a polite tone. "I hope to set my country free from all encumbrances and rule in a manner benefiting the people of North Korea."

"You have nuclear weapons and the ability to send them raining down on our cities. Your country has stolen technology, which is patented by U. S. companies. And you have recently taken actions disrupting the balance of the world economy. We can't tolerate your hostility to international rule of law."

"Please understand my position, Mr. Secretary. I don't want an American way of life for my people," Moon-ja said firmly. "I do not want to be a part of the capitalist system which now rules the world. I want nothing to do with the United States of America and will make every effort to block all attempts at influencing North Korea. I declare I will end all hostile actions towards America if you will end your police action, remove your military from our borders, end sanctions, and stop trying to influence anything which occurs in North Korea."

"Who are you to be talking to me like this?" demanded the Secretary. "You are a fifteen-year-old girl created in a test tube. You are not even human. Every civilized country on earth has banned genetic engineering of humans. Yet, I am here talking to the most engineered person ever made. You will agree to our terms."

"I will not," said Moon-ja confidently. "Not until you agree to end your influence on North Korea. How will you pay for all your military if you have nowhere to sell your debt?"

Another man laughed loudly and stepped forward.

Moon-ja turned to look at the source of the laughter.

"Allow me to introduce the Secretary of the Treasury," said the Secretary of State.

"You are all so naïve," the treasury secretary said, still chuckling. He pointed at Su-dae. "Hours ago, the banks where you hold securities were instructed to freeze your accounts. They have been designated as terrorist funds. Your sons are condemned as terrorists and hopefully arrested. The Chinese government has been asked to confiscate your power plants. The European markets are recovering nicely. It looks like the markets are recovering and should close higher." He folded his hands with a satisfied grin.

"Your only option is to sign the agreement or have sanctions increased," said the Secretary of State.

"I will address the United Nations," said Moon-ja in a forceful voice.

"You will not," the Secretary of State shouted with a wave of his arm. "You are just a little girl propped up as a puppet for a group of assassins. What can you know? Please leave."

Sun-hee stood beside Mr. Reed, stunned at the turn of events. The terrorist declaration thwarted Su-dae's dumping of the treasury securities. She watched as one security man took hold of Su-dae's arms from behind. Another grabbed her arm, and three moved towards Moon-ja.

"Don't touch the Premier," said Chun as he moved in front of Moon-ja, ready for a fight.

"You don't want to make Mr. Chun mad," said Theodore as he grabbed the security guard who held Sun-hee's arm. They struggled for a moment before the guard knocked Theodore across the side of the head with his pistol.

"Stop trying to force your will on us," Moon-ja said with a force that froze everyone in the room. "You think I am a weak little girl," Moon-ja yelled at the two officials. "All I want is a chance to lead the people of North Korea to a decent life. Stop interfering!" She turned and started for the door. "I am a human, Mr. Secretary. I'm as human as any person who has walked on this planet."

Mr. Chun darted in front of Moon-ja to open the door and looked out. "Clear," he said.

The sisters backed to the door as Su-dae helped Theodore to his feet. Sun-hee followed Moon-ja into the hallway, where the official who had first met them approached. "Two minutes until you are on, Madam Premier. This way." He waved and turned around.

The group made their way to the side of the stage. A sister held a handkerchief to Theodore's forehead. His wound was bleeding again.

Su-dae pulled Moon-ja and Sun-hee aside. "Eun-mi said to get them to vote to terminate the resolutions against North Korea."

"That is what China and Russia agreed to propose," replied Moon-ja.

"The podium is yours, Madam Premier," said a woman to Moon-ja as she pointed.

Moon-ja brushed her hair back, adjusted her dress, and looked at her sisters. Their eyes met, and the two nodded to Moon-ja.

With her head held high and taking little steps, Moon-ja glided across the stage. She grinned at the assembly through the lights, keeping her striking eyes wide open.

"Ladies and Gentlemen of the nations of our beloved planet," Moon-ja began, holding out her arms. "Thank you so much for allowing me to speak to you today. This is my message to you, the honored representatives of the nations of the world, and to all the people you represent. One family has ruled the Democratic People's Republic of Korea for eighty-two years." She paused. "I now carry a male child who will continue that rule for many years to come. North Korea is a nation with a history of strong filial leadership. Until my son is mature, I will hold the office of Premier and will lead the People of North Korea.

"The most crucial issue facing our people is freedom. We must be free of the war and sanctions the United Nations has placed on our nation. We sought to unify Korea seventy-eight years ago, and this assembly intervened. Their intervention prevented a unified Korea. Today, we recognize we are now two distinct nations on the Korean Peninsula. South Korea remains a puppet of capitalism, and we want nothing to do with them. Thus, we release South Korea to be a separate nation. The effort to unify the Korean People is at an end."

"Over the last few days, the Democratic People's Republic of Korea has made efforts to end our conflict with the United States. The United States of America refuses to end sanctions based on the resolutions adopted by the United Nations. They demanded we sign an agreement that would put North Korea under their economic control. Now in front of all the world, I reject their demands. I ask for an end to our conflict." She held up the one-page document. "I ask you, the great citizens of the world, to repeal the resolutions the United Nations invoked, and to impose sanctions upon the United States of America to pressure them to end their conflict and influence over the Democratic People's Republic of Korea."

The speaker walked from the other side of the stage. Moon-ja stepped aside as he stepped to the podium. He announced, "A resolution is now before the Security Council. Would those members please enter their votes?"

Sun-hee shook in anticipation and hoped for a miracle.

"We have the results," said the Speaker looking at his tablet. "The Security Council has unanimously resolved to NOT recognize Moon-ja as the Premier of the Democratic People's Republic of Korea because she is a genetically engineered person."

"What?" shouted Mr. Chun as he stepped onto the stage. "Moon-ja is the Premier," he bellowed at the assembly in a deep angry voice.

Sun-hee stepped forward and took Mr. Chun's arm. "Be calm, my son." Then she continued towards the podium.

Sun-hee met a stunned Moon-ja. "You are the Premier. The vote does not matter."

She turned to the Speaker. "May I, a citizen of North Korea, address the assembly?"

"You may," replied the Speaker as he stepped aside.

Sun-hee stroked her blue silk scarf, then swept the left side over her right shoulder and said, "Honored delegates to the United Nations. Seventy-eight years ago, Dr. Park established a school for the best children in North Korea. His goal was to have the Korean people respect themselves and gain the respect of other peoples and nations. The men and women in that school went on to be leaders in industry, medicine, science, and the economy. One of our group advised the Kim family for over seventy years."

"Our children and the following generations have been the backbone of most of North Korea's accomplishments. Our loyalty is to the Kim dynasty and the Democratic People's Republic of Korea. When Cloe Moon-ja became the bride of the Premier, I believed our influence on the direction of our country would increase. If Cloe Moon-ja teaches her son and heir what I taught her, then North Korea will be a nation you will easily respect. The unfortunate sequence of events leading to the death of Kim Jong-un, vaulted Cloe Moon-ja to the position of acting premier too soon. Yet, she is more capable of leading than any person in Korea. What happens too often in the history of humanity is we judge a person by their physical makeup, and not by their character, education, and accomplishments."

"I am old, and for my whole life have looked forward to living in a nation free from the control of other nations. I ask for your respect. Respect for me, for North Korea, and the new Premier. She is not your enemy."

The Speaker moved next to Sun-hee at the podium. He said, "A proposal is now up for a vote for the members of the Security Council. Would the members please enter their votes?"

Sun-hee looked over to her family. Su-dae smiled and gave her mother a nod of encouragement. The faces of Moon-ja, her sisters, and Mr. Chun showed defeat.

An eerie silence came over the auditorium. Sun-hee forced breaths in and out. Her eyes returned to the tablet held by the Secretary, who drummed his fingers lightly on the podium.

The tablet gave a small beep. The Secretary examined the tablet, glanced at Sun-hee, then turned to the microphone. "The vote on a resolution to terminate all previous sanctions against North Korea is fifteen to terminate, none to continue."

The Secretary of the United Nations stood next to Sun-hee and asked, "For the record, can I get your name?"

"I am Cha Sun-hee."

"Cha Sun-hee, do you have a title or a reason why you are the person to address the United Nations today on behalf of the Korean people?

Sun-hee paused for a moment then said into the microphone, "I am a prize-winner, Mr. Secretary. I won a prize."

81 — Epilogue - September 27 - 31, 2028

The flight attendant announced that lunch would be served shortly. Moon-ja turned around and stared at Sun-hee. "You did it, Mother. You accomplished what you wanted. You didn't need me."

"No, Moon-ja. I would not be here without you."

"I feel like a tool made for one purpose. Now that you achieved that purpose, my future is to raise the next Premier."

Sun-hee looked at the sadness in her daughter's eyes. "My dear daughter. You are correct. I dreamed of this moment. I used you to achieve it. From this moment, I release you from my expectations. Dream your own dreams, seek your own desires, be who you want to be."

"How can I? You, my brothers and sisters, the Korean people, and now the world expects me to lead."

"You can step aside. Any of your brothers or sisters are capable. Captain Gan wanted to lead. Let him be the Premier. You do what you want."

"You defined what I wanted and who I am. You never said I could do or be what I wanted. Right now, I don't know what I want," said Moon-ja, and she turned around.

Su-dae opened a bottle of champagne and poured a glass for Sun-hee.

Sun-hee said, "I don't understand how they all voted to reverse the resolutions. I thought the United States and their close allies would vote to continue sanctions."

Su-dae said in Japanese, "Oh, Mother. The vote was rigged. Eun-mi hacked the voting machines to give only positive votes. Unfortunately, the vote against Moon-ja occurred first."

"I hope the authorities do not discover Eun-mi's involvement," replied Sun-hee in Japanese.

Su-dae took another glass from the attendant, filled it, handed it to Moon-ja, and continued in Japanese. "Did you hear that, Madam Premier. The vote against you was rigged."

Moon-ja took the glass and continued in Japanese, "Rigged or not, they fear a *Yama no Megami*."

Su-dae held her glass up and said in Korean, "To the *San Yeosin*."

Moon-ja tapped the glass and smiled.

"Did I hear a toast to the Mountain Goddess?" asked Mr. Reed.

"You did," said Su-dae as she poured champagne for Mr. Chun and Mr. Reed. Then she held her glass high and spoke in Korean, "To my incredible mother."

"To our mother," said everyone.

Theodore said, "To Sunny. Like the rest of you, I would not be here without her."

Then Theodore Reed strolled down the aisle, chatting and making sure to tap glasses with everyone.

"Mr. Chun," said Sun-hee, "there are some things in my red bag I want to return to Mr. Reed. You'll find a helmet and some items packed inside. Can you get them?"

When Theodore returned to his seat, his great-grandfather's helmet and knives were waiting for him.

"I told you I had a few things Theodore left at the camp. It is time to return them," said Sun-hee.

"Oh, my! This is incredible! My father will freak out when he sees these. Thank you so much for holding on to these for all these years. I can't fathom how wonderful of a person you were to my family. How can I ever repay you?"

"We have what we truly wanted, freedom." Sun-hee sipped her champagne. "This is the first time I have tasted an alcoholic drink. I like it." She sipped some more and had a second glass with dinner.

After eating, she asked for a blanket. Then she cuddled up in her seat and stared out the window as the plane chased the sun across North America.

The puffy clouds look so different from above.

She imagined she was a cloud hovering over North Korea, protecting the people as she fell asleep.

Moon-ja talked with her three siblings, outlining how to proceed with changing North Korea. They concluded that they would have to get together with Hong-do when they landed.

Su-dae sent messages to halt the sale of treasury securities. Her son messaged back that the Chinese government refused to label them as terrorists. None of their assets in China were frozen or seized.

Mr. Reed taught Mr. Chun how to play poker and soon figured out Mr. Chun had as many brains as he had muscles. When Theodore's debt to Mr. Chun passed the million won mark, Theodore was smart enough to quit.

The plane started its descent for a landing in Pyongyang. The attendant tried to wake Sun-hee. Sun-hee did not respond. Then the attendant screamed as she touched Sun-hee's face. It was cold.

Mr. Reed leaped over and held his fingers to Sun-hee's neck. "There is no pulse."

Moon-ja rotated in her seat, took Sun-hee's head in her hands, and began to weep.

Su-dae screamed at the pilots, "Call for an ambulance to meet us when we land."

Mr. Chun stood over Moon-ja and cried.

***

Seo Young-ja entered the cave and hung Sun-hee's photo on the wall. Then, since there was no one left to hang hers when she passed, she hung her picture.

Hon-yong Jr. spent all week making the most magnificent casket he could think to make. He had trouble getting it to the elevator to take down to the valley until Mr. Chun arrived and carried it through the mineshafts and into the valley.

For hours, the elevator went up and down, transporting the family to the funeral. Theodore Reed III was on the last trip down.

The children Sun-hee bore, now in their seventies, stood at the front of the attendees. Cha Su-dae, Cha Hong-do, Cha So-min, Cha Eun-mi, and Cha Hon-yong Jr. were together for the first time in over fifty years.

Moon-ja stood before the crowd and spoke. "To quote Confucius, 'When things are investigated, then true knowledge is achieved; when true knowledge is achieved, then the will becomes sincere; when the will is sincere, then the heart is set right; when the heart is set right then the personal life is cultivated; when the personal life is cultivated, then the family life is regulated; when the family life is regulated, then the national life is orderly; and when the national life is orderly, then there is peace in this world.'"

"My mother sought truth through knowledge," Moon-ja continued. "It defined her will and her heart. She made the right decisions for herself, her family, and her country. The result was a path for our nation and peace to our people."

Theodore Reed the III stepped forward. "It has been said, 'Change in the world only occurs when a dedicated group of people gets together, determined to make that change.' I have come to understand that the House of Sanshin is such a group. But I must add, each group has one individual who, by their example, determines the direction for the whole. Cha Sun-hee was such a person.”

List of Characters

Note: In Korean culture the family name comes first. The name Cha Sun-hee would be Sun-hee Cha when referenced in the United States. This book uses the format for where the character is from.

Chapter 1

Cha Sue-dae; Mother of Cha Sun-hee.

Cha Sun-hee; Main character. Other characters are referenced as to their relationship to Sun-hee.

Pae Ai-yo; (Mrs. Pae) Friend and part time employer of Cha Sue-dae.

Chapter 2

Rim Seung-gin; (lieutenant) Assistant to General Park.

Kua Eun-young; (sergeant) Trainer and overseer of students.

Lim Joo-yun; Female student. Friend of Cha Sun-hee.

Seo Young-ja; Female student. Friend of Cha Sun-hee.

Ryoo Eun-seong; Female student. Friend of Cha Sun-hee.

Moon Choe-me; Female student. Friend of Cha Sun-hee.

Han Soo-hy; Female student.

Song Kyung-hee; Female student.

Suk Jong-hui; Female student.

Rhee Son-yong; Female student.

Youn Kum-ja; Female student.

Hung Mi-na; Female student.

Ryom Kyung-hwa; Female student.

Jo Yu-min; Female student.

San Sang-me; Female student.

Park Tae-song; (General) A doctor who is the Director of Medicine for North Korea.

Kim Il-sung; Premier of North Korea 1948-1994.

Chapter 4

Li Jong-soon; A professor of mathematics at

University of Pyongyang.

Ahn Ching-ying; (Nickname: Numbers) Male student and father of Sun-hee's fourth child.

San Hien-jin; (Nickname: Stinky) Male student.

Han Young-soo; (Nickname: The Stone) Male student and father of Sun-hee's first child.

Ho Hon-yong; (Nickname: Hammer) Male Student and father of Sun-hee's fifth child.

Chapter 5

Captain Kwang; (Captain) The commander of the compound.

Seok Yong-gak; (Nickname: The Strategist) Male student and father of Sun-hee's second child.

Chapter 6

So Jung-sip; Male student.

Chapter 7

I Kwong-ku; (Nickname, Unicorn) Male student and father of Sun-hee's third child.

Youj Mung-jo; Female student.

Chapter 8

San Hien-jin; Female student.

Chapter 9

Choe Chulsoon; (Nickname, Doc) Male student.

Noh Ki-Young: Male Student

Chapter 10

Maxim Bogdanov; (Max) Russian Doctor.

Aleksey Zaytesev; (Alek) Russian Doctor.

Shon In-jung; (Nickname, Skinny Beast) Male student.

Chapter 11

Mr. Yun; A builder.

Kwang Byeoung-keun; Male student.

Chapter 12

Jo Jin-taek; Korean soldier.

Chapter 14
Chae Dae-suk; Male student.

Chapter 15
Hung Young-Jee; Male student.
Theodore Reed; American Air force Pilot.

Chapter 17
Jeremy McLeod; American Air Force Pilot.

Chapter 19
Tsai Myung-hee; Female student.
Ryom Kyuung-hwa;Female student.
Jo Yu-min; Female student.
Shim Mi-kum; Female student.
John Peterson; American Army Sergeant.
Abraham Bryant; American Army Field Cook.
Lim Soo-kyung; (Mrs. Lim) Lim Joo-yun's mother.
Chun-ja; Housekeeper at the command house.

Chapter 20
Yun Chul; Male student.

Chapter 26
Ri Hea-jung; Female student.
Ma Chong-pil; Male Student
Yeo Wa-dae; (nickname, Waves) Male Student.

Chapter 27
Yi Yang-gae; A refugee. The Mother of Yi Si-ue.
Yi Si-ue; A girl born in the camp.

Chapter 28
Garrett Stallings; American in Tokyo.

Chapter 29
Ra Weon-kee; (nickname, Wires) Male Student.
Mrs. Ra; Ra Weon-kee's mother.
Mrs. Moon; Moon Choe-me's mother.

Chapter 32
Cha Hong-do; Sun-hee's second child, first son.

Chapter 33
Lieutenant Loo; South Korean soldier.
Major Johnson; American Army Major.

Chapter 35
Cha Seo-woo; Sun-hee's father's name.
Cha So-min; Sun-hee's third child, second daughter.

Chapter 36
General Ma; In charge of education.

Chapter 39
Chong Gil-hyung; (nickname, Bear) Male student.
Chou Sung-man; (nickname, Gears) Male student.
Chweh Han-gyong; Male student.

Chapter 40
Cha Eun-mi; Sun-hee's fourth child, second son.

Chapter 41
Ri Hea-jung; Female student
Cha Hon-yong; Sun-hee's fifth child, third son.

Chapter 42
Park Duk-bae; General Park's son with Chun-ja.

Chapter 50
Ryoo Tae-seon; Wife of Hong-yong Jr. Eun-seong's daughter.

Chapter 53
Yung-li; Choe-me's granddaughter.
Chweh; Chong-pil's son.

Chapter 54
Huang Jang-yop; Policy advisor to the Premier.